Elias Khoury

Gate of the Sun

Bab al-Shams

Translated from the Arabic by Humphrey Davies

archipelago books

Archipelago Books
25 Jay Street #203
Brooklyn, NY 11201
www.archipelagobooks.org

Maps drawn by Reginald Piggott.

Library of Congress Cataloging-in-Publication Data
Khoury, Elias.
Gate of the Sun / by Elias Khoury
translated from the Arabic by Humphrey Davies. – 1st ed.
p.cm.
ISBN: 0-9763950-2-9
I. Davies, Humphrey. II. Title.
PG7179.U45T7913 2005
891.8'538 – dc22   2005016693

First published with the title *Bab al-Shams* by Dâr-al-Adâb, Beirut, 1998.

The edition of the Koran quoted in this volume is *The Koran Interpreted*, translated
by Arthur J. Arberry, Oxford World Classics, Oxford University Press, 1998.

SECOND PRINTING

Distributed by Consortium Book Sales and Distribution
1045 Westgate Drive
St. Paul, MN 55114
www.cbsd.com

This publication was made possible with the support of Lannan Foundation,
the International Institute of Modern Letters, and with public funds from
the New York State Council on the Arts, a state agency.

NYSCA

He said, may Allah be pleased with him:
One day, Sheikh al-Junayd set out on a journey and while
traveling was overtaken by thirst. He found a well that was
too deep to draw water from, so he took off his sash, dangled it
into the well until it reached the water, and set about raising and
lowering it and squeezing it into his mouth. A villager appeared
and asked him, "Why do it so? Tell the water to rise, and drink with
your hands!" and the villager approached the edge of the well and
said to the water, "Rise, with God's permission," and it rose, and the
sheikh and the villager drank. Afterwards the sheikh turned to the
villager and asked, "Who are you?" "One of God's creatures," he
replied. "And who is your sheikh?" asked al-Junayd. "My sheikh
is al-Junayd, though I have yet to set eyes on him," replied
the man. "Then how did you attain these powers?" asked the
sheikh. "Through my faith in my sheikh," replied the man.

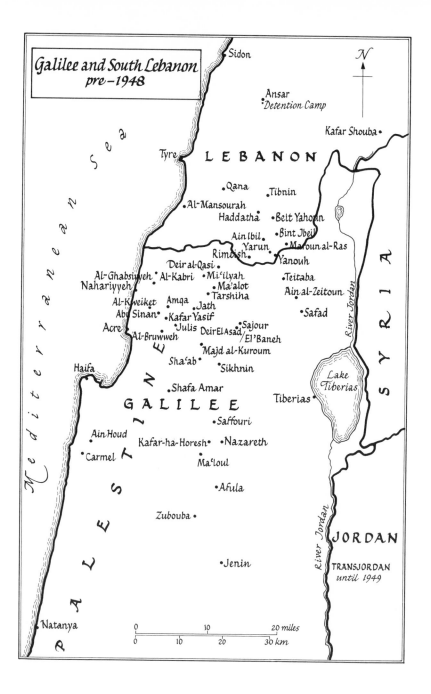

Galilee and South Lebanon
pre-1948

N

Mediterranean Sea

Sidon

Ansar
Detention Camp

Kafar Shouba

Tyre

LEBANON

Qana
Tibnin

Al-Mansourah
Haddatha
Beit Yahoun

Ain Ibil
Bint Jbeil

Yarun
Maroun al-Ras

Rimeish
Yanouh

Deir al-Qasi

Al-Ghabsiyeh
Al-Kabri
Mi'ilyah
Teitaba

Nahariyyeh
Ma'alot
Ain al-Zeitoun

Al-Kweiket
Amqa
Tarshiha

Abu Sinan
Jath
Safad

Acre
Kafar Yasif

Al-Bruwweh
Julis
Sajour

DeirEl Asad
El'Baneh

Sha'ab
Majd al-Kuroum

Sikhnin

Shafa Amar

GALILEE
Lake
Tiberias

Tiberias

Haifa

Saffouri

Ain Houd
Kafar-ha-Horesh
Nazareth

Carmel
Ma'loul

Afula

Zubouba

PALESTINE

SYRIA

River Jordan

River Jordan

JORDAN

TRANSJORDAN
until 1949

Jenin

Natanya

0   10   20 miles
0   10   20   30 km

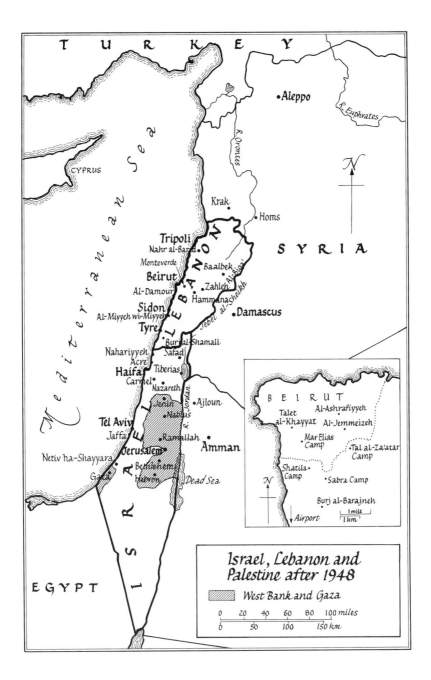

Israel, Lebanon and
Palestine after 1948

West Bank and Gaza

0   20   40   60   80   100 miles
0   50   100   150 km

Gate of the Sun

Bab al-Shams

Part One

> <

The Galilee Hospital

Umm Hassan is dead.

I saw everyone racing through the alleys of the camp and heard the sound of weeping. Everyone was spilling out of their houses, bent over to catch their tears, running.

Nabilah, Mahmoud al-Qasemi's wife, our mother, was dead. We called her *mother* because everyone born in the Shatila camp fell from their mother's guts into her hands.

I too had fallen into her hands, and I too ran the day she died.

Umm Hassan came from al-Kweikat, her village in Galilee, to become the only midwife in Shatila – a woman of uncertain age and without children. I only knew her when she was old, with stooped shoulders, a face full of creases, large eyes shining in a white square, and a white cloth covering her white hair.

Our neighbor, Sana', the wife of Karim al-Jashi the *kunafa** seller, said Umm Hassan dropped in on her the night before last and told her her death was coming.

"I heard its voice, daughter. Death whispers, and its voice is soft."

Speaking in her half-Bedouin accent she told Sana' about the messenger of death.

"The messenger came in the morning and told me to get ready."

And she told Sana' how she wanted to be prepared for burial.

"She took me by the hand," said Sana', "led me to her house, opened her wooden trunk, and showed me the white silk shroud. She told me she would

* A pastry.

bathe before she went to sleep: 'I'll die pure, and I want only you to wash me.'"

Umm Hassan is dead.

Everyone knew that this Monday morning, November 20th, 1995, was the time set for Nabilah, Fatimah's daughter, to meet death.

Everyone awoke and waited, but no one was brave enough to go to her house to discover she was dead. Umm Hassan had told everyone, and everyone believed her.

Only I was taken by surprise.

I stayed with you until eleven at night, and then, exhausted, I went to my room and slept. It was night, the camp was asleep, and no one told me.

But everyone else knew.

No one would question Umm Hassan because she always told the truth. Hadn't she been the only one to weep on the morning of June 5, 1967? Everyone was dancing in the streets, anticipating going home to Palestine, but she wept. She told everyone she'd decided to wear mourning. Everyone laughed and said Umm Hassan had gone mad. Throughout the six long days of the war she never opened the windows of her house; on the seventh, out she came to wipe away everyone's tears. She said she knew Palestine would not come back until all of us had died.

Over the course of her long life, Umm Hassan had buried her four children one after the other. They would come to her borne on planks, their clothes covered in blood. All she had left was a son called Naji, who lived in America. Though Naji wasn't her real son, he was: She had picked him up from beneath an olive tree on the Kabri-Tarshiha road and had fed him from her dry breasts, then returned him to his mother when they reached the village of Qana, in Lebanon.

Umm Hassan died today.

No one dared go into her house. About twenty women gathered to wait, then Sana' came and knocked on the door, but no one opened it. She pushed it, it opened, she went in and ran to the bedroom. Umm Hassan was sleeping, her head covered with her white headscarf. Sana' went over and took her by the shoulders, and the chill of death flowed into the hands of the *kunafa*-seller's wife, who screamed. The women entered, the weeping began, and everyone raced to the house.

I, too, would like to run with the others, go in with them, see Umm Hassan sleeping her eternal sleep and breathe in the smell of olives that clung to her small home.

But I didn't weep.

For three months I've been incapable of reacting. Only this man floating above his bed makes me feel the throb of life. For three months he's been laid out on his bed in Galilee Hospital, where I work as a doctor, or where I pretend that I'm a doctor. I sit next to him, and I try. Is he dead or alive? I don't know – am I helping or tormenting him? Should I tell him stories or listen to him?

For three months I've been in this room.

Today Umm Hassan died, and I want him to know, but he doesn't hear. I want him to come with me to her funeral, but he won't get up.

They said he fell into a coma.

An explosion in the brain causing permanent damage. A man lies in front of me, and I have no idea what to do. I'll just try not to let him rot while he's still alive, because I'm sure he's asleep, not dead.

But what difference does it make?

Is it true what Umm Hassan said about a sleeper being like a dead man – that the sleeper's soul leaves his body only to return when he wakes, but that the dead man's soul leaves and doesn't come back? Where is the soul of Yunes, son of Ibrahim, son of Suleiman al-Asadi? Has it left him for a distant place, or is it hovering above us in the hospital room, asking me not to go because the man is immersed in distant darknesses, afraid of the silence?

I swear I've no idea.

On her first visit Umm Hassan said that Yunes was in torment. She said he was in a different place from us.

"So what should I do?" I asked her.

"Do what he tells you," she answered.

"But he doesn't speak," I said.

"Oh yes, he does," she said, "and it's up to you to hear his voice."

And I don't hear it, I swear I don't, but I'm stuck to this chair, and I talk and talk.

Tell me, I beg of you, what should I do?

I sit by your side and listen to the sound of weeping coming through the window of your room. Can't you hear it?

Everyone else is weeping, so why don't you?

It's become our habit to look out for occasions to weep, for tears are dammed up behind our eyes. Umm Hassan has burst open our reservoir of tears. Why won't you get up and weep?

HEY, YOU!

How am I supposed to talk to you or with you or about you?

Should I tell you stories you already know, or be silent and let you go wherever it is you go? I come close to you, walking on tiptoe so as not to wake you, and then I laugh at myself because all I want is to wake you. I need one thing – one thing, dear God: that this man drowning in his own eyes should get up, open his eyes and say something.

But I'm lying.

Did you know you've turned me into a liar?

I say I want one thing, but I want thousands of things. I lie, God take pity on you, on me and on your poor mother. Yes, we forgot your mother. You told me all your stories, and you never told me how your mother died. You told about the death of your blind father and how you slipped into Galilee and attended his funeral. You stood on the hill above the village of Deir al-Asad, seeing but unseen, weeping but not weeping.

At the time I believed you. I believed that intuition had led you there to your house, hours before he died.

But now I don't.

At the time I was bewitched by your story. Now the spell is broken, and I no longer believe you.

But your mother?

Why didn't you say anything about her death?

Is your mother dead?

Do you remember the story of the icon of the Virgin Mary?

We were living through the civil war in Lebanon, and you were saying that war shouldn't be like that. You even advised me, when I came back from

Beijing as a doctor, not to take part in the war and asked me to go with you to Palestine.

"But Yunes, you don't go to fight. You go because of your wife."

You gave me a long lecture about the meaning of war and then said something about the picture of the Virgin Mary in your house, and that was when I asked you if your mother was Christian and how the sheikh of the village of Ain al-Zaitoun could have married a Christian woman. You explained that she wasn't a Christian but loved the Virgin and used to put her picture under her pillow. She'd made you love the Virgin, too, because she was the mistress of all the world's women and because her picture was beautiful – a woman bending her head over her son, born swaddled in his shroud.

"And what did the sheikh think?" I asked you.

It was then that you explained to me that your father, the sheikh, was blind, and that he never saw the picture at all.

When did Nahilah tell you of your mother's death?

Why don't you tell me? Is it because your wife said your mother had asked to be buried with the picture and this caused a problem in the village?

Why do you sleep like that and not answer?

You sleep like sleep itself. You sleep in sleep, and are drowning. The doctor said you had a blood clot in the brain, were clinically dead, and there was no hope. I refused to believe him.

I see you before me and can do nothing.

I hold conversations with you and tell you stories. I'll tell you everything. What do you say – I'll make tea, and we'll sit on the low chairs in front of your house and tell tales! You used to laugh at me because I don't smoke. You used to smoke your cigarette right to the end, chewing on the butt hanging between your lips and sucking in the smoke.

Now here I am. I close the door of your room. I sit next to you. I light a cigarette, draw the smoke deep into my lungs, and I tell you tales. And you don't answer.

Why don't you talk to me?

The tea's gone cold, and I'm tired. You're immersed in your breathing and don't care.

Please don't believe them.

Do you remember the day when you came to me and said that everyone was sick of you, and I couldn't dispel the sadness from your round pale face? What was I supposed to say? Should I have said your day had passed, or hadn't yet come? You'd have been even more upset. I couldn't lie to you. So I'm sad too, and my sadness is a deep breach in my soul that I can't repair, but I swear I don't want you to die.

Why did you lie to me?

Why did you tell me after the mourners had left that Nahilah's death didn't matter, because a woman only dies if her man stops loving her, and Nahilah hadn't died because you still loved her?

"She's here," you said, and you pointed at your eyes, wide open to show their dark gray. I was never able to identify the color of your eyes – when I asked you, you would say that Nahilah didn't know what color they were either, and that at Bab al-Shams she used to ask you about the colors of things.

You lied to me.

You convinced me that Nahilah hadn't died, and didn't finish the sentence. At the time I didn't take in what you'd said; I thought they were the beautiful words an old lover uses to heal his love. But death was in the other half of the sentence, because a man dies when his woman stops loving him, and you're dying because Nahilah stopped loving you when she died.

So here you are, drowsing.

Dear God, what drowsiness is this? And why do I feel a deathly drowsiness when I'm near you? I lie back in the chair and sleep. And when I get up in the middle of the night, I feel pain all over my body.

I come close to you, I see the air roiling around you, and I see that place I have not visited. I'd decided to go; everyone goes, so why not me? I'd go and have a look. I'd go and anchor the landmarks in my eyes. You used to tell me that you knew the sites because they were engraved on your eyes like indelible landmarks.

Where are the landmarks, my friend? How will I know the road, and who will guide me?

You told me about the caves dug out of the rocks. Is it true that you used to meet her there? Or were you lying to me? You said they were called Bab al-Shams – Gate of the Sun – and smiled and said you didn't mean the Shams I was in love with, or that terrible massacre at the Miyyeh wi-Miyyeh camp, where they killed her.

You told me I didn't love Shams and should forget her: "If you loved her, you'd avenge her. It can't be love, Son. You love a woman who doesn't love you, and that's an impossibility."

You don't understand. How can I avenge a woman who was killed because of another man?

"So she didn't love you," you said.

"She did but in her own way," I answered.

"Love has a thousand doors. But one-sided love isn't a door, it's a delusion."

I didn't tell you then that your love for Nahilah may have been a delusion too, because you only met her on journeys that resembled dreams.

I DRAW CLOSE to tell you that the moon is full. In al-Ghabsiyyeh, we love the moon, and we fear it. When it's full we don't sleep.

Get up and look at the moon.

You didn't tell me about your mother, but I'll tell you about mine. The truth is, I don't know much about her – she disappeared. They said she'd gone to her people in Amman, and when I was in Jordan in 1970, I looked for her, but that's another tale I'll tell you later.

I already told you about my mother, and I'll tell you about her again. When you were telling me about Bab al-Shams, you used to say that stories are like wine: They mature in the telling. Does that mean that the telling of a story is like the jar it's kept in? You used to tell the stories of Nahilah over and over, your eyes shining with the same desire.

"She cast a spell on me, that woman," you'd say.

But I know that the magician was you – how else did you persuade Nahilah to put up with you, reeking with the stink of travel?

My mother used to wake me while it was still night in the camp and whisper to me, and I'd get up to see the moon in its fullness, and not go back to sleep.

The woman from al-Kweikat said we were mad: "Ghabsiyyeh people are crazy, they're afraid of the moon." But we weren't afraid – though in fact, yes, we would stay awake all night. My mother wouldn't let me sleep. She'd tie a black scarf around her head and would ask me to look at the surface of the moon so I could find my dead father's face.

"Do you see him?" she'd ask.

I'd say that I saw him, though I swear I didn't. But now, can you believe it, now, after years and years, when I look at the face of the moon, I see my father's face, stained with blood. My mother said they killed him, left him in a heap at the door and left. She said he fell in a heap as though he weren't a man but a sack. And when she went over to him, she didn't see him. They took him and buried him in secret in the Martyrs' Cemetery. "Look at your father, and tell him what you want."

I used to look and not see, but I wouldn't say. Now I see, but what am I supposed to say?

Get up and look at the face of the moon! Do you see your wife? Do you see my father? Certainly you will never see my mother, and even if you saw her, you would never know her. Even I have forgotten her, forgotten her voice and her tears. The only thing I remember is the taste of the dough she used to make in the clay oven in front of our house. She would put chili pepper, oil, cumin, and onions on a piece of dough and bake it. Then she'd make tea and eat, and I'd eat with her, and we'd look at the moon. That burning taste is still hot on my tongue and in my eyes now when I look at the moon; I drink my tea, I look at the moon, and I see.

My mother told me that in my father's village they didn't sleep. When the moon grew round and sat on its throne in the sky, the whole village would wake up, and the blind singer would sit in the square and play on his single-string fiddle, singing to the night as though he were weeping. And I am weeping with drowsiness, and the taste of hot pepper, and what seem to be dreams.

The moon is full, my swimmer in white sheets. Get up and take a look and drink tea with me. Or didn't you people in Ain al-Zaitoun get up when the moon was full?

But you're not from Ain al-Zaitoun. Well, you are from Ain al-Zaitoun but your blind father moved to Deir al-Asad after the village was massacred in 1948.

You were born in Ain al-Zaitoun, and they called you Yunes. You told me that your blind father named you Yunes – Jonah – because, like Jonah, you'd beaten death.

You never told me about your mother; it was Amna who told me. She claimed to be your cousin on your father's side, and had come to help you set the house straight. She was also beautiful. Why did you get angry with me that day? I swear I didn't mean anything by it. I smiled – and you glowered, rushed out of the house and left me with her.

You came in and saw me sitting with Amna, who was giving me some water. She told me she knew everything about me because you had told her, and she asked me to watch out for you because she couldn't always come from Ain al-Hilweh to Shatila. I smiled at you and winked, and from that day on I never saw Amna at your house again. I swear I didn't mean anything. Well, I did mean something, but when all's said and done you're a man, so you shouldn't get angry. People are like that, they've been that way since Adam, God grant him peace, and people betray the ones they love; they betray them and they regret it; they betray them, because they love them, so what's the problem?

It's a terrible thing. Why did you tell Amna to stop visiting you? Was it because she loved you? I know – when I see a woman in love, I know. She overflows with love and becomes soft and undulating. Not men. Men are to be pitied because they don't know that softness that floods and leavens the muscles.

Amna loved you, but you refused to marry her. She told me about it, just as she told me other things she made me swear I'd never mention in front of you. I'm released from my oath now because you can't hear, and even if you could there'd be nothing you could do. All you would say is that Amna was a liar, and the debate would be closed.

Amna told me your whole story.

She told me about your father.

She said that Sheikh Ibrahim, son of Salem, son of Suleiman al-Asadi, was in his forties when he married, and that for twenty years his wife kept giving birth to children who would die a few days later because she was stricken with a nameless disease. Her nipples would get inflamed and collapse when the children started to nurse, and they'd die of hunger. Then you were born. You alone, Amna told me, were able to bite on a breast without a nipple. You would bite and suck, and your mother would scream in pain. So you were saved from death.

I didn't believe Amna because the story seems impossible. Why didn't your mother get medicine for her breasts? And why did the children die? Why didn't your father take the children to the women of the village to nurse?

I didn't believe Amna, but you confirmed what she said, which made me doubt it even more. You said that you were the only one to survive because you managed to grip a nippleless breast, and that your mother never failed to remind you of the pain she suffered. And when I asked you why your father didn't marry another woman, you put up your hand as though you didn't want me to raise that question – because your people, you told me, "marry only one woman only once, and that's the way it's been from the beginning."

I imagined a savage child with a big head and eager lips gobbling the breasts of a woman in tears.

Then you told me that the problem wasn't the absence of nipples. Your brothers and sisters died because they had a mysterious disease, which was transferred to them from their mother's inflamed breasts.

I see you now, I see that child, and I see its big head – its face within a flood of light. I see your mother writhing in pain and pleasure as she feels your lips grabbing at the milk. I can almost hear her sighs and see the pleasure fermenting in her drowsy, heavy eyes. I see you, I see your death, and I see the end.

Don't tell me you're going to die, please don't. Not death. Umm Hassan told me not to be afraid, and I'm not. She asked me to stay with you because no one would dare to break into the hospital to find me – even Umm Hassan believed I've turned your death into a hiding place for myself. Even Umm Hassan didn't understand that it's your death I'm trying to prevent, not my own. I'm not afraid of them, and, anyway, what do I have to do with Shams' death? Plus it's not right that that story should get in the way of yours, which is mythic.

I know you'll say, "Phooey to myths!" and I agree, but I beg you, don't die. For my sake, for your sake, so that they don't find me.

I'm lost. I'm lost and I'm afraid and I'm in despair and I'm wavering and I'm fidgety and I've remembered and I've forgotten.

I spend most of my time in your room. I finish my work at the hospital, and I come back to you. I sit at your side, I bathe you, massage you, put scent on you, sprinkle powder on you, and rub your body with ointment. I cover you and make sure you're asleep, and I talk to you. People think I'm talking to myself, like a madman. With you I've discovered many selves within myself, selves with whom I can maintain an eternal dialogue.

The thing is, I read in a book whose title I no longer remember that people in comas can have their consciousness restored by being talked to. Dr. Amjad said this was impossible. I know that what I read isn't scientific, but I'm trying, I'm trying to rouse you with words, so why won't you answer me? Just one word would be enough.

You're either incapable of speaking, or you don't want to, or you don't know how.

Which means you have to listen. I know you're sick of my stories, so I'm going to tell you your own. I'll return to you what you've given me. I'll tell them, and I'll see the shadow of a smile on your closed lips.

Do you hear my voice?

Do you see my words as shadows?

I'm tired of talking, too. I stop, and then the words come. They come like sweat oozing from my pores, and rather than hearing my voice, I hear yours coming out of my throat.

I sit next to you in silence. I listen to the rasp of your breathing, and I feel the tremor of tears, but I don't weep. I say, "That's it, I won't come back. What am I doing here? Nothing."

I sit with death and keep it company. It's difficult keeping death company, Father. You yourself told me about the three corpses in the olive grove. Please don't forget – you're a runaway, and a runaway doesn't forget. Do you remember what happened when you got to Ain al-Hilweh after you were released from prison? Do you remember how you fired your gun into the air and insulted everyone and they arrested you? When they'd set up tents that the wind blew through from both sides, you said to them, "We're not refugees. We're fugitives and nothing more. We fight and kill and are killed. But we're not refugees." You told the people that *refugee* meant something specific, and that the road to the villages of Galilee was open. Bearded and filthy. That's what the police report from Sidon says; you were carrying your rifle and muttering like a madman. The Lebanese officer wrote in his report that you were crazy and let you go. You listened in disbelief, but he bit his lip and winked before ordering you out of the police post. That day you screamed that you'd never leave jail without your rifle, so they forced you out. And you forced your way back in at night and got your rifle back, along with three other rifles from the guard post. With those rifles you began.

I don't want the beginning now. I want to tell you that fugitives never sleep. You told me how you used to sleep with one eye closed and the other one open for danger.

Where's your open eye so that you can see me?

I went over to you, opened your eyes and saw the whites. God, how white they were! I know you saw me searching for you because in those whites I could see all your shadows. Didn't you tell me about a man walking with his shadows on those distant roads? In your eyes I see the image of a man who neither lives nor dies.

Why don't you die?

No, please don't die! What will I do after you die? Remain hiding in the hospital? Leave the country?

Please, no! Death scares me.

Have you forgotten the olive grove, and that woman, and the three men?

You told me that the woman scared you. "All those wars, and I was never scared. But that woman, my God! She made my knees go weak and my face twitch. A woman sleeping beneath an olive tree. I went up to her. Her long hair covered her. I bent over, moved the hair aside and found that the woman was rigid with death, and her hair concealed a small child that slept curled up on top of her. That was the first time I saw death. I pulled back and lit a cigarette and sat in the sun, and there, behind a rock, I saw three other bodies."

You were with them and had no way of escaping, because that day the Israeli machine guns were cutting down anyone who slipped over, which is what they must have done and what you were returning from doing. You told me that you lived on olives for a week. You'd break them with sticks, steep them in water and eat their bitterness. "Olives aren't really bitter – their bitterness coats your mouth and tongue and you have to drink water after each one."

You couldn't dig a grave. You dug with your hands because you'd left your rifle buried in a cave three hours away from Deir al-Asad. You dug, but you couldn't make a grave that would hold the four of them. You dug a little grave for the child but then had second thoughts: Was it right to separate it from its mother? In the end you didn't bury any of them; you broke off olive branches, covered the bodies and decided to come back later with a pickaxe to dig them a grave. You covered them with olive branches and continued on your way to Lebanon. And all the many times you went back to Deir al-Asad, you never found a trace of them.

I'm with you now, and it's night. The electricity's off, the candle trembles with your shadows, and you don't open your eyes.

Open your eyes and tell me, have you forgotten my name? I'm Dr. Khalil. You told me I was just like your first son, Ibrahim, who died. Think of me as your son who didn't die. Why don't you open one eye and look at me? You're sick, Father. I'm going to call you *father*. I'm not going to call you by your name anymore.

What is your name?

In the camp they call you Abu Salem, in Ain al-Zaitoun: Abu Ibrahim, on long-distance missions: Abu Saleh, in Bab al-Shams: Yunes, in Deir al-Asad: *the man*, and in the Western Sector: Izz al-Din. Your names are many, and I don't know what to call you.

The first time we met, you were called Abu Salem, though I'm not sure of this, because I don't remember the first time, and you don't either. "Remember," you said to me, "you were alone in the boys' camp." My mother had gone to Jordan and left me with my grandmother. I was nine years old. I remember that she'd left me a piece of white paper on which she'd scrawled things I couldn't read; my mother didn't know how to read or write. I remember her dimly now. I remember a frightened woman hugging me, looking suspiciously at everyone, saying that they were going to kill us like they killed my father. I was afraid of her eyes; they had something deep in them that I couldn't look at. Fear, Father, sleeps in the eyes, and in the eyes of the woman who was my mother I saw a cold fear that I couldn't shed until I looked into the eyes of Shams.

I know you'll laugh and say I didn't love Shams and ask me to call you Abu Salem, because Salem – He who was saved – was saved from death, and we're not allowed to die.

You used to call Nahilah Umm Salem – Mother of Salem – telling her, in the cave or beneath the olive tree, that she should use the name of her second son, who had become her first.

To tell you the truth, I don't know the truth anymore. You never actually told me your story – it came out like this, in snatches. I wanted you to tell me the whole thing, but I didn't dare ask you to. No, didn't dare isn't accurate. It would be better to say that I didn't feel capable of asking you, or couldn't find an opportunity, or didn't realize the importance of the story.

The moon is full, Father.

I call you my father, but you're not my father. You said your hope was that Salem would become a doctor, but the circumstances – military rule, the curfew, poverty – didn't allow him to complete his studies and he became a mechanic. Now he's got a garage in Deir al-Asad and he speaks Hebrew and English.

You said to me, "Doctor, you're like a son to me. I picked you out when you were nine and I loved you, and I asked them at the boys' camp if I could take care of you, and you became my son. You've lost your parents, and I've lost my children. Come and be a son to me."

You took to referring to me as "my son, Dr. Khalil," though I'm not a doctor, as you know. Three months of training in China doesn't make you a doctor. You appointed me doctor to the camp and asked me to change my name the way the fedayeen do. But I didn't change my name, and the fedayeen left on Greek ships, and the only ones left here were you and me. The war ended, and I was no longer a doctor. In fact Dr. Amjad, the director of the hospital, asked me to work as a nurse. How could anybody accept that, going from doctor to nurse? I said no, but you came to my house, rebuked me, and asked me to report to the hospital immediately.

When you spoke, you'd open your eyes as wide as eyes can go. The words would come out of your eyes, and your voice would rise and I'd say nothing. I'd steal glances at your eyes, opened to the furthest limits of the earth.

In the office at the boys' camp, you'd stand spinning and spinning the globe and then would order it to stop. When the little ball stopped turning, you'd extend a finger and say, "That's Acre. Here's Tyre. The plain runs to here, and these are the villages of the Acre District. Here's Ain al-Zaitoun, and Deir al-Asad, and al-Birwa, and there's al-Ghabsiyyeh, and al-Kabri, and here's Tarshiha, and there's Bab al-Shams. We, kids, are from Ain al-Zaitoun. Ain al-Zaitoun is a little place, and the mountain surrounds it and protects it. Ain al-Zaitoun is the most beautiful village, but they destroyed it in '48. They bulldozed it after blowing up the houses, so we left it for Deir al-Asad. But me, I founded a village in a place no one knows, a village in the rocks where the sun enters and sleeps."

Dr. Amjad said he wasn't sure. The doctor said, and I say too, that you hear sounds but don't know what they are. Do the sounds enter your consciousness, or do they simply remain sounds?

The doctor said you don't see, and I didn't ask him what that means. Does it mean that you're in blackness, and is the blackness a color? Or do you exist in an absence of color? What does "absence of color" mean? Do you see that frightening blend of white and black that we call gray? If you don't see colors, that means you're not in blackness but in a place we don't know. Aren't you afraid of what you don't know?

You said you didn't fear death and that you knew fear only once, when you were living with the dead in the olive grove. You said that men die from fear, that fear is what is down below.

Are you "down below"? What do you see?

"It's a matter of arithmetic," you told me. "We are afraid because we live in illusion, since life is a long dream. People fear death, but they really should be frightened of what goes on before being born. Before they were born, they were in eternal darkness. But it's an illusion. The illusion makes us think that the living inherit the lives of all others. That's why history was invented. I'm not an intellectual, but I know that history is a trick to make people believe that we've been alive since the beginning and that we're the heirs of the dead. An illusion. People aren't heirs, and they don't have a history or anything of the sort. Life is a passage between two deaths. I'm not afraid of the second death because I wasn't afraid of the first."

"But history isn't an illusion," I answered. "And if it were, what would it be for?"

"What would what be for?"

"Why would we fight and die? Doesn't Palestine deserve our deaths? You're the one who taught me history, and now you tell me history is a ruse to evade death!"

That day, you laughed at me and told me that your father, the blind sheikh, used to talk that way, and "we ought to learn from our elders." I don't know if this discussion took place on a single occasion because we never had discussions; we'd just talk, and you wouldn't finish your sentences but would jump from one word to another without paying attention to cause and effect. But you laughed. When you laughed, it was like you were exploding from within yourself. Your laughter used to surprise me because I was convinced that heroes didn't laugh. I used to look at the photos of the martyrs hanging on the walls in the camp, and they weren't laughing. Their faces were frowning and closed, as though they held death prisoner within themselves.

But not you.

You were a hero, and you laughed at heroes. And the little creases that extend from the corners of your eyes created a space for smiles and laughter. You were a laughing hero – but all the same I wasn't convinced by your theories, or your father's, about death and history.

You answered me by saying that what was worth dying for was what we wanted to live for.

"Palestine isn't a cause. Well, all right, in some sense it is, but it isn't really, because the land doesn't move from its place. That land will remain, and the question isn't who will hold it, because it's an illusion to think that land can be held. No one can hold land when he's going to end up buried in it. It's the land that holds men and pulls them back toward it. I didn't fight, my dear friend, for the land or for history. I fought for the sake of a woman I loved."

I can't recall your exact words now. They were simple, transparent, and fluid. You speak as though you aren't speaking, and I speak as though I am. But I remember what you said about smells. We were sitting in front of the hospital drinking tea, it was the time of false spring. That year, spring arrived in February. The sun broke through the winter and tricked the earth, and yellow, white, and blue flowers emerged shyly from the rubble. That day you taught me how to smell nature. Putting your glass of tea aside, you stood up and filled your lungs with air and the aroma, holding it in your chest until your face started to turn red. When you sat down again and took a sip of tea and talked about the thyme and the jasmine and the columbine and the wildflowers, you said she was like the seasons. With each season she would come to your cave with a new smell. She would let down her long black hair, and the scents of flowers and herbs would fill the air. You said you were always enchanted by the new smells, as though she'd become a different woman.

"A woman, Son, is always new. Her smell reveals her. A woman is the aroma of the world, and when I was with her I learned to fill my lungs with the smell of the land."

That was when I understood what you'd told me about her death: Nahilah hadn't died, because her smell was still in you. But Umm Hassan has died. Don't you want to come with me to her funeral? Everyone is gathering at her house, except for her son, Naji, who's in America, as you know. I have to go. I want to carry Umm Hassan's bier, and I will fear no one.

Please get up. We'll go to Umm Hassan's funeral, and then you can go back to your children and die with them. Go, die with them, as Umm Hassan suggested, and set me free.

Do you remember Umm Hassan?

Umm Hassan was my professor of medicine. I was in the hospital when a pregnant woman was brought in; I'd never seen a woman give birth before. In China they had taught me how to bandage wounds and do simple operations, what was called "field medicine." But they didn't teach me real medicine.

The woman was writhing in front of me, and I could do nothing. Then I remembered Umm Hassan, and I sent for her, and she came. She managed the delivery and taught me everything. As she helped the woman, she explained everything to me like a doctor training a student. From then on I knew what to do, and I became sure enough of myself to deliver babies. But she deserves all the credit. Umm Hassan was the only certified midwife in al-Kweikat; she had British documents to prove it.

I can see her now.

She's putting the basin she was carrying on her head and bending over to pick up babies in the olive grove. In reality, she only picked up Naji, who became her son. I told you the story, remember? They were traveling inside Palestine because, having been driven out of al-Kweikat, they got lost in the fields and stopped on the edges of Deir al-Asad, and then they were driven from there, so they went to Tarshiha, which the Israeli planes came and burned, so they found themselves on the road to southern Lebanon, where Qana was their first stop. And on that road, a woman named Sara al-Khatib gave birth to a child with Umm Hassan at her side. Everyone was running, carrying their bundles on their heads, and Sara threw herself down under a tree writhing in pain. Umm Hassan washed the baby with hot water, wrapped him in old clothes and gave him to his mother.

Everyone walked on that "last journey," as the people of the villages of Galilee referred to their collective exodus to Lebanon. But it wasn't their last journey. In fact it was the start of wanderings in the wilderness whose end only God knows.

On that last journey, as Umm Hassan was walking with her basin on her head and her four children, her husband, her brothers, and their wives and children around her, she saw a bundle of old clothes discarded under an olive tree, and she realized they were the same clothes she'd used to wrap Sara's baby in. She bent down, picked up the child, put him in the basin, and named him Naji – Rescued. She offered him her dry breasts, then fed him sesame paste mixed with water. At the village of Qana, where they stopped for the first time, the boy's mother came, weeping and asking for her child back. Umm Hassan refused, but in the end, when she saw the milk bursting from the mother's breasts and spotting her dress, she gave him to her.

Umm Hassan said she'd named him Naji and his mother didn't have the right to change his name. Sara agreed, took the boy, offered him her breast, and went away.

"Naji's my only surviving child," said Umm Hassan. "He writes to me from America, God bless him. He's become a professor at the best university, he sends me letters and money, and I send him olive oil."

I see her walking and picking up babies and putting them in the basin on her head. It's as though she had picked me up, as though I were Naji, as though the taste of the sesame mixed with water still lingered in my mouth, as though – I don't know. I swear I don't know. Umm Hassan died this morning, and we have to bury her before the noon prayer, and you are sleeping as if oblivious to what Umm Hassan's death means for me, and for you, and for everyone in the camp.

Umm Hassan told me everything about Palestine. I asked her before she set off to visit her brother in al-Kweikat, or what's left of it, to pass by al-Ghabsiyyeh and tie a strip of cloth to a branch of the lotus tree near the mosque for me. I told her that my father had made an oath to do this and that he'd died before he could carry it out, but he'd passed it on to my mother, and my mother had passed it on to me before going to her people in Amman. I haven't been, and I didn't dare to ask you to do it. I was afraid you'd make fun of me and of my father's superstitions. I asked Umm Hassan to say a short prayer in the mosque and hang the piece of black cloth on the tree and light a candle for me.

When she returned, she gave me a branch heavy with oranges and told me she'd gone to the mosque to pray.

"Is a mosque defiled if they put animals in it?"

Umm Hassan didn't ask herself that question. She went into the mosque at al-Ghabsiyyeh, which had been taken over by cows, drove them out, performed her ablutions, and prayed. Then she went out to the lotus tree, hung a black ribbon on it, and lit two candles.

She said the tree was covered with pieces of cloth.

"I don't understand, Son. Your village is deserted. The roads have disappeared, and the houses aren't demolished but are collapsing and almost in ruins. I don't know why houses go like that when their people abandon them. An abandoned house is like an abandoned woman; it hunches over itself as though it were falling down. There's no sign of life in your village, except for the strips of cloth tied around the branches of the lotus tree and the melted candles spread around all the way to the mosque."

Umm Hassan said she'd been afraid of the tree when they told her about my uncle, Sheikh Aziz Yunes, and how he was found dead beneath it. But when she got close to it, she felt awe, and she knelt and wept and lit the candles.

She said she heard the rustling of the branches, full of the souls of the dead. "The souls of the dead live in trees," she said. "We have to return and shake the trees so that the souls fall and find peace in their graves."

I was about to cut an orange from the branch so that I could taste Palestine, but Umm Hassan yelled, "No! It's not for eating, it's Palestine." I was ashamed of myself and hung the branch on the wall of the living room in my house, and when you came to visit me and saw the moldy branch, you yelled, "What's that smell?" And I told you the story and watched you explode in anger.

"You should have eaten the oranges," you told me.

"But Umm Hassan stopped me and said they were from the homeland."

"Umm Hassan's senile," you answered. "You should have eaten the oranges, because the homeland is something we have to consume, not let consume us. We have to devour the oranges of Palestine and we have to devour Palestine and Galilee."

It came to me then that you were right, but the oranges were going bad. You went to the wall and pulled off the branch, and I took it from your hand and stood there confused, not knowing what to do with the decayed offering.

"What are you going to do with it?" you asked.

"Bury it."

"Why bury it?"

"I'm not going to throw it away, because it's from the homeland."

You took the branch out of my hand and threw it in the trash.

"Outrageous!" you said. "What are these old women's superstitions? Before hanging a scrap of the homeland up on the wall, it'd be better to knock the wall down and leave. We have to eat every last orange in the world and not be afraid, because the homeland isn't oranges. The homeland is us."

UMM HASSAN is waiting. Won't you come with me? I'm in a hurry now, so I won't tell you what she did in al-Kweikat.

Get up, my friend. God, you're impossible. The woman's dead, and everyone's at her house. I can hear them weeping through the hospital walls, and you hear nothing.

You're not coming? Okay, I'll go on my own. But tell me, why do you look like that – like a little baby swathed in white? For the last three months I've been watching you shrink. My God, if you could see yourself before you die. It's a shame you don't know what's going on, a shame you can't see how a man doesn't die but goes back to where he came from. I used to think the poets were lying when they said that a man returns to his mother's womb. But now I swear they weren't: A man becomes an infant again before he dies. Only infants die; all death is the death of infants – infants searching for their mothers' wombs, curling up like fetuses. And here you are, turning back into an infant, curling up on yourself, blind. If only you could see yourself.

I can't hear you properly. Why are you mumbling? Why are you moving your left hand? You want me to tell you about Nahilah? You already know the story, and no, I won't tell it again. Do you think of yourself as the hero in a love story? Why have you forgotten your other heroic roles? Or maybe they weren't so heroic. You told me, "Everyone thinks that the fighters are heroes, but that's not true. People fight the way they breathe or eat or go to the john. War is nothing special. All you need to be a fighter is to fight. Being a hero is something else; heroism doesn't exist, and even courage isn't anything special. A brave man can turn into a coward, and a coward can turn into a brave man. The important thing is – " You left it there.

I didn't ask what the important thing was. I knew what your reply would be, and I didn't want to hear it again. And now you want me to tell you some stories? No, I won't tell stories, not today. Today I'm busy. Have pity on me; get up and release me, please release me. I'm tired.

I'm tired of everything. I'm tired of your sickness and of how sad you look, I'm tired of the baby's round face suspended above your neck, I'm tired of praying for you.

Did you know that I pray?

My grandmother used to say that praying means laying down words like a carpet on the ground. I lay down my words so that you can walk on them.

Why don't you get up?

ONCE UPON a time there was a baby.

No, you don't like the story about Naji. You told me Naji was a dog because after everything Umm Hassan had done for him, he went off to America and left her poor and abandoned.

I see a frown on your face and black spots in your closed eyes. Okay, we won't start the story with Umm Hassan or Naji or America. I'll tell you another one.

Back to the beginning.

Do you remember when you used to say, "Back to the beginning!" and would stamp your foot? Do you remember what you did after Abdel Nasser resigned in '67? People gathered in the alleyways of the camp and wept; it was night, and humid, and they were like ghosts weeping in the darkness. You stood in their midst, spat on the ground, and said, "Back to the beginning!"

And after 1970, when you'd returned safely to the camp from the slaughter in the forests of Jerash and Ajloun,* you said to the woman who came to ask about her son, "Back to the beginning!" and left.

And after the Israelis went into Beirut, after each new thing that happened, you'd spit as though you were wiping out the past, and you'd say, "Back to the beginning!"

So, you want the beginning.

In the beginning, they didn't say "Once upon a time," they said something else. In the beginning they said, "Once upon a time, there was – or

---

* Liquidation by Jordanian forces of Palestinian troops based in Jordan.

there wasn't." Do you know why they said that? When I first read this expression in a book about ancient Arabic literature, it took me by surprise. Because, in the beginning, they didn't lie. They didn't know anything, but they didn't lie. They left things vague, preferring to use that *or* which makes things that were as though they weren't, and things that weren't as though they were. That way the story is put on the same footing as life, because a story is a life that didn't happen, and a life is a story that didn't get told.

Do you like this story?

It isn't real, you'll say, but I don't know any real stories, because my mother left me and went away before she could finish it. And the stories I know myself, you know, too.

Your eyes are alight with memories, and they're asking for the story's beginning.

The beginning of the story says that you were like a dead man, and there was no hope of reviving you. Dr. Amjad told me, "There's no hope" – but I wasn't convinced, and decided to try to treat you by talking to you.

Once upon a time, a long time ago, there was – or there wasn't – a young man called Yunes.

No. I have to start from the place you don't know, meaning from here, from the end, because the story can only start from its ending. I don't want it to be for you the way it was for me: I never knew the ends of stories because I would fall asleep before my mother got to them. You, however, are going to know the story starting with the ending.

The ending says that it was nine in the evening. I was sitting on the balcony of my house in the heat and humidity of August drinking a glass of arak. There's nothing like arak in the summer because it makes you burn hotter than the night. Each evening, I would nurse my sorrow and fear with arak. I was drinking on the balcony and eating a salted tomato and pistachios when I heard a violent banging on the door. Opening it, I found Amna, her face emerging from the shadows. All I could understand of what she said was that you were in the hospital. I thought you'd died, God forbid. Amna told me how you'd fainted and fallen to the ground like a piece of wood. I listened, waiting for her to say you'd died. I wasn't sad. I felt a space emptying in my heart, but I wasn't upset. I asked where you were. I tried to get through the door to go to you, but Amna wouldn't let me by. She stood rooted to the spot and talked. I tried to get out, but she blocked the door with her hand.

She said it had started the previous night, when you'd lost the ability to speak. She'd gone to visit you, and found you wandering around the place, muttering. She'd asked you what was wrong and you'd answered, but your tongue couldn't form the words.

"That's when I realized," Amna said. She ran to the hospital and told them, but nobody came. The nurse said she would send someone to look for Dr. Amjad, but Dr. Amjad didn't come.

"I stayed with him the whole night. Do you know what that means? He was wandering around his house and wouldn't settle down. He would raise his left hand and speak at the top of his lungs but you couldn't understand a word. I tried to calm him down. I sat him down and gave him a glass of aniseed tea. I led him to his bedroom, but when he saw the bed he went into a frenzy, and I ran in circles after him. He opened the front door and tried to leave. Look at my shoulder, my body's covered in bruises. No, he didn't hit me, but he was as strong as a bull, and I was running around after him in tears."

"Okay, okay, Amna," I said, and I tried to get past her so I could go to the hospital, but she blocked the way with her hand.

She said she'd been alone with you and that you'd scared her. She'd knelt down in front of you and beat her chest with her fist. She said you calmed down when you saw her kneeling. You looked at her as though you didn't understand, then fell to the ground.

At that point, I slipped between her hand and the door and went out.

Amna followed me, panting and talking, but I didn't listen. And at the hospital door, she said that doctors were bastards and that I was a doctor too and had no pity in my heart and that she'd waited for them to come, alone with you, until evening.

I went into the hospital and ran to the nurses' room so I could put on my white gown and go to you. Amna ran after me and said God would never forgive us. Then she disappeared.

You're upset with Amna because she doesn't come to visit you. Don't be angry with her. She doesn't know that you can hear and feel and are sad. She was convinced you'd died, so why should she come?

Who is Amna Abd al-Rahman really?

Is she a cousin of yours, as you told me? Were you in love with her? Why didn't you talk about her?

The fact is, my friend, you should tell me something about your women. You're a man surrounded by women, and there's something strange in your round pale face that inspires love; it's the face of a man who is loved. You always described yourself as a lover, but I think you hid your lovers. You only spoke about one woman, and even that one you only would talk about a little. Piecing the glimpses together, I turned it into a story. But you mentioned love only in passing. You jumped over the essential story as though it were a pool in which you might drown. Once I plucked up my courage and asked you where you made love with Nahilah. I didn't say her name, I just said "her," and you smiled. You were in a good mood that day. Your eyes shone, you raised your right hand in a vague gesture and said, "There. Among the rocks," and fell silent. It fell to me to collect your asides and mutterings and work them into a story to tell you.

Now you can't shut me up. I can say whatever I want and tell you that it's your story. My goal isn't to make one up. I'm only half a doctor awaiting death at the vengeful hands of Shams' family.

I promised I'd start with the ending, and the end will come when you've left this coffin of a bed. You'll get up, tall and broad shouldered, walking stick in hand, and you'll return to your country. You will go first to the cave of Bab al-Shams. You won't go to Nahilah's grave, as everyone expects. You'll go to Bab al-Shams, enter your village of caves, and disappear.

This is the only dignified ending to your story, which you'll never betray.

I know what you'll say and how you'll roll the word *betray* around in your mouth, before announcing that you had no choice. Your life was a series of betrayals. You'll say that in order for us not to betray, we have to change – that is, to betray.

You'll tell me how the adolescent you were during the sacred jihad alongside Abd al-Qadir,* God rest his soul, was related to the young man you became in the Arab Commando Brigades, and then in the Arab Nationalist Movement.

You'll say that the man you became in the Lebanon Regional Command of the Fatah Movement was a continuation of that same young man, but different from him in every way. You'll speak to me of the older man you became, the one dreaming of a new betrayal, because one has to begin somewhere.

Where were we?

Did you know that all this sitting in your room has made me incapable of concentrating? I jump from story to story, I lose the thread and forget where I began.

I was telling you about Amna. No, but Amna wasn't the point. I was telling you how they brought you to the hospital half-dead. We carried you into your room and put you on the bed. Your eyes were closed, and you were shivering with fever. They slipped an IV into your right hand, tying it first to the edge of the bed so the needle wouldn't rip the artery, you were shaking and twitching so much.

I stood there not knowing what to do. Alone in the room, I was listening to the nurses' voices in the corridor, taking in the smell. That was the first time I had really taken in the smell of Galilee Hospital. Why don't they clean the place? And why hadn't I noticed the smell before that day? I came to the hospital every day – it's true that I didn't really work, refusing the demotion from doctor to nurse – but I'd never smelled that horrible smell before. Tomorrow, I'll clean everything.

But the next day I didn't clean everything, and another day passed, and

---

* Abd al-Qadir Husseini, major figure in the Palestinian National Movement, died in combat in 1948.

after it another without my taking action. It seems I've gotten used to it. The smell is not a problem. Smells work their way into us, we absorb them, which is why they only exist at the beginning.

Let's return to the beginning.

I left your room in search of Dr. Amjad and found him sitting in his clinic, smoking, sipping his coffee, and reading the newspaper.

He invited me to sit down, but I remained standing.

"Please sit down. What's the matter with you?" he asked.

I asked him hesitantly about you.

"Blood clot on the brain."

"Treatment?"

"'No hope for a stroke,'" he recited.

"I can't believe it."

"It's in God's hands," he said. "Leave it, Dr. Khalil. It's over. I wouldn't give him more than seventy-two hours."

"What about a blood thinner? Didn't you give him a blood thinner?"

"There's no point. We did a scan on him and found that the hemorrhage has spread to more than half the brain, which means it's over."

"And the fever?"

I asked as though I didn't know, even though I did. It's amazing how one can become ignorant. Standing in front of Dr. Amjad, I forgot all my medical training and found myself behaving like an imbecile, as though I knew nothing.

I stood there asking and asking, and he answered me tersely, impatient with my questions, as though I were keeping him from something important.

Dr. Amjad explained that you would die within three days and asked me to contact your relatives about arrangements for the funeral, but instead of trying to get hold of Amna I returned to your room and began my work.

You have brought me back to the medicine that I hated and had forgotten. Don't be afraid of the fever. My opinion is that the clot occurred somewhere near the area of the fever in the brain, and the pressure is interfering with your body temperature, which means that the fever will disappear once the blood is drawn off.

Don't be afraid.

I disagreed with Dr. Amjad when he said that the shivering was your death tremor. You were shivering with fever, and the fever would go. As you see, I was right. But do you remember what Nurse Zainab did? She started massaging your chest. When I asked what she was doing, she said that she was helping your soul escape from your body.

"Don't you see how his soul is shaking?" she asked.

"That's fever, you idiot," I shouted, and chased her out of the room, locked the door and sat down, not knowing what to do.

During those first days I despaired. For three days I didn't leave your room. I changed your IV and put antibiotics in it; Dr. Amjad made fun of me, telling me that the fever had nothing to do with any inflammation.

But I wanted you to live – not because I'm a nonbeliever, as Nurse Zainab had thought – but because I don't want you to die in bed.

Do you remember what you told me when I visited to offer my condolences after Nahilah died? You received me calmly and offered me an unsweetened coffee. I asked you, as people offering condolences usually do, about the circumstances of her illness and her death, but you didn't give me any details. You said she'd died in the hospital in Nazareth. Then you started murmuring some verses by al-Mutanabbi.*

You recited the poetry as though you'd composed it yourself, and you said you'd never die here. You'd go and die over there.

"And if I die here, try to bury me over there."

"As you wish, Abu Salem," I said.

But then you looked at me strangely and said it was impossible, because you knew that your end would be a grave in the camp that would become a soccer field a few years later. You were talking about the mass grave of the

* Considered the greatest of Classical Arabic poets. (915–965)

victims of the 1982 Shatila massacre, where children now play soccer and trash is scattered all over the place. Then you went back to al-Mutanabbi's verses:

> *We make ready our swords and our spears*
> *And the Fates destroy us without a fight.*
> *We bury each other and the remains of those who came first*
> *Are trampled on by those who came later.*

That day – do you remember? – that day I suggested to you that you go to Deir al-Asad immediately and you said the time hadn't come and that you'd return when you were good and ready.

For three days I did the impossible to save you in your room. You'd open your bloodshot eyes, and I'd close them for you, because leaving them open endangers the cornea. The eye is not a mirror, it's a network of mirrors that must not be exposed to the air for too long or it's ruined. I focused all my attention on your eyes so that you wouldn't lose your sight. Because in those early days, I was certain that you would awaken from that sleep.

The strange thing is that, on the fourth day, when your temperature fell and you were lying quietly, I felt very afraid. I was certain the drop in your temperature would begin your return to consciousness. But stabilization led to lethargy. Now you never open your eyes. I've taken to opening them myself and passing my finger in front of them, but the pupils don't respond. Glaucoma has begun. The redness has been replaced by a bluish whiteness.

"He's entered a state of lethargy," said Dr. Amjad.

"What does that mean?" I asked.

"I don't know, but he'll stay like that until he dies."

"And when will he die?"

"I can't specify the hour, but he will die."

Dr. Amjad decided to substitute a feeding tube for the IV. At first I objected, but then I realized that he was right, the tube will put life back into your guts.

And I started to prepare your food for you myself. I replaced the hospital's ready-made yellow potion with bananas, milk, and honey that I mixed for you. For the last three months, you've been eating nothing else, like a baby.

Is it true that newborn infants are as happy as they look, or are they like you, opening their eyes in pain, refusing to take part in the life we're forcing on them? You've changed my thinking about being an infant. All the same, and despite the pain, I dream of having one, because a baby gives you the feeling that you'll live on through other people, that you won't die.

"That's a delusion," you'll say.

There, I agree with you, but I told Shams when I fell in love with her that I wanted nothing more than to have a child with her. A brown-skinned child that looked like her. No, it's not true that I was involved in her murder. I swear I had nothing to do with it. The problem wasn't with me but with Sameh Abu Diab. They killed her to avenge Sameh. I did nothing to hurt her. She told me she loved me and then left to kill Sameh. I loved her the way one loves, but she left and got herself killed. She killed him and then was killed, and that was that. I don't want to talk about her any more.

I'm worried about you. You've settled into death, it's as though you've turned your temporary coma into a permanent state.

Would you like to know what happened to me after you settled into this state of withdrawal?

To begin with, I was overwhelmed by a criminal impulse. I was obsessed with only one thought: of placing a pillow over your face and pressing down until you died of asphyxiation – that I should just kill you, cold-bloodedly and calmly. I felt real hatred for you. I pretended that I hated the world for what it had done to you, but that wasn't true. I didn't hate the world, or Fate, or God, I hated you – Yunes, Abu Salem, Izz al-Din, or whatever name fits you best as you lie here in this bed.

No, it's got nothing to do with wanting to murder my father, as the psychologists would claim. You're not my father. I already killed him long ago – and his image – after they killed him in front of our house. And I lived with my grandmother, who slept on her amazing pillow. I promised you I'd bring you the pillow, but I forgot. I'll bring it tomorrow. My grandmother's pillow doesn't look like a pillow anymore. It's turned into a heap of thorns. The flowers inside have faded and dried into thorns. My grandmother used to stuff her pillow with flowers, saying that when she rested her head on it she felt as though she'd returned to her village, and she'd make me rest my head on it. I would lay my head on her pillow and smell nothing but decay. I joined the fedayeen when I was nine years old to escape the flowers of al-Ghabsiyyeh that my grandmother would pick from the camp's dump. I hated the perfume of decay and ended up connecting the smell of Palestine with the smell of that pillow. I was convinced then – I still am – that my grandmother was afflicted with floral dementia, a widespread condition among Palestinian peasants who were driven from their villages.

The day her long final illness came, she summoned me to her side. I was in the village of Kafar Shouba in southern Lebanon, where the fedayeen had set up their first camp, when my uncle came and asked me to go to Beirut. In her house in the camp, the woman was dying on her pillow. When she saw me, her face lit up with a pale smile, and she gestured to the others to leave us alone. When everyone was gone, she asked me to sit down next to her on the bed. She whispered that she didn't own anything she could leave me but this – and she pointed to her pillow – and this – and she pointed to her watch – and this – and she pointed to her Koran.

She squeezed my hand tightly, as if holding onto life itself. She told me she missed my father. Then she closed her eyes and her breathing became irregular. I tried to pull my hand away, but I couldn't, so I yelled and the women came in and started weeping. She didn't die, however. I stayed for three days waiting for it to happen, then went back to Kafar Shouba. Two weeks later, I returned to Beirut for her funeral.

I don't know where I put the watch, the women in the camp decided to bury the Koran with her, but I still have the pillow. I thought of it because I was going to kill you with a pillow. Tomorrow I'll bring it to you before I throw it away; I must get rid of that pillow of flowers that reeks of decay. The strange thing is that no one who comes to my house notices the smell.

Even Shams didn't smell it. I'm the only one who can smell that secret odor that nauseates me.

I wanted to kill you with the pillow because I hated your incredible insistence on clinging to life, but I hesitated and became afraid, and that was the end of it.

Tomorrow I'll bring you my grandmother's pillow and open it so I can see what's inside. My grandmother used to change the flowers at the beginning of each season, and I think she expected me to continue the tradition. I want to open the pillow to see what happened to the flowers. Why does a person turn to dust when he dies, while an object decomposes and yet remains an object? Strange. Didn't God create us all from dust?

Tomorrow I'll open the pillow and let you know.

I wanted to suffocate you and then the desire faded. It was a passing feeling and never recurred, but I did feel it. How can I describe it? It was as though there were another person inside me who leapt out and made me capable of destroying everything. Whenever I became aware of that other person, I'd run out of your room and roam around the hospital. This would calm me down. Now I'm calm. Feeling that things around you and me are moving slowly, I've decided to kill some time by talking. Have you heard that terrifying expression "to kill time"? It's time that kills us, but we pretend it's the other way around!

So as to kill time and stop it from killing me, I've decided to examine you again.

At the beginning, that is, after you'd settled into your lethargy and the fever had left you, you smelled odd. I can't explain what I mean, because smells are the hardest things to describe. I'll just say it was the smell of an older man. It seems there are hormones that set different ages apart from one another. The smell of older men differs fundamentally from the smell of men in their prime, and especially from that of thirteen-year-old boys who start to give off a smell of maleness and sex. The smell of older men is different, quiet and pale. Like my grandmother's pillow, it's a disturbing scent. No, I wouldn't say it disgusted me – God forbid. But I was disturbed, and I decided I ought to bathe you twice a day – but the smell was stronger than the soap. Then the smell started to go away, and a new one took its place. No, I don't say this because I've become accustomed to your smell. It's a medical matter and has clearly to do with hormones. And I believe that – I don't know how – you've started a new life phase that I can't yet define but that I can discern through your smell.

And because one thing leads to another, as the Arabs say, I want to tell you that you're wrong, your theories about age and youth are a hundred percent erroneous. I remember I met you one rainy February morning when you were out jogging. I stopped you and told you that jogging after sixty was bad for the heart and lungs and that you should practice a lighter form of exercise, like walking, to lose weight and keep your arteries open. I told you older men should do older men's sports.

That day you invited me to have coffee at your house and subjected me to a long lecture on aging. "Listen, Son. My father was an old man – I knew him only as an old man. Do you know why? Because he was blind. A person will grow old at forty, not sixty, if he loses the two things that can't be replaced: his sight and his teeth. Being old means having your sight go and your teeth fall out. At forty, gray hair invades your head, your teeth start to rot, and your vision becomes dim, so you look like an old man. But inside you're still young; your age consists of how other people see you, it comes from your children. Yes, it's true: In addition to eyes and teeth, there are the children. We peasants marry early. I got married at fourteen, so just think how old my children and grandchildren were when I was forty. There's no such thing as being old these days, for two reasons. The first is the invention of glasses, so weak eyesight is no longer an issue, and the second is dentistry, so people don't have to have all their teeth out by the time they're seventy or eighty. Here I am today, with all my own teeth and glasses that let me read, so how can you call me an old man? Old age is an illusion. People get old from the inside, not the outside. So long as there's passion in your heart, it means you're not an old man."

On that occasion I meant to ask when you'd last seen her, but I felt shy.

I stood up and started looking at the pictures on the wall. Seven sons, three daughters, and fifteen grandchildren, and in the middle the photo of Ibrahim, who'd died as a baby. Twenty-five people, the first fruits of the adventure you forged.

You told me about Ghassan Kanafani.*

You told me he came to you with a letter of introduction from Dr. George Habash asking you to tell him your story. He would write it down. It was you who trained George Habash and Wadi' Haddad and Hani al-Hendi and everyone else in the first cadre. Why didn't you tell me what that first experiment was like? And also why you joined Fatah? Was it because of Abu Ali Iyad, as you told me, or because you were against plane hijackings? Or because you liked change?

Ghassan Kanafani came, you told him your story, he took notes, and then he didn't do anything. He didn't write your story.

Why didn't he write it? Did you really tell him your story? You never used to tell anyone your story because everyone knew it, so why bother?

Writers are strange. They don't know that people don't tell real stories because they're already known. Kanafani was different though. You told me you liked him and tried to tell him everything. But he didn't write anything. Do you know why?

It was the mid-fifties when he came to see you, and your story hadn't yet become a story. Hundreds of people were slipping across from Lebanon to Galilee. Some of them came back and some of them were killed by the bullets of the border guards. That, maybe, is why Kanafani didn't follow up on the story – because he was looking for mythic stories, and yours was just the story of a man in love. Where would be the symbolism in this love that had no place to root itself? How did you expect he would believe the story of your love for your wife? Is a man's love for his wife really worth writing about?

However, you became a legend without realizing it, and I want to assure

* Palestinian writer and spokesman for the Popular Front for the Liberation of Palestine. Assassinated by the Israeli secret service in Beirut in 1972.

you that if Kanafani hadn't been assassinated in Beirut by the Israelis in '72, if the car bomb hadn't ripped his body to shreds, he'd be sitting with you now in this room, trying to piece your story together.

Times have changed.

Then, you would have to have died in this cold bed to become a story. I know that you're laughing at me, and I agree – the important thing is not the story but the life. But what are we supposed to do when life tries to force us out? The important thing is life, and that's what I'm trying to get at with you. Why can't you understand? Why don't you get up now, shake death from your body, and leave the hospital?

You don't love the moon, and you don't love the blind singer, and you can't get up.

But moonlight is true light. What is this solar culture that's killing us? Only moonlight deserves to be called light. You told me about moonstroke. You said that in your village people feared it more than sunstroke, and you'd seek cover in the shade from the moon, not the sun.

The fact is, master, your theories on aging are faulty: It's not teeth and eyes, it's smell. Aging is that implacable death that paralyzes body and soul, and it always comes as a surprise. Of course, I agree that in your case the psychological factor was decisive: You became old in one fell swoop when Nahilah died – though, in fact, her death doesn't explain everything because other women still love you. Nevertheless, you got away.

Don't put your finger to your lips for silence. I can and will say whatever I like. You don't want me to talk about Mme. Nada Fayyad? Very well, I won't say a word – but she came yesterday and stood at the door to your room and wept. A woman of sixty, she came and stood at your door and refused to enter. This is the fourth time she's come in three months. Yesterday I ran after her and invited her in. I stopped her in the corridor, lit a cigarette, and offered it to her. She was weeping convulsively, mascara running into her eyes.

She said she didn't go into your room because she didn't want to see you like that. "Unbelievable!" she said. "How can it be? To hell with this world!"

I was surprised by her accent.

She told me she was from al-Ashrafiyyeh, in Beirut – her name was Nada Fayyad – she'd known you for a long time and used to work with you in the Fatah media office on al-Hamra Street.

Did you work in media? What did you have to do with media and journalists and intellectuals? You always used to say you were a peasant and didn't understand all that nonsense! Or is Mme. Nada lying?

She asked me if I was your son and said I looked a lot like you. Then she kissed me on the cheek and left. You must have seen her when she came in but didn't want to talk to her. Why don't you talk to her? Does she know about you and Nahilah? Or did you hide that story from her and give her a different account of your wife and children and journeys to your country?

Tell me the truth, confess you had a relationship with this woman. Maybe you even loved her. Tell me you loved her so I can believe the story of your other love. How do you expect me to believe you were faithful to one woman your whole life? Even Adam, peace be upon him, wasn't faithful to his only wife.

You had the habit of hiding your truth with a smile. When I asked you about other women, you had only one response: No. A big *no* would emerge from your lips. Now the secret is out: Amna and Nada and I don't know who else. One after another they will come, as though your illness has turned into a trap for scandals. I'll sit here with you and count your scandals.

Please don't get upset – I'm only describing the facts. Shams taught me to do this. She said she'd never lie to me. She said she'd lied to her husband and felt there was no reason to lie to me. She said she'd learned to lie after the long torment she'd lived through with him and had relished it because it had been her sole means of survival. Then she started to get sick of it. She said that when she lied successfully she felt she was disappearing. In the end she decided to run away so the lying and disappearing would stop. She said she wanted an innocent relationship with me. Then I discovered she was lying.

When I fell in love with her, she said she hated sex because her husband had raped her. I believed her and tried to build an innocent relationship with her. But, of course, I was lying to her: I used the phrase "an innocent relationship" so I could sleep with her. Then I discovered she was raping me.

I say she was raping me, but I'm lying. We lie because we can't find the words; words don't indicate specific things, which is why everyone understands them as they wish. I meant to say she enjoyed sex, as I did, which doesn't mean she raped me. On the contrary, it means we loved sex, reveling in it, laughing and frolicking. She would yell at the top of her voice – she said her husband had forbidden her to yell, and she loved me because of the yelling. She'd yell and I'd yell. I've no right to call that rape, so I withdraw what I said and apologize.

I'm certain Nahilah was different. You don't want me to talk about Nahilah? Very well, I'll shut up. With Shams, it was not a question of sex; I lost myself in that woman. And I wasted all those years of my life only to discover I'd been deceived. I don't concur with Shams' theory of love, that every love is a deception. She dominated me completely, and she knew it. Once, after disappearing for two months, she turned up as though she'd never been away, and instead of quarreling with her, I dissolved into her body. That was when I told her I was a lost cause, but she already knew it. She would disappear for days and weeks at a time, and then appear and tell me unbelievable stories that I believed. Now I've found out what a fool I was. Love makes a person naïve and drives him to believe the unbelievable.

The woman was amazing. After we'd made love and screamed and moaned, she'd light a cigarette, settle on the edge of the bed, and tell me about her adventures and her journeys. Amman, Algiers, Tunis. She'd tell me she saw me every day and heard my voice calling to her every morning. She'd ask me to repeat her name over and over again; she'd never get tired of hearing it. I'd sound her name once, twice, three times, a dozen times, then I'd stop, and I'd see her face crumple like a child's, so I'd start again, and we'd start making love again.

Then I discovered she was lying.

No – at that moment, when I was repeating her name, I knew, but I used to relish the lie. That's love – enjoying a lie, then waking up to the truth.

After the killing of Sameh Abu Diab, I looked everywhere for her. My first feeling was fear. I was afraid she'd kill me as she'd killed him. I told myself she was a madwoman who murdered her lovers. Instead of feeling jealousy or sorrow, I found fear. Instead of looking back over my relationship with this woman, I began shivering in my sleep.

Then she died.

No. Before she died, I went looking for her so I could warn her of her fate.

Do you believe me now? I know that the day her death became known you looked at me suspiciously and said, "Shame on you! That's not how a woman should be killed. A woman in love must never die."

I told you she was a killer. She killed the man she loved and then claimed she'd done it to revenge her honor because he'd deceived her. He'd promised to divorce his wife and marry her, but didn't do it.

I told you, "Shams is lying. I know her better than any of you."

"And why should she lie?" you asked me.

"Because she loved me."

You told me then that I was naïve, that we never could understand the logic of the heart, and the point of her relationship with me might have been to rid herself of the ghost of her love for Sameh. You explained to me that a lover takes refuge in other relationships in order to escape the incandescence of his passion. You despised me because I was the "other man," and you didn't believe I'd had nothing to do with the killing. It's true I appeared before the investigating committee in the Ain al-Hilweh camp, but I didn't participate in the massacre.

Now I call Shams' killing a massacre rather than an execution, as I used to. It was terrible. They tricked her, asking her to go to the Miyyeh wi-Miyyeh camp to be reconciled and to pay blood money, and they were waiting for her. A man with a machine gun came from each family; they hid themselves behind the mounds lining the highway, and when she arrived – you know what happened. There's no need to describe the shreds of woman stuck to the metal of the burned-out car.

Why am I talking about Shams when we're supposed to be talking about Mme. Nada Fayyad? Was Nada your way of escaping the incandescence of Nahilah?

You don't want me to talk about Nada? Okay, suggest another subject then.

I know you don't like talking about these things, and I never meant to end up here. I just wanted to tell you a story you didn't know. I must concentrate because one thing leads to another.

I was describing your physical condition to you. After they pulled out the IV needle, they put the feeding tube into your nose. Yesterday I decided to add a drug called L-Dopa that's used for epileptics and has proven effective for the comatose. This is something I should have done earlier. Why didn't I think of it sooner? Never mind. We'll have to wait a few days before we'll notice its effects.

I know you're in pain, and I can sense your rigidity in this white atmosphere. Here you are – wrapped in white, surrounded by dust and noise and incomprehensible murmurs.

I know that your back is hurting you. I promise you that will change; I'm rubbing your back with creams that will improve your circulation. I won't allow poor circulation to give you sores. There's no way around the pressure sores; we just need to deal with them quickly. Whatever we do, however much we massage you, we'll never be able to prevent the sores that come from lying motionless in bed.

We've inserted a permanent catheter. It has to be there or you'd be poisoned by your own urine, because instead of wetting yourself, as Nurse Zainab had expected, you are retaining everything. The catheter will most likely lead to an inflammation of the urethra. That's why we take your temperature every day. I know you hate it, but I have to do it. Please let me use the suppositories three times a week – even the milk is converted into shit.

God, how horrible we discover our bodies to be – a feeding tube at the top, a tube for waste below, and us in between.

Please don't despise yourself, I beg you. If only you knew how happy I was when I discovered it wasn't over, that your cells were still renewing themselves even in the midst of this death.

I'm cutting your hair, clipping your nails and shaving your beard, but the most important thing is your new odor, an odor of milk and powder almost like a baby's.

I'll describe how I spend my day with you, so you can relax and stop muttering.

I enter your room at 7 a.m., empty your catheter and clean your nails. Then I mop your room. After that I give you a bath with soap and water, for which I use an expensive soap that I bought myself, because here at the hospital they refuse to buy "Baby Johnson" claiming that it costs a lot and is supposed to be for babies. Then I change your white gown and call Zainab to help me lift you and sit you in the chair; she holds you up while I change the sheets. I don't want to give you more to worry about, but the sheets were a problem. What kind of hospital is this? They said they weren't responsible for sheets, so I had to buy three sets. I've asked Zainab to wash them, and I give her a small amount for the service. That way I don't have to worry anymore about changing the sheets every day. Next, I put you back in bed, get the mucus extractor (because you can't cough now), extract the mucus from your windpipe, clean the extractor, and rest a little.

At eight-thirty, I get your breakfast ready and feed it to you gently through your nose. At twelve-thirty, I prepare your lunch and, before feeding you, tip you a little on your side and wipe your face with a damp towel.

At five, I make your afternoon snack, which is a bit different because I mix honey into the milk, farm honey from the village of al-Sharqiyyeh in the south.

At nine, I rub your body with alcohol, then sprinkle talcum powder on it. When I find the beginnings of a bed sore, I stop rubbing and bathe you again. The evening bath isn't mandatory every day.

At nine-thirty, you eat dinner.

After dinner, I stay with you a while and tell you stories. Sometimes I'll fall asleep in my chair and wake up with a start at midnight. Or I'll leave you quietly and go to my room in the hospital, where I sleep.

My room is a problem.

They all think I sleep there because I'm scared and on the run. To tell you the truth, I am scared. Amin al-Sa'id came to see me three months ago. You know him: he was a comrade of mine in Fatah's Sons of Galilee brigade and now lives in the Rashidiyyeh camp near Tyre. He told me they'd decided to take special security measures because Shams' family had sent a bunch of their young men from Jordan to Lebanon to avenge their daughter, and he asked me to be careful. I told him I didn't care because I had a clear conscience. But, as you see, I'm stuck in this hospital and unable to leave.

The surprising thing, master, is how much you've changed. I won't tell you how much thinner you've gotten, since I'm sure you're aware of that. And your little paunch – which you hated so much you'd run five kilometers every day hoping to get rid of it – is gone. I think you've lost more than half your weight.

Zainab thinks that your new smell is the result of the soap, powder, and creams I use to massage you, but that's not true. You smell like a baby now because you eat what babies eat. Your smell is milky – a white smell on a white body.

I suspect you've started to shrink a little; maybe tomorrow I'll bring a tape measure. Don't be frightened, it's just your bones contracting because of the lack of movement or the cells not renewing themselves due to your age. Your bones are getting shorter and you're getting shorter, but so what? Don't get upset: Soon, when you get up, I'll organize a special diet full of vitamins for you and everything will be as it was, and better.

Do you hear me?

Why don't you say anything?

Didn't you like the story?

I know what you want now. You want me to leave you alone to sleep, and you want the radio. The bastards stole the radio. Last night I left it on all night. I thought it would keep you company while you were on your own, but they stole it.

I know who they are. They haven't forgotten their status and wealth during the revolution. Don't they know I'm the poorest guy here? True, I'm a nurse and a doctor, but I'm also a beggar. The golden days are over, but they haven't yet digested that we're back to square one – poor.

And you, have you forgotten those days?

Have you forgotten how Abu Jihad al-Wazir,* God rest his soul, would take a tattered scrap of paper and use it to disburse unimaginable sums to people in need of money? Indignant, I mentioned it to you, but you didn't agree with me. I told you so I could make the point that money had corrupted us and would destroy us, but you explained everything to me then and asked me not to say anything about Abu Jihad that I would regret later. "Two men, Son, represent all that's best among the martyrs – Abu Ali Iyad and Abu Jihad al-Wazir." Could you have had a premonition of his assassination in Tunis? Did you know about it then, or did you just see it coming? You said Abu Jihad used a tattered scrap of paper to disburse money to show his contempt for it, because money is nothing.

I'll buy you a new radio tomorrow.

What?

You don't want one?

You don't like listening to the news any more?

I'll buy you a tape player and some tapes. You love Fairouz, and I'll buy you some Fairouz songs, in particular the one that goes, "I'll see you coming under the cloudless sky, lost among the almond leaves." Tomorrow I'll bring you the cloudless sky and the almond leaves and Fairouz, and all the old songs of Mohammed Abd al-Wahhab. I'll bring "The wasted lover is spurned by his bed" – how I love Ahmad Shawqi, the prince of poets! Tomorrow I'll tell you the story of his relationship with the young singer Mohammed Abd al-Wahhab.

* Fatah leader, assassinated by the Israeli secret service April 15, 1988.

> *He was my lord, my soul was in his hands.*
> *He squandered it – God bless his hands!*

How I love love, Abu Salem! Tomorrow we'll sing and relive our loves. You'll love and I'll love – you and I, alone in the only hospital in a corner of the only camp in Beirut.

Recite this Surah with me:

> *Say, "I seek refuge in the Lord of men,*
> *the King of men,*
> *the God of men,*
> *from the evil of the slinking prompter*
> *who whispers in the hearts of men,*
> *of djinn and men." ** *

Say the verse. The Koran will comfort your heart.
I'm going now. Goodnight.

* Koran, Surah CXIV.

WHY DON'T you answer?

Why don't you want to tell me where the *good* is to be found?

Why would you believe me, anyway?

Last night I said goodnight, but I didn't go to sleep. Every night I say the same thing and don't go. I said goodnight because I was tired of everything. I sit with you and get upset. I sit and get fed up. I'm sick and tired of waiting. And I still can't sleep. I yawn, exhaustion fills my body as if all I need to do to drop off is put my head on the pillow, but I can't sleep.

Sleep is the most beautiful thing.

I lie down on the bed and close my eyes. The numbness that comes before sleep steals into my head . . . and then my body convulses, and I'm jolted awake. I light a cigarette, gaze at its glowing end in the dark, and my eyelids start to droop. I put out the cigarette, close my eyes, and let the phantoms take over. I think about Kafar Shouba; for ages now Kafar Shouba's been my sleeping companion. I lie down, and I go there and see the flares.

I was seventeen when I saw flares for the first time. At the time, I was a fedayeen fighter, one of the first cadre that came through Irneh in Syria to southern Lebanon to build the first fedayeen base.

I heard of Kafar Shouba on my way there, and the name stuck in my mind. In fact our base wasn't in Kafar Shouba but in an olive grove belonging to a neighboring village, al-Khreibeh. All the same, when in my drowsiness I travel back to those days, I go to Kafar Shouba.

I was the youngest. Actually, I'm not completely sure anymore, but in any case I was certainly too young for the job of political commissar that Abu Ali Iyad had handed me.

I was scared.

A political commissar has no right to be scared. I covered up my fear with a lot of talk, and the military commander of the base, a twenty-eight-year-old blond lieutenant named Abu al-Fida, used to call me the talk-a-lot-ical commissar.

I talked and talked because I wanted the fedayeen to acquire political consciousness: We wanted to liberate the individual, not just the land.

During those days – July of '69 – the Americans made it to the moon, and Armstrong walked on its white face.

That day, I remember, Abu al-Fida got very angry with me and punished me. Is that any way to deal with people – punishing a political commissar in front of his men for expressing an opinion?

In fact, as was the fashion in those days, I made no secret of my lack of faith. If man could go to the moon, that meant there was no God. May God the Exalted forgive me for such thoughts, but when I voiced them I only meant the concept. Atheism was just an idea, and I didn't express it because I believed in it but because it seemed logical, even though, along with the rest of the young men, I fasted during Ramadan and repeated Koranic verses to myself. How can you not repeat Koranic verses when confronted with death every day? What else can you say to death than, "Count not those who were slain in God's way as dead"? *

Abu al-Fida got angry with me and ordered me to hand over my weapon and crawl on the ground in front of the platoon. And I crawled. I won't lie to you and say I refused to carry out his order. I crawled, got filthy, and felt like an insect. I decided to hand in my resignation and join the fedayeen in the valley of al-Safi. Things heated up soon afterwards. The Israeli planes started shelling our positions, and we were too busy dealing with the slew of martyrs to remember Armstrong and his moon, my declarations and my atheism.

It was there that I discovered the incandescent flares. They lit up the sky, and I was able to see Palestine for the first time. The clustered bursts of

* Koran, Surah III, 169.

light spread across the shimmering olive trees. That's how I see them now, and I see you making your way alone, carrying your rifle through the hills and looking for a drop of water between the jagged rocks leading you toward Bab al-Shams, where Nahilah was waiting for you.

I see you making your way beneath the flares, feeling no fear.

How selective our memories are! Now I remember the light falling from flares, but then, after they had ignited the camp, after the flies had devoured me on the main street of Shatila, and after I had returned to this hospital with its pervasive stench of death, all I retained was the memory of fear.

That's the difference.

You remind me of the light, even though you're half-dead, while the corpses of the Shatila massacre make me think of death, however much they give the impression of living beings leaning against each other, petrified on the spot.

This is how I begin my journey toward sleep, watching the paths of the bright flares and the face of Abu al-Fida shining under the Doshka machine gun aimed at the sky. I run through the olive grove, take cover behind a rock, and fire. Then I find myself in al-Hama, taking part in general staff meetings and discussing military plans. Then I fall asleep. The memories come like swarms of ants invading my mind, and with their spiraling motion I sleep.

I lie on my bed and try to summon up the image of the ants, but it won't come. I think of Shams, I see her mutilated body, and sleep won't come. I think about love. Why didn't I go to Denmark with Siham? I see her walking in the streets of Copenhagen and turning around as though she's heard my footsteps. That was how our story, which isn't even really a story, began. She came to the hospital complaining of stomach pains. When she lay down and uncovered her belly, I trembled all over. A shimmering little sun appeared, coated with olive oil. I prescribed a painkiller and explained that the pains were just symptoms of nervous tension. From that day on, whenever I saw her on what was left of the roads of this devastated camp, she'd turn around and smile, because she'd heard my footsteps and knew I was hurrying to catch up with her. Our relationship developed through walking, turning, and smiling. Then she went abroad. Should I go to her? Or stay? Indeed, why should I stay? But what work would I find in Denmark?

Siham doesn't care because she doesn't understand that I'm almost forty and that it's difficult for someone of that age to begin again, starting from zero.

"But you're at zero now," she told me one day.

She's right. I have to acknowledge this zero in order to begin my life. But what do I mean by "begin my life"? When I say "begin," does it mean that everything I did before doesn't count?

I think of Siham and try to sleep. I go with her to Denmark and become a prince like Hamlet. Hamlet lived in a rotten state, and I live in a rotten state. Hamlet's father died, and my father died. True, my uncle didn't kill my father and marry my mother, but what happened to my mother was perhaps more horrible. Hamlet went mad because he was incapable of taking revenge, and I'm on the verge of going mad because someone wants to take revenge on me. Hamlet was a prince watching the world rot around him, and I, too, am watching mine rot. Hamlet went mad, so will I.

When you told me about Ibrahim, your eldest son, with his curly hair, black eyes and long eyelashes, Hamlet came to mind. You say Ibrahim, and I see Hamlet.

The image of Hamlet started to form when you told me of your son's death. At the time it amazed me that people could recall such painful things. Why wouldn't they forget? And a terrible thought crossed my mind – that people are only the phantoms of their memories. Ibrahim's story came up when you were telling me about the beneficial qualities of olive oil and how your mother never used any other remedy.

"Drugs never entered our house," you told me. "My mother treated herself and us with olive oil. If she felt a pain in her belly, she'd dip a piece of cotton wool in the oil jar and swallow it, and if my father came back from the fields with his feet covered in cuts, she'd dab oil on them, and if her son was crying in pain, she'd run to the demijohn of oil, for the perfect cure."

When Nahilah told you that three-year-old Ibrahim only liked to eat bread dipped in oil, you told her the boy was like his grandmother. He would dip his bread in oil and eat it with onions, only onions, never any thyme or *labneh*.* Only onions – but he liked honey, too.

You didn't know your son.

His mother brought him to the cave several times, and you saw him swaddled in his diapers by candlelight, but you didn't really see him. All that stuck in your memory was a white face and half-closed eyes. You loved him, of course – could any man not love his firstborn son? You would hold him in your arms and kiss him and then, when his mother came close, forget about him. When he got a little older, Nahilah no longer brought him to the cave.

She would describe him to her husband and imitate his walk, his move-ments, and his words, but she adamantly refused to bring him to the cave. She said he could understand now and talk, and that the child shouldn't be exposed to danger. The village was full of informers. You'd agree with her, ask her to imitate the way he talked, and then forget the boy in your fever-ish efforts to hold onto time as it drained out of the cave. You'd bury your head in her hair and tell her you wanted to sleep with your head resting there, but you wouldn't sleep.

One day, when Nahilah was telling him about her son, Yunes left the cave. He left his wife with her talk and went off. Nahilah knew he'd go to the house, but she didn't go after him. Later she'll tell him she'd been rooted to the spot with fear.

Yunes reached the house, pushed open the old wooden door, went into his wife's room, turned on the electric light, and saw for himself. The boy was sleeping on his left side, his head resting on his hand, which was curled under the pillow, and his curly black hair covered his face.

Years after that visit, he would tell his wife that when he stood in front of the bed, he forgot where he was and was overwhelmed by beauty. He would tell her that beauty was curly hair flowing over a sleeping face on its pillow.

Yunes doesn't recall how long he'd stood there before hearing his

* A soft, yogurt cheese.

mother's footsteps. The old woman had been awakened by the light; she climbed out of bed and went toward the bedroom, asking Nahilah if something had happened.

"When I heard her, I turned off the light," he told his wife, "and tiptoed out of the house."

Nahilah would tell him that his mother never stopped interrogating her.

"Your mother hates me," she said. "You know she's hated me since day one because she was convinced I was to blame for the mess-up that forced her to cut my finger and bloody the bed sheet, and for the rest of her life she would say she never felt such shame as on that night. But the night you visited, everything changed. I came back, and she was sitting in my room waiting for me. I saw something gentle in her eyes. I opened the door – it was four in the morning – and I heard her voice. She was walking up and down in the room talking to herself. I came in as the last shadows before dawn were slipping from the house.

"'Was it him?' she asked. 'He was here, and you were with him?'

"I asked her to keep her voice down, afraid she'd wake Ibrahim. She lowered it, but it still seemed loud. She shook with excitement as she talked, her words tumbling over one another. She didn't ask me anything, and I don't remember what she said. Then she calmed down. She went to the kitchen and returned with two cups of tea and sat down on the floor. I was sleepy and felt my body slipping away. I drank the tea quickly so I could go to bed. Looking at me affectionately, she told me not to worry, she'd take care of Ibrahim when he woke up.

"'Go and get some sleep,' she said.

"I felt her eyes boring into my belly – from that night on, her gaze always fell on my belly first. I lay down on my bed. She came and sat on the edge of it and asked me to take her there with me. She didn't ask me where I went, or how, or where 'there' was.

"'Tell Yunes his mother wants to see him before she dies. I know he doesn't have much time, Daughter, but tell him.'"

Nahilah told Yunes, but he warned her, "Don't bring that woman here. I'll go and see her."

He didn't go, though, except when his father died, and after he'd been, his mother said it was like she hadn't seen him.

You didn't go, you told me, because after Ibrahim's accident you were no longer capable of going. "How could you expect me to enter that house after Ibrahim died?"

"His mother," you said. "His poor mother. I saw how Nahilah died and came to life again. I somehow knew he'd died; nobody told me, I swear. I heard his voice calling for help. I went and found that he was dead. After my only visit to the house, when I saw him sleeping, a special bond grew between us. You could say I started to love him, and I started to find a place in my pack for small presents. Nahilah didn't understand at first why I insisted she dress him in the pajamas I'd stuffed into the pack. She said they were too big for him, so I asked her to shorten them, and when I explained why, she laughed. She said I was crazy, wanting my son and me to wear the same pajamas. Then she took things one step further. She started buying us the same outfits. I told her I wouldn't wear Israeli clothes, and she said they weren't, she sewed them herself. She said, 'This shirt's just like Ibrahim's,' and that when I wore it I looked amazingly like my son. She would make us matching clothes and say that when Ibrahim grew up we'd be like twins. I started wearing my clothes and imagining my son wearing his. She'd dress him, and then speak to him as if he were me. We became like one man divided in two, one half in the cave, the other at home."

That was your favorite game.

Nahilah used to say that when she missed her husband, she'd dress Ibrahim in his pajamas, and that would take care of it. And Yunes would tell her that when he didn't change his shirt for a while, it meant he was longing for her and her son. "See, the shirt's torn and I haven't changed it. That means I really am homesick. Plus it means you need to make us some new clothes."

Clothes became the prime subject of the meetings of husband and wife in that cave suspended above the village of Deir al-Asad. The husband would bring cloth from Lebanon and the wife would sew it while protesting that she didn't want to turn into a tailor, she had to take care of the unborn child growing in her belly.

"I started holding conversations with my son without realizing what I was doing. He became part of me. Even after Nahilah delivered our second son, Salem, and in spite of all the problems associated with the birth, we never forgot the clothes game."

Yunes said he somehow knew.

"I was in Lebanon, hiding out at Nezar al-Saffouri's house, God bless him, when I had that dream. I dreamt I saw Nahilah mourning my death. I saw myself lodged in the pit of al-Birwa, and Nahilah was standing at the edge of the pit trying to get me out, weeping. I was telling her to go back to the house, I don't know how I was speaking because I was dead, or how I was able to see into the pit where I was, but I saw my pajamas.

"It was five in the morning and raining heavily. I got dressed and decided to go to Deir al-Asad. The dream had frightened me a lot because I had it more than once. I awoke in a panic, put on my clothes and set off. At Nezar's house, I remembered I was seeing the dream for the third time, each time repeated detail for detail. The two times before, I'd seen it in prison and thought it was a hallucination caused by the torture, because in prison you become incapable of distinguishing between sleeping and waking. That morning I got up in a panic and heard the slosh of the rain, and I decided to go. I thought it was my father, that the old man had died and I had to go. I don't know; when I thought of my father's death, I felt relief, even though I'd grown to love the blind sheikh in his last days. But a father's death comes quietly.

"Nezar al-Saffouri also awoke in a panic, tried to stop me from leaving, and said they'd kill me this time, that I'd never be able to stand the torture. I was worn out after three months in prison. I don't know where they held me – I was in an underground vault, in darkness, damp and cold. I only saw the interrogator's face once. The cold got into my body, and the pain, the pain of cold bones, crushed me from the inside. When cold gets into your bones, it turns you into solidified bits of agony. It was as though my skeleton had turned into shards of ice inside my body.

"You know, I used to hope I'd be beaten because it was my only way of getting a little warmth. I'd look forward to the beating huddle and rush to it. They must have noticed how I enjoyed the warmth while they were punching and kicking me, so they decided to do something different.

"I was laid out in the middle of the beating circle, with three men above me kicking every part of my body, while I rolled among their feet, unseeing. Just the boots, the boots above my cheeks and eyes. The interrogator came in, and the boots withdrew from my face. They stood me up – I couldn't do it on my own – and one of them propped me up against the wall with his arm around my neck while the other started hitting me on my mouth with a chain wrapped around his fist, and the floodgates of pain opened. I remember the interrogator's voice as he told me to swallow. I spat and gagged, and the man held my mouth shut with his hand to force me to swallow my shattered teeth.

"The Lebanese interrogator spoke to me in a fake Palestinian accent as though he were making fun of me, and he threatened me. Then he said they were going to let me go, and they knew everything and God help me if I tried to cross the Lebanon–Israel border again because they'd make me swallow all my teeth.

"I listened but didn't answer. No, not because I was afraid of him, really. I just couldn't talk without my front teeth.

"Nezar took me to a dentist, a friend of ours, who put in a temporary bridge and advised me to rest for a month before he put in a permanent one.

"Nezar didn't ask me why I was wearing a torn shirt; his only concern was to stop me from going out. I told him I wouldn't be long but that I had to go, and I set off. That day I was wearing the torn blue shirt I'd been wearing in the dream of the pit of al-Birwa. I found the shirt in the bottom of my pack – I'm the only man in the world who lives out of a bag: I put all that I possess in my bag, and it goes wherever I go.

"I won't describe how I got there, because you'd never believe me. It's true the distance between southern Lebanon and the village of Tarshiha in Galilee is short and you can do it, walking, in four or five hours, but in those days it took about twenty hours because we had to avoid the Israeli patrols.

I don't remember how, but I flew. Now, as I'm telling you the story, I see myself as though I weren't walking – no, I swear I was moving over the ground as though I were skating, and I arrived at noon.

"I went to my cave at Bab al-Shams thinking I'd wait until evening and then go to the house, and I found her there, waiting for me."

"You're too late," she said.

Yunes didn't hear and didn't see. Nahilah stood with her back to the entrance of the cave. The cave was dark, and the sunlight splintered against his eyes so he couldn't see a thing. A wavering shadow appeared and what looked like bowed shoulders.

She said she'd spent the whole night waiting for him.

She said she wanted to die.

She said she had died.

And her words blended into her moans.

"She wasn't weeping," said Yunes. "I didn't hear sobbing or screaming. I heard moaning like that of a wounded animal. I went to her. She shook me off and fell to the ground. Then I understood, and I started to rip up my shirt.

"She whispered, 'Ibrahim.' Silence and the madness of sorrow struck me, and I heard a low moaning coming from every pore of her body.

"I tried to question her but she wouldn't reply. I sat down on the ground and reached out to her shaking body, but she moved away. She opened her mouth to say something, and a grating, gasping sound emerged, as though she were in her death throes.

"Poor Nahilah, she stayed that way for more than a year. For a year her eyes were swollen with unspilled tears. Her milk dried up, and Salem, our second son, almost died.

"To tell the truth, I couldn't understand her behavior. Is it possible for a mother to lose her instincts, to refuse to let her second son live, as though she wanted him to join the first?

"Her milk dried up, but she went on feeding Salem as though nothing were wrong, and my mother didn't notice. The child wept night and day. She would give him her breast, and he would fall silent for a while. Then he would start crying again. My mother finally discovered the truth when he wouldn't stop crying even as he was nursing.

"Do you know what my mother did?

"She stole the child. She snatched him away and took him to Umm Sab', Nabil al-Khatib's wife, and asked her to suckle him and keep him with her. My mother was afraid the old story would happen all over again, and my children would die just as hers had.

"Poor Nahilah. Mothers, my friend, are really something."

I didn't ask you then what you did, and how you bore the death of your son that you so resembled. "You look like him," Nahilah used to say, when she found you sad in the cave because she hadn't cooked you *mihammara* and *kibbeh nayyeh*. She said it wasn't just your features and clothes but also in the way you moved. This would make you laugh, and you'd accept the dish of leftover food she'd brought from home after hearing the tap of your hand on the kitchen window.

I didn't ask you because this time you seemed like someone who was just telling the story. You told me how you'd spent two months in the wild out of fear for your wife. You tried to calm her down and told her that Salem had to stay with Umm Sab' so he could survive. She would speak disjointedly and say your mother was a liar, that her milk hadn't dried up, that she was going to die. You spent two months wandering in the woods, going to see her three times a week, and taking her to Bab al-Shams.

After staying with her for two months, you went back to Lebanon because the temporary bridge the dentist had given you was starting to crumble. You wanted to forget: More than a year went by before you returned to Galilee. You told me you were delayed by your various preoccupations and that you were getting things ready for the first groups of fedayeen, but I didn't believe you. I believe you fled because you had no solution. A wife on the edge of madness, inconsolable, what could you do? You fled as men always do. Manliness, or what we call manliness, consists of flight, because inside all the bluster and bullying and big words, there's a refusal to face up to life.

You went back to her after more than a year. You were embarrassed and timid, but you went back, knocked on the window and sprinted off to your cave.

She came.

She was like a new woman. Her hair was long and tied back; she smelled of a mixture of coffee beans and thyme, and her face was just like the face of Ibrahim, whose sleeping face you'd known only from photographs, with his curls spread across his pillow.

You said the woman had come to resemble her dead son and that when you smelled the coffee beans and the thyme rising from her hair, you fell into that feeling that never left you. You said that when you returned to Lebanon after that visit, you were like a lost man, talking without thinking, moving like a sleepwalker, unaware of your own existence except when you were on your way to Bab al-Shams.

"That's real love, Abu Salem."

You refused to acknowledge this blazing truth and said that something inside you, something that had come out into the open after being secret, made you incapable of putting up with other people, and that you were like a wolf that prefers to live in the open.

During that time, Yunes lived in the forest for sixteen continuous months. He didn't tell Nahilah he was nearby. He would visit her twice a week, amazing her with his ability to traverse such distances and dangers. He didn't tell her he had no distances to traverse, only time – the time that became his cross during the days and nights of waiting.

You told Dr. Mu'een al-Tarshahani, who was in charge of the training camp you'd set up at Meisaloun near Damascus, that you were going on a long surveillance trip. "I'll be away for a few months, maybe a year. Don't look for me, and don't issue any statements. I won't die, I'll come back."

At the time, Dr. Mu'een thought you'd been hit by "Return fever," that disease that spread among the Palestinians at the beginning of the fifties and led hundreds of them to their deaths as they tried to cross the Lebanese border on the way back to their villages. He tried to dissuade you, saying that the Return would come after the liberation.

"But I'm not going back," you told him. "I'm going to scout out the land, and I'll come back so that we can return together."

Dr. Mu'een explained that those who succeeded in reaching their objective couldn't live decent lives because they were treated as "resident absentees" and were permitted neither to work nor to move around.

"No communiqué. No death notice. I'm coming back."

And you left.

There you were, pretending that you wanted to explore Galilee inch by inch, but you were lying. You didn't explore Galilee. On the contrary, you just kept hovering around Deir al-Asad and making a circuit of Sha'ab, al-Kabri and al-Ghabsiyyeh. You lived among the ruins of villages and would go into the abandoned houses and rummage for food. You'd pounce on what people had left behind and savor the vintage olive oil. You said oil's like wine, the longer it matures in its jars the smoother it gets. And then you gave me your views on bread. You made me taste the bread you ate when you were on your own during those long months, kneading the dough and cutting it and frying the little pieces in olive oil. You said you'd gotten used to that kind of bread, and you made it now in the camp whenever you felt nostalgic.

"But it's bad for you and raises your cholesterol," I said tasting its burning flavor.

"We don't get high cholesterol. Peasants are cholesterol-proof."

A year of living without shelter around Deir al-Asad.

A year of solitude and waiting.

You spoke to no one. No one lent you a sympathetic ear. People had other things to worry about, they danced with death every day.

Who remembers that woman?

You told me you prayed that God would bless you with forgetfulness and that you didn't want to remember her, but she kept slipping into your thoughts, like a phantom.

She was alone – a woman alone wandering among the destroyed graves of al-Kabri. But they weren't graves: The Israeli army didn't leave one stone on top of another in al-Kabri after its occupation.

The woman was picking things up and putting them in a bag on her back. Yunes approached her. At first she looked like an animal walking on all fours. Her long hair covered her face, and she was muttering. Yunes moved toward her carefully, ready to fire his rifle. Then she turned and looked him in the eye.

"My hands were shaking and I nearly dropped the rifle," he told his wife. "She seemed to have thought I was an Israeli soldier, and when I got close to her she slung her bag over her shoulder and started running. I stayed where I was and looked around but saw nothing on the ground. I found dried bones, which I thought belonged to dead animals. I thought to catch up with her to ask her what she was doing, but she bolted as fast as an animal. When Nahilah told me who she was, I went back to the place, gathered the remaining bones and buried them in a deep hole."

The woman's story terrified the whole of Galilee.

In those days, Galilee quaked with fear – houses demolished, people lost, villages abandoned and everything in shambles.

In those days, the woman's voice was like a wind whistling at the windows. People became afraid and called her the Madwoman of al-Kabri; she crept along the ground, leapt from field to field, her bag of bones on her back.

It was said that she gathered the bones of the dead and dug graves for them on the hilltops. When she died, the bones from her bag were scattered in the square at Deir al-Asad, and people came running and gathered them up and made a common grave for them. The Madwoman of al-Kabri was buried next to the bones she'd been carrying.

Who was that woman?

No one knows, but people learned her story from her bag.

Yunes said he met the madwoman of the bones and spoke to her, and that she wasn't as mad as people said. "She gave me wild chicory to eat. She was looking for wild chicory, not bones. What happened was that she stayed behind in al-Kabri after the Jews demolished it to avenge the victims of Kherbet-Jeddin. The woman didn't run away with the others because they'd left her behind."

"In those days we forgot our own children," said Umm Hassan when I asked her about the Madwoman of al-Kabri.

"In those days, Son, we left everything. We left the dead unburied and fled."

IN THOSE DAYS the people lived with fear, military rule, and the death of border crossers. People no longer knew who they were or who their families were or where their villages were. And there was her voice. She would go around at night and wail, like a whistling wind colliding with the tottering houses.

All that the people saw in the square at Deir al-Asad was a dead woman. She was dead and spread-eagled, her arms outstretched like a cross, her black peasant dress torn over her corpse, her empty bag at her side, bones everywhere.

Ahmad al-Shatti, the sheikh of the mosque at Deir al-Asad, stood next to the corpse and ordered the women to leave. Then he wrapped it in a black cloth and asked the children to gather the bones; he placed them on top of the corpse. "The children of Deir al-Asad will never forget it," Rabi' told me at our military base in Kafar Shouba. Rabi' was a strange young man who laughed all the time. Even when Abu Na'el al-Tirawi was killed by a bullet from his own machine gun, Rabi' laughed instead of crying like the rest of us. Abu Na'el was the first dead person I'd ever seen. I'd only seen my dead father through my mother's description. I saw Abu Na'el dying and the blood spurting from his stomach while we stood around him not knowing what to do. We carried him to the car, and on the way to the hospital he screamed that he didn't want to die. He was dying and screaming that he didn't want to. Then suddenly he went stiff, his body slumped, and his face disappeared behind the mask of death.

I don't know how Rabi' escaped from Israel, but I do remember his terror-stricken eyes as he said he hadn't forgotten the bones. "Sheikh Ahmad al-Shatti was sure they were human bones but we children thought they were animal bones. That's why we played with them until the sheikh made us put them on top of the corpse. There was a single human skull in the madwoman's bag, and this the sheikh wouldn't let us touch. He took it and put it in a bag of its own, and the rumor went around among the children that he'd taken the skull to his house to use in magic séances."

Rabi' left Kafar Shouba and joined one of the Hebrew-Arabic translation bureaus belonging to the resistance. He died during the Israeli bombardment of Beirut's al-Fakahani district in 1981.

YUNES WAS sure that the madwoman collected people's bones and put them in her bag. He believed that she'd been killed by mistake, that the Israelis had killed her during the sweeps ordered by Prime Minister David Ben Gurion in 1951.

In those days the villages of Galilee were haunted by border crossers at night, and there were clear orders to shoot anything that moved.

The madwoman used to move around at night, alone, like the ghost of the dead she carried in her bag. People were afraid of her. Nobody saw her and everybody saw her, wearing her long black dress and walking among the patches of darkness.

WHEN YOU told me the story of those long months spent among the abandoned houses, the night ghosts and the sound of the Israeli guns harvesting people, you told me everything except the word I was waiting to hear.

Are you scared of the word *love*?

I am, I swear; that's why I can't sleep: Frightened people can't sleep. I lie on my bed, and I ask the memories to come like swarms of ants, and I follow their spiraling motion. I think of Shams, and I get scared.

What if I couldn't open my eyes again? What if I slept and didn't get up? What if they came here and killed me? I'm scared.

No, not of them, nor of the rumors, which I don't believe. I'm scared of sleep, of the distance it erases between my dreams and my reality. I can't tell the difference anymore, I swear I can't tell the difference. I talk about things that happened to me and then discover they were dreams.

And you, do you have dreams?

Scientists say the brain never stops producing thoughts and images. What do you imagine? Do you see your story the way I paint it for you?

Anyway, I'm scared. There are rumors all over the camp. They say Shams' gang will take revenge on everyone who took part in her murder. I'm ready to explain that I had nothing to do with it, but where are they?

Is it true they killed Abu Ali Zayed in the Ain al-Hilweh camp? Why did they kill him? Because he whistled? Can a man be killed because he whistled? They say he was standing at the entrance to the Miyyeh wi-Miyyeh camp and that when he saw Shams' car he put two fingers under his tongue and whistled. And the bullets rained down.

They'll kill me, too.

I didn't do anything. They took me to court, I gave my testimony, and that's it.

I'm sure they're just rumors. Dr. Amjad and the crippled nurse think I'm hiding in your room because I'm afraid of them, and two days ago I heard Nurse Zainab telling Dr. Amjad she wouldn't try to stop them if they came. I gathered she was talking about me.

You know I don't live here out of fear of Shams' ghost or her gang. I'm here so you're not on your own and I'm not either. What kind of person would leave a hero like you to rot in his bed? And I hate being on my own with no one to talk to. What kind of days are these, enveloped in silence? No one knows anyone else or talks to anyone else. Even death doesn't unite us. Even death has changed; it has become just death.

I lie on my bed, open my eyes and stare into the darkness. I look at the ceiling, and it seems to get closer, as though it were about to fall and bury me beneath the rubble. But the darkness isn't black, and now I'm discovering the colors of darkness and seeing them. I extinguish the candle and see the colors of the dark, for there's no such thing as darkness: It's a mixture of sleeping colors that we discover, little by little. Now I'm discovering them, little by little.

I won't describe the darkness to you, because I hate describing things. Ever since I was in school I've hated describing things. The teacher would give us an essay to write: Describe a rainy day. And I wouldn't know how, because I hate comparing things. Things can only be described in their own terms, and when we compare them, we forget them. A girl's face is like a girl's face and not like the moon. The whiteness and the roundness and everything else are different. When we say that a girl's face is like the moon, we forget the girl. We make the description so that we can forget, and I don't like to forget. Rain is like rain, isn't that enough? Isn't it enough that it should rain for us to smell the smell of winter?

I don't know how to describe things even though I know a lot of pre-Islamic poems. Nothing is more beautiful than the poetry of Imru' al-Qais – king, poet, lover, drunk, debauché, quasi-prophet, but I have a problem with his descriptions. "Her breast smooth as a looking glass" . . . How, I mean, can a woman's breast possibly be like a mirror? It won't do. Isn't he saying in effect that he's not seeing her, he's just seeing himself? And that he's not making love to her but to himself? Which would lead us to a terrible conclusion about our ancient poets. Of course Imru' al-Qais wasn't a sodomite, nor was al-Mutanabbi; it's the description that's at fault.

All the same, I love ancient poetry, and I love al-Mutanabbi. I love the melody that makes the words turn inside their rhythms and rhymes. I love the rhythm and the way things resonate with one another and the reverberation of the words. When I recite that poetry, I feel an intoxication equaled only by the intoxication I feel when I listen to Umm Kalsoum. It's what we call *tarab*. We're a people of an exalted state, and *tarab* is beyond description, so how can I describe things to you when I don't know how?

I don't sleep, and I don't describe, and I don't feel *tarab*, and I don't recite poetry. Because I'm afraid, and fear doesn't sleep.

Tell me about fear.

I know you don't use that word. You'll say that you *withdrew*, because you use words to play tricks with the truth. That's the game that you play with your memories – you play tricks and say what you want without naming it.

I know you want me to leave after this night of weariness, insomnia, and darkness. I'll go; just tell me how Ibrahim died.

Nahilah told the story two ways, and you believed both.

The first time around, she lied to you because she was afraid you'd do something stupid. Then she told you the truth because she could tell from your eyes that you were going to do something stupid anyway, so she preferred you to do something meaningfully stupid.

Yunes went into the cave, the sun burning his sweat and fatigue-rimmed eyes, and he saw her. She was a motionless shadow in the back of the cave, her back turned to the entrance, and she was motionless. She heard his footsteps and smelled the smell of travel, but she didn't turn around. Yunes went toward her and saw that she was staggering, as though she had waited for him to come before falling to the ground.

He saw her shoulders, outlined by shadows, shaking as though she were weeping. He went up to her, gasping for breath as if all the distances he had traversed and that had been imprisoned in his lungs were about to explode. When he tried to grasp her by her shoulders, she started moaning and let out a single name.

Yunes tried to make her explain, but she wouldn't stop repeating "Ibrahim," which had become a part of her moaning. He tried to ask about his father, but she didn't answer and burst into a long fit of weeping that grew louder before being choked off.

She said the boy died because she had been unable to take him to the hospital at Acre.

"His head fell forward while he was eating. He said his head was ringing with pain."

She tied cloth around his head and rubbed oil on his neck, but the pain didn't stop. He held his temples as though hugging himself and writhed in pain. So she decided to take him to the hospital in Acre.

Nahilah went to the headquarters of the military governor to ask for a pass and was subjected to a long interrogation. When she returned to her house without a permit, she found her son in the throes of death with the blind sheikh whispering the last rites.

"They didn't put the sack over my head, but they threw me into a dark-ened room," she said, "and left me there for more than three hours. They then took me into the office of a short man who spoke with an Iraqi accent. I told him my son was sick, but he wouldn't stop asking about you. I wept and he threatened me. I said the boy was dying and he asked me to cooper-ate with them and questioned me about the border crossers. Then he said he couldn't give me a permit if I didn't bring him a medical certificate to prove my son was sick."

"There's no doctor in the village," I told him.

"Those are my orders," he said. "If you don't cooperate with us, we won't cooperate with you."

WHEN NAHILAH finished her story, she saw how calm your face was. Your panting had stopped, and you looked at her suspiciously, as though you were accusing her. She saw how calmly you took the news as you sat down, lit a cigarette, asked about Salem and told her you'd be away for a long time.

She understood you'd never come back.

You asked about the new Israeli settlement that was being built near Deir al-Asad. Then you stood up, said you'd have your revenge and walked out. She grabbed you by the hand, brought you back into the cave and told the story over again.

She said Ibrahim had been playing with the other children.

She said the new settlement had sprung up like a weed, and they'd fenced off the land they'd confiscated with barbed wire while everyone looked on, seeing their land shrinking and slipping out of their hands, unable to do anything.

She said, "They took the land and we watched like someone watching his own death in a mirror."

She said, "You know how children are. They were playing close to the wire and talking to the Yemeni immigrants in Hebrew – our children speak Hebrew – and the immigrants were answering them in an odd Arabic; our children know their language and they don't know ours. Ibrahim had been playing with them, and they brought him to me. God, he was trembling. They said a huge stone had fallen on him. I don't know how to describe it; his head was crushed, and blood was dripping from it. I left him in the house and ran to ask for a permit to take him to the hospital in Acre, and at the military governor's headquarters they made me wait for more than three hours in a darkened room, the Iraqi threatening to beat me during the interrogation. He said they knew you came, that their men were better lovers than you, and that they'd kill you and leave you in the square at Deir al-Asad to make an example of you. And he asked for information about you while I pleaded for the permit.

"And when I got back to the house, Ibrahim was dead, and your father was whispering the last rites."

You sat down, lit a cigarette, and put a thousand and one questions to her. You wanted to know whether they'd killed him or he'd died accidentally; had they thrown the stone at him, or had he just gotten in the way of it.

Nahilah didn't know.

You got up and said that you'd kill their children as they'd killed your son. "Tomorrow you'll trill with joy, because we'll have our revenge."

For three nights you circled the barbed wire. You had your rifle and ten hand grenades, and you decided to tie the grenades together, throw them into the Jewish settlement's workshop, and, when they exploded, fire at the settlers.

It was night.

The spotlight revolved, tracking the wire fence, and Yunes hid in the olive grove close by. He started moving closer, crawling on his stomach. He got the chain of grenades ready and tied them to a detonator, deciding to throw them into the big hall where Yemeni Jewish families slept practically on top of one another. He wanted to kill, just to kill. When you described the event to Dr. Mu'een, you said that during your third pass you imagined the dead bodies piled on top of one another and felt your heart drink deep.

"I was thirsty; revenge is like thirst. I would drink, and my thirst would increase, so that when the time came and I began to crawl, a refreshing coolness filled my heart. When everything was about to happen, the thirst disappeared, and I set out not with revenge in my mind but out of a sense of duty, because I'd promised Nahilah."

Yunes never told the story of what actually happened.

He said later that it was impossible to carry out the operation successfully, that he had realized the huge losses the villages would incur as a result of the predictable Israeli response.

He crawled toward the fence, and after the spotlight had passed over him a number of times, heard the sound of firing and dogs barking. He flattened himself to the ground. Then he decided to run, not paying the slightest heed to the spotlight. Bullets flying around him, he disappeared into the olive grove, and instead of hiding there until morning, he kept going until he reached the Lebanese border.

He said later that he decided not to go through with the operation because it was an individual act of revenge and because the Israelis would take it out on the Arab villages. But he never spoke of the fear that paralyzed him or why he fled all the way to Lebanon.

Now I have a right to be afraid.

But not Yunes; Yunes wasn't afraid, his heart never wavered. Yunes "withdrew" because he was a hero. I, on the other hand, am hiding in his room because I'm a coward. Have you noticed how things have changed? Those days were heroic days, these are not. Yunes got scared, so he became a hero; I'm scared, so I've become a coward.

When Yunes returned to Bab al-Shams, he didn't tell Nahilah about the revenge that never happened. But me – the crippled nurse looks at me with contempt because she's waiting for me to justify my stay at the hospital. Shams was killed, and I'm expected to pay the price for a crime I didn't commit.

I don't sleep.

And you – could you sleep after you postponed your revenge?

You want a story!

I know you'd like to change the subject, you don't agree with my way of telling the story of your son's death and your revenge. You'll ask me to tell it a different way. Maybe I should say, for example, that the moment you got close to the barbed wire, you understood that individual revenge was worthless and decided to go back to Lebanon to organize the fedayeen so we could start the war.

"It wasn't a war. It was more like a dream. Don't believe, Son, that the Jews won the war in '48. In '48, we didn't fight. We didn't know what we were doing. They won because we didn't fight, and they didn't fight either, they just won. It was like a dream."

You'll say you chose war instead of revenge, and I have to believe you. Everyone will believe you, and they'll say you were right, and I'm trying to camouflage my fear within yours.

You weren't afraid that night of March 1951.

And I'm not afraid now!

When Yunes told how his son Ibrahim died in 1951, he spoke a lot about Nahilah's suffering. He never spoke of his own suffering, only of his thirst for revenge.

"Didn't you feel pain?" I asked him.

"Didn't you want to die? Didn't you die?"

"I don't understand, because I'm only afraid of one thing," I once told Shams, transported by our love. "I'm afraid of children."

When we made love, she'd scream that it was the sea. She was next to me and over me and under me, swimming. She said she was swimming in the sea, the waves cascading from inside her. She would rise and bend and stretch and circle, saying it was the waves. And I would fly over her or under her or through her, flying above her undulating blue sea.

"You are all the men in the world," she said. "I sleep with you as if I'm with all the men I've known and not known." I'd soar above her listening to her words, trying to put off the moment of union. I'd tell her to go a little more slowly because I wanted to smell the sky, but she would pull me into her sea and submerge me and push me to the limits of sorrow.

"You're my man and all men."

I didn't understand the expanses of her passion and her desire to control her body. She would massage her body and grasp her breasts and swoon. I'd watch her swoon and it was as though she weren't with me, or as though she were in a distant dream, a sort of island encircled by waves.

I didn't dare ask her to marry me because I believed her. She said she was a free woman and would never marry again. I believed her and understood her and agreed with her, despite feeling that burning sensation that could only be extinguished by making her my own.

I agreed with her because I was powerless and didn't dare force her to choose between marrying me and leaving me, for the idea of not seeing her was more painful than death.

Then I found out she'd killed Sameh because he'd refused to marry her. They said she'd stood over his body and pronounced, so everyone could hear, "I give myself to you in marriage," before fleeing.

That's what they said at the interrogation, when they detained me. I was silent. I was incapable of speech because I felt betrayal and fear. It was there, in the eyes of the committee members, I discovered she'd been sentenced to die. The head of the committee was in a hurry, as though he wanted to use me as new evidence to justify the decision to kill her.

The committee eyed me with contempt as the duped lover, though I wasn't duped – but what could I say? I used to smell the other men on her body, but it never occurred to me that she loved another man the way I loved her. There – with him – she would have said nothing and been on the verge of tears as she listened to him saying that with her he was sleeping with all of womankind.

I understand her, I swear I do: The only solution to love is murder. I never came close to committing the crime, but I did long for her death, because death ends everything, as it did that day.

Shams is a hero because she put an end to her own problem. But me, I'm just a man who grew horns, as the head of the investigating committee said, thinking he was making a joke everyone could appreciate.

I refused to answer their questions. All I said was that I was convinced she was "not a normal woman." I know I was hard on her, but what could I say? I had to say something, and those words spilled from my mouth. As for all the other things I'm supposed to have said, they're not true. Liars! I never said anything about orgies. My God – how could we have held orgies in my house when it was surrounded by all those other wrecked houses? They put words into my mouth so as to come up with additional justifications for killing Shams. All I said was that she was my friend and that she was a woman of many moods. I heard their laughter and the joke about my horns.

The head of the committee ordered my release because I was pathetic. "A pathetic guy, no harm to anyone," he said.

Pathetic means stupid, and I wasn't stupid. I wanted to tell them that love isn't foolishness, but I didn't say anything. I left and went looking for Shams, and I was arrested again before being released and allowed to return to Beirut.

This isn't what I wanted to say. I wanted to tell you that when I was caught up in that wave, I would dream of having a child and, at the same time, was terrified. I told Shams that the most horrible thing that could happen to a person was to lose a son or daughter. Even though I live amid this desolate people that has grown accustomed to losing its children, I can't imagine myself in that situation.

Shams laughed and told me about her daughter, Dalal, in Jordan, and about how missing her was like having her guts ripped open.

And when I asked Yunes about the death of his son, he told me about Nahilah.

The woman almost went mad. All the people of Deir al-Asad said the woman lost her mind. She would roam the outskirts of the village as though chasing her own death – going into areas the military governor had placed out of bounds (almost everywhere was out of bounds). She'd roam and roam. Then she would return home exhausted and sleep. She'd never worry about her second son, Salem, whom his grandmother had smuggled out of the house.

It took Nahilah months and months to return to her senses after she gave birth to her daughter, Noor, "Light." The girl's name wasn't originally Noor: Her grandmother named her Fatimah, but Yunes said her name was Noor because he'd seen Ibrahim in a dream reciting verses from the Surah of the Koran called "Noor."

"Listen to what he was saying." Nahilah looked and saw a halo of light around Yunes' head as he recited:

> *God is the Light of the heavens and the earth;*
> *the likeness of His Light is as a niche wherein is a lamp*
> *(the lamp in a glass, the glass as it were a glittering star)*
> *kindled from a Blessed Tree,*
> *an olive that is neither of the East nor of the West*
> *whose oil wellnigh would shine, even if no fire touched it;*
> *Light upon Light;*
> *(God guides to His Light whom He will).* *

Yunes said he'd been able to bear his son's death because he hadn't believed it. "When you don't see, you don't believe. I used to tell Nahilah that Ibrahim would come back once he'd tired of playing with death. For me, I swear to you, Ibrahim is still alive, I'm waiting for him."

I CAME INTO your room today laughing. Nurse Zainab had made me laugh by telling me how a woman had smacked Dr. Amjad. I'd thought that Amjad Hussein was a respectable man. I don't know where they dug him up to play the doctor here. Some say Mme. Wedad, the director of the Red Crescent, got him the job because he's a relative of hers. But he's not one of us, because he didn't fight with us and the Israelis didn't detain him at Ansar. So where does he come from? Don't ask me now why I didn't go to the Biqa' when

---

* Koran, Surah XXIV, 35.

our battalion withdrew from al-Nabatiyyeh during the Israeli incursion – that's just the way it happened. I withdrew with the battalion and went to Ain al-Hilweh, and that's where I was arrested. A month later they released me and I found myself going to Beirut. I've no idea, however, where you disappeared to. You told me that when you learned the Israelis had gone into Beirut, you fled to the village of Batshay and hid there with the priest.

"The priest's an old friend of mine, he thinks I'm a Christian," you told me.

Me, on the other hand, they tied up to a barred window that looked like a cage, blindfolded me, wound what felt like ropes around me, and took me to the Israeli prison before I was moved to Ansar.

I won't tell you right now what I told everyone about our life in the detention camp. In Ansar, I lost fifty pounds, I was frail and sick. Everyone was at the camp except Dr. Amjad. Even Abu Mohammed al-Rahhal, president of the Workers' Federation, left sick and died two months later. I haven't told you this dream he used to tell us every day. I don't know what happened to Abu Mohammed in the detention camp. There were thousands of us in the middle of a bare field surrounded by barbed wire, "treating our cares with our cares," as we used to say – all of us except Abu Mohammed, who went from one tent to another, telling the same dream.

"Yesterday," he'd say, "I had a dream," and he'd repeat the same dream, until it became a joke.

"Yesterday I had a dream that I was, I don't know how, standing on the pavement with my manhood (he used this odd term for his member) sticking out, and it was – and I apologize for mentioning it – long, very long, longer than the street from side to side, and an Israeli tank came along and drove over it."

"Did the tank cut it off, Abu Mohammed?"

"Did it hurt a lot?"

Abu Mohammed would say he was afraid he was going to die, because "when a man sees his manhood cut off in a dream, it means he's going to die."

"Where did you get that from, Abu Mohammed?"

"I read it in Ibn Sirin's *Dreams*," he answered.

"And who's this Ibn Sirin? An interpreter of dreams about reproductive organs?"

"God forbid! Ibn Sirin was a great Sufi and a great scholar, and his dream interpretations are never wrong."

Anyway Ibn Sirin was right, because Abu Mohammed died. This Dr. Amjad, though, wasn't with us at Ansar, and no Israeli tank cut off his manhood. But he's here; a respectable man, obsessive about cleanliness. I've never seen such a clean man. He lives in the middle of this shit and streams of cologne flow from him. He washes his hands with soap, then dabbles them with cologne and turns his nose up at everything. I don't know what to make of him. You haven't seen him, so I'll have to describe him to you (even though I don't like descriptions): bald, short, thin, with an oval face, high cheekbones, small eyes. He wears glasses with gold frames that don't flatter his dark complexion, and his pipe never leaves his mouth. He has very narrow shoulders, and he speaks fast, looking off into the distance to make what he says seem important.

He wasn't with us in the war or the detention camp, and I don't understand why he's working in the hospital here. He says he's half-Palestinian because his mother's Syrian, from the region of Aleppo, and he doesn't speak Palestinian Arabic but a funny dialect that's a mixture of Classical and Lebanese.

Zainab told me today about a pious Muslim woman wearing a headscarf who struck him because he tried to make a pass at her.

"I heard the woman's scream, then the sound of slapping. The woman came out, threatening to return with her husband, and the doctor started pleading with her in an embarrassed voice. Later the woman emerged with her husband, who was carrying a bag of medicine, and the doctor thanked the husband, practically falling over himself he was bowing so low."

Today I'm happy. Dr. Amjad was humiliated, and I want to savor the thought of him bowing in front of the husband, groveling like a dog. I want to have a quiet cigarette and think about life. What more do you want from me today? I've bathed and fed you. We sucked out the mucus and everything else. Today I'm happy.

I DON'T KNOW any stories. Where am I supposed to get stories when I'm a prisoner in this hospital? Okay, I'll tell you the story of the cotton swab. You're the one who told it to me, I'm certain of that. You know, when I heard the story, I was very aroused, even though I pretended to be disgusted and went into a long tirade defending women's rights, saying that such degradation of our women was the root of our failures, our paralysis, and our defeats. But when I fell asleep, I was possessed by the demon of sex. That's all I will say.

In those days, as the story goes, in a small village in Galilee called Ain al-Zaitoun, Sheikh Ibrahim Ibn Suleiman al-Asadi decided his only son should marry. The boy had reached adulthood, his beard sprouting at fourteen. The blind sheikh urged his wife to find a bride for her son quickly, for the sheikh had one foot in the grave, and he wanted to see his grandchildren before dying.

The wife was of the same mind. She, too, wanted her son to marry so that he'd settle down, find himself work, and put an end to his long absences and his life in the mountains with the sacred warriors.

The story is that the young man, who was called Yunes, had no objection to the idea, and when his mother told him she was going to ask for the hand of Nahilah, the daughter of Mohammed al-Shawwah, he agreed, even though he'd never met the girl. He said yes because he liked her name and in his mind drew himself a picture of a fair skinned girl with long black hair, wide eyes, broad cheeks, full hips, and round breasts. He fantasized about a woman sleeping next to him and letting him into her treasures.

But Yunes got a surprise. His wife wasn't a woman, she was a twelve-year-old girl. The girl wasn't fair skinned; her complexion was the color of wheat, her hair wasn't long but like tufts of black wool stuck to her head, and her hips weren't . . .

More than ten years later, when he was about to make love with her at Bab al-Shams, he discovered that he was mistaken. The girl was a woman, and fair-skinned, and her eyes were large, her hair long and black, and she was overflowing with secrets and treasures.

He said, on that occasion, that she'd changed.

And she laughed at him because he hadn't seen what was in front of him. "Now, after I've had children and have become fat and flabby, you come to me and say I'm beautiful? Now, after all the hard times, you see that . . . You men! Men are blind, even when they can see."

But Yunes insisted, and embraced the roundness of her hips and saw the bright sky in her broad, high brow and ate Turkish delight from her long, slim, smooth fingers.

He told her he could smell Turkish delight on her neck. He would open his pack after making love to her and would pull out a tin of Turkish delight while she made tea. Then he'd sit hunched up inside the curve of her body as she lay on the rug, and she'd feed him, the fine white sugar falling onto his chest. He told her he loved eating Turkish delight from her fingers because they were as white as the sweet, which was the best thing the Turks had left behind when they left our country, and because her smell was musky, like the white cubes that melted in his mouth.

IN THOSE DAYS, as the story goes, the world was at war, and when there's war, things take on a different shape. The air was different, the smells were different, and the people were different. War became a ghost that seeped into people's clothes and walked among them.

Ain al-Zaitoun, in those days, was a small village sleeping on the pillow of war. Everything in it rippled. The people hurled themselves into the electrified air and tasted war. Nobody called anything by its real name, war itself didn't resemble its own name. Everyone thought it would be like the war tales of their ancestors, where mighty armies were defeated, locusts ate up the fields, and famine and pestilence spread through the land. They didn't know that this time the war without a name was them.

The blind sheikh told his wife that words had lost their meaning, so he had decided to be silent. From day to day, he withdrew deeper into his silence, which was broken only by his morning mutterings while he'd recite Koranic verses.

The blind sheikh told his wife that he could see, even though his eyes were closed, and he couldn't explain why he had come to fear the water.

Weeping, the woman told her son that the old man had gone senile. She said she was ashamed in front of the other people and begged her son to come back from the mountains with the fighters of the sacred jihad to look after his father.

The blind sheikh told his wife he couldn't bear to live any longer now that they'd appointed a new sheikh to be imam of the village mosque. He said an imam couldn't be deposed and that he'd never abandon his Sufi companions in the village of Sha'ab. And he said that Ain al-Zaitoun would be destroyed because it had rejected the blessings of its Lord.

He explained everything to his wife, but he couldn't explain to her why he'd come to fear the water. He said that water was dirty and that when he touched it he felt something sticky, as though his hand were plunging into dead putrefying bodies, and that ablutions could be performed with dust, and that dust . . .

He took to using dust to wash with.

The woman would look at him, her heart torn to pieces. The sheikh would go out into his garden carrying a container, squat as though he were preparing to pray, fill the container with dust and go into the bedroom. He would remove his clothes and bathe with the dust, which stuck to his body as he moved and sighed.

The sheikh said he was afraid of the color of water.

"Water doesn't have a color," said his wife.

"You don't know, and nobody knows, but the water has its own color, like gluey blood that slides over the body and sticks to it."

At the time, Ain al-Zaitoun was preoccupied with the story of its blind sheikh who bathed with dust. It had no idea that after a little while the dust bath would move to the neighboring village, Deir al-Asad, and that the sheikh would die in his new village.

Ain al-Zaitoun was built on the shoulder of a hill. It didn't look much like a real village. Its rectangular square was long and sloping, and didn't look much like a real square. Its houses were built of mud and rose up above one another in piles above neighboring terraces. To the left lay the Honey Spring, Nab' al-Asal, which the village drank from and which the villagers said was sweeter than honey.

Ain al-Zaitoun was suspended between the land and the sky, and Sheikh Ibrahim, son of Salem, had been the imam of its mosque since he was nineteen years old.

Everyone looked like everyone else in Ain al-Zaitoun, and they all belonged to the Asadi clan, the Asadis being poor peasants who had come from the marshes of the Euphrates in southern Iraq during the seventeenth century. No one knows how or why they came. The blind sheikh said they weren't Asadis and didn't come from Iraq, but the Asadi name got attached to them because they worked as hired laborers on the lands of a feudal landlord of the Asadi clan who had come from there. It was said that the landlord's descendants had sold the land to the Lebanese family of Sursuq toward the end of the nineteenth century. The question of land sales in Palestine has "no end and no beginning," as they say. As to how the Asadi came to possess the lands of Ain al-Zaitoun, no one has any idea. Did he purchase these wide and extensive holdings, or was he a brave fighter in the army of Ahmad al-Jazzar – the governor of Acre who defeated Bonaparte – to whom the governor granted lands in Marj Ibn Amir, along with a group of villages including Ain al-Zaitoun, Deir al-Asad, and Sha'ab? Or did he flee Acre with a band of horsemen following the governor's death, and were they the ones who occupied the land? The blind sheikh didn't know, but he preferred the story with the band of horsemen, so he could say that the native inhabitants of Ain al-Zaitoun were originally cavalrymen with the Asadi sheikh in Acre and had come with him to the village to establish it, and that it came to be known by this name, which had nothing to do with them because they were originally from the districts surrounding Acre – "though we're all sons of Adam, and Adam was created from dust."

As for the Sursuq family, it's even more complicated.

Did the Sursuqs buy the land, or was it given to them as a fiefdom because they were friends of the Turkish governor of Beirut?

The inhabitants of Ain al-Zaitoun never saw anyone from the Sursuq family. It was Kazem al-Beiruti, a man dressed in Western clothes and wearing a fez, who used to come after each harvest, count the sacks of wheat, and take half. The peasants parted with half their crop of wheat and maize without protest. The olives, however, were a different story; Kazem al-Beiruti didn't dare demand the owner's share of olives or oil. "The oil belongs to him who sows it," the blind sheikh told Ahmad Ibn Mahmoud to his face when he came demanding his share.

When the disturbances in Palestine spread during 1936, the inhabitants of Ain al-Zaitoun refused to give Kazem al-Beiruti anything. Ahmad Ibn Mahmoud chased him away after humiliating him in public by knocking his fez off his head with his stick, trampling it underfoot and announcing the return of the land to its rightful owners. And Ahmad Ibn Mahmoud al-Asadi declared himself, as head of the clan, sole legal heir of the original al-Asadi, taking the fertile lands belonging to the village and giving the peasants of his family the liberty to cultivate the land without paying the owner's share. However, he tried to take some of the olives and oil, and this was what caused problems between him and Sheikh Ibrahim.

Ahmad Ibn Mahmoud was one of the local leaders of the Revolution of '36. It's said that he met Izz al-Din al-Qassam,* and that he was injured in the revolution. He declared that anyone who sold land to the Jews was a traitor who must be killed.

Yunes doesn't know why Ahmad was killed, because he's convinced he didn't sell land to the Jews, and that, in fact, he didn't have any land to sell

---

* Legendary figure of the national Palestinian movement, died in combat in 1935.

since he'd taken the land he controlled by force, and the deeds were in the Sursuq family's possession.

When Ahmad was killed by the revolutionaries' bullets, Yunes, who was then seventeen, didn't understand why. Despite the rumors, he wasn't the one who'd killed his cousin, and he was sure that Ahmad, who'd become the leader of the village, hadn't sold land to the Jews. True, he was domineering, arrogant and rude; and true, he hated Yunes and would say that the youth had abandoned his father, mother, and wife to beggary while he worked as a bandit in the name of the revolution; and true, he beat his two wives terribly and treated everyone with contempt, but why had he been killed?

Yunes was convinced that Ahmad hadn't been a traitor. Everyone hated him, even his children. The strange thing was that at his funeral his wives yelled as though they were being beaten. Surrounded by their children, the two women wept, moaned, pleaded with him to get up, swearing they would never leave the house again. Everyone was dumbfounded. No one mourned the loss of this shit (this is what his relatives called him privately), but everyone was amazed at his wives' behavior and how unconvinced they seemed that the man had died. They appeared to be afraid he might rise up, see they weren't weeping enough, and shower them with blows.

Ahmad died without anyone knowing who killed him, but the way he was killed seemed to indicate that he was a collaborator or had sold land. The killer came to his house at night, knocked on the door, shot him, and left. Then, when the killer got to Nab' al-Asal, he fired two shots into the air. The two shots gave the impression that Ahmad had been executed rather than murdered for some personal or family reason. Suspicion hung over Yunes because of the quarrel between Ahmad and Sheikh Ibrahim, which had ended with the sheikh's being expelled from his position at the mosque.

It was Ahmad who engineered the replacement for Sheikh Ibrahim, convincing everybody by saying that the sheikh was blind and unable to teach his pupils reading and writing, that he'd begun forgetting the names and verses of the Koran, and could no longer conduct prayers decently. Once shamefully dismissed from his responsibilities, Sheikh Ibrahim became a beggar, at a loss as to how to provide for his family.

Into the house of Sheikh Ibrahim came Nahilah, the twelve-year-old daughter of Mohammed al-Shawwah. They had asked for her for Yunes because her family was the poorest in the village. Her father, who had died when she was six, had had only girls, and her mother had inherited nothing from her husband. She took up work in the fields, and Ahmad didn't let her keep the land her husband had worked because women, in his view, "should never be entrusted with land." So she ended up working on Ahmad's land and as a servant in his house and was beaten along with his wives. When Yunes' mother decided to arrange a marriage for her son, she consulted one of Ahmad's wives, who advised her to go to Nahilah's mother: "Go and take your pick – five poor, fatherless girls who need someone to give them a respectable home." She went to choose, but Nahilah's mother wouldn't let her.

"If you want a bride for your son, take this one," she said, pointing to Nahilah, and there was no further discussion.

"This one" was Nahilah.

Yunes will never forget the wedding, and the wedding night.

How could he forget when he could smell the blood for days and days and would hate himself until the day he died?

How could he forget the girl's face as she shook with fear?

How could he forget his mother closing the door behind them and waiting?

How could he forget that he fell asleep with the girl next to him in the bed, and didn't take off his clothes?

How could he forget the high-pitched *youyous* of joy outside and the mother waving a white handkerchief with a spot of blood on it to announce the girl's virginity and purity?

How could he forget that room, with its bittersweet smell?

The mother took the girl without argument. She wanted a wife for her son. Marriage would steady the boy and force him to come back home.

The sheikh took the girl without argument, because he'd grieved over his son and wanted a grandson. He had wanted his son to be a sheikh, a scholar and a Sufi, but all the boy could cite from the Koran was the first chapter. He sent him to the elementary school in Sha'ab, but instead of studying he made off with the others into the mountains. He'd picked up a rifle and started moving from village to village, taking part in attacks on British army patrols.

Yunes could see that his father and mother were sunk in poverty, but he had no concept of what that meant. He must have wanted to escape from the company of that old man who cursed fate and sat all day in front of his house, and who'd go every Friday morning to the mosque of Salah al-Din in the village square, where, without fail, an incident would arise that would result in his being thrown out. During that time, Kamel al-Asadi led the worshippers. This Kamel was neither a sheikh nor a scholar. He hadn't learned the Koran by heart, he hadn't studied in a religious school, and he didn't take part in the devotions of the Sufis who'd built themselves a modest mosque in Sha'ab dedicated to the Yashrati master of whom Sheikh Ibrahim was one of the first disciples.

They said, "Let's get him married," so they got him married.

And Yunes accepted. He heard the name Nahilah and accepted. He gave his mother ten Palestinian lira – God knows where he got them – for the wedding, the dowry, and the rest.

And the wedding took place.

The boy sat down among the men. The ceremony almost got ugly: Sheikh Ibrahim threw Sheikh Kamel out and performed the rites himself, after which there were *youyous* of joy. Nahilah entered the house. The *youyous* mounted, and the young man was receiving congratulations when the door opened and the girl entered, holding her fingers out in front of her with a lit candle on each one. She was covered from head to toe by a robe behind whose colors her face was lost.

Yunes didn't see her.

He saw a girl on the verge of collapse, swaying as though dancing, approaching the chair on which her husband was seated, and then kneeling. The candles shone in Yunes' face, the flames dazzled his eyes, and he didn't see.

Yunes doesn't remember how long she knelt, for time seemed eternal that day; his eyes burned with something like tears, his shadow swayed on the walls, and the *youyous* pounded in his ears.

He would never say he was afraid. He would say instead that when his shadow leapt up in front of him that night he didn't recognize it, as though it were the shadow of some other young man, lengthening and breaking off and barging around against the ceiling and among the guests and against the walls. And he would say too that when he bent over to extinguish the candles, his mother stopped him and made him sit still again and asked him to smile. Then his mother knelt next to the girl, took hold of her right arm and pulled her up, and the two of them walked among the guests as the showers of rice started to fall on them. Sheikh Sa'id Ma'lawi stood up, struck his tambourine and shouted, "God lives!" and the cry was taken up by five bearded men who had come from Sha'ab at the behest of the great Yashrati, sheikh of the Yashrati Shadhili order, to bless Sheikh Ibrahim's son's marriage and recite the prayers that would help him follow the path of righteousness like his father before him.

The woman and the girl disappeared into the bedroom. After what seemed like a long while, they returned carrying olives and grapes. The girl tossed the olives one by one to the guests while the woman bent down and laid a large cluster of white grapes before the girl's feet and asked her to walk on them. The girl took off her slippers, raised her right foot with care and stepped on the grapes; then she raised the other foot and walked on them.

Yunes, telling me of his love for white grapes as we drank a "tear" of arak once at his house, said that the women sitting in the reception room rose from their places and started laying clusters of white grapes before the bride, and that she walked on them, the tears of the grapes soaking the ground.

He said he saw the tears. "Wine is the tears of grapes. That's why we say 'a tear of arak' – not because we want to drink it in small quantities, and not because we put the arak in the small flask we call a *batha*, which is tear-shaped, but because when the grapes are pressed, the juice oozes out like tears, drop by drop."

Years later, when Yunes and Nahilah were in the cave at Bab al-Shams and night fell, Nahilah lit a candle she had hidden behind a rock she called the pantry. Yunes leapt up and brought out ten bunches of grapes he'd cut from the vines scattered around Deir al-Asad, and he spread these on the ground and asked her to walk on them.

"Take off your shoes and walk. Today I'll marry you according to the law of the Prophet."

She said that that day the man was mad with love. She bent over, re-moved her head scarf, placed the grapes on it, wrapped them up and pushed the bundle to one side. She told Yunes that at the wedding, she'd only stepped on one bunch, that she hated walking on grapes, that she'd slipped and narrowly escaped death because the grape juice had clung to her heels, and that when it came time to marry her daughters, she'd never ask them to walk on grapes – what a shameful idea!

Nahilah walked on the grapes, which exploded beneath her small, bare feet, then went into the bedroom and did not come out again.

"You know the rest," Yunes said. "My mother right by the door and me inside. What are these awful customs? You have to fuck for their sake, strip off your clothes and get it over with in a hurry so they don't get bored wait-ing outside."

But I don't know the rest, Father, and you're lying when you say the rest was the way it usually is.

You didn't tell me everything; I know, because Abu Ma'rouf filled me in.

Abu Ma'rouf was a pleasant man I met in 1969 in the Nahr al-Barid camp in northern Lebanon, after the commander of the base at Kafar Shouba had thrown me out for being an atheist. I had gone to Nahr al-Barid as politi-cal commissar for the camp militia, when clashes broke out between us and the Lebanese army. The November cold was intense and made our bones ache. They put me and Abu Ma'rouf on the forward road block, which was supposed to be a lookout position. We were opposite a hill occupied by the army, and it was our job to engage the enemy briefly if the camp were attacked before withdrawing, in other words, to delay their advance as much as possible so that the other groups could block the roads leading to the camp.

A naïve plan, you'll say.

It wasn't even a plan, I'll answer, but I'm not interested at the moment in a critique of our military experiences, which I've never understood much about. I wanted to inform you that the rest was not "the way it usually is."

Abu Ma'rouf was a grown man.

In those days, before we reached the age of twenty, we wondered at the way these men would come and fight with us. We thought they must be brave, if only because they were what we imagined men should be like. Abu Ma'rouf was in his forties. A thick black moustache covered his upper lip and curled into his mouth. He would take hold of the Degtyaref machine gun, wrap the ammunition belt around his neck and waist, and sit in silence. I gathered that he was from the village of Saffouri, that his wife and children lived in the Ain al-Hilweh camp, that he had fought in '48, and that he didn't believe Palestine would ever exist again.

I never asked him why, in that case, he was fighting. In those days I believed that the "people's war" (that's what we called it, inspired by the Chinese model) would liberate Palestine. These days, the issue's become more complicated, even though I do believe that Palestine will return, in some form.

Abu Ma'rouf, that silent man from whose lips I would have to wrest words almost by force, told me a story similar to yours.

You'll be surprised, since you never met Abu Ma'rouf al-Abid, and Ain al-Zaitoun isn't near Saffouri. All the same, this man made me understand your generation's stories about women, which can be summed up in the one about the cotton swab. Yes, the cotton swab. Don't tell me I'm making this story up to upset you. I swear I'm not making up a word of it. But I finally understood.

It was four in the morning. We'd gone more than two days without sleep, wasting away in the trench under the November drizzle, with the cold stealing into our bones.

He said he was going to warm himself up by talking about women, since nothing warmed a man's bones like a woman's body. He told the story of his first night with his wife from Saffouri. At the time, I didn't ask him any questions, and that may be why he got going. He said that women would warm us up – what was I to say? Then I got scared. I thought maybe he was one of *those* and would eventually make his move. The man wanted me to keep quiet so he could talk, so I listened, but I didn't believe him. Now I know that I should have believed him, because the story of Abu Ma'rouf and his first wife, who died in Saffouri, could well be your story, too.

Abu Ma'rouf said his first wife died during the Israeli bombing of Saffouri on July 15, 1948, and that it was Abu Mahmoud's fault, the village's commander in the sacred jihad: "After the fall of Shafa Amar and the displacement of more than three thousand of its inhabitants to our village, he should have realized that the battle was over, but he insisted on staying put. We gathered in the square in front of the mosque, and he said we could hang on for a week and then the Arab Liberation Army, which was based at Nazareth, would come. But we didn't hang on. In fact, I can't remember if we even fought. The planes came. Three of them circled above the village, dropped barrels filled with fire and gunpowder, and the houses started to collapse."

He said he watched how the houses would blast open, the doors and windows would fly out, and then the flames would rise. He said his wife and three children died in their house: "I was at the roadblock at the entrance to the village, and when I heard the bombing, I ran toward the house. They said I got scared, but no, I wasn't scared for myself, I was afraid for her and the children. I ran to the village carrying my English rifle, and when I got to the house, the flames were everywhere. I didn't even have time to bury them. I was driven, with the rest of those who escaped, from Saffouri to al-Ramah, from al-Ramah to al-Bqei'a, from al-Bqei'a to Sahmatah to Deir al-Qasi, and finally, to Bint Jbeil in Lebanon.

"We spent three days in the fields around al-Ramah, where we had nothing and almost died of hunger. My mother asked me to go back to her house in the village to get a little flour and cracked wheat. I found the village empty and didn't see any Jews. I met three old men and a woman with a crooked back. They said they'd given up, they didn't know where to go. One of them was a relative of mine, Ahmad al-Abid. I was stunned that his son hadn't taken him with him and asked if he wanted to come with me. He raised his head to say no, and then I realized he'd stayed behind because he was sick; he was spitting and coughing, and his eyes were running. I went to my mother's house. The door was open and everything was in its place, untouched. I grabbed a bag of flour and left. On the way back, they fired at me, and I left the bag in the field. Later we found out that the three old men and the woman had been killed. We were in the fields near al-Ramah when we heard the news. It seems Ahmad's son went back to look for his father and found the four bodies lying in the road.

"We never fought. Now we say we fought and that Palestine was lost because the Arab countries betrayed us. That's not true. Palestine was lost because we didn't fight. We were like idiots; we would take our rifles and wait for them in our villages, and when they came with their motorized units and their heavy machine guns and their airplanes, we were beaten without a fight."

Later, he remarried in Lebanon and had seven children. He'd named the first three after his children who'd died there, but his first wife was still in his bones. "She was like fire," he said. "She would ignite me whenever she came near me."

She had been fourteen and he fifteen.

"Impossible! At that age!"

He started laughing, the tears pouring from his eyes from the cold. Then he told me about the cotton swab.

How to tell you the story, Father? Abu Ma'rouf said incredible things, but I believed them – perhaps because we were alone in that trench, perhaps because of the dawn, the changing colors of first light, perhaps because my bones were cold. I don't know.

He said, "After the wedding party was over – and as you know, a wedding, my friend, is no joke – we went inside. You know, I swear I had no idea. Well, no, of course, I used to practice the secret habit and I'd played around with my buddies and everything, but getting married is different. As soon as I entered the bedroom, I saw her. She was young, seated on the edge of the bed all wrapped up in her clothes, and crying. I sat down beside her, my body feeling icy all over. She told me she liked sewing and embroidery and that she'd made all her wedding clothes. Then she started to yawn. She lay back on the bed, and I stretched out beside her. She didn't take her clothes off, and I didn't take mine off either. I went to sleep. Or no, before I dropped off I got on top of her, and as soon as I was on top of her it happened. I came and got it all over my trousers. Then I lay down next to her. I think we must have dropped off quickly because I woke up to a loud knocking on the door. I opened it and found my mother asking for the sheet. Then she rushed into the room, pulled out the sheet from under the girl and ran out. We heard the trills of joy. My mother told me later she'd wiped the sheet with chicken blood and that she'd wished the earth would have opened up and swallowed her."

Abu Ma'rouf said that two days later he went into his bedroom and found the girl naked, and everything went fine.

"Do you know what my mother did, two days later? She took the poor girl into the bathroom, stripped off her clothes and started inspecting her body minutely, touching her everywhere. The girl didn't know what to do – laugh at the tickling or scream at the pain of my mother's pinches. Then my mother scrubbed her with scented soap, poured water over her, and dried her off. She brought a cotton swab and asked her to open her thighs; then she placed the swab there and told her, 'Tonight take off your clothes and wait for him in bed. Take hold of his member and insert it here where the cotton is. Put a pillow under your behind and lift up your legs.'

"When I got into bed and lifted the coverlet so I could lie down, I found her naked. She gestured to me to take off my robe, so I took it off, the sweat dripping off my face and eyes, and I stretched out beside her and did nothing. She stretched out her hand, took hold of my thing and pulled me toward her, and I found myself on top of her, with her holding onto it with both hands and tugging. I was bathed in sweat and fear. She stretched her hand to the place where the swab was and placed it there, and I found myself getting bigger and bigger and bigger. Then I was inside her, and I got bigger inside her and learned the secret of life. She put her hands on my shoulders and screamed. That was the night I really came for the first time. Before that it wasn't the same. That night my whole being was there, inside her.

"When I rolled off of her, I saw that blood had stained the sheet, and that she was searching for something like a madwoman. She searched the whole bed, afraid the swab was lost. I looked with her for a bit, then dropped off, so exhausted I didn't hear her questions. The next morning she said she'd found the swab but I don't think she had. I think my mother had just reassured her it wouldn't do her any harm."

Abu Ma'rouf said he'd never forget the taste of her.

"And your second wife?" I asked him.

"At first I didn't want to get married again; Umm Ma'rouf had been part of my flesh. But my mother, God rest her soul, knew better than I. She knew a man shouldn't remain alone or he'd mate with the devil, so she convinced me to marry the second Umm Ma'rouf, a refugee girl from Sha'ab, like us. I married her in Ain al-Hilweh, and she bore me seven children."

"And what happened," I asked.

"Shame on you – you can't ask things like that. With the second one, I knew what to do, and everything went fine from the first night."

"Did you tell her about the piece of cotton?"

"Of course not. You don't understand women. You must never tell a woman about the others. If a woman doesn't think she's the center of your life, she'll become miserable and make your life miserable, too."

Abu Ma'rouf's story amazed me. I thought it wasn't possible, and then forgot all about it.

But now I see it could be true. I see you before me, and I see Nahilah, I see everything. I can see you, a child, going into the bedroom, playing around with the young girl, then falling asleep beside her. I won't say you were innocent, but you just didn't know how. Your mother arrives. She takes the girl to the bathroom. She soaps her and pours water over her, then puts the cotton in her – and you discover the secret of life through a little piece of white cotton.

I know you won't like this story, you'll think it's a slur on your manhood. You prefer to talk about grapes and tears of arak and the dance of a girl adorned in candles before her groom, and you'd rather not admit that you didn't know what to do.

Would you like to deny the whole thing?

Fine. I'll agree with you. I won't say you lay down beside her in your clothes like Abu Ma'rouf did. Maybe you took off your clothes and made the poor girl take hers off, too, and you didn't know how to do it and your mother had to make do with a little drop of blood from her finger on the sheet. Then she waited seven nights for you two and finally was forced to put the cotton swab inside the girl to guide you to the place.

"It's not true," you'll say.

Okay. So where is the truth? Tell me, since I'm still confused about the dates. Did Ibrahim die in 1951 at three, meaning he was born in 1948? What was going on between 1943, when you got married, and 1948, the year your first child was born?

Didn't your wife get pregnant?

Would you put up with a wife that couldn't get pregnant? Why didn't you divorce her? Your mother used to say she was still a child and would get pregnant when she matured. So Nahilah didn't mature until 1948?

Did you love her?

No, you didn't. You yourself said you only learned to love her a long while after you married her, when your visits to her came to be your whole life.

So what was it?

You'll tell me it was the war, and you paid no attention. You're confusing me – I don't understand a thing, I swear to you. Your story seems muddled and mysterious. And my presence in this hospital seems like a dream, but I know I'm not dreaming because I can't sleep anymore.

Say something, Father – I've had enough of all this. Say something, just one word, then die if you want, or do whatever you please, or you could tell me if you need something.

Okay, okay, fine. It wasn't thanks to a piece of cotton that your marriage was consummated, and it never crossed your mind to divorce your wife for not having children right away, you didn't experience terror facing the Jewish settlement, you didn't kill Ahmad Ibn Mahmoud, and you didn't cry when you had toothaches . . .

Happy now?

Satisfied and sound asleep? I swear you're a lucky man. What have you got to worry about? You sleep like a baby beside death – death doesn't dare touch you.

Death is afraid of you, you'll say, or you used to say.

But me, right now I'm not in the mood to listen to heroics. Do as you like – die or don't die, dream or don't dream, it's up to you.

How DID we get here?

Honestly I don't understand how things took this course, why they happened – or didn't happen – like they did. I don't understand why I stayed here, why I didn't leave with them. I don't understand how, you . . .

Who says I had to stay?

I'm not talking about the hospital. The hospital, that's you, and I couldn't abandon you even if I weren't a frightened fugitive or hadn't fallen into Shams' trap.

I'm talking about Beirut. I didn't have to stay in Beirut as I claimed to Shams. I told her I felt I had to stay and that it just wasn't possible for us to leave the people here, to turn our backs on them and go.

But I was lying.

Well no, I wasn't lying. At that moment, with Shams, I believed what I said. But I don't know anymore. I was with her in my house here in the camp; I closed the windows tightly so no one would see us. The cold was intense, but I didn't feel it. My body was shivering with heat. I wanted to prostrate myself in front of her. She was beautiful and naked, wrapped in a white sheet, her long hair beaded with drops of water. I wanted to kneel down and place my head on her belly. Everything inside me was quivering. And there was the thirst that can never be quenched.

I wanted to kneel, rub my head all over her feet and pour myself out in front of her. But instead of kneeling, those stupid words came from my lips.

She asked me why I didn't go with the others, and I answered and waited. I heard her laugh. She turned around in the white sheet, sat down on the bed, and started laughing. She didn't say my words had bewitched her, the way words are supposed to in moments of passion.

She laughed and said she was hungry.

I suggested we make something at home and asked if she wanted me to make her some pasta as usual.

She yawned and said, "Whatever you want."

She stretched her hand behind her back and the sheet fell away from her brown breasts, still wet from the bath. I leapt toward her, but she raised her hand and said, "No. I'm hungry." I ran to the kitchen and started frying cauliflower and making *taratur* sauce.

"You're the champion at *taratur*," she used to say, licking the last of the white sauce, made from sesame paste, limes, and garlic, from her fingers.

She said she didn't like fried cauliflower, but the *taratur* was fantastic.

I didn't say . . . well yes, in fact, I did repeat that sentence of mine for her ears. I said I felt that I had to stay because we couldn't leave the people here. She laughed again and said she'd eaten enough and wanted to sleep. She pushed the tray to one side, put her head on the cushion, and slept.

At that moment I told her I wanted to stay because I wanted to impress her. But now, no. I feel there's no reason for me to stay. I stayed here without rhyme or reason, just to stay. I don't know where you were those days. The truth is I didn't ask about you. I was like someone who'd been hypnotized. I picked up my bag, took my Kalashnikov, barrel pointed to the ground, and made my way to the municipal stadium in Beirut to leave with the rest. And there, in the middle of the crowd and the long, wan faces, I made up my mind to go back to the camp.

You'll remember how the fedayeen left Beirut during the siege.

You said you were against leaving. "Better death!" you told me. "Leave under the guard of the Americans and Israelis? Never!" But you were the first to set off. You went to that Christian village and hid yourself there and made up that story about the priest who thought you were a Christian who hid you in his house. I believed you at the time. At the time I, too, claimed to have refused to leave – "Shame on you, my friend! Like the Turkish army? Never! We can never leave Beirut!" But, at the same time, I was convinced that we had to leave. We were defeated, and we had to withdraw as defeated armies do. On my way to the stadium, I imagined myself part of a

Greek epic setting out on a new, Palestinian Odyssey. I'm not sure if I imagined that Odyssey then or I'm just saying that now because Mahmoud Darwish wrote a long poem about such an odyssey, even though he didn't get on the Greek boats that would carry the Palestinians to their new wilderness either.

I put on my military uniform, picked up my small pack, took my rifle, and went. It felt like I was ripping the place from my skin. I turned around and saw the camp looking like a block of stone. Suddenly the camp became a mound of ruins, a place unfit for habitation, and I decided to leave it forever. What would I do in the camp after the fedayeen had pulled out? Would I end my life there, meaninglessly, the same way I'd lived all those years doctoring the sick when I wasn't really a doctor, loving a woman I didn't really love? At that time I was on the verge of marrying plump, light-skinned Nuha, who worked with us at the Red Crescent. The only thing Nuha wanted was to get married. She'd take me to her parents' house at the camp entrance near the open space that later became the common grave, and there we'd eat and I'd see in her mother's eyes a phantom called marriage. I don't know how I came to find myself half-married without realizing it. Then came the Israeli invasion and the decision to move us out of Beirut.

I looked back and I saw the heap of stones called the Shatila camp, and I started running in the direction of the stadium. I was afraid that Nuha would come, persuade me to stay, and take me to her parents' house. I reached the stadium convinced she'd be there. I ducked down, blending in with the crowd so she wouldn't see me. I didn't want her, and I had no desire to stay or to get married. I would raise my head from time to time and steal a look, so I could spot her before she saw me and could run away. But I didn't see her. Instead of relaxing, setting my concerns aside, and looking for my friends, however, I was seized with anxiety, as though her absence had struck terror in me. I didn't want her to come, and she didn't, yet I found myself searching for her.

You remember those days – women and tears and rice and shots fired into the air. I never saw anything like it in my life – a defeated army withdrawing like victors! That burning Beirut summer was cooled with tears; August scorched the earth, the people, and the tears with its savage sun. And I searched for Nuha. I thought, it's impossible – Nuha's given up her life's best bet after all that? She was bound to come and ask me to promise to marry her, and I'd agree, and then forget her. But where was she? I walked through the crowds like a stranger, because if your mother doesn't come to say goodbye, it's not a real goodbye. Mothers filled the place, and the young men were eating and weeping. Food and tears, that was the farewell. Mothers opening bundles of food wrapped in cloths and young men eating, *youyous* and bullets.

At that moment, Abu Salem, I thought of my mother. At that moment I loved her and forgave her and said I wished she were there. But where was she? At that point I didn't know she was in Ramallah. At the municipal stadium, I was sure my mother would come, that she'd suddenly appear at Nuha's side and unwrap a bundle of food in front of me, and I'd eat and weep like everyone else.

I stood there alone, and nobody came.

Then I don't know what happened to me – I looked at the people, and they seemed like ghosts.

I already told you about the siege, about the hospital, and about death – how we lived with death without taking it in. I stayed in the hospital for a month treating the dead, eating eggplant, and watching the Israeli planes launch bombing raids like they were competing in fireworks displays. I lived with death, but I couldn't absorb it. They all died. They came, and as soon as we'd put them in beds, they died. Strange days. Do you remember how we used to talk about the walking dead? Did I tell you about Ahmad Jasim? The man was hit in the throat near the museum, but he kept going. He fell to the ground, then got up like a chicken with its throat slit and, to the astonishment of his comrades, set off in the direction of the Israeli army positions. After about ten meters, he fell down dead, motionless. They picked him up and brought him to the hospital. I examined him and ordered them to take his body to the morgue. "The morgue?" shrieked one of his comrades. "Why the morgue?"

"Because he's dead," I said.

"Dead? That's impossible!" the man cried.

I ordered Abu Ahmad to take him to the morgue.

Then the yelling started. They seized the body, picked it up and left. I tried to explain that he was dead and that walking after being hit didn't mean anything because it was just an involuntary reflex, but they called me names, wrapped him in a woolen blanket, and went off with him.

We lived three months with death without believing it. But in the middle of the stadium, I finally believed it. They all seemed dead, eating and firing into the air and weeping.

Just as I came to the stadium running, so I left it running.

I won't tell you how I looked for Nuha like a madman. God, why didn't she come? It was just that my tears wouldn't flow. I hated this farewell of theirs – why were they eating and weeping and shooting? There shouldn't have been a farewell. At that instant I was ready to buy a farewell for myself at any cost. I wanted to weep as they wept and shoot as they were shooting.

But she didn't come.

What had happened to Nuha? Had she understood that I didn't want her anymore? Had love ended along with the siege?

Why the tears? I ask you. Your closed eyes are soaking in bluish white. I opened your eyes and put a few drops in. Do you know what the drops are called? Artificial Tears. They call drops for washing out the eyes "tears." People go to the pharmacy and actually buy tears, while we can barely hold ours back.

"Tears are our remedy," my mother used to say.

My mother used to cry beneath the beating rain that crackled on the zinc sheets we'd made into a roof for our crumbling house in the camp. She'd cry and say that tears were a remedy for the eyes. She'd cry and get scared. Then she fled to Jordan and left me with my grandmother and the flower pillow. I told you about my grandmother's pillow, so why should I repeat the story now? I just wanted to say that I bought this eyedropper made in England so I could put tears in your eyes, which are dry as kindling. Brother, cry at least once. Cry for your fate and mine, I beg you – you don't know the importance of tears. The best thing for the eyes are tears, tears are indispensable. They are the water that washes the eye, the protein that nourishes it, and the lubrication that allows the eyelids to slide over it.

You've made me cry, but you refuse to cry yourself.

I administer the drops, wait for your tears and feel the tears rise up in my own eyes. I'm not weeping for you; I'm weeping for Umm Hassan, not because she died but because she left me the videocassette.

SANA', THE WIFE of the *kunafa*-seller, came. She came and stood by the open door of your room and knocked. I was sitting here reading Jabra Ibrahim Jabra's novel *In Search of Walid Mas'oud*. I was fascinated by Walid Mas'oud, the Palestinian who disappeared leaving a mysterious tape in his car, to unravel the riddle of which Jabra had to write a long and beautiful novel. I love Jabra because he writes like an aristocrat – his sentences are elitist and beautiful. It's true he was poor when he was a child, but he wrote like real writers, with expressive, literary sentences. You have to read them the way you read literature, not the way I'm talking to you now.

Sana' knocked and didn't enter. I put my book aside, stood up, and asked her in, but she stood by the door and gave me the cassette.

"This is what Umm Hassan left you," she said. "Umm Hassan entrusted me with this tape to give to you."

I took the videotape and offered her a cigarette, which she smoked greedily. I used to think that veiled women didn't smoke, but Sana' talked and stammered, gulping down the smoke between syllables.

I didn't understand about the cassette, because Umm Hassan had visited Galilee three years before, and when she returned she brought me a branch of oranges and told me of her visit to al-Ghabsiyyeh, where she'd lit a candle under the lotus tree and prayed two prostrations in the mosque.

Sana' said Umm Hassan had visited al-Kweikat again, six months before, and had seen her house and made up her mind to die. Every day she'd watch this cassette and tell stories while others joined her in her lamentation, her sorrow, and her memories.

"She stopped sleeping," said Sana'. "She came to me and said she'd heard the call of death, because she couldn't sleep. Sobs clung to her voice, and she told me to give you this tape. I don't know what you'll see on it. It's falling apart it's been used so often, but she left it for you."

I thanked Sana', nodding goodbye to her, but she didn't move, as if she were stuck to the door. Then she spoke. She blew smoke in my face and her eyes filled with tears.

Sana' told me about that journey. At first I couldn't understand a thing. Then the words started transforming themselves into pictures. She spoke about Fawzi, Umm Hassan's brother, and about the village of Abu Sinan, stammering and repeating herself as though she had no control over her lips. Then she got to the point.

"I won't tell you to take good care of it," said Sana'. "That cassette – I mean, you know . . ."

"God rest her soul," I said.

"God rest all our souls," said the pious woman and started to go. After taking two hesitant steps, she came back and said, "Please, Doctor, take good care of the cassette."

Is it true?

Can it be that a woman died because she met another woman?

Umm Hassan's story shook me to the core, not just because she died, but because she thought of me and left me this tape.

What could have happened in al-Kweikat for the woman to die?

You know Umm Hassan better than I do and you know her courage. She left al-Kweikat when she was twenty-five carrying her son, Hassan, on her back and holding her daughters, Salema and Hanan, by the hand. They walked from al-Kweikat to Yarka. In the olive orchards of Yarka, when the wife of Qasem Ahmad Sa'id discovered that what she was carrying in her arms was a pillow rather than her baby son, she started wailing. Her husband was sitting on the ground like an imbecile while she implored him, "Go and get the boy!" But the man was incapable of getting to his feet. The mother moaned like a wounded animal, and the husband sat motionless, but Umm Hassan – do you know what she did? Umm Hassan went back on her own. She left her children with Samirah, the wife of Qasem Ahmad Sa'id, went back to the village, and took the child from the hands of the Jews. She didn't tell anyone what she'd seen or what the Palmach* men were doing to al-Kweikat. She returned exhausted, gasping, as though all the air in the world couldn't fill her lungs. She set the child down in front of its mother, took her own children, and went to the olive tree that her husband and brothers were beneath. Samirah ran to her to kiss her hand, but Umm Hassan looked at her with contempt and pushed her away.

Umm Hassan didn't think she'd done anything extraordinary. She'd gone and got the child, and that was all there was to it. No one considered her a heroine. In those days, surprise had disappeared from people's faces; sorrow alone wrapped itself around them, like an overcoat full of holes.

Al-Kweikat fell to the Jews without our knowing it. On the night of June 9, 1948, everyone came out of their houses in their nightclothes. The shelling was heavy, and the artillery thundered into the night of the unsleeping village. People took their children and fled through the fields to the neighboring villages of Yarka and Deir al-Qasi, and from Deir al-Qasi to Abu Sinan and Ya'thur, and on from there. Abu Hassan drove four head of sheep and three of goats along the road, but the flock died at Ya'thur, and Umm Hassan wept for the animals as a mother weeps for her children.

"God, I wept, Son! How I mourned those animals! How could they be gone as though they'd never been? Wiped off the face of the earth, dead. How were we supposed to live?"

But Umm Hassan lived long enough to bury her sons one after the other.

Sana' said Umm Hassan never stopped weeping. She'd put on the cassette and would weep and tell everyone the story of the two visits she'd made over there. "Dear God, people. What we've lived through and seen. Would that we'd neither seen nor lived through such things!"

Sana' said that she died of grief over her house.

"She knew?" I asked.

* Striking force of the Haganah, consisting of nine assault companies throughout Galilee and Jerusalem. Palmach leaders included Yigal Allon, Moshe Dayan, and Yitchak Rabin.

"I've no idea," she answered. "Maybe it was because she saw it for her-self. Hearing's not like seeing."

And you, Father – did you know these things? Why didn't you tell Umm Hassan what had happened to al-Kweikat? Didn't you spend your days and nights in those demolished villages? Why didn't you tell the woman that the Jews had occupied her house?

"Why the fuss?" you'll say. "Umm Hassan didn't die because she saw the house. She died because her hour had come."

THAT'S WHAT you would have said if I'd told you about Umm Hassan's house.

Umm Hassan said she'd gone there. It was her second visit to her brother Fawzi's house in Abu Sinan.

"My family fled from al-Kweikat to Abu Sinan and stayed there. What a shame that my husband didn't want to listen to my father. He preferred to stay with his own family; his brothers had decided to go to Lebanon, so he went with them. My father disagreed. He hid with his wife and children and grandchildren in the olive groves for more than a year. Then he appeared in Abu Sinan and stayed there. I don't know how they managed. My father used to grow watermelons. After the Israelis moved in, the watermelons belonged to them. They were signed on as construction workers and got by. Then my father bought a plot of land and built a house. It was to my father's house in Abu Sinan that I went, and there I found my brother, sick. He had pneumonia, and we feared for his life. That's why we didn't go to al-Kweikat. Was I supposed to go on my own? I went to Deir al-Asad and Sha'ab and visited our relatives there, but al-Kweikat had been demolished, and my brother was sick. All the same, once when we were coming back from Sha'ab and my nephew was driving me in his little car, I begged him to go by al-Kweikat. "No, Auntie," he said. "There are only Jews," and kept going. I begged him, but he wouldn't agree. We went on the road parallel to the village, but I couldn't see a thing."

"The second time was different," said Umm Hassan.

"My brother was in excellent health, and he took me to al-Kweikat. I asked him to do it, and at first he said the same thing as his son, but later he agreed. We went and he took his son, Rami, who had a video camera. He's the one who filmed the tape, God love him. We went into al-Kweikat, and I didn't recognize it until we got to the house."

What should I say about Umm Hassan?

Should I mention the tears, or the memories, or say nothing?

Seated in the backseat of the little blue Volkswagen, she was looking out the window and seeing nothing.

"We're here," said Fawzi.

Her brother got out of the car and held out his hand to help her out. Umm Hassan moved her stout body forward but couldn't raise her head. She seemed unable to do so, as though her breasts were pulling her down toward the ground. She was bent over and rooted to the spot.

"Come on, Sister."

Fawzi helped her out of the car. She remained doubled over, then put her hand to her waist and stood upright.

He pointed to the house, but she couldn't see a thing.

Her tears flowed silently. She wiped them away with her sleeve and listened to her brother's explanations while his son played around with the camera.

"They demolished every single house, and built the Beyt ha-Emek settlement – except for the new houses, the ones that were built on the hill."

Umm Hassan's house had been one of the new ones up on the hill.

"All the houses were demolished," said the brother.

"And mine?" murmured Umm Hassan.

"There it is," he said.

They were about twenty meters from the house. The branches of the eucalyptus tree were swaying. But Umm Hassan could see nothing. He took her by the arm and they walked. Then suddenly she saw it all.

"It's as if no time has passed."

Of what time was she talking about, Father? Can we find it in the videocassette tapes that have become our only entertainment? The Shatila camp has turned into Camp Video. The videocassettes circulate among the houses, and people sit around their television sets, they remember and tell stories. They tell stories about what they see, and out of the glimpses of the villages they build villages. Don't they ever get sick of repeating the same stories? Umm Hassan never slept, and, until her death, she would tell stories, until all the tears had drained from her eyes.

She said that suddenly everything came back to her. She went up to the front door but didn't press the buzzer. She stood back a little and walked around the house. She sat on the ground with her back against the eucalyptus tree as she used to do. She'd been afraid of the tree, so she'd turn her back on it. Her husband would make fun of her for turning her back on the horizon and looking only at the stones and the walls. Her brother took her by the hand and helped her up. Again, it was difficult for her to stand, as though she were rooted to the ground. Her brother dragged her to the door and pressed the buzzer. No one opened, so he pressed it a second time. The ringing reverberated louder and louder in Umm Hassan's ears; everything seemed to be pounding, her body was trembling, her pulse racing. The brother stood waiting.

The door finally opened.

A woman appeared: about fifty years old, dark complexion, large eyes, black hair streaked with gray.

Fawzi said something in Hebrew.

"Why are you speaking to me in Hebrew? Speak to me in Arabic," said the woman with a strong Lebanese accent.

"Excuse me, Madam. Is your husband here?" asked Fawzi.

"No, he's not here. Is everything all right? Please come in."

She opened the door wider.

"You know Arabic," Umm Hassan whispered as she entered. "You're an Arab, Sister – aren't you?"

"No, I'm not an Arab," said the woman.

"You've studied Arabic?" asked Umm Hassan.

"No, I studied Hebrew, but I haven't forgotten my Arabic. Come in, come in."

They entered the house. Umm Hassan said – like everyone else who's gone back to see their former homes – "Everything was in its place. Everything was just how it used to be, even the earthenware water jug."

"God of all the worlds," sighed Umm Hassan, "what would Umm Isa have said if she'd visited her house in Jerusalem? Poor Umm Isa. In her last days she spoke about just one thing – the saucepan of zucchini. Umm Isa left her house in Katamon in Jerusalem without turning off the flame under the saucepan of zucchini."

"I can smell burning. The saucepan. I must go and turn off the flame," she would say to Umm Hassan, who nursed her during her last illness. And Umm Hassan, who had felt pity for the dying woman, stood in her own house in front of the earthenware water jug that was still where it had been, smelled the zucchini in Umm Isa's saucepan, and said that everything was in its place except for those people who had come in and sat down right where we'd been sitting.

The Israeli woman left her in front of the water jug and returned with a pot of Turkish coffee. She poured three cups and sat calmly watching these strangers whose hands trembled as they held their coffee. Before Umm Hassan could open her mouth to ask a thing, the Israeli woman said, "It's your house, isn't it?"

"How did you know?" asked Umm Hassan.

"I've been waiting for you for a long time. Welcome."

Umm Hassan took a sip from her cup. The aroma of the coffee overwhelmed her, and she burst into sobs.

The Israeli woman lit a cigarette and blew the smoke into the air, gazing into space.

Fawzi went out into the garden where Rami was playing with the video camera, filming everything.

The two women remained alone in the living room, one weeping, the other smoking in silence.

The Israeli turned and wanted to say something, but didn't. Umm Hassan wiped away her tears and went over to the water jug, which stood on a side table in the living room.

"The jug," said Umm Hassan.

"I found it here, and I don't use it. Take it if you want."

"Thank you, no."

Umm Hassan went over to the jug, picked it up, and tucked it under her arm; then she went back to the Israeli woman and handed it to her.

"Thank you," said the Palestinian, "I don't want it. I'm giving it to you. Take it."

"Thank you," said the Israeli, who took the jug and returned it to its place.

The silence was broken – the two women burst out laughing. Umm Hassan started looking around the house. She stood in front of the bedroom but didn't go in. Next she went to the kitchen. In the sink were piles of dirty dishes. Umm Hassan turned on the tap and watched the water flow out, and the Israeli woman ran in saying, "I'm so sorry, it's a mess." Umm Hassan turned off the tap and said, laughing, "I didn't leave the dirty dishes. That was you."

The two women went out into the garden.

The Israeli woman gave Umm Hassan her arm and told her about the place. She told her about the orange grove where Iraqi Jews worked, the new irrigation projects the government had started, their fear of the Katyusha rockets, and about how difficult life was. Umm Hassan listened and looked and said one word: "Paradise. Paradise. Palestine's a paradise." When the Israeli woman asked her what she was saying, she answered, "Nothing. I was just saying that we call it an *orchard*, not a *grove*. This is an orange orchard. How wonderful, how wonderful."

"Yes, an orchard," said the Israeli.

Then Umm Hassan began telling the Israeli woman about the place.

"Where's the spring?" asked Umm Hassan.

"What spring?"

Umm Hassan told her the story of her spring and how she'd discovered water in the field next to the house. When her husband had built the house, close to the eucalyptus tree, there had been no water. It was Umm Hassan who had discovered it. And one day she saw water welling up from the ground. She told the men, "We must dig here," and they dug, and water came gushing out. So they built a little stone wall around the spring, and it became known as Umm Hassan's spring.

"Where's the spring?" she asked.

The Israeli woman couldn't answer. "There was a spring here," she said, "but they dug an artesian well around it and laid some pipes. Could that be it?"

"No, it's a natural spring," said Umm Hassan, and told how they'd decided to plant apple trees after they discovered the water. But the war.

Umm Hassan guided the woman to where her spring had been.

She didn't find it. Where it had been, she found a well walled with pipes and iron with a small tap on each side. Umm Hassan bent over to open the tap, and when the water gushed out, splashed her face and neck, sprinkled the water on her hair and clothes, and drank.

"Drink," she said. "Water sweeter than honey."

The Israeli woman bent over and washed her hands, and then turned off the tap without drinking.

"This is the most delicious water in the world."

The Israeli woman turned on the tap again, drank a little and smiled.

Later Umm Hassan would say the Israelis don't drink water, just fizzy drinks. "They only drink out of bottles, even though Palestine's water is the best in the world."

In vain we tried to explain to her that they drink mineral water not fizzy drinks and that the people of Beirut have started to drink water out of plastic bottles, too, but she stuck to her guns and said, "They don't drink water. I saw them with my own eyes. You want me to question what I saw with my own eyes?"

After they'd had a drink, the two women walked around the house. Umm

Hassan told the woman about the eucalyptus tree and the olive grove and pointed out the stone that looks like the head of an ox. She took her around behind the house and showed her the cave on the other side of the hill.

Umm Hassan talked and the other woman discovered, astonished that she'd never noticed the ox's head, or had even gone into the cave. Then Umm Hassan told her how she'd learned her profession as a midwife from her grandmother on her father's side, Maryam, and that she had an official license from the British government. She recounted how she'd gotten married at fifteen "to chase away the chickens from the front of the house," as her mother-in-law had said when she'd asked for her hand.

Umm Hassan told her stories, strolling from place to place, and the Jewish woman followed along behind, listening and nodding her head but not uttering a word.

Umm Hassan would tell her guests that she had seen her life dissolving in front of her: "What's life? Like a pinch of salt in water, it just melts away." She slipped back as though no time had passed. She saw again the young woman who'd gone to live in her new home. At twenty, she told her husband that she wanted a house of their own – "I'm no good for chasing chickens anymore and I am no longer a little girl." They got the land and built the house with their own hands, and she discovered the spring and the cave and the ox's head, and became the midwife for the whole district of Acre.

The women went back inside the house and sat in silence.

Umm Hassan got up and went into the bedroom. She looked at the bed that occupied the center of the room. It was the first bed she'd slept on in her life. At home with her family, and then in her husband's house, she'd slept on bedding on the floor, folding it up each morning and tucking it away at the far end of the room. But in this house the bed couldn't be folded up.

"A room just for sleeping in," her husband had said.

The other woman sleeps here every night, thought Umm Hassan, with her husband, in the same bed, in the same room, in the same house, in the same – No, not in the same village: The village didn't exist anymore. Umm Hassan could no longer see the close-packed houses of the village – the houses were gone. Nothing was left of al-Kweikat.

When she finished her tour of the house, Umm Hassan wept. She sat in the living room and wept. Her brother came in to hurry her up so they could return to Abu Sinan and found her weeping. He wept, too, and the son with the camera wept.

"Do you know what she said to me?"

Umm Hassan would relate the same conversation every day, adding a word here, deleting one there, choking back her tears.

"She asked me, 'Where are you from?'

"From al-Kweikat, I told her. This is my house and this is my jug and this is my sofa, and the olive trees and the cactus and the land and the spring – everything."

"'No, no. Where are you living now?'

"'In Shatila.'

"'Where's Shatila.'

"'It's a camp.'

"'Where's the camp?'

"'In Lebanon.'

"'Where in Lebanon?'

"'In Beirut, near Sports City.'"

When the Jewish woman heard the word Beirut, she gave a start and her manner changed completely.

"You're from Beirut?" she cried, the words tumbling out of her mouth and her eyes filling with tears.

"Listen, Sister," the Jewish woman said. "I'm from Beirut too, from Wadi Abu Jmil. You know Wadi Abu Jmil, the Jewish district in the center? They brought me from there when I was twelve. I left Beirut and came to this dreary, bleak land. Do you know the Ecole de l'Alliance Israélite? To the right of the school there's a three-story building that used to be owned by a Polish Jew named Elie Bron. I'm from there."

"You're from Beirut?" Umm Hassan said in amazement.

"Yes, Beirut."

"How did that happen?"

"What do you mean, how did that happen? I've no idea. You're living in

Beirut and you've come here to cry? I'm the one who should be crying. Get up, my friend, and go. Send me to Beirut and take this wretched land back."

Umm Hassan said she talked with the Israeli woman for a long time.

The woman's name was Ella Dweik. Hers was Nabilah, daughter of al-Khatib from the family of al-Habit – the fallen – wife of Mahmoud al-Qasemi. Al-Habit isn't the family's real name, but my grandfather used to spend all day sitting down so they used to call him that. Our real ancestor was Iskandar, and before Iskandar there was al-Khatib.

Nabilah al-Habit talked of al-Kweikat.

Ella Dweik spoke of Beirut.

Ella said then that she'd married an agricultural engineer who worked there, that they'd been given the house, that she hadn't had any children. Her husband was Iraqi, from the outskirts of Baghdad; she'd always wanted to see Baghdad. She had a brother who worked in Tel Aviv, but she never saw him.

Umm Hassan told her about Beirut. About the sea and the Manara Corniche, the shops on Hamra Street, the wealth and the beauty and the cars. She said the war hadn't been able to destroy Beirut. It had destroyed a lot, but Beirut was still as it had always been.

Umm Hassan said that there, in al-Kweikat, she saw once again the Beirut that she didn't know very well. "All I know is Umm Isa's house on America Street, near the Clémenceau cinema."

"In al-Kweikat I saw Beirut, but I don't live in Beirut, I live in the camp. The camp? It's a grouping of villages piled up one on top of another."

The Jewish woman stood up.

When someone stands up, it means it's time for the guest to leave. Umm Hassan didn't grasp the meaning of the signal, however; when her brother said they had to go, she looked at him in amazement and didn't respond.

"And now, what can I do for you?" said Ella.

"Nothing, nothing," said Umm Hassan as she began ponderously to get up.

The Jewish woman took the earthenware jug and gave it to Umm Hassan without a word. Umm Hassan took it without looking and went back with her brother to his house in Abu Sinan.

"The jug is still in its place," said Sana'.

Umm Hassan said nobody should move it and that she was sorry she'd brought it with her, it should have stayed in its own house.

"Then what?" I asked Sana'.

"'Then what?'" she said. "She died in the camp, and the Jewish woman is still living in her house."

Can you imagine, Father, that Umm Hassan would die weeping for the earthenware jug she brought with her from her house? That she'd die because a woman said to her, "Damn al-Kweikat! Take it!" Why didn't she take it? Why didn't she tell this woman she was welcome to the whole camp, the whole of Wadi Abu Jmil, the whole world?

Umm Hassan said she wept over what had happened to her. "The Jewish woman bought my silence with the jug and her stories about her mute childhood, and I came back to the misery and poverty of the camp. She has the house and I'm here. What's the point?"

So the story was turned into a videotape that's now mine. Rami didn't film the conversation between the two women. He made the camera roam over the house and around the land and the olive orchard. But it's a beautiful tape, made up of lots of snapshots joined together. I'd have preferred a panorama, but never mind, we can imagine the scene as we watch. We've become a video nation. Should I be watching the tape every night, weeping and eventually dying from it? Or should I be filming you and turning you into a video that can make the rounds of the houses? What should I film though? Should I ask someone to play you as a young man? I might be able to play that role myself, what do you think? Mme. Claire already asked me if I were your son. I'd be able to say that I am and that I might play the role of you as a young man. But I'm not an actor, acting is a difficult profession! I wish I did know how to act, I'd have reenacted Shams' crime, and the interrogators wouldn't have laughed at me and humiliated me with their pity.

"Pity is the ugliest thing," you used to say. "We must not pity ourselves. Once a man pities himself, he's doomed."

But I'm very sorry to have to tell you now that I pity you. I swear you stir more pity than Umm Hassan's earthenware jug or that mute Jewish woman.

The Jewish woman told Umm Hassan she hadn't forgotten her Arabic and said she'd been struck dumb when she came to Israel.

"I was on my own, the only child from Lebanon; they all spoke Hebrew. I went for five months without saying a word in class. I didn't dare talk to anyone, I didn't answer the teachers' questions, and I refused to read out loud. Five months. Then I opened my mouth. It was as though I'd tried, in my silence, to become part of these people I didn't know. French was my first language because at the Ecole Alliance in Beirut we were taught Arabic, like all other school children in Lebanon, but our language in school and at home was French. I knew a little Hebrew because we also studied it at school, though we never liked it. I also learned Hebrew at the Maabarot, but in the classroom, in the midst of all the children, I was struck dumb before I could speak like them."

She told Umm Hassan how she'd lived in the Maabarot, where they'd sprayed the Sephardic Jews with insecticide, as though they were animals, before admitting them to the stone barracks. She cried when they'd forced her to take off her clothes; a blond woman approached her with the long, cylindrical sprayer and showered every part of her body mercilessly. Her father, a man in his fifties, began howling when they ordered him to remove his red fez and the men started kicking it around like a soccer ball. He chased after it while the soldiers horsed around and laughed. When he could see that his fez was destroyed, he started howling, repeating, "There is no god but God," so they assumed he was a Muslim and subjected him to a prolonged interrogation before asking him to remove his clothes and spraying him – letting him get used to standing naked, without a fez, forever.

Ella Dweik told Umm Hassan al-Habit her story. And Umm Hassan told everyone that she'd wept.

"May the Lord punish me for how I cried. 'Take this bleak, dreary land,' she told me, 'and send me back to Wadi Abu Jmil, send me back to the Elie Bron building!'"

"And what did you say, Umm Hassan?"

"What could I say? Nothing. I began to weep."

Did you know, Father, that the medical profession is against pity? You can't be a doctor and feel pity for your patients. That's why I'm a failure as a doctor. In fact, I'm not a doctor. I came to the profession by accident. It never occurred to me to be a doctor until the Chinese doctor – a woman – decided for me. It was by her decree. She ordered my military training stopped and enrolled me in medical school. I don't like medicine. I found myself in China and had to acquiesce. But the way people regarded my new profession won me over. They call you a *hakim* – a wise man – and think you're a magician. I think that magic aura was what made Shams love me. Don't say Shams didn't love me – she loved me in her own fashion, but she loved me. I'm convinced her death contains a riddle that needs to be solved. The riddle will only be solved after the emotional shock has passed along with my self-imposed imprisonment in this accursed hospital. There's dirt everywhere. The walls of the room are no longer white, the paint is peeling and yellowed, and something is smeared on them. I scrubbed them with soap, but it made no difference.

What do you say to Denmark?

You know Dr. No'man al-Natour? I don't know him, but he wrote an article that made me weep. I didn't weep for old Acre, which has nearly collapsed, but I wept over the key.

Shall I tell you what happened to No'man?

He went to Acre – he can visit Israel because he has a Danish passport. He boarded a plane at the Copenhagen airport and got off at Lod. He disembarked like any ordinary passenger, presented his passport to the security man and waited. The man took the passport, examined it closely and asked Dr. No'man to wait. He waited for about a quarter of an hour, and then a young woman in military uniform arrived. She returned the passport to him and apologized, smiling. He took his passport and went out to the baggage claim, got his suitcase, which he later discovered had been opened and carefully searched, and left the airport.

These formalities had no impact on him because he was already in a dreadful state, everything shaking inside him. He thought he'd have a heart attack the moment he stepped off the airplane but was surprised to find himself behaving like an ordinary traveler, as though this weren't his own country.

He left the airport and got a taxi, which took him to Jerusalem. He spent the night in a hotel in the Arab quarter and in the morning, instead of touring old Jerusalem as the tourists do, he took a taxi to Acre, where he alighted in the square close to the Jazzar mosque. He walked and walked and walked, lost and alone in his own city. He said he wanted to find his house without help. He was like me – born outside of Palestine with no memories of his country except what his mother had told him. No'man walked, got lost in the alleys, stopped and scrutinized the houses, and walked some more. At last he found the house. He said he knew it as soon as he saw it. He knocked on the door and was greeted, as Umm Hassan had been, in Arabic, but they weren't Jews, they were Palestinians.

He went into the house, greeted everyone and sat down.

The woman went to make coffee. He got up and started to look around, refusing the company of the man of the house. As he went through the rooms, No'man recalled his mother's words, and they became his guide. He came to the kitchen and there he saw his mother standing in front of the big saucepan of cracked wheat. No'man said that in the Yarmouk camp near Damascus, where he'd been born, they ate nothing but cracked wheat. His mother would stand in their small kitchen in front of the saucepan, and No'man would hold onto the hem of her dress and cry.

But in the spacious kitchen in Acre, it wasn't his mother he saw, but a solitary child, standing in front of the Palestinian's wife, who was making coffee. The woman tiptoed out when she saw No'man wiping away his tears.

They drank coffee, and the Palestinian explained to No'man that he'd been waiting for him for a long time, that he'd rented the house from the official in charge of absentee property after they'd thrown him out of his own house, and that he was ready to leave whenever No'man's family wanted.

No'man listened without uttering a word, as though he'd forgotten how to speak.

The Palestinian tried to explain their circumstances and the difficulties of their life and to reassure No'man that he didn't want the house but had been forced to rent it because his own house had been demolished.

No'man stood up and excused himself.

"Stay for lunch – the house is yours," said the man.

"No. Thank you," said No'man, and left.

No'man didn't look back, and he never returned. He wrote that he regretted not having gone back. Before, he'd needed to preserve the image of the house in his head, but now that image had evaporated, and nothing was left but the words of his mother that had engraved it in his memory.

No'man said he walked and walked, and then he heard the Palestinian man shouting, so he turned and saw the man running after him, waving something in his hand.

"The key. I forgot to give you the key to the house. Take it, it's yours."

"There's no need," said No'man. "We still have the old key in Damascus."

Dr. No'man returned to Denmark, the key is still in Damascus, Umm Isa died muttering about the saucepan of zucchini, and her son, Isa, is in Meknes looking for the keys.

Umm Isa used to talk about her son as though he belonged to a different world, as though he were dead, which is what Umm Hassan thought when she heard Umm Isa talking about her son almost as if she were in mourning. Then she found out that Dr. Isa Safiyyeh wasn't dead – he was living in Meknes, a faraway city in Morocco, where he taught Arabic literature at the university.

He'd been seduced by a woman from Meknes, said Umm Isa. "He met her in New York, where he was teaching, and fell in love. I saw her once when they visited me in Beirut. Damn her, how beautiful she was! Huge eyes and long, smooth black hair, and with something strange about her. She put a spell on him for sure. I know women, and I know that that one had shown him the fish that talks."

Umm Hassan agreed, even though she didn't believe in the existence of a magic fish in a woman's private parts. Also, she didn't give a damn about "Dr." Isa, who did his doctoring in literature instead of becoming a real doctor and helping people. But then again, who knows, "maybe our Christian brothers from Jerusalem have a fish we don't know about."

"The woman from Meknes took Isa to her country, and they left me by myself in Beirut. Why don't they come and live with me here? Isa writes to me, but the letters don't arrive during wartime, and in the last one he said he was collecting keys. God help us, now we're collecting the keys of the Andalusians! He said the descendants of the people of Andalusia who were chased out of their country and who migrated to Meknes still keep the keys to their houses in Andalusia, and he's rounding up keys to put on an exhibition and wants to write a book about them. Here, read it, Umm Hassan."

Umm Hassan's sight was failing, and she could no longer read, the words looking to her like little jumbled-up insects. Umm Isa asked if she'd read it, and Umm Hassan nodded her head as though she had.

"What do you make of that? He said he wants to collect their keys and write a book! He says we have to collect the keys of our houses in Jerusalem. What do you make of it? Collect our keys, when the doors are already broken!"

Umm Hassan told me the story of Dr. Isa Safiyyeh's keys when I asked her where I could find Dr. No'man, since she knows everybody. I told her I didn't want to collect keys, I wanted to ask him about emigrating to Denmark, but she didn't believe me. She thought that I too had been struck by key fever and told me that our house in al-Ghabsiyyeh didn't have a door and wasn't even a house anymore because the weeds had devoured it.

I'm not interested in keys. That sort of sentimentality doesn't concern me. I was only thinking about emigrating, and I said Denmark because lots of the young men from the camp have gone there. And I thought of Dr. No'man because he was a doctor like me. I thought he might be able to get me a job in one of the hospitals over there. But I forgot about it and stayed here.

Umm Hassan said, "Stay in your own house here and forget about keys."

Can we call these wretched shacks in the camp houses?

Everything here is collapsing, wouldn't you agree, dear Abu Salem?

Do you know, master, where you are now?

You think you're in the hospital, but you're mistaken. This isn't a hospital, it just resembles a hospital. Everything here isn't itself but a simulacrum of itself. We say *house* but we don't live in houses, we live in places that resemble houses. We say *Beirut* but we aren't really in Beirut, we're in a semblance of Beirut. I say *doctor* but I'm not a doctor, I'm just pretending to be one. Even the camp itself – we say we're in the Shatila camp, but after the War of the Camps and the destruction of eighty percent of Shatila's houses, it's no longer a camp, it's just a semblance of a camp – you get the idea, the boring semblances go on and on.

You don't like what I'm saying?

Look around you. It shouldn't take long to convince you that it's true.

Let me walk you around the place.

This is a hospital. You are in the Galilee Hospital. But it's – what can I say? It's better I don't say. Come on, let's start with this room.

A tiny room, four meters by three, with an iron bed next to which is a bedside table on which are a box of Kleenex and a mucus extractor (a round glass instrument connected to a tube). To the left, opposite the bed, is a white metal cupboard. You think everything is white in this room, but in fact nothing is white. Things were white, but now they've taken on other colors – yellowish white, flaking walls, a cupboard discolored with rust, a ceiling covered in stains where the paint has blistered and burst because of damp, neglect, and shelling.

A white stained with yellow and gray, a yellow stained with gray, a gray stained with white or . . .

You don't care, but I'm disgusted by the sight. You'll say I worked here for years and never let on at all that it bothered me, so what has changed?

Nothing has changed except that I've become like a patient myself, and a patient can't put up with such things. As you can see, when a doctor starts to feel like a patient, it's the end for medicine. And medicine has come to an end, dear Mr. Yunes, Izz al-Din, Abu Salem, or I-don't-know-what. In the past you were content with all the names people had for you, you'd shrug it off. And when I asked you your real name, you gestured broadly and said, "Forget all that, call me whatever you like." And when I insisted, you told me your name was Adam: "We're all children of Adam, so why should we be called by any other name?"

I found out the truth without your telling me. I found it out by chance. You were telling the story when I came to visit and your relatives from Ain al-Hilweh were there. When I saw them I tried to leave, but you told me to sit down, saying that Dr. Khalil was family, and went on with your story.

You said your father had first wanted to call you Asad. Lion. So you would have been Asad al-Asadi, Lion of the Lions, and everybody would have been terrified of you. He did name you Asad but changed his mind after a couple of days because he was scared of his cousin Asad al-Asadi, a village notable who'd indicated displeasure at his name being given to the poorest of the poor in the family. So he named you Yunes. Jonah. He chose Yunes to protect you from death in the belly of the whale, but your mother didn't like the name, so she chose Izz al-Din and your father agreed. Or so the woman thought, and she started calling you Izz al-Din while your father was still calling you Yunes. Then he decided to put an end to the litany and said that the name Abd al-Wahid was better. He started calling you Abd al-Wahid, and you and everybody else got confused. In the end, the teacher at the primary school didn't know what to do, so he went to the blind sheikh to clarify matters, on which occasion the sheikh pronounced his theory on names: "All names are pseudonyms – the only true name is Adam. God gave this name to man because the name and the thing named were one. He was called Adam because he was taken from the *adeem* – the skin – of the earth, and the earth is one just as man is one. Even after his fall from Paradise, Adam, peace be upon him, gave no thought to the matter of names. He called his first son Adam and his second Adam and so on until the fatal day, until the day of the first murder. When Cain killed his brother, Abel, Adam had to resort to pseudonyms to distinguish between the murderer and the murdered. So Gabriel inspired him with the names he gave to every Adam in his line so things wouldn't get mixed up and the names get lost."

"All our names are pseudonyms," the sheikh told the schoolteacher. "They have no value, and you may therefore call my son whatever you like, but knowing that his name and your name and the names of everyone else are one. Call him Adam if you like, or Yunes or Izz al-Din or Abd al-Wahid or Wolf . . . Why don't we call him Wolf? Now there's a name that never came to mind before!"

You told your relatives you only discovered the wisdom of your father's words during the revolution. You were the only sacred warrior, and later the only fedayeen fighter, who wasn't obliged to take an assumed name. You used all your names, and they were all real and all assumed at the same time.

I brushed against the essence of your secret, master, and understood that truth isn't real, it's just a matter of convention; names are conventions, truth's a convention, and so is everything else.

When your relatives left your house, I asked you for the truth and you said you'd been telling the truth. Listening to you, I'd thought you'd been making the story up as you went along, perhaps to make yourself even more mysterious, but you assured me you'd told them the truth and that to this day you still didn't know your real name. Then you told me the men were your relatives from Ain al-Zaitoun and lived in the Ain al-Hilweh camp and had come to invite you to be the head of an Asadi clan association they'd decided to form, and that the business of the names was the only thing you could think of to make them drop the idea. "Names and families and sects have no meaning. Go back to Adam," you told them as they left. So they left with gloomy faces. They'd wanted you to be head of the association because you were the family's only hero, but as you were pouring the tea and stirring in the sugar you said, "There are no heroes. We all come from Adam, and Adam was made of mud."

Come with me then, Adam, to your hospital room. There's only one small window, which is covered with a metal grille like in a prison cell. The yellow – or sometime-yellow – door opens onto the corridor, from which comes the sharp smell of ammonia. Why the smell? Zainab says it's to kill germs, but I'm convinced there are germs nesting in every cranny here. That's why I bought us some cleaning supplies and clean your room every day. I wipe it down with soap and water, making sure that the smell of the soap gets into every corner. But no matter what I do, the smell of ammonia seeps back in and threatens to choke us. I thought of washing the corridor at night but gave up on the idea since it would be impossible to clean the hospital on my own, and everyone else seems to be used to the smell.

We're leaving your room now for the corridor, where you can see rooms just like yours on both sides. But you are the only patient with a private room. Why this special treatment? That's something I won't go into. You think you're here because they respect your history, and that's what I tell myself too so I can put up with the situation. The truth, however, is very different.

When they brought you here, Dr. Amjad threw up his hands and said, "There is no power and no strength but with God." Everyone dealt with you as though you were dead so they didn't allocate you a room. Zainab understood you were to be left in the emergency room until you died – they left you lying there and went away. When I saw you in that state, with the flies hovering around you as though you were a corpse, I rushed to the doctors' room, put on a white gown and ordered Zainab to follow me. She didn't. Zainab, who throughout the war used to tremble at my orders, looked at me with contempt when I told her to prepare a room for you.

"No, Khalil. Dr. Amjad said to leave him."

"I'm the doctor and I'm telling you . . ."

The bitch! She left my sentence hanging in the air and turned her back and went off. So I stayed with you on my own.

You were primed for death – lying on the ground on a yellow foam pad and shivering. And the flies. I started shooing the flies away and yelling. I left you and went in search of Zainab, ordered her to follow me, and went back to you. Even Amin, the young man in charge of the emergency room, had disappeared. I became obsessed with finding Amin. Where was Amin? I started yelling for him, and then a hand came from behind and covered my mouth.

"Shush, shush. Snap out of it, Khalil."

Dr. Amjad covered my mouth with his hand and dragged me to his examining room on the first floor, where he explained to me that Amin had disappeared and started telling me a strange story about the killing of Kayed, the Fatah official in Beirut, and the Kurdish woman, and the car, going into an exhaustive analysis of the political assassinations that had taken place recently in Beirut.

You remember Kayed.

He was quiet and gentle and brave – you don't know that he's dead. No, you should know – Kayed died two weeks before your stroke. He was the last to be killed. Is it true he married a Kurdish woman before he died? And if he did marry her, why did he make a date to meet her at Talet al-Khayyat near the television building? Who makes an appointment with his own wife to meet on the road? And where did his new Japanese car vanish to?

"They buy luxury cars instead of spending money on equipping the hospitals," said Dr. Amjad. "The Kurdish woman stole the car. She was a spy and inveigled him into meeting her and they assassinated him. And it seems Amin had something to do with the affair."

Amjad was speaking, and I was trembling.

Amjad was telling his stories, and you're prostrate down below.

Amjad was analyzing Kayed's killing, and when I tried to get in a word his hand would come and cover my mouth.

When we're puzzled we always say, "*Cherchez la femme!*" and the problem is soon resolved. I'm convinced this Kurdish woman doesn't exist but is a figment of the young Iraqi who calls himself Kazem.

Do you know Kazem? He was Kayed's personal bodyguard. He came by twice to see you, claiming he wanted to see how you were doing. But he didn't know you. He came to clear his conscience; I'm sure he was involved in the assassination. But why would he come to visit me? I have nothing to do with all that. It's true, Kayed was my friend, but I wasn't his only friend, why choose me to tell the story of the Kurdish girl to? Did he want to get me involved? Or maybe he's part of the plot against my life. Does he know Shams' family? Did he come to check the place out? I don't want my imagination to gallop out of control because it has nothing to do with me, and Kazem has immigrated to Sweden. He said he was waiting to get refugee status but I didn't sympathize, and I made sure he understood that. Then he stopped coming to see me and we were finally free of him.

I know, but I haven't told anyone. The girl that Kayed loved wasn't Kurdish, she was a Jordanian from Karak, a student at the American University in Beirut studying engineering. Kayed did love her. I met her with him a number of times. She was tall and fair and had mesmerizing eyes. They weren't large like the eyes we usually describe as beautiful, but they were mesmerizing. And her name was Afifa.

She smiled as she introduced herself to me: "An old name that isn't used much now." She said her father, who'd been living in Beirut for twenty years, had named her Afifa after her mother, who was living alone in Ma'daba, and that she'd discovered that her uncle on her mother's side was a priest named Nasri who lived in Deir al-Seidnaya near Damascus and painted beautiful icons. Her eyes watered – no, they didn't water, but they had something of that watery blue in them. Kayed loved her and said she bossed him around: "People from Karak are always bossy."

There was no Kurdish woman. Kayed was in love with a girl from Karak and all his friends knew about it, but that wasn't why he was killed. It's true that after falling for Afifa he abandoned many of the security precautions that Fatah officials in Beirut had to take in the wake of the decision to liquidate the Palestinian political presence in the city, but his death had nothing to do with love. It was connected with something else, and I don't think the Israelis had anything to do with it.

But where did the car pass?

This Dr. Amjad rubbed me the wrong way. Where did he get all this information? Is it true the so-called Kurdish woman stole the car? She suggested they meet in front of the television building and, when he arrived, asked him to get out of the car so she could tell him something. He was killed getting out of the car. A man fired five bullets at him from a silenced revolver, and the Kurdish woman disappeared, with the car.

Was the whole thing just a car theft?

But why did he get out?

Didn't he know his life was in danger?

If we are to believe our Dr. Amjad's version, Kayed was supposed to drive just past the television building, and the Kurdish woman should have gotten into the car beside him.

How could that be? He stops his car, gets out and dies? Where was his Iraqi bodyguard, Kazem, and what did Amin have to do with it?

Kazem told me with a wink that he didn't make it to the rendezvous: "You know, meetings of that sort require privacy."

Privacy! What privacy is there in the street at eleven in the morning? They're all lying, and Kazem has disappeared. He came to say goodbye because he was traveling and to "see how *Uncle Yunes* was doing"!

I never heard anyone else use this *Uncle*. You're *Brother*, Abu Salem, Yunes, or Izz al-Din – you're only *Uncle* to people who don't know you. The easiest trick in the book to get close to someone. *Uncle* and *Hajj* are titles we give to men over fifty when we don't know what we're supposed to call them. Out of laziness. Our language is a very lazy language. We don't dig deep for the names of things; we name them on the run, and it's up to the listener to figure things out, he is supposed to know what you mean so he can understand you; otherwise misunderstandings abound.

That's the word I was looking for. What happened between Dr. Amjad and me was a misunderstanding.

Dr. Amjad was talking about the disappearance of Amin after Kayed's killing and presented an exhaustive analysis to prove that Amin had a relationship with the Kurdish woman, as though I cared.

"She would come here to visit him and I think . . . I think the last time she came in the Japanese car, so Amin killed him and not Kazem. He killed him for the woman and the car. It's an expensive car as you know – Mazda, *full automatic*. I'm sure it was the car, but I don't know anymore."

Dr. Amjad doesn't know but he wants me to know. I didn't say anything, gave no support to his hypotheses, and didn't tell him about the girl from Karak who's studying at the American University. I wish I could contact her; she's really fantastically beautiful, or not beautiful but striking (now look at the precision of the word *striking*, meaning more than pretty and implying presence and authority).

God rest your soul, Kayed, but on the occasions when I met her I never saw her as being bossy. She had a certain indescribable delicacy. Her neck was long and smooth, and around it she'd wear a silver necklace with the Throne Surah, or so I thought until Kayed told me that it was a picture of the Virgin Mary. He said the girl from Karak loved the Virgin and would tell him not to be afraid because she had made a vow on his behalf to the Mother of Light. I didn't ask who this "Mother of Light" was, guessing it must be one of the countless names of the Holy Virgin.

I'd like to see her again, but not to clear things up, since they're beyond being cleared up at this point. No, I want to contemplate her beauty. Shameless, really. Instead of mourning my friend, Kayed, and bemoaning his horrible death, I desire his girlfriend. They left him on the pavement in Talet al-Khayyat for more than five hours before taking him to the hospital. A man lying in a pool of blood. The passersby looked on without wanting to see. For five hours under the Beirut sun, Kayed was in agony. Well, there you are. But I'm still not sure why I desire his girlfriend. My desire isn't sexual; I desire to see her. Men are traitors from the beginning, from the moment they discover their names. To know your name is to be a traitor. Wasn't that your blind father's theory about names?

Where were we? It seems I've become like Dr. Amjad. All doctors must be that way: I've left you lying here to amuse myself with the story of Kayed.

That day I swear I could have committed murder. But it was as if I were hypnotized, virtually paralyzed and mute. I was asking for Amin when a hand covered my mouth; then Dr. Amjad got deep into the analysis of Kayed's assassination and started mulling over the possible explanations and asserting the involvement of Israeli intelligence. But that wasn't enough. If he'd stopped there, this eruption would never have come, involuntarily, from deep inside me. Zainab told me that I roared, and that Dr. Amjad fled, terrified. It was when he launched into his contemptible tales about women that I let loose. You know how we men are. Amjad was talking about Kayed and the Kurdish woman when he suddenly switched to his sexual experiences with Kurdish women. How vulgar! He said a Kurdish woman used to call him every day on the phone, sigh into the receiver, and tell him the color of her panties.

That was when I exploded.

I didn't explode for your sake but for the sake of that woman he'd invented.

He said she would sigh into the telephone, but he didn't say what he was doing – how he would sigh and masturbate and leap like an ape from one line to another.

Plus, how dare he talk about Kurdish women that way? Even if we suppose that one Kurdish woman did that, is it thinkable to write them all off? I hate this stupid machismo. I think it's a cover up for men's deep-seated impotence.

I exploded, howling and bellowing like a wounded bull. Dr. Amjad fled, and Zainab came running. Zainab's stupid, and I could have done without further proof of it. She's not really a nurse, all she can do is take blood pressure and give injections. Not grasping that I was shouting because of you, she ran to get me a glass of water and started to calm me down. The idiot! I threw the glass on the ground, grabbed her hand, and dragged her over to you. She found a woolen blanket, and I covered you with it.

"What are we going to do with him?" she asked, looking at me like an imbecile.

"Quickly, quickly! Let's get him into a room."

It was then that Zainab let out that Dr. Amjad had said you were to be left alone because there was no hope.

I told her to shut up and help me.

We tried to carry you, but it was impossible because the yellow foam mat on which they'd thrown you down wasn't rigid. I ordered Zainab to bring a stretcher and she ran off.

From the moment I yelled at her, Zainab changed completely. She started running blindly every time she heard an order from me. I'd give an order and she'd set off running like a fool. I could hear her clattering around everywhere – on the stairs, in the room, in the corridors. I could hear, but I couldn't see a thing. All she brought was a woolen blanket with a moldy smell. So I picked you up – I couldn't wait any longer. I committed an unforgivable medical sin. I picked you up and put you over my shoulder folded in half. You were heavy and shaking. God, how heavy people are when they're dying, or approaching death, as though, as Umm Hassan explained to me, the soul were a means of combating gravity and half your soul had left your body. I took you out of the emergency room and climbed up toward the first floor. Zainab was waiting on the landing to say there weren't any empty rooms. I climbed up to the second and last floor and took you into Room 208, which you now occupy. I put you into bed and ordered Zainab to take the second bed out of the room.

Now you're in a first-class room. It's clean and attractive and organized. Forget about the colors – it's impossible to preserve the original color of walls and doors in a place that's been eaten away by moisture. There's no solution to the humidity in Beirut, which is between eighty-five and ninety percent most of the time. However, it's less a matter of humidity and more of the water pipes and sewage mains. The hospital was bombarded dozens of times, and each time they repaired it from the outside, that's to say, patched the holes in the walls and sealed off the water that was spurting from the pipes at the joints. The place needs a complete overhaul, which is impossible at the moment. The pipes leak, the damp stains the walls, and the smell, a mixture of Nurse Zainab's ammonia and standing water, seeps everywhere.

All's well.

I say "all's well" because I know you're in a place that's relatively safe from all those smells, because soap, insecticides, cologne, and powder fill your room with the aroma of paradise.

Of course, everything's relative. It's a relative aroma in a relative paradise in a relative hospital in a relative camp in a relative city. That'll do.

Everything is relative. Even the Arabic calligraphy that I've hung on the wall above you is relative, since it isn't a work of art in the precise meaning of the term, though it is beautiful. I brought it from my house because Shams refused to take it. A beautiful work with the name of the Almighty written in Kufic script. I like that script. I see its angular forms as redrawing the boundaries of the world, and I see it curving and rounding everything off. It's true it's not a curved script, but everything's round in the end. *Allah* in Kufic lettering is above your head because Shams didn't grasp the picture's artistic value when I offered it to her. She looked at it with something approaching revulsion, said, "You want to make me into one of those women who cover their hair?" and laughed treacherously.

When Shams laughed, she laughed treacherously. I would smell the scent of another man on her breath and "avert my gaze" as they say. I would feel that I was with her and not with her. I would see them all hovering around the two of us and I would try to push them away so I could see her. Then I would forget them, and the betrayal, when I slid into her undulating body.

Shams laughed treacherously.

We were at my place, I told her I had a gift for her. I went to the bedroom to get the canvas rolled up in white paper. She tore off the paper, full of curiosity. Then the picture with the Kufic lettering shone out.

"Beautiful. A beautiful work," I said. "Don't you love Arabic calligraphy?"

She looked closely at it, read it carefully, then pulled back.

"You want to turn me into one of those women who cover their hair?"

Shams thought I was prodding her to believe in God and gave me a lecture on her personal view of the divine and of existence. I'll spare you her theories about the united nature of existence and how God is present in everything and so on.

She didn't take the picture because she imagined I wanted her to adopt the head scarf in preparation for marriage. She spoke of her conviction concerning the liberation of women.

I can assure you that such thoughts never had crossed my mind! I bought the thing because I love Arabic calligraphy, that's all, and I wanted to give her a nice present.

This drawing, my dear Abu Salem, cost more than fifty dollars, and it's the most beautiful thing in my house. Shams didn't take it and I didn't hang it up because it wasn't for me. I said to myself, I'll hang it in the living room when Shams comes and lives with me. But she died. I therefore decided I deserved the present and ought to hang it on the wall above my bed. Then things heated up: There was talk of a list of people to be killed and of Shams' relatives seeking revenge. Apparently my name was at the top of the list. So I forgot about the drawing, and everything else.

But then, after having put you to bed and cleaned everything up, I went home to get a few things and remembered it. Something told me that it belonged here. *Allah* in Kufic letters wraps you in its aura and protects you.

I didn't bring the map of Palestine or the posters of martyrs. Nothing. Those don't mean a thing here. Do you remember how we used to tremble in front of those posters, how we were convinced that the martyrs were about to burst through the colored paper and jump out at us? Those posters were an integral part of our life, and we filled the walls of the camp and the city with them, dreaming that one day our own pictures would appear on similar ones. All of us dreamed of seeing our faces outlined in bright red and with the martyr's halo. There was a contradiction here to which we paid no attention: We wanted to have our faces on the posters but also wanted to see them – we wanted to become martyrs without dying!

Tell me, how were we able to separate the image of death from death? How did we attain this absolute faith in life?

All that I know is that after the massacre I grew to hate the posters of martyrs. I won't tell you what happened, about the swarms of flies that almost devoured me – it's not the right moment for those sorts of memories. They need the right moment. We can't just toss off memories like that, we don't have the right to remember any which way.

I brought you the picture, saying to myself that the name of *Allah* in Kufic lettering would remain however circumstances and conditions changed. The photographs and posters were ephemeral, but the name of the Almighty will be eternally present before our eyes.

You don't like the word *eternally*. You used to say, "What small minds the Jews have! What is this silly slogan of theirs – 'Jerusalem, Eternal Capital of the Jewish State'! Anyone who talks of eternity exits history, for eternity is history's opposite; something that's eternal doesn't exist. We even ate our gods. During our Age of Ignorance, we – we Arabs – would model gods out of dates and then eat them, because hunger is more important than eternity. And now they come and tell us that Jerusalem is an eternal capital? What kind of shit is that? It's foolish – which means that they are becoming like us, defeatable."

You said we'd never defeat them: On the contrary, we needed to help them defeat themselves. No one is defeated from the outside; every defeat is internal. Ever since they raised the banner of eternity, they've fallen into the whirlpool of defeat, and it's up to us to keep them going in this direction.

You didn't tell me how we were supposed to keep them going. So far, the only people we've helped to defeat have been ourselves – carpeting our land with our blood for the Israelis, so that they could walk over it like victors.

Things have changed, Father.

If you'd become sick, God forbid, ten years ago, I wouldn't have brought you this drawing. I would have hung a map of Galilee above your head, to show how proud I was of you. You are the pride of us all. You made our country that we'd never seen come to life within us; you traced our dream with your footsteps.

Now it's not the dream I put up but the reality.

Allah in Kufic lettering is the one absolute reality we can depend on.

No, I won't let you speak.

You're in a mysterious place now and approaching the moment when nothing but faith can help you. Please, don't blaspheme. You're a believer, your father was a Sufi sheikh.

You'd like to say – though I won't let you – you'd like to say that someone who's lived your life can depend on nothing and that even gods change; our forefathers used to worship other gods.

Be quiet, please – I don't want to listen to your theory of temporariness. It's time for the temporary to become permanent. It's time for you to relax. I've had enough of your theories, but you don't care. I believe you're lying. You, too, are sick of the temporary and can't take it anymore. The proof? May I remind you of Adnan Abu Odeh?

I know you don't like to recall this affair because it scares you. Have you forgotten the day you came back from visiting him, trembling, and came to ask me for sleeping pills?

You came to me, doubled over, as though you were looking for death. Why don't you want to face the truth? Why don't you admit you feared for your life and not Adnan's? And why, after I gave you those pills, did you go back to mocking everything?

Heroes aren't supposed to behave that way.

A hero has to remain a hero. It's a crying shame – you all abandoned Adnan, forgot him, and all you remember now is his legend. As for the man himself, he went to his fate without anyone batting an eye.

You're acting all macho now because you've forgotten. Have you really forgotten Adnan?

Adnan Abu Odeh came back to the Burj al-Barajneh camp after twenty years in Israeli prisons. He came back a hero. You went to welcome him because he was a comrade, a friend, a lifelong acquaintance. You always used to speak of him as The Hero.

What happened to The Hero?

It was 1960. You were five fighters on one of your first operations inside Galilee. Adnan was taken prisoner, three others died, and you survived. What were the names of the three martyrs? Even you've forgotten – you were telling me about that fedayeen operation and you hesitated and said, "Khaled al-Shatti. No, Khaldoun. No, Jamal . . ." Even you couldn't remember anymore. You survived and they died. Death isn't a good enough reason to forget, but you did.

You survived, you told me, because you "withdrew" forward after you'd fallen into the Israeli ambush, while your comrades "withdrew" backward, as soldiers normally do. They came under fire from two sides and died, while you continued your journey to Bab al-Shams. Adnan didn't die even though he received appalling wounds in his stomach. The Israelis took him prisoner and treated him in the hospital before putting him on trial.

You'd tell the story tirelessly, as though it were your own. Then you suddenly stopped going to see him after he came back, and no longer talked about him.

Adnan stood up in court and said what he had to say.

He said he didn't recognize the court's authority: He was a fedayeen fighter, not a saboteur.

"This is my land and the land of my fathers and my grandfathers," he said, refusing to answer any questions. They asked him about you, but he said nothing.

During the interrogation, he spoke of the three others because he'd seen them die in front of him, but he didn't say one word about you. Although the Israeli interrogator informed him of your death, he didn't believe it. The interrogator showed him the Lebanese newspaper; the Fatah leadership had issued a statement announcing the death of four martyrs. But Adnan didn't believe it because he'd seen you move forward and disappear (which doesn't change the fact that that statement in the papers was a terrible error, because it exposed you and led Nahilah to prison).

You realized Nahilah had been arrested when she stopped visiting you in your cave. You stayed in your hideout for more than a month, only going out at night to nourish yourself with wild herbs and to fill your flask with dirty water from the irrigation ditch.

You lived for five months at Bab al-Shams, which became a prison for you, and you almost went insane. You sat all day long without moving, not daring to sleep or go out. You became like a vegetable. Have you forgotten how a man can become a vegetable? How his thoughts can be wiped out, his words disappear, and his head become an empty pot full of ringing noises and incomprehensible sounds?

When Dr. Amjad informed me you'd entered a vegetative state and there was no hope, I couldn't understand his pessimism: You'd already been through a vegetative state once and emerged on the other side.

Nahilah woke to their violent knocking, and, when they failed to find you, they took her for a weeklong interrogation. Leaving the prison, she found the village surrounded and realized they'd let her out as bait to lure you with. She acted out her celebrated play and buried you, praying for your absent corpse and receiving condolences while she wept and wailed and smeared ashes on her face. Nahilah's excessive carrying on drove your mother crazy – the old woman couldn't see why she was behaving that way. She understood the play had to be staged to save you, but Nahilah turned the play into something serious. She wept as women weep. She lamented and wailed and fainted. She let down her hair and tore her clothes in front of everybody.

"This isn't how we mourn martyrs," everyone told her. "Shame on you, Umm Salem! Shame on you! Yunes is a martyr."

But Nahilah paid no attention to the sanctity of martyrs. She wept for you until she could weep no more, and her sorrow was mighty unto death. And death came. Your mother believed Nahilah caused your father's death. After the death of his only son – meaning yours – he went into a coma that lasted three years, then he slept in his bed for a good month, and when he finally got up, started using dirt again to perform his ablutions. Then he died.

"Nahilah killed him," your mother told everyone.

Your mother tried to explain to him that what Nahilah was doing was just an act, but he couldn't understand. She would speak to him, but he wouldn't reply; she would look at his face, but all she saw were his closed eyes; she would tell him you were alive, but he would shake his head and moan.

In the past his wife had been able to understand him from the slightest movement of his eyebrows. After your death, however, his eyebrows stopped moving, and she felt she was talking to herself as he sat there in front of her utterly apathetic.

Why did Nahilah act this way?

Was she worried about you? Did she hate you? What was it?

Did she reach into herself "where the tears are," as the Sufi sheikh would say to his ring of disciples? "In our depths is nothing but water. We go back to the water to weep. We are born in water, we are drawn toward water, and we die when our water runs dry," he would say. He'd always repeat the words of a certain Sufi imam: "The sea is the bed of the earth and tears are the bed of man." Having finished their chanting and whirling, the dervishes would fall to the ground and weep – that's what the Sha'ab Sufi chapter did. Sheikh Ibrahim, son of Suleiman al-Asadi, would go every Thursday evening from Deir al-Asad to Sha'ab to lead the séance; he'd return home, borne by his disciples, his eyes – red as burning embers – closed.

But Nahilah?

Why did she act that way, knowing that you were still alive?

I know why: Nahilah was weeping for herself, for others like her, out of resentment.

"She wept for love," you would say if you could.

No, Abu Salem. Nahilah returned to the source of her tears to find herself again. She lived her life alone among the blind, the refugees, and the dead. Then you'd turn up at Bab al-Shams, place grapes beneath her feet and go away again, leaving her sad, abandoned, and pregnant.

What did you expect her to do?

Wait for you?

Languish?

You'd love to believe that she did nothing but wait for you. A woman who filled her days with bearing children and waiting for her husband who didn't come. And when he did come, he'd breeze in secretly, once a month, or every three months, or whenever he could.

Nahilah got fed up with her life between an old blind man, his maniacal wife obsessed with cleanliness, and the children, always hungry, still crawling around on all fours.

And on top of that, you would have wanted her to rejoice to see you and stretch out on the floor upon your second sun hidden inside the cave?

Nahilah left the prison barefoot and when she got to her front door fell to the ground in tears. People thought the blind sheikh had died, so they raced over, only to find her weeping for you. Everyone in Deir al-Asad had learned of your death because Israeli radio had broadcast the military communiqué, but the villagers hadn't dared to think of holding a big funeral. They mourned you in silence and told one another that Nahilah had been relieved of all the torment, the childbearing, the oppression, prison, and interrogation.

People rushed over and found Nahilah collapsed at her door lamenting and rolling her head from side to side in the dirt. When they gathered around her, she stood up and said, "The funeral is tomorrow. Tomorrow we'll pray for his soul in the mosque," and she went inside.

It was a wake beyond compare. Her weeping made everyone else weep. "As though he were Imam Hussein," people said. "As though we were performing the rites of Ashura." Food was served, coffee was prepared, turbaned sheikhs came from all over, and chanting circles formed. Nahilah went unveiled to where the men were gathered and recounted the news of your death. "They killed him and left him gasping with thirst. Three bullets to the chest. He fell to the ground, and they fell upon him. He asked for water, and the officer kicked him in the face." Then she wept and the men's tears fell, while the blind sheikh sat in the place of honor and red streaks, like tears, furrowed his creased, aged skin.

The village turned into a place of lamentation, and your mother said, "Enough!"

But Nahilah wouldn't be silent. Three days of tears and lamentation. Even the Israeli officer who came to monitor the wake stood there dumfounded. Did he believe Nahilah's tears, call himself a liar and doubt what he knew to be the facts? Can weeping deceive the eyes?

You think she did all that to protect you from them. As though the Jews didn't know you'd escaped and were probably hiding somewhere in Galilee.

No, that's not the case. It was about weeping.

The woman wept because she needed to weep. Nahilah needed a false death in order to cry because a real death doesn't make us cry, it demolishes us. Have you forgotten how the death of her son Ibrahim annihilated her? Have you forgotten how she was incapable of weeping and sank into moaning?

You, Abu Salem, were merely the pretext for all those tears brought up from the depths of waters imprisoned there for a thousand years.

No, she didn't weep for you.

During the false funeral and even later, you were holed up in your distant cave. You and the night – a long night, thick and gluey, a night without color or eyes.

When Nahilah finally came to the cave of Bab al-Shams, she was afraid of you; you were lying on the ground like a corpse. She arrived with food, water, and clean clothes, found you lying on your belly. Your foul smell, like that of a dead animal, filled the cave. She tried to wake you. She listened to your rasping breath. She tried again to wake you, trying to pull you up by your shoulders, but kept falling back down. She held your head in her hands and spoke to you; your head kept falling back down, and she kept pulling it back up. When you opened your eyes, you didn't see her. She said she'd brought you food, and you moaned. Then you turned over and tried to sit up. You pulled yourself onto your hands and knees. Finally managing to sit up, you looked around, frightened.

"It's me. Nahilah."

You started peering around, terrified, while she tried to convince you that you had to wash and change your clothes.

Nahilah told you later that you were in that state for at least two hours before coming to your senses. After she succeeded in stripping off your clothes, she bathed you in cold water. That was the only chaste bath that took place in Bab al-Shams.

She covered you with soap, her long black dress was soaked, clinging to the curves of her body. And, instead of leaping out of the water like a fish, you let her bathe you, covered in soapsuds, weeping.

Nahilah didn't say that you wept, but she felt you were on the verge of tears. She said it wasn't you. It was as though you were another man, as though the fear had almost paralyzed you and made you surrender.

Later, when you came back to yourself, you'd deny all that, claiming that you hadn't slept for four weeks and that when you heard the sound of Nahilah's footsteps, you felt safe and gave in to sleep.

I don't know what to believe.

Sleep or fear?

Should I believe Nahilah, who saw her husband disintegrating, or the husband who claims he was sleeping peacefully to the sound of his wife's footsteps?

I've thought about the story of the cave a lot since you went into a coma, and about your fate and that of Adnan. I've thought about those long weeks in the cave and your sleeping while your wife tried to wake you. I wish I could ask Nahilah about it. Nahilah knows the secret, but you, you're locked up tight, like all men. You've turned your life into a closed book, like a circle.

How am I to bear the death of Shams and my fear, if not through telling stories?

But you, what are you afraid of?

Why did you always tell the story of your life as though it were only the story of your journey over there?

You'll say I talk about Bab al-Shams because I'm in love: "You're in love, and you want to use my story to fill in the gaps of your own, to paper over your disillusion with the woman who betrayed you."

Please, don't speak of betrayal – I don't believe in it. If they hadn't humiliated me the way they did, digging around in my hair for cuckold's horns, staring me down, I wouldn't have cared.

No, I'm not using your story to complete my own. I lost my own life right at the beginning, when my mother left me and escaped to Jordan. But you, you won everything.

The state you're in now resembles your former state in the cave. The only difference is that your beloved won't come and save you from death, so I have to find a woman for you. What do you say to Mme. Fayyad?

"Mme. Fayyad only exists in your imagination," you'll say.

But I saw her with my own eyes! She came to the hospital and kissed me. I know you don't want me to go down this road but before I shut up I want to ask you why you didn't tell me what went on in the cave during those weeks.

When I asked you, you replied that you'd sat and waited, that nothing happened.

Is waiting nothing? You must be mocking me; waiting is everything. We spend our whole lives waiting, and you say "nothing" as though you wanted to dismiss the entire meaning of our existence.

Get up now and tell me the rest of the story.

The story isn't yours, it's Adnan's. Get up and tell me the story of your friend Adnan. You tell it much better than I do.

ADNAN HEARD the sentence of thirty years in prison and burst out laughing. So the judge added another ten for contempt of court.

Before the sentence, Adnan stood in the dock and put his hands on the bars like a caged animal. He struck the bars and shouted and cursed, so the judge ordered his hands tied behind his back, at which point he decided to remain silent. The judge asked questions, and Adnan said nothing. Then the blond Israeli woman lawyer, the only Israeli one who dared defend

Adnan, explained the reason for Adnan's silence, so they untied him. He said only one thing before being sentenced: "This is the land of my father and my forefathers. I am neither a saboteur nor an infiltrator. I have returned to my land."

When the judge announced the sentence, Adnan burst out laughing and slapped his hands together as though he'd just heard a good joke. The judge asked him what he thought he was doing.

"Nothing. Nothing at all. But do you really think your state is going to last another thirty years?"

The judge listened to the translation of the defendant's words, and, as they were leaving, Adnan began yelling, "Thirty years! Your state won't last, and I'll put you all on trial as war criminals."

The judge came back to the stand and added ten years for contempt of court, while Adnan kept up his gesturing and fooling around, as if he were dancing in the Israeli clink.

That's how you told me the story. You weren't at the trial, naturally, and the events of the trial weren't published in the Arab papers, but you knew all that from your private sources – whose source is known to none!

Tell me, now, why did you return in such a state from visiting Adnan, when he was freed after the celebrated prisoner exchange in '83?

Were you afraid? Of what?

Were you afraid of his illness?

I told you he had a neurological disorder and that neurological disorders could be treated, but you continued to feign ignorance.

Adnan was mentally disturbed, which doesn't mean he'd gone crazy. He returned as a semi-imbecile; that's the correct term to describe his condition. He spoke calmly and with self-possession. He recognized everybody and knew the names of all the members of his family, even the grandchildren who'd been born during his long absence. He knew them and embraced them as grandfathers do their grandchildren.

He spoke slowly and calmly, that's all.

After a few days, however, he began to lose his head. He would have unexpected outbursts and speak to people as though he were talking to the Israeli jailers, jabbering in Hebrew. Then, a bit later, he lost the use of language completely; he'd bellow and run into the streets naked.

You returned from your last visit to him in the Burj al-Barajneh camp defeated, in despair. You asked me for sleeping pills and decided to stop going to see him. His son, Jamil, wanted to send him to the mental hospital. You objected and even wept. Everyone saw you weep. You told them, "Impossible! Adnan is a hero, and heroes aren't locked up in a lunatic asylum." It's said you pulled out your gun and tried to shoot him. People intervened to stop you, saying it was a sin. "The real sin is that he won't die. The sin is that he should live like this, you bastards."

Why didn't you tell me you pulled out your gun? And why didn't you kill him? Why did you let them take him away to the Dar al-Ajazah Institution? Did you believe that place was the same as a hospital? I swear it wouldn't even be suitable for a beast. The patients there are crammed together like animals, they live a thousand deaths each day.

This time, allow me to give another version of the facts.

With your permission, I won't let Adnan end this way. I'll tell you what happened in a different way.

Yunes, Abu Salem al-Asadi, went to visit his friend Adnan Abu Odeh in the Burj al-Barajneh camp. This wasn't his first visit since his release from the Israeli prison where Adnan had spent eighteen years. Yunes was at the head of the group that welcomed him home. He danced, fired his rifle into the air, and slaughtered sheep in his honor. He'd embraced Adnan and told everyone, "Hug him, smell the aroma of Palestine!"

Everybody sat in the Abu Odeh clan's guest hall eating lamb and rice and drinking coffee, and Adnan said nothing except for a few words that were lost among the ecstatic *youyous* of the women – and even the men, that day. The camp was flooded with a sea of colors – the women wore their multi-color peasant dresses and poured out onto the dusty streets of the camp as though they were back on the streets of their own villages.

When the party was over and everyone had departed, Adnan went back home with his family and sat down among his children and grandchildren. He embraced them all and kept repeating, "Praise be to God!"

Everyone laughed when Yunes related the events of the trial.

"Stand up, Adnan, and tell us the story!" said Yunes.

Adnan didn't stand up, or tell them the story, or laugh, or clap; he didn't repeat for them what he'd told the judge: "Do you really think your state is going to last another thirty years?"

Yunes told the story and everyone laughed, while Adnan remained immersed in his deep silence.

"You see, Adnan, twenty years have passed. There's still plenty of time to go!"

At that moment Adnan began to manifest strange symptoms. He would raise his voice, then fall silent. He spoke an incomplete sentence and mixed in Hebrew words.

Yunes thought he was just tired. "Let the man rest," he said. "He's exhausted."

He said goodbye to Adnan and promised to visit him in the next few days.

A week later, news began to arrive of Adnan's madness, but Yunes refused to believe it. He went back to his friend's house to see for himself – he saw and wept and returned distraught.

But things didn't end there.

One morning, Adnan's son, Jamil, came to Yunes to inform him of the family's decision to move Adnan to the mental institution and asked him to get a report from a doctor at the Palestinian Red Crescent.

This is where Dr. Khalil – that would be me – comes in. He went to the Burj al-Barajneh camp, examined Adnan and said he was suffering from depression and in need of long-term neurological treatment, but there was no need to put him into a hospital. Adnan's condition worsened, however, to the point where he would leave the house naked. The writing was on the wall, and Jamil came to me for help. I explained my diagnosis and the man exploded, shouting that he couldn't take it any longer and that he'd made up his mind and it didn't matter whether I wrote the report or not.

Yunes decided to intervene.

He went to Burj al-Barajneh and knocked on Adnan's door. Jamil welcomed him, then started complaining and telling him stories. Yunes told him to be quiet.

Yunes went into the living room where Adnan was sitting in his pajamas listening to Umm Kalsoum's "I'm Waiting for You" on the radio and swaying to the music. Yunes greeted his old friend. But Adnan remained absorbed in Umm Kalsoum, as though unaware of him.

Yunes pulled out his gun, fired one shot at Adnan's head and shouted, "I declare you a martyr."

Then he bent over his blood-covered friend and embraced him, weeping and saying, "It wasn't me that killed you, it was Israel."

Adnan died a martyr. They printed his photo on big red posters, and he had a huge funeral the likes of which had never been seen before.

Don't you think this ending's much better than yours?

You should have killed him the way they do a wounded stallion instead of letting him be taken there.

Instead, you came to me asking for sleeping pills and left your friend to die a gruesome death in that place.

I saw him there, and I know he spent his final days screaming and then in a coma having shock treatments, but I never told you because you were busy and only wanted to hear what made you feel good.

As far as you were concerned, Adnan ended in the courtroom with his "This is the land of my father and my forefathers." You'd clap your hands and laugh, saying, "Thirty years! God bless you, Adnan. There's still plenty of time to go, Adnan. The years have passed, and we're still in the camp."

"It was time that pushed Adnan over the edge," you told me. "Don't count the years. We need to forget. The years pass, that doesn't matter. Twenty, thirty, forty, fifty, a hundred years, what's the difference?"

You let Adnan die like a dog in the hospital, and his son didn't have the courage to announce his death. The Abu Odeh family didn't take part in his funeral. They buried him secretly, as though there'd been a scandal. Even you, his lifelong friend, didn't go to his funeral.

Now do you understand my confusion?

The temporary confuses me because it scares me.

"Everything's temporary," you told me when we met after the disaster in '82. And during the long siege at Shatila in '85, you said it was temporary. "Listen, we have no choice. However dire the circumstances are, we have to keep on living or we'll simply disappear."

I know your views, your eloquence, and your ability to make the impossible sound reasonable.

But what would happen if we were to remain in this temporary world forever?

Do you believe, for example, that your present condition is temporary?

Do you believe that I'll stay here in your temporary world trying in vain to wake you, telling you stories I don't know, traveling with you to a country that I've never seen?

What kind of a game is this? You're dying right in front of me, so I'll take you to an imaginary country!

"Don't say *imaginary!*" I can hear you protesting. "It's more real than reality."

Very well, my friend. I'll take you to a real country. Then what? I can't stand any more illusions. I want something other than these stories stuffed with heroic deeds. I can't live forever within the walls of fiction.

Should I tell you about myself?

There's nothing to tell. I have nothing to say except that I'm a prisoner. I'm a prisoner of this hospital. Like all prisoners, I live on memories. Prison is a storytelling school: Here we can go wherever we want, twist our memory however we please. Right now, I'm playing with your memory and mine. I forget about the danger hanging over my life, I play with yours, and I try to wake you up. The fact is I no longer care whether or not you wake up; your return to life doesn't matter anymore. But I don't want you to die, because if you die, what will become of me? Would I go back to being a nurse or wait for death at home?

So, you're right.

You were always right: The temporary is preferable to the permanent, or the temporary is the permanent. When the temporary comes to an end, so does everything else. I'm in your temporary world now: I visit your country, live your life and make imaginary journeys. I'm your temporary doctor who isn't really a doctor. Do you believe I became a doctor? Do you believe three months' study in China can make someone a doctor?

Would you like to hear about China?

I'll give you a bath first, then order a dish of beans from Abu Jaber's next door, then after dinner, I'll tell you. I'm starving and the hospital food is foul. Believe me, you eat better than I do. You can't taste anything now because you're fed through your nose, but the taste of bananas with milk is delicious. Our food, on the other hand, is vile, and I'm forced to eat it. What else can I eat? Do you think I'm going to pay for a dish of beans every day? I had to fight a huge battle to get Dr. Amjad to take me back onto the hospital payroll as a mere nurse, at a miserable salary. He claims I'm not working and you don't need a full-time nurse and all I do is take care of you.

That bastard of a doctor only agreed to pay me half a salary after Zainab intervened and told him his conduct was unjustified "because Dr. Khalil was a founder of this hospital, and he has a right to return to it." She used the word *doctor* after hesitating and eyeing me like an idiot, as though she had really gone above and beyond the call of duty.

Do you know how much I make?

I make two hundred thousand Lebanese lira a month, or the equivalent of a mere one hundred and twenty U.S. dollars. A doctor for a hundred dollars, what a bargain! It's not even enough to cover the cost of cigarettes, tea, and arak. And I only drink arak rarely because it's gotten expensive.

What age are we living in?

"We were willing to take the shit, but the shit thought it was too good for us," as they say. Between you and me, Amjad's right. He found out I wasn't a doctor, so he offered me a job as a nurse. I refused. And when I agreed, he made me half a nurse!

Do you believe I'm a doctor?

You encouraged me when I came back from China to work as a doctor, telling me revolutionary medicine was better than regular medicine.

But how sad it is when revolutions come to an end! The end of a revolution's the ugliest thing there is. A revolution is like a person: It gets senile and rambles and wets itself.

What matters is that revolutionary medicine no longer exists. The revolution's over, medicine's gone back to being medicine, and I was only a temporary doctor.

And now I'm returning to my real self.

But what is my real self?

I have no idea. I know I became a doctor by accident, because I fractured my spine. I don't remember how the accident happened – we were in the Burjawi district, whose main street forms a tongue descending from al-Ashrafiyyeh in East Beirut to Ras al-Nab' in the west, a stretch we were able to occupy to announce that we were liberating Beirut.

It was Lebanon's civil war.

When the war began, I remembered Amman and how we were thrown out without having lost; in September of '70 we were defeated without a war and left for the forests of Jerash and Ajloun, and that was the end of it. Amman – today it seems like a dream; Black September was my dream. We called that September black to convey its significance, but Amman was white, and there I discovered the whiteness of death. Death is white, white as these sheets that you're wrapped up in in your iron bed.

I was just a kid at the time. I fought in the district of al-Weibdeh near the Fatah office. To tell you the truth, I'd been enthusiastic about going to Amman so I could look for my mother, but that's a long story I'll tell you later.

The war in Beirut was different and went on for a long time. When it started, I thought it would be Amman all over again, and the fighting wouldn't go on for more than a few weeks and then we'd withdraw somewhere. But I was wrong, Lebanon blew up in our faces. An entire country reduced to splinters, and we found ourselves running around among the shattered fragments of districts, cities, villages, sects.

I won't provide an analysis of the Lebanese civil war right now, but it terrified me. It terrified me that the belly of a city could burst open and its guts spill out and its streets be transformed into borders for dismembered communities. Everything came apart during the years of the civil war; even I was split into innumerable personae. Our political discourse and alliances changed from one day to the next, from support for the Left to support for the Muslims, from the Muslims to the Christians, and from the Shatila massacre, carried out by Israelis and Phalangists in '82, to the siege-massacre of '85, carried out by the Amal movement with the support of Syria.

How can this war be believed?

I see it pass in front of me like a mysterious dream, like a cloud that envelops me from head to foot. I was able to swallow an amazing number of contradictory slogans: Words were cheap at the time, as was blood, which is why we didn't notice the abyss we were sliding into. None of us noticed, not even you. I know you hated that war and said it wasn't a war. With due respect, I disagree because I don't think you can apply the concept of blame to history. History is neutral, I tell you – only to hear you answer, "No! Either we dish out blame where blame is due, or we become mere victims." I don't want to get caught up in that argument since, as you can see, nowadays I tend to agree with you, but you'll have to explain one thing to me. Some day soon, when you wake from your long sleep, you must explain to me how clouds can so fill someone's head that he goes to his own death without noticing.

In the war, the Khalil who's sitting in front of you now was the hero of al-Burjawi. No, I'm lying. I wasn't a hero. I was with the young fighters when we occupied that salient that climbs toward al-Ashrafiyyeh, and that's where I fell: The world flipped upside-down, I couldn't hear a sound, and I understood that death has no meaning, and we can die without realizing it.

Like all fedayeen, I expected to die and didn't care. I thought that when I died, I'd die like a hero, meaning I'd look death in the eye before I closed mine. But when the world flipped upside down in al-Burjawi and I fell, I didn't look at death. Death occupied me without my realizing. It was only in the hospital that I found out four of my comrades had been killed, and then I was stricken with the crazy fear that I'd die without knowing I was dead.

If you were alive, my dear friend, you'd laugh and tell me that no one knows he's dying when he's dying. But it's not true, I've seen them dying and knowing. A doctor sees a lot, and I've seen them trembling, terrified of death, and then dying.

It's not true that the dying don't know; if they didn't, death would lose its meaning and become like a dream. When death loses its meaning, life loses its meaning, and we enter a labyrinth from which there is no exit.

Tell me, when you were struck dumb and fell, did you know you were dying?

Of course not. I'm sure you didn't. In medical terms, the moment you lost the power of speech, you became worried because Amna couldn't understand what you were saying. You thought she'd gone deaf, so you raised your voice and tried to express yourself with gestures. Then, with the second stroke, you lost consciousness. Now look at you, lying here, not aware of a thing.

For me, too, when the world turned upside down, I didn't regain consciousness for three days. The doctor at the American University Hospital in Beirut said I had to remain motionless for a week. My L6 vertebra was crushed to powder, and to escape semiparalysis, the only cure was to lie motionless.

If I told you the pain was unbearable, I'd be lying. The pain was appalling, as pain always is, but it could be withstood. It was like a hand of steel gripping my chest and neck. I was paralyzed, my chest was constricted, my breathing was shallow, and pain ran through every part of my body. But I knew I wasn't going to die and that if I did, I'd die with my comrades who'd been killed by the heat from the B7s. The B7 was our secret weapon – a small rocket-propelled grenade carried on the shoulder capable of piercing tank armor because it gave off two thousand degrees of heat.

We were in our hiding place in an old house in al-Burjawi when the grenade fell on us and we ignited. They told us later that our bodies were completely charred, that I was black as charcoal. They thought I was dead and took me to the hospital morgue, but a nurse then noticed I was breathing so they moved me to the emergency room. They worked for hours to remove the black coating incrusted on my skin; you can still see a trace of it on my shoulder.

The doctor said my life wasn't in danger; the only real fear was that I'd be paralyzed, but I'd probably "escape clean" – and he made a gesture with his fingers like popping an almond from its skin. I wasn't afraid of paralysis. I was sure it wouldn't happen to me. But the idea that I'd die without knowing struck terror into me. Everyone knowing and not me. Everyone weeping and not the dead man. A true masquerade, the masquerade of death.

I got better, of course. After a week I got out of bed completely healed; I even forgot the pain. Pain is the only thing we forget. We're capable of revisiting many things, and may even be moved by certain sensations, but not pain. We either have pain or we don't – there's no halfway house. Pain is when it's there, and when it's not, it doesn't exist. The only feeling it leaves is of lightness, the ability to fly.

Why am I telling you about my back?

Is it because the pain came back since Shams' death?

Shams has nothing to do with it. God knows, when I was with her I didn't notice my back. I was like a god. With her I experienced love in the way you described it. You said God had made a mistake with men; he'd created them with all the necessary parts except one, which there is no doing without and whose importance we only discover when we truly need it.

But why am I telling you about the missing part now? I started out telling you about China.

Could it be because that was where I became aware of how ponderous my body was and discovered I was unfit for war? Do you know what it means to be unfit for war during a war?

I won't take up more of your time with this. I sense you're tired of my stories and would prefer to have me take you back to Bab al-Shams, to that day when you wept for love and told Nahilah you felt impotent.

"Women possess it, this missing organ," you told me. "I discovered there that women possess it; it's their entire body, while I'm incomplete, incomplete and impotent."

Nahilah looked at you in astonishment. She had a hard time believing in this sense of impotence that you were voicing, because you were insatiable. She thought you were talking about sexual impotence and burst out laughing. After such a journey of the body through the realms of ecstasy, you stop and tell her you're lacking something! She felt she'd been purified inside and out, luminous, embodied, that her eyes were two mirrors reflecting the world!

You tried to explain, but she didn't understand. You explained that you needed another part because the sexual organ was not an instrument of love. It was its doorway, but when the chasm opened you needed another part, for which you were searching in vain.

Nahilah thought you were saying all that as a preamble to making love again, and she had no objection; she was always ready, always ardent, always waiting. So she said, "Come here." But you didn't want to. You'd just been trying to tell her about your amazing discovery. But of course, you went to her; and there, amid the waves of her body, you discovered that women surpass men because the woman's body itself is the part a man doesn't have, because she's a wave without end.

I won't tell you now the details of that night at Bab al-Shams. First China. Let's make a short journey to China, then we'll go back to the cave.

In China I discovered I was unfit for war and metamorphosed from an officer into a doctor. I studied medicine in spite of myself, because I had no other option.

In Classical Arabic mixed with colloquial Egyptian, the woman told me I was unfit for war and should go back to my country or join the doctors' course. I accepted even though the idea of studying medicine had never crossed my mind. Like the rest of my generation, I'd had no serious schooling. After elementary school we joined the cadet camps of the various military forces. We set off to change the world and found ourselves soldiers. We were like the soldiers in any ordinary army, the only difference being that we talked about politics, especially me. I started my active military life as an officer, a political commissar with the commandos of al-Assifa because I loved literature. I used to memorize long passages of what I read. I liked Jurji Zeidan and Naguib Mahfouz, but my favorite was Ghassan Kanafani. I learned *Men in the Sun* by heart, like a poem. Then I broadened my horizons and memorized whole sections of Russian novels, especially Dostoevsky's *The Idiot*. How I felt for Prince Mishkin! How sweet he was, caught between his two lovers! How wonderful his naiveté, like that of the Christ! I'd read *The Idiot* and would never tire of it. How I wished I could be like him!

No. When I stood before the investigating committee, I didn't feel like an idiot; I felt humiliated. Being an idiot is not the same as being humiliated. It's a position one takes. But there I stood before them humiliated, and I lost my ability to defend myself.

Literature was my refuge. In the days of Kafar Shouba, when we were exposed to the aerial bombardment, sheltered only by the branches of the olive trees, those books were my refuge. To stay alive, I would imitate their heroes and would speak their language.

I became a political commissar because I loved literature, I became a soldier because I was like everyone else, and I became a doctor because I had no choice.

It happened because of my back: After a week I was completely recovered and rejoined my battalion, which had been transferred to fight at Sanin mountain. There among the snows of Lebanon I grew to hate the war and love that white mountain. I lived in the mire of blood-spattered snow.

Blood stained the snow on both sides of the front, which stretched to the horizon. I understood why my mother had fled the camp. There we don't see, we remember. We remember things we never experienced because we take on the memories of others. We pile ourselves on top of one another and smell the olive groves and the orange orchards.

At Sanin I realized that those far horizons were an extension of man and that if God hadn't made these curves, we'd die and our bodies would turn into coffins.

I was in Sanin when Colonel Yahya from the Mobilization and Organization Department came and informed me that I'd been chosen to join a training course for battalion commanders in China.

And I went.

From Sanin to China in one straight shot. "Seek knowledge, though it be from China," the Prophet said. I descended from the highest mountain in Lebanon to the lowest point in the world and there my final destiny was decided. "No soul knows in what land it shall die."*

It never occurred to me that I'd switch from military to medical school. Such are destiny and fate. My destiny was not to be a soldier, and my fate took me where it willed. I understood that that fall on the Burjawi steps had determined my future, and once I accepted my future as a doctor in the armed forces, things began to change. Now I'm no longer a doctor and it's up to me to decide whether I remain a nurse. I prefer something else but I don't know what it would be. You'll say it was my fault, that I should have left with the others in '82, you'll blame me for having left the stadium and gone home.

When I recall my moments at the stadium, where the fedayeen gathered amidst rice and *youyous*, I don't know what happened to me. I had no justification for staying in Beirut. I had no family, only Nuha, who I didn't want.

"You should have gone with them," Zainab said when she learned they'd decided I wasn't a doctor and had to work as a trainee nurse.

Do you see the significance of the insult, Father? A trainee nurse! After all those years of being treated as a doctor, I've become a miserable servant in the hospital whose founding physician I once was. But let's suppose I had gone with the fedayeen, where would I find myself today?

I'd probably be in Gaza, and my status would be ambiguous. Do you think they'd have accepted me as a doctor there? Our leaders, as I understand it, are setting up a legal authority, and this authority needs educated people, crooks, merchants, contractors, business men, and security services.

* Koran, Surah XXXI, 34.

Our role has come to an end; they won't be needing fedayeen anymore. If I'd gone with them, I'd have to choose between working as a nurse or joining one of the intelligence groups. My destiny would be in limbo.

We've ended up in limbo, dear friend. Our lives have become a burden to us.

The decision to return to Shatila from the stadium wasn't a mistake. It's true it wasn't a conscious decision, but, like all critical decisions, we take them, or they take us, and that's the end of the matter.

In China I had no choice, I had to accept my role as a doctor because after two weeks of intensive nonstop military training, the doctor discovered I was unfit for war. She didn't take me into the X-ray room or subject me to medical tests; she simply looked at me and understood everything.

I went to see her bare chested as my comrades had done. She looked at me attentively, walked around me, asked me to bend over, put her finger on the place where it hurt and pressed. I screamed in pain.

"When did your spinal chord get broken?" she asked.

"What? . . . Two months ago."

She asked me to bend over again, brought her face close to the place where it hurt, and I don't know what she did, but I could feel her hot breath scorching my bones. Then she went back behind the desk and asked me to get dressed and wait.

After everyone had left, she came and sat down beside me. She was wearing khaki pants, a khaki shirt, and a khaki cap. All I could see of her was a small face and Mongol eyes. I couldn't work out her age; I had guessed about thirty, but then someone mentioned she was in her fifties. I have no idea.

She sat down beside me and explained that my broken spine had knitted in such a way that to continue training, or any military work, was out of the question. The pain might erupt again at any moment. This meant that I had to get ready to go home.

I tried to explain that she was cutting off my future and that I had to continue military training at any cost.

She patted my hand to reassure me – the only time my hand touched a

Chinese woman's. She advised me to go back to Palestine to work with the peasants, saying that her most beautiful memories were of the time when she'd worked in the countryside.

"But I can't go back."

"Of course you can."

"If I go back, I won't work with the peasants because we're not living in our own country and because there aren't any peasants . . ."

My response stunned her. I explained that we were a people of refugees, and she was even more stunned. I said we were orchestrating our revolution from the outside, surrounding our land because we were unable to enter it.

"You are surrounding the cities," she said, looking relieved, "as we did on the Long March."

"No," I said. "We're surrounding the countryside because we're outside our country."

Numerous questions flitted across her face, but she didn't say anything more; she didn't understand how you could surround the countryside or how there could be no peasants. She asked me to pack my bags, so I left the clinic and went back to the barracks as though nothing had happened.

The next morning, I went out to join the lineup as usual, but the trainer, who was accompanied by a social worker who spoke Classical Arabic, ordered me to leave. I went back to my room to wait to go home, but instead of sending me to Beirut, they took me to another camp, where I spent the training period in a field hospital belonging to the Chinese People's Army. It seems that what I'd said had had some effect on the doctor. Medical training wasn't very different from military training. We drank the same water, ate the same food, ran in morning lineups and practiced using medical instruments as though they were weapons. The only difference was the language.

In the military camp, we used Arabic, while in the field hospital, it was English. It's true that I don't know the language very well, but I could understand everything. The truth is I learned English in China! Imagine the paradox; imagine that I learned the importance of drinking water warm in English! In China they always drink their water tepid, almost hot. That's why no one gets fat there. You open your eyes in the morning, and you're desperate for a drink of cold water. But you get warm water, so you drink and you drink and you're still thirsty. For the first few days, I was thirsty all the time. The more I drank, the thirstier I would get. Then I became accustomed to their water, discovered the secret and grew to like it. Warm water enters you as if through your pores: You drink as though you aren't drinking, as if the water were already inside you. To this day I yearn for warm water, but I don't drink it anymore the way I used to during the first days after I returned to Beirut. Perhaps the climate is the reason. The climate is what makes our men fat.

After the first days in China, we were overwhelmed by the feeling that we were outsiders. This happened when we visited the tunnels of Beijing – there were tunnels everywhere, tunnels full of rice and wheat depots, tunnels amazingly camouflaged. Once we went into a small shop to buy clothes. The salesman stood up and pushed aside piles of khaki garments, and we found ourselves descending into a tunnel more than thirty meters deep, equipped for people to live in for months.

An underground universe. A universe of war, a universe of history. In China we learned how a human being could live in history. How can I describe history to you?

Some middle school children came one day to take part in our military training. We competed with them at target practice with Simonov rifles. It's a useless rifle, or that's what we think here, but over there they respect the Simonov enormously, because it's the rifle that played such an important role in bringing American planes down in Vietnam.

The point is that Chinese kids, not more than fifteen years old, beat professional officers at target practice! That was our first lesson – respect your weapon. Of course, you'll say, we forgot everything the moment we returned to Beirut, but that's not true. I didn't forget everything, but I wasn't able to keep things up on my own. How can you convince people from here to drink water warm? How can you teach them to respect an ordinary rifle when Kalashnikovs are dirt cheap, along with Belgian and American rifles and all the others?

This isn't what I wanted to tell you.

I wanted to try to describe for you the sight of the people doing their morning exercises. I know this is difficult to believe, but I saw it with my own eyes. At seven in the morning, in the streets, music blasts out of loud-speakers scattered everywhere, and millions of men, women, and children of all ages pour into the streets for their calisthenics. The entire Chinese people doing morning stretches!

Can you imagine how these scenes affected us?

First the warm water, then the Simonov children, then the morning exercises, then the soybean that would swell up in water that we ate, and then the long, thin bag of rice that every Chinese soldier would wrap around his neck and waist.

It took us into history.

Now, that's history.

Today I might have another reaction, but at the time we were intoxicated by the wine of revolution. Imagine with me a billion Chinese men, women, and children doing their street exercises each morning. Imagine the tunnels and the grain and the ideas of Chairman Mao Tse Tung.

I was convinced and bewitched.

No, I can't say I was convinced one hundred percent, but I started repeating phrases to myself as though they were prayers: "Chairman Mao Tse Tung, a thousand years more." Of course, Mao died, and stayed good and dead, and the Cultural Revolution ended, the crimes were revealed, and these things no longer stir up the same sort of emotions in us.

But during those days, Father, we felt we were making history. We behaved and talked as though we were heroes in novels without authors, novels we all knew and which we narrated every day. We ended up not speaking when we spoke but reciting lines we'd learned by heart. We would ask and we knew the answer and our memories would speak through us. It was as though we were mimicking ourselves; yes, mimicking ourselves.

Now, that's history.

It drags you to two contradictory places: where you're everything and where you're nothing. You are both a monster and an angel, you kill with the feeling that you're the one dying, you seek gratification and fear it, you become your own god.

History is our becoming gods and monsters at the same time.

I say it because I lived it. No, it's not about China, it's about us. I don't want to desecrate anyone's memory, but you know Ali Rabeh? The martyr, Ali Rabeh, who we mourned so bitterly?

Ali Rabeh was the hero of Maroun al-Ras in '78. He didn't run from the Israelis who swept over our positions in their first incursion into Lebanon. Ali Rabeh, along with a small group of others, stuck it out and fought and became a hero. We thought he'd died because in those days we used to assume that anyone who didn't withdraw was a dead man. Our term for running away was *withdrawing*. Ali Rabeh came back alive, told his story, and became a hero.

I saw an unrecognizable monster emerge from inside Ali Rabeh. We were fighting in the district of al-Burjawi – this was before my fall and before China and before I became a doctor. Abu George was there. This Abu George wasn't important enough to be mentioned in the history books. He was just an ordinary citizen living on the ground floor of a three-story building located at the crossroads that divides al-Burjawi in half – a protected half and a half exposed to gunfire from the Phalangists who occupied the tall buildings of al-Ashrafiyyeh opposite. He was our friend. From his accent, I could tell that he was from Syria, from the village of Maaloula where the houses seem to grow out of the rock and the people still speak Aramaic and pray in the language of Christ.

Abu George lived alone, cooked alone, and listened to the radio alone. He'd look at us with sleepy eyes. He was short and chubby with a broad brow and a round white face full of wrinkles. He never spoke with us about politics; he'd tell us about his son, who'd emigrated to Canada, and his daughter, Mary, who lived in Paris. He said he couldn't abandon the house because it held memories of his wife, who'd died there as a young woman, and that he also hated the idea of emigrating to Europe: "Better the tares of your village than the Crusaders' wheat," he'd say. Then he'd watch us rushing up to the roof in our khakis and weighed down with arms and he'd say, "My my, what fine tares!"

Abu George didn't object to our squatting in the third story of his building, where Ali assembled a Doshka cannon. When he invited us down for coffee, he seemed pleased to study our arms and say: "My my, what fine tares!"

I'm certain that the man didn't like us or, if *like* isn't the appropriate word here, didn't think much of us, and that was his right, not to mention the fact that we hardly inspired admiration. Now, in fact, I'd say we inspired pity – the way we'd talk, set up ambushes, build bunkers, shoot, and drop dead.

In al-Burjawi, our wounded dropped by the dozen. It was unthinkable to turn the street into a second front: Anyone who occupies al-Burjawi has to get all the way to al-Nasira in the center of al-Ashrafiyyeh or *withdraw*. We stayed on, however, so we could die. It wasn't our decision, as you know; we were just troops, potential martyrs.

One day, after Ali had finished his morning coffee with Abu George, he thanked him and was already climbing the stairs to the third floor when he heard Abu George say, as he had dozens of times before, "My my, what fine tares!"

"So we're tares, you son of a bitch?" Ali yelled.

Without warning, he started beating Abu George savagely. Ali must have been harassed that day – or maybe even terrorized – I could see fire in his eyes. He was beating the life out of him. Abu George was doubled over, shielding his head with his hands and moaning as Ali kicked him.

"Spy, traitor, where's your communications setup?" Ali shouted at the top of his lungs, panting and swinging punches.

This had nothing to do with Abu George, the man was innocent, far from a spy. It's true that he wasn't enthusiastic about our cause or our war, and it's true that a tinge of contempt could be detected in his gaze, but he was neutral.

Ali, on the other hand . . .

Ali was a monster. What caused his eruption was never clear; it was as though there were a monster inside him, as though the war had become a spirit that possessed him. We were afraid he'd kill the man. It wasn't just a beating, it was murder. Ali was killing Abu George with his bare hands, his feet, his brown, full face and his curly hair. He devoured him.

We feared for Abu George. We all feared for him.

"And what did you do?" you'll ask me.

Nothing, I'll tell you. We froze and looked on and didn't say a word. We waited for Ali to finish, we saw that Abu George had come out of it alive, we finally opened our mouths.

We weren't petrified because we were afraid of Ali. No, we stood and watched as though we, too, had become like Ali, as though we were watching a wrestling match.

All the others said they'd been afraid for Abu George, but I was more afraid for Ali. I could see that he'd turned into another man, a man I didn't know, a monster.

History, dear Abu Salem, extracts from our inner selves people we don't know, people whose presence we don't dare acknowledge. In China I found myself in history and felt capable of doing anything; I wasn't afraid of myself or for myself because I couldn't see. When you're surrounded by mirrors on every side, you lose your ability to see, and the monster of history makes you its prey.

Abu George survived.

Ali suddenly calmed down and left. Abu George slowly began to pull himself together, as if he were gathering his scattered limbs. He managed to get up, took a few things: a pair of trousers, a shirt, some underwear, and left muttering a few incomprehensible words under his breath. I think he was cursing us in Aramaic, a language usually used for prayer.

In China we opened the book of history and learned the art of war and the art of seizing an opportunity. Our Chinese trainer told us that the central idea in a war of the people is to exploit advantage: to withdraw when victory is impossible, to attack in large numbers, to concentrate our forces and wipe out the enemy. To guarantee victory in a battle, we have to be greater in number and better armed than our enemy.

By exploiting advantage, we can delude our enemy into thinking we are capable of permanent victory.

He'd use the word *victory*, and we'd hear it and feel victorious, as though words could cast magic spells – for words are either magic or they should be thrown into the wastebasket. *Revolution* is the same thing – a magic word with magic powers.

We started discussing things we knew by heart, fighting as though we'd fought before and dying as though we were mimicking our own deaths.

God, what times!

I speak of those times as though they were over, but actually that's both true and false. We're "caught," as Major Mamdouh used to say. We're caught and have no alternatives. We get out of one tight place only to crawl into another. "All that's wrought is caught," as they say. That's how history works: When you have no alternatives, you get caught and twist in the breeze in spite of yourself.

I sit before you with Major Mamdouh's words resonating in my ears. I'm stuck here, so are you, and so is Dr. Amjad, and everyone else. And Mamdouh? I believe he got out of his tight spot because he managed to get a visa for Paris. But what became of him? Did he become a millionaire and live an easy life? Of course not. Mamdouh got to France, married for the sake of getting married (as he said in the only letter he sent his mother), and died of a heart attack. *No soul knows in what land it shall die.*

We were talking about history and I don't want to upset you with Major Mamdouh's tragic end – even though it wasn't a tragedy – tragedy calls for tears while Mamdouh's death made me laugh. Imagine, a man who spent all his time searching for a way out of the trap and then, when he gets out, dies! Mamdouh died in '81, so one year before the Israeli incursion into Lebanon – a year before his appointment with death. If Mamdouh had remained stuck with us in Beirut, he would have died in '82 as thousands did, but he postponed his appointment.

I go back to China to say that history bewitched me during those two weeks of intensive military training. I discovered how it was possible to open the book of history, enter it, and be the reader and the read at the same time. This is the illusion that revolution creates for us. It makes us believe we're both the individual and the mirror, and it leads to terrible things.

I'd fallen under the spell, until the day the doctor said I was unfit to continue training and told me to pack my bags to go back to my country. But instead of taking me back to Beirut, they took me to another camp and pronounced me a doctor.

I won't bother you with the ins and outs of Chinese medicine, which I never learned – I remember almost nothing of it, particularly not the names of herbs, which our teacher knew only in Chinese. But I discovered the human body. I discovered the existence of an interconnecting natural logic with a precise regime that controls our bodies. Through the body I discovered the soul of things, the links between our bodies and nature, and the limitlessness of man.

You'll say these philosophical theories I'm repeating are an attempt to cover up my ignorance of medicine. Not true. I'm convinced of these things and that's why I'm treating you according to my own methods. Of course, you're not the issue; Dr. Amjad was right when he pronounced you a vegetable. But I'm convinced that the soul has its own laws and that the body is a vessel for the soul. I'm trying to rouse you with my stories because I'm certain that the soul can, if it wants, wake a sleeping body.

In China, in spite of everything, and in spite of the madness of history raging in my head, I learned the most valuable thing in my life. I learned that each of our bodies holds the entire history of the human race. Your body is your history. I'm the living proof. Look at me. Can't you see the pain tearing at me? The Chinese doctor was right. The break in my spinal column, dormant for many years, has suddenly come back to life. The pain is everywhere, and painkillers are useless.

Our body is our history, dear friend. Take a look at your history in your wasting body and tell me, wouldn't it be better if you got up and shook off death?

I learned medicine in China and returned to Lebanon, a doctor, understanding nothing of medicine beyond its general principles, but speaking English!

After I transferred out of the training course, I was taken to a field hospital belonging to the Chinese People's Army, where a tall man – the Chinese are not all short, as we have a tendency to think – asked me if I spoke English. He asked me in English, so I answered, "Yes." I used to think I knew English, which we studied in the UNWRA schools*. So they put me with a group of trainees, most of them Africans. The training doctor taught the course in English. I didn't understand a thing. Well, actually, I understood a little bit, so I decided to pretend I was following everything. I learned to parrot everything that was said in front of me and ended up learning the language. I discovered I was no worse than the others. To speak English, you don't really have to know it; this is the source of its power. With amazing speed I retained the doctor's lectures and came back from China rattling on in English, tossing in a few medical terms to convince people that I was a real doctor. Everything was fine.

What I can't forget is that, when I spoke English in China, I felt I wasn't myself. Sometimes I'd be my Chinese professor or my African colleague, or I'd imitate the Pakistani. Oh, our group was composed of ten students, eight from Nigeria, me, and a Pakistani. The Pakistani knew more than we did; he said he'd been a student at the medical school in Karachi, had been thrown out because of his political activism and had come to China to study the science of revolution. He didn't want to study medicine, but they'd forced him to join this course before training him for guerrilla warfare.

I'd imitate him and feel myself becoming another person inside the English language. I'd react as they did – especially like the Pakistani, who would change totally when he got excited, stretching his mouth so that he looked like the heroes in American films when they scream, *Fuck!*

I figured out something very important. I realized that when I spoke, I

* Schools managed by the UN agency for Palestinian refugees.

was imitating others. Every word I spoke in English had to pass through the image of another person, as if the person speaking weren't me. And when I returned to Beirut and started speaking Arabic again, I found myself again, I found the Khalil I'd left behind.

In China I discovered that when I spoke the language of others I became like them. This isn't true, of course. But what if it were? What if, even in Arabic, I was imitating others? And that the only difference was that here I no longer knew who it was I was imitating? We learn our mother tongues from our mothers, imitating them, but we forget that. As we forget, we become ourselves; we speak and believe that we're the ones who are speaking.

Now I've begun to understand your feelings about your father's voice. You told me that sometimes you felt that the voice emerging from your throat was that of the blind sheikh: "It's amazing, but I began to look like him, and when I spoke I started to feel it was he who was using my tongue."

No, no, I don't agree with that theory. It's true we imitate, but we shape our own language as we shape our own lives. I don't know my father. All I remember is a shadow, and I can't tell you now – or in twenty years – that it's that shadow's voice that emerges from my throat.

Of course we imitate, but we forget, and forgetting is a blessing. Without forgetting we would all die of fright and abuse. Memory is the process of organizing what to forget, and what we're doing now, you and me, is organizing our forgetting. We talk about things and forget other things. We remember in order to forget, this is the essence of the game. But don't you dare die now! You have to finish organizing your forgetting first, so that I can remember afterwards.

Even now, when I say the word *fuck*, I see the Pakistani with his distended mouth, white teeth, and fine oblong jaw like the beak of a bird; I feel his voice in my throat, and I can smell China.

I studied medicine for three months and then returned to Beirut carrying with me a new language as well as an education in drinking warm water and in the performance of simple field operations such as removing bullets, bandaging wounds, treating fractures, giving injections and so on.

I passed as a doctor. I worked in a field hospital in Tyre, would stretch my mouth while repeating the Pakistani's words, and became a doctor. Time's wheel has turned, as they say, and now here I am, a temporary doctor, in a temporary hospital, in a temporary country. Everything inside me is waiting for something else. These waiting periods breed and erase each other, push each other out of the way and interact.

I look at my life and see images. I see a man who looks like me, and I see men who don't look like me, but I don't see myself. It's strange how we deal with life. We go to one place and find ourselves in another. We search for one thing and find something else. Alternatives pile up on top of us. In place of Nuha came Siham. In place of Siham came Shams, and in place of Shams I don't know. But now I have to wise up and marry. I'm forty years old, and at forty you either get married or life becomes hell. When a man says he "has to" get married, it means he's reached rock bottom. Marriage is supposed to happen without that "has to."

No. With Shams, marriage never occurred to me because I was living like someone under a spell. Now when I remember that magic, I see another man. The Khalil sitting in front of you isn't Shams' Khalil. Shams' Khalil was different. He didn't eat, because love suppresses the appetite; he didn't speak, because love has no language; and he didn't mind waiting. When she was there, her presence filled him up, and when she wasn't, the waiting filled him up.

Then the love went.

The only thing that destroys love is death. Death is the only cure for love. It ought to have been me. It ought to have been me who killed her. I'm the one who . . . But I didn't.

Now I'm looking for a substitute. I'm not looking for a woman like Shams but for any woman. How good it is to find a woman in your bed! But my bed remains empty, and I can't ask anyone to help me find a woman. A woman is something you have to find for yourself.

Betrayed, a cuckold, and in search of a woman?

So what? All men are betrayed and all of them are cuckolds. I know.

There, in the house of the Green Sheikh, I realized this. I suffered and wept for Shams.

I went through moments of great weakness. Shams was dead, and rumors of a death list were everywhere. I decided to go to them. Abd al-Latif with his one good eye took me to the house of Sheikh Hashim, who they called the Green Sheikh. I took off my shoes and joined their circle and twisted and swayed with the chanting, invoking with them God's name in their *dhkir* ritual. I let my breathing be guided by the hand of the sheikh who conducted us to the final ecstasy where we touched the universal Presence. I twirled with them, experienced the intoxication, and my tears flowed involuntarily. The sheikh asked me to stay behind after the others had dispersed and said he was pleased with me, letting me know that the time to repent had come. He accepted me as a disciple in his order. He gave me a book by the great Yashrati sheikh and told me to come and see him whenever I wished.

On my second visit, when I went to ask him about the story of Reem at Sha'ab, which I'd heard from everyone, I saw his wife pound on the door of their house, cursing the sheikh. He refused to open the door.

Then I learned the truth.

She was sixty-three years old. Seated on the bench outside her sister's house, she told the story, to those who wanted to hear, of how she'd gone in and found the sheikh panting with the wife of one of his disciples in his arms.

"I saw it," the woman went on, "and her cuckolded mule of a husband didn't want to believe me. He said I was crazy and drove his wife home."

The Green Sheikh's wife said that when she saw them she started screaming. Everyone, including the woman's husband, rushed over, and the hullabaloo commenced. She continued: "Then the Green Sheikh raised his hand, everyone fell silent, and he declared, 'You are repudiated.' He managed to convince everyone that I was crazy, and ordered me out of the house. I tried to tell them the truth, but no one believed me. A man in his seventies, the old lecher: I saw him hugging the woman to his fat belly while he panted like a dog! They all said I was crazy. The husband took his wife away and spat on me. He should have spat on himself and on her."

In the house of the Green Sheikh, I understood that Shams hadn't betrayed me. She'd been under a man's spell, or under I don't know what . . . I left the Sufi circle and never went back.

I understood Shams, but I was very angry with her for not having told me about her relationship with that other man. I'd have advised her not to kill him. But she was right; only death can put an end to love. By killing her love, she revealed who was the more courageous of the two of us. Me, I waited for my love to die. And with death came death. With death love evaporates and turns into nothing.

I don't care about people. They pity me because they don't understand anything. They pity me because I loved her, because she betrayed me, because I fear her ghost and because – I don't know. For my part, I don't care. Anyway, I'm in China. The hospital sent me back to China, where I was able to work on my English. I can't be a doctor just in Arabic, and without warm water! There I was reborn. There, when everything seemed to end, when they decreed I couldn't continue my military training, everything began. Khalil the officer was swept away, and in came Khalil the doctor. Instead of going to war, I went to the hospital. And today Khalil the doctor has been swept away again, and in has come Khalil the nurse.

Do you know what Dr. Amjad said?

He invited me into his office and started rambling incoherently. He sat behind the desk and spoke as though he were the director of a hospital. Of course, he is the director of a hospital, but come on! A hospital without the minimum necessities – no hygiene, no medication, nothing – it's almost a prison. And this empty head stammers in front of me, saying I really should work full time. He stretches out his words, hesitates and leaves half of them suspended in midair before snatching them back and continuing. He trips over the letter *R*, saying, "You're a *nu'se*, and you have to work as a *nu'se*. It's impossible. Things can't go on this way." I tried to explain the conditions under which I was working and how you take up all my time.

"All your time!" he said mockingly. "The fact is, we've started to worry for your sanity, doctor, talking to yourself all the time. You think we don't know what you do in that room? You think talking's a cure? If talking were a cure, we'd have liberated Palestine long ago. No, it's impossible."

I told him I took half a salary and was content with that, and he told me that what I called a half-salary was a full salary now that the Red Crescent's funding had been cut off.

"The money evaporated with Kuwait's oil, Dr. Khalil. There is no money. There's war and America, but the oil has gone, and the Arabs have gone bankrupt, and the revolution has gone bankrupt and your salary isn't half a salary, so you'll have to choose between working with us as director of nursing on a full-time basis and leaving the hospital."

He said the hospital wasn't a place of asylum, that he only wanted what was best for me, and he had respect for my past accomplishments. "But you have to do something. Don't be afraid, you're under our protection."

I didn't answer. He was trying to manipulate me, to make it clear that he knew the ins and outs of the Shams affair. All the same, I was on the verge of refusing his offer when he hung a threat over you.

"We'll take care of Yunes," he said. "Anyway, he no longer needs attention and the question of whether he should stay here is still on the table. I'm in the process of getting his papers ready for his transfer to Dar al-Ajazah.* People like him are put there, not in a hospital. His condition's hopeless, and clinically he's dead."

Do you see what that son-of-a-bitch doctor wants? He wants to throw you into a home. Yunes – Abu Salem, Izz al-Din, Adam – is to end up in Dar al-Ajazah? May lightening strike him! Do you know what this means? Listen to me, please. I didn't promise Amjad that I'd consider the proposal seriously out of concern for myself. After all, what can they do to me? It's God that decides when we die. I said I'd consider the proposal because the idea of that place struck terror in my heart. Do you know what moving you

---

* Literally: Home for the Elderly.

> 167 <

there would mean? You would rot alive – yes, you'd rot and the worms and the ulcers would devour you. I didn't tell you about Adnan because I didn't want to upset you, but I'm the only one who visited him, because they sent for me, and while I was there Dr. Karim Jaber showed me something horrifying.

"I'm not a relative of the patient," I told him.

"Precisely," he answered. "We reviewed his medical file and found the report you wrote, and we'd like to discuss his condition with you."

When I said I knew nothing about neurological diseases, he eyed me with distaste and corrected me: Mr. Adnan's illness was not neurological but psychiatric. He was suffering from schizophrenia and received electric shock therapy.

I'll spare you the excruciating details of the doctor's diagnosis since I was certain he understood absolutely nothing. He invited me to see Adnan and we walked through the place, which could have been called anything but a hospital.

Heaps of lunatics, the smells of lunatics, the sounds of lunatics.

Moans from every corner.

Moans rising like smoke.

In front of the cluster of slums that previously was the Sabra camp, there stands a dingy yellow building enclosed on all sides called Dar al-Ajazah.

In this enclosure, which isn't part of our world, I walked and walked until I got to a room that looked nothing like other rooms and saw an old man tied up in chains; they told me it was Adnan.

We walked through the first floor, where the larger wards are. "Here," said Dr. Karim, "is where we put the nondangerous patients."

We walked among them. They clung to our clothes as though they wanted something they couldn't articulate. The musty smell of food and the sight of the patients in their soiled white garments gave the impression that the rooms hadn't been aired for years.

I told Dr. Karim that I could barely breathe because of the poor ventilation, but he just patted me on the shoulder, saying that the hospital had been built to the proper standards and was equivalent to the best in Europe.

"And the odor?" I asked.

"Oh, that's nothing," he said. "It's the natural odor of a group of people. Any indiscriminate mixture of humans or animals gives off a strong and penetrating odor, that's all."

We continued through the halls, which opened onto the patients' rooms, and I noticed that they were all in pajamas. I wanted to ask why they weren't wearing clothes, but I held back.

We went up to the second floor, and there I saw!

On the first floor the conditions were more or less humane. The patients' rooms opened onto relatively large halls, and they could choose to stay with their companions in the hall or sit in their rooms, in each of which were four beds.

Upstairs was unbelievable.

We came first to a large ward full of cots with metal sides. "These are the incapacitated," he said. Then we turned right and entered the hall of horrors. I saw thirty children tied to their beds, immobilized. "These are the mentally retarded," he said with a smile.

"But this is torture," I said.

"It's better this way, for them and for us," he replied.

He led me down the long corridor and said we were coming to the "dangerous" ward.

There I saw Adnan.

It wasn't a ward, or a hall, or a room. It was a cluster of small, dark cells, and Adnan was tied with a metal chain to a bed fenced with metal bars. He was snoring.

The doctor went up to him and tried to wake him. "Adnan! Adnan!" he said.

The patient fidgeted and his snoring grew more staccato.

The doctor put his hand on the black metal siding surrounding Adnan's bed and launched into a lengthy explanation of his case. He said they'd made a mistake. "It seems the doctor on duty didn't read Adnan's medical file carefully and had him tied down. You understand, the man had spent twenty years in solitary confinement under restraint, and when he saw the restraints here he went into convulsions, so the doctor was forced to give him shock therapy. Then he had him tied to his bed, and his condition began to deteriorate. He wouldn't stop screaming and trying to attack the nurses, and he's very lucky they didn't kill him. These errors can occur, of course, but as soon as I got back, I took things in hand. As you can see, there's not much hope and his condition's getting worse."

"But he's still tied up!" I said.

"Of course, of course," answered the doctor. "I was away, as I told you, and I had no choice but to tie him up so he wouldn't endanger himself and the nurses."

"You ordered this?"

"Yes, Sir, absolutely. As you can see, the physician can be forced to take harsh measures. What could I do? As soon as I undid his restraints, he started beating one of the nurses and fractured his hand. So I ordered him to be taken back to shock therapy and tied down."

"But he's half-dead now!"

"Precisely. That's why I called you in," replied Dr. Karim. "I don't think he'll get up again after the last shock treatment. I'd like you to get in touch with his family and explain the situation to them so they can come visit him before he dies. Maybe if he sees one of his children he'll improve a little. Can you get in touch with them?"

That's where Dr. Amjad wants to send you – to the place where they chained Adnan up, tortured and killed him; to the place where Adnan hovered on the verge of death for six months between the shock-therapy room and his cell before taking his last breath.

"Impossible!" I said to Amjad.

I told him I'd give the matter some thought, gave him the impression that I would accept, and then implored him to leave you here. I said it was a scandal. I begged. I insisted that it was out of the question.

I talked and talked and talked, I forget now what I said. I begged him not to transfer you to the home, and he promised to reconsider, so I felt better. I left his office in good spirits, but now I am sad.

I'm here before you confused, scared, despairing.

But in Amjad's office I was pleased that he would reconsider the situation, which meant that I'd remain here, and if I stay you stay, or vice versa.

When he does reconsider, he'll realize that he can't expel you from the hospital because that would be shameful. True, the hospital resembles a prison, and true, we're both prisoners here, but it's better than dying.

But no.

I shouldn't have given in to his conditions. I should have threatened him, don't you think?

In your room I saw the scene with new eyes, and I imagined what I should have said and said it, or basically did.

It was 9 a.m. and I'd finished giving you your morning bath and was standing in front of the window drinking tea and smoking an American cigarette when I found Zainab in the room.

She said Dr. Amjad was expecting me.

I threw my cigarette out the window, put the teacup on the table and followed her. The doctor was reading the newspaper. He moved it a little to one side, said, "Please sit down," and went on with his reading. I accepted his kind invitation, sat down, and waited. But he didn't interrupt his reading, muttering in disapproval as he read. Finally he threw the paper onto the desk, greeted me, and fell silent again.

"Nice to see you," I said.

"Can I do anything for you?" he said.

"Thanks. Zainab told me you wanted to see me."

"Ah yes," he said. "How's the old fellow doing?"

"Better," I said.

I told him about the drops, of your reaction when I pricked your hand with a needle, of the clear signs of improvement.

He took off his dark glasses – I forgot to tell you, he wears dark glasses when he reads. Strange. I'm sure this doctor doesn't have a clue about either medicine or politics, but what can we do? "God's the Boss," as they say. He took off his dark glasses, blew pipe smoke in my face, and announced my new duties as a full-time head nurse.

I objected.

I explained the importance of my work with you and was getting up to go when he informed me of the decision to transfer you to the home.

I tried to say something but couldn't. My tongue was as heavy in my mouth as a log. Then the words burst out. I said that transferring you meant throwing you onto the garbage dump and leaving you to die, and that I knew the place was neither a *home* nor a hospital but a purgatory for the living and the tortured.

Amjad, however, insisted on having his way.

"Do you have any idea what you're doing?" I asked.

"Of course, I'm doing my duty. The hospital isn't set up for a case like Yunes'. People like him die in their own homes."

"There's nobody there," I said.

"I know. That's why we'll be transferring him to Dar al-Ajazah," he said.

"Impossible!" I yelled. "You don't know what you're saying."

"On the contrary, I know better than you do."

"You know nothing."

"I'm doing my duty. There's no room for pity in our profession."

"Pity! You're an imbecile. You don't know what Yunes represents."

"Yunes! What does Yunes represent?"

"He's a symbol."

"And how can we treat symbols?" he asked. "There's no place for symbols in a hospital. The place for symbols is in books."

"But he's a hero! A hero doesn't end up in a cemetery for the living dead."

"But he's finished."

When I heard the word *finished*, everything tipped over the edge. I don't remember exactly what spilled out of me – that you were the first, that you were Adam, that nobody was going to touch you, that I'd kill anyone who got near you.

The doctor tried to calm me down, but I got more and more excited.

He said he was the one who made the decisions here.

I said, "No. No one decides."

I snatched the newspaper out of his hands and started ripping it into little shreds and putting them in my mouth. I chewed them up and spat them out and shouted. I kept on ripping and spitting away, and the doctor shrank back behind his desk until only his head remained visible. Then it disappeared and his body grew smaller and smaller in the chair until it vanished entirely as though the desk had swallowed it.

I left him under the desk and stormed out of his office. A stormy exit: a hurricane.

And I came back to you.

I'm sure now that you'll stay put even though I didn't say what I meant to in Amjad's office.

Tell me, how is it possible? How could Amjad dare speak of you that way? Is he completely out of it? Everyone knows your story. Doesn't it mean anything to him or what? Has he lost his memory? Are we a people without a memory? Maybe he's just out of it, but I bet he's not. What's come over him? What's come over all of us? In the end, there's nothing left but the end. You and me, in a world that's hurling us into oblivion.

You're fortunate, Yunes.

Can you imagine where you'd be without me?

If you were in my shoes, and only if you were in my shoes, you'd understand that the worst is yet to come. I know, you want me to tell you about the political situation at the moment. I hate politics because I can no longer understand what's going on. I just want to live. I run from my death into yours and from my self to your corpse. What can a corpse do?

You can't save me and I can't heal you, so what are we doing here? I'm in the hospital and you're in prison – no, I'm in prison and you're in the hospital – and memories flow. Do you expect me to make myself a life out of memories?

I know, you don't like memories. You don't remember because you're alive. You've spent your whole life playing cat and mouse with death, and you're not convinced the end has come, you're not ready to sit on the sidelines and remember. "We only remember the dead," you said to me once, but no, I completely disagree with you about that. I remember through you so I can stay alive. I want to know. At least know.

Like all the other children who grew up in the camps, I heard all the stories, but I never understood. Do you imagine it's enough to tell us we weren't defeated in 1948 – because we never fought – to make us accept the dog's life we've led since we were born? Do you imagine I believed my grandmother? Why did my mother run away? Why did my grandmother tell me my mother had gone to see her family and would come back? She didn't come back. I went to Jordan to look for her and couldn't find a trace of her, as though she'd evaporated into thin air. That's how it works for us: Things disappear rather than appear, as in a dream.

Now, within this long dream in the hospital, I want you to tell me the story. I'll tell it to you, and you can make comments. I'll tell it, and you'll speak to me. But before that I want to tell you a secret, but please don't get angry. I watched the video Umm Hassan brought, and I saw al-Ghabsiyyeh. I saw the mosque and the lotus tree and the roads smothered in weeds, and I felt nothing. I felt no more than I felt when I went to the center of Beirut devastated by the civil war and saw the vegetation wrapped around the soaring buildings and the ruined walls. No, that's not true. In the middle of Beirut, I almost wept – I did weep. But while watching Umm Hassan's film, I felt a breath of hot air slap me. Why do you want me to weep for the ruins of history? Tell me, how did you abandon them there? How did you manage that? How did you live in two places at once, inside two histories and two loves? I won't take your sincerity at face value nor your enigmatic talk about women. All I want is to understand why Nahilah didn't come with you to Lebanon. How could you have abandoned her? How could you have lived out your story and let it grow and grow to the point of killing you?

My question, dear master, is: Why?

Why are we here? Why this prison? Why do I have no one left but you, and you no one but me? Why am I so alone?

I know you're not able to answer, not because you're sick or because you're suspended between life and death, but because you don't know the answer.

Tell me, for God's sake, tell me, why didn't you insist that your wife come with you to Lebanon? Why did Nahilah refuse to come?

She said that she wanted to stay behind with the blind sheikh but you didn't believe her. Yet you abandoned her and left. You left her and you left your oldest son, who died. It's because your father told you, "Go, my son, and leave her here. We're drained after so many moves; we don't have the energy to pick up and move again."

The old blind man, who'd moved from village to village and from olive grove to olive grove until fortune brought him to Deir al-Asad to die, told you he didn't have the energy to move, and you believed him?

Why did you believe him?

Why didn't you tell them?

Why did you turn your back on them and go?

I know you were one man straying from village to village along with the other lost souls, that you were wanderers in despair. But what did you do after the fall of Tarshiha? Why didn't you go to Lebanon with the fighters? You made your way into the hills of al-Kabri and fought with the Yemenis, and then returned to Sha'ab and found the village empty. You looked for them everywhere. A month later you found them in Deir al-Asad, living in half a house, and instead of looking after them you left again, abandoned them.

Tell me, what came over you?

Fill me in.

Whenever I ask you what happened, you start mixing events up, jumping from month to month and from village to village, as though time had melted away among the stones of the demolished villages. My grandmother used to tell me stories as though she were tearing them into shreds; instead of gathering them together, she'd rip them apart, and I understood nothing. I never was able to understand why our village fell or how.

I can understand my grandmother, I can forgive her her pillow that reeks of decay. But you, you who fought in '36, who took part in all the wars, why don't you know?

Do you want me to believe my grandmother, to lay my head on her pillow of dried flowers and say, "This is al-Ghabsiyyeh"? Do you want me to be like her and close my eyes? Her only son came back, and she didn't see him at all. She was standing under the olive tree, undoing her hair and swaying in sorrow, when her son, my father, came back carrying a sack of vegetables, but she didn't see him. The boy, who had just slipped through a shower of bullets, grasped his mother's dress, and the two of them burst into tears together, she because she'd lost him and he from seeing her weep that way.

I won't tell you about my father who died in a heap on the threshold of his house. They assassinated him and left him there. I didn't see it myself. My mother and his mother were there, and when I see him now it's with my mother's and my grandmother's eyes. I see him dying in a pool of his own blood like a slaughtered lamb, and I see white.

But no, it didn't happen that way.

The sky fell to the earth, my grandmother told me, describing the terrible exodus into the fields. The sky fell to earth, the stars turned to stones, and everything went black.

Tell me about that blackness. I don't want the usual song about the betrayal by the Arab armies in the '48 war – I've had enough of armies. What did you do? Why are you here and they're there? And why did fate finally bring us together now?

I won't go back as far as Ain al-Zaitoun because our story begins where the story of Ain al-Zaitoun ends.

That was on the night of May 1 of '48. You'll never forget this date because you tattooed it with a piece of smoldering iron onto your left wrist. On that day Ain al-Zaitoun was wiped out of existence. The Israelis entered the village and demolished it house by house. It's as though it had never been. Later, they planted a pine forest on the site of the village.

Where were you on May 1?

I know you were organizing the defense of Sha'ab. You had been summoned by Abu Is'af and you'd gone, not expecting an attack on the village. The sacred jihad battalions were reorganizing themselves after the volunteer Arab Liberation Army, led by the Lebanese Fawzi al-Qawuqji, decided to enter Galilee.

Suddenly the village was overrun and destroyed; you couldn't find it.

As you were coming home, with your English rifle slung over your shoulder, you saw Palmach men everywhere but you didn't do a thing; you didn't fire a single shot. You took a bit of iron, heated it in the fire and scratched the date on your left wrist. Then you ran off to the fields, heard how the village had fallen, and swore vengeance.

Ain al-Zaitoun marked the major turning point of the war in Galilee. On the night of May 1, 1948, a Palmach unit with mules carrying ammunition advanced on Ain al-Zaitoun via the hill of al-Dweirat, which overlooks the village from the north, and from the hill the Palmach men rolled barrels of explosives down onto the village.

Umm Suleiman said, weeping, that they'd killed your father.

In the olive grove, you saw their forlorn wandering ghosts. You grabbed Umm Suleiman by the shoulder, but she didn't stop. She kept going, and you kept trying to catch up with her.

"Umm Suleiman, it's me, Yunes," you yelled.

Then she turned around and saw you, but she didn't stop. She said, "They killed your father. Go look for your mother and your wife up ahead."

You took off running and spotted your mother and Nahilah in the crowd. Drops of salty sweat mixed with your tears as you searched for your son. You got close to them and saw that your mother was leading the blind sheikh and Nahilah was walking next to them, carrying the child.

You walked beside them and didn't say a word. You didn't ask about your father's death because you could see he was alive. You'll tell me you were lost, mistaking the living for the dead and the dead for the living. Everything got tangled up, and you spent years after this first great disaster, the *Nakba*,* trying to draw a line between the dead and the living.

Your father didn't die. Umm Suleiman was mistaken, and you didn't ask about it. But when you reached Sha'ab and the Khatib family house, you tried to discover what had actually happened. Upon seeing Umm Suleiman sitting in the doorway of the mosque with her hands clasped like a young schoolgirl, you told her that the sheikh hadn't died, and she looked at you as though she didn't know you. People began gathering in the courtyard of the mosque and Hamed Ali Hassan arrived.

Hamed Ali Hassan's clothes were dripping with blood when he reached the courtyard of the mosque of Sha'ab. Hamed was in his early twenties with green eyes like those of his dark-skinned Bedouin mother. He left the village when he'd found himself alone with bombs exploding around him.

Hamed Ali stopped in the courtyard of the mosque and said that Rashid Khalil Hassan had been killed.

"We went back," said Hamed. "We were six young men from the Hassan family. We wanted to get the money buried in the courtyard of our house. Rashid was the first to enter the village: He was hit by a bullet in the neck and fell. Bullets rained down on us from all sides, and we were driven off. We have to go back to bury Rashid."

He sat down. Your mother ran over and gave him some water. No one else moved. No one got up and said, "Come on. Let's go get the body."

They were in the courtyard of the mosque of Sha'ab, wrapped in their astonishment like ghosts in long black mantles.

It was there that you found out what had happened.

On the morning of May 2, the armed men withdrew from the village and people were penned up inside their houses, trapped by the gunfire. When

* Literally: Catastrophe. Massive expulsion and exodus in 1948 of approximately 750,000 Palestinians.

the Palmach soldiers arrived, they ordered the people to gather in the courtyard of Mahmoud Hamed's house.

Umm Suleiman had hid in the stable near her house, then finally decided to join the others in the courtyard, carrying a makeshift white flag.

"What can I say, Son? We were standing there, and they were firing over our heads. We started to crouch down, some of us kneeling, some squatting, some lying flat on the ground. Then Yusef Ibrahim al-Hajjar stood up. His wife was beside him, and she tried to pull him down, but he stood. He raised his hands as though surrendering, but the firing didn't stop. Yusef Ibrahim al-Hajjar went toward the soldiers, bearing the seventy-five years of his life on the shoulders of his huge body.

"'I want to say something. Listen to me.

"'We surrender. Our village has fallen, and our men are defeated, and we surrender and expect to be treated humanely. Pay attention now. We are captives, and you must treat us the way captured civilians are treated in wartime. We're not begging for your sympathy. We are requesting it and will repay it. If you treat us well, we'll repay your good deed with many more. Tomorrow, as you know, Arab armies will enter Palestine and we'll defeat you and then we'll treat you as you treat us today. It would be better for you that we come to an understanding. I have said what I must, as God is my witness.'

"A young officer approached Yusef and slapped him across the face. Then he pulled out his revolver and fired at Yusef's head, and the man's brains scattered over the ground. None of us moved. Even his wife remained kneeling. Then the soldiers chose about forty young men and drove them ahead of them, and after they disappeared from sight, we heard firing. They killed the young men and then drove us like sheep toward the valley of al-Karrar, where we gathered before setting off toward Sha'ab."

As they talked you looked for Hanna Kamil Mousa. Hanna was the leader of the village militia and closer to you than a brother. You'd met Abd al-Qadir Husseini with him in Saffouri, and you were inseparable.

"Where's Hanna?" you yelled.

Ahmad Hamed told you he'd seen him.

"I was hiding in the house," he said, "before I decided that it would be better to give myself up. So I went out and walked along the street where the Hamed clan lived, making my way to the square. Before I got to Abu Sultan Hamed's house, they grabbed me and started dragging me along: I'd put up my hands in surrender, but they dragged me along as though they'd captured me. It was behind the square that I saw him. He was in the oak tree. I don't know if he was alive because they wouldn't let me get near him. One of them had a tight grip on my neck and was pulling me along as if he'd tied a rope around it. I couldn't resist. I had no intention of resisting, I just wanted to stop in front of the oak, but they wouldn't let me. Then they led me to the square where they had just killed Yusef Ibrahim al-Hajjar. They'd done the same with the sheikh, your father – didn't your mother tell you? Where is the blind man? Have they taken him away?

"Hanna Kamil Mousa is still crucified on the tree. Go and get him down, Son. I wish I could come with you. I don't know where his family is. They've probably come to Sha'ab. Perhaps they went to Amqa, lots of people went toward Amqa. Go to Amqa, maybe you'll find his mother or father there. Tell them Ahmad Hamed saw him crucified, and we have to get him down from the oak."

You left him midsentence and rushed to the Khatib house to confirm, for the umpteenth time, that your father was alive. You found the sheikh sitting in the courtyard drinking coffee and talking about the terrible events of the First World War!

You were gone for three weeks. Everyone believed you'd gone to Ain al-Zaitoun to get Hanna down from his cross, and when you came back you didn't tell anyone about what you'd seen.

Tell me, is it true they crucified him? And what does it mean that they crucified him? Did they drive nails through his hands? Did they tie him to the tree with a rope and then kill him? Or did they tie him there and leave him to die, the way the Romans did with their slaves?

You don't know, because when you slunk into the village and went to the oak tree, you found no one.

Was Ahmad hallucinating?

Or were you no longer able to see?

Perhaps, my friend, you weren't capable of seeing your father walking beside your mother and wife in this exodus.

"It was as if I could see only darkness," you told me.

Is it true that the area around the spring was strewn with the bodies of the forty young men who were killed there in cold blood?

Is it true that instead of burying the dead they used a bulldozer to push them into a communal pit, which didn't get covered over properly so that people's remains stuck out, mixed with earth?

Is it true that their demolition of the village was meant as revenge for Kherbet-Jeddin?

Saleh al-Jashi claimed you didn't take part in the battle at Kherbet-Jeddin. I know he's lying, and in any case, no one in the camp believes anything he says since the strange scene he made in '72 following the Munich operation. People saw something they'd never seen before – a father jealous of his dead son!

Everyone raced to his house to offer their condolences after his son Husam was killed at the Munich airport, but instead of talking about Husam, he couldn't stop talking about himself and his own acts of heroism, about how he'd killed seventy Israelis in the battle at Kherbet-Jeddin.

Of course you remember the Black September operation and the kidnapping of Israel's Olympic athletes in Munich. I know what you think about that kind of operation, and I know you were one of the few who dared take a stand against the hijacking of airplanes, the operations abroad, and the killing of civilians. People said your position sprang from your fears for your wife and children in Galilee, but you said no, and you were right. I'm completely convinced of your position now, even though at the time I believed you only wanted to protect your family. As you used to say, "If you want to win a war, you don't go in for acrobatics, and if you don't respect the lives of others, you don't have the right to defend your own."

Saleh al-Jashi claimed you didn't take part in the battle of Kherbet-Jeddin. We didn't believe him, though. That old hunchbacked man with a large nose sat in his house receiving condolences and congratulations on his son's martyrdom, and seized the occasion to recount his own glories and those of the bands that came from al-Kweikat and Sha'ab and Ain al-Zaitoun to support the fighters of al-Kabri. And when someone asked about you, he raised his finger and said, no, he didn't remember you being with them. Puffing out his chest, he told the story of the ambush: "The people of al-Kabri won't forget the victory they tasted at Kherbet-Jeddin! If we'd fought throughout Palestine the way we did at al-Kabri, we wouldn't have lost the country!"

"But we're fighting now," a voice said. A youth, one of Husam's comrades.

"We'll see, my son. We'll see what you can do." Then Saleh al-Jashi started telling us about the Israeli convoy that fell into the ambush.

I want to ask you, was the fall of Ain al-Zaitoun, al-Kabri, and al-Birwa revenge for Kherbet-Jeddin?

Umm Hassan said she went past there on her way to al-Kweikat and amid the ruins saw a burned-out bus and the remains of an armored car; the Israelis had set up a monument to their dead.

"What about us – what will we put up there?" I asked her.

"What will we put up?" she asked in surprise.

"After the liberation, I mean," I said.

She looked at me with half-closed eyes as though she didn't understand what I was getting at. Then she laughed.

Umm Hassan's right. We'll never put up anything – we can't even manage a decent burial ground, let alone a monument. For the fifteen hundred individuals who fell at Sabra and Shatila, we built nothing. The mass grave has turned into a field where children play soccer. Some even say that the whole of Shatila will be razed soon.

Monuments aren't important, only the living count. But why did Abu Husam claim you didn't take part in the battle, and why, instead of weeping for his son, did he sit like a puffed-up cockerel boasting of his heroic deeds?

Tell me what really happened.

I don't want to listen to that cripple boasting that a hand grenade went off in his pocket and didn't kill him. I didn't believe the story, but you confirmed it, laughing, "The poor man was frightened for his manhood. Blood was spurting out of him, and he put his hand between his thighs, and when he was sure the injury was elsewhere he started jumping for joy before fainting from the pain. We were a band of fighters on our way to al-Birwa. Saleh al-Jashi was hanging out of the window of the bus when the grenade went off in his pocket and he fell. We took him back to al-Kabri and continued on to al-Birwa. Then he met up with us again at the Sha'ab garrison after he'd become crippled."

That was in May of '48.

Al-Kabri had been in turmoil for two months. At the beginning of February, a band of Israelis attacked the village and tried to blow up the house of Fares Sarhan, a member of the Arab Higher Committee. The attack failed, and the band that made it to Sarhan's house would've been wiped out if they hadn't withdrawn under a hail of bullets.

On the same day, the commander of al-Kabri's militia, Ibrahim Ya'qub, saw a Jewish armored car leave Jeddin at the head of a convoy of vehicles in the direction of the main road that leads to Safad via Nahariyyeh. He rushed to Alloush, commander of the Arab Liberation Army in the area, to ask him for help, but Alloush refused because he hadn't received any orders.

Ibrahim gathered the fighters and divided them in two, the first group in the area of al-Rayyis, two kilometers southwest of al-Kabri, and a group at the cemetery.

The first group blocked the road with rocks and stones while the second set up an ambush in the cemetery under the command of Saleh al-Jashi.

The Israeli convoy stopped where the road was blocked but didn't retreat. The armored car pulled back and the bulldozer moved forward, followed by three armored cars, two trucks, and a bus.

Then all hell broke loose.

The battle began at noon. After the bulldozer succeeded in clearing a way, Saleh threw a hand grenade, but it didn't explode. He threw another, and it made a terrible noise and produced a lot of dust, but the convoy continued to advance. Suddenly one of the armored cars turned and burst into flame. How did it catch fire? No one knows. Did a third grenade hit it or did it collide with the pile of rocks at the crossroads and catch fire?

Saleh didn't know.

But he does know that the convoy halted in its tracks and the firing started. It was a bloodbath. The firing went on until dawn.

Sitting in his house among the mourners, Saleh described what happened:

"They began getting out of the armored cars and tried to spread out among the olive trees while we fired at them with our rifles. We had English rifles, some hand grenades, and one Sten gun. Not one of them got away. They couldn't fight, and they didn't raise a white flag. We fired and received occasional fire from the windows of the bus or from the perimeter of the ambush. The firing didn't stop until we'd killed every last one of them.

"In the morning, the British came to remove the bodies. I stayed up the whole night in the cemetery with a few young men from al-Birwa and Sha'ab who'd come to lend their support. The rest gathered the arms of the Israelis and went home to sleep. General Ismail Safwat, chief of staff of the Arab Liberation Army, came, was photographed in front of the destroyed Israeli vehicles, before confiscating our stash of arms, from which he gave us back eleven rifles and seven boxes of ammunition.

"What kind of army was that? And what kind of liberation?"

Didn't anyone ask him what they did after the battle?

Didn't they expect a counterattack? Did they prepare for one?

But tell me, dear friend, what did Khalil Kallas do, commander of the group of thirty ALA men stationed near Fares Sarhan's house in al-Kabri?

"*Withdrew*," you'll say.

"When?" I'll ask.

"Three days before the village fell."

"Why?"

"Because he knew."

"And you? You all didn't know?"

Abu Husam said they were taken by surprise by the attack on al-Kabri.

However, Fawziyyeh, the widow of Mohammed Ahmad Hassan and wife of Ali Kamel, knew, because she left the village the day that the ALA men left.

Fawziyyeh, whose husband died in the battle of Jeddin, didn't remarry for twenty years, and Ali Kamel, her second husband, discovered that she was a virgin.

Her first husband died in the battle of Jeddin without taking part in it. He was a cameleer, transporting goods among the villages. On that day in March 1948, he was returning from Kafar Yasif to al-Kabri when he passed by the Israeli ambush pinned under the gunfire of the village militia. He was hit and died. The man fell, but the camel continued on its way to the village, ambling along in its own blood, until it reached its owner's house, where it collapsed.

Fawziyyeh said the camel was hit in the hump and belly, and the militia men ate it to celebrate their victory. "No one paid any attention to my tragedy. I was seventeen years old and hadn't been married more than a month. My husband died, and they slaughtered the camel and ate it. They invited me to eat with them. I won't deny that I joined them, but I could taste death, and from that day I haven't eaten meat, not even on feast days or holidays. When I see meat, I see the body of Mohammed Ahmad Hassan and feel faint. I didn't touch meat again until I married Ali Kamel twenty years later. Poor thing, he couldn't believe his eyes when he saw that I was a virgin. He was a widower, like me. When he took me, and he saw the blood, he went crazy – he kissed me and laughed and danced. I was frightened, I swear I was frightened. I mean, how could it be? It was as if I'd never been married and blood had never spotted the sheets in al-Kabri. He wanted to say a few things about Mohammed Ahmad Hassan, but no, I assure you, Mohammed was a real man, it was just that I had turned back into a virgin. My virginity came back when I saw them eating the camel and wiping the grease from their hands.

"Ali Kamel, poor Ali, couldn't make sense of it. He went to the doctor and came back reassured. The doctor told him it meant I hadn't had sex since the death of my first husband. But how could I have? I was living in a hovel with my father in Shatila, and he watched me like a hawk. He even stopped me from working in the embroidery workshop – he said he'd rather die of hunger than see his daughter go out to work. Then this widower with no teeth comes along and tells everyone he's taken my maidenhood! But it's not true; Mohammed was the one. Ali was like glue – he'd stick to my body and lick me like a piece of chocolate. Umm Hassan laughed at him when he told her he wanted a child. She explained that I wasn't a virgin and that his seed was weak, but he didn't get it. A man over sixty and a woman in her forties, and he wants children!"

Fawziyyeh was sitting apart from the others at the wake, and al-Kabri rose up before everyone's eyes. Abu Husam spoke of his exploits while the village faded like an old photo.

"But we left the dead behind, and that was shameful," said an elderly man as he got up to leave.

Umm Sa'ad Radi wasn't at the wake to tell her story.

Amina Mohammed Mousa – Umm Sa'ad Radi – died a month before Husam was martyred. If she'd been there, she'd have told you; she would have stopped the flood of nostalgia and memories.

If Umm Sa'ad Radi had been there she'd have said: "My husband and I left al-Kabri the day before it fell. We were on the Kabri-Tarshiha road and they slaughtered us. I wasn't able to dig a grave for my husband. I see him in my dreams, stretched out in the ground. He sits up and tries to speak, but he has no voice.

"We were on the road when darkness fell. My husband decided we should spend the night in the fields, and we slept under an olive tree. At dawn, as my husband was getting ready to say his prayers, our friend, Raja, passed and urged us to flee. He said the Jews were getting very close. My husband finished his prayers, and we kept going toward Tarshiha, where we ran into them. They were approaching al-Kabri from the north and the south. We were stopped, searched, and taken in an armored car to our village.

"They left us in the square; I could see the troops dancing and singing and eating. A Jewish officer came over to us, chewing on bread wrapped in brown paper and started asking us questions. He pointed his rifle at my husband's neck and asked in good Arabic, 'You're from al-Kabri?'

"'No,' I answered. 'We're from al-Sheikh Dawoud.'

"'I'm not asking you, I'm asking him,' he said.

"'We're from al-Sheikh Dawoud,' my husband repeated, his voice shaking.

"At that instant, a man with a sackcloth bag over his head came over. I recognized him – it was Ali Abd al-Aziz. The bag had two holes for his eyes, and one for his lips. Ali nodded; he was breathing through his mouth, the bag was stuck to his nose, and he was puffing as though he were about to choke. I knew him from his nose, from the way the bag clung to his face.

"The bastard nodded his head, and I recognized him.

"'You're from al-Kabri,' said the officer after the man with the bag over his head had confirmed it for him.

"They took my husband, along with Ibrahim Dabaja, Hussein al-Khubeizeh, Osman As'ad Abdallah, and Khalil al-Timlawi, and left the women in the square. We stood motionless while they danced and sang and ate around us. Then the officer came over and said he would have liked to bring my husband back to me except that he'd been killed. He also told me not to cry. Then he showed me a picture of Fares Sarhan and asked if I knew him.

"'Tell Fares we'll occupy all of Palestine and catch up with him in Lebanon.'

"I burst into tears, but they weren't real tears. Real tears found me on the second day when I saw my husband's body and tried to carry it to the cemetery and couldn't. That's when I cried, the tears gushing even from my mouth.

"The officer raised his rifle and ordered us to leave the square. We slept in the fields, and in the morning Umm Hassan and I returned to al-Kabri and saw the chickens in the streets. I don't know who'd let them out. Their feathers were ruffled and they were making strange noises. Umm Hassan tried to round them up. I don't know what we were thinking of, but we started rounding up the chickens. Then I got scared. Scared of the chickens. They seemed wild and were making such strange noises. I fled to the spring. I was thirsty, so I left Umm Hassan rounding up the chickens and fled. On the way I found Umm Mustafa. She hugged me and started sobbing: 'Go gather up your husband, he's dead.' She took me by the hand and we ran to the square.

"I found him there, lying on his stomach. He had been shot in the back of his head. The sun! The sun burned into everything. What, dear God, was I to do? I carried him into the shade. No, I dragged him into the shade. I didn't dare turn him over. I left him like that, took hold of his feet and pulled him into the shade. I looked around. Umm Mustafa had disappeared, and Umm Hassan was still over there with the chickens. I went looking for her and I found her in the street, bleeding, with the chickens hopping around her. I pushed her ahead of me to where my husband was. Upon seeing him, she calmed down, went off, and came back with a plank. We turned him over onto his back and carried him to the cemetery, but we weren't able to dig a grave for him. We pushed some earth to the side and buried him above his mother's bones. To this day I pray, haunted that I wasn't able to bury him properly. We didn't wash him because he's a martyr, and martyrs are purified by their own blood. And besides, dear God, how were we to wash him in such conditions?

"But the chickens!

"I don't know what got into the chickens.

"I went back to my house on my own and stayed in al-Kabri five days not daring to go out – you could still hear scattered shots. On the sixth day, I went out. I found blood everywhere and couldn't see the chickens. I'm sure they'd shot them all and eaten them. I didn't see a single chicken. I went to Umm Hussein's house. Where was her husband? Her husband was with mine and had to be buried, too. The door of her house was off its hinges, and no one was inside. I looked around for her and stumbled upon old Abu Salim, a seventy-five-year-old man, who said he was looking for his son. He kept saying he'd lost his son and needed my help, and it was only then that I came to my senses again.

"Suddenly, I could see straight. I was someone else during those five days I'd spent hidden in my house after burying my husband. I remember nothing, or I remember that I fried some dough and ate it. I was completely lost, as though the soul of some other woman had entered my body. Five days that ran together like one single day, or one hour!

"When I found Abu Salim and walked through the deserted streets with him in search of his lost son, I came back to myself.

"I took the old man's hand and brought him with me to Tarshiha. I told him he was the one who was lost, not his son. He went with me and didn't say a thing. He bowed his head and went like a little child. At the entrance to Tarshiha, I saw my sister and rushed over to her. Then I couldn't find the old man again. His son said he looked for him everywhere but in vain. I swear I don't know. Maybe he went back to al-Kabri and died there."

Umm Sa'ad Radi died before the families of the district of Acre assembled at Abu Husam's house to congratulate him on the glorious death of his son.

If she'd been there she'd have told everyone her story, and told Abu Husam to stop boasting of his fictive heroic deeds.

I visited her a few days before her death. She wasn't sick; it was more as if her life force were draining away. I prescribed some vitamins even though I knew they wouldn't do any good. But I did my duty; a doctor has to do his duty to the end – he is the guardian of the spark of life. I'm the guardian of your life force, dear Abu Salem; I won't abandon you. It's my duty to defend the life in you against all odds.

With Umm Sa'ad Radi I did my duty. Radi was there, a man of about sixty, his children and grandchildren with him, hovering around his mother's bed, afraid of death.

Umm Sa'ad Radi spoke in a low voice, almost inaudibly. "His grave," she said, almost as if she could see him shaking the earth off his bones, raising his head a little, then sitting up with his pale, cracked face and looking at her as though in reproach. The woman kept repeating, "His grave. Go to his grave."

She died in fear. She lived her whole life in fear, waiting at the entrance of the fedayeen camp for the fighters coming back or going to southern Lebanon and imploring one after another: "I beg you, go to the cemetery at al-Kabri."

And the young men would shake their heads and run off as though to escape her words.

"The grave is the fourth on the right, near the oak tree. You'll recognize it, my son. Just dig a little and you'll find him. I wasn't able to dig deep enough. Make sure his head's aimed toward the *Qibla*,* and if it isn't, I beg you, move him into the correct position. God will reward you."

Everyone promised her but no one went. Who would be so stupid as to venture to the cemetery at al-Kabri? And who would go scratching around in a grave?

Even you, Father, made promises to her and lied, telling her you weren't able to travel that far. Even you didn't dare speak the truth – that al-Kabri no longer existed, the cemetery had been erased, the oak tree cut down, the olive groves uprooted, and palms and pines had been planted in their place.

Abu Salem never told her he hadn't looked for the grave, and he never told her the story of the madwoman of al-Kabri and the bag of bones thrown down in the square at Deir al-Asad. He listened to her like all the others, and like all the others he nodded hurriedly and went on.

Umm Sa'ad Radi said she wanted nothing. "They took Palestine? Let them have it. I just want to visit the grave to make sure I buried him correctly. I don't care about al-Kabri or anywhere else, they're all going to disappear. They took them? They can have them. But they should give us the grave at least."

Abu Salem agrees but says nothing.

* Toward Mecca.

And we say nothing.

All of us were afraid; we didn't dare visit her and give her a proper answer.

Why? A good question.

Why didn't we lie to the woman and let her die with her mind at peace?

Why didn't anyone dare release her from the ghost of the man sitting in his grave gazing at her from the sockets of his eyes, moving his head as though he wanted to say something?

Why didn't we lie to her?

We're not even capable of lying. Incapable of war, incapable of lying, incapable of truth.

Umm Sa'ad Radi wasn't there, and she didn't tell her story.

As for you, Abu Salem, you were sitting in the midst of them, calm and silent. Everybody knew you'd taken to criticizing everything, and no one took you seriously anymore. You were bitter, they said. Even I thought so. You'd become dismissive; we thought you felt beaten down because the route over there had been blocked. After the fedayeen were thrown out of Jordan in 1970, we only had the Lebanese front, and it was swarming with fighters. They told us we had to climb Mount Hermon to protect Palestine from vanishing, so we climbed it and set the ice on fire with our fighting and our blood. This made your route to Bab al-Shams difficult, if not impossible. However, I know you managed to make your way through and slipped into your village many times, but that's another story. I'll save it for tomorrow.

But today.

Now, on that day, you got up and explained things to us. The house of Abu Husam al-Jashi was sailing along on memories; the stories were flying from people's mouths. Everyone told some story or other and believed what he wanted to remember.

And the curses rained down on Kallas and Alloush: How could the Arab Liberation Army have withdrawn? How could they have betrayed us? How?

Then your quiet voice came from the corner of the room, cutting through all the others. You were holding a thin stick resembling a long pen in your hand, and you drew imaginary lines and circles on the dark red carpet. You said that Galilee had collapsed.

"The whole of Galilee collapsed between operations Dekel and Hiram, and we had no idea."

The Dekel plan began with the occupation of Kaswan on July 9, 1948. Then al-Mukur, al-Jdeideh, Abu Sinan, Kafar Yasif, and al-Kweikat were occupied. On July 13, they occupied Nazareth, and then Ma'loul, linking Kafar ha-Horesh with the rest of the settlements south of Nazareth. On July 15, an Israeli unit moved from Shafa Amr to occupy Saffouri, and a broad mopping-up operation followed that led to the occupation of al-Birwa.

"What did we do after the fall of al-Birwa? We were besieged in Sha'ab. Every village and city in Galilee fell during the war, except Sha'ab. We stayed there until the end of Operation Hiram on October 28, where, in the space of sixty hours, the whole of Galilee had fallen."

"We never . . ." said Yunes.

He stood up like a man I didn't recognize, uttered half a sentence and sat down again without finishing it. He put his head in his hands and closed his eyes.

He resembled a man, somebody I didn't know. When we call someone we know "a man," it means we don't recognize him anymore, or he's taken us by surprise. That's why a wife addresses her husband as "Man" – because she doesn't know him.

And Nahilah, what did she call you?

You never told me your wife's names for you, but I don't think she addressed you as "Man" despite the fact that she was completely in the dark about her husband.

This man, his head crowned with white, stood up and tried to respond to this woman. All the woman said was what we'd been saying every day, what we'll always say because it's easiest.

"So, they sold out," said the woman.

But instead of letting the words slide past, as words usually do on such occasions, you stood up and said, "We never . . ." and fell silent. And everyone else fell silent.

Yunes used Classical Arabic on that occasion, as though he felt himself to be an orator or wanted to say the final and unanswerable word. So he said, "We never . . ." in Classical Arabic and sat down.

I would like to know, what stopped you? You waited for the teardrop to be caught in Nuha's eye before speaking. You stood up twice and started to tell the story of what happened to you in Sha'ab, your last war. You said that all the villages fell except for Sha'ab: "We evacuated Sha'ab because defending it was impossible after the rest of Galilee had fallen. Sha'ab isn't a country, it's just a village."

You said you understood the meaning of the word *country* after the fall of Sha'ab. A country isn't oranges or olives, or the mosque of al-Jazzar in Acre. A country is falling into the abyss, feeling that you are part of the whole, and dying because it has died. In those villages running down to the sea from northern Galilee to the west, no one thought of what it would mean for everything to fall. The villages fell, and we ran from one to another as though we were on the sea jumping from one boat to another, the boats sinking, and us with them. No one was able to conceive of what the fall would mean, and the people fell because everything fell.

You talked and talked; you were at boiling point, almost exploding, and we couldn't grasp what you were trying to get at, and why you said that Palestine no longer existed.

"Palestine was the cities – Haifa, Jaffa, Jerusalem, and Acre. In them we could feel something called Palestine. The villages were like all villages. It was the cities that fell quickly, and we discovered that we didn't know where we were. The truth is that those who occupied Palestine made us discover the country as we were losing it. No, it wasn't only the fault of the Arab armies and the ALA; we were all at fault because we didn't know. And by the time we knew, everything was over. We found out at the end.

"Listen. All of them sold out, and we want to buy it back. We tried to buy it back, but we were defeated, defeated utterly.

"Listen. They were less traitors than miserable wretches because they were ignorant; they didn't know what was really happening. Would you believe me if I said that none of us – not I, not Abu Is'af – knew their plans or understood the logic of their war? We didn't know the difference between the Palmach and the Stern Gang.*

"Why call it a war when you aren't really fighting?"

"We thought we were fighting to defend our homes. But not them; they didn't have any villages to defend. They were an army that advanced and retreated freely, as armies do.

"We didn't put up a defense. At Sha'ab we discovered we were incapable of defending our homes. My house in Ain al-Zaitoun disappeared into thin air; all the houses in the village were blown up the moment they entered. I fought at Sha'ab, even though it wasn't my village.

"We fought and fought. Don't believe all that lying history. We have to go back there to fight, but I'm here. That's enough for now."

Do you remember how Abu Husam got up, all macho, and said that it made him angry to hear that kind of talk. "The Arab Liberation Army never fought. The Arab armies just entered Palestine to protect the borders that had been drawn and left us on our own."

You tried to explain that we fought but we didn't know. When you fight and don't know, it's as though you aren't fighting. But no one wanted to listen. Only Nuha. Do you remember Nuha? She was there. She came and sat close to you and stared at the imaginary map you'd drawn on the dark red carpet. Then she took the stick from your hand, redrew the map of Galilee and asked you about al-Birwa.

That was the day I fell in love with Nuha and a one-sided love story began that only turned to real love six years later, when she came to the hospital to ask for my help in looking after her dying grandmother.

After Nuha finished drawing her map, she turned to you and asked, "Why?"

I think I saw a tear suspended in the corner of her eye, and that tear was the start of a love story, a love that began with a teardrop that didn't fall and

* Jewish terrorist organization formed in '39.

ended in the municipal stadium under a downpour of tears that soaked eyes and faces.

But Nuha, when she fell in love with me years later, denied the story of the tear. She said she hadn't cried, but she'd felt pity for all of you because you were living on memories, and the past was your only pillar of support.

Looking at the map, she asked you – her voice halting and punctuated by white spaces, as though emotion were staining her words with silence:

"Why did you believe Mahdi?"

The room exploded in silence.

Is it true, Father, that al-Birwa fell because you believed Mahdi, Jasem, and the ALA division stationed at Tal al-Layyat?

Answer me. I don't want anecdotes but a clear-cut answer.

I know you don't know the answers. I can see you with the eyes of those days. You were an impulsive young man – that's how everyone who knew you describes you. Despite that, or because of it, you succeeded – you and the division from Sha'ab – in breaking through to al-Birwa and taking it back.

But, to be accurate, before the breakthrough and the recovery, al-Birwa had fallen without a fight.

Sun-dust enveloped the fields, the wheat glittering in that golden light that precedes the harvest. And the village was afraid. After the fall of Acre, the villages of al-Mukur, al-Jdeideh, Julis, Kafar Yasif, and Abu Sinan surrendered, leaving al-Birwa floating in the wind.

And they attacked.

No one was ready. Our ambushes were laughable. Now we've figured out how to do things, and we have an impressive numbers of fedayeen. But then we were forty men and Father Jebran. The priest of al-Birwa didn't negotiate with the Jews for a surrender, that's a lie. He negotiated for our return – this issue has sparked great debate.

Nuha's grandmother, who came to be known as Umm al-Hajar,* would tell the story and say, "If only!"

---

*Literally: Mother of Stone.

"If only we'd believed Father Jebran! We were nothing, my daughter – just forty men and up above, at Tal al-Layyat, more than a hundred soldiers of the ALA under their leader, Mahdi, who used to come down like a monkey asking for chickens. We named him Lieutenant Chicken Mahdi and would hand them over. What are a few chickens? Let them eat and good health to them! The important thing was for the village to survive – better a village without chickens than chickens without a village. But the chickens did no good, my dear, because when the Jews attacked, Chicken Mahdi didn't fight."

They were forty. They'd sent their wives and children into the surrounding fields and sat in their ambushes waiting. The Jews chose to attack from the west at sunset, so the sun would be in the peasants' eyes. Three armored vehicles advanced under a heavy cannon bombardment but were brought to a halt. Then the Jews retreated and dug themselves in, renewing the attack at dawn.

"We ran," said Nuha's father. "Yes, we ran. We had no means of defense and the army up above us didn't fire a single shot. I said to Mahdi, 'Aren't you even going to defend your chickens?' He replied, 'No orders.' The village fell and we left everything behind. The ALA didn't even try to save the chickens."

Nuha said her father had always lived with sorrow in his heart: He said his greatest wish was not to kill the Jews but to kill Chicken Mahdi.

It would be lawful to kill Mahdi, isn't that right, Father? It would be lawful to kill him not because he didn't fight with you, but because after you took the village back he gave the order for you to withdraw and join your women and children because the ALA would protect the village. And you believed him.

Why did you believe Mahdi?

Yunes said he didn't believe Mahdi, "but what could we do?"

"Listen, my daughter. They occupied the village, so the fedayeen withdrew and joined their families in the fields nearby. They slept and lived under the olive trees, waiting for an end to their sufferings. When they got hungry, they decided to take back their village. The Jews occupied the village on June 10, 1948, and we waited in the fields for two weeks. Then we came together – people from al-Birwa, Sha'ab, al-Ba'neh, and Deir al-Asad – and decided to liberate the village. The wheat and maize were waiting to be harvested, and people couldn't find even a dry crust for sustenance.

"The fighters gathered at Tal al-Layyat, and there the Iraqi officer Jasem stood up and made a speech. He said the ALA didn't have orders to help, but they were wholeheartedly with the villagers and would be praying for their success.

"Our attack began. We attacked the village from three directions – Jebel al-Tawil in the north, Sha'ab in the southeast, and Tal al-Layyat in the east – and we won.

"We won because they were taken by surprise and didn't fight. They did just as we'd done: Instead of resisting, they ran away to Abu Laban. So we entered the village. Of course, they fired at us for a while, but it seems their numbers were very small so they withdrew.

"In al-Birwa we found everything in its place and Father Jebran there to greet us.

"He said, 'You should have agreed with me and given me time to finish negotiating with them, but this is better. God has granted us victory.'

"The priest suggested we harvest the wheat before they came back, and we agreed. We were inspecting the village and the houses when we heard *youyous* coming from the house of Ahmad Isma'il Sa'ad. When we got there, we found everyone's clothes stuffed into bags and placed in the center of the patio. People were attempting to pick out their own clothes from the jumble. I swear no one knows what he took and what he left behind. The clothes were all mixed up, and we couldn't make heads nor tails of them. The priest kept telling us to leave the clothes and go out to the fields. Saniyyeh, the wife of Ahmad Isma'il Sa'ad, let out a celebratory trill and we all laughed; it was a rag wedding – we discovered our clothes were only rags. Why would the Jews take rags? And us, too – why were our clothes rags? We celebrated. I can hardly describe it, my dear – clothes were flying through the air, and everyone was trying things on and pulling them off. Everyone wore every-one else's things, and we came together and were joyous. That was our vic-tory celebration, but we couldn't enjoy it because we heard gunfire from the direction of the threshing ground, so we thought the counterattack must have begun. Leaving our rags, we ran to get our rifles, and we found Darwish's son, Mahmoud (not the poet Mahmoud Darwish, who was only six years old then and hardly knew how to talk – it was his cousin, I think) standing in the middle of the field, firing his gun in the air and pointing to the threshing floor. There we discovered the sacks: A large part of the wheat harvest had been placed in sacks in the middle of the threshing floor. We started gathering the sacks while Salim As'ad stood by in a British police officer's uniform, which he'd never parted with, next to seven harvesters the Jews had left when they fled.

"We climbed over the harvesters, but then the shooting started, and the dying, too.

"We left the harvesters, picked up the sacks of wheat, and rushed toward the village; the women began to leave ahead of us.

"Bullets, women leaving with sacks of wheat on their heads, men spread-ing out to their positions – the men decided to stay in the village after they'd been joined by eleven fighters from the village of Aqraba who announced they were deserting the ALA."

"We were like drunkards," said Nuha's father.

He said he was drunk on the scent of the wheat, on the sun-dust.

"Can you get drunk on dust?" she asked Yunes.

Yunes said that Mahdi committed suicide in Tarshiha. "It wasn't his fault, my son. Mahdi was just carrying out orders. In Lebanon we found out that Mahdi had died. When he heard the final order to withdraw, he said, 'Shame on the Arabs,' pulled out his revolver, shot himself in the head, and died.

"At some point, Mahdi came and said, 'Okay. Go away and rest up with your families.' And Mahdi was right – the big push was over. We rushed to al-Birwa and liberated it, and then we returned to our villages. Thirty-five men, too exhausted to move.

"When we talk about these battles, you think of us as disciplined soldiers, but that wasn't at all the case.

"Listen.

"After we liberated al-Birwa, three United Nations officers arrived carrying white flags and asked to negotiate with our commanding officer.

"'But we don't have a commanding officer,' said Salim As'ad.

"'We're just peasants,' said Nabil Hourani. 'We don't have a leader, we're just peasants who want to harvest our crop and go back to our houses. Would you rather we died of hunger?'

"'But you broke the truce,' said the Swedish officer.

"'What truce, Sir? We've got nothing to do with the war. We wanted to go back to our village, so we went.'

"The Swedish officer asked our permission to search the village and go to Tal al-Layyat to meet with the commanding officer of the ALA, but we refused. We were afraid of spies working for the Jews, so we insisted that the officers leave the village.

"We weren't an army. We were just ordinary people. More than half the fighters knew nothing about fighting, I swear. For them, war was shooting at the enemy. We'd stand in a row and fire; we knew nothing about the art of war. That's why, when Mahdi came and asked the fighters to withdraw and leave the village in the hands of the ALA, we agreed without thinking. The peasants did what they set out to do, took part of their crop and handed the village over to the regular army.

"Forty aging men and women who refused to leave their houses was all that was left in al-Birwa, plus a young man named Tanios al-Khouri, who wanted to stay with his uncle, the village priest. Later he was killed when the Jews came back to occupy the village.

"The shelling started and no one knew what was happening because they found the Israelis in the village square, but there was no sign of the ALA. The Jews started blowing up houses and then asked everyone to assemble in the square. They discovered that there were only old people, the priest, and his nephew left in the village. Tanios had been helping his uncle in the church and was preparing to join the order himself, and when the village fell, the priest dressed him in a black cassock identical to his own, and they joined the others in the square.

"An Israeli officer came forward and took the youth by his hand, dragged him out of the crowd and ordered him to take off his cassock. The youth hesitated a little, then took it off under the officer's steely gaze and stood trembling in his underwear. The July sun struck their faces, the dust spread over the village while Tanios trembled with cold. The priest tried to say something, but the shots tore over their heads.

"The officer ordered Tanios to walk in front of him. He walked until they reached the sycamore tree at the edge of the square. There the officer fired a single shot from his revolver. Returning to the little clump of people, he ordered them to get into a truck. Everyone rushed toward the truck; not even Father Jebran looked back at his dead nephew. But before the priest reached the truck, he fell, striking his head on a stone. He started bleeding, and the blood seemed to rouse him from his stupor. He stood, or tried to stand, staggering as though he were about to fall, and then regained his balance. Instead of continuing his dash for the truck, he turned and walked back to the tree, where he knelt and started to pray.

"The truck took off, and no one knows what happened to Father Jebran. He wasn't seen again. He didn't catch up with everyone at al-Jdeideh, and no one saw him at the village of Kafar Yasif. Maybe he fell near his nephew. Maybe they killed him. We just don't know. Some say he went to stay with the Shufani family (who were distant relatives) in Ma'aliyya, where he changed his name and stepped down from the priesthood.

"The old people were dumped at Kafar Yasif, and the priest disappeared.

"When the Israelis entered al-Birwa, they blew it up house by house. They didn't take our clothes and rags. They were like madmen. They blew up the houses and began bulldozing them; they trampled the wheat and felled the olive trees with dynamite. I don't know why they hate olives."

Actually, why do they hate olives?

You told me about Ain Houd and the peasants they chased out of their village, which was renamed En Hud. The peasants wandered the hills of

Jebel Karmal, where they built a new village, which they named after their old village.

You were telling me about them because you wanted to explain your theory about the secret population that stayed behind over there.

"I wasn't the only one," you said. "We were a whole people living in secret villages."

You told me how the Israelis changed the original village into an artists' colony and how the peasants live in their new, officially unrecognized village with no paved streets, no water, no electricity, nothing. You said there were dozens of these secret villages.

And you asked yourself why the Israelis hate olive trees. You mentioned how they planted cypress trees in the middle of the olives groves at Ain Houd, and how the olive trees were ruined and died under the onslaught of the cypresses, which swallowed them up.

How can they eat without olive oil? We live on olive oil, we're a people of olive oil, but them, they cut down the olive trees and plant palm trees. Why do they love palms so much?

"Poor little Tanios," Nuha's father went on. "They killed him right in front of us, and God, what a sight he was. He arrived in the square all puffed up in his uncle's cassock. The uncle was short and fat, but Tanios was tall and slender. Tanios went out with the priest, in his short cassock that ballooned out like a ghost. We could see his legs, covered with thick, curly black hair. He had to take off the cassock and was shivering as he walked; then we heard the fatal shot and everything went dark. Sweat filled our eyes, and we could hardly see – when you're scared, you sweat an incredible amount. Sweat was dripping into our eyes, and Father Jebran wiped the blood from his forehead. He knelt in front of his nephew's body under the tree, made the sign of the cross over the thin young man, then stretched his arms out under the tree as though he'd become a tree himself or as though he were crucifying himself against the air, while the village collapsed."

Tell me, Yunes, how, why, did you believe Mahdi? Did you have to believe him?

We shouldn't have believed him, you'll say. "We believed him because we had no choice at the time. Only the priest suggested reconciliation with the Jews, but who could guarantee that it wouldn't turn out with us as it did at al-Kabri? The priest said he'd be the guarantor, but he wasn't even able to save his nephew's life."

Nuha, who told me the story of al-Birwa, wouldn't accept this. Nuha was different from Shams and would only allow me a small peck on the corner of her mouth, whose taste I'd steal as I listened to the endless story of al-Birwa.

One time she said she'd seen the rags in a dream.

Another time she said that Father Jebran had put the cassock on Ahmad Yasin, the grain measurer, who hadn't withdrawn with the others because he wanted to steal one of the harvesters the Jews had left behind on the threshing floor, and that the officer recognized Ahmad and ordered him to take off his cassock and killed him. And that the priest didn't go back to the body under the tree but that an Israeli soldier pushed him and he fell and his head was cut open, so they dragged him away and killed him as well as Ahmad. And her grandmother, who witnessed the scene, swears that Father Jebran didn't have a nephew named Tanios and that the young man disguised in the cassock was the son of the grain measurer.

"Al-Birwa, it's gone," said Nuha. "All I see are the shadows of the houses drawn in my grandmother's eyes." This grandmother was the cause of all their trouble. "She turned my father into a stone. She killed him, killed everything inside him. Like all the mothers who kill their sons, out of love. I lived with him. He lay there in our house like a stone."

Nuha said her grandmother walked and walked until her feet were swollen. When the truck dumped them in al-Jdeideh, she refused to enter the village and started searching for her children. She got down from the truck and walked. She went to al-Damoun and from there to Sekhnen and from Sekhnen to al-Ramah and then on to Ya'thur. In Ya'thur she found her son and his family, and they crossed over into Lebanon, where she found her four other children.

Her grandmother walked alone, entered the villages and slept in the open. She entered the villages a stranger and left them a stranger, and all she ate was bread moistened with water. She ate so she could walk, and she walked so she could look, and she looked but she didn't find.

Nuha said the pain etched on her grandmother's face frightened her. A woman etched with pain and stories. "She didn't love us; she loved only my father. She seemed in a perpetual state of shock that he was still alive. Every day – every day, I promise you – she'd squeeze him to make sure he was still among the living. She didn't want him to work; when they settled in the camp near Beirut and he found work in a chocolate factory, she refused. 'You stay in the house and we'll work,' she said. 'You're the pillar of the house; it will fall down without you.' My mother couldn't understand her mother-in-law – a woman stopping her son from working, not wanting him to leave the tin shack, so that no harm might come to him while we were all dying of shame and hunger? He'd sit next to his mother and they would listen to the radio and analyze the news and whisper to one another. She'd make plans, and he'd agree with her. Then they decided to go back to al-Birwa, and so we returned."

The story as Nuha related it to me was as distorted as her grandmother's memory. Nuha was a child and her grandmother an old woman. The child couldn't remember, and the old woman couldn't speak. The grandmother would raise her hand and point upward as though invoking the help of mysterious powers and all Nuha would see was dust.

"I was two years old," she said, "so I can't remember anything. I remember vague images, an old woman speechless in the house, my father looking at her with hatred. My father hardened into stone. He would enter the house in silence and leave it in silence. My brothers and sisters and I called him the Stone, that's what he was. My father spoke in '68, after his son died in Ghour al-Safi in Jordan during the battle for al-Karameh, but his speech was shrouded in silence. He spoke like someone who never spoke, and he would never raise his voice, as though he were afraid of something. My father tried several times to work. He tried at the soft-drink factory. Then he became a taxi driver, but they put him in jail because he didn't have a work permit. He tried to get that impossible permit, but didn't succeed. As you know a Palestinian can only work clandestinely in Lebanon, and a driver can't work clandestinely. He loved to drive. Since he was a child he'd loved cars, but it was difficult for him to buy one, so he decided he'd work as a driver. He wasted his time running around in pursuit of a work permit that never came. We only survived because it was easier than dying.

"My mother worked as a seamstress. She wasn't a very good seamstress, but she managed to make a living with the women in the camp. She sewed a little and earned a little, and we survived. The Stone would leave the house every morning and not come back until evening. He wouldn't speak to us, and he'd even refuse to eat with us. My mother had a relief card so she'd go at the beginning of each month to get flour, milk, and cooking oil from the agency. But he wouldn't touch it. I don't know how he got by. He wouldn't ask my mother for money, and he didn't steal like most of the men in the camp did. He'd get up at dawn, drink his coffee before we woke up, and leave for the day. My mother would beg him to taste the food she'd prepared, but he'd flatly refuse. He'd turn away from her, open his newspaper, and read. My father wasn't illiterate, he was semiliterate and could sound out words. He'd learned to read from the newspapers. He'd sit and read in silence. We'd see his lips moving but couldn't hear a sound. He would read without a sound and speak without a sound and come and go without a sound."

"I heard the story just from my grandmother," said Nuha. "I thought she was rambling like all old people, but it was the truth."

"We went back, my love, but it was hopeless," she told me. She said they'd demolished al-Birwa and she couldn't stand to live in any other village, so she decided to move back to Lebanon. Her son left them in the fields outside the village and went to Kafar Yasif; then he came back to tell them that they should all go there.

"But I couldn't agree to live in Kafar Yasif; I wanted al-Birwa. I said we should go back and live with the people of al-Birwa that were left, go back and cultivate our land. What were we supposed to do for work in Kafar Yasif? Your father said he'd met Sa'ad's son who worked in the building trade, and he'd promised him a job. I said no, and I picked you up and started walking. Your mother caught up with me with your brother, Amir, leaving your father standing there. He screamed at us; he wanted us to stay with him, but we left. We found him again here in the camp. I thought he'd stayed behind. I said, 'Let him stay, it's his destiny, but I can't,' and your mother caught up with me, and he screamed at us, but we couldn't hear his voice, as though it couldn't make it out of his mouth. I think he caught up with us, and when we got to the camp he went into the bathroom, then he left the house and turned into stone. Our feet were sore, and all we wanted to do was sleep, but he went out. I was right. I mean, how could we go back to al-Birwa when al-Birwa no longer existed? What were we to do? Go to another village and become refugees in our own country? No, my dear."

Nuha said she'd pieced the story of their return together from scraps of stories. She could picture the scene as though she were remembering it herself. Going back, her mother told her, was difficult, but people did return. "Suddenly, all the members of a family would disappear, and we'd know they'd returned. Your father was like a madman, hunting for scraps of news and abusing your mother. One morning in April of '51, he told us, 'Come on, we're going back.' We didn't take anything with us. We returned as we'd left, with nothing but our clothes, two flasks of water, a bundle of bread, some potatoes, and some boiled eggs. We got a taxi to Tyre and another to Rimeish, and from there, we started our march to al-Birwa. Going back was easy. We went around the villages and walked in the rough. The Stone walked as though on the palm of his hand – he'd stretch his hand out in front of him and read from his palm, he said everything was written there. We walked behind him in silence, your grandmother carrying you, me carrying your brother, and the Stone walking ahead of us. Finally we arrived. We'd walked the whole night and arrived at dawn. At the outskirts of the village, he told us to wait under an olive tree.

"There, the Stone started walking in an odd way. He bent over as though he were getting ready for a fight and started leaping until he disappeared from our view. Your grandmother went crazy. She started to go after him, but he waved her off, placing his finger on his lips to ask her to be quiet. Then he disappeared.

"And us, what were we to do? How could I wait when I had this half-paralyzed old woman with me? Suddenly the strength left your grandmother. All the way there, she'd been like a horse, but at the outskirts of the village her knees gave out and she collapsed, dripping with sweat. She was carrying you in her arms and the sweat dripped onto you. You started crying, and I took you from her and gave you my breast. No, you weren't still breast feeding, you were two years old and I'd weaned you more than a year before, but for some reason, I took you from her arms, wiped the old woman's sweat off you and gave you my breast. You stopped crying and fell into a deep sleep.

"The Stone returned.

"The sun was starting to set and your grandmother was sitting on her own under an isolated olive tree. Upon seeing her son, she struggled to stand up but couldn't, so she crawled. We helped her to sit up; her eyes fixed on her son's lips.

"We sat around him. He drank some water, ate a boiled egg, and asked us to wait for him before making his way toward the olive grove and disappearing again.

"He came back the next morning and said he was going to Kafar Yasif.

"We understood.

"The old woman bowed her head and began sobbing. I tried to question him. I asked him about my father's house – I thought, Never mind; if our house has been demolished, we can go and live in my father's house. 'Listen, woman,' he said, 'I'm going to Kafar Yasif.' And we understood. I said to him, 'They demolished all the houses, right?' And he said, 'Yes.'

"When I heard the word *yes* I fell to the ground. I couldn't see; everything had gone black. The Stone tried to bring me around.

"He explained everything to me.

"'Al-Birwa is dead,' he said. 'You stay here, I'll go.'

"He didn't wait for nightfall. He said he'd go, and he went. His head must have been hurting him because he kept putting his hands to his temples and pressing. He ordered us not to move from where we were.

"We waited for three days and nights. April was cold, and we had only brought two woolen blankets. The four of us slept under them, the old woman shivering and talking in her sleep. We weren't hungry. I had brought some bread, and your grandmother gathered thyme and some seeds from the land that we ate also.

"On the third night, the old woman disappeared.

"I woke up and didn't find her with us under the blankets. I looked everywhere, but she'd disappeared.

"The Stone came back to tell us that we had to go to Kafar Yasif in the night, everything was arranged. Al-Birwa had been completely demolished, and the Jews had built the settlement of Achihud on top of it. Kafar Yasif was the only solution.

"I told him about his mother's disappearance.

"'She's over there,' he said. 'I know her. I'll go and get her, and don't you move from here.'

"I wanted to tell him not to go, but I didn't dare. How can you tell someone to abandon his mother? I begged him to wait for night to fall, but he didn't answer. He left and didn't return until sunset. He said he'd seen her and that she'd refused to come back with him. She was sitting alone on top of the ruins.

"A ruined village, and a woman sitting on top of the remains of her house, and a man trying to persuade her to go with him, and her stubborn silence. He talked, and she remained silent. He'd ask her to come with him, but she'd pay no attention.

"He said he'd told her about Kafar Yasif, that he'd found a house and that everything would be all right. She continued to refuse.

"He slept with us that night, got up at dawn and brought her back. He brought her back like a prisoner and said, 'Let's go to Kafar Yasif.' I started getting ready. I folded the blankets and was checking around the huge olive tree among whose roots we'd been sleeping when I heard the old woman say, 'No.' She picked you up and started walking in the direction of Lebanon."

Nuha said her grandmother had told her about three young men who'd approached her and how they'd pelted her with stones. She'd told them she was so-and-so, the daughter of so-and-so and that this was her house, so they pelted her with stones.

"'I told them I was staying.'

"'I told them this was my house, why did you destroy my house?'

"'I told them they were stupid because they'd cut down so many olive trees.'

"'I told them these were Roman olive trees. How could anyone dare cut down Christ's olive trees? These were Father Jebran's olive trees.'

"'I told them lots of things.'

"She said she told them she didn't care – 'You took the land – take it. You took the fields and the olives and everything else – take them. But I want to live here. I'll put up a tent and live here. It's better than the camp. The air is clean here. Take everything and leave me the air.'

"The three young men backed away and started throwing stones at her.

"'They were afraid,' she said.

"The stones started raining down on her and piled up around her and she became a bundle of wounds.

"She said they spoke Arabic to her. They spoke like the Yemeni headman she'd met in '47 when she wandered into the Jewish settlement near Tiberias by mistake.

"'At first they came over to me and seemed kind. They weren't aggressive. But when I told them I was so-and-so, daughter of so-and-so, they began inching away. They drew back one step for every one of my words. Then suddenly they all bent over as if they'd received some kind of signal and the stones started raining down.'

"The old woman sat under the olive tree and my mother went to get a rag and a flask of water so she could clean her wounds. At the same time the Stone was telling them about Kafar Yasif and the house Sa'ad's son had found and the job in his workshop. He said, 'We're here now and we can't go back to Lebanon.' He said, 'We'll live in Kafar Yasif, then we'll see.' He talked and talked and talked; the old woman sat on the ground looking into the distance. She didn't tell them what had happened to her. She didn't say she'd tried to talk to the Yemenis. She didn't say she'd talked about a tent she was going to put up in the ruins of al-Birwa. She was like a tree with its branches broken. Suddenly she got up, picked up two-year-old Nuha, and set off in the direction of Lebanon."

Nuha's mother said she'd caught up with her mother-in-law. "I took your brother by the hand and we started running after her. The Stone stood like a stone. And we found ourselves in the camp."

What do you make of Nuha's story?

Naturally, Nuha didn't describe her grandmother as looking like a tree with its branches broken. I added that detail to describe the old woman, both her psychological state and her bleeding wounds. Nuha wasn't that troubled by the story; she just told it to me in passing when she was explaining her own situation. She doesn't believe in the possibility of our returning to Palestine. "If we go back, we won't find Palestine, we'll find another country. Why are we fighting and dying? Should we be fighting for something only to find ourselves somewhere else? It would be better to marry and emigrate elsewhere."

She cried a lot when her grandmother died. She told me how her father started to speak after his son was martyred in the battle of al-Karameh. She said that even though he didn't talk, he didn't stop fathering children.

"Wouldn't you agree that the man was a bit strange – not talking to his wife but sleeping with her every night?" I tried to ask Nuha about her grandmother's story, but she said she didn't know and didn't care. Nuha loved Egyptian soap operas and said she had to get out of this cesspit – that's what she called the camp. Her father, whom I met numerous times at their house, was very nice to me. He was a strange man, eyes hanging vacantly in his face, always clicking his prayer beads and talking about everything. He knew a lot about agriculture, medicine, politics, and Palestinian history. He talked to me a lot about my father, about how his death had been his first calamity in the camp.

In fact I wanted to marry Nuha, but then I don't know what happened. I started to feel stifled when I was with her. We couldn't find anything to talk about. She'd tell me about her soap operas and their heroes and I'd get bored. Even my desire for those little stolen pecks started to fade.

I never told you the story of Nuha and her grandmother before because I thought it wouldn't interest you. You didn't talk much about the past except incidentally; the past would come up in the form of illustrative examples, not as lived reality. Then you were transformed into the unique symbol in the stories of the camp people, the symbol of those who kept slipping back there. You know you weren't the only man who'd go over there and come back. Thousands went, and maybe some of them are still going over now. I know of at least three cases of married men whose stories are like yours. They go over, leave their women pregnant and come back to the camp. The story of Hamad intrigued me. I'll tell it to you later; I'm tired now, and the woman of al-Birwa has wrung out my heart.

The first time I heard the story from Nuha, it made no impression on me. I was absorbed by the story of the Stone and paid no attention to the grandmother. Now it occurs to me that this woman (who was called Khadijeh) was remarkable. I wish I'd known her better. I only saw her once, when she was sick. A woman I saw only once but whom I found more beautiful than her granddaughter who tried to seduce me into marriage.

I forgot to mention that Nuha was white, whiter than any woman I've ever seen. Her skin was so white, the whiteness almost seemed to be bursting out from inside her. She thought she was beautiful just because she was so white. She was a bit short and plump, but her whiteness made up for everything.

I was taken by her whiteness, I won't deny it, but I never discovered beauty until I met Shams. I discovered then the secret of the color of wheat.

Brown tinged with yellow is the highest color because its nuances are infinite. Nuha's whiteness, on the other hand, blocked my spirit – no, I'm talking through my hat, saying anything that comes into my head. Please don't believe all that . . . I have nothing against white, but I did suddenly stop loving her. All my feelings evaporated, and when I looked at her I could no longer see her. I only felt something for her at the stadium, when I stood there with hundreds of fedayeen waiting for the Greek ships that were to take them from Beirut into their new exile. I searched for her but couldn't find her. Do you know what that feels like – to leave when there's no one to bid you farewell? I searched for her and didn't leave. I went back home, not because she didn't come and not because I wanted her; I went back because I felt the utter nonsense of it all. Everything had become absurd, so I couldn't bring myself to go away with everyone else; a journey has to be more than just a journey, and I noticed, after the siege and the defeat, that I wasn't capable of such things, so I went home and never saw Nuha again. I forgot her. I forgot what that girl I'd loved looked like. Now, when I try to recall her, I see her as a blurred image, a shapeless woman. I see her white face, and I see her lips quivering on the verge of tears, and I see her grandmother Khadijeh.

I think that I fell in love with Nuha in the image of her grandmother.

Try to imagine with me the woman of al-Birwa.

A woman walking alone through the rubble of her village looking for the stones that were once her house. A woman alone, her head covered with a black scarf, hunched up in that emptiness that stretches all the way to God, among the hills and valleys of Galilee, within the circle of a red sun that crawls over the ground, passing slowly and carrying with it the shadows of all things.

All the woman saw was shadows. She was alone. They came and she spoke to them. It may be that she didn't say the exact words her granddaughter related. Maybe they didn't understand her language.

Nuha said they were Yemenis, and Yemenis understand the Palestinian dialect, or a lot of its words anyway. But probably they didn't understand a thing. When she spoke they were terrified, because they thought she was a spirit who'd come out of the tree, and they started to throw stones at her. They were just adolescents, so they didn't call the Border Guard from the kibbutz that had been built on top of al-Birwa.

Maybe. I don't know.

Anything's possible.

But why wouldn't she agree to go to Kafar Yasif?

Was it because . . . ?

She probably regretted it afterwards, that must be why she didn't tell her story to anyone, unlike Umm Hassan, who never stopped telling people the story of the woman of Wadi Abu Jmil.

The woman of al-Birwa said nothing.

And I'm telling you now to prove that you weren't the only hero, or the only living martyr.

Don't worry, you'll die in peace. But I want you to know before you die that this protracted death of yours has turned our life upside down. Did you have to sink into this death for your memory, and mine, and everyone else's, to explode? You've been stricken with a brainstorm, and I'm stricken with a storm of memories.

You're dying, and I'm dying.

God, it's not about Shams, or Dr. Amjad, or this Beirut that no longer looks like Beirut. It's to do with me staying here and starting work in the hospital tomorrow. Don't be scared. I won't leave you. I'll continue to work with you as usual and tell you stories and give you the latest.

Think about me a bit, and you'll see I can't take it anymore.

True, nobody cares anymore, and nobody believes anyone. Those who got used to me as a doctor will get used to me as a nurse. But me – how can I adjust to this new me that I'm being forced to accept?

We'll find out tomorrow.

But before tomorrow comes, I want you to tell me who the woman of Sha'ab was.

I want the story from you. I've heard it dozens of times from different people, but I'm not convinced. In the Ain al-Hilweh camp I got to know

Mohammed al-Khatib, who claimed that the woman of Sha'ab was his mother, Fatimah. Then I met a man from the Fa'our clan who said his mother, Salma, was the woman of Sha'ab. And then, of course, there's that legend about the woman called Reem, to whom the story became attached.

Let's go back to the beginning.

You went back to Ain al-Zaitoun only to find the village demolished. At that point you were with Abu Is'af on a mission to carry weapons to Galilee from Syria. I don't want to hear now about the humiliations you suffered trying to find weapons and about how Colonel Safwat treated you like shit, saying you weren't a regular army and that he wasn't about to throw away the few weapons he had on peasants who were known for their cowardice and slyness.

That was how the "general of the defeat" – as he'd become known to the fighters who withdrew to Lebanon to the beat of the Arab leaders' mendacious war drums – talked to you.

You returned, you and Abu Is'af, empty-handed. You left Abu Is'af in Sha'ab and continued on to Ain al-Zaitoun, discovering that the village had fallen without a shot being fired to defend it, and that your friend and twin Hanna Kamil Mousa had died crucified on an oak tree.

You all ended up in Sha'ab, and you only left after the whole of Galilee had fallen.

Now tell me about the woman. I know that the story of Palestine of your generation is a rough one, and that we can find a thousand ways to tell it, but Sha'ab, and that woman, and the men of Zabbouba: I want to hear about them from you.

You left Ain al-Zaitoun and went running to Sha'ab. You told me you ran there even though you went by car. What matters is that you got hold of a house in Sha'ab because the headman, Mohammed Ali al-Khatib, gave it to you, telling you he'd built it for his son, Ali, and that he considered you another son.

Sha'ab became your new village and it was there that you saw the miracle.

I don't want to hear the history of the village, because I'm not interested in the brawl that broke out between the Fa'our and Khatib clans in '35 and how it grew during the great revolt of '36 when the Khatib clan avenged the murder of Shaker al-Khatib by killing Rashid al-Fa'our, headman of the eastern quarter, and how all of you – you were still very young – took action. You came with the revolutionaries and imposed a settlement, which was concluded on the threshing floor, where they slaughtered more than forty sheep and people came from all the neighboring villages to eat and offer their congratulations.

I don't want to get into the labyrinth of families and subclans of which I understand nothing. I know you always cited the example of the Sha'ab settlement when you were conducting training courses for fighters. Instead of theorizing about the Sha'ab war, as we did, you'd tell stories and cite examples. And instead of asserting that the family and tribalism had to be transcended, you'd explain to the fighters how you succeeded during the Revolution of '36 in fusing families together, and you'd cite the example of Sha'ab.

You'd tell them about the moon.

Your moon wasn't the full moon of my mother's; yours never became totally full. I think I read the fable of the moon in a Chinese book translated into Arabic, but it sounded more beautiful coming from your mouth than from any book: "The moon is full only one day a month. On all the other days it's either getting bigger or smaller. Life's the same. Stability is the exception, change the rule." You'd ask the boys to follow the movement of the moon on training nights so they could get some practical political culture instead of book culture, which goes in through the eye and out at the ear.

Now tell me about Sha'ab.

Was it Abu Is'af who made the arrangements with the headman for you to have a house, the leader of the Sha'ab garrison thus guaranteeing that you'd stay with him?

You found yourself in the Sha'ab garrison after you'd failed – yes, failed – to form the mobile military unit you'd dreamed of. The war was speeding up, and the Arab armies that entered Palestine in 1948 were being defeated by the larger, better-armed Israeli army in record time. God, who'd have believed it? Six hundred thousand Israelis put together an army larger than all seven Arab armies combined!

You started military patrols, you begged weapons, you took part in the battles of al-Birwa and al-Zib, but the rapid fall of the villages and hamlets of Galilee made it impossible for you to move and turned you into a garrison of not more than two hundred fighters centered on the little village called Sha'ab. Later, the garrison would end up in prison in Syria and its heroic deeds would disappear among the flood of displaced people who invaded the fields and groves.

All the stories of the exodus have collected now in your eyes – shut over the teardrops I put in them – and in place of heroism I see sorrow and hear the voice of my grandmother telling about the woman who sewed up the pita bread. I'm listening to the story of the woman in the fields of Beit Jann, and I see my grandmother miming the story, screwing up her eyes so she can put the imaginary thread into the eye of the imaginary needle, then taking the imaginary pita bread in her hand, cutting it in two and starting to sew it up.

"The woman sewed the pita bread, and the boy was crying. She gave him the whole pita and asked him to be quiet, but he tore it in two and began crying again. So the mother killed her son!"

I see the exodus in your eyes and I hear my grandmother's voice, which has dwindled into a low mutter full of ghosts.

"We reached Beit Jann, but we didn't go into the Druze village because we were afraid."

She tells me about fear and the Druze, and I swallow the pita bread stuffed with fried potatoes and feel the potatoes sticking to the roof of my mouth, as though I'm going to suffocate.

No, I'm not complaining about the potatoes – they were my favorite. I loved fried potatoes and still do. They were incomparably better than the boiled plants my grandmother cooked. She'd leave the camp for who-knows-where and come back loaded down with all kinds of greens, wash them, cook them, and we'd eat. The taste was – how can I describe it? – a green taste, and the stew would form a lump in my mouth. My grandmother would say that it was healthy food: "We're peasants, and this is peasant food." I'd beg her to fry me some potatoes; the smell of potatoes gives you an appetite, but those cooked weeds had neither odor nor taste; it felt like you were chewing something that had already been chewed.

You don't like fried potatoes, I know. You prefer them grilled and seasoned with olive oil. Now I've come to like olive oil, but when my grandmother, who cooked everything in it, was around it tasted waxy to me and I didn't like it, but I couldn't say so in front of her. How can you say that sort of thing to a woman if she doesn't see it? She used to live here as though she were over there. She refused to use electricity because they didn't have it in her village – can you believe it? She didn't want to get used to things that didn't exist there because she was going to go back! If only she'd known what Galilee had become! But she died before she knew anything.

You won't believe the story of the pita bread, just as you didn't believe the story of Umm Hassan and Naji, whom she picked up and put in the basin. You believe, as I'd like to, that we don't kill our own children and throw them under trees. You like things clear and simple. The murderer is a known quantity, and the victim, too, and it's up to us to see that justice is done. Unfortunately, my brother, it wasn't as simple as us and them. It was something else that's hard to define.

I'm not here to define things. I have a mission. As usual I'll fail and as usual I won't believe I've failed; I'll claim I succeeded or put the blame on others. Ah, habit! If only we could walk away from it! If only I could shed this past that hovers like a blue ghost in your room! Come to think of it, why do I see things as blue? Why do I see Shams looking at me with a blue face as though she were about to kill me?

If I could, I'd go to Shams' family and tell them the truth and let them do what they want. I'm innocent of her murder, of her love, of everything, because I'm an imbecile. If I hadn't been made a fool of . . . everything might have been different.

Tell me, who in the story of Shams wasn't made a fool of?

She killed him, the bitch! She told him, "I give myself to you in marriage," and then she killed him.

She loved him, and he loved her, but, like me, he felt she would slip out of his hands. Is it possible for a man to marry a woman who leaves someone else's bed to go to him?

Why did she kill him?

Was the fact that he'd lied to her enough to make her kill him?

We all lie, so it really seems unreasonable. Just imagine – if the penalty for lying were death, there'd be no one left alive on the surface of the earth.

Now I've started to doubt everything. I'm not sure it was a matter of honor. Shams is the first woman in the history of the Arab world to kill a man because he was unfaithful and tricked her.

But let's slow down . . .

Did she kill him?

They said she killed him in public. Everyone saw her, but does that mean anything? What if everyone's lying? What if everyone just believed what they'd heard from everyone else, who had heard what they'd heard from others?

No, that's impossible. If that were true, my whole life might have been an unbearable lie, which it is anyway. Shams lied to me, and everyone is lying to me now. Death threats are being passed on to me, and I'm afraid of a lie. When you're afraid of a lie, it means your life is a lie, don't you think?

I'm scared and I hide in the hospital, and the memories pour down on me and I have no idea what to do with them. What would you say to a novel-writing project? I know you'll tell me I don't know how to write novels. I agree, and I'd add that no one knows how to write because anything you say comes apart when you write it down and turns into symbols and signs, cold and bereft of life. Writing is confusion; tell me, who can write the confusions of life? It's a state between life and death that no one dares enter. I won't dare enter that state, I say this only because like all doctors and failures, I've become a writer. Do you know why Chekhov wrote? Because he was a failed doctor. I imagine that by becoming a writer he was able to find the solution to his crisis. But I'm not like him; I'm a successful doctor, and everyone will see how I was able to rescue you from the Valley of Death.

I'm certain she killed him, because I know her and I know how death shone in her eyes. I used to think it was love that changed her eyes from gray to green, then back to gray, but it was death. Gray-green is the color of death. Shams used to talk about death because she knew it. My grandmother didn't.

Shahineh didn't dare say the child had died. She said they went by Beit Jann and were afraid. The airplanes were roaring above their heads, and when night fell their journey to Lebanon began.

My grandmother said she found herself in the middle of a group of about thirty women, old men, and children from the village of al-Safsaf wandering the hills looking for the Lebanese border. "With my daughters and my son, we walked with them. I don't know how we ended up in that terrified group. We were afraid, too, but not like them. When they spoke they whispered. When we got to Beit Jann, they refused to go into the place. Their leader said they'd rob us and ordered us to continue marching. I told him not to be afraid, but he told me to shut up, and we left. When we got to Lebanon, we'd lost our voices because the old man had made us whisper so much."

It seems that on that journey my grandmother's voice became husky. I forgot to tell you that my grandmother had this husky voice, like it was coming out of a well deep inside her, which made it seem broad and full of holes.

"The child began crying from hunger. A child of three or four sobbing and whining that he was hungry, while everybody looked askance at his mother and asked her to make him shut up. The woman didn't know what to do. She picked him up and started shushing him, but he wouldn't let up. And there was an old man . . . I'll never forget that old man."

My grandmother always used to threaten me with the old man of al-Safsaf. When I refused to eat her greens, she'd tell me she'd ask the old man of al-Safsaf to come and strangle me at night, and I'd be scared and chew my prechewed roughage.

She said she realized why they were so terrified when they reached Tarshiha. There their fear disappeared and they ate and wept, and the old man told the story of the white sheets.

"We received them with white sheets. We went out waving the sheets as a sign of surrender, but they started firing over our heads. Then they ordered us to gather in the square. They chose sixty men of various ages, tied their hands behind their backs with rope and stood them in a row. Sixty men of various ages standing like a wall threaded together by the rope linking their hands. Then they opened fire. The sound of the machine guns deafened us, and the men dropped. The people gathered in the square fled into the fields. Death enveloped us."

"After we reached Tarshiha, he became a different man," said my grandmother. "But on the road, during those silent nights, he was a monster. A tall, thin man with a hunchback. His moustache looked like it had been drawn with a pen. His hair was gray, his moustache black, and he ordered us about furiously. We could see the sinews of his small, veiny hands as he motioned to us to be silent."

My grandmother said she gave the mother the one pita bread she had underneath her dress. She said she was afraid of the old man because he was determined to kill the child if he kept crying. The woman tried her best to make her son shut up – holding his hand, lifting him up, carrying him, putting him back down on the ground, letting him walk between her legs; but the child wouldn't stop crying. The woman took the round loaf from my grandmother and divided it in two. She gave her son half and the other half she gave back to my grandmother. But the boy refused; he wanted a whole pita and started crying again. The old man came up to him and took hold of his clothes and started shaking him. My grandmother rushed over and gave her half to the mother, who gave it to her son. But the boy wanted a whole pita, not two halves. The woman put the two halves together, extracted a needle and thread from the front of her dress, threaded the needle, and started sewing up the pita bread.

My grandmother said she saw things as though they were wrapped in shadows. The meager crescent moon that would slip out from among the branches of the trees turned people into colliding shadows. I listened to the story and was scared of my grandmother's husky voice, which swallowed up the scene and made it a story of djinn and afrits.

The woman sewed up the pita bread and gave it to the boy, and he stopped crying. He took it joyfully, until he discovered that it wasn't a normal pita. The woman had sewn it hastily in the dark and hadn't made the stitches tight. The boy took the bread and the stitches started to pull apart – the gap between the two halves widening. And he started to cry again. He held the pita up to give back to his mother and cried.

The old man came forward, took the pita bread, put it in his mouth, and started gobbling it down. He swallowed more than half of it along with the thread and went over to the woman.

"Kill it," he hissed at her.

"Throw it down the well," said a woman's voice from the within the shadowed crowd.

"Give it to me. I'll take care of it," said the old man.

He went toward the child, whose screams grew louder and louder. The woman took a wool blanket, wrapped her son in it and picked him up. She put his head on her shoulder and kept pulling him down onto it as she walked, stifling the child's cries with the blanket. The old man walked behind them; my grandmother said he walked behind the woman and kept pushing the child's head down onto its mother's shoulder.

In Tarshiha the mother put her son down on the ground. She pulled back the blanket and started weeping. The child was blue. But the old man changed when they reached the last Palestinian village and started looking for his daughter, eagerly asking people about a short, fat woman with five children.

My grandmother said the people of Tarshiha brought them food, but the man refused to eat. He became a different person. The veins disappeared from his face and hands, his body slumped, and he started weeping and asking to die.

"And the child?" I asked.

"What child?"

"The child with the pita bread."

"I don't know."

She said she didn't know, though she knew the boy had died.

Its mother killed it – do you hear, Father? – its mother killed it because she was afraid of the old man, who was afraid of the Jews. The mother didn't carry her child on her breast, and she didn't support his head on her shoulder the way my grandmother had told me. She wrapped him in the blanket and sat on him until he died.

That's the way our relative, Umm Fawzi, told it. Umm Fawzi said they walked for five days without a sound so the Jews wouldn't hear them, and when the boy cried his mother killed him because the old man threatened to kill them both.

"Umm Fawzi's raving," said my grandmother.

You'll say I'm raving, too, because you don't like hearing the story about the boy, or the story about the people of Saleheh, who were executed wrapped in their bed sheets. The Jews wrapped more than seventy men in the white sheets they'd been carrying as a sign of surrender and fired on them, and the sheets spurted blood.

You don't want to hear about anything except heroism, and you think you're the *heroes' hero*. Listen then to the story of another hero, a mixture of you and your father, a hero who didn't fight. A man from a village called Mi'ar. It's close to your new village. His name was Rakan Abboud.

When Mi'ar fell, after the rest of his family had gone, the man refused to leave his village and stayed on with his wife. This is what Nadia told me. Do you know Nadia? Didn't you meet her? She was in charge of the People's Committee in the camp. Nadia said the Jews drove her grandfather out along with two other men from the village three months after they'd occupied it. The two men died on the road, near Jenin, but Nadia's grandfather, who was in his eighties, went to Aleppo and stayed with someone he knew there. Then he joined Nadia's father in the camp in Baalbek.

"My grandfather had become unbearable," said Nadia. "He hated Baalbek. He hated its snow and its cold. He used to scream that he didn't want to die there, so my father decided to move to the camp in Burj al-Shamali near Tyre. We lived in a shack there, like everyone else. His condition got frighteningly worse. He'd go out at night and only come back at dawn. Then he informed my father he'd decided to go back to Mi'ar to look for his wife. That was in 1950, and we were waiting. All my father did was listen to the radio and set dates for the Return. Each month he'd say our time would come next month. My father tried to stop him and begged him to wait one more month, but the man had made up his mind. One day, he managed to hire a guide and a donkey and left.

"He made it to his house – imagine! – knocked on the door, and a woman opened it. The poor man thought she must be a spirit and ran off, tripping over himself. He left Mi'ar, never to return. He spent what remained of his life in the fields. My grandmother, who lived in Majd al-Kuroum, found out and began her long search for him. She looked for him for more than a year. When she found him, the poor man had completely lost his sight, so she took him to Majd al-Kuroum, where he died."

Nadia went on at great length about how her grandfather died. She told how he lived his last days like a thief, a blind, feeble thief. Despite this, his wife had to hide him from the police so he wouldn't be expelled like others who'd got back in. He'd gone to see his village and his wife, but he saw nothing. He lived in secret, and his presence was made public only when he died.

Blind and feeble, living in secret – but when he died, people wept openly. All those people who'd now become the people of Majd al-Kuroum wept. You know the villages aren't the old villages anymore: They've become full of abandoned houses inhabited by refugees from other villages. The people were all mixed together. The people in Majd al-Kuroum didn't know the blind old man. They knew that Fathiyyeh Abboud was hiding "Lebanon" in her house. They called him Lebanon because he'd come from there. When the secret got out, the whole village wept for the blind man. He didn't die in his own house surrounded by children and grandchildren; he didn't die, as most die, in the platitude of memories. He went back and died in the secrecy of that town living under the secrecy of military rule, curfew, and the footprints of those who slipped back in.

"That was a blind old man, nothing like me," you'll say. "I didn't go back to end my life wrapped in memories. I went back to start again, to remember the way, so I could love my wife."

Nice words, my dear friend, and everything you say is correct. And I'm not going to talk to you about the beginnings of the fedayeen, which coincided with your journeys to Deir al-Asad and the routine births of your children.

Tell me, how did Sha'ab fall?

Very well, tell me how Sha'ab didn't fall.

Without heroics, please. I'd like to find out who the woman of Sha'ab was. Nahilah, or who?

Who was that woman who stood up six days after the village fell and said she was going to go back? The men tried to stop her, but she'd already left, and you had to catch up with her.

Did people get confused and mix up the woman who carried a jerry can of arak on her head with the woman who led them in liberating their village?

And why didn't you tell me about the smuggling of arak? Because it was shameful? What's shameful about smuggling arak from Lebanon to Palestine? Is it because you don't want to acknowledge that the Lebanese arak they make in Zahleh is the best in the world? Or are you embarrassed because the smugglers made use of the Revolution of '36 and became revolutionaries in their own way?

Reem belonged to the Sa'ad family, which was famous for smuggling. It was the smugglers' sheikh, Hassan Sa'ad, who came up with the brilliant idea to smuggle arak on the heads of women. He'd place jerry cans of arak on the heads of the women so it appeared they were carrying water.

The column set off, crossed the Lebanese border, and came to the outskirts of Tarshiha. The column was composed of eight women in long peasant dresses and, for protection, three armed men, Hassan Sa'ad at their head.

A column of eight women, moving rhythmically as though they were coming from the well, armed men at the rear, and Hassan Sa'ad about three hundred meters ahead to scout out the unpaved road joining Tarshiha to al-Kabri.

Hassan came back suddenly, having spotted a British patrol. He ordered the women to scatter in the fields, and the women began to run. All of them ran except Reem. It appears she was paralyzed with fear. Hassan shouted, but Reem stayed frozen to the spot. Hassan pulled out his revolver and fired at the jerry can. Reem bolted, the arak pouring down over her face and clothes. Then she fell. Apparently she'd drunk a large quantity of the triple-strength arak, or maybe it was just the fumes. The girl staggered and fell. Hassan tried to hold her up, but he couldn't, so he left her and hid in the field by the road. Having heard the shot, the patrol approached and found the girl awash in arak. They tried to question her and searched at the sides of the road but didn't find anyone. One of the soldiers went over to her, held out his hand to help her up . . . and bullets rang out. Hassan had seen the soldier going up to Reem so he fired, and the battle was launched.

This is where accounts differ.

Some people say Hassan killed three members of the patrol and took Reem and fled with her to Sha'ab, others that Hassan fired into the air so no one was hit, and that the soldiers had simply retreated, thinking they'd fallen into an ambush set by revolutionaries. That's how Reem managed to escape and reach Hassan, even though she tripped over her long, wet dress.

Hassan became a hero. When he arrived at the village, he was treated like a revolutionary.

Even Reem believed in his heroism and fell in love with him. Their love persisted for more than five years, Reem's father refusing to marry his daughter to her smuggler cousin and Reem refusing marriage to any other suitor. Things grew even more inflamed when Reem threw tradition to the winds and declared in front of everybody in the *madafé** of Shaker al-

*Great reception hall.

Khatib, and to the councillor of the Western Quarter, that she loved Hassan and would never belong to anyone else. The old story of blood feuding would have been repeated if Abu Is'af hadn't intervened by claiming that Hassan had become a sacred warrior and that he would vouch for his character.

And so Reem married her hero, Hassan.

Reem of the jerry can full of arak became Reem the heroine. Incredible as it may seem, most people attribute the decision to return to Sha'ab to her.

Yet, it's the truth.

Please tell me, wasn't Nahilah the woman of Sha'ab?

Nahilah rose. She gave the impression that she was at the end of her rope: a woman with an infant in her arms, faced at every turn by a blind man and his wife. Her first village had been demolished, and her second was occupied.

Nahilah rose, and Reem joined her.

But why did people say it was Reem?

Was it because that woman, who'd carried the jerry can of arak and staggered under the shot fired by the man she loved, lost everything the moment they entered the village?

Her husband, Hassan, was the first to join her and to plunge into battle. And he was the first martyr.

Reem was at the front beside Nahilah, and Hassan was behind them. On that day in July 1948, Reem came to the end. After the village was liberated and her husband died, she took her three children and went to Deir al-Asad. From there she fled to Syria, and nothing more was heard of her. She lived in the Yarmouk camp outside Damascus and ceased to be of interest to all of you.

What puzzles me is why everybody forgets all the other stories but remembers Reem and her decision to enter the village?

They forgot Hassan, the smuggler-martyr, they forgot Nahilah, who led the march, and they forgot you, too. There is no mention of you in the battle of Sha'ab. Nobody ever told me anything about you. They all said you were there, but you weren't what people were interested in. What they were interested in was your father, the blind sheikh, who refused to leave again after the village had been liberated. He said he couldn't because he had responsibilities at the mosque. You begged him to leave, but he refused. You begged him and you begged your mother and you begged Nahilah. Your decision was clear: No one but militiamen were to stay behind in Sha'ab. The residents were to take their belongings and leave because it was no longer possible to live in the village, which was under constant fire from the Jews posted at Mi'ar.

But your father refused, and then he refused again when you decided to withdraw to Lebanon.

Let's get back to Sha'ab.

I'll try to put together the fragments I've heard from you and others. When I make a mistake, correct me. I won't begin at the beginning because I'm not like you. I can't say "In the beginning . . ."

I'll start after the fall of al-Birwa, with the story of Mustafa al-Tayyar.

After you'd mobilized all the men and matériel, you liberated al-Birwa, seizing weapons, ammunition, and harvesters. Then Mahdi, the commanding officer of the ALA detachment, arrived and his men surrounded you. "Everything on the ground!" Mahdi cried. He wanted to confiscate the weapons and claim he was the hero of the liberation.

You were dumbstruck. The battle of al-Birwa was your first offensive. You'd tried to coordinate your fire and organize the assault; you'd put great effort into mobilization and were exhausted from the victory, your first; and along comes this officer whose soldiers hadn't fired a single bullet, yelling, "Everything on the ground!"

Up jumped Mustafa al-Tayyar, a fighter from al-Birwa who'd die in the last battle between the Yemeni volunteers and the Israeli army, which took place on the hills of al-Kabri.

Al-Tayyar bolted up and yelled, "We're the Arabs and you're the Jews," and threw himself down on the ground holding the machine gun Ali Hassan al-Jammal had pulled out of the Jewish redoubt during the battle.

The Iraqi sergeant Dandan intervened and said, "This won't do. An Arab doesn't kill another Arab." He prevented a massacre. Things were worked out, and they took half the weapons.

Mahdi came back afterward and convinced you to leave al-Birwa and hand it over to the ALA. And you let him persuade you! You abandoned al-Birwa only for it to be surrendered to the Jews twenty-four hours later without a fight. And Dandan stands up and says, "An Arab doesn't kill another Arab!" Poor people! Say you agreed with Mahdi because it was impossible to stay, because you were exhausted, and the village was surrounded on all sides; so you abandoned it before the ALA did the same.

After al-Birwa fell, you only had Sha'ab.

And Sha'ab didn't survive either.

On July 21, 1948, the shelling of Sha'ab began, from the direction of al-Birwa. Then an infantry unit advanced from Mi'ar and swept through the village. The first shelling was intermittent but accurate. Ten minutes after the first shell fell on the threshing floors, the second one fell on the houses of Ali Mousa and Rashid al-Hajj Hassan, destroying them. The villagers started fleeing in all directions. In the midst of the chaos, everyone found themselves on the outside of the village except for a small group of fighters concentrated in al-Abbasiyyeh on the eastern side of the village.

On July 21, Sha'ab fell for the first time, without a fight!

The ALA, concentrated in Tal al-Layyat, Majd al-Kuroum, and al-Ramah, didn't intervene. It seems the Israeli attack took everyone by surprise. War was everywhere, and it took you by surprise!

The village collapsed before its defenders fired a single shot, and the Jews came in.

You said you lived those six days in the fields and could see Sha'ab from a distance. It was as though the village had fallen into the valley. Sha'ab is hemmed in by hills on all sides, and had become a valley of death. After the fall of al-Birwa and Mi'ar, Sha'ab was under fire, and the only way to protect it was by concerted military action. Abu Is'af tried to organize the fighters. He divided them into four detachments and assigned each one the task of protecting one of the village borders, but he didn't leave a central force capable of responding to emergencies.

Practically speaking, there was no battle.

The shelling and screaming caused terrible confusion among the peasants and the fighters, and the battle ended before it had begun.

In the fields, the Sha'ab fighters discovered they were impotent. Attempts at surveillance and infiltration were useless. "We can't attack," said Abu Is'af, "without preparatory shelling, and we don't have any artillery." He assigned the task of contacting the ALA to assure artillery support to Yunes.

Yunes went to Tal al-Layyat and entered into impossible negotiations with Mahdi and Jasem. Every plan he proposed was rejected on the grounds that it would cause huge losses to both peasants and fighters.

"I suggested an attack from Tal al-Layyat, and they said the artillery at Mi'ar would wipe us out. I suggested an attack from the fields to the east, and they said they'd discover us and wipe us out before we arrived. I suggested that the ALA unit move, to give the impression that the attack would come from their positions while we attacked from the east, and they said they had no order to move. All my plans were refused, and their suggestion was to reflect and wait. I told them, 'You're the army. You propose something and we'll carry it out.' They said, 'Of course, but we're waiting for orders.' I said we couldn't stand around waiting. They said, 'In war, you have to obey orders.'

"I said, they said . . .

"My mission ended in failure. I went back to the field where everyone was waiting for me. Everybody thought I'd returned with the order to liberate Sha'ab in my pocket. When I told them, their faces darkened but they made no comment, as though I were telling them about some other village."

The table for breaking the fast was set at sunset. They were starving, miserable, yet nevertheless keeping the fast.

When I ask you about the meal, you'll tell me you were tired but not hungry. You'll tell me you never used to feel real hunger unless you were with her, after you'd made love to her in the cave of Bab al-Shams. On ordinary days you didn't feel hungry, you ate just to fill your stomach. On that day, however, you did try to eat from that meager table. There was almost nothing – greens and weeds. There wasn't even any bread.

Perhaps that was the reason.

Why didn't you tell me the Jews attacked Sha'ab precisely at sunset in the month of Ramadan, as the villagers were all around their tables, breaking the fast? The shelling started, your defenses collapsed, and you were defeated. Hungry, you fled to the fields in that terrible chaos; then, as you were fleeing, you saw the flames springing up in the middle of the village. You thought they were burning the village, and this added to your panic and drove you out into the neighboring fields.

When Yunes got back, he found everyone eating. He was hungry, but he didn't eat. He put his hand out, and before the food reached his mouth, he threw it down and said, "We'll attack on our own." There followed a long, noisy, involved discussion about military plans, but there was no plan. Only Yunes' blind father said, "There's no hope. Everything's lost." People saw the tears falling from his closed eyes while the gathering broke up without a decision. That night everyone slept like the dead, even those who'd taken it upon themselves to act as guards; in the face of the despair, the fear, and the hunger, only the door of sleep remained open.

In the morning, the two women were struck by something resembling madness.

They were discussing ways of getting water from the spring, when suddenly a hubbub arose and everyone saw Nahilah and Reem leaving.

Nahilah said she couldn't take it any longer.

Reem said death would be more honorable.

The women set off behind them. Abu Is'af and Khalil Suleiman Abd al-

Mu'ti tried to stop them, but they were like a torrent sweeping everything in its path.

"At the outskirts of the village, we started to fire. We attacked without a plan. We were running and firing at random. It wasn't a battle, it was like a Bedouin brawl, and we found ourselves in the village with the Jews gone. A few of our people were dead, first among them, Reem's Hassan. I can't describe the battle because it wasn't a battle, it was a charge. We were back into the village in less than an hour. Afterward we found out that Dandan's group of Yemeni and Iraqi volunteers in the ALA had mutinied against their commander when we started our attack and opened fire from their positions at Tal al-Layyat, deluding the Jews into thinking there was a coordinated attack. Then Dandan and his men came to join us, after they'd been thrown out of the army."

Yunes said that when he met Abu Is'af more than twenty years later, he was astonished to hear the Sha'ab garrison leader's version of the story.

"Abu Is'af is more than a brother to me. Being comrades in arms is something time can't erase, as you know well. Your comrade in arms can turn up, after twenty years, and you discover he still has his place in your heart. Abu Is'af came and we sat and drank tea, and the conversation took us back to '48.

"He said the Israelis threw white powder into the square at Sha'ab as they withdrew, that they set fire to it to frighten us. When he saw the fire, feeling that he couldn't bear one more retreat, he threw himself into it and discovered that it was just flames.

"I remember things differently – the fire started when they occupied the village, not when they withdrew. But that's not important.

"Abu Is'af knew very well that I was the military official in charge of the whole South Lebanon sector, but he still treated me as though I were a junior officer, raising his hand and expecting me to be silent, like in '48.

"I was silent so as not to upset him. After all, Abu Is'af is truly dedicated to the struggle, and I respect him immensely. When we disagreed over the flame powder, and he started to get upset, I lied and claimed he was right. I recounted how I had followed him, how I, too, had thrown myself into the flames. I let him tell whatever stories he liked in front of his sister and grandchildren – how he caught on fire himself and how all the other fighters did the same, and this terrified the Jews."

"We were like demons," said Abu Is'af, "like demons that spring from the heart of a fire, and they fled, leaving their arms on the battlefield."

I ASKED YOU about the woman of Sha'ab, and you told me about the flames. Fine, but now I want a clear explanation of why you said that Sha'ab didn't fall.

What did happen?

What were you doing there?

"The truth," said Yunes, "is that after we'd liberated the village, we buried the four martyrs and met on the threshing floor. We decided that the women, children, and old men should leave and that only the militiamen should stay. Everyone agreed. In the morning, all the women, old men, and children left, except for my father and mother, and Nahilah.

"My father said he'd never go, that he was going to stay so he could conduct prayers. And my mother said she'd never leave him. And Nahilah stayed with the two of them. Then we learned that many of the older men had stayed behind secretly, or had come back secretly.

"That's how Sha'ab became a den for fighters and a retreat for old people – about two hundred fighters and more than a hundred old men and women.

"We waited for three months, the women coming into the village at night to get provisions. We stood guard, awaiting a major offensive, but they launched only limited attacks. The first was on July 27, the day after the liberation of the village. The attacks continued through August and September, but I can't say there was even an all-out invasion. They'd open fire without any real attempt at advancing. We provoked them into fighting on several occasions, even though our ammunition was low. Then we withdrew."

You withdrew, just like that, for no reason?

"No, we withdrew because it became impossible to stay any longer. On

November 29, 1948, the Jews bombed Tarshiha from the air. Then the bombardment expanded to include al-Jish and al-Bqei'a, and the ALA began its withdrawal to Lebanon. Jasem came to Sha'ab and said, 'Friends, they've betrayed us all. The Sha'ab garrison must withdraw before they close the Lebanese border.' We realized that everything had collapsed.

"That day, Abu Is'af made the decision and said, 'We'll withdraw. If everyone else withdraws and we're left on our own, it won't work.' He said, 'We'll go now, then come back.'

"I told him, 'If we go, we'll never come back.'

"'What do you suggest?' he asked.

"'Nothing,' I said.

"He said, 'We'll withdraw, then come back.'

"So we withdrew. All the fighters withdrew with their arms.

"But the old people refused to withdraw.

"Hussein al-Fa'our, who was to die later in the mud of Zabbouba, said, 'Take your arms and go. We're going to stay in our village. They can't do anything to us. We're old people; they have nothing to gain by killing us.'

"But they killed them.

"Nahilah told me about the massacre of the old people in the village and how the Israeli officer called Avraham came in and ordered them all to gather near the pond. He stood among them like an officer inspecting his troops, as though they were a military lineup. He even ordered al-Hajj Mousa Darwish, who was disabled, to be brought from his house. It was his wife's fault. She told the Israeli officer she'd left her husband in the house because he was disabled. She told him about her husband because she was afraid they were going to blow up the houses, as they'd done in al-Birwa. The officer ordered her to get him. She said she couldn't carry him on her own and a man volunteered to help her, but the officer waved his rifle in his face and said no. She went on her own and came back dragging her husband along the ground. She wept as she dragged him. The woman was dragging her husband and the officer was smiling, pleased with himself. We could see his white teeth. There was something strange about the whiteness of his teeth. When the woman had brought her husband to the officer, al-Hajj Mousa Darwish gave a loud snort, black liquid gushed from his mouth, and he died.

"The officer saw nothing; it was as if he hadn't seen the man die. Instead he started pointing at various men. Anyone the finger pointed to had to move to the other side. He chose about twenty old men. Then he pointed at Yunes' blind father. The man didn't see the finger, so the officer pulled out his revolver. Yunes' mother screamed 'No!', went over to her husband, and led him to where the others stood before returning to her place. A truck came and the officer ordered them to get in. My mother ran up and took hold of my father's hand and explained that he was blind.

"'Get back, woman,' the officer yelled.

"Nahilah ran over, her son in her arms, and took told of the blind sheikh's hand.

"'Get back, all of you,' shouted the officer.

"They didn't get back. They took my father and went back to the pond where most of the people were, and the truck set off. The Israelis started firing over the heads of the people, who scattered into the fields looking for new villages or the Lebanese border.

"The story of Zabbouba, my son, is the real embodiment of our tragedy," said Yunes.

No more was heard of the twenty men that the officer's finger had put onto the truck until Marwan al-Fa'our appeared in Lebanon. Marwan al-Fa'our was the only one to survive what we would later come to call the Massacre of the Mud.

Marwan al-Fa'our told of the rain.

"It was a diluvial downpour and the truck forged through it. We reached Zabbouba, close to Jenin on the Jordanian border. They made us get down from the truck, ordered to us to cross to the Arab side, and started firing over our heads."

It was a march of rain, death, and mud.

The mud covered the ground, and the rain was like ropes. Cold, darkness, and fear. Twenty men walking, sliding, grabbing at the ropes of rain hung down from the sky and falling down. They'd try to rise, and they'd get stuck in the mud.

Twenty men hanging onto ropes of rain, sobbing and coughing, trying to walk but sliding and sticking in the mud.

The mud was like glue.

They stuck to the ground. They fell and the mud swallowed them.

The ropes of water falling from the sky began to turn to mud.

And the dying started.

That's how the men of Sha'ab died in the Massacre of the Mud, which took place on a certain day in December of '48.

The Sha'ab garrison congregated and withdrew in orderly fashion in the direction of the Lebanese border.

The detachment commanded by Dandan, however, left them and joined the Yemenis concentrated in the hills of al-Kabri, where the last battle took place and all the Yemenis and Iraqis died. That was where Dandan, and Abdallah, and al-Mosulli died.

The Sha'ab garrison congregated at Beit Yahoun and Ain Ibil and started making forays from Jesr al-Mansourah.

An army unit surrounded them, disarmed them, and ordered them to join the Ajnadayn Brigade near Damascus. There they were put in prison.

Yunes came to the Ain al-Hilweh camp from the prison, stood up, and screamed among the tents, "We're not refugees!"

The rest you know, Father.

Shall I tell you the rest? Why should I tell you when you already know everything?

On the other hand, you don't know what happened to Abd al-Mu'ti.

Abd al-Mu'ti died yesterday, here in the hospital. He breathed his last after suffering an angina attack. We tried to treat him, but he died.

What can you do for a man of seventy who's decided to die? Let him go – it's better for him and for us. We tried to save him, but in vain. "It was the will of God Almighty."

When they brought him in, he was having a hard time breathing, opening his mouth as though there weren't enough air, or as though his spirit were seeking a way out of his body.

A new booby trap for me, I thought, because Sha'ab men refuse to die. Then I remembered you are not from Sha'ab, which meant that he wasn't like you and so wouldn't repeat this drama. On top of that, I realized he wasn't a relative of yours, as I'd first thought based on your resemblance. Actually, you don't look alike at all; but you old men all become infants again – you all resemble each another at first glance, but the resemblance is only in our heads.

Abd al-Mu'ti died and took his story with him.

He was like a broken record when it came to his towering courage during the long siege of the Shatila camp. And you were the reason, because you – I don't know why you took such pleasure in that story of the nuclear bomb that you made up with the Lebanese woman journalist to break the siege of the camp.

I wasn't in the camp for the entire siege because I'd been given the mission of going out for antibiotics, which we needed desperately, and when I came back I found that the routes into the camp had been closed off once and for all. That was the day I met Shams, in our office in the Mar Elias camp, and she took over the mission. She said she could get things in through her private network, and she took the antibiotics and disappeared. Then I learned that she'd entered the camp and had stayed there for about two months, leaving again after a dispute with its military commander, Ali Abu Toq. It was after she left the camp that our love began. She'd come to Mar Elias, sit with us in her uniform, draw maps and talk about her impossible plans for breaking the siege of Shatila. That was when my passion was ignited. I didn't make a declaration or a move. I just waited. When she would come, that burning passion that erupts from deep inside the rib cage would hit me and cut off my breathing. It seems she noticed, because she behaved like she'd noticed. At the time I thought she was trying to convey her lack of interest, but I found out later that this sort of sideways way of showing interest was her way. She'd glance at me obliquely, as though desire had made its abode in the corners of her eyes.

My love for Shams started with the antibiotics, in Mar Elias. I didn't run away during the siege, as was said; I was on a mission. And anyway, when I came back, no one looked on me as a traitor. The camp had been wiped out, and none of the siege fighters were left. Even Shams refused to stay in Shatila and joined the fighters of Ain al-Hilweh, using a village east of Sidon as her base.

I didn't return to the camp because I was afraid to take part in the fighting in Maghdousheh but because I'd lost any desire for war. War is an urge, as you used to say. You said that war burned inside you and you couldn't wait for the Arabs to complete their military arrangements so you joined Fatah, and fought the way you wanted to.

In those days I didn't like fighting anymore. What was I supposed to do east of Sidon? Plus why continue with the war of Lebanon when it wasn't a war anymore? I will never say, as you do, that it wasn't ever a war, that it was a trap we set with our own hands and fell into. I disagree. We got into the civil war in Lebanon because all roads were closed to us and because it was our duty to bring the world down on the heads of its masters. That's what I believed in '75. But after the fall of Shatila in '87 and our conversion into bands fighting around Sidon, I was no longer convinced.

Abd al-Mu'ti was different.

His war urge never died.

During the siege, when the camp was surrounded by men from the Amal movement, when everyone was on the verge of collapse, Abd al-Mu'ti picked up his Czech rifle and hunkered down in one of the forward positions. The young fighters felt sorry for him being so old, but he was as alert as an ape. The years had left no trace on his well-defined body, white moustache, and bald head. His rifle fire used to reassure us because it signified that we were still capable of resistance.

Abd al-Mu'ti said he fought so they wouldn't give him another "sunbath."

Before we get into "sunbathing," do you remember what Abd al-Mu'ti did during the siege?

You were all cut off and half-starved and your morale was pitiful. So Abd al-Mu'ti decided to use his secret weapon. He telephoned the Agence France Presse office in Beirut and talked to a woman, asking her to repeat her name several times before he gave her the news. He said he wanted to be sure of her identity. She said her name was Jamila Ibrahim and that she was Lebanese, from Zahleh.

You listened to him stupefied. He made up a story about a meeting to be held by the fighters in the camp to discuss the situation. He said that the fighters had decided to ask a religious authority for a fatwa permitting the consumption of human flesh. "We're dying of starvation. We've eaten the cats and the dogs, and there's nothing left to eat, and the militias surrounding us have no mercy, so what are we to do? We've decided to eat the flesh of our fallen comrades, and we're asking for a fatwa to allow it."

He said they couldn't call from the camp and asked the journalist to contact a religious authority, promising to call her back in an hour.

An hour later, the news that shook the world was out. Abd al-Mu'ti called Jamila, and she told him of the good news that Sheikh Kamel al-Sammour had ruled that it was permissible to eat human flesh in situations of urgent necessity. Agence France Presse sent the news out over its international network of television and radio stations, and the world press went into an uproar.

The people of Shatila didn't eat human flesh, and the Syrian army that was surrounding the area ordered the Amal militias to make a partial lifting of the siege.

I entered the camp after Abd al-Mu'ti's bombshell. I went in with medicine and rations, and there I met Jamila Ibrahim.

The journalist came to the camp looking for Abd al-Mu'ti. She came carrying a cooking pot full of delicious food – God, how good her food was! A pot of cracked wheat, cooked cracked wheat with mutton and onions and chickpeas piled on top, plus a big container of milk.

Jamila said she'd cooked it for Abd al-Mu'ti, and everyone ate. When she saw the number of people hovering around the pot, she said she was ashamed; if she'd known Abd al-Mu'ti was going to invite the whole camp she'd have made more. Abd al-Mu'ti told her, his mouth full of cracked wheat, that he was going to repeat the miracle of the fishes. "Didn't your prophet make five fishes feed a thousand people?"

We ate and laughed, and Jamila's round face was flooded with happiness. I never saw a woman so happy. She didn't touch the food herself, and Abd al-Mu'ti sat next to her and tried to make her eat from his hand, as though they were two old friends, and she called him "my partner" because he'd written the news dispatch with her that led to the raising of the siege, and he called her "my partner" because she'd cooked for him.

Where is Jamila now?

I ought to contact her to tell her of Abd al-Mu'ti's death, but what if she doesn't remember him? What if she talks to me as though the pot of cracked wheat never existed?

I won't get in touch with her, but how I wish she'd bring another pot of cracked wheat. The man is dead, and death calls for food; nothing stimulates hunger like death.

Abd al-Mu'ti is dead and, with him, died the story of al-Ba'neh and its square and his stubborn refusal to stay inside his house in the camp.

"I'll fight and I'll die, but I'll never let that happen again."

Abd al-Mu'ti said, "After Sha'ab, we fled to the forests of al-Ba'neh and lived there. We turned our blankets into tents. We'd throw the blanket over the branch of a tree, tie it to the ground, and that would be half a tent. We lived in those half-tents for more than a month. Then al-Ba'neh and Deir al-Asad fell. We knew they'd fallen when the Jews surrounded us and brought us to the square at al-Ba'neh. Al-Ba'neh doesn't really have a square; I don't know another village in the world like it – the square of al-Ba'neh is shared with Deir al-Asad, as though they were one village. They gathered us up in the square and left us crucified under the sun. That was the first time I'd heard the term *sunbath*. A man next to me said, 'They're going to give us a sunbath before they kill us.' I found out the full horror of what it meant later in the Ansar detention camp. In that vast camp, which the Israelis built after the occupation of '82, sunbathing was a basic means of torture. They tie your arms and legs and throw you down in the sun, so you twist and turn and roll, trying to get a moment's relief from the burning. That would be from sunrise to sunset. Then the officer comes and gives the order for your arms and legs to be untied and asks you to stand up, and you discover you can't do anything. The sun has set under your skin, and fire has made its home inside you. Sunset is tribulation and death. When the sun disappears on the horizon, the burning inside begins, as though the sun had gone to its rest in your bones instead of in the sea.

"We were in the square of al-Ba'neh and there was the sun, and the man said, 'They'll give us a sunbath before they kill us.' I didn't understand what he meant until they killed us.

"We were a vast mass of humanity writhing under the sun and waiting for death. Later we discovered that we were to spend the rest of our lives in such a sunbath. What do you call the refugee camp? Now you see houses, but early on the camp consisted of a group of tents. Then later, after we'd built huts, they allowed us to put roofs over them. It was said that if we put actual roofs on our houses, we'd forget Palestine, so we put up zinc sheets. Do you know what zinc sheets do to you under the Beirut sun? Do you know what it means to be under zinc at night, after it's absorbed the sun all day?

"In the square of al-Ba'neh – Deir al-Asad they left us to bathe in the sun all day long after they'd separated out the women. They ordered the women to go to Lebanon and left us out to burn.

"Two men I didn't know asked permission to fetch water, and the officer told them to follow him. They walked toward the spring. We heard the sound of two bullets. The officer returned, and the men didn't. After that no one dared to say he was thirsty.

"After more than an hour an old man stood up and asked for water. The officer looked at him with contempt, pulled out his revolver, brought the barrel close to the man's forehead, placed it between his eyes but didn't fire. The old man started to tremble. I was sure he was going to kill him, but he didn't. The officer put his revolver in his belt, and the man went on trembling for a long, long time.

"Then they searched us and stole everything – money, watches, and rings. Then the soldiers pulled back, and we saw the officer's hand rise and fall. The soldiers were dragging away the men tapped by the officer's hand. The hand fell on more than two hundred men, who were loaded onto trucks that took them in the direction of al-Ramah. To this day we don't know what happened to them. Soon after, they ordered us to go to Lebanon. The shooting started. We found ourselves in the fields with our wives and our children, and we walked for endless hours. We walked until we got to the village of Sajour, where we slept in the fields; we continued our journey in the morning to Beit Jann. There the Druze gave us food. We walked for more than two days before we got to Lebanon.

"My son, Hamed, was ten and had been hit in his right knee. I wrapped his knee and carried him on my shoulders, but eventually I became exhausted and put him down – he had to walk. By the time we reached Lebanon, he was crippled.

"Sahirah, the daughter of Ibrahim al-Hajj Hassan, gave birth to a girl in the fields of Sajour. God knows what had happened to her; she pulled out a little girl from under her skirt and began dancing – saying that she would name her Sahirah.

"Ibrahim al-Hajj Hassan tried to calm his daughter, but the woman didn't care. She danced like she was at a wedding party and said she could hear drums beating in her ears. She said she wouldn't stop dancing until her husband came back. Alas! How was he going to come back after they'd taken him to al-Ramah?

"Sahirah kept dancing until we reached Lebanon, where they said she'd gone crazy, though only God knows the truth.

"Do you understand, my son, why I don't want to stay home? I'm an old man who fights because I prefer death to a sunbath. They gave me a sunbath in al-Ba'neh in '48, and they gave me another in Ansar in '82, and now I've had enough – I'd rather die than face another."

You are dying, Abd al-Mu'ti.

Your rigid body slackens. Your features return to you; your face clears, the wrinkles are wiped from your broad brow, and the cloud over your eyes parts.

I STAND.

What am I to say to this man I call my father but is not my father?

I open his eyes, put "tears" in them, but he doesn't weep.

Abd al-Mu'ti dies, and you don't weep. You're dying, and you don't weep.

I bring you news and tell you stories and you don't hear. Tell me, Abd al-Mu'ti, what to do. Take me with you on your journey, for I yearn to see all of you. I live among you and I yearn for you, and you are somewhere else.

Weep a little, Father. Just one sob and everything will be over. One sob and you'll live. But you don't want to, or you no longer want to, or you've lost your will. And I'm with you and not with you. I'm busy, I have to check on the other patients; that's what Dr. Amjad has decided. Don't be scared, I won't leave you for long. I'll just slip over, check on them and come back to your side.

And afterward what?

Indeed, will there be an afterward?

For three months I've been telling you stories, some of which I know and some of which I don't. And you're incapable of correcting my errors, so I make mistakes once in a while. Freedom, Father, is being able to make mistakes. Now I feel free because with you I can make as many mistakes as I like and retract my mistakes whenever I like, and tell story after story.

My throat's dry from so much talking. I'm dried up, I've become desiccated.

I feel water coming out with my words and spotting the ground around me. I feel I'm drowning in my own water. Do you want me to drown? Reach out your hand, I beg you, reach out your hand and rescue me from the pool of storytelling in whose waters I'm drowning. I'm a prisoner who possesses nothing but the stories he makes up about his freedom. I'm a prisoner of the hospital and a prisoner of the story. I'm drowning. Water surrounds me. I swallow water and swallow words and tell the story.

What do you want from me?

I've told you all your stories, of the past and of the present, yet you remain unreachable.

Now you know the whole story, but I don't. Can you believe that? I've told you a story I don't know. I understand nothing; things are collapsing inside my head. I've almost forgotten all of your names, I mix them all together.

You know everything, but I don't.

I don't know, but I have to know so I can tell. But I don't know the story; I'll have to go back to the beginning to look for it. What do you think?

You want the beginning? This time, though, I'll tell it the way I like; I won't subject it to your distorted memory or to the phantoms that hover above your closed eyes. I'll tell you everything, but not now. I have to go now. I'll turn on the radio so you can listen to Fairouz. Her voice calms the nerves and spreads its lilac shade over the eyes. I'll leave you in the shade of lilacs and go.

Part Two

> <

Nahilah's Death

I WANT to apologize.

I know that nothing can excuse my leaving you on your own these past two weeks. Forgive me, please, and try to understand. I don't want you to think for a moment that I'm like them – certainly not, Father. I despise positions of responsibility, and my new one is of no importance. I don't know what came over me the other night. After leaving you, I went to my room to sleep. And when I was in bed, I began to suffocate – all of a sudden I couldn't breathe. I lay down on my bed, and, without realizing what I was doing, started searching for the oxygen bottle I'd put in your room in case of an emergency. While I was sleeping, everything became constricted. I woke up, my heart was racing, I was bathed in sweat, and the air . . . the air wasn't sufficient anymore. I started breathing heavily, gasping for air, but there was no air. I felt a tingling sensation in my head, in my left hand, my belly, and my back. I tried to get up. I raised my head, managed to sit up, and tried to turn on the light, but there was no electricity. I supported my head with my hand. There was the dark. A thick darkness was drawing closer. I raised my hand to push it away, but my right hand was completely paralyzed. Everything was murky, and there was no oxygen. I thought, "I'm going to die." But instead of lying on my back and waiting for the angel of death, I leapt out of bed like a madman, ran toward the window, threw my head out and started gulping down the air. I ate all the air in the world, but the world's air wasn't enough. I dressed quickly and left my room. I walked down the corridor and down the stairs to the ground floor and then climbed back up. It was what one might call the Night of the Stairs. I jogged up them and down them, panting and running, as though I wanted to prove to myself that I was still alive. Imagine the scene: a man on his own in the darkness running and panting and gasping, running up and down the stairs dozens of times so he wouldn't die. And it was just at that moment when my decision came to me. I went back to my room and lay down on the bed.

So, at last, Khalil Ayyoub – the same one who stands before you – has become head nurse at the Galilee Hospital. I accepted Dr. Amjad's proposition and went to tell him the next morning.

Forgive me.

These two weeks flew by. I swear I couldn't find the time to scratch my head. I asked Zainab to look after you, but I don't know why I couldn't do it myself. I'd get to the door of your room and instead of going in I'd hesitate, as if a wall had gone up in front of me.

It has nothing to do with my new position; I'm not like that, as you know. But I somehow felt I was floating, and I thought that maybe, just maybe, my fear would come to an end and I could go home. I miss my house and my grandmother's cushion and the smell of decayed flowers. I told myself I would go back, but I didn't. I swear it was only when the French delegation came that I dared go out into the streets of the camp. I found Salim then – and I'll tell you more about him – but my uselessness and my fear drove me back to the hospital.

Will you forgive me?

I came back to you, organized everything, and convinced myself that leaving the hospital wasn't worth it. We're back to our old routine: I bathe you and perfume you and take care of you. I'll tell you the entire story from the beginning, just as I promised I would two weeks ago. That was when I left you, sure that I'd see you in the morning, but the oxygen night happened. In the morning, I went to see Dr. Amjad in his office. I knocked on the door, went in, and stood there. As usual he had his feet up on the desk and was reading a newspaper, and, as usual, he pretended he hadn't noticed me.

I stood there like an idiot and coughed, the smoke from his pipe rising from behind the newspaper, obscuring his face.

"I accept, Doctor," I said. "Dr. Amjad . . . Dr. Amjad . . . I . . ."

He moved the paper aside.

"Hello, hello! Please do sit down. I didn't see you."

"I accept the job," I said.

He removed his feet from the desk, folded his paper, lifted his finger and raised his voice: "You'll assume your duties immediately." Then he rang the bell on his desk and Zainab came in.

"He's responsible for everything from now on," he said.

Dr. Amjad hid behind the newspaper again and Zainab stood there nailed to the spot, with no idea what to do.

"But, Doctor . . ." she said.

"You're still here?" he asked from behind the newspaper.

I asked him to brief me a bit on my new job.

"Later, later," he said. "Go with Zainab and take over."

So I took over.

You might think that I took over the administration of a hospital! It's true that I am, practically speaking, the hospital's director, now that Dr. Amjad has found that by appointing me he has an excuse to absent himself from work on a permanent basis. So, just like that, I'm back to being a doctor, the way I used to be, but . . . This *but* says it all. I'm a doctor, but Dr. Amjad's the real doctor! I examine, diagnose, and prescribe medicine – everything, but the patients say they're waiting for the doctor's opinion. And when the doctor comes, he doesn't have an opinion. He agrees with my diagnosis and my prescription, but the patients wait for him just the same. One would think the only thing they have faith in is a diploma. I swear he knows nothing, but never mind, it's better this way: I make the decisions without assuming the responsibility.

I took over the administration of the hospital and am in charge of three nurses. Zainab – you know her; Kamil, who stole the radio but who's a nice kid (he has a beautiful voice and knows all the songs of Abd al-Halim Hafiz by heart) and who's waiting for a visa so he can leave the country; and the Egyptian, Hamdi, who's not a nurse, but we say that he is so the hospital won't seem empty. Can you imagine an enormous hospital with more than forty beds and only two nurses! Hamdi's also started helping us move patients and take care of them, even though basically he's a guard. And there's Kamelya the cook, who's told me she's decided to leave the hospital at the end of the month. We added Kamelya to the nurses' list, too, and I've begun teaching her the basics.

So things were moving along.

I'd managed to get things under control to a certain extent, and that was my mistake, because when things are under control we discover what's wrong – and here everything is wrong. There's no medicine, no serums, nothing. It's as though we aren't in a hospital, and, in fact, we aren't. We're in a white building suspended in the air, and I'm its head nurse and its director. As I attempt to organize things, I am becoming more and more aware of the impossibility and precariousness of the task. When I accepted my new duties, I thought I'd find a solution to my problem, but now my problem has become part of the hospital's.

Hamdi, the Egyptian, was shown the door. Dr. Amjad threw Hamdi out without warning and replaced him with a Syrian youth called Omar. Poor Hamdi was crying as he got his things together.

"What are you crying for?" I asked him. "Go and look for work. You barely earn enough to eat here." He said he'd gone back to Egypt and that they'd thrown him out because he didn't have a work permit.

"I don't have a work permit either," I told him.

He explained that he'd been here three years and that he'd come to Beirut through a smuggler in Damascus since Egyptians don't need a visa to get into Syria. He'd coughed up seven hundred dollars for the Syrian smuggler who got him to Beirut. He'd thought that Beirut would be a stop on his way to Germany. He said he didn't want to leave because he needed two thousand dollars to procure a visa for a European country from which he'd then slip into Germany. Now he'd be deported back to Egypt and return to his village penniless, so how would he get married?

The Syrian, Omar, talks to no one. He's supposed to work as a guard and custodian but he doesn't guard anything and he doesn't clean. He has a little car that he traipses around in all day, and he returns to the hospital only to sleep.

Dr. Amjad told me to leave him alone.

"Don't bother him. He's free to do what he wants. You must understand, there's no need to explain these things. We have to accept them and that's all. They made me get rid of the Egyptian and dug up this fellow to keep an eye on the hospital. So you'll just have to keep your mouth shut and swallow the rest."

"The rest" means that we live in a place filled with security services, each of which is keeping an eye on the other, and we're supposed to deal with them as though we don't know. I don't have any dealings with Omar, and practically speaking it's Kamelya who guards the hospital at night. She stands at the entrance, lets people in, writes down their names, and that's all.

We don't need much of a staff. True, we have fifteen patients, but their families take care of everything. They change the sheets, bring food and clean the rooms. I don't understand why they bring anyone to this hospital; they'd be better off at home. But they feel safe here, or they use it as an excuse to get out of the house. All we offer is free medicine; any cure is in God's hands.

I'll spare you the details of this strange world that I find myself in because you're tired and need your rest.

I've come back to you now, and everything's going to be as it was. Your condition isn't great because of the ulcers. Zainab looked after you while I was away, but she didn't do everything I used to do. She gave you a bath every two days, which is why the ulcers on your back have gotten so bad. Don't worry, they'll go away in less than a week, and you'll be my spoiled child again. I'll bathe you twice a day and won't forget your ointment – everything will be fine.

Will you forgive me?

I swear you're better company than any of the others. I see them roaming and muttering as if they were dead. We aren't dead though, we're seeking the aroma of life and are waiting.

I know you're waiting for the end, but I assure you, as I have in the past, that the end can only be a man disappearing into the cave of Bab al-Shams.

I'm optimistic, Salim As'ad has promised to find a waterbed for you. By sleeping on water, you'll find that your body will return to you.

I forgot to tell you about Salim As'ad.

The kid is driving me insane. I met him by chance, and now he's coming to my office every day asking for work. He's a good-looking guy, and strange, always on the verge of flying away. When he gets up to say good-bye, I feel that he's not going to walk away but fly off. He stands in front of me holding out his hand; I hold out mine, shake his quickly, and then step back.

"Any work, Doctor?"

"I'm not a doctor, and I don't have any work."

He smiles, stands up, shakes my hand again, gets ready to fly off, and leaves.

The young man fascinates me, and I'm prepared to do anything to find him a job. What do you say I appoint him to look after the records? We need someone to put the hospital's files in order. I know Amjad will never agree, but I'll make him give in, in spite of himself.

Why am I telling you about Salim As'ad?

Because he dumbfounds me and has convinced me that anything's possible?

Salim As'ad has taught me that deception is life.

Listen. I was in my office (I now have my own office and a telephone) when Zainab came and announced that there was a group of foreigners asking for the doctor. Amjad, as usual, wasn't around. I told her to bring them in. Why not? Foreigners wanting a doctor, and I am one.

There were three of them, two men and a woman. They spoke to me in French, so I answered them in my Chinese-English, so they switched to French-English, and we understood one another.

The tall, bald one, who seemed to be their leader, said they were a group of French artists who'd come to Beirut to visit Shatila. They said they'd met Abu Akram, the Popular Front official in the camp, who'd advised them to visit the hospital. They wanted to learn about the camp.

Zainab offered them tea, they lit cigarettes, and I was caressed by the toasty aroma of French tobacco.

Their leader said they were members of a theater troupe and were getting ready to put on a play by a French writer called Jean Genet – *Quatre heures à Chatila*. Before starting rehearsals they'd decided to come to Beirut to acquaint themselves with Shatila. He introduced me to the French woman, who was going to be the sole actress in the show.

"It's a monodrama," he told me.

The woman smiled and said her name was Catherine. She had light skin and her short black hair could hardly keep still on her head. Everything about her seemed to be on the verge of coming apart, as though her limbs were joined together artificially. She shot glances at me, and all around her, with dancing eyes.

"The actress," said the tall bald guy.

"It's a play with just one actor," he said, pointing at Catherine. "She tells the story alone on the stage."

"A play without actors?" I asked.

"Just one. We wanted to preserve the spirit of the text; we wouldn't want to do violence to the work of Jean Genet. You know Genet, I'm sure."

I nodded, though it was the first time I'd heard the name.

"He's the French writer who lived with the fedayeen in Jordan and wrote a beautiful book about them called *Un Captif amoureux*. Did you ever meet him?"

"No, I never met him, but I've heard a lot about him."

"Have you read his books?"

"No, I haven't, but I know the sort of thing he wrote."

"He's a great writer," said the bald man. "He wrote a stunningly beautiful text about the Shatila massacre."

"I know."

"And he was a supporter of yours."

"I know."

"So that's why we're asking for your help."

"For *my* help?"

"Mr. Abu Akram suggested we begin our tour with the hospital. He said that talking to Dr. . . ." He pulled a piece of paper out of his pocket and read the name: "Dr. Amjad. You're Dr. Amjad?"

"No, I'm Dr. Khalil."

"And you're in charge?"

"More or less."

"And Dr. Amjad, will we meet him? Mr. Akram said he was a knowledge-able man."

"Tomorrow, if you come by at the same time, he'll be here."

I said tomorrow even though I knew he wouldn't come either today or tomorrow because he'd managed to get himself a job at Dr. Arbid's hospital in Beirut, where he would be paid a real salary, not like here – but what was I to say? We don't hang out our dirty laundry in front of foreigners!

The tall bald man said he wanted to ask a few questions, but the actress got up and said something to him in French with a commanding air.

The man apologized and asked me, if it were possible, to accompany them on their tour. "Catherine would rather we see things for ourselves before asking questions."

"But I can't leave the hospital."

"Please," he said.

He said *please* knowing that I'd agree. These foreigners think that just visiting us is such a big sacrifice that we'll agree to anything they ask. I don't adhere to that school of thought, but it occurred to me that it would be an opportunity to get out of this godforsaken hospital. I'd been a prisoner here for three months, and it was about time I got out to try my chances. It would be a kind of protection to be with three French tourists: No one would dare kill me in front of them. So, I bolstered my courage and agreed. I asked them to wait so I could take care of a few things. I rang the bell, Zainab came, I asked her to bring them some coffee, and I left them. I felt like a little boy going on an outing. I took a shower, put on clean clothes, and went back to them. The girl smiled at me; it seemed she'd noticed the change in my appearance and could smell the scent of soap my white hair gave off.

"Let's go," I said. "But what do you want to see?"

"Everything," said the girl.

The bald man said he'd like to speak to families of the victims if possible. I understood him to mean the victims of the massacre of '82, not the ones that came later.

"The cemetery," said the second man, whose name I learned, when we lost him in the alleys of the camp, was Daniel. He was the set designer and spoke a little Arabic.

"The cemetery," said Daniel.

I explained that the victims' mass grave no longer existed because it fell outside the boundaries when the camp was made smaller during the War of the Camps. I also explained that the grave of the martyrs who were killed after the massacre was now inside the mosque. I asked them which one we should start with.

"You decide, and we'll follow you," said their leader.

We left the hospital. I'd made up my mind to walk in the middle of them; Daniel was in front while the short, curvaceous girl kept moving around, walking around us and raising the pen she was holding to her lips as though she wanted to say something. When we got to the main street, I said, "In this street, the bodies were piled up, in the surrounding alleys, too." The girl came up close to me, raised her pen to her lips and repeated, "In this street." Then she leaned against me, put her head on my shoulder, and held the pose. I tried to move away a little, for that sort of thing is frowned upon in the camp, but she didn't move. I thought she must be weeping because I could feel her shaking against my shoulder. I turned toward her, and her head fell onto my chest. Then I took her by the shoulders, pushed her back, and said: "Let's go."

Daniel asked me about the "vertical" bodies: He said that Jean Genet had described the bodies as being "vertical."

"Of course, of course," I answered. "That happened here." I didn't tell them about the flies; I couldn't bring myself to. I didn't say anything, even though I'd been determined to tell them the story. While I was taking my shower, I'd told myself that the story of the flies would be the high point of the visit. I'd tell them how I left the hospital and how the flares fired by the Israeli army had lit up the night, turning it into a day of blood and fear.

I TOLD THE armed men who broke into the hospital that I was Turkish. I spoke English to them and told them I was a Turkish doctor and couldn't permit them to violate the sanctity of the hospital. And they believed me! You know what they did to the Palestinian nurses, but me they believed, or forgot about. So I ran away from the hospital. I know I should have stayed, but I left crazed into that night illuminated with fire. Dear God, all I remember of that night are the shadows. I ran, and the houses would emerge from the darkness into the light and then fall back again into darkness. I ran to Umm Hassan's house, trembling with fear. I'm telling you now, and I'm ashamed of myself. A man can become, in an instant, what he truly is and then forget. I've forgotten those tears that turned me into drops of water at Umm Hassan's. Umm Hassan cried, too, but she never reminded me of my weeping and my fear, not even on the day when we finally succeeded in building a wall around the mass grave. You remember how the women congregated and wailed, and how Umm Hassan upbraided them, saying: "No tears! Let's thank God we were able to bring them together in death as fate had brought them together in life!"

She said it was forbidden to weep, and everyone fell silent.

Then Umm Ahmad al-Sa'di let out a long *youyou* and cried, "We won, everybody. We won, and we have a grave." Umm Ahmad al-Sa'di, who was trilling and leaping about, had lost her seven children, her husband, and her mother in the massacre; all she had left was her daughter, Dunya. She trilled and leapt, and the tears started. Everybody left the grave and gathered around the woman.

Umm Ahmad al-Sa'di held more sorrow than the grave. She said that her belly was a grave. She said she could smell death in her guts, could smell blood.

The people gathered around Umm Ahmad, whose daughter was standing there, leaning on her crutches. I saw Dunya again today. She was just a pair of eyes suspended in an oval, wan face, eyes that looked as though they'd fallen from some distant place and got stuck in that sand-colored face. A yellowish ochre shade of sand. Leaning on her crutches, she stood wide-eyed, looking around, hoping someone might speak to her. I went over and asked how things were. She said she was looking for work, and I suggested the hospital, but she said she'd spent two years in hospitals and couldn't stand them. She said she wanted to go to Tunis and asked if I could do anything.

At that point I didn't yet know her story. For me she wasn't much more than a lump of bloody flesh thrown down in the emergency room. I tried to treat her, before proposing that she be moved to the American University Hospital because we didn't have the means to treat her. She was a wreck. Fractures in the chest and pelvis. Blood and holes everywhere. They moved her to the American University Hospital, where she stayed for about two years, and it never occurred to me to visit her; like all the others, I was flabbergasted by her mother's loss. Umm Ahmad was the story, and the strange thing is that the woman never mentioned her daughter, as though Dunya had died along with the others.

Dunya was standing next to the wall. I asked how things were, and she asked about the possibility of going to Tunis to work in one of the Palestine Liberation Organization's offices.

When I left, she joined me.

She said, "I'll walk with you to the hospital."

"I'll walk with you to your house," I responded.

She smiled and said she was strong now. I asked about her injuries, and she said she didn't remember anything, or rather, she remembered running through the street, and when she woke up, she was in the hospital.

She told me how the men from the Lebanese Red Cross had discovered she wasn't dead. They were at the entrance to the mass grave, sprinkling quicklime on the bodies, when a fat man discovered her, picked her up, and rushed with her to the hospital. He stood in front of me sobbing like a child.

"Doctor, doctor, not dead. Still alive, doctor."

They threw you down in the emergency room, and that fat young Lebanese man – his white gown almost busting at the seams – begged me to go with him, saying we had to dig around at the grave site: "We may have buried people who're still alive. Please, Doctor, come with me." I went with him, and there was the smell and the flies. All I remember are the flies. I didn't see the bodies. They were sprinkling quicklime over the piled-up, puffed-up corpses, and the flies were buzzing and making insane sounds. The man in white led me by the hand and I doubled over frightened of the flies. They were like a cloud or a woolen cover of black and yellow buzzing. I bent over and let him guide me, jumping over the corpses. I jumped, too. I let go of his hand and fell down and rolled over in that white stuff and got up again clinging to the ground and to the lime and ran toward the hospital. I ran turning and looking back afraid that he might have been following me. I ran with the quicklime dripping from me. I wiped my eyes with my hands so I could see. The flies were creeping into my hair and taking up residence in the depths of me. I wiped my hair and my face and I kept running. When Zainab saw me enter the hospital, she fled. In those days, Abu Salem, we used to fear the dead. We didn't fear those who killed them, but we feared the people who'd been killed. We feared the quicklime. We were afraid they'd rise up and come toward us, covered with quicklime, shaded beneath their cloud of flies.

That's how the camp lived, and the people died. We covered them with quicklime to kill the germs and wiped away their features before throwing them into the hole, which later became a soccer field.

I didn't tell these stories to Catherine and her group, and I didn't tell them about Dunya. I walked with them through the streets of the camp and took them to the mass grave, which is outside the camp borders now, and there they saw three children playing soccer. Catherine went up to the fence and laid her head on it. I thought she was going to cry, but she didn't.

"Is that really the grave?" she asked me.

I nodded, but her dancing eyes and short black hair seemed not to believe me. The tall man, whose name I've forgotten, asked me about the numbers.

"Fifteen hundred," I said.

I told them about the wall and said we'd built one around the grave, but that it had been destroyed during the War of the Camps and replaced with this fence.

The tall man said he wanted to talk to people.

"Of course, of course," I said.

We went back to the main street and took the first turn on the right. We found children running through the alleys and women sitting in front of their houses washing vegetables and talking. We stopped in front of one of the houses.

"Come in, come in," said the woman.

"Thank you," I said. "I have a delegation of French actors with me, and they'd like to talk with you a little."

"Welcome, Dr. Khalil. It's been ages! How are you? I hope your mind's at peace."

Oh no, I thought, what I was afraid of is happening. Now she'll ask me about Shams, and I'll have to lie. But she didn't, thank God; I ignored her words and explained that the French visitors wanted her to tell them about the massacre.

When the woman heard the word *massacre*, her face fell.

"No, Son. We're not a cinema. No."

The woman went into her house and closed the door in our faces.

I was embarrassed because I'd told the French group that the people here loved guests and spoke naturally, and that we only had to knock on the door and go in.

After the first door was closed in our faces, all the others were, too, and no one wanted to speak to us.

The fourth and last woman whose door we knocked on was very kind, but she, too, said she had nothing to tell us.

"My story? No, Dr. Khalil. I don't want to talk about my children. Come and talk to me about something else. Not my children." Then she came up close to me and whispered, "Don't tell them what I'm going to tell you now, it's a secret. Can you keep a secret? Every time I talk about them, or say something to them, they come to me at night. I hear their voices speaking like the wind. I can't make out what they're saying, but I know them from their voices. I know they don't want me to talk about them. Maybe whenever I talk about them they remember the massacre. The dead remember, and their memories hurt like knives."

"You're right, Sister. Do whatever you like," I told her and made a sign to the visitors to leave.

"No, please. Have some tea!"

We drank tea in a living room whose walls were covered from top to bottom with photographs banded with black ribbons. Catherine got up and bent over the sofa to examine one of the photos close up. It showed a girl of about ten standing with her short skirt riding up a little on her left thigh. She was wearing sandals and playing with her braid. Catherine bent even closer until her face was almost touching the picture, but the woman pulled her back and said, "Sit down." Catherine almost fell over, but she sat down silently. When we left, however, the tall man asked me what the woman had said to Catherine. I told him she'd asked her to sit down and keep away from the picture.

"Why?" he asked me.

"I don't know," I said.

"We're bothering them, I can understand," he said.

"We shouldn't have come," said Catherine.

Then Daniel disappeared. We left the house, walked on a little, and he was no longer with us.

"Where's Daniel?" I asked.

The tall man said Daniel was like that; he had to explore places by himself.

"Do you want to wait for him?" I asked.

"No need," said the tall man. "He'll figure out how to get back to the hospital on his own."

"Is that all?" asked Catherine.

"There's the mosque that was turned into a cemetery," I said, and explained that during the long siege we'd turned the mosque into a cemetery because the original cemetery had been occupied and destroyed.

"I don't want to go. *Nous sommes des voyeurs*," Catherine said to the tall man, who tried to translate what she had said, to the effect that it was the tragedy of intellectuals and artists that they had to go and look and react, and then they'd forget. When he read Jean Genet's text on the massacre, he said, he felt as though he'd been struck by lightning; he said he hadn't read the words, he'd seen them – the words emerged from the pages and moved around his room. That was why he'd decided to come here: "I had to see the people so the words would go back into the book and become just words again."

I didn't get into a discussion with him because I couldn't understand what lay behind all that finickiness of his. I understood the meaning of *voyeurs* and said one didn't have to be an intellectual to be a voyeur; we're all voyeurs. Voyeurism is one of the human race's greatest pleasures; uncovering what others want to hide justifies our own mistakes and makes life more bearable.

Catherine said the people were right. "Why should they talk to us? Why should they give us information? Who are we to them? It's not right."

I didn't tell them what the fourth woman had said to me; I felt I had no right to reveal her secret. I also felt a certain pride, believe me, for when we suppress pain it shows we know its meaning. Nothing equals pain as much as the suppression of it.

On our way back to the hospital, we met Abu Akram, and he invited us to the Popular Front office, where I was introduced to Salim As'ad.

You agree that holding your tongue is a noble stand to take, don't you?

They were right not to talk. How could they, after all? We don't tell these tales to each other, so why should we tell them to foreigners? What's the point? And those voices – is it true that the voices of the dead flow through the alleys of the camp?

And Dunya? Why do I keep seeing Dunya, with her wide eyes, in front of the tall French man, speaking to him?

I don't know Dunya. Behind the cemetery fence, I encountered her eyes, suspended in her face. I'd promised to try to work something out for her in Tunis, and then forgot the matter. Later I discovered that Dunya *was* the matter, all because of Dr. Muna Abd al-Karim, professor of psychiatry at the Lebanese University. Professor Muna works with the Association for the Disabled in the camp, and Dunya was a regular visitor. We thought Dunya had found a job for herself, but she hadn't been working, she'd been talking. Foreign journalists would come and Professor Muna would take them to his office, where Dunya would tell her story with Professor Muna translating. Dunya had become a new kind of storyteller, one who tells stories only to foreigners, and she had become a story herself. I don't have any objections – everyone's free to do as they please – but a month after the Carlton Hotel Women's Conference, they brought her here to the hospital and Dr. Amjad refused to receive her. He said that there was nothing he could do for her, that she was untreatable, but Salim As'ad and I admitted her by force. She's living now in a room on the second floor, close to yours. Her situation is precarious because her pelvis has been shattered again. I think there must be some problem with her bones because they're disintegrating. Today Dunya looks like a corpse and needs a private nurse. Her mother visits her every day but instead of helping us, she weeps. And Dunya says nothing. Her eyes, suspended in her thin, wan face, look without seeing, silent.

Dunya talked too much – it was Professor Muna's fault. He had made her into a tool for *fund raising*. Let's contemplate this expression that has entered our language from America. In order to collect money, we need pity, and Dunya could cry on command. Professor Muna Abd al-Karim would make her tell her story, and the *fund raising* went forward. I don't know what's come over us since the Israeli invasion of '82: Every intellectual and activist has started talking about nothing but the international organizations that give out money. The activists have turned into thieves, Abu Salem, with all this *fund raising* going into their own pockets. Maybe they're right! I swear I don't know anymore.

But no.

This has nothing to do with Professor Muna. The psychologist was just doing her job, and maybe she believed that Dunya, being asked to tell her story so often, had turned into an actress. Acting isn't confession and has no impact on the actor's life. It seems, however, that Dunya wasn't acting; she was really telling her story.

I saw her. I was watching the Women's Conference on television when they announced a "Palestinian testimony," and I saw Dunya come forward, on crutches. Her feet struck the ground hard, her pelvis swiveled, she walked slowly and calmly. She was neither hurried nor embarrassed, as though she'd learned her role well. She reached the podium, supported her weight on it, and let the crutches fall with a clatter. Dunya paid no attention either to the noise or to the man who hurried to pick the crutches up. She looked straight ahead and started speaking. And she amazed me. This woman was telling a completely different story. I'd no idea she'd been . . . had no idea how she could have hidden all these things from us and could now be saying them in front of these foreigners. She spoke in English, sometimes slipping into Arabic, which Professor Muna would hasten to translate.

"I ran," she said. "Then they raped me." She said *raped me* in English and then stopped, to let the hall fill with silence.

"They came into the house and started firing. We were wearing our night clothes and sitting in the living room. Our house has two rooms, one for sleeping and the other for the television. When we heard the explosions, we all went into the television room. The electricity had been cut, but we found ourselves going there without thinking, to listen to the news."

She said that her whole family was around the television when armed men entered carrying flashlights. "The light from the flashlights was terrifying. We were seated around the silent television with a single candle lit. Then the ropes of light burst in, and the firing. I fled. I went to the door, which the armed men had ripped off before entering. I walked away slowly without looking behind me, I didn't run. I saw the flares, like little suns. I walked and I walked, then I felt something hot in my right thigh. I started running, or I felt I was running, but I wasn't. I was moving very slowly in fact. I heard the machine-gun fire as though it were exploding in my ear."

Dunya said she was running in place when he brought her down. "I thought I'd fallen, but it was that man. I didn't see his face. The flares didn't seem to give light, as though they were enveloping the darkened faces with light rather than lighting up their features. He fell on top of me. They all fell on top of me. I'd reached the corner of the main street. From our house to the main street was about ten meters. I was in front of Abu Sa'adu's shop when I fell and the faces fell on top of me. *They raped me* and I felt nothing. I thought that the hotness that exploded from my right thigh was blood. Everything was hot, everything was black, everything was . . . I can't tell you long it went on. I was like someone in a coma. I saw without seeing, felt without feeling."

Dunya's face filled the small screen; she seemed to have black rings around her eyes. She spoke and spoke, in a flat, white voice without any trace of emotion, as though she were telling some other woman's story. As though it had nothing to do with her.

Later I learned from Professor Muna that all Dunya did was relate what had happened to her and yet her listeners would be taken by surprise each time by some new thing she hadn't mentioned on previous occasions. The journalists and representatives of international humanitarian organizations would come, and Dunya would sit in the office of the Association for the Disabled in the camp and speak, and Professor Muna would translate what Dunya didn't know how to say in English.

Dunya became a story telling its own story.

When Professor Muna came to the hospital to visit her, she said she understood now. "Dunya collapsed because she stopped speaking after the Carlton conference. That was the first and last time she spoke about the gang rape. The story went around the camp, her mother got very angry, and everyone . . . well, you know the people here better than me, Doctor."

Professor Muna also said she'd been disappointed. "A German journalist said he wanted to do a piece about the camp and the trauma of the massacre. I told him about Dunya and he asked to meet her. She came, but she didn't say a word. She told me the pain in her pelvis had come back and was so terrible she couldn't talk through it. I begged her because I'd told the German journalist about her, and he was very interested. He wanted to hear a story from a victim, but the victim wouldn't talk. I tried to persuade her, but she shook her head, tears flooding from her eyes, so I left her alone and apologized to the journalist, who was very sad because he wouldn't be able to use Dunya's story in his article. Then her mother came and told me that Dunya couldn't get out of bed and asked me to get her into the American University Hospital. We don't have a *budget*, Doctor, for such cases, so I advised her to put her in Galilee Hospital, and you know the rest."

Dunya lies on her bed sleeping with her eyes open, or so Salim As'ad informed me before he disappeared. He said he went into her room to check because he thought he'd heard a moan, and he saw her swathed in the woolen blanket up to her neck and eyes . . . her eyes were open in the darkness, and a white light was coming out of them.

Thinking she was awake, Salim said he'd approached her. "I came closer," he said, "but she didn't move. I bent down and whispered her name, but she didn't answer. I put my ear close to her nose, and her deep, slow breathing brushed my ear. She was asleep with both eyes open. Is that possible, Doctor?"

Salim said he'd been frightened and wanted to ask my opinion, which is, of course, that it's impossible; no one can sleep with their eyes open. But I don't know anymore, anything's possible these days. Isn't your own death a clinical reality, Father, except that you won't die? Everything's become strange. Tell me, is it true the voices of the dead fill the streets at night? I don't believe such superstitious nonsense, but we weren't able even to collect the names of the dead properly. The community committee met and decided to make a list of names. We gathered lots of names but still couldn't arrive at a final record. Differences arose among the various political organizations and the project folded. We don't have the names of our dead, we only have figures. We put figures next to figures, subtract them, add them, multiply them – that's our life. Even the Lebanese journalist, Georges Baroudi, who came to the camp and asked for a list of the names of the victims and learned that we didn't have a complete list, said that would complicate things. He suggested that a memorial be erected to the martyrs. You know how those intellectuals think: They imagine they can solve the problems of their consciences with statues, poems, or novels. I told him that memorials were impossible here because we didn't know what would happen to us or the camp tomorrow. But he insisted. He came back a few days later with a Lebanese sculptor, in shorts, sporting a straw hat. They roamed around the camp together, then walked to the grave. The women rushed over, yelling and hurling abuse. In those days we were still capable of defending our dead. Only when you intervened did the brawl come to a halt. You dispersed the women, invited Baroudi and the sculptor for coffee, and explained that no one was allowed to walk over graves. They apologized profusely and told you the details of their project, and you asked them to contact me to coordinate it.

More than three weeks later, Baroudi came back and told me that a committee of Lebanese artists and intellectuals had been formed to prepare plans for the Martyrs' Garden.

"We're going to call it the Martyrs' Garden – what do you think?" he asked.

I said the name was fine and asked him for details of the project. He said the committee hadn't finalized the plans yet and promised to discuss them with me and the community committee before work started. Then he told me he was writing a book about the Shatila massacre. He said there were only two books about the massacre, both by Israelis. One was by a journalist, Amnon Kapeliouk, and the other, the report of Israel's Kahane Commission. "Don't you think it's shameful that we don't write our own history?" he asked. Baroudi told me he'd translated the Kahane Report into Arabic, but he felt that we should write a book that would gather eyewitness accounts together.

He invited me to lunch at Rayyis'* restaurant in the Jemmeizeh quarter so I said to myself, Why not? We drank arak and ate a good, cheap Lebanese stew. My attention was drawn to the Lebanese man they call Shoukri. He was sitting at a table surrounded by customers, peeling enormous quantities of garlic. Baroudi told me Rayyis' was the best popular restaurant in Beirut, that he went there regularly to meet a group of young men who'd fought in the ranks of the Lebanese forces, and that he'd heard the story from Boss Josèph, who'd taken part in the massacre himself. What he had in mind was to arrange an encounter between Boss Josèph and me. "A Dialogue between the Executioner and the Victim" would be the first chapter of the book.

He asked me what I thought.

I said I didn't know because I didn't know about that kind of book, but it might be a good idea.

We sat and waited, but Boss Josèph never appeared. Baroudi ordered some food and arak, and then he took me on a tour of al-Ashrafiyyeh and told me about the massacre as it had been described by Boss Josèph.

Are you in the mood to hear it? Or are you in some other place and would prefer me to tell you about Salim? I think you liked the story about Salim because he was a pleasant young man, bright, and a real son of a bitch.

Where was I?

Abu Akram came by and invited us to drink tea at the Popular Front office. The tall bald man hesitated, he was waiting for Daniel.

"Where's Daniel?" asked Abu Akram.

"I don't know. We lost him in the camp," said the tall man.

"I'll send someone to look for him. Please come with me."

* Rayyis: president, or boss.

So we went with him.

In the office, I had to translate.

Abu Akram delivered a brief lecture in his awkward English on the sufferings of the Palestinian people. He was followed by a man I hadn't met before; his stomach hung down over his leather belt, the smoke from his cigarette filtering through his thick moustache; he held forth. The tall man and Catherine found their attention wandering, and I translated a bit. I skipped the slogans because they bored me, and also because they sounded ridiculous in English. China taught me a valuable lesson. There I was required to translate whatever I said in Arabic into English, and I discovered that I could dispense with half the expressions we use. Even my way of speaking changed: I started to avoid the lengthy introductions we usually put in front of whatever we have to say and went straight to the point instead.

The fat man's speech resisted translation. How was I to translate the words for suffering, torment, oppression, and persecution that the man used, one after the other? He'd string together adjectives without indicating what he was describing, so I summarized his long Arabic sentences in brief English ones.

He interrupted me to say, "I said more than that."

"It doesn't matter," I told him. "English is a condensed language."

"But you cut out half my speech. How do you expect them to understand our sufferings when you cut them out?"

He looked at the tall man and asked if he understood what he was trying to say.

"Translate, Son, translate. Ask him if he understood what I was trying to say."

"I understood," said the tall man in response to my translation, adding that the aim of their visit was to acquire knowledge. He didn't say one word to indicate solidarity, as Abu Akram and the fat man expected he would. He said he'd come to learn so he'd be able to transfer an accurate picture to the stage.

Salim was sitting behind the room's only table, while Abu Akram, the fat orator, and the rest of us sat on low sofas against the walls. Salim said nothing during the speeches; his glances moved between the French woman and me. But when we'd subsided into silence and were sipping our coffee, he asked me, without any preliminaries, why I didn't dye my hair!

"Why should I dye it?"

"To make you young again," he said.

"I am young. I don't need to prove it."

You know that my hair started to go white when I was twenty-one. My grandmother, God rest her soul, told me it was in the family, that my father's hair was completely white before he was twenty-five.

My grandmother said my father had loved his white hair because it made him look old and young at the same time. She also told me she'd insisted on washing his hair before he was buried. She got a bowl of water and washed his hair, which had been stained with his blood, until it was white as snow. And she wept. My grandmother said she didn't weep until the hair was shining white once more. It was then that she understood her son was dead, and she plunged into a bout of weeping; her tears only dried up when she died. I wasn't in the house when she died. They sent me a message to tell me the end was coming, and I came up from the south. She gave me the cushion and the watch and the Koran, but she didn't die. Her last days dragged on, so I went back to the base in the south. She died in my absence.

Salim asked me why I didn't use a shampoo to dye my hair. He said he had a wonderful French shampoo. "Would you like to try it?"

"No, thank you."

"I use it, look at my hair."

"You?"

"Certainly. I've been using it for eighteen years."

"You!"

He said the shampoo had removed all traces of white from his hair. He then told me his story.

Now that's a story, I said to myself. No one had agreed to describe his experience of the massacre to the French people, so I asked if he'd let me translate this into English.

Salim said he could speak English if he wanted to and didn't need me to translate, but he didn't want to tell them his story.

When Salim said his hair had turned white, Abu Akram shrugged his shoulders as though he already knew and looked at me in amazement, as though I should have known, too.

I asked him apologetically how his hair had come to be white, and he smoothed it with his right hand and said it had turned white during the massacre.

"How old were you?" I asked.

"Five," he said. He said his mother had picked him up; they had both been bleeding, and his mother had run through the fire.

"There wasn't a fire," I said.

"Oh yes there was," he said. "The fire was everywhere, and we jumped over it."

"It was the flares," said Abu Akram.

"No," said Salim.

"Of course," said the fat man. "What's the problem? Everyone tells the story his own way. There wasn't any fire, Son, it was the flares, but you were young, how would you know."

"I know alright," said Salim and pointed at his head.

He said his mother ran with him, picked him up and ran, and they were shooting in all directions. He'd clung to her neck, then suddenly, everything went sticky and bloody, and he'd come to in the hospital with his hair as white as snow. The nurses had been afraid of him.

"In America I shaved my head."

He said he'd gone to America with his mother after all the members of his family had been killed. "My mother emigrated to join her sister in Detroit and took me with her. That was in '84, but they refused to give me a resident's visa. I stayed with her for two years in secret, then I came back. She told me, 'You go back to Lebanon and I'll send for you when they give me a Green Card.'"

"And did she send for you?"

"No. I waited and waited but it was no use. Abu Akram is my father's first cousin. He took me in and is letting me live in this office until my mother sends for me. I wrote her letters, but I received no responses. It seems the Americans don't like white hair, or she's forgotten about me. God knows where she is now. I asked to meet the American ambassador in Beirut. I phoned the embassy several times, but they never gave me an appointment, I don't know why, even though I spoke Classical English to them."

"There's no such thing as Classical English," I said.

"What are you talking about, man? All the languages are the same. There's colloquial Arabic and Classical Arabic and there's colloquial English and Classical English, am I right?"

"No," I said, "but it doesn't matter."

"Do you want some shampoo?"

He got up and fetched a black leather case, opened it, and took out a number of bottles.

"I sell shampoo to keep myself busy."

He went over to the actress and indicated that she should buy some. Catherine took a bottle and seemed embarrassed, not knowing what she should do.

I snatched the bottle from her and gave it back to Salim.

"Forget it. Try it on someone else."

"Let them make up their own minds, brother. Maybe they would have bought some."

"Leave it alone, Son. Forget it," I scolded him in a loud voice.

"Why don't you buy some, Doctor, and dye your hair," said Salim.

"What's he saying," asked the tall man.

"He's selling dye," I answered, and quickly told him the story of Salim's white hair.

"Don't tell him," said Salim. "If you want, I'll tell him myself. But did you believe my story? I only tell it to sell shampoo."

I looked at Abu Akram and saw his lips curling in a kind of smile, and his small white teeth – as white as those of a young child – appeared.

"What? What?" asked Catherine.

"Buy the shampoo, and I'll tell you," said Salim.

The girl took the bottle of shampoo and asked how much it was.

"It doesn't matter," said Salim. "Pay whatever you want."

Catherine took a hundred-franc note out of her little purse and gave it to Salim. Salim took the note, looked at it for a while, then handed it back to Catherine and turned to me, "No, Brother. I was just joking."

"Which part was the joke," I asked him, "the shampoo or the white hair?"

"You guess."

Salim took the bottle from Catherine, put it back in his leather case, said goodbye, and went off.

Abu Akram then explained that Salim joked around all the time, treating his tragedy as comedy; he is alone in life and needs work.

"What did he study?" I asked him.

"Nothing, my friend," he said. "We're all children of the revolution, and what can you study in the revolution?"

"Tell him to come and see me at the hospital. Maybe I can find him some work. But is his story true?"

"Of course, of course," said Abu Akram. "He's the only one of his family to have survived."

"What about his mother?" I asked.

"His mother died, but he insists on saying she picked him up and escaped with him. She didn't pick him up. They found him under the bodies; they pushed the bodies away and took him to the hospital, and there they discovered that every hair on his head had turned white."

"And America?"

"What America, Brother? His aunt lives in Detroit, that's all. Do you think someone like Salim or like us can get a visa for America? Out of the question! He just loves the cinema. He sees Al Pacino's films dozens of times each and learns the dialogue by heart. He puts the films on the video machine and says the words along with the actors. That's how he learned English – monkey see, monkey do."

"And the shampoo?" I asked.

"That's a different story," he said. "The shampoo came after the Ekza.

Do you know what he was doing for a living last year? He'd go out to al-Fakahani with a bunch of small bottles, stand in the middle of the road and shout, 'Ekza for pain! Ekza for rheumatism! Ekza for impotence!' He'd invented a medicine he called Ekza and he'd package it in empty bottles and sell the bottles for three thousand lira each.

"'Ekza!' he'd shout, opening a bottle and drinking the contents in front of everyone. 'Drink and get well! Rub it on where it hurts and the pain will go away!' And people bought the stuff. Then they arrested him.

"They took him to the police station on the new highway, where he confessed that Ekza was a mixture of water and soya oil, and that it was harmless. The officer smiled and told Salim that he'd overlook it this time on condition that he didn't do it again. But instead of leaving, Salim took out a bottle and offered it to the officer saying he'd give him a good price and sell him the bottle for two thousand, now he'd become his friend, and that Ekza cured everything, especially constipation.

"The officer lost his temper and ordered him to be beaten and put in jail. They practically beat him to death and left him to rot for more than a month.

"When he returned to the camp, he said they'd released him because they were scared of him and his hair that had turned white overnight.

"After his ordeal in jail, Salim decided not to leave the camp. He stopped making and selling Ekza and started selling shampoo. Yesterday, if you'd seen him, you'd have understood how he works."

"And is it real shampoo?" I asked.

"I don't know," said Abu Akram, "but he stands in front of the mosque, washes his hair, and people buy."

"What's he saying?" asked the tall man.

As I told him the story of the shampoo, I was looking at Catherine, expecting a reaction, when we heard a racket outside the door. The bodyguard Abu Akram had sent to look for Daniel had returned with him. Daniel came in with three children larking around while he handed out chewing gum and chocolates and they argued over them.

"Get the children out of here!" shouted Abu Akram.

"Where were you?" I asked.

"Walking around," he said. "And, as you can see, I like children."

The tall man stood up and Catherine got ready to go; it seemed they'd lost interest. They didn't ask for more information about Salim.

Abu Akram asked if I'd taken them to the mosque-cemetery.

I said no.

"I'll take them," he said. "Thank you, Doctor."

I was on the verge of leaving when Catherine asked me what Abu Akram wanted.

"He'll take you to the cemetery," I said.

"But we've already seen the cemetery," said the tall man.

"The one at the mosque," I said, and explained how we'd turned the mosque into a cemetery during the siege.

"Another cemetery!" exclaimed Catherine, and her lower lip started to tremble. "I don't want to, I don't want to. I want to go back to the hotel."

I told Abu Akram that our friends were tired and it would be better to take them back to the hotel, but Abu Akram insisted and asked me to translate what he said. He started talking about death, and about how we as a people regarded the dead as holy, and that if Shatila hadn't stood fast during the siege, the Gaza and West Bank *intifada** would never have happened.

I interrupted and said I wasn't going to translate. "Can't you see, my friend, the woman's crying and the man's trying to calm her down, with his pale face and his bald spot shining with sweat? Drop it and let them go."

I heard the girl whisper to the tall man that she wouldn't do the part: "I'm scared. I won't do the part, and I want to go back to the hotel."

I translated this to Abu Akram, and the fat man said he understood and went over to pat her on the shoulder. The moment his hand touched her, she trembled and pulled back, as though she'd received an electric shock, and I saw a sort of fear mixed with disgust in her eyes.

* Uprising of the Palestinian people, launched in early December 1987.

I left them there and walked out without saying goodbye.

Shit!

Is this what things have come to? They're afraid of the victim! Instead of treating the patient, they fear him, and when they see, they close their eyes. They read books and write them. It's the books that are the lies.

But why does the image of Catherine stick in my mind? Perhaps because she's young and inarticulate, or perhaps because of her short hair, cropped like a boy's. I must have felt something for her, especially when her lower lip started trembling. It started when I translated parts of the anecdote about Salim, and especially the part about how he used to stand in front of everybody and dye his hair in order to sell the shampoo. Catherine didn't laugh like me and Abu Akram and the tall man. Her face seemed obscured by a dark veil, as if she'd seen us playing out our own deaths. I think she thought we were beasts. How can we take all that and not implode?

In fact, Father, wouldn't it be better if nobody saw us? Otherwise, why would they want to build a wall around the camp? The Lebanese journalist I told you about spoke to me about the wall. He said the government would soon complete the rebuilding of Sports City, which was demolished by Israeli planes, and that Beirut was going to host the next Arab Games, and it would be better for the Arab athletes if they didn't see.

They solve the problem by covering their eyes. And maybe they're right! In this place, we're a kind of a dirty secret. A permanent dirty secret you can only cover over by forgetting it.

"I'd like to forget, too," I told Baroudi when he invited me to Rayyis' restaurant.

I'd prefer to forget, and my encounter with Boss Josèph changed nothing because I'm not seeking revenge.

Can you believe it? The man invites me to meet with one of the butchers of Shatila, and I tell him there's no point because I don't hate them.

"There is a point," said the journalist. "I want you to come because I'm going to write about reconciliation and forgiveness."

"But I haven't forgiven him or the others," I answered.

"Never mind, never mind. What matters is how you feel."

"And what about how he feels?" I asked.

"About what who feels?" he asked me.

"This Josèph that I don't know."

I went out of curiosity, since I don't know East Beirut, and I'd never had the chance to meet someone we'd fought. The civil war had become a long dream, as though it had never happened. I can feel it under my skin, but I don't believe it. Only the images remain. Even our massacre here in the camp and the flies that hunted me down I see as though they were photos, as though I weren't remembering but watching. I don't feel anything but astonishment. Strange, isn't it? Strange that war should pass like a dream.

What do you think?

If you could speak, you'd say that the whole of life seems like a dream. Maybe in your long sleep you're floating over the surface of things, as eyes do over pictures.

We went to Rayyis' restaurant and waited, but he didn't come.

We sat at a table for four. The journalist ordered two glasses of arak and some hummus and tabouleh, and we waited. Then a group of young men came in. Their hair was cut like youths in the Lebanese Forces.

"Nasri!" yelled Baroudi, who jumped up from his seat to embrace him.

"What are you doing here?" asked Nasri.

"What am I doing? I'm getting drunk," answered Baroudi.

"Come and get drunk with us," said Nasri.

"I can't. I have a guest. And we're waiting for Boss Josèph."

I found myself at their table. There were six young men and a young brunette in a very short skirt and a low-cut blouse. It seemed to me she must have been Nasri's girlfriend because whenever she got the chance she'd put her hand in his.

They laughed and drank and ate and told jokes. I tried to match their mood, but I couldn't, it was as though my mouth were blocked with a stone, or I was ashamed of my Palestinian accent.

Baroudi broke the ice and told them who I really was: "I forgot to tell you that Dr. Khalil works for the Palestine Red Crescent in Shatila."

"Welcome, welcome," said Nasri. "You're Palestinian?"

"Yes, yes."

"From Shatila?"

"Yes. Yes, I live in Shatila, but I'm originally from Galilee."

"I know Galilee well," he said, and he started to tell me, to the delight of his companions, about a training course for parachutists that he'd taken part in in Galilee.

"Have you visited Palestine?"

"No."

"I know it well. You have a beautiful country. It's a lot like Lebanon, but the Jews have fixed it up, and it's in good shape. The way it's organized is astonishing – gardens, water, swimming pools. You'd think you were in Europe."

He said they'd done their training in a Palestinian village. The village was just as it had been, but weeds had sprouted up everywhere.

"What was the name of the village?" I asked.

"I don't know. They didn't tell us, and we didn't ask."

"It was a small village," said another youth, called Maro. "In the center of it, there was a big rock."

Nasri said he'd fired at a tree, to amuse himself, and the Israeli trainer had scolded him and told him that he was lucky he'd missed because in Israel they loved trees and forbade anyone to cut them down or do them any harm.

"They're taking care of our trees," I said.

"If only you could see it, the whole area is planted with pine trees. God, how lovely the pines are! You'd think you were in Lebanon."

"Pine trees! But it's an area for olives."

"The Jews don't like olive trees. It's either pines or palms."

"They killed the trees," I said.

"No. They uprooted them and replanted."

Nasri would throw in a few Hebrew words that I didn't understand to prove that what he was saying was true. He said he'd been a fool because he'd believed in the war, and that this war was meaningless. He was leaving for America soon to continue his studies in computer engineering.

The strange thing was that I listened to this young man who'd jumped with his parachute over Galilee without feeling any hatred. I'd imagined that if I ever met one of those people, I wouldn't be able to hold myself back, but there I was drinking arak and laughing at their jokes and watching the girl as she tried to hold Nasri's hand and he pulled it out of hers, while Baroudi observed me and looked at his watch and grumbled because Josèph was late.

"That Josèph of yours is full of shit," one of them said. He started telling tales of Josèph's cowardice, telling how during the battle of the Holiday Inn,* he threw himself from the fourth floor to escape and ran on a broken leg.

"A dopehead and an asshole," said another.

"Look how he's ended up – calling himself a boss, just when there aren't any bosses left," said Nasri.

I felt a desire to defend Boss Josèph. I thought it wasn't fair to talk about him behind his back and that if he were there, he'd show them what being a boss meant. And as to his being a coward, I didn't believe it, especially after what my writer friend had told me about how particularly brutal he'd been during the Shatila massacre. However, I preferred to remain silent. I was in a strange position. How can I describe it? I really can't say there had been no crimes. We, too, killed and destroyed, but at that moment I sensed the banality of evil. Evil has no meaning, and we were just its tools. We're nothing. We make war and kill and die, and we're nothing – just fuel for a huge machine whose name is War. I said to myself, It's impossible. Especially with this Nasri, I felt as though I were standing in front of a mirror, as though he resembled me! If I'd been able to talk, I'd have talked more than he did, but a big stone stopped up my mouth. Then the stone started

---

* Battle for control of the hotel strip in West Beirut in October 1975.

crumbling to the rhythm of the girl's hand that reached out for Nasri's hand and then pulled back. He was drinking arak in a special way: He'd suck the glass, leave a little of the white liquid on its lip and then lick it off. He had fair skin and broad shoulders. I think he must have been a body builder because his chest rippled under his blue shirt. He kept coming back to the story of the parachute training and what he'd felt while flying over Israel.

He'd say *Israel* and look at me apologetically: "Sorry, sorry – *Palestine* – is that better?" He said he'd flown over Palestine and would look at me with eyes full of irony and complicity.

After my third glass I asked about the war: "What do you feel now?"

"Nothing at all," said Nasri. "And you?"

"I feel sad," I said.

Nasri said he didn't feel regret or sorrow for his friends who'd died in the war. "That's life," he said, shrugging his shoulders indifferently.

"But you were defeated," I said.

"And you were defeated," he said.

"Not exactly," I said.

"Tell me about your life in the camps, and then talk to me about victory and defeat."

"I'll tell you about my death," I said. "You killed me."

"We killed you, and you killed us. That's what I was trying to explain to you," said Nasri. "We were defeated, and you were defeated."

"All of us were defeated," said Maro, raising his glass. "Knock it back, boys – a toast to defeat."

The young men raised their glasses and drained them to the last drop.

"We have to go. It was good to meet you, Doctor. Don't be upset, we'll talk some more," said Nasri, who asked for the bill and paid it. Then they all left.

I wanted to – but didn't – mention the *intifada* and say, "It's true we were defeated, but the game's not over." But that stone stopped up my mouth.

Nasri paid and left, and I was embarrassed because my friend the writer didn't even take out his wallet.

I felt nauseous among the stacks of empty dishes, but I wasn't drunk. I'd only drunk three glasses of arak, but it was the emotion. I looked at my watch and said Josèph wasn't coming.

"How about a coffee?" asked Baroudi.

I said, "Great," and raised my hand to order, but Baroudi pulled it down. "Not here," he said. "Let's go to a café."

I sat next to him in his red Renault, and he took me through streets I didn't know. That's how I finally became acquainted with al-Ashrafiyyeh, East Beirut's Christian quarter that they also call Little Mountain. He switched the car's tape recorder to the Fairouz song, "Old Jerusalem."

"We're enemies," I said to Baroudi.

"Don't worry about it," he answered me. "It's all bullshit."

Then we entered a beautiful street. It was how I imagined the streets of Haifa. My grandmother told me tales of the city by the sea, where the streets were shaded by trees and jasmine and there was the scent of frangipani. "We're in the Circassian quarter," Baroudi said. "This is where the rich people live. They were just translators for the foreign consuls in the days of the Ottomans, and look at their palaces now!"

He said he dreamt of having a house here.

He said that during the illness of his aged father, who was now dead, he'd come to walk with him every day in this street. His father loved to walk here. "I want to die and take these colors with me to the grave," he would say. Then Baroudi told me a strange story about a woman his father had been in love with before he married his mother. He spoke of an old hunchbacked woman who lived close to the cemetery: "She was ten years older than my father, worked as a seamstress and spent her money on him. She had no family; her only brother had died when he was young. My father didn't marry her. His family forced him to marry his cousin, my mother. The strange thing was that this woman encouraged him to get married. He went on loving her even when she grew old and her back was bent, but he would send me to see her because his heart could no longer bear to see her in her miserable old age. A woman with a hunched back, who wore black clothes, and walked as though she were crawling – as though she'd turned into a tortoise. I was afraid of her; I'd place the basket of food at the entrance to her house, knock on the door, and flee. She'd yell at me to come in, but I was scared of the tortoise shell that had sprouted on her back."

He stopped the car, turned to me, and said, "And you?"

"And me what?"

"What about your father?"

"My father died a long time ago, and I don't remember him."

Before we got to the café, he pointed out the cemetery of Mar Mitri. I saw what looked like marble palaces adorned with statuettes of angels and doves taking flight.

"These are their tombs," he said.

"Whose tombs?"

"The tombs of the owners of the palaces we saw along the avenue."

"Those are tombs!"

"Indeed, my friend. They live in palaces, and they're buried in palaces. It's the way of the world."

We sat in Joachim's Café close to Sasin Square in al-Ashrafiyyeh, whose name has been changed to Phalange Martyrs' Square. In the middle of the square is a memorial to the victims of the explosion of the House of Phalanges on the day of the Feast of the Cross, September 14, 1982, when President-elect Bashir Jmayil met his end. The base of the monument bears a large photograph of Jmayil crossed with gray lines. His assassination, a few days before he was to assume the post of President of the Lebanese Republic, was the declared pretext for the Shatila massacre. It was said that his men committed the massacre, in coordination with the Israeli army because they were so blinded by sorrow for their leader.

Pointing to the monument, Baroudi said the massacre was an instinctive act of revenge, and he just wished Boss Josèph had come so I could hear his version of the events.

I said I knew very well what had happened; I didn't need Josèph to tell me because I'd been there.

"You know nothing," he said and told me what Josèph would have told me. As I listened, the cold crept into my bones, as though the words were bits of ice dropping onto my spine.

What did he hope to achieve?

I'd believed at first that he sympathized with us and wanted to build a memorial to the victims. Then he brings me to this café and talks to me as though he were Josèph.

When I think of him now I can only see him in the form of Josèph. After that trip to al-Ashrafiyyeh, he disappeared. He gave me a lift to the entrance of the camp and promised he'd come back with the plan for the memorial garden, but he didn't. The war started up again, and with it the long siege that destroyed the camp and the cemetery and the memories of the massacre. As with all disasters, the only thing that can make one forget a massacre is an even bigger massacre, and we're a people whose fate is to be forgotten as a result of its accumulated calamities. Massacre erases massacre, and all that remains in the memory is the smell of blood.

Baroudi disappeared; he never contacted me again. I phoned the newspaper where he worked a number of times but didn't find him. The switchboard operator said he wasn't in even though I was sure he was there. I didn't want anything from him, I just wanted him to publish our news, for in those days I was living within two deserts: My little desert was the blockade, and my big desert was Shams.

I left the camp to get some antibiotics, got held up in Mar Elias, and couldn't go back to Shatila. In the Mar Elias camp I met Shams and was smitten, and then she disappeared. When I think of that day, Father, I feel ashamed, but I wasn't interested in the fate of the camp, I was running after the shadow of that woman. Something inside me was stronger than I was. Something made me forget everything and nailed me to the cross of her eyes. I was like a madman. You understand; you must have gone through a similar experience with Nahilah. Like me, you weren't married. Okay, well, let's say that your marriage wasn't like a marriage. You didn't possess the woman you loved in such a way that could quench your thirst, and you were suspended between places just as I was during the siege. I used to feel a cruel loneliness, that's why I phoned Georges Baroudi, but he avoided me because he didn't want to get involved.

That day at Joachim's Café, however, Baroudi forgot himself and assumed the character of Josèph. At first I thought he was going on the way he was because he was drunk, but then again maybe he was with them in the camp! How, though? He was an intellectual, a writer, a journalist, and those people don't go to war or get involved; they observe death and write about it, believing they've experienced death.

On that rainy day, however, he was different.

I forgot to mention it was raining and in Beirut, as in Haifa, the rain comes down like ropes, then suddenly stops. I almost said the man was raining! I can see him in front of me through the café window, the ropes of rain around his thick lips, the smoke rising from his cigarette abandoned in the ashtray; his words hurt my ears, and the sloosh of the rain drowning the road that descends from Place Sasin to the church of Our Lady of the Entry.

Why did he tell me all that?

I'm certain he wasn't seeking my reactions – a drunk doesn't observe a drunk. So why? Because he was one of them? Did he want to confess? Christians confess in front of a priest. Their confessions are like the self-criticism sessions I learned in China and tried to apply here. It was ridiculous. I'd call a self-criticism session and start with myself to encourage the others, and the meeting would end in jokes. No one was capable of assuming responsibility for his mistakes, and they'd all find justifications for their actions and blame others. To put an end to the joking around and the obnoxiousness, I'd be forced to agree with them that we hadn't made any mistakes at all, even in the case of the village of al-Aishiyyeh in South Lebanon, which we entered in the summer of '75 after a grueling battle with the Phalangists. Our commanding officer ordered the armed fighters who'd surrendered to stand against a wall and executed them all with machine guns. The execution of prisoners is forbidden, as you know, by the laws of the Fatah Movement, but we found justifications for the criminal error that we'd committed. We said we were taking revenge for the massacres that had been committed against us, that civil wars always involved massacres, etc. Rasim, the militia commander, God rest his soul, went as far as citing Sholokhov's novel *And Quiet Flows the Don*, saying that during the civil war in Russia the Bolsheviks would ask their captives to take off their clothes before executing them so they wouldn't get torn by the bullets. Standing naked in the snow, shivering, they waited their turn to be executed, before falling into the graves they'd dug with their own hands.

"We're more merciful than the Bolsheviks," said Rasim. "We aren't forcing them to dig their own graves or take off their clothes."

That was when I became convinced that self-criticism was useless, since everything will be found to have its motives, its pretexts, its special circumstances, and so on.

Sitting in the café, Georges Baroudi took advantage of the rhythm of the rain with its long ropes to confess. He said he'd recorded more than three hours of confessions by Boss Josèph and wanted to publish them in a book that he'd call *The Banality of Man*. He said he'd brought a tape recorder with him to record our conversation, and that he'd make that the introduction to his book. But Josèph didn't come, so he asked me to tell him my version of what happened, so he could put the two versions into the book. "A page for you and a page for him – what do you think? The killer and the killed in conversation."

"But I wasn't killed," I said.

"You represent the dead," he said.

"The dead don't talk and they don't have representatives," I said.

"Aren't you a Palestinian like them? Look at Israel; it represents the victims of the Holocaust."

"That's the difference," I said. "I don't believe victims have representatives, that they . . . that they . . ."

"You understand nothing," he said.

I told him his project didn't make sense, that you couldn't sit the victim down next to the perpetrator. "Your book will be as banal as its title." Then I burst out laughing.

At that instant, the man before me was transformed. Even his white face became tinged with green. He said, as though it were Josèph speaking, "They took us to the airport – I was leading a detachment of twenty boys. We were wasted. Bashir died and Abu Mash'al gave me a load of cocaine and asked me to distribute it to the boys. We were sniffing cocaine like a snack, as if we were eating pistachios. Then we went down to the camp and began. We didn't take any prisoners and there was no face-to-face combat. We went into the houses, sprayed them with bullets, stabbed and killed. It was like a party, like we were at scouts' camp dancing around the campfire. The fireworks came from above, from the flares the Israelis were sending up, and we were down below having a party."

"A party," he said!

Boss Josèph had come across three children. He'd asked one of his comrades to help him grab them. He'd asked his comrade to push them together on a table. "I took out my revolver. I wanted to find out how far a shot from a Magnum could go. One of the children slipped off onto the floor. The light was burning our eyes, and I asked my comrade to turn his face away. He didn't understand what I wanted, so he let go of the two children and left the house. I went up to them. I wanted to tie them up and then move back from them but I couldn't find a rope, so I jammed them together, put the muzzle of the revolver close to the head of the first one, and fired. My bullet went through both heads, so they died right off. I didn't see the blood, I couldn't see it, in that strange Israeli light. When I left the house, I came across the third child, the one who'd fallen. I stepped back and fired at this small moving thing, and it came to a sudden stop where it was."

At this point Monsieur Georges got into a complicated analysis of Boss Josèph's state of mind, saying he wasn't aware of what he was doing and so couldn't be considered responsible for his crime, and he got into a complex theory about death. Then he asked me if I'd killed anyone.

"Listen, Monsieur Georges, I'm a fighter, your friend is a butcher. Can't you tell the difference between a criminal and a soldier?"

"You're right, you're right, but I want to know."

"What do you want to know?"

"I'm asking you if you've ever killed anyone and what you felt afterward."

In the middle of this maelstrom, he asks me if I've killed anyone! Where does this man live?

"Of course," I said. I said it simply, even though I'd never asked myself that question before. I hadn't killed anyone, in the sense of getting close to an unarmed man and firing at him and seeing him die. But I said with a simplicity that astonished Monsieur Georges that I'd killed.

He asked me about my feelings.

"What feelings? There are no feelings."

Imagine, Abu Salem. Imagine if Monsieur Georges came to you and asked you the same question. How would you answer him? For sure you'd throw him out of your house and tell him to go to hell. What kind of questions are these? Doesn't this genius know that death means nothing, all his talk of blood instinct means nothing, it's just literary talk? In war, we kill like we breathe. Killing means not thinking about killing, just shooting.

Is it possible that someone would come along in the middle of the whirlwind of this war and ask me about my feelings when I kill?

First of all, I haven't killed.

Second of all, even if I'd killed, there would have been no feelings.

And finally, I'm a fighter. Either I die or I live. What am I supposed to do?

Monsieur Georges wanted to focus on the first experience. He said he was starting to understand my response, because anything could become a habit, and habitual behavior loses its impact.

"Tell me about the first time," he said.

"There wasn't a first time," I said.

"No, no, try to remember."

"The first time I saw a man die, he was screaming that he wanted to die."

That was my first time.

Do you remember your first time, master?

I think that this kind of question leads nowhere.

When Monsieur Georges asked me about my first time, I could only remember myself as a cadet. I could see myself running with the other boys with shaved heads and crying out: "We'll die, we'll die, but we will never submit!"

The trainer running in front of us shouting, "We'll die," and us behind him, our mouths full of the fruit of death. That was my first experience – putting death in my mouth like a piece of gum, chewing on it, running with it to the end of the world and then spitting it out. But Monsieur Georges wanted to know my feelings when I killed a man – so I asked him about his feelings. He said he'd never fought in his life. I don't understand how a man can be an intellectual and a writer and let war go on right next to him and not try to find out what it's like.

He said his first time was when he truly saw, and then he told me the story of the barrels in the camp Jisr al-Basha.

He told me he went with them to provide press coverage and saw how they forced their prisoners to get into the barrels. He said the fall of the Tal al-Za'atar and Jisr al-Basha camps had been barbaric.

I told him I didn't want to hear about it – about the barrels that seeped blood, or the prisoners rolling around inside the barrels, or the rapes, the killings, or the eating of human flesh.

I have enough to deal with as it is.

I told him I hated myself now. I hated myself for the way I'd stood spellbound in front of that yellow poster designed by an Italian artist – I've forgotten his name – as a salute to the martyrs of Tal al-Za'atar. I hate those three thousand vertical lines the artist put on his poster. I hate our way of celebrating death. The number of our dead was our distinguishing feature – the more deaths, the more important we became.

I said I no longer liked our way of playing with death.

He said death was a symbolic number and numbers had been the sole stable element since the dawn of history. "Numbers are magic," he said. "Nothing fascinates men more than numbers; that's why death expressed in numbers turns into a magic formula."

We left the café. He gave me a lift to the entrance of the camp and went away. I don't know what he wrote in his newspaper about the meeting with Boss Josèph that never took place; I lost interest the moment I got back to the camp. Even the idea of reconciliation stopped making any sense: The reconciliation has happened without happening, as should be clear from my telling you about the incident without getting upset.

The reconciliation happened when Dunya became the victim of her own story; when her story was transformed into a scandal, the woman fell from grace and all that was left were her two eyes suspended in the emptiness of her sand-colored face.

I believe she became separated from her own story when she agreed to participate in Professor Muna's game. I saw her on TV; I saw how she bent over the microphone after the horrible clatter of her crutches hitting the ground. And she was lying, I swear she was lying. How can you rape a girl with a shattered pelvis? She said she'd been hit in her right thigh, meaning her pelvis, and then that she fell and they threw themselves on top of her – which is impossible. But that was the story the public wanted to hear. Rape is a symbol. I'm not talking just about Arabs but about everyone on earth. Man connects war with rape. Victory signifies the victor raping the defeated enemy's women; it's only complete when the women are subjected to rape. This isn't something that happens in reality, of course; it's a fantasy. No! God forbid – Dunya didn't say she was raped because she wanted that. I don't accept the superficial, simplistic point of view that so many men hold about women wanting to be raped; rape is one of the most savage and painful things there is. Dunya said she was raped to please the psychologists, the sociologists, and the journalists, who were expecting to hear that word from her. She said it, and they relaxed.

That's the problem with the Lebanese war. It entered the world's imagination pre-packaged as insanity. When we say that its insanity was normal, the same insanity as in any war, our listeners feel thwarted and think we're lying. Even Boss Josèph's story – I won't say it didn't happen; it probably did, and there may have been worse outrages. The issue isn't what happened but how we report and remember it.

I'm convinced that if Boss Josèph had come to the restaurant and told the story to me, he would've been compelled to introduce fundamental modifications. He was used to telling it in front of people who believe that what happened in the camps was heroic. With me, however, he wouldn't have been able to talk about heroism. He would have had to describe what he did in a cold and neutral, maybe even apologetic, fashion. And that would've changed everything; even the significance of that bullet penetrating the heads of two children thrown down on a table in a house somewhere in the camp would have changed.

I will never forget how the clusters of flies hovered over me and pursued me. I won't forget the buzzing blue flies over those bodies acting as reservoirs for all the death in the world. I won't forget how we stepped over the distended vertical bodies, holding our noses.

I told Monsieur Georges that "the first time" didn't exist, that there was a beginning only in stories.

You used to say, "Back to the beginning." You would talk, and we'd listen. It was enough for us to hear your footsteps for "the beginning" to return, for things to get started.

Not now.

Now there's no one, there's no beginning.

The issue is war, and war has no beginning.

I was willing to meet Boss Josèph even though I felt no curiosity about him. I was willing to meet him because I'd learned the secret of war. This secret is the mirror. I know no one will agree with me, and they'll say I talk like this because I'm afraid, but it's not true. If you're afraid, you don't say your enemy is your mirror, you run away from him.

I agreed to meet with Boss Josèph despite the fact that I didn't expect to hear anything I didn't already know. The man would start – as indeed he did start – with cocaine. He'd say he took huge amounts of cocaine before going to the camp, so he'd be exonerated from responsibility for his acts. He'd say the Israelis lit the place up and that his superior, who was sitting with the Israeli officers on the roof of the Kuwaiti embassy overlooking the camp, expected something extra special from him. He'd say that when he entered the darkened camp, he was stumbling on the stones and the flares blinded him, which made him fire randomly, without thinking. When he entered that particular house and opened fire and saw people collapsing on the sofas where they were sitting, he felt a strange intoxication, and that he never meant to kill the two children but was just joking around with his buddy about the effectiveness of the gun and then he killed them, just like that, without thinking.

This is something about us that you won't understand, Father.

You didn't get caught up in your war the way we did in ours. You went to war, but we didn't. Our situation was more like yours when you were in Sha'ab, except that we couldn't withdraw. Do you remember Sha'ab after you took it back from the Jews? Did you hesitate even once? Of course not. The only time you hesitated was when the ALA informed you of the decision to withdraw before the Lebanese borders closed. Then you hesitated, but you withdrew with the rest. When you met Nahilah, you told her you'd made a mistake and asked her to stay because you thought it would be possible to correct that mistake quickly enough.

Do you remember those long months after Ibrahim died?

Do you remember how many decisions you made and how often you swore you'd stay? You lived in caves. The earth, the rocks, the trees and the wild animals were your companions, and you said you'd never leave. And when you recovered from the shock of your son's death, you went back to Lebanon and began forging your own path as a permanent journey between the two Galilees. You'd go from Lebanese Galilee in the south to Palestinian Galilee in the north. You created your existence, like a story.

But we moved from war to war. We didn't fight a war, Father, we lived war. For us war became numbers added to numbers.

When the Lebanese war ended, I didn't realize it had. The war ended but didn't end, which is why I didn't pay any attention to the question of what and how our life would be afterwards.

My expedition to that restaurant in al-Ashrafiyyeh permitted me to meet my enemies, but unfortunately I didn't feel they were my enemies. At Rayyis' restaurant it was as if I were in front of a mirror and were seeing my own image. No, I'm not defending them. If the war began again, I'd fight them again. Despite that, I want to say that the real war begins when your enemy becomes your mirror so that you kill him in order to kill yourself. That's what history is. Can you see the sordidness and inanity of history? History is inane because it dislikes victors and defeats everybody.

Take yourself. When you told the tale of your journeys and your wars, when you saw that woman kneeling close to the Roman olive tree in the middle of the red sphere of the sun, you were designing your mirror. You saw your own image in their mirrors. No, I'm not equating executioner and victim. But I do see a mirror broken into two halves, which can only be mended by joining the parts together. Dear God, this is the tragedy: to see two halves that come together only in war and ruination.

I say these things to you, and you can do nothing nailed there to your bed, which has become your ship on the sea of death. I hear you saying no and telling me the story of Nahilah before the Israeli investigator.

"I'm a prostitute. Write that I'm a prostitute, what more do you want from me?"

Please tell me that story again, I like it so much. The first time you told it to me you didn't say the word *prostitute*. You said she said, "I'm a pro . . ." And when I asked what that meant you burst out laughing and said, "Prostitute. You've always been stubborn, you don't understand much, do you?"

I asked you, "What did she say? Did she say *pro* . . . or *prostitute*?"

"She said *prostitute*. She said the word the way it is. A mouthful, huh?"

Nahilah was pregnant with her fourth child: Ibrahim had died, Samir was two, Noor nine months, and Nahilah found herself pregnant once again.

Noor saved her. After the birth of her daughter, Nahilah recovered from her sorrow, and the chronicle of her never-ending pregnancy began: Her beauty would round out, her long black hair flowed down her back, and she'd sway as she walked. When pregnant, it seemed as if she were filled with a secret light that radiated from her face and eyes.

You told me that your lust for her would explode whenever you saw her belly growing round. Nahilah would get as round as a ripe apple and give off a smell of thyme mixed with green apples. She would ripen. When she came to you pregnant at the cave of Bab al-Shams, she'd be overflowing with love and drowsiness.

The incident with the Israeli military investigator occurred nine months after Noor was born. Your mother went to register the girl and get an Israeli identity card for her. They refused to register her.

The Israeli registrar asked for the father's name, and the old woman said it was registered on the headman's document as Yunes Ibrahim al-Asadi.

The registrar said he wouldn't register the girl until he'd seen her father. This happened even though your mother had brought an official document from the headman of Deir al-Asad and had thought that registering Noor would be a mere formality. But the Israeli official insisted on the father coming, so the old woman took the document and went back home.

Nahilah told the headman and all the men of the village that she wouldn't register the girl. "Forget it," she said. "I'm the one responsible for my children." From that moment, Nahilah ceased to be an ordinary woman in the eyes of the villagers: She began to mix with the men and sit in their councils.

Soon after, some soldiers came and escorted her to an interrogation. They entered the house, turned it upside down, and found nothing except the blind sheikh, his wife, and two young children. They took Nahilah and put her in a dark solitary-confinement cell for three days before starting to ask her questions.

At the time the Israelis hadn't yet developed the art of torture with chairs; they invented that after invading Lebanon. This consists of tying the detainee to a chair and letting him sit there for a week with a black bag over his head. The detainee remains tied to the chair inside the darkness of the bag. Soldiers lift the bag once a day to give the prisoner a crust of bread and a mouthful of water, and they take him, with his head still covered, to the bathroom once a day. Eventually the prisoner forgets who he is, his joints stiffen up, and he's crushed by the darkness. By the time he's taken to the interrogation, he's lost all sensation in his body, and his back feels like a sack of stones he's carrying on his spine. He stands before the interrogator staggering, on the verge of collapse.

In those days the Israelis didn't have a particular way of dealing with women. The first charge against Nahilah was that she'd had two children, and the second charge was that she was pregnant. After three days in a solitary-confinement cell, they summoned her for interrogation.

There were three interrogators in the room. The first sat at a small metal desk and the other two on either side of him. Nahilah, handcuffed, stood.

The first one asked her her name.

"My name is Nahilah, wife of Yunes Ibrahim." Then, she exclaimed, "Oh! It's so nice!"

"What's so nice?"

"The light," she said. "The light, Sir. Glory be to God, three days in the darkness and then the light came. Praise God, praise God!"

The interrogator began questioning her in Classical Arabic and Nahilah stared out the window and didn't respond.

"Can't you hear?" yelled the interrogator.

"Yes, I can hear. I just can't understand."

"You've been charged, and the charges are serious."

"What are the charges?"

"You're pregnant, right?"

Nahilah burst out laughing, and the two assistant interrogators looked at her with fury in their eyes. One of them got up, slapped her, and started questioning her in Moroccan dialect. Nahilah couldn't understand a word; the Moroccan words spewed from the interrogator's mouth, fell on her ears, and wouldn't go in.

The man sat down again, and Nahilah was left standing, the slap ringing in her left ear. After a short silence, the interrogator with the Classical tongue, sitting at his desk, said he'd been patient long enough.

"I'm at your service, Sir," said Nahilah.

"You're pregnant, right?"

"Yes, Sir."

"So?" asked the interrogator.

"So, I'm pregnant, you're right. Is there a law against pregnancy in your state? Do we need a permit from the military governor to have children? If so we'll ask next time. I didn't know there was such a law."

"No! No!" bellowed the interrogator.

"Okay, what do you want? I confess that I'm pregnant. Satisfied? Can I go home?"

"We're asking about him," said the interrogator.

"Who?"

"Your husband, Yunes. Is Yunes your husband?"

"What's Yunes got to do with it?"

"We're asking you, where is Yunes?"

"I don't know anything about him."

"How?"

"How what?"

"How did you get pregnant?"

"The same way as every other woman on earth."

"So it's him, then."

"Who?"

"Your husband."

". . ."

"He's your husband, isn't he?"

". . ."

"Why don't you answer?"

". . ."

"Answer and get it over with."

"I'm embarrassed."

"Embarrassed? Forget modesty and answer me."

"Okay."

"So Yunes is the father of your child."

"I don't think so."

"You'll only confess under duress. We have methods you can't imagine, and we'll force you to tell us everything."

He looked to his assistants and said, "Take her."

"No, no!" she screamed. "I'll confess."

"Excellent," said the interrogator. "I'm listening. Please go ahead."

"I've been pregnant for four months."

"Fine. Continue."

"That's all, Sir. You ask, and I'll answer."

"Where's your husband?"

"I don't know."

"Is he the father of the child in your belly?"

"No. No, I don't think so."

"It's not him? Then who is it?"

"No, it's not Yunes."

"Who then?"

"I don't know."

"You don't know?"

"Right. I don't know. Or at least I'm not sure."

"You're not sure! What does that mean? You mean you're a . . . ?"

"Yes, I am. I can do as I like. What's it to you, Brother? I'm a prostitute. What, there aren't any prostitutes in your respectable state? Count me in their ranks and let me go."

The interrogator spoke with his companions in Hebrew; they seemed suspicious.

"I confess I'm a prostitute; I don't know who the father is."

"Do you know the child's father?"

"No."

"Who do you think it might be?"

"Everybody. Nobody. What kind of a question is that, Sir? Can a woman like me be asked who she thinks it might be? It's shameful!"

"So it's not Yunes?"

"No."

"And how can your uncle, the respected sheikh, accept a fallen woman under his roof?"

"Go ask him."

Nahilah sat down on the ground, cuffs on her hands, laughter fluttering across her face, in the midst of that bizarre interrogation, which took place in three languages. She sat and told them calmly: "After having destroyed everything, how dare you now attempt to defend honor and morals?

"You destroyed the sheikh's house twice, Sir: once in Ain al-Zaitoun and again in Sha'ab. Here, it isn't his house, it's mine. This is my house, and I support him and his wife. I can do what I like."

"Stand up, whore!" screamed the interrogator.

Nahilah rose sluggishly in the silence.

"Are there any more questions? I'm tired, and the children are alone in the house with the old people."

"You won't say where Yunes is?"

"I don't know anything about him."

"And you acknowledge that you work as a whore?"

"I'm free to do as I like. You can think what you like, but I don't work and I don't take money for prostituting myself."

"Disgraceful!"

"Disgraceful! You stole our country and drove out its people, and now you come and give us lessons in morals? We're free to do as we like, Sir. No one has the right to ask me about my sex life."

The interrogator wasn't convinced but he didn't want to pursue the matter. What could he do with a peasant woman who stood in front of him and told him she was a prostitute? He spat on the floor and ordered her released.

When Nahilah got back to the house, she let out *youyous* of joy, and everyone gathered around her. That day, she told them, she'd become Yunes' bride: "Before I was arrested, I didn't deserve to be his wife. Now, though, I'm his wife and the mother of his children." She told them what she'd said to the interrogator, and the villagers laughed until they cried. They laughed and wept while Yunes' mother offered everyone glasses of sugared rosewater, and from time to time would trill with joy.

You told the story, but you didn't finish it.

The story, Father, doesn't end with a woman standing alone before the interrogator and protecting you in such an inventive way – a woman wrapping herself in disgrace to protect your life while wrapping you in her love.

You used to tell portions of the story and look at me to see my astonishment and admiration, and I was astonished and admiring – all our stories are like that: They make you laugh and cry and squeeze joy from sorrow.

But let's look in the mirror.

I don't want to rewrite our history, but tell me. You say you didn't understand, and that in '48 all of you slipped helter-skelter from your villages into the darkness. And Umm Hassan says she carried her basin on her head and went from village to village, from olive grove to olive grove, without ever knowing where she was going.

During that time – no, before that – when you were a young man in the Revolution of '36 and afterward, tell me, did you know anything about them?

You were peasants and didn't know anything, you'll reply.

Where was Palestine? You'll agree that Galilee wasn't the issue. Galilee has its magic because it's "Galilee of the Nations," as they call it in books. Today we've become "the Nations of Galilee" – nations, the *others*, or the *goyim*, as the Jews call us.

But tell me, what did the nationalist movement posted in the cities do apart from demonstrate against Jewish immigration?

I'm not saying you weren't right. But in those days, when the Nazi beast was exterminating the Jews of Europe, what did you know about the world?

I'm not saying – no, don't worry. I believe, like you, that this country must belong to its people, and there is no moral, political, humanitarian, or religious justification that would permit the expulsion of an entire people from its country and the transformation of what remained of them into second-class citizens. So, no, don't worry. This Palestine, no matter how many names they give it, will always be Palestinian. But tell me, in the faces of people being driven to slaughter, don't you see something resembling your own?

Don't tell me you didn't know, and above all, don't say that it wasn't our fault.

You and I and every human being on the face of the planet should have known and not stood by in silence, should have prevented that beast from destroying its victims in that barbaric, unprecedented manner. Not because the victims were Jews but because their death meant the death of humanity within us.

I'm not saying we should have done something. Maybe what we should have done was understand, but we – you – were outside history, so you became its second victim.

I don't mean to give sermons, even though I have been giving a few. The settlers who set up the early *koubbaniyye*, or "companies," and who are still setting up settlements today in Jerusalem, the West Bank, and Gaza, don't resemble those who died. The settlers were soldiers who possessed the means to kill us – as indeed they did, and as they'll kill themselves as well.

But the ones who died, they're like Nahilah and Umm Hassan.

I see Umm Hassan wandering in the fields among the thousands of others without homes. I see her, and I hear the whistle of the train. I know there weren't any trains in Galilee; they came later, in Lebanon and Syria, when the refugees were rounded up and distributed around the various suburbs, which then turned into camps.

The whistle rings in my ears. I see the people being led toward the final trains. I see the trains, and I shudder. Then I see myself loaded into a basin and carried on a woman's head.

I confess I'm scared.

I'm scared of a history that has only one version. History has dozens of versions, and for it to ossify into one leads only to death.

We mustn't see ourselves only in their mirror, for they're prisoners of one story, as though the story had abbreviated and ossified them.

Please, Father – we mustn't become just one story. Even you, even Nahilah – please let me liberate you from your love story, for I see you as a man who betrays and repents and loves and fears and dies. Believe me, this is the only way if we're not to ossify and die.

You haven't ossified into one story. You will die, but you'll be free. Free of everything, even free of your own story.

Salim As'ad taught me the meaning of freedom.

I was preoccupied with the French visitors when he pointed to his head, described the child he'd been and led me to the story of the shampoo. Salim would stand in front of the mosque that had been turned into a cemetery, expose his white hair and wash it in front of everyone, claiming to perform a miracle.

"The old man made young again!" he'd shout.

People would press in around him. There was nothing magical or exotic – everyone knew that the white hair would turn black, that the old man before them would become young again. His back was hunched, his legs shook, and his voice cracked as he invited everyone to the show, which took place at five o'clock on the first Thursday of every month. He'd stand there and ask one of the onlookers to help him pour the water over his head. The old man would groan, he'd apply the shampoo, rub it in well, pour on more water, and all of a sudden there he was, prancing around, a young man again. The tremor in his legs was gone, his voice was loud and clear, and his head was covered in black hair. "The old man's return to his youth! A shampoo for every part of the body! I'm the old man who returned to his youth – wash your limbs with it and they'll be young again, every part of you will be young again. Try it once, you'll never regret it." And he'd start handing the little bottles out to the onlookers and taking their money.

Women, old men, and children would gather in the courtyard of the mosque to watch the miracle of the old man returned to his youth.

As you can see, there's nothing to it as a story except that it's a trite representation of the massacre.

Then I saw him for myself.

I went to the mosque out of curiosity, no more. I overcame my fear and isolation, and I went. The youth bewitched me. He played his part amazingly well.

He comes forward, his back hunched, walking in circles and moaning. Then he draws an imaginary circle around himself and walks around and around inside it. He goes around in circles without getting tired until the number of onlookers is sufficient. Then the show begins.

A voice like a death rattle. A back hunched and broken. A face – the face is the real genius. He turns and swallows his face, sucking in his lips and swallowing them so that it becomes a mask, as though he's put on the mask of old age. His eyes sink into the skull, his mouth widens, his gums become toothless. He goes around in circles, groaning, his legs shaking, staggering, almost falling but not falling. Then says in a low voice, "My children, my children. Your old father is about to die. Come, my children." He puts out his hand like a beggar and asks for help. One of the younger spectators comes forward, and the old man shows him the bucket of water. The young man picks up the bucket, the old man bends over until his head is almost touching the ground, and the young man pours the water over the old man's head as he totters under its force. Then he puts his hand into his pocket, pulls out a little bottle, puts a small amount of the green liquid on his hand, and shows it to the people before rubbing it onto his head. He groans and trembles. He asks for more water. His voice disappears. He opens and closes his mouth as if he wants to speak but can't, as if he's pleading for help. A woman goes up to him and offers him water from a bottle she's carrying. He drinks a little, then breaks into a fit of coughing resembling sobs. He raises both hands, and the young man comes forward and pours water over his head again. The water gushes, and the old man drowns. The pool of water around him widens. He gets down on all fours and splashes around in the water, his head dripping. Then suddenly he leaps up – he's young again, and he shouts, "The old man's returned to his youth! A shampoo for every part of the body! Especially . . . especially . . ." and he gestures toward his crotch. "Welcome, welcome to eternal youth!" he cries. Then he starts passing around his little bottles, while everybody laughs and claps and shoves and pays.

The French actors should have come to see this play, *The Old Man's Return to his Youth*. "This is the play of the massacre," I'd have told Catherine if she'd been standing at my side watching Salim's transformation from youth to old age and from old age to youth, as though he were purchasing his life by performing it.

I went up to him, bought a bottle and laughed. When the crowd had dispersed and he'd paid the young man with the bucket and the woman with the bottle their share, he saw that I was still standing there.

"See, Doctor. You liked us."

I took his hand and asked him to come to the hospital the following day to start work.

"You can work," I said, "but without these antics."

"Whatever you say, Doctor," he said, selling me another bottle.

"I have to sell all the bottles before moving to my new job," he said.

He took five thousand lira and said he would come the next day. And he came. He worked here for about a month and turned the place upside down: He stole medicines and sold them, he flirted with Zainab, he told anecdotes, and he went into the patients' rooms and sold them medicines he'd made himself from herbs that he claimed were more effective than the ones we used.

I knew all about it but was incapable of reining him in. He had amazing powers of persuasion and claimed that what he was doing was in the patients' interest.

"There's no such thing as illness, Doctor," he'd say. "Half of all illness is psychological, and the other half is poverty. I'm treating them psychologically. Leave me alone, and you'll see the results."

I left him alone because I didn't know what else to do about him.

"What does a patient need? I make them laugh; they die laughing. What's the problem?"

He even tried to joke around with you, so I explained to him that such things stopped here, at the door to your room, and to Dunya's. But he didn't want to understand, or rather, he understood as far as you were concerned, and he stayed away from your room, but it was different with Dunya. He'd go into her room and do his act and sell her mother weird and wonderful things. She was happy and said that her daughter had finally smiled.

"It's the first time she's smiled, Doctor. Please don't stop him from coming to her room." She said Dunya responded to the medicine Dr. Salim prescribed for her.

"Dr. Who?" I asked.

"Dr. Salim. Really, he's better than all the other doctors!" said the mother.

When I asked him about the amazing medicine he'd made for Dunya, he looked at me from behind the mask of the old man I'd seen in front of the mosque.

"Leave me in peace. You don't understand."

And I didn't.

If I'd understood, I wouldn't have been taken by surprise when he disappeared. He stayed about a month before disappearing, and I never saw him again. I don't think he went back to doing his play in front of the mosque.

Zainab said he'd said he wanted to go to the Ain al-Hilweh camp, where he planned to marry his cousin.

"What will he do for a living there?" I asked.

"Nothing," she said.

"I know," I said. "He'll act the old man there. He'll find a new audience."

"No," she said. "He'll live in his father-in-law's house. He told me her father works in Saudi Arabia and sends them dollars, and he was going to live like a king there."

HAVE YOU accepted my apology?

Salim As'ad bewitched me with his stories and his play and his white hair. He bewitched me and made me forget you. You will, no doubt, appreciate what a battle I got into with Dr. Amjad over creating a job for him. Amjad refused, saying that the budget wouldn't cover it and that Salim As'ad would turn the hospital into a circus, but I insisted and won.

I won, meaning I lost, because he didn't want to work. He worked for a month and then left without saying goodbye. What did I do to him? Nothing at all. I let him do as he pleased, just forbade him to go near your room. That was all. But he's a louse – really a louse – who doesn't want to work. He's gotten used to being unemployed and putting on a show and bullying people into giving him money. What more could I have done for him than I did?

"This isn't a hospital." Every time I made any comment about his behavior, he'd look at me in astonishment, shrug his shoulders and say, "This isn't a hospital."

Once he came into my office.

"What, Salim?" I asked.

"I have some bottles, Doctor. Haven't you made up your mind yet about changing the color of your hair?"

"Get away from me. Leave me alone so I can work."

"Work!"

"Yes. Please leave me alone."

"Work, Doctor? You think you're working, but you're a fool (sorry, Doctor, I say whatever pops into my head). You're a fool, and you're cheating everybody by making them believe they're in a real hospital. You sell them things you don't have. I'm better than you, I sell them the real thing, the white-haired man who gets rid of his white hair and feels like he's become young again. But you give them nothing, just a continuation of the lie. Stop lying, please; stop lying and let people get on with their lives."

Is it true, Father, that I deceive people?

Have I been deceiving you?

You, too, would prefer things to be solved by Salim As'ad's methods, with a little bottle containing a liquid made of soap and herbs. But where am I going to find a liquid that will restore consciousness to your paralyzed brain?

No, no, don't believe Salim.

Salim is just a game, just a play, just a show. The real thing is hiding here, in these two rooms. You're here, and Dunya's there. Dunya's dying, and you're dying. She can no longer tell her story, and you can no longer stand yours since Nahilah's death.

And I'm a play actor.

I'm the real actor, not Salim. I'm acting out your story, and Dunya's story, and Salim's story. I'm acting out all your stories.

If Salim had understood what goes on in this room, he wouldn't have gone away. I'm convinced that the story about him marrying his cousin isn't true; I bet he'll come back the first Thursday of every month to perform his play in front of the mosque so he can purchase an imaginary old age with his youth to help him face these times.

Salim left, and I didn't look for him.

I'm here, and I have a lot of work to see to. I've returned to you, as you see. I'll come three times a day and spend most of my time in your room. I'll supervise the distribution of morning tasks before coming back here, just like before. I'll tell your story, you'll tell mine – and we'll wait.

I'LL TELL YOU everything, from the beginning.

We're back at the beginning.

At the beginning, I see my father. I see him and I don't see him, for Yasin Ayyoub died before I could set eyes on him. I see him as a photograph hung on the wall, a big photograph with a brown frame. He stands in the frame, against the wall, looking into the distance. His tie with its vague intertwined patterns hangs down like a long tongue. Above it are his stern face, his sculpted chin, and his tired eyes. I'd like to ask him about his death. My mother went away and never told me, and my grandmother died before I could find out.

Why did they kill him in '59? Why did they throw him down in a heap in front of the house, after his white hair had become stained with blood?

That was when everything came to an end: The civil war that had set Lebanon on fire in '58 had subsided, the reconciliation was concluded between the Christians and the Muslims, the U.S. Marines withdrew, and the commander of the Lebanese army, Fouad Shehab, was elected president of the republic. Everything went back to the way it had been before, except for us. Everyone was celebrating peace and life, while my grandmother celebrated the death of her son!

You're the only one who knows his story, so why don't you tell it to me?

Before you – that is, before this endless illness and coma of yours – I wasn't interested in him, I didn't love him. I'd look at his picture without seeing it, and if my grandmother hadn't been so obstinate, the picture would be dead.

Shahineh, Yasin's mother, had a theory about photos. She thought they died if we didn't water them. She'd wipe the dust from the glass over my father's photo with a damp rag and place a container full of flowers and sweet-smelling herbs beneath it, saying that the picture lived off the water and the nice scent. She'd pick basil and damask roses and put them in vases underneath the picture. Bending over it with a damp rag, she'd talk with her son. My grandmother would talk to the man hanging on the wall and hear his voice, and I'd laugh at her and fear her.

"You'll understand when you grow up," she'd say.

I grew up and didn't understand.

Maybe the picture died because I didn't water it. Maybe it died the day my grandmother died. Maybe it ought to have been buried with her. I was young and didn't care; even her death happened without my feeling it. I didn't shed a single tear for her. I arrived after they'd buried her, so I returned to my base in southern Lebanon, and it was there that the pain struck me. Can you imagine, I waited a month to feel the sorrow? On the day itself, I didn't feel any sorrow – it was as though I'd been hypnotized. I remember sitting. I remember that I took the pillow and the watch. I remember that I put the watch on my wrist and discovered it was broken. I tried to wind it but the spring wouldn't move. So I took the watch off and threw it in a drawer and forgot about it.

Can it be that my grandmother wore a broken watch all those years – as though she'd killed the time on her wrist? Did she occasionally look at her watch?

I don't know because I didn't see her during her last days. I came and stayed for a stretch of her suffering, then came again after she was dead; I threw her watch into a drawer before returning to my base.

It was there, at the base, that fierce sorrow hit me, and I didn't dare tell anyone why I was sad. How could I? You're living in the midst of young men who fall in battle every day and you mourn for an old woman who waters her son's picture, tells delirious tales, and sleeps on a pillow of flowers?

The sorrow struck me fiercely. Her voice came and went among dreams filled with horror and empty picture frames. At the time, I didn't admit to myself that my sorrow was for her.

Today, faced with your perpetual sleep, I understand my sorrow.

There at the base we built in the olive grove at al-Khreibeh, death came and spoke to me. My sorrow was indescribable, as though I'd lost the meaning of life, as though my life had been dependent on this woman who'd departed, on her tall tales and memories.

On that day I was possessed by an intimation of death, and I became convinced I was going to die because she had died. However, it was my duty to come back to life – that's what I told myself then, and that's what I told myself after the massacre of the camp in '82. I didn't go to Tunis with the others because I was afraid of the death I saw on the faces of those who were saying goodbye. I stayed here and lived death. Then along came your illness to bring me back to the beginning. When I'm with you, master, I feel as though everything is still at its beginning, my life hasn't started yet, your story is still before me to try to unravel, and my father has come back to me, as though he'd stepped down from the picture on the wall and is speaking to me.

Do you know what I did yesterday?

I let you sleep and went home. I lit a candle, took a wet rag, and wiped the picture, telling it I'd come back tomorrow with flowers and basil. I didn't go back, however. It was an absurd thing to do, don't you think? There, beneath the picture, I understood why my grandmother said I was like him, because in fact I really do look like him. I don't know why I used to hate myself when my grandmother told me I was like him. Perhaps because I was afraid of dying like he had.

Where is my mother now?

Even her photos have disappeared from the house. My grandmother said she'd run away and taken her pictures with her. Maybe my mother was afraid of what my grandmother might do to them. Maybe she was afraid the old woman would find a way of talking to the pictures and somehow compel her – Najwah, wife of Yasin – to come home. Or no, maybe my grandmother tore the pictures up so all that would be left to me would be his picture, which spoke to her. My grandmother would say she heard him order this or that to be done, and I believed her. She'd attribute all her orders to him. Which is why I detested the picture and detested her and detested my father.

I told you I looked like him, and I hated myself because of that. No longer. But in those days, when the white was starting to invade my hair, I felt a terrible hatred for that man, and for myself, but I didn't dye my hair. I don't possess Salim's degree of irony. Maybe if my life had started like his, with the Shatila massacre, I'd have become an actor like him. But let's slow down – I also started my life with a massacre; what else would you call my father's murder? True, I was young and can hardly remember anything, but I can still imagine the scene. What my grandmother told me about his death turned into images that haunt me.

I sit and talk to you and hear that man's voice coming from my heart. What does one call that? The first sign of old age? Maybe. I stand at the crossroads of my forties, and at this crossroads the image of that man who left me so he could die still imposes itself on me, and always will.

Shouldn't he have given some thought to his son's fate, which was to be decided by two women – one who'd run away and another who'd collapse under the weight of her memories? Shouldn't you all have given this some thought?

Before going on about my father, and before getting to the beginning, I want to tell you that the temperature you've had isn't a cause for concern. Don't be afraid and don't fidget about on the feather pillow I put under your head. The miracle finally has occurred: I've managed to buy you a waterbed. I bought it with my own money, with Salim As'ad acting as the intermediary. It was the last job he did at the hospital before he took off for who-knows-where. He went and bought the waterbed, brought it to the hospital and gave me back twenty thousand lira.

"From you, Doctor, I'd never take a commission," he said.

He took a hundred dollars from me and gave me back only twenty thousand lira, and everything was settled.*

---

*One dollar is equivalent to approximately 1500 Lebanese lira.

This bed will help. Your bed sores will heal because waterbeds don't stick to people's bodies like ordinary beds do. In the beginning, I substituted a cotton mattress for the hospital mattress, which is made out of foam. Cotton is more comfortable, but it's soft. As soon as you start sleeping on cotton, the mattress fills with lumps. I thought of cotton because I was afraid of the heat of the wool we normally stuff our mattresses with.

And look at the result.

I left you for three weeks only to come back and find you covered in sores. Then I thought of the waterbed, and Salim As'ad solved the problem. He said he could rustle one up, and he did. Nothing to worry about from now on. The cause of your fever this time is the ulcers, not the catheter. All the same, I've decided to give you a rest from the catheter for a while – I can't do more than that. I left you for four hours without one so you'd feel your freedom again. But more than that means blood poisoning so I put it back, in spite of your objections. I expect your temperature to decrease gradually with the ointments and the antibiotics I've mixed into your food. Don't be afraid, we'll start over, like before. I'll bathe you twice a day, apply the ointments, put powder on your ulcers and perfume you. Rest easy, Father, and don't be afraid. I say *father* and think of how you used to call me *nephew*. When you came to visit us at home or dropped in on the cadets' camp, you used to hug me and say, "This one's a champ, a champ like his father." Now you've figured out that I'm not a champion like my father. I'm just a semi-unemployed nurse in a hospital suspended in a void. Also, I don't resemble him in any way except for my prematurely white hair, my stooped shoulders, and my height. My mother used to say: "Poor boy, he'll grow up short. He'll be no taller than a water pipe." And my grandmother would rebuke her and shout, "No. He's like Yasin. Yasin was that way, then suddenly he shot up and became as tall as a spear." She'd talk of the *Nakba*: "The *Nakba* shortened our lives and stunted our growth, too, all except Yasin. Suddenly the short boy became like a spear. We got to Lebanon after all that torment, and there I suddenly noticed, God knows how I'd failed to see it – I opened my eyes and there he was, tall and beautiful.

Amazing how he grew up like that. This boy's like his father, you know nothing about our family!"

My mother knew nothing and would curse the luck that had brought her here and say she hated Beirut, and hated this camp, and hated al-Ghabsiyyeh and its people, and didn't know why she'd married man who was destined to die.

Should I tell you how my father married her?

Or maybe these things don't interest you. You prefer stories of heroes and heroic deeds. You'd probably rather hear the story of how the man died on the threshold of his house.

But I don't know that story.

Listen. I'm going to tell you a story I don't know. My story isn't beautiful like yours, but I'll tell it so we don't get bored.

I know you're fed up with me. This way we can save some time and kill it before it kills us. I'm certain you can hear and are laughing to yourself and want to say lots and lots of things. Never mind, Father, say what you like, or say nothing at all; what matters is that you arise from this sleep. I'm certain you'll wake up one day and discover that I bathed you in words, and washed your wounds with memories.

Fine words, you'll say, but I don't like them.

You like words when they're like a knife's edge. You used to make fun of people's speech, of how instead of stating their opinions directly they take refuge in euphemisms and metaphors. "Words must wound," you'll say. But where do you want me to find you words that wound? All our words are circular. From the beginning, which is to say since Adam, our language has been circular. No matter how hard we try to break its circles, we find ourselves falling into new ones. So bear with me and play the game. Come, let's circle with our words. Let's circle around the sun, let's circle around the camp, let's circle around Galilee, let's circle around Nahilah and Shams and around all the names. Let's circle with names, let's circle without names. Let's circle and come back to the beginning. Come back with me to the beginning, so we can get to the opening of the story.

I see the opening as a long dress. I don't know if it belonged to my mother or my grandmother. Two slender women covered from head to toe by long, ample, black dresses. Two women waiting, sitting on the doorstep of the house with me between them not knowing which is my mother and which my grandmother.

When I was little, I had two names and two mothers. My first mother called me Khalil and my second mother called me Yasin. The first told me stories about the death of her man, the second about the loss of her child after the village fell. Both stories belong to me, and I juggle them, becoming both child and man. You'll understand what I'm saying because you yourself are living the moment that everyone yearns for: You're in your second childhood – helpless as a child, speechless as a child, resigned as a child. Ah, how good you smell! Didn't I tell you we'd go back to the beginning? Your childhood smell has come back to you, your childhood has come back to you. Even your shape has started to change. I'm convinced you've started to get shorter, that you've lost a lot of weight, and that you've returned to that mysterious moment that confuses our memory when we try to recapture our childhood.

Put out your hand so I can prove it to you.

I open your hand and place my finger in its palm; your hand closes over my finger. Do you know what that means?

It's the first test we give a child at the moment of its birth. It's an involuntary reflex. So now you're at that stage: You've become a child again, and instead of being my father you've become my son. I open your hand again, and you have the same reaction, and I'm as proud of you as any father of his child. I play with you and hug you, and you surrender to the game and play and squirm. I hug you and breathe you in; your smell fills my nose. It isn't the smell of soap and ointment and powder; there's something that comes from deep inside you, a new smell that transports you to the first sproutings of childhood, to an ageless age, where we find the beginnings of speech.

I can return there, too, and see those mysterious days that I lived between two mothers. Najwah went away to her family and left me with Shahineh, daughter of Rabbah al-Awad – the leader of Ghabsiyyeh's militia – and wife of Khalil Ayyoub, who was killed in '36 when he was a bodyguard for his wife's father in the revolution. I see the two as one woman. They looked as alike as sisters, the same dark complexion, small eyes, high forehead and long hair rippling black. When Shahineh died, I felt that Najwah had died, too. I won't talk to you about Najwah now because I know nothing about her. I do know that I looked for her once. I went to Jordan and looked for the wife of Ayyoub and daughter of Fayyad in the Wahdat camp but could find no trace of her. Then I got that mysterious letter from Sameh's wife in Ramallah. Then nothing.

I asked you why my father died, and you didn't answer me.

I asked my grandmother, and she said he had been killed because he was destined to die like his father.

"Dear God! How could the dream come twice?" she asked. "And both times, the man dies." The first time was in '36, when I saw, as a dreamer sees, this light go out, and the second time was in '59, when the light went out again. How can I describe what I saw to you, my son? A light like no other light, a light white and brilliant. It was over me as I sat on the ground. The light came in through the window and drew closer and closer to me. I got up and moved toward it, and when I got there, I saw the face of your grandfather, Khalil. 'What's the matter, man?' I asked, and his face started to crumble into bits like glass. He came to me and hugged me, and suddenly he went out. People, like lights, go out. The light that came from the faces of your father and grandfather went out before my eyes, and I said to myself, 'He is dead.'"

Both times, my grandmother saw a light that went out. She never tired of retelling her dream, which took the place of the actual story.

"Al-Ghabsiyyeh was like a light, and it went out," said my grandmother as she listened to her son-in-law telling of his visit to the village.

"Al-Ghabsiyyeh went out," said Shahineh. "I was alone that day. My late father and my husband were commanding the militia, and I had Yasin and his brothers with me. Suddenly they attacked. The Jews broke into the village from the north and southeast. They occupied the house of Osman As'ad Abdallah in the southern part of the village and seized him with his son. Then the shelling started, and we fled."

My grandmother told how a man fell from the minaret of the mosque. She said she saw him falling like a bird. His name was Dawoud Ibrahim. In the midst of the bombardment and the chaos, he climbed to the highest point of the mosque to hang a white rag on the minaret to announce the village's surrender. She said she saw him there at the top waving it in his hand. Then he hung the rag, but it fell. He picked it up, looking into the distance, toward the source of the shelling, as though he wished they'd stop firing for a while. As he tried to hang up the rag again, he was struck by a bullet in his chest and fell like a bird. He hugged his arms to his chest and plummeted. My grandmother said that when she saw him she understood how birds die, that Dawoud was like a bird. She gathered together her children and ran with the others, scared of the tall trees – she kept glancing upward as she ran, scared that people would fall from the trees.

She kept running until she reached the fields of Amqa, where she lived for a while with her children beneath the olive trees.

My grandmother said she lost all her relatives and her father disappeared.

I'm sure that you must know my grandfather because he joined up with you after the fall of al-Ghabsiyyeh on May 21, 1948. He went to Sha'ab and stayed there with your garrison until it was dismantled and you were all arrested. He died in prison in Syria. You got out and went to the Ain al-Hilweh camp, where you put on an unforgettable show of madness that allowed you to move in on the police post and seize their rifles before disappearing.

The story I want to tell you is that of my father in Amqa.

I swear it's as though I were the one who lived the story. My grandmother told it to me hundreds of times, and every time she'd say to me, "You did such and such," and then would catch herself and say, "May God forgive me, I was starting to get you and your father mixed up." I'd enter the story and correct the details because she'd forget names or mix them up. Even the name of Aziz Ayyoub, my father's uncle, that nobody from al-Ghabsiyyeh could possibly forget, slipped her mind when she was telling me the story of my father and the donkey.

They were in Amqa.

My grandmother was living under the olive trees, like everyone else, with her four children: three daughters and Yasin.

Let's suppose now that I'm her son, by whose name she used to call me. I'm her son, and I'll tell you the story.

I was short and round, and no one could believe that I was really twelve years old; they thought I was just a child until the day I returned with the sack of vegetables.

We were hungry. Do you know what we ate during that long month? Almost nothing: bread, thyme, and weeds. Then the bread ran out. Can you imagine a whole people living without bread? We'd gather greens and weeds, and we'd eat them and still be hungry. We slept under the trees, we'd spread woolen blankets over the branches of the olive trees for protection, and we waited. My mother wasn't afraid. The olive trees weren't so tall that she had to be afraid of dead men falling out of them. Her father let her know he'd joined the Sha'ab garrison and asked her to stay put with her children until he came and took them to Sha'ab. But he didn't come, and she couldn't take it any longer. She told her children that hunger had made her ache for her village and she'd decided to go back to gather some vegetables from her field and bring back some flour and oil. She told her children to stick together and to be careful while she was away.

So I volunteered.

"Yasin volunteered," said my grandmother, "and insisted on coming with me. I refused and asked him to stay with his sisters. 'You stay, and I'll go,' he said, and to cut a long story short, Yasin came with me."

We walked with the others who were going to the village, each one with sack in hand. My mother had a donkey she'd gotten from a relative in Amqa. We kept walking until we reached al-Sheikh Dawoud. There the firing started from the rampart that dominates the village. The Jews were hiding behind the barrier, and the firing began. People got scared and ran back toward al-Kweikat and Amqa. I lost my mother, she'd gone off with the donkey toward Amqa, while I kept going toward al-Kweikat, running and shouting. Then, suddenly, there was a man standing in the middle of the road behind his donkey that was moving straight into the line of fire. "Help, Uncle Aziz!" I say, and he says, "Get behind me," as if the donkey were a shield. I got behind him, and, after a while, the firing stopped. I left Aziz and his donkey and went down toward the valley. He told me he was going to al-Ghabsiyyeh to stay there. "I'm the guardian of the mosque," he said, "and I won't leave it. Come with me." "I want my mother," I told him, and I left him and went down the valley. I heard firing and thought, Uncle Aziz is dead and started crying, and when I saw my mother I told them Uncle Aziz had died behind his donkey, and everyone believed me.

But Uncle Aziz, as you know, Father, didn't die. He remained dead in the memory of the people of al-Ghabsiyyeh until '72, when my sister's husband returned from his visit and told the amazing stories of Uncle Aziz. Then people found out that my father had lied, that he hadn't seen Uncle Aziz dead. Yasin died before his son-in-law's visit to the village, so he won't be able to tell you about it. So I'll tell you about it, but not just now.

Where were we?

We left Yasin in the valley of al-Kweikat, crying from fear. Then the bullets became fewer. "I pulled myself together and climbed in the direction of Amqa. On the way, I found a bundle of okra and vegetables. Someone must have thrown his bundle down and fled for his life when he heard the shots. I picked the sack up with difficulty; in fact, I couldn't really lift it, so I dragged it and the vegetables started spilling out onto the ground. Then I slung the sack onto my back and set off."

Shahineh reached the olive groves of Amqa and said she'd lost her son at al-Sheikh Dawoud and had fled along with everyone else. She'd led the donkey through the valleys looking for her son; she held on to the donkey's halter and cried out her son's name. On the outskirts of Amqa, she had to admit that she had truly lost him and, fearing that she might lose the donkey, too, she returned it to its owners before she went back to stand in front of her blanket-tent, waiting and weeping.

She said she was weeping and didn't see him.

Yasin returned carrying the bundle of vegetables he'd found in the valley of al-Kweikat. He was small and bent over – the bundle hid him completely.

"I was tired, my back was bent, and the vegetables were on top of me – I was all sweat and okra pods. I made it to the entrance of the olive grove at Amqa with the okra spilling everywhere. I was exhausted and couldn't believe I'd made it. Instead of throwing the bundle down and running toward my mother, I stood where I was with my back nearly breaking, inching toward her with tiny steps. She was tall and thin and kept waving her hands about and crying while everyone looked on and wept with her. Everyone was rooted to where they were while I drew closer, the bundle of vegetables still on top of me, until I reached her. Then I threw the bundle down on the ground and stood up. Everyone said, 'Yasin's here! Yasin's here!' They all saw me except for her. She kept crying and waving her arms around, and I didn't know what I was supposed to do. I grabbed hold of her long black dress and started tugging on it. She bent down and saw me and fell to the ground as if she'd fainted, and everyone went and got water and sprinkled it on her face."

My grandmother said that when she saw her son, she lost her voice and couldn't remember anything after that.

She was the only one not to see him. When she recovered from her faint, Yasin and his three sisters were around her. He opened the bundle on the ground and told her he'd gathered all these things: "I went and harvested the land, and I wasn't afraid of the Jews." The mother slowly got up, asked her daughters to start the fire beneath the stew pot, and the bustle of cooking began.

My grandmother said they attacked the village at dawn.

The village was half-empty because after the fall of al-Kabri and what happened to its inhabitants we'd understood that everything was over. "But my father, God bless his dust in its foreign grave, didn't leave," said my grandmother. "He stayed with the militiamen, so we stayed. Do you know, Son, I don't know where they buried my father. They said he was killed in the military camp, trying to escape from prison."

My grandmother said she went to look for him in al-Neirab camp in Aleppo. She paid her uncle and his children a visit, who lived in strange barracks the French army had built. They were squashed on top of one another like flies, in long, oblong rooms. Her husband's brother, Azmi, said he wasn't sure, but he thought they'd buried him in the Yarmouk camp and suggested she forget the matter.

"The man's dead," Azmi said, "so we can say he died in Palestine."

But Shahineh wasn't convinced.

"Forget it, Shahineh, and look after your children."

But Shahineh didn't forget it.

She went to the Yarmouk camp and visited Abu Is'af, the commander of the Sha'ab garrison, who was living in the camp alone under a sort of house arrest.

In his tiny house, which consisted of one room without a bathroom, Abu Is'af told her he'd heard shots, but he wasn't sure if the man had died. He said the military camp they'd been in resembled a prison.

"They took our weapons and said the war was over. We said, 'Okay, then we'll go back to our wives and children.' They said no, you will stay as our guests. You know what Arab hospitality is like: We were prisoners without a prison, we were like people abandoned in the desert. In fact, we were in the desert. Then your father disappeared and we heard shots, but we didn't know then that it was him. He did disappear, however. God rest your soul, Rabbah al-Awad, you were the reason for our release. After he disappeared, we went on a hunger strike. Yunes was the one who proclaimed the hunger strike and yelled in the officer's face, 'A strike to the death!' Then they let us go. Everyone went back to his family except for me. They said that in view of my military experience, it had been decided to put me 'at the disposal of the leadership.' Imagine the situation that I find myself in at my age! I'm at the disposal of the leadership, I don't have a latrine to use, and I'm not allowed to visit my children in Ain al-Hilweh. Go, daughter, and take care of your son: Rabbah is a martyr and is buried God-knows-where. Forget his grave and look after the living. Go, God keep you, and if you pass by Ain al-Hilweh, ask for my son Is'af and tell him his father wants to see him before he dies."

My grandmother said she was convinced.

"Listen well, Daughter," said Abu Is'af. "Death is destiny. Someone who was destined to die in Palestine and wasn't able to, will die somewhere else."

He said he'd wanted to die there himself because "Palestine is closer to paradise."

My grandmother said she stayed in al-Ghabsiyyeh and didn't want to move out with the others three days before the battle because her father was fighting there, but he soon disappeared. "I waited for him at the house during the shelling, but he never came. So I got myself and the children ready and left. They were bombarding as we fled, the houses were collapsing. They died: Mohammed Abd al-Hamid and his wife Fathiyyeh, Ahmad al-Dawoud, Fayyad al-Dawoud; I saw them lying in the street, as though they had been hurled out of their houses." She said, "The houses were still standing, but their roofs had flown off."

I didn't want to believe my grandmother. The story of that birdman who fell from the minaret with his hands folded across his chest seemed like an image that had broken loose from memory and alighted in the woman's consciousness.

"That's history," you'll tell me.

But I'm not concerned with history anymore. My story with you, Abu Salem, isn't an attempt to recapture history. I want to understand why we're here, prisoners in this hospital. I want to understand why I can't free myself from you and from my memory. In becoming the head nurse, I've returned to the position I deserve, as the hospital's effective director.

Is that because the hospital isn't a hospital any longer, that, in fact, it's been turned into something less than a clinic?

Or because I saw in you an image of my own death and rushed toward death to talk with it?

Or because, deep down, I'm afraid of Shams? I'll tell you her story later, then you'll understand why I'm afraid. I'm not afraid of death but of Shams, yes – of her, of her hoarse voice when it shudders with anger and passion, and of her body marked by sex, men, and death.

I don't believe my grandmother, and I don't believe history either, but that day I found myself wearing the name my grandmother had given me. She'd dressed me in the name of her dead son, ruffling my hair and weeping for her husband who'd died in the Revolution of '36 in the neighboring village of al-Nahar, and whom they brought back to her in a shroud, so that she was unable to see him.

My grandmother said she smelled the same odor when Yasin died.

"He was basted in his blood, and the odor of it escaped from the cracks of his disintegrating body until the whole house was filled with it, there in al-Ghabsiyyeh and here in the camp."

"Like that smell, Grandmother?" I asked sarcastically, pointing to the pillow.

"It was our smell. The smell of the al-Awad family, the smell of blood mixed with the scents of flowers and herbs."

She ran to her pillow.

"Smell it," she said.

I clasped the pillow to my chest and took in a deep whiff of it; I chuckled and snorted at once.

"It's the smell of henna, Grandma. It's the smell of your head. Did my grandfather dye his hair with henna?!"

She snatched the pillow away from me angrily. "You don't understand anything," she said. "When you grow up, you'll understand what I'm saying – the same dream and the same smell. They brought my husband and his smell came off him and filled me up. They took him into the house for a few minutes and stopped me from going to the grave. They carried him around the house and asked me to let out some ecstatic *youyous*, but I didn't, not because I don't believe in God, as they claimed, but because I couldn't. The smell had overwhelmed me, and I could feel it creeping into my bones and inhabiting them. You have to trill for martyrs, and I've trilled for many. In fact, our lives are punctuated by *youyous*. We're all martyrs, Son. But when they brought him to the house, I couldn't; his smell reigned everywhere."

She recounted my father's death.

When she recounted his death, she'd rise and enact the crime. The truth of the matter is that the story changed after my mother disappeared. When my mother was here, she was the one who'd tell the story. My mother would speak, and my grandmother would sigh. My mother would say the man fell like a sack, motionless, as though he'd died before they shot him.

My mother said she opened the door, with Yasin behind her, and saw three men. Yasin said, "Is everything okay? Please come in." One of them pulled out his revolver and fired three bullets. She said she was standing in front of him, saw the gun and heard the shots. She said that everything happened very fast – they shot him and left.

"I turned and saw him on the ground, motionless. I bent over him. His mother came and pushed me away. Then everyone came."

My mother said my sister died two weeks after my father. "He took my daughter and went away," she said, "so what am I doing still here?"

I don't remember my younger sister, Fatmah. My grandmother said she was pink and blond and white, like the middle of the day, and that the Jew, Aslan Durziyyeh, when he visited us, couldn't believe she was my father's daughter, she was so beautiful and white. The old woman yawns and raises her hands to her head as though she's going to throw the days behind her. "God bless him, Aslan Durziyyeh. I don't know what's become of him."

My grandmother doesn't remember my sister well. I ask her and she says she doesn't know. "I told Najwah, 'You take care of Fatmah, and Khalil's mine,'" so the work was divided between the two women from Fatmah's birth. But Fatmah died; she was struck by an intestinal infection.

"We got up in the morning, and she was like a piece of cold wood. Your mother picked her up and ran with her to the doctor. He told her she'd dehydrated."

I lived alone. My mother stayed up at night, waiting for the moon of al-Ghabsiyyeh that she never saw, and my grandmother wept and called me Yasin. Between the two women I listened to stories I thought were mine and got confused. I would tell stories about my father as though I were telling them about myself. I'd imagine him through my mother's eyes and see him fall like a sack. Then I'd see him in my grandmother's words, see the blood staining his white hair as he convulsed between life and death on the threshold of our house.

But why did they kill him?

The papers wrote that he'd been killed because he'd resisted the police patrol that came to arrest him. My mother said he was behind her when he went to the door and didn't possess any weapons. And my grandmother says the weapons were there, but they didn't find any. "They came the next day and turned the house upside down. I'm the daughter of Rabbah al-Awad and you think they're going to find the rifle? The rifle's there, Son, and when you grow up you'll take it. But they were liars. He didn't resist. If he'd resisted, he'd have killed them all. He went out to greet them because he didn't know they'd come to kill him. The sons of bitches."

My grandmother doesn't know why they killed him.

You, Father, on the other hand, know everything.

My grandmother said you showed up at the funeral when no one was expecting you, appearing among the mourners and raising your hand in the victory sign. You'd covered your face with your *kufiyyeh*.* In those days, the *kufiyyeh* hadn't yet become our emblem; we didn't have an emblem. You came with the *kufiyyeh* covering your face and head and you shouted "God is most great!" and everyone shouted the same thing. Then you disappeared.

---

* Head scarf, usually black and white.

Tell me about those days. Tell me how you held onto the courage of the beginning after all that had happened.

You'll tell me that in those days you weren't aware of the beginning. You continued your journeys over there as though things hadn't been interrupted, as though what had been etched on our bodies hadn't been etched on yours. You moved among the forests and hills of Galilee, continuing your life and returning to the camp. You appeared only to disappear.

I know that things weren't as simple as they appeared.

I know you were a wolf and like all wolves didn't like to settle down in one place. In the early years, you felt a strange wildness and a killing loneliness.

But my father.

Why did he die that way?

Why didn't he go with you?

Why did he leave me?

Dr. Amjad is wrong. Do you know what he told Zainab? He said: "Khalil is going through a psychological crisis driven by the need to find his father; leave him with that corpse until he's had enough."

He spoke of you as a corpse, of me as an idiot, and of our story as nonsense. The son of a bitch! I wish I could rip away that shell he hides behind! Camouflaged behind those thick glasses of his, he's so sure he's discovered meaning in his life by chasing after money. I know he's a thief. He steals here, and he works at another hospital, where he dons the skin of the all-knowing, all-understanding doctor – but he doesn't know a thing. No one who hasn't crossed a desert like the desert of Shams can know anything about life.

Excuse me, Father, if I say that love is not as you describe it. Love is feeling yourself to be lost and unanchored. Love is dying because you can't hold on to the woman you love. Shams would slip through my hands, and she made a fool of me, saying that she wanted me, then taking off for some other man. That's love – an emptiness suddenly filled, or a fullness that empties and melts into thin air. With her I learned to see myself and love my body.

Before, I knew nothing. I thought that love was Nuha, her mother's cooking, and her father's throat clearing, desire that wakes and then dies away. But Shams taught me to be a man, how to die in her arms and cease to exist. Please don't laugh. I don't remember if I became aroused with her the way men do, the way I would when I took hold of my member and discharged it with my hand. With her I didn't have a member. Naturally, I'd become aroused but – how can I put it? – it was more like melting and coming out of the water. We'd bathe in the water of desire and dissolve – but the desire never died. Her water . . . her water would burst forth like a spring emerging from the depths of the earth, and I'd drown.

That's what Amjad doesn't know, since, if he had known love, his life would've been ravaged as mine has been.

How can you expect me to fix my life now that she is dead?

Should I tell you a secret? My secret, Father, is that now, when her ghost comes to haunt me, I feel the same desire that used to take me into her limitless world, and I tremble with lust, and I'm afraid.

But why?

I used to think that Sameh's death would be swept under the carpet the way we've swept so many hundreds of deaths under the carpet. Why did they sentence her to death?

Was it because . . . ?

Or because she . . . ?

But I knew she was going to die, because I could see death lurking in her eyes. You were the one who told me about the death that blazes from people's eyes. Do you remember that girl, what was her name? Dalal? Yes, Dalal al-Maghribi. Do you remember the suicide operation she carried out in Tel Aviv, convulsing the camp as though it had been struck by an earthquake? We were unable to believe that Dalal, that melancholy, meek girl who worked in the sewing workshop, had been capable of commanding a boat that would set her down in Haifa, of kidnapping an Israeli bus full of passengers and dying that way.

That day you told me you'd seen death in her eyes and explained that you could tell the fighter who was going to die from his eyes, since death covers the eyes like an invisible film and the fighter is bewitched by his own death before he dies, and so goes obediently. I remembered the Lebanese youth, Mohammed Shbaro, who we called Talal. You don't know him because you weren't with us during the Lebanese war. That was our war, Abu Salem. I say that in all sorrow because whenever I talk about memories of the Lebanese war, I feel as though my face is falling to the ground and shattering. I could see death in the eyes of that young man, who we called the Engineer because he was a student at the Jesuit University in Beirut. He'd put on his thick glasses, wrap the patterned *kufiyyeh* around his neck, and go out looking for death. He died in Sanin because he'd decided to die. He didn't have to die, but you might say he was trailing behind his eyes. The image of the Engineer resurfaced when you were telling me about the connection between my father's death and his eyes. I know you'll say that my father carried his death in his eyes, I know that it wasn't your fault, or Adnan's, God rest his soul. In those days you were all in a hurry to carry out armed operations, and the central authority that emerged from the Lebanese civil war of '58 had decided to teach you a lesson. My father was the lesson. They came and killed him to deter you, but in vain. My father died and my mother paid the price.

Did my father understand the danger he'd put himself in? Why didn't he hide? Why didn't he flee the house? Why didn't he get his weapon and fire before he died?

He fell like a sack, as my mother said, or he flailed around in his blood like a rooster with its throat cut, as my grandmother said, or he was a hero, as all of you said.

But shouldn't he have worried about us?

I know you didn't worry about your children, but why didn't he?

Tell me, what was this life you led? You left your children with a woman on her own over there, and you were between here and there, wearing your heroism on your sleeve the way heroes do.

Tell me, is that what heroism's about? You abandon your children to fear and despair and march off to die?

I told you I hated my father and lived alone with my grandmother. Do you know what it means for a person to live in a vacuum? Do you know why my mother left me, and where she went?

You want the beginning!

That's the beginning. The beginning, Father, is death. In the beginning my father died, and my mother disappeared. My grandmother knows why she disappeared, and I'm certain she encouraged her to flee; she may have even given her a push. After the death of my little sister, Fatmah, my mother spent five years with us, weeping. Then she disappeared. I don't remember the day because I didn't notice her absence. Then it seemed as though it had always been that way. My grandmother said my mother had gone to visit relatives in Jordan, and the visit had turned into a long one. The woman disappeared as though she'd never been, and when I became aware of her absence, it was too late. I used to long for her at night. Just at night, I used to feel like something was gnawing at my chest. I'd get up from the mattress and go to hers, and not find her. I'd sleep next to her when she wasn't there. Then my grandmother decided to rearrange the house. She bought two beds, one for her and one for me, and my mother didn't have a place anymore, and I could no longer go to her mattress at night to sleep next to her or smell the scent of her hair. No, no, nothing happened the way it was supposed to happen, like my coming back to the house, for example, and not finding her, bawling, rousing the neighbors and everyone setting out to search for her; my grandmother bawling, surrounded by women giving me pitying looks, and one of them saying, "Poor boy, no father and no mother!" No, nothing like that. I told you, I don't remember the day she disappeared because I didn't notice, and then I sort of got used to it. My grandmother never told me what had happened, but I understood my mother wasn't going to come back.

"She's gone to her family," the old woman said.

"Aren't we her family?" I'd asked her in amazement.

I don't remember if she answered, or had ever wanted to speak about the matter. My mother's phantom would hover over me at night, and the pain would gnaw at me. Then the light would come and she'd disappear.

Yes, I lived an ordinary life. I thought that everyone was like everyone else and all houses were like all other houses. I was sure that the memories of this faraway razed village were memory itself, and that my grandmother and my aunts were all the women there were.

But why were my aunts like that? Why did they refer to me as "Najwah's son"? Was it because I was dark-skinned like her or because they wanted to erase the image of my father from their lives?

My grandmother said that Lebanon was, in spite of everything, the beginning of a change for the better. She said her daughters married in Lebanon within two years: "We came to Lebanon, my daughters got married, each one went her own way, and I'm still waiting to find my own path."

"And what's your path, Grandma?"

"My path is the one that will take us back."

"Where will we go back to, Grandma?"

"We'll go back to al-Ghabsiyyeh."

"When are we going to go?"

"How should I know? But my heart tells me I'm not going to die here. I'm going to go back and put my head next to that man's and close my eyes and rest."

"We get no rest," she said. "Since that day, we've been going from place to place like gypsies." She said she picked up her children and ran. She said she saw the man fall from the minaret like a bird. She said she heard the screams of the dead, but she didn't look back and found herself in the midst of throngs of people on the outskirts of Amqa, and there, among the olive trees, she set up her tent made from two woolen blankets and lived for three months. Then she found herself among those going from Amqa to Yanouh, and from Yanouh to Tarshiha, and from Tarshiha to Deir al-Qasi, and from Deir al-Qasi to Beit Lif, and from Beit Lif to al-Mansourah, and from al-Mansourah to al-Rashidiyyeh, and from al-Rashidiyyeh to Burj al-Barajneh, and from Burj al-Barajneh to Shatila.

My grandmother said the journey had been long and that she'd believed the exodus from one village to the next would eventually bring her back to al-Ghabsiyyeh, but she found herself in Lebanon. And in Lebanon, fate took her three daughters by storm and they married, and she was left on her own with her husband-son until she married him to Najwah.

I saw my grandmother's sisters only rarely. My grandmother used to visit them three times a week at the Ain al-Hilweh camp, but she didn't take me with her, and they didn't come to us. Though, in those last days, when I was summoned from the south as she succumbed to her final illness, I went to see her and they were seated around her. She gestured to them to leave the room. They went out, indignation written all over their faces, and I was left alone with her. That was the day she gave me her bequest. She tried to say something but couldn't, the words emerging in fragments from her lips like unconnected letters. The words broke up into letters and the letters rang in my ears as I bent over her trying to understand, but all I could understand was that these things were for me: the watch that didn't work, the pillow of flowers, and the Koran. I nodded to show I accepted them, she put her hand on my head to bless me, and I heard her say, "Yasin." I pulled away. At the moment of truth, the woman revealed the secret of her relationship with me: she didn't know that I wasn't Yasin, that I didn't love Yasin and that I didn't want to be him. I'm a different man, and I don't resemble that photograph. I'm not a picture hung on the wall. At that moment I hated everything, and I decided to leave the base in the south and go abroad. I don't want to die the way my father died, and I don't want to become the captive of this mysterious village I've never seen or of al-Ghabsiyyeh's moon when it's full or of the man who hanged himself from the lotus tree.

I left her room after putting the watch in my pocket and let my aunt Munirah take the Koran from my hand. I sat in the living room listening to my aunt's husband.

"What's this?"

He questioned me about my grandmother Umm Yasin's bequest. Taking me by the hand and sitting me down next to him, he started telling his story. A man of about forty-five with a bald patch that shone as though he rubbed it with olive oil, and a face full of pimples and pock marks, and a hand that trembled, holding a lit cigarette.

"Come and listen," he said. "This is a story you must hear."

Ahmad Ali al-Jashi began his story. I forgot about my grandmother dying in the next room, my hatred for Yasin, and my decision to go abroad, and I traveled with his words. Like a small child, that bald man told me with his eyes and his tears what his words could not. He spoke of his uncle Mohammed, who now lives in Kafar Yasif, and how he'd visited him the previous month and they'd gone together to al-Ghabsiyyeh.

I tell you, my dear friend, when I listened to Umm Hassan telling the same story before she died, I saw things flickering in front of me as though I knew the place. At the time I didn't understand my feeling of having already lived that moment, of already knowing the story.

Umm Hassan told me about the lotus tree, and about the candles and the cattle that fill the village mosque, and I shook my head as though I already knew what she was telling me and what she was about to tell me. The fact is, it was this man who turned into a child before me with his eyes and his tears; he's the one who took me there, fed me prickly pears and gave me water to drink from "the Bubbler."

My grandmother's dying in her room, I'm fidgeting inside my hatred of the place, the people, the prayers and the incense, and this bald man takes me by the hand, sits me down at his side and forces me to listen to his story. Then my grandmother dies, and I forget the story. And after about twenty years, along comes Umm Hassan and tells me the same story, which makes me see the man's words as though I'd actually been there. I see the village square and its narrow streets, and I follow the words of Umm Hassan in my memory, interrupting her to say, "No. The Bubbler isn't near the mosque, Umm Hassan. The Bubbler's near the orchards." She'd respond: "How foolish I am! I'm getting al-Ghabsiyyeh mixed up with al-Kweikat," bringing her hand to my brow, caressing my face, and then leaving me.

The man said he went to visit his uncle in the village of Kafar Yasif and that it was very easy to do. The uncle got him a permit, he went to Jordan by car, crossed the bridge, and found himself standing in front of his uncle and his nephews, who took him to Kafar Yasif.

The man said he visited the whole of Palestine – Haifa, Jaffa, Acre, Jerusalem, Tel Aviv, everywhere. But he wanted to tell me about al-Ghabsiyyeh. He said the moment he arrived in the square at al-Ghabsiyyeh, he fell to the ground spontaneously. "I started kissing the ground, and my tears were falling. I stayed like that for about five minutes, then I told my uncle, 'I want to see our house.' 'You won't recognize your house,' he said to me. We stood in the square, and I walked toward the west. There was grass all around me and they'd planted pines to hide the features of the place. My uncle said, 'Don't go. There are vipers and scorpions.' I walked through the plants, and the houses looked as though they'd been planted in the middle of the green grass. I stopped in front of our house but didn't go in. The stone walls were still intact, but the roof was gone and there was grass growing inside the house and out of the walls themselves, as though the grass were eating the walls. I rested my head on the wall, and I felt a hand on my shoulder. I jumped. My uncle said, 'Let's go.' I told him, 'This is our house.' 'I know,' he said. 'But we have come back to live here.' 'It's forbidden,' he said. 'Even visits are forbidden. Come on, let's go, Son.' And we left. There were nettles on my clothes. I don't know why nettles grow so well inside houses. I told my uncle, 'We have an orchard. I want to see it.' I turned northward, and he walked at my side. I told him, 'Please, don't show me the way, Uncle,' and he said, 'Very well.' I arrived at a rusty iron gate, looked around, and sensed it was there. There's a way of recognizing our orchard. It has a *muzawi* winter fig tree whose fruit is shaped like pears. I saw the fig tree and told him, 'This is our orchard.' My uncle picked a fig – fig season was past – saying to me, 'A bit of what's yours.' I ate the fig, and afterward we picked a few prickly pears and ate them. Then he said, 'Come on, let's go back.' I said, 'No.' There's a gap in the wall between our orchard and the Hammad family's orchard. I used to slip through and steal pomegranates from them. I searched and found the opening, and I slipped through and found myself, as if by magic, in front of the pomegranate tree. I started picking. The tree was full of fruit. I told him, 'Come and pick with me.' As I was picking, I could hear my uncle's voice calling for me and asking, 'Where did you go through?' And I answered, 'Through the gap in the wall.' 'I don't see a gap,' he said. I took off my coat, filled it with pomegranates, and told him, 'Here I come.' And guess what happened – I couldn't find the gap either, as though the wall had closed up before my eyes. He was shouting from one side and I was shouting from the other, carrying the coat full of pomegranates and telling him to be patient. He was searching for me and I was searching for him. I don't know how much time passed, but I stopped hearing his foot-steps, and his voice disappeared. I was afraid. I thought, I'm on my own, and if the Jews come now, what would I say? I threw the pomegranates aside, keeping one with me, which I put in the pocket of my coat, and I shouted to him, 'Let's meet at the mosque!'"

Ahmad Ali al-Jashi told me how he'd gone around the whole village before reaching the mosque, and how he'd been afraid the weeds would devour him, and how he heard something panting and it scared him, and how he decided never to go back to al-Ghabsiyyeh again.

"Then I found the gap in the wall," he said.

He said he walked a lot but kept looking back, for the pomegranate tree was his only landmark in the middle of that obliterated landscape. He returned to the tree, walked three steps backward and found himself in front of the opening. He jumped through it and was in their orchard. From there he returned to the mosque to find his uncle waiting for him.

Ahmad Ali al-Jashi said al-Ghabsiyyeh was the way it had always been.

He said it had been waiting for him.

He said most of the olive and carob trees had been cut down, but we'd plant new ones.

He said it wouldn't take much work. We'd pick ourselves up and go. What could they do to us? We'd pitch our tents there the same as we'd pitched them here and wait until we'd rebuilt the houses that had been knocked down.

He said they hadn't really been knocked down, it was just the earthen roofs that had collapsed, and we could rebuild them in days.

He said and he said and he said, his bald patch shining like oil, and I listened to him with half an ear. I thought, People like that never tire of repeating the same thing, they live in the past. Why don't we pay attention to our present? Why must we remain prisoners of a past that overshadows us?

Then he asked me about the base in South Lebanon and said that, if I wanted, he could come down there so we could go to al-Ghabsiyyeh together. "It won't be a military operation," he said. "Fighting isn't the point. I'll take you there so you can see your village. Wouldn't you like to see your village?"

When he said the words *your village*, we heard a wail from my grandmother's room and realized the woman was dead. None of the men moved, but their tears flowed copiously, as though they'd been waiting for a signal, and the signal had come from my grandmother's room. No one said a word, and no one went into the room. They were sure the end they'd been waiting for had come, and the crying began.

My aunt's husband wiped the tears away with his hand and whispered into my ear his suspect question: "What are you going to do with the house?"

"What house?" I asked, thinking he was continuing the conversation about our houses in the village.

"This house," he said.

"Nothing," I said.

"You don't want to sell it?" he asked.

"Why would I want to sell it?"

"Because you live on the base, and my son is coming next year to study at the university in Beirut. I'll buy it."

"No, I'm not going to sell my house."

He said he was ready to give me whatever sum I named on the spot.

I told him that I didn't need money, and I wasn't going to sell my house.

The man stood up, joined the men's circle, and resumed his weeping. Then my aunt came out of the room, silenced everyone with a flourish of her hand and announced that the woman wasn't dead. The sobbing came to a sudden halt, the men returned to their conversation, and my uncle his story. Me, I decided to go back to the base. It seemed the woman was never going to die, and I had to get back.

My grandmother died in my absence, as my father had.

Why does the memory of my father come back when I want to root it out?

The fact is, I did root it out long ago and had forgotten about it, and the only reason it's come back is you, because you want the story to go "back to the beginning." I don't know the beginning of the story. It's not mine; I didn't move from village to village, or go back to the field in Amqa carrying a bundle of vegetables on my back, or hide among the stalks, and I don't know Aslan Durziyyeh and his son, Simon, or the story of the crime in Wadi Abu Jmil.

All the same, he comes back and haunts me.

It's as though that woman who raised me on the smell of decaying flowers had slipped me into the skin of another man and handed me another name. It's as though I'd become the Other that I'd never been.

My grandmother said the days passed. "I was like everyone else. I worked the land my husband had left me. Actually, I worked the land before and after he died – he, God bless him, was a fighter, meaning that he'd leave me and go off. If I hadn't cultivated the land and looked after the olive trees, well, we'd have died of hunger. God rest his soul, he was full of talk, a peasant who didn't know how to work the land and whose head was stuffed with gunpowder and weapons. We peasants don't fight. I told them we don't know how to fight, that the Arab armies were going to come lead the battles. But he didn't want to listen to me. He would take off and occasionally return from further and further away, and then he died, and that was the end of him. It was my father's fault. He was their commander, and he married me to Khalil without consulting me. One day, he came to say that they'd read the first surah of the Koran, the *Fatihah*, and that the wedding would be the next day. The wedding took place and I had a god-awful time. I lived with him for five years, bore three girls and a boy, and then my husband went off. The girls worked with me in the fields, and the boy we sent to the school in Acre."

When Yasin finished his Koran lessons in the village, his mother sent him to Acre, where he joined the fourth grade class of its elementary school. In Acre, he stayed at the house of Yusef Effendi Tobil. This Yusef Tobil owned the oil press in the village and a small shop in Acre, and only came to the village in October and November, when he would press his olives and those of the peasants and then return to Acre.

"Your father, God rest his soul, would help with the oil pressing and then go back to Acre. He only studied in Acre for two years. He'd come to the village every Friday. He'd pass by the mosque and say his prayers before coming to the house, where he'd open his books and read. I barely saw him. I'd ask him about his life in Acre, and he'd read in a loud voice to make me stop talking. I tried to read his books, but I couldn't. We knew how to read the Koran: We could open the Koran and read easily, but the books your father brought were impossible. My daughters and I tried to read them, but we couldn't, even though they were written in Arabic. In those days, God help me, I used to think there was an Arabic language for men and another for women. Our language was the verses and chapters of the Koran, and God knows where theirs came from. Yusef Effendi, God bless him, persuaded me to send my son to school. He said, 'Your son's a beacon of intelligence, Shahineh, and he must go with me to Acre.' I told him, 'The boy'll be scared there because he's never seen the sea in his life.' Yusef Effendi laughed and said the sea was the most beautiful thing in the world, and he'd teach him to swim. 'The sea of life is harder than the sea of Acre,' he said and took the boy. Yasin lived with them as though he were a member of the family, eating with them and sleeping in their house. He would go to school in the morning and help Mr. Yusef in his shop in the afternoon. I thought the boy would do as well in life as he did in school, but, poor boy, he only studied in Acre for two years. Then the catastrophes began: The war came to Galilee, and we started running from village to village until we reached Lebanon."

My father, dear Yunes, didn't understand what was going on. He was young and short and plump. He carried the vegetables on his back and stood watching his mother cry, and then resumed the exodus with her until they reached Tarshiha, and in Tarshiha he died. No, he didn't die, but he saw death with his own eyes when the house collapsed on his head as the Israeli planes bombarded the town.

"In Tarshiha we lived in the house of Ali Hammoud, who'd fought with my father," said my grandmother. "Yasin stopped going to school, and I worked in the olive groves with Ali Hammoud's wives, and we waited for the ALA, of which there was news everywhere, and we said to ourselves, 'Things are fine.' How were they fine? We lived like dogs. True, Ali Hammoud offered us a house, and true, we worked in the olive groves, but God, we were so hungry. I never slept a night in Tarshiha with a full stomach. You know, Son, from the day we left the village, I've not once gone to sleep with a full stomach. I eat and I don't feel full, like there's a leak at the bottom of my stomach. I have no appetite, and my stomach hurts I'm so hungry."

My grandmother's appetite was never satisfied. She'd say she wasn't hungry, put the plate in front of me and sit watching me. Then, all of a sudden, she'd swoop down on my plate, devour everything without coming up for air and say she'd eaten nothing. The woman was a strange case. She'd only eat from my plate, devouring every last crumb, would put her hand on her stomach and moan, and then start eating again. I used to think she'd taken to eating that way as a sort of compensation after my father's murder. Then I found out that her hunger came from further back, and that she had treated his food the same way she did mine. I remember the story of the string stew only vaguely, but my paternal aunts, on their rare visits, used to talk about little else, starting with laughter and ending up in a sort of quarrel.

"You loved Yasin more than us," one of the aunts would say.

"God forgive you," Shahineh would reply. "It wasn't like that at all. I used to make string stew because the boy was short and we were poor, not like now."

You hear her? As though we weren't poor now. We say we used to be poor so that we don't have to face our present reality. But the main thing is that she had this strange way of cooking. She'd make a stew the way everyone else did, she'd fry bits of meat with onions before adding the vegetables, but she'd take the bits of raw meat, thread them on a string and tie the ends together before frying them. When the family sat down at the table, she'd pull the meat string out of the pot and say, "This is for Yasin." I don't know what happened next. Did my father eat the meat while his sisters looked on, their eyes glazed with desire? Or did he distribute the bits of meat among them? Or did he leave the string untouched, to be devoured by his mother?

My grandmother only stopped cooking string stew when my mother left. I vaguely remember those days. I remember how I hated the string on my plate. I remember that I wouldn't touch it, and my grandmother would try to force me to eat it and I'd refuse. Maybe I ate it once or twice, or a dozen times, I don't know, but the taste of string stuck between my teeth has never left me.

My grandmother stopped threading the meat after my mother left, and I didn't think of it again until one of the fighters with us at Kafar Shouba told us about his mother's string stew, which was just like my grandmother's. In the fedayeen camps we ate lots of meat, and Abu Ahmad used to take my share, saying that I didn't understand anything about food because I hadn't tried string stew, and I'd say that I hated the taste of meat precisely because of string stew. Abu Ahmad would eat in an extraordinary way – but was his real name Abu Ahmad? In those days, our names were all made up anyway. I wasn't called Khalil, I was Abu Khaled, even though I'd wanted to call myself Guevara. The fact is, I love Guevara, and whenever I see his picture, I see the light in his eyes as something holy. I think that he, like Mohammed or that Talal you told me about, had his death lurking in his eyes, which is why they were beautiful and radiant. I wanted to call myself Guevara but discovered someone else had beaten me to it. Amir al-Faisal said, "We'll call you Abu Khaled." Then the Abu Khaleds multiplied.

Gamal Abd al-Nasir was the first Abu Khaled because he called his oldest son Khaled, and when he died in '70, the young men all wanted to name themselves after him, so we were everywhere. I was the first Abu Khaled in South Lebanon, but following the September massacres in Jordan, a wave of fighters fleeing from there swept in and we couldn't distinguish among all the Abu Khaleds anymore. My name thus became Abu Khaled Khalil, and gradually the Abu Khaled part dropped off. To this day, however, I still turn when I hear the name Abu Khaled, even though I know people have forgotten that's what I used to be called.

Meat was Abu Ahmad's only joy. He'd leap onto the supply truck, pick up the meat platter, put it under a tree, pull out the knives, and start cutting it up, singing. He sang to the meat because meat was *the* food, as he would say. I despised him. Or not exactly despised him but felt disgust when he would eat raw meat and invite me to join him.

"That's disgusting," I'd tell him.

"What's disgusting is your not eating it. Don't you know what Imru' al-Qais said were the three most beautiful things in the world – 'Eating flesh, riding flesh, and putting flesh into flesh'?" – he'd say, his tongue, extended to lick his lips, mixing with the red meat that he was chewing.

"All our lives, brother, the only meat we ate was string. We used to fight over the string and the little scraps of meat that clung to it. Now we are really eating. Long live the Revolution – the best thing about this revolution is the meat. It's the Revolution of Meat!"

He'd chew on the raw meat and start preparing *maqloubeh*. We ate *maqloubeh* once a month, when the supplies arrived, and Abu Ahmad would put huge quantities of meat on top of the rice cooked with eggplant or cauliflower; everyone at the base dove into the meat of the revolution. Our revolution was rich while our people are poor, that was the tragedy. The problem's over today – the revolution's moved on, leaving nothing here in the camp but a consuming poverty. I don't know if people have gone back to their old habit of cooking meat on a string because I live on my own, and so do you. And I don't like meat, I prefer lentils and cracked wheat and broad beans, and you like olives.

I know the story. You don't have to tell me what your mother did with black olives, how she would slice them over bread cooked in the peasants' clay oven and say they were chicken breasts and that olives were tastier than chicken. I know the story, and I don't feel like spelling out the virtues of olives again, or talking about the Roman olive tree that served as a shelter during the winter, inside whose huge hollow trunk you'd spend the day before continuing your journey to Bab al-Shams.

As a doctor, I acknowledge the beneficial properties of olive oil, but I can't agree with your mother's theory about dentistry. I'm still not convinced by her belief that ground olive pits make a good painkiller for a toothache. A handful of cloves will act as a painkiller, and arak will do the job, but olive pits – impossible! It seems your mother found a solution to her poverty by transforming olives into something similar to Salim As'ad's little Ekza bottle. No, my friend, olive pits are useless as a medicine, and olive leaves are useless for fumigating houses. Were we – were you – that poor in Palestine? Were we too poor to buy a handful of incense? Was it poverty that made your blind father take dry olive leaves and use them as incense when he led the Sufi devotions every Thursday night? They'd use dry olive leaves for incense: The men would gather around the blind sheikh, who stood in the middle of the circle clapping his hands and saying, "There is no god but God," and the circle would start to rotate. Then you'd come, carrying a vessel full of dry olive leaves with three lit coals placed on top of them. You'd give the vessel to your father and step back while he'd try to make you join the others – you'd run away and stand at the far end of the room, near the door, where the women were gathered, and you'd watch for a while before leaving quietly. The sheikh would blow on the coals, the coals would ignite the olive leaves, and the incense would rise. The circle would begin revolving faster, and the men would fall down until the tambourine player himself fell to the ground, shouting "Succor! Succor! *Madad!*"

The smoke blinded you, Father. Your incense wasn't incense, it was smoke, which blinded you and made you fall down. Your poverty, however, allowed you to transform olives into an entire way of life. You transformed them into meat, chicken, incense, and medicine. Explain to me now, why all this nostalgia for those days of poverty? Why did my grandmother hug her pillow and take such care to change the flower heads she stuffed it with, saying it was the smell of al-Ghabsiyyeh? Have you forgotten how poor you were there? Or do you feel sentimental about it? Or is memory a sickness – a strange sickness that afflicts a whole people? A sickness that has made you imagine things and build your entire lives on the illusions of memory? I still remember the song we chanted at our bases in South Lebanon. Listen to these words and think with me about the meaning of illusion:

> *Abd al-Qadir pitched a tent*
> *Above the tent were orange groves*
> *Feyadeen I am, my father too*
> *Together, we go out to battle!*

Imagine with me how Abd al-Qadir saw his life: He'd become a refugee, so he set up his orange groves on top of his tent and sat underneath singing songs. That's how we express our nostalgia. We believe an orange grove is just above the tent and that the homeland was an orange grove! We feel sentimental about our poverty and our demolished villages to the point of forgetting ourselves and, finally, dying.

But not me.

Never! You know my commitment to and faith in our right to our country. I just talk that way. We're not in a meeting or at a lecture. We're conversing, so let the stories take us where they will.

Where were we?

I was trying to pull together for you scraps of the story of my father. They were in Tarshiha, and that's where Yasin died. Not really died but fell beneath death's wing and survived. It was after Qal'at Jeddin fell into the hands of the Jews. "We took refuge at Tarshiha while waiting to return to our villages," said my grandmother. "But instead of us getting closer to our villages, the Jews got closer to us. Jeddin fell, and Tarshiha was exposed to regular bombardments."

One day – the day Yasin came to call the day of his true death – the planes started shelling Tarshiha: "I was in the market and suddenly found myself running with the crowd. I holed up in Ahmad Shirayh's shop, and suddenly the shop started shaking and the walls toppling, and there was smoke everywhere. A bomb fell into the shop and demolished it. Everyone died. I was standing in the only corner that wasn't demolished, with rubble above me, below me, and all around me – and the dead. I started groaning. I don't know if I was in pain, but the groaning emerged from deep inside me. Then I felt a hand pulling me. Everything was on top of everything else. They picked me up, shouting 'God is most great!' and I found I hadn't died."

Yasin said that when he discovered he was still alive, he started running in the direction of the house they'd been staying in. The mother had gotten everything ready and was standing with her three daughters, and they'd lifted the woolen blankets and pots and pans onto their heads waiting for Yasin. The second they saw him, their new march began.

"My mother didn't ask me where I'd been or why I was covered with dust. She was in a hurry. She set off, my sisters behind her, and me behind everybody, until we got to Deir al-Qasi. There we couldn't find a house, so my mother set up her tent beneath the olive trees and made up her mind yet again that this life was intolerable and that she'd go to her village to get provisions.

"My sister, Munirah, said, 'No, I'll go.'

"My mother protested, but the matter was settled, and Munirah and I and a girl whose name I can't remember – a friend of my sister's who lived under a woolen blanket near ours – set off. We went down to the Acre plain and hid in the cornfields. The cornstalks were more than a meter and a half tall. We had just begun picking okra, cucumbers, and tomatoes when, suddenly, a man carrying a rifle came toward us and took the vegetables away from the girls by force. The vegetable guard was Jew named Melikha. We knew him, and he knew my sister – so why did he get out his weapon and threaten us and confiscate the vegetables we'd taken from our own land? I watched my sister hand over everything and raise her hands. Then she looked back to warn me and left. This alerted him to my presence. I'd been standing stock still, preparing myself to put my hands up so Melikha wouldn't kill me, but I found myself throwing my sack to the ground and running as I heard the sound of shots. I ran and ran, and when I reached my sister and her friend, I felt something hot trickling down my left thigh, which at that moment I didn't know was blood. But my sister tore my shirt and tied up the wound and ran in front of me, crying. It wasn't an actual wound in the true sense of the word; it was gunpowder from the double-barreled shotgun the guard had fired. It had burned through my trousers and several grains of buckshot had lodged in my left thigh. There was blood everywhere. My sister tied up my wound, and we ran back to our tent without picking anything. That was my second heroic deed. The first time I was the only person who managed to get vegetables from al-Ghabsiyyeh, and the second time I returned wounded like a martyr. I can't describe what my mother did when she saw the blood covering my trousers."

"What can I tell you about him, my dear?" my grandmother would say. "Your father was a hero. I saw him and I saw the blood, and I ran to him, my tears flying ahead of me – my only son dying for the sake of a handful of okra – and started screaming: 'the Jews killed him, I killed him! I've killed my son. Come, everyone, and see!' I didn't stop when I discovered the injury was trivial. I gave him a wedding, as they do for martyrs. I belted out *you-yous* and wailed and waved above me his blood-stained trousers. I did what all the mothers of martyrs did, I thanked God. I brandished the trousers over my head, and our neighbor, Umm Kamel, came and sprinkled me with vapors of incense and sprinkled the trousers and sprinkled you. I thought, This is my slice of martyrdom. I did what the mothers of martyrs do so I might spare myself later. I thought, My son has died. That means he'll never die again after today. But he betrayed me and betrayed his wife and betrayed you. He left us and died on the doorstep of this house that I built with my tears. God help me, in Deir al-Qasi I thought death would not come back and that I could escape from it with my children, but it caught up with me here and snatched away my son and left me on my own with this boy who's the spitting image of Yasin. My son was scared of the vegetable guard. He feared for his life – they were killing all the young men. He didn't put his hands up to surrender in order to escape death. At the door, seeing the revolver pointing at him, he tried to put his hands up, but he didn't have enough time, and they didn't let him surrender. They killed him."

Why did they kill him?

My grandmother asked you why, and I'm asking you, too.

Wouldn't it have been better if he'd died in the cornfields? Was it necessary for him to go through that long agony from Deir al-Qasi to Beit Lif and from Beit Lif to al-Mansourah and from al-Mansourah to al-Rashidiyyeh and from al-Rashidiyyeh to Shatila, and to death?

My grandmother hated bananas.

No one in the world hates bananas, but Shahineh hated them.

You don't know the story of this woman and bananas because you don't know how she would use banana leaves to cover the floor of her tent in the al-Rashidiyyeh camp. Banana leaves were the only thing they could find to protect them from the rain that was inundating them. You weren't there to see how the banana leaves covered them, and you weren't there to see how Nahilah stole her own food and the food for her children from her confiscated land.

You were nowhere. You'd entered your secret world that made you think that things were the way they'd always been, while Shahineh was spreading the floor of her tent with banana leaves and eating dust, and Nahilah was stealing olives from her confiscated land, before your father, the sheikh, returned to his post and started receiving his livelihood from the Deir al-Asad Mosque Endowment. You may or may not know that there was no such endowment or anyone to make one – the Israelis had confiscated all the lands. The sheikh convinced himself about the endowment so he wouldn't have to acknowledge that he'd become a beggar, a beggar living off the donations of people who were poorer than himself but were embarrassed to look into his sightless eyes and by the belly of his daughter-in-law, always swollen with children.

My grandmother hated bananas, and Nahilah hated the endowment and went to work in the *moshav* the Yemeni Jews had built along the edges of the rubble of the village of al-Birwa. You don't know these things. You'll ask why she didn't let you know. Do you have to be told in order to know? I'd like to believe you and forgive you now, because you didn't know how we lived, how they lived, but tell me, what did you do for them and for us? Why did you let us go through such hell?

I hear your laughter breaking through the veil of your death. You're laughing and dragging on your cigarette until it burns down to nothing, and you raise your hand with a nonchalant gesture. Your voice shouts out, "Hell? You, Khalil, are talking to me about hell? What do you know about hell?"

And I hear, coming from the depths of your voice, the voice of Yasin, bringing with it the stories of the banana leaves that covered the ground and the roof of the tent so that those inside wouldn't drown.

My grandmother said she entered Lebanon on a donkey. "We hired a donkey to cross the Lebanese border. We had to abandon everything on the spot, we weren't allowed to bring anything with us." But in fact, my grandmother brought her jewelry, which allowed her to live reasonably during the first few years in Lebanon.

She said she'd been in Deir al-Qasi. All the people were asleep in their tents, but she couldn't get to sleep. She said she felt as though everything were lost. It was night and the stars were like red spots in the sky, and the sounds of distant howling mixed with scattered gunfire and silence. The armed young men who guarded Deir al-Qasi's tents stuck close to the olive trees as though fear had petrified them to the spot.

A woman on her own, sitting in front of her shelter of olive branches, seeing nothing but darkness. A dead husband, four small children, a father whose whereabouts were known only to God, an unsure future, and a village that had died. My grandmother said that during those moments, when night was concealed in her eyes, she realized that al-Ghabsiyyeh was dead and that she had to do something to save her own life and that of her children, and she remembered that she'd left her gold jewelry and twenty Palestinian lira, which were her entire dowry, in the bottom of a chest.

The woman sat in front of her tent, the howling around her, the night covering her, the tears flowing from her eyes. Then she found herself in front of her eldest daughter, Munirah. Munirah was sixteen years old and greatly resembled her mother. Shahineh went up to her sleeping daughter and shook her gently. The girl woke with a start.

"Get up! Get up!" said her mother.

The mother took her daughter's hand and led her out of the tent. Outside the girl listened to her mother but understood nothing.

"I don't understand a thing," said Munirah.

The mother explained her plan to her daughter. She hadn't had a plan when she'd awakened her, she hadn't known what she was going to say to her; she just wanted to break her solitude and speak to someone about the loss of her dowry. But instead of complaining, she found herself laying out the plan to her daughter. She said she was going to go there at dawn to get her money and her jewelry, and that if anything bad should happen, God forbid, she was to go with her brother and sisters where everyone else went. If they go to Lebanon: "Go with them and ask about your grandfather, Rabbah al-Awad. You grandfather's still alive, he's fighting now with the others, I don't know where. Look for him, and he'll take care of you." Munirah proposed that she go instead of her mother, but her mother refused. "No, Daughter. I'll go on my own. You're still young, and your life's ahead of you. Just don't forget to ask for your grandfather. His name's Rabbah, Rabbah al-Awad, and he's with the Sha'ab garrison now, and everyone knows him. Wait for me until tomorrow night. I'll come back tonight, but something may hold me up. Wait two nights for me. If I'm not back, something will have happened. Forget me, go with the others, and put your trust in God."

Munirah said she understood and went into the tent and fell into a deep sleep. Shahineh couldn't believe her eyes. How could the girl sleep after what her mother had just told her? Shahineh went into the tent again and bent over Munirah, who was breathing quietly.

Shahineh put a crust of bread inside the front of her dress and set off. It was dark. Shahineh didn't know what time it was, but the veil of night was breaking to reveal dim colors. She walked and walked, and no one appeared to stop her – not the camp guards, who kept close to the olive trees, nor the Jews, who had invaded the villages and spread out over the hills. She walked alone on paths she knew. She bent over and stumbled and almost fell but caught herself. She walked for about two hours. Distances in Galilee aren't great – as you once told me, Galilee is like the palm of a hand. She walked until she reached the Bubbler. She bent over the water, washed her hands and her face, drank, and entered the village.

The spring called the Bubbler isn't more than two kilometers from al-Ghabsiyyeh, but it was the longest leg of her journey. She walked and walked and never arrived. Shahineh knew the road and could have done it with her eyes closed since she was used to fetching water from the Bubbler every day – but what did every day have to do with that day? Her head felt heavy, as though she were carrying three water jars on it. She kept going, weighed down by her head; her fear welled up and out of her mouth in the form of labored breathing.

Many years later, she'd tell me that this adventure had taught her to see.

"You know, Son, it was there that I saw. Before I hadn't seen, and after I left the village I didn't see again."

"And what did you see, Grandma?"

"I saw everything there. It's difficult to explain, my boy. With one look I saw all the houses and all the trees, as though my eyes had pierced the walls and could see everything."

On her journey to al-Ghabsiyyeh, Shahineh walked bent over. She bent over to avoid the branches of the olive trees, she bent over because of the night, she bent over out of fear, she bent over for water from the Bubbler, and she bent over for the lotus tree. When she passed the mosque, however, she suddenly straightened up. She held her head high and walked calmly into the village as though she'd never left it. Her frightened panting subsided, and she saw everything. She saw the houses and the trees and the orchards, and she heard the voices of the people and the cries of the children. The woman walked calmly toward her house. The door was open.

She ran into the room, opened the chest, and reached in. There she found her money and her jewelry – her gold signet ring, her twisted bracelets, and her necklace of pearls. She put everything inside the front of her dress and decided to go back. No. She was famished. She took the crust of bread out of the front of her dress and started to gnaw on it. Then she hurried to the kitchen, found the bread in its place, looked around for the molasses, mixed it with tahini and stood in the kitchen eating. She ate three pieces of bread with tahini, and then made some tea. She sat and drank and began to feel sleepy. Overcome by drowsiness, she stood up heavily and found herself stretched out on the bed slipping into unconsciousness. She slept like someone who doesn't know she's asleep – that's how she'd describe it later. She didn't shut the door and she didn't take off her clothes. She lay down as she was, her hands sticky with molasses, and drowsiness overcame her. When she awoke, darkness had started to steal into the house. She opened her eyes and was completely disoriented.

"I was lost, I didn't know where I was."

For a moment, she didn't dare move. She opened her eyes and went rigid.

"I slept on the only bed we owned. My husband, God rest his soul, bought a brass bed unlike any in the whole village. I didn't sleep on it after he died, because, in our day, the bed was for the man. He'd sleep on the bed, and I'd sleep on a mattress on the floor. Then he started asking me to sleep in the bed next to him. He said it was because he loved me. In our day, Son, no one used that word. A husband loved his wife, but he wouldn't tell her. But your grandfather Khalil, he made me sleep up there."

That day Shahineh slept on the brass bed. "I hadn't slept in the bed since his death. It was his bed. I used to make it every day and wash the sheets once a week, but I never slept in it. That day, though, when my eyes grew heavy with sleep, I threw myself down on it and slept. You can imagine what it was like when I woke up and saw darkness everywhere. For an instant I didn't know where I was; it was as though my husband had never died, the village hadn't fallen, and the children weren't waiting in a field in Deir al-Qasi. I forgot everything and found myself at home. When I remembered where I was and where I'd come from, I was struck by fear and started shivering. I jumped off the bed, patted my chest, found the jewellery in its place and thought I'd better go back."

Shahineh said she regretted one thing. "I'm sorry I didn't make the bed. In my fear and haste, it was like I didn't care. I know my husband was angry with me: I dreamt of him, Son. We were here in the camp, and he came to me in a dream and said, 'Even so, Shahineh, is that any way to leave my bed? Where am I going to rest now?' I went to the Green Sheikh, God set him straight, and told him about my dream, and he reassured me and said the dead don't return to their houses, and that my husband was a martyr, and the martyrs are in Heaven, and he asked me to come and visit him from time to time. I didn't visit him, though. I'd seen that look in his eye; praise God, I didn't visit him even once. He looked me up and down and licked his lips, saying, 'The martyrs are in Heaven, where there's ease, and houris. Your husband, Shahineh, is enjoying his fill of the houris now.' As he said *houris*, he licked his lips as though he were, God forbid . . . ! Is that how to behave with martyrs' widows? I mean, who did that old lecher think he was? No, dear God, I spit on his beard and the beards of all like him. He picks up the Book of God and then looks with that lustful look?"

Shahineh said she came to her senses and started to shiver.

"I got up, drank some water, and left."

She said the village was empty – no one. Not a sound, nothing. Only the wind whispering to the branches of the trees and the sound of her footsteps.

In front of the mosque, she heard someone quietly clearing his throat. She threw herself on the ground, and saw the man coming.

"Who's there?" whispered the man.

Shahineh couldn't find her voice to reply. She tried to make herself as small as she could. The White Sheikh was coming toward her, carrying what looked like a rifle in his hand.

Shahineh said she closed her eyes and started reciting the Throne Verse in her heart to conjure away the Evil One when a stick tapped her and she heard her name.

"Get up, Shahineh my daughter. What are you doing here?"

She opened her eyes and screamed, "I seek refuge with God against Satan – I beg you, please not me! Don't take me, Aziz! Please, I have children."

He held out his stick as though he wanted her to take hold of it to raise herself up.

"What's the matter, Daughter? I'm Uncle Aziz Ayyoub."

"But you're dead, Uncle. Leave me alone. I have children."

"Me, dead! Have you gone crazy? Did you ever hear of a dead man talking? Here I am in front of you. Get up."

"I beheld my uncle, Sheikh Aziz Ayyoub, and discovered that Yasin had lied to me. Aziz Ayyoub hadn't died; there he was, taking me inside the mosque, lighting a fire, giving me tea, and asking after my children. But you know, Son, not one person believed me. They said I'd seen a ghost. Even his daughter, Safiyyeh, laughed at me and said that he was dead and gone, but I'm sure. I saw him, and he gave me tea and said he couldn't leave the village because he had to guard the mosque and the tree."

Nobody believed her, Father. Even I didn't believe her, and, finally, she started to doubt herself. Poor grandmother. She died before Umm Hassan returned from her journey over there and confirmed the man wasn't a ghost, and that he died in a strange way.

Aziz Ayyoub told Shahineh they'd been guarding the tree for five generations and they couldn't abandon it. "I asked my wife to stay on here, but she refused because she was afraid of the Jews. 'What can the Jews do?' I asked her. 'The worst has already happened.' And she said, 'I'm afraid of Deir Yasin.'"*

Sheikh Aziz said he wasn't afraid. "I'm the fifth generation and I won't leave the lotus tree. Who will look after the holy saints? Who will pray in the mosque? Who will wash the graves?"

Shahineh listened to what the man said as though she were in a dream,

---

*On the night of April 9, 1948, Begin's Irgun Zvei Leumi and the Stern Gang surrounded Deir Yasin. The residents were given 15 minutes to evacuate before the village was attacked. Approximately 250 people were killed.

and in dreams words have no meaning. "He asked me to tell his wife he was still alive. I didn't ask him anything. It was very strange – whenever I was about to ask him something, I'd hear the answer before I could ask. Merciful and Compassionate God, it was as though he could read my heart. He said the Jews came from time to time. A patrol of three armed soldiers would come, roam around the village, then go into the houses and loot the gold. 'You found your gold by God's will, my daughter, but the gold's disappeared. They think I'm insane. When they see me, they run away, so I climb the minaret and say the call to prayer; the call frightens them and protects me. Off with you now, Daughter. Go to your children.'"

My grandmother said the journey back to the fields of Deir al-Qasi was as quick as a flash. "I ran the whole way. I ran, without looking back once. I felt there was someone running behind me. I couldn't hear a thing, as though my ears had been blocked by the wind. I ran and the wind carried me until I arrived. I arrived at our camp and saw my four children sitting there, waiting for me. I arrived and threw myself among them. I took them into the tent and told them to sleep. They leaned close to one another in silence. It was then that I smelled myself. It was sweat; it had stained my clothes, and the smell of it spread inside the tent. I was embarrassed and asked Munirah to get up and help me wash. That day I divided the wealth between the two of us. I put ten lira into the front of my dress and ten into the front of hers. I took the signet ring and the pearl necklace and gave her the twisted bracelets. With this money we were able to live for a whole year in Qana before my girls had to go and work in the stone quarries."

You don't know Aziz Ayyoub, Father, you never told me anything about him or about the life he led alone in our village. Didn't you visit al-Ghabsiyyeh? Didn't you hear the story of the holy saint who was killed? If it weren't for Umm Hassan, I'd have known nothing. You ought to have heard her telling me. How wonderful Umm Hassan was – I wish she'd been my mother! At least I'd sleep comfortably. Did you know I'm afraid of sleeping? I told you, I'm scared of sleeping and waking up to find myself in a strange land whose language I can't speak. I'm scared I won't wake up. I'm scared I won't find my house or I won't find you or I won't find the hospital or I don't know what.

With Umm Hassan I would have slept. My grandmother used to scare me at night. I'd hear the sound of her footsteps in the house as though she couldn't sleep and couldn't let me sleep. She'd walk and walk, then come to my bed and ask me if I was asleep. I'd awaken with a jolt to find her at my side saying she'd remembered something, and she'd start to repeat her tedious stories about Yasin, of his life and of his death, on and on.

With Umm Hassan, sleep comes to you. With her you feel the world is stable, not about to be dislodged. Oh, where are you now, Umm Hassan? And where's the nursing certificate you kept from the days of the British Mandate? Umm Hassan told me about my grandfather's uncle, Aziz Ayyoub. She said he'd become a saint and that people made oaths in his name and that he could cure illnesses. She said that during her visit to her brother in al-Jdeideh, she'd remembered her promise to my grandmother to visit al-Ghabsiyyeh and light a candle under the lotus tree.

Have you seen the lotus tree, Father?

Have you tasted its fruit?

Umm Hassan said its fruit was called *doum* and were like medlars, or even more delicious than medlars.

Umm Hassan told the people in Jdeideh that she had to go al-Ghabsiyyeh to fulfill her vow under the lotus tree, and she went on her own because her brother was afraid to go with her. He told her that since the Ayyoub incident and the building of his tomb there, the Israelis had started to clamp down and stop people from visiting the village. Al-Ghabsiyyeh was a military area, and if anyone was found there they were taken to prison and had to pay a huge fine.

Her brother took her to the village of al-Nahar and showed her the way. She said that when she reached the tree, she made a prostration. She saw melted candles and ribbons hung over the delicate small leaves, which covered the branches. She made a prostration there and then entered the mosque, where she knelt in a corner and prayed.

When she returned, she told me about Ayyoub.

She said the people in al-Jdeideh talked about him. They told her about a white man with a white beard and white clothes who guarded a tree and talked to its branches. People would come from the surrounding villages to fulfill their vows to the tree and see the man. Umm Hassan told them it was Aziz. "It's Aziz," she'd say. "No. His name's Ayyoub," they'd say.

Umm Hassan said Aziz cleaned the mosque every day. The Israeli settlement that had been built on the edge of al-Ghabsiyyeh used the mosque as a cow pen. Ayyoub would get up every day and start cleaning the mosque first thing, picking up the dung with his hands and throwing it into the fields. Then he'd sprinkle water and pray.

Umm Hassan said that at first the people thought he was Jewish, for he resembled the Iraqi Jews who were common in the area and had set up the settlement of Netiv ha-Shayyara. They thought he was the guard for the cow pen. Then they discovered the truth because whenever more than three women gathered around the lotus tree, he'd climb the minaret and give the call to prayer. Many, both men and women, had attempted to talk to him, but he wouldn't speak. He seemed to be from another world, a spirit, with his eyes sunken in his oval face and his shoulders that drooped as though his body were no longer capable of holding them up.

"That's Aziz Ayyoub," said Umm Hassan, and she told them his wife and children lived in the Burj al-Shamali camp near Tyre, and that she'd seen his son, who'd grown into a fine man and worked as a broker for the lemon growers in Tyre.

The people of al-Jdeideh couldn't believe that their Ayyoub was this Aziz Ayyoub.

Their Ayyoub was a phantom; our Aziz was a man.

Their Ayyoub was a saint; our Aziz died when the young Yasin left him and fled into the valley.

Ayyoub, or Aziz Ayyoub, lived his life a solitary phantom in a village inhabited by ghosts. He lived alone close to the tree and the mosque, sleeping in the mosque with the cows and eating plants that grew on the land and the remains of provisions that had been left behind in the abandoned houses. They'd see him walking through the fields or sitting under the lotus tree or praying in the mosque or giving the call to prayer. His clothes were a brilliant white, as though all the muck that surrounded him left no mark.

People called him White Ayyoub.

After lighting their candles under the tree, they'd approach him hoping for a blessing, but he'd walk away. No one could touch him. Umm Hassan didn't know how they knew his name. "He didn't speak to anyone, he didn't respond, so how did they know? This, my son, I'm not able to tell you. They said he was as pure as an angel, that he'd clean out the mosque and become even more immaculate."

Umm Hassan says she thinks a good number the stories circulating about Ayyoub are just fantasies. The mosque wasn't used continuously as a cow pen, most likely the Jews kept their cattle there during the winter. She didn't think they'd leave their cows with Ayyoub.

"Ayyoub went mad," said Umm Hassan. "How could anybody live alone among those ruins and not lose his mind? If he hadn't lost his mind, he'd have left al-Ghabsiyyeh and gone to live in another village, any other village, among people."

"But that's not the point of the story, Son," said Umm Hassan. "The point is that Aziz Ayyoub became a saint after he died."

One day a woman came to the lotus tree to fulfil a vow, and she saw him. She threw down her candles and ran to al-Jdeideh, and everyone came. Ayyoub was dead beneath the holy tree, his neck tied to a rope, the rope on the ground, as though the man had fallen from a branch of the tree. At one end of the rope was Ayyoub's neck, which had turned thin and black, and at the other end was a branch of the lotus tree that had been torn from its mother and had fallen to the ground.

"No one touch him," someone said. "The man committed suicide, and suicide is an impure act."

The people backed away from the body of White Ayyoub, whispering in strangled voices. One woman left the throng, went over to the corpse, took off her headscarf, and covered the face of the dead man. Then she knelt bareheaded and started to weep.

"They killed him," said the kneeling woman. "They killed the guardian of the lotus tree. It's a sign."

Sheikh Abd al-Ahad, imam of the Jdeideh mosque, said that Ayyoub hadn't committed suicide. "Ayyoub is a martyr, my friends."

The sheikh gave orders to take the body into the mosque, where it was washed and wrapped in a shroud. The burial took place beside the lotus tree, where they built Ayyoub a tomb.

"Now, Son, when you go to al-Ghabsiyyeh, you'll see cacti everywhere. Only the cactus bears witness to our endurance. And there next to the tree, you'll see the tomb of Ayyoub. The tree is lush and beautiful and green. Ah, how beautiful lotus trees are! Have you ever seen a lotus tree in your life? Of course you haven't. Your generation hasn't seen anything. There, Son, sleeps Aziz Ayyoub, Saint Ayyoub. People visit his tomb and leave him gifts and votive offerings, and he answers their prayers. I saw the tomb. A small tomb with a window. I leaned my head down and shouted, 'Aziz! Can you hear me? Dear beloved one, you truly have earned your name!* You rose above an entire people. You ended your life on the tree you guarded. Aziz, Dear Saint, Beloved of God!' That's how the people invoke him, Son. They come from all around; they put their heads near the window and call, 'Ayyoub!'"

Umm Hassan said she thought Aziz Ayyoub had committed suicide. "A man all alone, afflicted by madness, what was he to do? But he was transformed into a sheikh, and they swear by his name and await his blessings. Poor humans!"

Even though Umm Hassan didn't believe that Aziz Ayyoub had become a saint, in her last days, she'd swear by his name and ask me to tell her the story of how I'd stood with my father behind the donkey, and how Aziz

* Aziz literally means beloved, or dear.

grabbed the donkey's tail and told my father to stand behind him. I'd describe the scene to her and she'd burst into laughter: "What was that? Did I think the donkey would act as a barrier and protect them from the bullets?"

As you see, dear master, things have become mixed up in my mind just like in yours. I had nothing to do with it: It was Yasin, my father, who stood behind the donkey. But, you see, I've been infected by Umm Hassan and have started talking about these people as though I knew them all personally. But Ayyoub did become a saint. What do saints do to become saints? Nothing, I suppose, because people invent them. People invent wonders and believe in them because they need them. True as that is, it changes nothing. Ayyoub's a saint, whether we willed it or not.

Aziz was guardian of the mosque and the lotus tree and the cemetery. He'd inherited his profession from his father, who'd inherited it from his father, who'd inherited it from his father, who . . . until you run out of fathers. Every day he filled his water jar, washed the graves, cleaned the mosque, walked around the lotus tree, and slept.

"A man who sleeps in a cemetery." That was how Umm Hassan described him.

And the man who slept in a cemetery started curing the sick, helping women get pregnant, bringing back those who had gone away, and finding husbands for girls.

Ayyoub gave his name to the tree, which became known as the Tree of Ayyoub.

Now I understand why you get things mixed up, Father. I asked you about the lotus tree, and you answered that there was no such thing as a lotus tree in al-Ghabsiyyeh, and that the people of Deir al-Asad used to talk of a tree called an *Ayyoubi* but you didn't know what kind of tree that was.

The tree, Father, is the lotus, and its guardian is Ayyoub – a man who hanged himself from its branches, so the tree proclaimed him a saint.

"Listen, Khalil," said Umm Hassan. "It could be that he hung himself, or it could be that the man tied the rope around his neck and climbed onto a branch of the tree to put an end to his misery and loneliness, but the tree took pity on him and broke so as not to allow him to commit the defilement of suicide. The tree, which is ruled by a saint, proclaimed him a saint, so now it has two saints, the first one, whose name we don't know, and Ayyoub, of our village, whose name was Aziz. The sheikh of al-Jdeideh has a different opinion. He believes the Israelis strangled him, then tied a rope around his neck to make people think he'd committed suicide. 'Why should he commit suicide?' the sheikh asked me. 'The man chose to live alone in the service of God – they killed him. They killed him because they wanted to uproot the tree, but we'll never let them do that. I'll appoint a new guard, for the tree and the tomb.'"

The sheikh of al-Jdeideh didn't appoint a guard as he'd promised Umm Hassan, and the tomb remained alone, but no one lifted a hand against the sacred tree.

Would you like me to make a vow to Ayyoub for your recovery?

I'm certain you know Aziz Ayyoub. You may not have liked him because he wasn't a fighter. You told me you despised anybody who didn't carry a gun: "The country was slipping away before our eyes, and they sat there doing nothing." Aziz Ayyoub didn't carry a gun, and he didn't fight, but look what he became and what we've become. He's now a saint to whom people make vows, and we're on our own.

Leave Aziz Ayyoub in his tomb and come with me to look for Shahineh. We left her in front of her tent in Deir al-Qasi. She went into the tent and lay down next to her children after her long journey to al-Ghabsiyyeh. And before she fell asleep, she smelled her own sweat, left the tent and asked Munirah to help her bathe. Later she divided her wealth into two halves, and managed to live off it for more than a year.

From Deir al-Qasi to Beit Lif, from Beit Lif to al-Mansourah, from al-Mansourah to Qana. Shahineh told how the people were like locusts: "The Israeli planes sailed overhead while we scurried through the emptiness looking for a refuge, until we reached al-Mansourah. There we crossed the border, the noise stopped, and the terror was extinguished. We found ourselves in Qana, and there we rented a house from the Atiyyeh family. Yasin went to school, and the girls and I sat in the house, and I spent all my money. Qana was beautiful and quiet, like our village in Palestine."

My grandmother didn't tell me much about Qana because she believed her exile only really began when they gathered everyone together in the camps around Tyre.

"In Qana, we weren't in exile, or refugees. We were waiting."

Do you know what waiting, and the hope of return, meant to these people, Abu Salem? Of course you don't. However, the story of the buffalo of al-Khalsah astonished me. When my grandmother told me the story, I thought she was telling me something like the stories grownups tell children that they don't expect them to believe. The story concerns a man called Abu Aref, a Bedouin of the village of al-Khalsah, belonging to the tribe of Heyb. He came to Qana along with everyone else and stayed there with his wife and five daughters. And he brought his buffalo. Seven buffalo cows, God protect them. "We all drank their milk, for the man used to give it away to everybody. He refused to sell it, saying the buffalo were an offering to al-Khalsah – 'When we go back, we can buy and sell.' He was generous and stubborn, like all Bedouin. When spring came, the season when buffalo become fertile, people saw the man leading his herd toward the south. His wife said he was crazy because he believed the buffalo could only conceive in al-Khalsah, and he'd agreed with a cousin of his to hand the buffalo over to him at the Lebanese-Palestinian border on the condition that he return them two weeks later. The man set off for the border, and his wife stood in the square at Qana to bid him farewell, mourning him and mourning the buffalo, but the man would have nothing to do with her. Then the buffalo disappeared from view, and everyone forgot about the matter."

My grandmother said Abu Aref returned alone, cowering, his spirit broken. He wouldn't speak. "He was bathed in tears, and we didn't dare ask him anything. He returned alone, without the buffalo."

"We've lost everything," said Umm Aref.

Abu Aref drove his buffalo to al-Khalsah because he was convinced the buffalo could only conceive on the land where they were raised, and, at the border post, the firing started. The buffalo sank to the ground, their blood splashing the sky, and Abu Aref stood there in the midst of the massacre.

He told his wife he was standing at the border making signs to his cousin when the firing started.

He said he ran from buffalo to buffalo. He said it was all blood. He said he raised his hands and screamed, but they were killed anyway.

He said his dog of a cousin never turned up. He said he'd taken off his white *kufiyyeh* and raised it as a sign of surrender, then started running with it from buffalo to buffalo, trying to staunch their wounds, the *kufiyyeh* becoming drenched in blood. He said he raised the stained *kufiyyeh* and shouted and begged, but they didn't stop. "The ground was covered in blood, the buffalo were dying, and I was weeping. Why didn't they kill me too? I wiped my face with the blood-soaked *kufiyyeh* and sat down among the buffalo."

The man returned to his wife cowering, frightened. He returned without his buffalo, carrying the blood-stained *kufiyyeh* and the marks of despair.

That was Qana.

My father went to the school, and my grandmother got out her Palestinian lira and spent them one by one, then sold her gold bracelets and her necklace; she didn't, however, sell the signet ring, which remained on her finger until her death. I think my aunt Munirah took it. I don't know. She sold everything and then started working with her daughters crushing stone in the village. Waiting was no longer viable. The borders were closed; people had entered a labyrinth. The Lebanese police came and said they had an order to gather the Palestinians into the camp at al-Rashidiyyeh. This was when the agony began. They drove Abu Aref, tied up with ropes, whipping him while he bellowed that he couldn't bear to be taken away from his buffalo.

They brought everyone together in the village square, put them onto trucks and trains, and moved them away from the borders of their country.

My grandmother said the agony started in the camp. "They dumped us on the seashore in winter. The wind blew hard from all directions, and we were left in the dark."

She said she couldn't remember daylight. "During those days, everything was black. Even the rain was black, Son.

"We drowned in the mud. Your poor father, God rest his soul, was only knee-high. Afraid for him, I told the girls to watch out for Yasin because he'd drown in the mud. I'd yell and hear nothing; my voice flew away in the wind. God, what terrible days those were!"

How can I tell you of those days, Father, when I didn't experience them myself and my father never spoke of them? My father died before we reached the age when fathers tell their sons their stories.

They were known as "the banana days."

The only shelter people could find was under big, dry banana leaves. They'd buy ten leaves for five Lebanese piasters and make roofs for their tents and spread the leaves on the ground.

"They were the banana days," said Shahineh.

When Shahineh spoke about those days, you had the feeling that she wasn't telling of the past – it was as though time had stopped. She told of the crowded buses, of the wooden pattens they wore as protection from the hot sand, of the tents in which the wind was a permanent occupant, of the rain that penetrated the bone.

She told of moving from Qana and of how the Lebanese officer came, surrounded by his men, and ordered the Palestinians to congregate in the square, of how he whipped Abu Aref until he was soaked in blood.

"We only had banana leaves," she said.

"We spread the leaves over the ground and covered the roofs and the sides of the tents with them, and lived with the rottenness. The leaves rotted, and we rotted beneath them and on top of them."

It was then that Shahineh decided Yasin's schooling was over, and it was time for him to work.

"No, that's not true," she said. "I begged him not to leave school. I said we'd live off the rations we were allotted with the relief card." But he refused. He found work in the sheet-metal factory at Mina al-Hesn, which landed him in prison, though that's another story.

Shahineh told of three months in the camp before their departure to Beirut. She and her children lived for about two months in an old Beirut house that had belonged to the Hammouds – a family of fighters from '36 – before moving to the camp at Shatila.

Shahineh met Ahmad Hammoud in the Rashidiyyeh camp. He was one of a group of young men who came from Beirut to distribute relief supplies to the refugees, and when he found out that she was the daughter of the '36 fighter Rabbah al-Awad, he bent down and kissed her hand. Two days later, he returned with his father and asked Shahineh to come to Beirut.

"So we went to Beirut, and lived about two months in their beautiful house, but, it must be said, people get on each other's nerves."

My grandmother never told me about her stay in that house or why people get on each other's nerves. She simply said she'd taken her children and gone to Shatila, set up her tent there, and lived. From the tent, to the concrete room roofed with canvas, to the corrugated iron roof, to the "roof of the revolution" – she had to wait twenty years, until '68, to get a concrete roof. The concrete roof came with the revolution and the fedayeen. Only then was the woman able to get any sleep. She said that until then, she hadn't been able to sleep at night because she felt she was sleeping in the open.

My mother told me nothing.

She moved within her silence, which she wore like a cocoon. When I remember her now, I see her as an evanescent phantom.

She was there and not there, as though she weren't my mother, as though she were a stranger living with us. She disappeared and left the story to my grandmother.

I wasn't very interested in the story. You might think that to gather the stories of al-Ghabsiyyeh, I had to search and ask around, but it's not true. The stories came to me without my having to chase them. My grandmother used to drown me in stories, as though she had nothing to do but talk. When I was with her, I'd yawn and fall asleep, and the stories would cover me. Now I feel that I have to push the stories aside in order to see clearly, for all I see is spots, as though that woman's stories were like colored spots drifting around me. I don't know a whole story; even the story of Abu Aref's buffalo I don't know entirely – why did the Israelis open fire on the buffalo and leave the man alone; why did they leave him standing in the midst of the carnage?

My grandmother said his wife didn't believe him. "He disappeared for a month and then returned saying they'd killed his buffalo! Abu Aref lied to us because he didn't dare to tell the truth of his disgrace. He said he wanted his buffalo to conceive in al-Khalsah, and his cousin would meet him at the border and take them from him, then return them after a week. Fine. But he didn't come back after a week, or after the massacre. He was away for a month. Then he came back carrying his *kufiyyeh* and saying the Israelis had killed them."

"I'm certain the Jews didn't kill them," said his wife. "Why would they kill them? They'd take them. And how could they have killed the buffalo and not him with them? I would have been rid of him! No, the Jews didn't kill the buffalo. I'm certain his cousin stole them. Took them and disappeared. The man must have waited a month at the border, then despaired and had no choice but to make up the story of the buffalo massacre. Everything foolish we do, we blame on the Jews. No, the Jews didn't kill them. And all of this for what? We could have sold them and lived off the money."

My grandmother said Umm Aref grieved for her buffalo as much as if her husband had died. She'd insult him and grieve at the same time, weep and get furious, while the man behaved like an imbecile, carrying his *kufiyyeh* around and showing it to people in Qana. Everyone believed him and cursed the times. Everyone believed him except his wife, who knew him better than anyone else.

"So what do think, my boy?" asked my grandmother.

I said I didn't know because I'd only seen buffalo in Egyptian films and didn't know we'd raised them in Palestine.

"Did we raise buffalo?" I asked her.

"Us, no. We raised sheep, cows, and chickens. The people of al-Khalsah are Bedouin, they raise buffalo, not us."

And she started telling me the story of Abu Aref again.

"You told me that story, Grandma."

"So what? I told it to you, and I'll tell it again. Talk is just flapping the lips. If we don't talk, what are we to do?"

"The man was a pain in the ass and a fool. Wouldn't it have been better to slaughter them and eat them? In those days we were dying for a bit of meat. All we had to eat was *midardara* – lentils, rice, and fried onions."

"But I like *midardara*, Grandma."

What did they eat, there in their village in Palestine? I'm convinced *midardara* was the only thing they ate. But my grandmother always had an answer "under her arm," as they say. Over there everything had a different taste. "Our olive oil was the real thing. You could live on it and nothing else, and there were so many things you could use it for."

Have I told you what Shahineh did to my father on their wedding night? She made him drink a coffee cup full of olive oil before going in to my mother. "I made him drink oil. Oil's good for sex. One day soon, Son, God willing, one day soon, at your wedding, I'll give you oil to drink the way I did your father, and later you'll say, 'Shahineh knew, God rest her soul!'"

Father, I don't know Shahineh's story well enough to be able to tell it to you. The stories are like drops of oil floating on the surface of memory. I try to link them up, but they don't want to be linked. I don't know much about my aunts. All I can tell you about is the husband of one of them, the one with the bald patch that looked like it was polished with olive oil. I've already told you about him, so there's no point in repeating it. I hate things that repeat, but things do repeat, infinitely.

Would you like to hear the story of my father and the Jew?

I'll tell it to you, but don't ask about the details. You can ask my grandmother tomorrow – I mean, a long time from now when you meet over in the other world. You should ask her because she knows it better than I do, she'll tell you the story of the rabbi with all the details. All I know are the broad outlines, which I'll try to tell you.

I apologize.

Again, I return to you with apologies. I'll give you your bath now and feed you, and then I'll tell you the story of the rabbi. Tell me you're comfortable – your temperature's gone down, and everything's back to normal; all that's left is this small sore on the sole of your left foot.

Tell me, what do you think of the waterbed?

If Salim As'ad, God send him good fortune, did nothing else in his life but come up with this mattress for us, his heavenly reward will still be great.

I was apologizing because I had to attend to other matters. I just witnessed a sad scene, but instead of crying I burst into laughter. Something like tears were flowing inside me while I was laughing, and I could only settle the matter the way Abd al-Wahid al-Khatib wanted it settled.

Do you know him?

I doubt it. I didn't meet him until his son put him in the hospital a month ago. He arrived in a bad state; he was suffering terribly. I examined him along with Dr. Amjad and suggested having him transferred to al-Hamshari Hospital in Ain al-Hilweh so he could have X-rays taken. We don't have any equipment here – even the lab has closed. We're more of a hotel. The patients come, they sleep, and we provide them with the minimum of care. Nevertheless, we continue to call this building suspended in a vacuum a hospital.

So Abd al-Wahid came, and I examined him. My diagnosis was liver cancer. But Dr. Amjad disagreed, as usual. He said the man was suffering from the onset of cirrhosis of the liver and prescribed some medication. I suggested to his son to take him to al-Hamshari to be sure. Father and son left with Amjad's prescription and my advice, and it seems that after a few days of Amjad's medication, they decided to go to al-Hamshari Hospital. There the man underwent exams that showed he was suffering from liver cancer. They came back to me carrying the report. They'd undoubtedly read the report and discovered the case was hopeless, since it ends with the recommendation that the patient be taken home to rest with strong painkillers.

I read the report while the two men sat in my office, their eyes trained on my lips. People are strange! They think doctors are magicians. What was I supposed to do for them?

"You must take the medication regularly," I told the sick man.

I told the son he could phone me if there were any developments.

The son made a move to go, but Abd al-Wahid didn't budge and asked me, with trembling lips, "Aren't you going to put me in the hospital, Doctor?"

"No," I said. "Your condition doesn't warrant it."

As he spoke, he bit his lower lip; he was wrung with pain, and his eyes were tearing. I don't know what the eyes have to do with the liver, but I could see death like a bleariness covering his eyes. And the man with his red face, his little potbelly and his sixty years didn't want to leave the hospital.

"I don't want to. No. I'll die," he said.

"How long we live is up to God," I said. I didn't hide it from him that his case was serious because I believe the patient has a right to know.

"How much time do I have?"

"I don't know," I said. "Probably not much."

"Why won't you treat me here?"

I explained that we didn't have the means to treat him and that, anyway, his case didn't require a hospital.

He said he didn't want to go home: "You're a hospital, and it's your duty to treat me." He looked at his son for support, but the son stood in silence and looked at me with complicit eyes, as though . . . I won't say he was glad his father's end was near, but he was indifferent.

I stood up to mark the end of the consultation, and then, without any preamble, the son began abusing me. He said he wouldn't take his father because it was the hospital's duty to care for difficult cases, and he threatened me, saying he'd hold me responsible for any harm that might come to his father.

I had to explain our situation again and tell him how, since the Israeli invasion of '82 and the massacres, blockades, and destruction that had come with it, we no longer had the necessary equipment.

"Why do you call it a hospital?" screamed the son.

"You're right," I told him. "But do you want to change the name of the place now? Go and take care of your father."

The son took his father and left, and I forgot about the incident. I didn't even tell you about it.

Yesterday there was a surprise. I was in your room when I heard Zainab scream. I went out and found myself face-to-face with Abd al-Wahid. He had come to the hospital barefoot and in his pajamas. I saw the man standing there and Zainab on the ground, pulling her skirt over her thighs while he mumbled incomprehensibly.

Zainab said he'd shoved her and tried to go up to the rooms.

From where he drew the strength when he was already in the jaws of the angel of death I don't know. I only know he ran into the hospital and started climbing the stairs to the rooms. Zainab, running after him, tried to ask him what he wanted, and he responded with an incomprehensible babble, almost a howling, and when she tried to stop him he shoved her to the ground.

When he saw me, he ran toward me shouting, "I beg you, Doctor, put me back in the hospital." He grabbed my hand and tried to kiss it, saying he didn't want to die.

"Don't treat me if you don't want to," he said. "But I don't want to die. People don't die in hospitals. I implore you, Doctor, for pity's sake, don't send me to die at home."

It was then, Father, that I burst into tears inside but started to laugh. I was laughing, Zainab got up, and the man was trembling. When I asked Zainab to prepare him a room, he seemed to fly with joy. I saw him climbing the stairs behind Zainab, in his dirty white pajamas, his feet hardly touching the stairs, as though I'd saved his life or promised him a place in Paradise.

Believe me, I never saw such joy in all my life. Naturally, nothing changed. His joy disappeared when he lay down on the bed and the pain renewed its onslaught. His son's wife came to be with him. I think he heard his wife ask me when he would die and then start grumbling when she heard me say she had to take care of him and give him his painkillers regularly.

"Regularly!" she exclaimed, not having expected to hear this word. "You mean I have to stay here all the time?" she said, gesturing in my face.

"Of course," I said. "Everyone knows that here it's up to the family to look after the patient."

"We'll take him home," she said. "Home's better."

When the man heard the word *home*, he started to cry.

I said, "No. Abd al-Wahid has to stay in the hospital."

Hearing my reply, he relaxed on the bed and eased himself into his pain, as though he'd found comfort.

Abd al-Wahid, Father, will die in flight from his death. He'll die without knowing it. He didn't want to stare death in the face; he came here so he could close his eyes before dying.

No, please.

Please don't misunderstand me. I just wanted to apologize because I neglected you for a while, and I don't mean to compare you to him or to my father. I don't know if my father saw his death in the muzzle of the gun or whether he shut his eyes before he died. I told you, I don't know much about the man. My mother said one thing and my grandmother another, and I'm not that interested in the subject. I just want to know why my mother ran away.

You don't know a thing about my mother, so listen at least to what I'm about to tell you. My mother ran away because she'd gotten into a bad marriage, because of a certain Jew. This is how my grandmother told it – my grandmother who seemed somewhat pacified after my mother ran away. From then on, my father's horrendous death no longer constituted the mainspring of her life. From then on, she relaxed, tenderness softened her face, and she never stopped abusing this Jew. I was young and incapable of making sense of things, so I didn't understand that when she abused "the Jew" she was talking about a specific person. Later I discovered that "the Jew" was the catalyst for my father's marriage to Najwah, my mother.

My grandmother said my father had to go to work young. His sisters were married and the UNWRA assistance wasn't enough, not to mention that he hadn't done well at school. So he started work at Shukri's pharmacy in Bab Idris. Then he found work in a sheet-metal factory at Mina al-Hesn that belonged to two Jews, Aslan Durziyyeh and Sa'id Lawi. That was where the scandal occurred.

My grandmother said they arrested my father and threw him in jail for more than two weeks. "Poor thing, he was just a child. True, he was tall and mature, but he was only sixteen. He liked reading a lot but was a trouble-maker at school, so he went to work. At the pharmacy, his wages were a joke: seven lira a week, and he worked from dawn to dusk. I asked him to put up with it so he could learn something useful."

The young man who was my father was fascinated by Beirut, especially by Abu Afif's restaurant on al-Burj Square, not far from where he worked. He'd leave the camp at six in the morning, walk from Shatila to al-Burj Square, and arrive at work at half past six. Then he cleaned the shop before opening for customers at seven.

On the way, he'd pass in front of Abu Afif's, which was at the intersection, and the smell of beans, onions, oil, and mint would make him feel hungry. He'd sit on the edge of the pavement opposite, spread out the food he'd brought with him and wolf it down. The food his mother had prepared was divided into two, half for breakfast and half for lunch, and consisted of squares of bread baked and sprinkled with thyme or pounded spices, three boiled eggs, two rounds of pita bread, and a tomato. But the young man seated on the pavement in front of the restaurant would smell the food and see the men sitting at the small tables inside devouring their meals, and he'd finish off all the food he'd brought with him. He'd eat breakfast and lunch together and would never feel satisfied. And when he went back to the house, at seven in the evening, he'd be overcome by hunger again, he'd gulp down his dinner quickly so he could go out into the alleys of the camp.

My grandmother didn't know that my father longed for a dish of beans, but when she found out, she orchestrated a surprise. She woke him at five one morning, after laying out a special table with beans, mint, onions, tomatoes, and a pitcher of tea. The boy got up and looked at his mother's table with neither hunger nor appetite. He ate to please her, telling her the smell over there was different. Then he took his picnic and left. When he came back that evening, my grandmother discovered that he hadn't touched his food. He confessed that he'd eaten beans at the restaurant. He said he hadn't been able to resist. He'd gone into Abu Afif's at ten in the morning and had eaten two plates of beans and paid a whole lira. He said his stomach hurt, and he felt guilty, but the restaurant beans were tastier than the ones she made at home. "Then he started eating beans at Abu Afif's every Friday morning, and he remained faithful to his dish of beans until the day he died, God rest his soul."

But it wasn't really the dish of beans that fascinated my father, it was the city. A new world stood before him, anonymous. And he wanted to know everything. I don't know about how well educated he was, but in his room I found a box full of books. There were novels by Jurji Zeidan on the history of the Arabs, and the books of Taha Hussein, as well as a collection of yellowing Egyptian magazines. My grandmother said that if my father had finished his education, he'd have been a great scholar. But all mothers say the same, right? I'm the only one who has none of that self-confidence mothers can give.

I won't talk to you about my mother now but about why my father married her. What happened was that after about a year of working at Shukri's pharmacy, my father left to work in the sheet-metal factory at Mina al-Hesn.

After Emile Shukri threw him out for being rude to the customers, the young man roamed the streets of Beirut. My grandmother said he denied the accusation and said he'd never pestered customers for tips, and she believed him because he never came back at the end of the week with anything but the six and a half lira, his wages minus the cost of the weekly dish of beans.

"But he smoked," I told her. "Where did he get the money to buy cigarettes?"

"How should I know?" she asked.

My father was shown the door because of tips. Mr. Emile didn't like it: "You can't insist with a customer. If he gives you a quarter of a lira, how can you tell him it's not enough? The customer's free to give you what he wants." It seems, though, that my father insulted one of the customers, so that was the end.

He hung around in the streets. Heading down toward the sea, he kept on until he reached the Bahri restaurant, and from there walked in the direction of al-Zaitouneh. In the Mina al-Hesn district he went into a gas station to ask if they needed help, and there he saw a small notice announcing positions for workers in the sheet-metal factory.

"I went into the workshop through the old arch at the entrance and saw a man wearing a fez and a long, open gown. I asked if they needed workers. He looked me up and down and asked where I was from. When I said Palestine, he took me inside and said, 'Get started.'"

It was because of the workshop that my father went to prison.

The sheet-metal factory owned by the Jews Aslan Durziyyeh and Sa'id Lawi was small and employed about twenty young men, most of whom were Lebanese Christians. The two owners differed in every respect. Aslan Durziyyeh loved the workers and mixed with them. He even invited my father to his house in Wadi Abu Jmil once Yasin got to know his son Simon, and they'd started going to the movies together. Sa'id Lawi, who wore Western dress, was tough on the workers and would dock their wages if they were even a few minutes late.

I won't tell you about the work because I don't know what it was like. What I know is that my father told my mother he'd visit the Durziyyeh family at their home in Wadi Abu Jmil and that they used to feed him lamb-sausage sandwiches and that Simon had suggested he work with him in a dairy that Simon managed close to the fish market. But everything came to an end when the Lebanese police surrounded the factory and arrested all the young men who worked there.

That was 1953, the year when Rabbi Ya'qoub Elfiyyeh was stabbed to death in his home in Wadi Abu Jmil. It seems the police suspected that the gang responsible for the crime consisted of workers at the sheet-metal factory owned by Durziyyeh and Lawi, so they raided the place and took all the young men in for interrogation.

"Your father went straight from the prison to his wedding," said my grandmother.

The story spread through the camp. At the beginning, the newspapers hinted that the presence of three Palestinians among those arrested pointed to it being a revenge killing. You know how they make a big thing out of any crime committed by a Palestinian in Lebanon, so you can imagine when the victim was a rabbi.

The investigation turned up some amazing facts. The rabbi's wife gave everything away, confessing that her husband had been involved in abnormal relationships with seven young men and had fallen madly in love with the Greek, Dimitri Alefteriades, and had kept him overnight in his bed despite his wife's objections.

So the investigation turned to Alefteriades, who confessed before the investigating magistrate, Lt. Colonel Tanyous al-Tawil, that he, along with seven of his comrades, had stabbed the rabbi to death. Dimitri said he'd wanted to get rid of the rabbi, who'd forced him to have sex with the young man, Salim Hneineh, in front of him and hadn't paid him the money he'd promised. He said that he'd hated the rabbi but had had sex with him and had gone along with his wishes out of greed.

Dimitri wept in the courtroom and swore he was innocent and that he'd killed the rabbi unintentionally. The judge, however, accepted the view of the public prosecutor, who asserted that the crime was premeditated and that seven young men had taken part, led by Dimitri.

Naturally, my father was released a long while before the trial. But the details of the sodomy spread through the camp, and my grandmother felt she had to get her son married. She went to visit her daughter in Ain al-Hilweh the day before my father was let out of prison. There she met Najwah and her father, and the father broached the subject. She didn't mention to him that the groom was in prison for a sex crime, and he didn't ask what the groom did for a living. He just confirmed that he owned land in al-Ghabsiyyeh, for in those days people didn't believe the land was lost.

So my father left prison and went straight to his wedding.

It goes without saying that he lost his job, since Aslan Durziyyeh closed his factory after the scandal and devoted himself to prayer, and my father went on visiting him at his house and eating lamb-sausage sandwiches with him. Aslan Durziyyeh even visited my father in the camp when my sister was born. After the events of '58, however, he emigrated to Israel.

It was the rabbi's wife who became the story!

She came to the courtroom and spat in Dimitri's face as he stood handcuffed in the dock, cursed her husband who had soiled the reputation of the Children of Israel, and said that Beirut would burn like Sodom. She said she didn't know what would become of her: "I'm alone and have no children, and I can't stay in my house, which is filled with the stench of sin." She said she wasn't asking for anything, but she was ruined: "I'm completely ruined, Your Honor. I don't have the strength to stay here in Beirut or the courage to migrate to the Land of Israel. What am I supposed to tell them there? That I'm the widow of the rabbi who was murdered in the bed of adultery and sodomy?"

The judge ordered that she be removed from the courtroom because in those days it was forbidden to pronounce the name of the State of Israel, and there was this woman saying that Beirut was going to turn into the new Sodom and that she didn't dare migrate to the land of her ancestors because she would be turned into a pillar of salt. "I am the pillar of salt, Your Honor, who announces the burning of your city," said the woman before the policemen dragged her out of the courtroom.

The upshot was that my father married the girl from al-Tirah.

Najwah Hani Fayyad was fourteen years old when she married Yasin. Her father put her in my grandmother's hands. He took the dowry and left, and the girl entered our house as the wife of Yasin, who'd found himself work in a sheet-metal factory called The Light Metals Company, in the Bir al-Abed district, owned by the Palestinian Badi' Boulis.

I know nothing about my mother's family. My grandmother said her mother had died and her father agreed to the marriage quickly because he'd found a job in Kuwait and didn't want to take his daughter there with his second wife and her children.

"The wedding was like any other wedding – a party, a procession, *you-yous*, and the usual fuss. But the girl remained a stranger among us, and your father changed after he got married. It was all the fault of the girl from al-Tirah. He would come home in the evening after work, close the door of his room, and read for hours. She'd sit with me in the house doing nothing – I swear she did nothing. I'd do all the cooking, wash the clothes, wash the dishes, everything. Even you, Son: I looked after you, and your father took no interest. He began staying away from home a lot and not coming back until the morning. It seems he left his job. I think Adnan Abu Odeh put ideas into his head. Then Najwah had her daughter, and Yasin died, and his daughter followed him."

TELL ME about those days. My grandmother didn't know much. Tell me about the beginning and how you formed the first groups of fedayeen, why my father died, why you disappeared, and why Adnan left the camp.

Tell me why Najwah disappeared.

In Jordan no one knew her address. It was as though she'd melted into thin air. My grandmother said she'd gone to her family in Amman, but she didn't have family. Her father was in Kuwait. So where was she? The subject didn't interest me much because when she disappeared, I was a child, and when I grew older, I held a grudge against her and didn't pay much attention to her story. Then I met Samih and his wife, Samya. You didn't meet Samih Barakeh; you hate intellectuals, especially the ones who come and visit the fighters, theorize and philosophize, and then go back to their comfortable homes.

I first met Samih in '73 when clashes erupted between the army and the camps. He came to the camp with a group of workers from the Palestine Research Center. They toured the camp and then all went home. Except for him. Samih stayed for more than ten days, we were posted in the same positions and we became friends. I liked him a lot. There was great suffering in his face, which was broad and brown and etched with pain. He told me he was waiting for Samya to come from America so they could get married in Beirut. He said he'd fallen in love with her in Ramallah and then had gone to prison, and in the meantime, she had to leave with her family for Detroit, which has the world's largest concentration of inhabitants of Ramallah. I asked why he didn't go to her, complete his education in America, and marry her there. He told me he had his hands full here because he wanted to liberate Palestine. He spoke of his lengthy imprisonment in Hebron and of his dream of living with Samya in the stone house he'd inherited from his father in Ramallah. Samya did come and marry him, and now she lives in the stone house in Ramallah while Samih sleeps in his grave.

Samih said he was arrested for the first time in October of '67.

He was distributing pamphlets against the Israeli occupation in the city. "In prison," he said, "the Israeli officer taught me the most important lesson of my life. He interrogated me with a copy of the pamphlet in his hand and flung questions at me. At first I said I'd been reading the pamphlet and had nothing to do with distributing it, when in fact I was the one who'd written it, which called on schools to strike in protest against the occupation. He looked me in the eye and said I was a coward. He said that if he were in my place, and if his country were occupied, he wouldn't go around distributing pamphlets – that would be shameful – he'd be distributing bombs instead. I confessed I was the one who'd written the pamphlet, and then he grew even more contemptuous and said I deserved to be beaten. I finished my one-year sentence in Ramallah, and when I came out, we started the real resistance. We began organizing a network for Fatah, but they arrested us before we could undertake any operations. They seized one of the members of the network who'd gone to Jordan and had come back in clandestinely, with explosives. And it was in the second prison that I learned my lesson."

Samih said he'd been in the Hebron prison.

"It was February; it was bitter cold, and snowing. They took me to the interrogator, who ordered me to take off my clothes. Around the interrogator were four men with rippling muscles. I took off my shirt. 'Go on,' he said. I took off my vest. 'Your trousers,' he said. I hesitated, but a punch in the face that made my nose bleed persuaded me. I took off my trousers and my shoes and stood naked except for my underpants. With a wave of the hand, the interrogator ordered them to take me away, and we went through the door of the prison and walked to a high mound. It was icy. I was certain they were going to kill me and dump me on the ice as food for the birds. At the top of the mound, the beating started. They attacked my entire body. They used their hands and their feet and their leather belts. They threw me down on the ground and kicked me and stamped on my face, my blood turning into icy red spots. At first I screamed with pain, and I heard the interrogator say, 'Coward.' I remembered the first interrogator and the contempt in his eyes as he flung the political pamphlet in my face, and I went dumb. They beat me, and I swallowed blood and groans. I rolled naked in the ice, and my skin was torn from me. The beating stopped after a stretch that seemed interminable, and they took me back to the prison. At the door to the interrogator's room, where they ordered me to go in and get my clothes, I understood everything."

Samih said he understood.

The naked, bleeding man stood at the door. He heard the order to enter so he could be given his clothes. The naked man turned to the interrogator, took hold of the sleeve of his thick coat, and said to him, "Please, Sir, don't go."

The interrogator turned in disgust. He tried to pull his arm away, but Samih tightened his grip and said, "Please, Sir. I want to tell you something."

"Quickly, quickly," said the interrogator.

Samih swallowed his blood and saliva and little bits that he later realized were pieces of his teeth and said, "Listen, Sir. Listen to me well. I didn't cry out. You beat me and stamped on me, and I didn't cry out even once.

Next time, when you fall into my hands, please don't cry out. I can't stand pity."

Samih didn't know what happened after he said that because he woke up in solitary confinement. When he returned to the common wing, he told the other prisoners only part of his story. He told of the beating on the mound but didn't tell them what happened afterwards in the interrogator's room. He said his words had to remain a secret between him and the interrogator.

"What do you think?" he asked me.

"Do you know the interrogator's name?" I asked him.

"No."

"So?"

"Any one of them will do."

"And if he cries out?"

"I'll kill him."

Samih died in Tunis, and his wife returned to Ramallah. I learned that he died in his small house in Menzah VI. It's said he died of shock at the Israeli invasion of Lebanon in '82, but I'm not convinced that was the reason. I mean, after all those who were killed fighting and in massacres, along comes someone who dies of sentiment! It's too much. But in her letter, Samya said that heart disease ran in Samih's family and his two brothers died of angina before reaching the age of fifty.

Samih said that nothing – not the ice, not the solitary confinement – frightened him as much as the day the prisoners beat him. "In the cell I lost all sense of time. But when the prisoners beat me, I lost my soul."

He said he opened his eyes to find himself in darkness.

The cell was very small, and the darkness extended into every corner. He tried to stand, and his head hit the ceiling. He sat and began to suffocate.

"There wasn't enough air," he said, and he almost went mad worrying about it. He struck the walls of the cell with his fists and discovered that he couldn't find where the door was. The walls seemed to be covered in seamless iron in which the door was lost.

He said he was suffocating, that he opened his mouth wide to capture the air.

He said he felt a terrible thirst inside. This was true thirst: True thirst is having no air.

He said it took a while to get used to the lack of air. Then, once he'd regulated his breathing, he relaxed a little and tamed the darkness.

"Do you know what darkness means?" he asked. "No one knows the meaning of the darkness of the grave. Darkness can't be described. A gluey emptiness creeps over your body and seals your eyes and your pores."

He said he no longer knew who or where he was. Time was lost and with it the man. "To regain my sense of time, I started to count. Eureka! I thought. I opened my ten fingers and started counting. On the count of sixty, I reached a minute. I'd count sixty minutes and reach an hour. But I began to get confused. Had I reached two hours, or was it more? I'd go back to the beginning and count over again. I'd count and the numbers would get confused, and then I couldn't go on any longer and passed into silence."

He said he waited for daybreak, when they brought him water and food.

He said that the day didn't come. "I didn't have a watch, I had nothing. I was alone in the darkness, with the darkness."

He said he hit his head on the walls. He said he bled and screamed until he was hoarse. He said he only wanted one thing from them, that they tell him what day and what time it was.

As Samih told his story, the fear would steal into his words, and he'd shudder and say, "That's the worst torment, being deprived of time. Eternity is true agony."

I asked him what he felt when they took him out of the dark. He was silent for a long time before saying that he felt the beauty of old age. "The prisoner doesn't see himself in the mirror; there are no mirrors there. His only mirror is the eyes of other prisoners." When he saw his own image in the eyes of the other prisoners, who were struck with terror at how he'd aged, he felt comforted.

"And the beating?" I asked.

"That was my mistake," he said.

Do you know what Samih did when he left solitary confinement? He joined the prisoners' Sufi circle. He said he started joining in their prayers and their ritual *dhikr*. In fact, he became close to their sheikh, Hamid al-Khalili, until they found out he wasn't a Muslim.

"When Sheikh Hamid found out I was a Christian, I was terrified," said Samih. "On the mound I wasn't afraid. I thought I'd die on the ice, so I surrendered to the ice; it inhabited my eyes and took me into the whiteness of death. With the sheikh it was a different matter. I think an informer told the sheikh I was a Christian; he said he'd seen my mother with the other visitors, and she was wearing a cross around her neck."

"Is it true?" asked the sheikh.

Samih didn't know what to answer. All he could do was confess. They pounced on him, but the sheikh raised his hand and they stopped in their tracks. The sheikh approached him.

"I said yes. I couldn't find words to justify my position. How could I, how could I tell him that after the darkness of solitary confinement, I felt the need to be among them?

"He asked me if I was mocking them.

"I said, 'No, no, I swear.'

"In the midst of the devotees, as their fury took shape around me, a murmur spread. I wished I were dead.

"The sheikh questioned me and I tried to explain, but my words were the cause of my downfall.

"I said I was Christian, but also not, that I believed in God and loved Christ, but still I was . . .

"'A communist, maybe?' said the sheikh.

"I told him I was a member of Fatah.

"'So you're an atheist,' said the sheikh."

This was where Samih made the mistake that almost cost him his life. He said he saw religion as a social phenomenon, an ethic. He said he loved Arabic literature and knew the Koran and pre-Islamic poetry by heart, and wanted to join in their experience.

"But that's not what you told us at the beginning," said the sheikh.

The sheikh held his hand up and said, "What do you think, brothers?" The brothers, however, rather than responding, attacked. The sheikh managed to extricate himself, but Samih fell beneath their blows and howls.

"On the ice," said Samih, "when I saw death, I didn't open my mouth. But there, I screamed and wept and was afraid. The circles revolved around me and by the time I opened my eyes, I was in solitary confinement. Then they took me to a new communal cell, where I found Sheikh Hamid, and we became friends.

"I explained to him and he explained to me. He wanted to convert me to Islam, and I wanted to convince him of the mixture of secularism, humanism, and Marxism that I believed in. We parted ways without him converting me or me convincing him, but he came to understand that I hadn't been mocking them and that I loved religious ritual."

Samih was an intellectual. He'd had two books published, plus a number of articles. He had his own particular theory on Israel, basically that it would collapse from within and that the moment of liberation was near. He'd mention dates. He was convinced that Israel would collapse at the end of the eighties as a result of its internal contradictions. It was difficult to discuss anything with him because he knew everything. He read Hebrew and English and kept an amazing amount of numbers in his head, which he would toss down in front of you so you could do nothing but agree. Naturally, his predictions didn't come true. The only part that came true was that his remains were transported to Ramallah, where he was buried in his family's grave. Samya was the one who arranged it.

I've told you about Samih so I can tell you about Samya. Samya was an ordinary woman, or at least that's what she led us to believe in Beirut. She did nothing other than wait for her husband. In the space of two years, she bore two children and cooked a lot. When I visited them at home, I'd see her sitting on the edge of the sofa as though ready to get up at any moment. She sat with us but gave the impression of being elsewhere. I was told she changed a lot after Samih died. She arranged for herself and the children to return to Ramallah because she had American citizenship. She'd worked as a librarian and became the official in charge of the Ramallah organization during the *intifada*. It was as though Samih's death had liberated her from waiting and had driven her to forge a new life.

My existence was jarred by Samya's mysterious letter.

I was in Shatila, during the first siege, when a young man called Nadim al-Jamal joined us. He was a friend of the camp commandant, Ali Abu Toq.

Nadim al-Jamal said he had a letter for me from a woman called Samya Barakeh whom he'd met by chance in Amman, where she was returning from a conference in Stockholm. When she found out he was going to see me in Beirut, she asked him to delay until the next morning and brought him a letter for me.

I believed that Samya had never listened to me because although she'd sit with us at their place, she always gave the impression of not really being present. Her husband would ask questions and I'd respond, but she would never intervene. Samih would always talk about his dream of writing a book without a beginning or an end. "An epic," he called it, an epic of the Palestinian people, which he'd start by recounting the details of the great expulsion of '48. He said we didn't know our own history, and we needed to gather the stories of every village so they'd remain alive in our memory. Samih would talk to me about his theories and dreams, and I had nothing to tell him. Well, I did tell him about our village, and my grandmother's stories, and my father's death and my mother's disappearance. With him, or because of his questions, I became acquainted with the stories of my family, put events together and drew a picture of al-Ghabsiyyeh, which I hadn't known. I put so much into getting the story ready that I came to know the village house by house. And during all that time, Samya sat there in silence.

I opened Samya's letter and read it.

To start with, she wrote about her longing for Beirut. Then she informed me of Samih's death and about the difficulties of life in Ramallah. I don't have the letter any longer to read to you because we tore up all our papers when we were afraid the camp would fall. I wish I hadn't torn it up, because it was my only evidence that my mother wasn't a ghost or a story made up by my grandmother. My mother is a real woman, not a phantom belonging to the mysterious world of childhood. I followed orders and tore up the letter; Abu Toq called us together during the siege and ordered us to tear up everything. "I don't want documents falling into their hands," he said. I tore the letter up, but before doing so I wrote down the telephone number Samya had put at the end. I must have tried that number a dozen times, and every time I got a recorded message saying it was out of service. Did I copy it wrong? Or were the numbers on that little piece of paper I kept in the back pocket of my trousers erased or illegible?

Sanya wrote that she'd met my mother, Najwah, and that she had wept and wept when Samya told her she knew me and had kissed her and held her close, so she might breathe in the smell of me. Samya wrote that she'd met my mother in the hospital in Ramallah, that she wore a headscarf, and she was working as a nurse.

Samya was waiting for her son outside the operating room where he was having his appendix taken out when a dark-skinned nurse wearing a white headscarf came over to reassure her.

"Your mother's beautiful, Dr. Khalil," she wrote. I wish I had the letter, but it's gone and I can't get in touch with Samya because the number was either erased or written down wrong.

My mother's there, a nurse like me! Samya wrote that she knew her because she was a nurse. "Nurses look alike, and she resembles you a lot." I'm at a loss. What if I found my mother? I don't want her now, and I don't love her. But why? Why should her ghost come and inhabit this room with me? My grandmother didn't describe her to me, and all I can remember is her brown arm. I used to put my lips on her arm and kiss it. All that's left of that woman for me is the image of a face nuzzling her arm, two eyes fixed on it, a mouth caressing the vast, soft brownness.

Samya's letter brought me this new picture of a woman, a woman who covered her hair and worked as a nurse in Ramallah. My mother emerged from the letter looking like any other woman, and when your mother comes to resemble any other woman, she's not your mother anymore. What strange kind of a relationship is this that depends on an illusion? But everything's like that. Isn't Shams an illusion? My problem with Shams is that the illusion won't die. When they killed her, they didn't kill her image. I haven't told you what I found out afterwards. When Shams was ambushed, she opened the door of her car and was about to get out. The upper half of her body hung outside the open door while the lower half remained inside the car. The number of bullets that poured into her was terrible. More than sixty machine guns firing at once. Her body was torn apart and scattered. Little bits flew through the air and pelted trees and houses. After they'd finished, the pieces were collected in two plastic bags and buried.

As far as I'm concerned Shams didn't die, for when the body is torn apart there is no death. I wish she'd died, but she didn't. And I'm incapable of loving another woman. No, I'm not saying that I won't ever be unfaithful, because everyone is unfaithful, but I can't . . . The problem is not my betrayals but my permanent feeling of being unfaithful. I wish she'd died. No, it's not possible to compare your situation with mine. You died when your wife died, but my wife wasn't my wife, she was another man's wife, and when she died her smell invaded and took hold of me. When her image comes to me, I'm overwhelmed by that feeling that my rib cage is burning. I get up from my bed and stand in the dark and drink it in. I drink in the dark and rub it into my chest, and the memories possess me.

I WAS TELLING you about my mother, and what has Shams to do with that?

I told you I lost my mother, then found her in Samya's letter, then lost her again. All I know is that my father married Najwah after the incident with the Jew, then took a new job in the factory belonging to the Palestinian Badi' Boulis, and then died.

My father married Najwah by chance. If he hadn't worked in the factory belonging to the Jew in Mina al-Hesn, and if the rabbi hadn't been murdered, and if my father hadn't been arrested, and if Najwah's father hadn't been on a visit to Ain al-Hilweh, my father wouldn't have married at such an early age. You know, I feel as though he were my older brother. He was eighteen years older than me. Now do you understand why I hated him, and hated my white hair and my face with its bulging cheekbones and long jaw? I don't want people to look at me as if I were him. The truth is that that sort of look stopped existing after the Shatila massacre – as if everyone had died, as if that massacre, with its more than fifteen hundred victims, had wiped out the memory of faces, as if death had wiped out our eyes and our faces, and we've become featureless.

It was chance, as I told you. Chance was his story.

Explain to me how that young man could work for a Jew after all that had happened? Please don't talk to me about tolerance; say something else.

Listen! I'll tell you this story, and it's up to you to believe it or not. Do you remember Alia Hammoud, the director of the camp kindergarten? Alia asked me to give a lecture to the teachers at the kindergarten on preventive health. So I went. When we were having tea after the lecture, one of the teachers started talking about her problems with a child named Khaled Shana'a. She said he was obnoxious and she couldn't put up with his being in her class any longer. He was full of turbulence and anxiety, and she asked Alia's permission to expel him from the class. Alia told her to be silent. The teacher continued complaining, at which point Alia said to her in a controlled voice that she couldn't expel him and suggested that the teacher try being gentle and caring with him. When the teacher indicated her dissatisfaction with the director's suggestion, Alia's voice rose.

"Do you know who Khaled is? He's the grandson of a great man."

She was speaking of the '48 occupation of her village, which was located in the district of Safad, and of how a group of young men had been taken and then crushed by a bulldozer; Khaled Shana'a, the child's grandfather, was the only one to survive. She also mentioned how, after the villagers crossed the Lebanese border and took up residence in the village of Yaroun, Khaled was the only one to return to Teitaba. He stole into the village on his own, went to his house, opened the door, and everything exploded. The man opened his door and found himself thrown to the ground, blood gushing from him. He pulled himself together, returned to Yaroun, and spent the rest of his life blind.

"He's a hero," said Alia. "His grandfather is a hero, and I won't expel his grandson."

The teacher couldn't understand where the heroism lay in the story, since she was one of the ones who'd escaped from the Tal al-Za'atar camp, where, during the siege of the camp, which had ended with the massacre of its inhabitants, she'd seen for herself how heroes die and their acts of heroism disappear.

"I don't want to hear such stories," said the teacher, leaving.

But Alia went on. She said her mother still remembered Salim Nisan, the Jewish cloth seller who came to Teitaba before it fell and said, "Muslims, don't go anywhere! We're all in the same boat!" The cloth seller had originally been from Aleppo. He carried his goods over his shoulder and went through the Arab villages selling without getting paid. He carried a big ledger in which he recorded debts, and people paid what they could – a jerry can of oil, a dozen eggs, and everyone loved him. He'd go into people's houses, eat their food, and flirt with the women; his sixty years made him seem like an innocuous old man. He'd laugh and tell jokes, and the women would surround him laughing and choose their cloth.

Alia was astonished when her mother told her that a number of the women of Teitaba crossed the border to pay him what they owed.

I didn't ask Alia how the women of Teitaba knew where to find Salim Nisan once the border between Lebanon and Palestine had become a reality.

I listened to the story as one would to a love story, and I didn't ask Alia for the details of the meeting between the women of Teitaba and Salim Nisan.

"We helped Salim Nisan out and that teacher won't help Khaled Shana'a out. Is that any way to do things?"

COME, LET'S get back to our story and ask what that young man, my father, who was one of the first members of the fedayeen groups to initiate the struggle against Israel, wanted by working in Mina al-Hesn. Was he drawn to his enemies? Were they his enemies?

Today the Durziyyeh family lives in Israel. I found that out from my aunt's husband, who told me, as he was telling me about al-Ghabsiyyeh, that he'd gone to see them in Haifa and had visited Simon at his falafel and humus restaurant. Simon had been gracious to him and had asked him about the circumstances of my father's death.

What did my aunt's husband have to do with Simon Durziyyeh? Did he also work in the sheet-metal factory with my father, or did he visit him there to see how he was doing, or what? I don't understand a thing anymore! My aunt's husband said Simon took him on a tour through the whole of Palestine and that he visited Tel Aviv and Nahariyyeh and Safad and was amazed at everything he saw, to the point of almost believing he was in a European country.

Is it true, Father, that they've created a European country?

I've tired you out, and I'm tired too.

I've told you story after story, but my mother's secret remains a secret. The only thing I got out of Samya's mysterious letter was that she'd gotten remarried and had gone to live with her husband in Ramallah, where she discovered that he was already married. And that she became a nurse.

That's all.

Catherine came half an hour ago. Do you remember her? The French actress I told you about? She said she'd got in a taxi and asked the driver to take her to Galilee Hospital. When he told her there was no such hospital, she explained that she wanted to go to Shatila. The driver was reluctant, but she paid him ten dollars so he brought her to the door of the hospital, muttering under his breath.

I ordered a cup of Turkish coffee for her, and she drank it down in one gulp, wrinkling her face because the coffee burned her tongue. She sat in silence and then asked me why people hated the Palestinians. I didn't know what to say. Should I have told her about the fragmentation caused by the Civil War? Or say what Nahilah said to the Israeli officer: "We're the Jews' Jews. Now we'll see what the Jews do to their Jews." I don't agree with these phrases we use so easily every day. I can understand Nahilah because she was over there, where a Palestinian finds himself face to face with a racism like that toward the Jews in Europe. But not here. We're in an Arab country and speak the same language.

Catherine said she'd decided not to act in the play, that she'd feel ridiculous if she did. She asked my opinion.

She said she was afraid, and that they had no right. Then she burst into tears.

I wanted to invite her to dinner and talk with her, but she said she couldn't play this role because that much horror couldn't be put into a play.

Why did Catherine come to my office and then leave?

These questions are unimportant, Father, but our whole life is composed of unimportant questions that pile up on top of one another and stifle us.

I want to rest now.

I'm getting tired of talking and of death and of my mother and of you. I want to lay my head on the pillow and travel wherever I wish.

But please explain the secret of my father's death.

My grandmother told me they were wearing civilian clothes, and my mother said they were soldiers. And what do you say?

Do you believe we can construct our country out of these ambiguous stories? And why do we have to construct it? People inherit their countries as they inherit their languages. Why do we, of all the peoples of the world, have to invent our country every day so everything isn't lost and we find we've fallen into eternal sleep?

It's Umm Hassan.

She came to the hospital to visit you three weeks before she died and said you had to be taken back there.

She came into the room and looked at you out of the corners of her small, sharp eyes. I was sitting in this eternal chair I sit in, and she gestured to me. "What?" I asked, and she put her finger to her lips and made me follow her out.

In the corridor she spoke in a low voice, almost a whisper. When I asked her why she was talking that way, she said, "So he won't hear."

"They can hear. I know them," she said.

She talked about your planet, which no longer resembled ours. She said you were in torment and mustn't be disturbed. "Talking's no good anymore, my son," she said. "He has to be taken back over there."

Umm Hassan took me into the corridor and whispered that it was necessary to take you back to your country.

"How terrible!" she said. "He's become like Aziz Ayyoub. You can't let him die alone here."

She said you were in this state because you refused to die alone. "Shame on you, my son, shame. The man spends his life over there and you want him to die here, in this bed? No, no, impossible. Get in touch with his children."

I told her I didn't know how to get in touch with his children in Deir al-Asad. She said I should contact Amna, that she would know what to do. I told her Amna had disappeared. She said she knew where she lived in Ain al-Hilweh and would go to her and come back with your children's telephone number so we could contact them and organize your Return.

"He has to die there. It's a sin. I know him. He'll never die here."

She put her hand on my shoulder and said you were like Aziz Ayyoub, who died hanging from the branches of the lotus tree.

I told her Aziz Ayyoub had committed suicide and there was no basis for comparison.

She said no. "Saints don't commit suicide. They killed him to get rid of him."

"But he wasn't causing any problems, so why should they have killed him?" I asked.

"You don't know anything," she said. "They killed him by hanging him from the tree, and if it hadn't been for God's wisdom and the tree's kindness, people would've thought he'd committed suicide. I didn't see him, Son, but people told me: His eyes were open, the rope was around his neck, and he was lying on his back like a piece of wood, like this Yunes. No, Son. A man can't die among men. A man needs a woman to die. Women are different, they're stronger and can die on their own if they want to. But a man needs women so he can die. Aziz Ayyoub died that way because he was alone. His wife left him and took her children to Lebanon. I don't understand why he lived that way. He said he was the guardian of the tree and of the mosque and of the graves, and he couldn't abandon them. Who's guarding the tree now? God is its guardian. I went there and I saw how the tree guards the whole of Galilee. The tree is the guardian, so why do we guard it? And this Yunes, Abu Salem, look at him. He's shrinking and becoming a child again. Look at his face and eyes. His face is the size of a child's palm, which means he wants his mother. Why are you keeping him here? Don't you see how he's shrinking? Take him to his mother, my son, and let him die in her house. Tomorrow I'll go to Amna and get their telephone number and we'll send him back. I know him better than you. He was a stubborn man; we called him 'the billy goat.' When he came back from over there, he stank like a billy goat, and we'd know Yunes had come back. How that poor woman could stand it I don't know. A woman is a deep secret."

Umm Hassan placed her hand over her mouth to hide her smile, then she drowned in laughter. When I say *drowned*, I mean it: She fell into her choked-off, silent roar of laughter, and her white headscarf slid onto her shoulders. Suddenly, she put her scarf back on, lowered her hand, and wiped away her smile.

I told her Nahilah would bathe you the moment you arrived at the cave of Bab al-Shams.

"Alas!" she sighed, turning her face away as though to close the subject.

I told her about the cave and about the village you built inside the caverns of Deir al-Asad. She said she knew those caves, which opened their mouths like ravening animals, and knew that no one ever went into them. "Those caves are haunted, my son."

She told me about the goat that got lost in one of the caves of Deir al-Asad and reappeared in Ramallah.

"It's the truth, Son. In Ramallah. And it was white. Its hair had turned white as though it had seen something terrible." She said people had seen strange things in its eyes, so they shot it dead and no one dared eat its meat. "And now you come along after all this time and tell me that Yunes lived in those caves and used to bathe there. No, my son. I know better. He'd take her into the fields. Who told you about the caves? Yunes would go to his house, tap on the windowpane and wait for her. She'd come out and follow him, and he'd take her to the fields, and that was where those things happened. Not in the cave. Impossible."

I told her that it was you who'd told me about it, and I tried to explain how Nahilah had fixed up the cave, how she'd brought mats and the mattress and the wooden chest and the primus stove and so on, but it seems it's impossible to convince Umm Hassan of anything she thinks she already knows.

Then I understood.

This is your secret, Father. Your secret is your obscurity. Your secret is your multiple names and your mysterious lives. You are the Wolf of Galilee, and why should the wolf reveal his secrets? You yourself chose the name Wolf: You told me you wanted to be a wolf so the wolves wouldn't eat you. You were a wolf enveloped in its secret. No one knew your secret or penetrated Bab al-Shams, which you made into a house, a village, a country.

I told Umm Hassan that the Ramallah goat resembled my mother. Najwah seemed to have disappeared down a tunnel from here to there. She disappeared from Beirut only to appear in a hospital in Ramallah wearing her white nurse's outfit.

"No, my son, no," said Umm Hassan.

"What could your mother do in the face of your grandmother's madness? It was Shahineh who destroyed her, and all the people of the camp were witnesses. After the death of your little sister, the life of your mother became hell. Your grandmother, God rest her soul, was an excellent woman, but she was the reason. Was Najwah responsible for the death of your father? She didn't know anyone here, she was from Tira, near Haifa, and had come on a visit to Lebanon. Your grandmother sunk her claws into her and managed to persuade her father to give his daughter to her son, who worked in that workshop that stank of scandal and filth. She wouldn't let her touch anything in the house. She'd do the dishes, and the old woman would come along, sniff the dishes and the pots, and wash them again. She'd mop the floor, and your grandmother would mop it again behind her, cursing the filth. Your mother, my son, is no Ramallah goat; your mother is an unhappy creature, God help her. Her family must have truly tormented her to make her agree to marry the Bedouin and live with him in Ramallah."

"The Bedouin! What Bedouin?" I asked.

"Yes, the Bedouin. Abu al-Qasem had come to Amman and saw her at Ashrafiyyeh Hospital, where she worked, so he went to her family and asked for her hand, and they agreed right away without asking her because her stepmother wanted to get rid of her."

Umm Hassan said that in Ramallah, Najwah found out that the Bedouin was married to another woman, and she lived in misery and humiliation. The Bedouin married her and then regretted it because his first wife, who was also his first cousin, turned the whole clan against him, so that Najwah became a sort of secret wife, which was why she was forced to work in the hospital.

I asked Umm Hassan how she knew all this.

She said that everybody knew.

"But I didn't know."

"The husband's the last to know."

But I'm not her husband, and I don't understand. Why didn't anyone tell me about my mother? When I'd ask my grandmother, she'd shut down, locking her face with the key of silence. I had to wait for that mysterious letter from Ramallah to know, and still I didn't know. I tore up the letter, I lost Samya's telephone number, and I lost the name of the Bedouin in Ramallah. Even Umm Hassan didn't know the Bedouin's name even though she knew everything. She told me about my uncle Aziz and about his days and nights in the ruins of al-Ghabsiyyeh. "He lived alone for more than twenty years, dividing his time between the tree, the mosque, and the graves. He'd stand in front of the lotus tree, talking to it and listening to it. He knew everything because the tree used to tell him. When people came from the surrounding villages to visit the tree, he'd disappear. He wouldn't talk to them or go near them. They'd see him like a distant ghost wrapped in the shadows of his white mantle. They'd greet him and he'd respond with a nod. They'd bend over the roots of the tree and light their candles before tying their strips of cloth and ribbons to the branches and departing."

I told her that he'd committed suicide, that he was mad: "Who could live alone for twenty years and not go mad?"

Her face lit up, seemingly in agreement, but then she said, "No, no, Son. He's a saintly man; people make offerings to him and call his name when praying for their children."

But I'm tired of saints and heroes and wolves. My father's a hero and you're a wolf, and I'm lost in the middle. I see my father's death in yours and in your newfound childhood I see his. It's very strange! I see you both, but I don't see myself, it's as though I'm no longer here and everything around me is unreal, as though I've become a shadow of the lives of two men I don't know. It's true, I don't know you. You I know only through this childlike death of yours, and him only through a picture on a wall. Even Shams, Shams who I loved to the point of wanting to be her assassin, Shams whose vengeful ghost I fear, seems to be no more than the ghost of that woman who disappeared and became a white goat in a hospital in Ramallah.

I can't believe Umm Hassan and her saintly Aziz Ayyoub, or my grandmother and the evil spell that was the cause of my father's murder. Instead of telling me about the first fedayeen in whose ranks my father died, Shahineh told me about the cave and its curse.

Shahineh would contemplate the photo of the dead man; she'd wipe it with water to keep it fresh and would talk about the cave of al-Ghabsiyyeh.

She said she'd known that Yasin would die and that a woman was going to kill him.

"May God curse me," she'd say, "I married him off and thought nothing of it. I was terrified by the business of the rabbi, so I married him to that girl from Tira. I paid no attention to her eyes. Her eyes had something of that fear I saw after the business with the cave."

My grandmother said it was called Aisha's Cave. Aisha's Cave is to the north of the village, on the high ground that separates al-Ghabsiyyeh from al-Kabri.

My grandmother said that my paternal uncle, Mohammed Abdallah Ayyoub, was a religious scholar and a Sufi, and he had power over the djinn. "One day he sent his son Mahmoud and a boy called Sa'id with my son, Yasin, to the cave, telling them, 'When you arrive, read this paper. A black dog will appear. Do not fear it, for it is possessed by the djinni that rules the cave, and watch out if you're afraid!'"

My grandmother said Mohammed Abdallah Ayyoub wanted to test the three young men in preparation for their initiation into his Sufi circle.

"At the cave, it happened as he had said, for as soon as Mahmoud had finished reading the paper, the black dog appeared. Mahmoud was afraid and started to run. The dog struck him with its tail, knocked him down and then pounced on him. In the meantime, Sa'id and Yasin managed to get away. Then we don't know what happened. Mahmoud had a fever for three days, and when his temperature went down, he left his father's house carrying a stick. He knocked on the first door he came to, and when they opened it, he rushed at the people and beat them with the stick. He was like a madman. No, he had truly gone mad. He kept going from house to house beating and smashing until the men of the village managed to tie him up. He was sent to the insane asylum in Acre. I don't know what the Jews did with him after the fall of Acre. During those days, people forgot themselves and their children, so how could they remember the insane? We were living in apocalyptic times. We rushed about in the fields to save our skins, but not one of us was saved, not one.

"I saw death in the eyes of my son. Yasin came back from the cave utterly transformed. I saw death hovering over him and knew he was going to die. And when he married Najwah, I saw death in her eyes, but somehow I took no notice, God curse us human beings. I saw death, but I wanted to release him from those rumors that clung to him after the incident of the Greek boy and the rabbi. So I decided to get him married and paid no attention, and he died."

This is how things become linked in the mind of a senile old woman. The whole business of the cave is meaningless. Fantasies, Father. Fantasies, Son. We invent stories of our misery and then believe them. We'll believe anything so as not to see. We cover our eyes and set off, and then we bump into each other.

Umm Hassan believed the story of the cave never took place and that my grandmother was crazy, persecuting my mother for no reason and forcing her to run away into God's vast world.

But Umm Hassan knows that God's world is narrow and that "eventually, all men meet."

My mother fled from Beirut to Amman and then from Amman to Ramallah. She disappeared as completely as if she'd gone into your cave, dear friend. Which reminds me: Tell me about the cave. Umm Hassan said the Deir al-Asad cave was uninhabitable, so where's the Bab al-Shams you spoke about? Where is that village that stretches through interlinked caves, "a village that's bigger, I swear, than Ain al-Zaitoun," as you used to say? "I proposed, 'Come on, let's look for caves in Galilee and bring back the refugees.

A cave is better than a tent, or a house of corrugated iron, or banana leaf walls.' But they didn't agree. Members of the Organization said it was a pipe dream. An entire people can't live in caves. They told me to go look for caves for the fedayeen and I saw the sarcasm in their expressions, so I didn't look. I arranged my cave for myself and by myself and lived in it."

Do you want me to take you back there, as Umm Hassan suggested?

"Go to his house, Son, and look. You may find their telephone number. Call them. Call his children, and they'll work things out through the Red Cross."

I don't think Umm Hassan's suggestion is practical. I'm not selfish, and it's not that I'm afraid. To hell with this life. Whenever I think of you, I feel eyes boring into my back, eyes saying I'm scared. No, I'm not scared. Does Umm Hassan think I haven't tried to contact your children? Do you remember that first day, Father, when Amna came to tell me of your fall? That same day I asked her to contact your children, and she did. She said she did.

"What did they say?"

"Nothing."

I didn't ask what *nothing* meant. Nothing means nothing.

She said nothing, and I didn't comment. At the time it never occurred to me that you might live. Being sure you'd die, I didn't think of sending you over there. What for? I don't believe they want you anymore. This is what things have come to.

In describing your other planet, Umm Hassan told me you could see God.

"Pay attention, my son," she said. "Pay attention to his movements. We may learn something from them. People like him see God."

"How's that, Umm Hassan?"

"I don't know, my son, but I'm sure of it."

She told me about an old woman in Acre that she'd known before everything happened. Whenever the woman awakened from her stupor, she'd tell people of strange things, and then they'd happen. "It was like she saw

God, my son. I was there, training as a nurse, and this woman, who was halfway between life and death, would fall unconscious for a few days and say these strange things when she awoke. For instance, she'd say that so-and-so's husband was going to die. The man's wife would be nearby and would laugh it off, but when she went home, the prophecy would turn out to be true. They all started to fear her; her children and grandchildren sat around her deathbed trembling with fear, and they only relaxed when she died – as if a stone had been lifted from their chests. To tell you the truth, Khalil, I think they killed her. They were scared of her cottony words, her quavering voice, and her white hair. I think one of them smothered her with a pillow because she turned blue in death. But I didn't say anything. I returned to the village, dying with fear. And I'm telling you now, this man, Yunes Abu Salem, is in the same place. Take him back home and let's be done with it."

CAN YOU hear me?

What's happening to you?

You know, you're really starting to look like Na'im, Noor's son. I know you'd rather look like Ibrahim, your first son and your twin, but unfortunately you don't look like him; you look like one of your grandsons. When I went to your house I saw a picture of Na'im. I was shocked, it was as if I were seeing you in front of me! I didn't go to your house because of Umm Hassan. I did search for the telephone number out of curiosity though, but didn't find it. No, I went for the pictures. And there I saw you the way you really are. What a setup, my dear friend! Two rooms and a kitchen and a bathroom. The first room for guests, with a traditional carpet spread on the floor, three sofas, a small table, a radio, a television and a video player, and one photo on the wall. I went up to the photo and saw a group of children circled around an old woman. It's her, I thought. I moved closer because I couldn't distinguish the features. Their features were almost obliterated, as though time had wiped them away – or not time, the photographer. The photographer had taken the picture from a distance in order to get that throng of twenty-five children around the woman into the frame. The result was a crowd of indistinguishable children. I smiled at them. You don't know them; to you they're just numbers and names, these grandchildren of yours whose names you won't tell me. Wait, you did tell me about Nahilah No. 2, Noor's daughter; you told me you loved her particularly. Which one is she?

I WENT INTO the bedroom, and there I saw them all. It's like a studio. Seven photos frame to frame on the wall and, above the bed, a large photo of Nahilah. An amazing number of small photos of children of various ages hung on the other wall. A world of photographs. A strange world. I don't know how you managed to sleep amid all that life.

Tell me, did you sleep?

During the long nights of the Lebanese civil war, when there was no electricity, did you light a candle in your room and see them transformed into shadow puppets flickering on the walls?

Weren't you afraid?

They frightened me, those photographs. I entered your bedroom in the early evening. The clock said five and it wasn't dark yet, but there wasn't enough light. I tried the switch – no electricity. I seemed to be floating with the photos in the dark. I went up to them, one by one, and discovered your secret world, a world of photographs hung from the cords of memory. The photographs seemed to move. I heard low voices emanating from the walls and was afraid.

Where did all those photos come from?

When you went, did you go for Nahilah or for the pictures?

Tell me how you could live with their pictures. How could you restrain yourself from going to their houses and breathing in their smells, one after another?

I hear laughter in your eyes, you're telling me you did see them. You had gone into the house and kissed them one after another. It was the day that your father, the blind sheikh, died.

During that terrible winter of '68, the likes of which Galilee hadn't seen for a hundred years, Yunes arrived at his cave in the pouring rain, exhausted and soaked. The wolf arrived at his cave covered in mud and with every part of him knocking against the other. He lit a candle and searched for dry clothes in the caverns he'd made into his home, and all he could find were a shirt and a wool sweater. He undressed, put the dry clothes on over his wet body, and left the cave. He headed to the right, behind the hill that hid his cave from the village, and ran into the masses of mud that were sliding down with the rain, forming torrents of mud and water. He fell into the torrent, swallowing a lot of mud before getting back on his feet and continuing on his way. He reached his house, gave his three knocks on the window, and left. But she ran after him, grabbed him by the arm, and led him into the house he hadn't entered for twenty years. The blind sheikh was laid out on the ground, dying. He saw his mother beside the sleeping man, whose mattress had been placed on the floor. When his mother saw him, a sort of scream emerged from deep inside her. She stood and opened her arms, tried to go toward him, doubled over and sunk down again onto the floor. Yunes went up to her and kissed her on the head. She took him in her arms and squeezed him, and the water started to run off him. The mother wept while the water dripped from his clothes, and Nahilah stood there.

"Now you come?" said the mother.

Nahilah took him to the bedroom, undressed him, dried him with a large white towel, wrapped his naked body, and fetched hot oil and rubbed his back, his belly, and all his limbs with it.

"You're going to get sick," she said. "What made you come?"

She rubbed him with the hot oil and left him to bring dry clothes, and when she returned she found the water exuding from his pores. He was naked, he was shivering. Droplets of water oozed from his limbs – water streamed onto the floor, a man enveloped in water as though it dwelt in his bones. She dried him again and told him how the blind sheikh had fallen into a coma three days before and how they'd given him nothing but a few drops of water dripped into his mouth, and that since the evening before he'd been shaking with fever.

Yunes left the room, drops of water clinging to his feet, and approached the prone man. He bent over Ibrahim, kissed him and left, saying nothing to his mother, who was reciting verses from the Koran, her eyes drifting in the emptiness.

Yunes returned to his cave, he was hungry but could find nothing to eat. He sat alone smoking. Then she came. She was wrapped in a long woolen blanket dripping with water that gave off a smell of mold. Nahilah cast the blanket aside and sat down. She said she'd brought him three boiled eggs, two sweet potatoes, two pieces of bread, and an onion. He took the food from her and devoured it. He'd tear off a corner of the bread, stuff it with onions, sweet potatoes, and eggs, and swallow the whole thing without chewing. By the time she'd made him his glass of tea, he'd polished off the lot. She told him the man had died and that she was tired and was going to go back to help his mother prepare for the funeral.

She stood up, wrapped herself in the woolen blanket, and bade him farewell. He grabbed her by the waist, threw her to the ground, and made love to her. At the time, Nahilah didn't understand why he'd behaved that way. She'd come with the intention of bringing him food, informing him of his father's death, and returning. He'd listened to her weep for his father without shedding a tear himself while he was busy eating. And when she got up to go, he threw her down on the soggy, musty blanket, and took her. He was like an animal mounting its mate. He was like he'd been in the beginning, an ignorant kid who didn't know how to love. On that stormy night he mounted her. Nahilah tried to refuse, but he was on top of her. She tried to move so he could penetrate her, but he came. In an instant, the hot fluid spurted and spread across her dress. She tried to get up, but he clung to her neck and broke out into loud sobs. She stayed motionless and cradled his head, and his sobs grew even greater. "Let me go, my love," she said. "I have to go to your mother. The poor woman's alone with the dead man and the children."

Instead of moving aside and letting her go, he hung on to her. His body covered her entirely, his chest on her chest, his belly on her belly, his feet on her feet. She had to shove him several times before she succeeded in freeing herself. She got up, straightened her clothes and departed, swathed in the damp blanket. Nahilah couldn't understand how he'd lain with her without her removing any of her clothes. He hadn't penetrated her, she thought on her way back through the black night spotted with drops of rain the size of cherries.

At eleven the next morning, the sun was wrapping itself around the hills of Deir al-Asad and spreading itself over Galilee. The procession moved off from the house of Sheikh Ibrahim al-Asadi toward the mosque. After the prayer, they carried the bier to the village cemetery. The men walking behind the bier, which was raised up to the height of outstretched arms, bent their heads, covered with their white *kufiyyehs*, as they tried to avoid the mud and the puddles, and kept up a loud buzz of prayers.

Opposite the hill on which the village cemetery lay, Yunes stood alone, holding his rifle and hiding behind a tall palm tree that he would call from that moment on, "Sheikh Ibrahim's palm." There the men turned into ripples of water around the bier as they circled it to the sound of Sufi chanting, their voices reaching Yunes: "*Madad! Madad!* Succor! Messenger of God, Beloved of God, People of the House, You whom we adore." He seized his rifle, raised it in the air, and placed his finger on the trigger to bid the sheikh farewell with a salute. Instead, he lowered it and pointed its muzzle at the ground, bent over where he stood, and started to sing with the others as he had done when he was a child, when his father had taken him from Ain al-Zaitoun to Sha'ab. There, in the little mosque, the young Yunes would let himself be transported by the rhythm of the men as they spun around their blind sheikh, singing, shouting and dancing. And now, Yunes wanted to revolve with them and merge with their voices, but he stood still where he was and listened to the voice of the child he'd been.

The funeral rites came to an end, earth was thrown over the sheikh, everybody dispersed, and Yunes returned to his cave, where he stayed for a week, never leaving it. Then Nahilah came and took you to the house. You walked behind her like a sleepwalker, and when you arrived you were a little nervous and said you shouldn't go in, so she dragged you inside. In the courtyard, the children were playing, but you didn't go to them. You went in and sat down in the living room; your mother came and sat down beside you, took your hand, and said nothing.

You were sitting next to your mother when you heard Nahilah's voice calling the seven children into the house. She'd call to each of them by name, then say, "Shoo!" as though she were herding chickens rather than children. They came in and saw you. None of them came over to you, and you didn't open your arms the way a father who sees his children is supposed to do. They came in and you stayed where you were. They came in and drew back and stood in a single row, pressing against the wall as though they were afraid of you. Silently, you got up, approached them, knelt, and kissed them one after the other. Then you stood up and left. Noor, who was fourteen, cried "Dad!" as you went away.

That was your only meeting with your children, and when you recalled it, you spoke of it as a dream – "as though it never happened." When you told me about your father's funeral and how you'd taken part, you said that the barbed wire and the electric border fences hadn't stopped you from bidding him farewell.

AND YESTERDAY, I stood in your room, under the avalanche of pictures – I saw them all. I saw your children and your grandchildren with their backs to the wall, waiting for you to get up and approach them on your knees and kiss them. I heard Noor's voice and saw your mother's death-inhabited eyes. You told me your mother died two months after your father and that you didn't go to her funeral.

That day, after you'd kissed them, you returned to Lebanon. You came back once more on a short visit before disappearing for more than a year because of your preoccupations and the tense situation on the border. In the meantime, everything had changed. Salem had started work with his brother Mirwan in Mr. Haim's garage in Haifa, and Noor was about to announce her engagement to Isa al-Kashif, who worked as a construction worker before becoming a contractor in the Arab villages, and Nahilah was exhausted.

"I'm worn out with poverty and the daily grind," she said.

You were together in the olive grove next to your cave, sitting beneath the summer moon that shed its light on the green leaves, giving them a blue shimmer. You waited for her there because she'd told you, "Beneath the tree." You tapped on the window and were about to leave when Nahilah appeared behind the glass and said, "Beneath the Roman tree." You thought she meant the enormous old tree with the hollow trunk, the one that yields a small fruit with a special taste.

You love olives.

All of us love olives, especially those little green ones Nahilah used to cover with coarse salt in a cloth bag and recommend you place – the moment you reached your house – in a glass jar filled with water so the salt would melt and rise, white and raw, to the top, and into which you were to throw a few bay leaves, leaving the jar for a month before eating them.

You kept those olives for celebrations. You'd celebrate with your olives in Shatila, taking a handful from the jar and steeping them in garlic, lemon, and oil, and drinking a glass of arak while listening to Saleh Abd al-Hayy singing, "My beloved, he tells me what to do," taking your ritual to its pinnacle. You called those moments the ultimate prayer. You'd . . . no, I won't say the truth now so that I don't spoil your memories, which you construct to please yourself. But when I listened to you talking about those Roman olive trees, planted before the time of Christ, saying they had an irradicable hidden bitterness, a bitterness that gave one an appetite for life, and then going on at length about those huge trees with the hollow trunks which they called Roman because they're as old as the Romans, I'd imagine you with another woman. Please don't get upset. You know I'm telling the truth, or what would the visits of those two women mean? The first I told you about. She came, and then disappeared. The second would come every Thursday at four in the afternoon. She still has a certain beauty, especially in her fine jaw and the two creases that crossed her cheeks. Her name is Claire; she introduced herself as Claire Midawwar. She came into your room and sat down. I was cleaning the mucus extractor. She didn't pay the least bit of attention to me. She made me feel out of place, so I left the room, and when I came back an hour later, she was gone.

She continued to come at her regular time and I continued to leave her alone with you. Last week, however, she was late. Do you know why I haven't spoken of her until today? Because she'd become a part of our life here in the hospital, a routine one pays no attention to until it stops. Last week I became aware of her because she was late, and I decided to wait for her to ask her who she was. I put on a clean white gown and thought to wear my glasses, which I usually forget in my pocket since I haven't gotten used to the idea of putting on glasses. As soon as she entered the room, I went over to her to shake hands.

"I'm Dr. Khalil Ayyoub."

"Pleased to meet you, Doctor," she answered, sitting down again.

"I haven't had the pleasure of making your acquaintance," I said.

"I'm a friend," she said. "An old friend."

I got into a stop-and-go conversation with her about conditions in the city, but she didn't seem to want to talk, as though I were stealing the time she'd set aside for you. Despite her irritation with my questions and her abrupt and evasive answers, I decided to be impertinent. I sat on the second chair and leaned forward a little as if to follow what she was saying. As soon as she saw me sit down, she put her hand on her hip as though she were about to stand up. Before the gesture could be transformed into the arch of the back that precedes the moment of rising, I got a question in. I asked her, point-blank, what her relationship to you was.

"When did your relationship with him start, Madame . . . ?"

I left my question hanging in the air, and the shock took the wind out of her sails. Looking at me with startled eyes, she said, "Claire. Claire Midawwar."

"Have you known him for a long time?"

"A very long time," she said and got up.

"Tell me about him," I said.

She picked up her bag and said she was going. "Look after him, and may God make him well."

Mme. Claire didn't come that week, and it's possible that she'll never come back again. It's my fault, but I couldn't help but ask her. I saw her coming once a week and I imagined her with you, eating Roman olives dripping with lemon juice and oil.

Eating Nahilah's olives with another woman!

I don't understand anymore.

You'll ask me about the French actress, I know. But no, I swear there's nothing between us. I just felt a strange tenderness.

You'll ask me about my visit to her at the Hotel Napoléon on Hamra Street.

I didn't mean to visit her. I was feeling stifled here, so I went. I'm not going to tell you any more now. I'll behave like Claire Midawwar, who went away without telling me a thing.

Tell me, is Claire the woman you sought shelter with during the Israeli invasion of '82? You claimed that you'd fled to a priest's house! Was she the priest? Got you! I've got you now, and it's up to me to decipher what you said. Everything needs translating. Everything that's said is a riddle or a euphemism that needs to be interpreted. Now I must reinterpret you from the beginning. I'll take apart your disjointed phrases to see what's inside them and will put you back together again to get at your truth.

Can I get at your truth?

What does your truth mean?

I don't know, but I'll discover things that had never crossed my mind.

"And you?" you'll ask.

"Me?"

"Yes, you. What about you?"

"Nothing."

"And the French actress?"

"Nothing."

"And Shams? Where is she?"

Please don't say anything about Shams. I promise, I'll forget about Claire and the olives dripping with lemon juice and everything else, but please, not Shams.

So let's close this chapter and return to the summer moon and Nahilah.

> 398 <

That night, the moon was bright in the skies of Galilee. Yunes tapped on the windowpane and left, but he heard her whisper. He turned and saw her standing at the window, the moonlight pouring down onto her long black hair. He went closer and she said, "The Roman tree. Go on ahead and meet me at the Roman tree."

He went to the tree, wondering why she didn't want to go to the cave, guessing that she might be indisposed, because at that time of the month, she'd come to him at Bab al-Shams and ask him to go out with her into the fields, and he'd stubbornly refuse. The game would end with him kissing every crevice of her body while she screamed at him, "Stop it! Stop it! It's a taboo!" and he'd give way before this taboo and be content with expending himself between her small breasts.

He went to the Roman tree, but instead of waiting for her beneath it, he got inside its huge, hollow trunk, which was wide enough to hold more than three people, and the idea rushed into his head that he could possess her there. He hid in the trunk, held his breath, and heard her circling the tree looking for him. She was like a small child lost in the fields. His love caught fire. He waited until she was close to the opening of the trunk, pulled her to him and brought her inside, while she trembled with fright and called on God for protection. He drew her to him.

"It's me. Don't be afraid."

She yielded to his hands, and kisses, and his hot breath that enveloped her, while saying: "No, no."

He pulled her closer, his back against the trunk, and tried to lift her dress. She pulled back, and her head struck the trunk. The pain made her groan. He tried to take a look, but she pushed him away with both hands and slipped outside. He followed her, reaching out like a blind man searching for something to grope.

"Listen," she said and sat down.

"Sit there," and she pointed.

He asked about her head.

"It's nothing. Nothing."

She spread the provisions she'd bought out in front of them. "I brought you some chicory and *midardara*."

"No," she said, escaping his grasp. "Today you have to listen."

He listened as he ate, the femininity of the moon creeping inside him and chilling his body. She talked and was born through her own words. That day the seventh Nahilah was born.

The first Nahilah was his young wife that he didn't know, because he was in the mountains with the fighters.

The second Nahilah was the beautiful woman who was born in the cave of Bab al-Shams as she trod the grapes and married her husband.

The third Nahilah was the mother of Ibrahim, the eldest who died.

The fourth Nahilah was the mother of Noor that Yunes clung to in the cave and called Umm Noor, Mother of Light, whenever she came to him with light shining from her eyes.

The fifth Nahilah was the heroine of the funeral who came out of prison to announce the death of her husband and lamented in front of everybody.

The sixth Nahilah was the mother of all those children who filled the square at Deir al-Asad.

And on that night, the seventh Nahilah was born.

Beneath the olive tree whose branches were drenched in the green moon of Galilee, the seventh Nahilah was born. She was approaching forty, wrinkles ran down her long neck, and sorrow extended from her eyes to her cheeks.

The seventh Nahilah had grown exhausted with all there was to exhaust her. A woman alone and poor.

"You know nothing at all," she said. "Sit down and listen. I'm worn out, Yunes, you have no idea. You know nothing at all. Tell me, who are you?"

Did she ask him "who are you?" or was it enough to recount her torments? Did he see himself mirrored in her words?

Yunes sat down and discovered he knew nothing. He'd been concerned only with his Nahilahs, as though he'd married seven women who were different in every way but united by one thing: waiting.

All of a sudden, Yunes saw his life as scattered fragments – from Palestine to Lebanon, from Lebanon to Syria, from one prison to another.

He had lived for his long journeys to Galilee, when he had to get through the barbed wire, past the dangers and the Border Guard and the machine guns that mowed down border crossers.

He'd built up political and military cells composed of the tattered remnants of men who wanted to get back to their land. He'd joined various organizations. He'd started as an Arab nationalist with the Heroes of the Return and the Youths of Revenge and moved on to Fatah after meeting Abu Ali Iyad, and there, he became an official in the Western Sector.

"I was living in a no man's land," he told Nahilah, "as though I weren't living, and you were here on your own, and I did nothing for you. Come with me to Lebanon."

She said no. "The children have grown up, and it's over. What do you want me to do in Lebanon? Live in the camp? Become a refugee? No. You come back here. I know you can't because they'll kill you or put you in prison here. You can't come and I can't either. You're my husband, and I'm your wife. What kind of life is this, Abu Salem?"

The green moon cast its light over Yunes, and the story stole into his eyes and drowned them in a sort of drowsiness. It wasn't tears; things rooted themselves in his eyes and spread out before him, and he became like a blind man who sees. He had been seeing without understanding. This was Yunes' state in the presence of the seventh Nahilah – hearing and seeing and dissolving in the light of the moon that emanated, pure and green, from the woman's eyes.

She spoke of the world she'd divided into two halves, her life she put into little compartments, her children. She didn't talk about the little compartment of fear, she didn't talk about how the children – their children – wore her down with their questions and their fearful eyes. She didn't say she'd waited for him to say, "Come with me," and that she'd thought he hadn't said it because of his parents, so she'd waited, and when they'd died, leaving was no longer possible. She said only that things weren't as impossible anymore, that Salem and Mirwan had started working in Mr. Haim's garage in Haifa, and that they were happy. Then a certain hesitancy began to punctuate her speech, stretches of silence began inserting themselves between words.

"You don't know," Nahilah said. "You don't know anything. You think life is those distances you cross to come to me, carrying the smell of the forest. And you say you're a lone wolf. But my dearest, it's not a matter of the smell of the wolf or the smell of wild thyme or of the Roman olive tree, it's a matter of people who've become strangers to each other. Do you know who we are at least? Do you know what happened to us when we found ourselves being led by a blind man? Your mother saved him from death, she yanked him out of their midst, and the Israeli soldier looked right through her. She said she asked God to blind them so they wouldn't see her. Then they killed them all. You know what happened at Sha'ab. We found ourselves with bullets flying over our heads – no, before we fled, they led the men in front of the pond, the Israeli officer was shouting: 'To Lebanon!' Your mother took your father by the hand and tried to lead him to where the officer was pointing, but your father walked in the opposite direction. So we followed him. A blind man leading two women and a child toward the unknown. 'Go with the others,' your mother told me, but I didn't go. I was afraid to leave them, afraid to meet you in Lebanon, afraid of you and of those crowds racing against one another and stomping over one another, and I said, 'No, I'll stay with you.' So we walked. Night came, but the sheikh didn't notice. It was the first time the sheikh failed to distinguish between night and day. Your mother said that was the day the sheikh went blind. You know your father better than me. The sheikh knew the times for prayer by the way the sunlight fell upon his closed eyes, but that night he lost the ability to distinguish. Two women walking behind a blind man, in the blackness of the night, in a devastated land. We walked for endless hours. Then the sheikh stopped and said, 'We've reached Deir al-Asad. Take me to the mosque.' The sheikh had decided that Deir al-Asad was his new village, and in the morning your mother went to the headman, who was related to your father; his name was Awwad. But the headman pretended he didn't know them. In those days, no one knew anyone anymore; we'd all become strangers. The village sheikh intervened. He came to the mosque and told your mother there were plenty of abandoned houses, and that they should go to any house. We went to the first house we found, and it was beautiful, close to the caves that came to be known as Bab al-Shams, and surrounded by an olive grove. It was the house of Ahmad Karim al-Asadi, who had fled to Lebanon with his family at the time of the unforgettable incident in the village square when everybody lay down in the road to stop the Israeli bulldozers. Ahmad Karim al-Asadi didn't join them in the square. Like many others, he fled. So we moved into the house; it became ours. And the village became our village.

"Yes Sir, we were strangers. Your father became a beggar. We went to live in this house not knowing what else to do and discovered, with the villagers, that the land had gone. The village wasn't a village anymore – the peasants' land wasn't theirs anymore, so they were nothing, like you in Lebanon and Syria and I-don't-know-where. No land, no rifles, and no horses – the men were no longer men. When a woman tried to pick her olives from her grove, they would detain her and make her throw them away – the land now belonged to the State. Nobody was left with work except for thieves. Yes, we stole from our own land and lived like thieves. I don't know how many stayed behind. I stayed because I followed the blind man, and others fled because they ran like blind men."

"There were more than a hundred thousand of you," said Yunes.

"We became strangers to one another. The villages were all mixed up together. The Bedouins moved into Sha'ab, we were in Deir al-Asad, and al-Ba'neh filled up with people from who-knows-where. We were no longer at home, and the villages weren't villages any more. We no longer felt we were in our own country. You knew only the bullets that flew over your heads, of the blood that flowed, and of the young men reaped by death. We could no longer move from place to place. Going from one village to another required a military permit. We weren't even allowed to visit al-

Ba'neh, which was only a stone's throw away. It was as though they'd built imaginary walls between the villages. And the people turned into thieves, or something like thieves, going into their fields at night and stealing their own crops. Strangers stealing from strangers. I would look around me and see nothing but emptiness, as though we had dug graves for ourselves in the air and had been buried in them. I hated everyone. I hated them all: the ones driven to take jobs working for their enemies, building settlements for the new immigrants with their own hands. We hated each other, idiotically, for no reason. Yes, we are an idiotic and naïve people. We buried our land with our own hands. Instead of digging the soil to make the plants grow and provide food for our livestock, we dug the foundations for houses to be built on the ruins of our own. We labored without daring to look each another in the eye, as though we were embarrassed to.

"What could we do? Nothing. We worked so we wouldn't die.

"Then you came.

"You made your way through the blockade of hate that surrounded us, and knocked on my window. Did you think you were Qays looking for Layla among the ruins? You poor thing, I swear I hated you as much as I did myself. I was afraid you'd take me with you to Lebanon. I didn't want to have anything to do with you because I didn't know you, and you scared me. All I had in the world was the blind man, who used to go every day to the mosque and try and convince everyone that he was the sheikh of the Shadhliyya order. They would take pity on him and throw him a few piasters, which weren't even enough to buy bread with. There was no trace of my mother. It was as though the earth had split and swallowed up my sisters. Do you know anything about my family? Are they in Lebanon? I never asked you about them and you never mentioned them, as though we had a tacit agreement to forget about them. At the beginning I used to see my mother in my dreams. I'd see her sinking into green water and when I woke up, choking, it felt is if my neck had been in a vise. Gradually their images started to disappear. I know they're somewhere but I've forgotten them. I hated my mother. How could she have married me to a man who wasn't even a man, and when I was only a child? How could they have abandoned me to roam from place to place and stopped taking care of me? All I had left was the blind beggar, who succeeded – by some miracle – in turning himself into a real sheikh and acquiring disciples.

"And you came.

"I was starting to get used to my new life when you returned to us bearing a promise. Why did you promise you'd all come back? Why did you make me believe you, even though you knew otherwise – don't deny it. You knew it was history and that history's a dog. You'd bring me books and go away. And I'd read. I read all the novels and the poetry, and I learned the stories by heart. Do you know what I used to do? I used to copy the books by hand. I wrote out Ghassan Kanafani's *Men in the Sun* longhand innumerable times.

"And what else?

"Your father was fierce as a hawk. He said, 'We'll die before we let our women work for the Jews.' And he didn't let me. My belly would swell up and I'd swell up and my children filled the house. I swelled up so I wouldn't die. I'd get pregnant and I'd feel the life beating in my belly. The plenitude."

Nahilah talked and talked.

She talked of the death of Ibrahim and of her madness.

She talked of Salem, who was stolen by his grandmother so he wouldn't die of hunger because of his mother's dry breasts.

She talked of Noor and of the other children who are now adults.

She talked and talked, and Yunes put his head in his hands, sitting against the Roman olive tree on the ground that stretched to the horizon of the green summer moon.

She talked of a country that didn't look like itself, and of people who refused to look in mirrors so they wouldn't see their own faces, and of abandoned villages . . . She said she no longer believed this world founded on destruction would last: "We lived in expectation of something that would come, as though we weren't in a real place.

> 405 <

"That's why I loved you," she said.

"Do you remember the day you came to me and married me all over again? You spread your clothes on the ground, in that cold cave, and asked me to walk over the grapes. There I felt something real. There things were real. But not here. I fell in love with you in that place you called Bab al-Shams. I'd come to you as though I'd been sleeping on thorns, for in the house in Deir al-Asad, which had become our house, and among the furniture and the pots and pans left by its owners, I felt afraid, and strange, and insecure, drinking out of their cups and cooking in their saucepans. What do the Jews who live in our houses feel? I just couldn't do it, even knowing that I'll give everything back the moment they ask for it. I've lived all this time in the house of al-Asadi, who fled to Lebanon, but I was no longer myself.

"In truth, who am I? And who are you?

"Only Ibrahim made me feel I was alive, but he died. They killed him, or it was his destiny to die – I don't know. I don't cry for Ibrahim, I cry for myself.

"You know.

"At one point, I decided to work, work at anything, work as a maid – but where? I went to Haifa. I'd never been to Haifa in my life. I got on a bus and went, and I walked the streets aimlessly. In Haifa, I got lost. No, not because of the language. I speak their language, I learned it with my children. I speak it as well as they do, or even better. I got lost because I felt like a stranger. On the way from here to there, I saw all the houses that have sprouted up; I felt like I was in a foreign country. And in Haifa, I saw the city. God, Haifa's beautiful: a mountain that runs down into the sea, and a sea that embraces the mountain as though it were rising to meet it. But what good does beauty do? Is it true that Beirut looks like Haifa? You haven't told me about Beirut, but Haifa is beautiful. I wish we could live there with the children. I went looking for work without saying anything to the sheikh or his wife. In any case, by that time the sheikh already wasn't taking in what was said to him. He performed his ablutions with dust and lived in his own distant world. He'd talk to strange beings that only he could see. I went on my own to find a solution to our money problems, which became serious once the sheikh became confined to the house. But I couldn't find work. And you didn't care and didn't know and didn't come. And when you finally came, you'd give me the little bit of money you had on you. I didn't tell you it wasn't enough; I didn't want to upset you. But the village isn't a village anymore. It's become part of a large city that sprawls from the heights of Galilee to Acre. A city of ghosts. The village has died and the city has died, and we are trying to . . . And you knew nothing. I told the military interrogator, 'I'm free to do as I please, and it's no business of yours.' I told him, 'You're stronger and richer, but you're an impossibility that can't last forever.' I don't know where I got those words, how I was able to say what I said about the Jews. I told him, 'You were tormented, but your torment doesn't give you the right to torment us.' I told him, 'We are suffering in our guts.' He asked me about my swollen belly and my pregnancy and the children, so I told him, 'Pain generates pain, Sir. You don't know the meaning of pain that attacks the guts.' He made fun of me for what I said. He said, 'Go to Lebanon, where your husband is.' And I said, 'My husband isn't in Lebanon; I don't know where he is, and I'm not going anywhere. You, Sir, go to Poland where you came from, or stay here, but leave me alone. You come here and then ask me to leave? Why?' I didn't know how to argue with them. When the interrogator was with me, I pretended you were in front of me and thought, If Yunes were here, he'd know how to make them shut up. When you talk, you convince me of everything. Do you remember the first days in the cave – we'd make love, then you'd light your cigarette and start to talk. You'd talk about politics, and I didn't understand politics; I was waiting for you to take me in your arms and cover me with your body, for you to pull out the thorns that had attached themselves to my soul. But all you'd talk about was politics and how you all were ready to liberate the land, and you'd tell me about Gamal Abdel Nasser, who was like Saladin. I believed you. I told the military interrogator about Saladin. He laughed, baring his large white teeth, and said, 'You Arabs are living in a daydream.' I didn't understand what he meant by that, but I told him, 'We're not Arabs.' Tell me, why here in Israel don't they call the other Arabs Arabs? They call the Egyptians Egyptians, the Syrians Syrians, the Lebanese Lebanese, not Arabs. Are we the only Arabs? 'We're Palestinians, Sir,' I told him, and he said, 'Just a daydream.' I agree we're Arabs; if we aren't, what are we? But I said we're not Arabs to annoy him, because I didn't understand what *daydream* meant.

"Then later I understood.

"My whole life is a daydream.

"You imagine I was waiting for you because I was dazzled by your man-liness? No, Yunes. I was waiting for you to talk, to escape the daydream that was swallowing my life. But you didn't listen. You'd tell of your adventures, and of the magic nights that bewitched you, but you knew nothing.

"I didn't tell you what the young men here in the village did. I was afraid you'd get upset. On the first of each month, they'd knock on my door and throw down a small cloth bundle. I'd open it and find money, and that was what we lived on. Do you think your blind father supported us – a family of ten mouths? Did you think we were waiting for your visits and the few pen-nies you brought to get by? No, Abu Salem. We were waiting for the little cloth bundle; I neither knew nor wished to know who threw it nor how they collected the money.

"Don't tell me they were your comrades because we both know they had nothing to do with you.

"I waited for you to give me the feeling that my life was real. Can you believe it? I lived my life without being convinced it was really life? Maybe everybody feels that way, maybe all our lives are like mine, I don't know. But I'm exhausted."

The seventh Nahilah said she was afraid.

"I'm getting scared now. Noor will get married, and Salem and Mirwan will go to work every day in Mr. Haim's garage, but what will become of us?

"I'm afraid for your children. I don't know how they'll live. I don't under-stand them. They live these things as though they were ordinary things and this reality as though it were the only reality. Do you know what Salem said? That he was going to open a garage in Deir al-Asad. I told him Deir al-Asad wasn't our village, and he laughed. He said he dreamed of going to America. And Noor, how lovely she is! She's going to get married, and the younger children are in school and I'm afraid for them. You've never really been interested in them. You only ask about their health. You don't care about their studies or their future. Do you think they'll wait for you, their lives suspended in a vacuum like mine was waiting for your Saladin to put things back the way they were? Things will never go back to the way they were. Don't misunderstand me: I'm not saying . . . I have Israeli citizenship, of course, and I vote for the Arab Communist party for the Knesset, and I attend the meetings and demonstrations, in an attempt to preserve what's left of our land.

"I told the interrogator that they were like an isolated fortress from the days of the crusades, they were destined to fade away.

"I told him we'd paid the full price and had been destroyed. 'You've taken us to the bottom, and beneath the bottom there's nothing. You'll go down with us – we'll show you around down there, and you'll taste the fire that burns us.'

"Don't misunderstand me, Yunes, but I want to assure my children's future. I want them to build houses, and find work, and marry, and live. I want the illusions to end, I want . . ."

He didn't let her finish the sentence.

Yunes understood that she didn't want him anymore, understood that she was tired of him and his journeys through the unknown. He understood, and at that moment, he discovered that he'd talked about his journeys over there more than he'd actually gone on them, and that his life, too, was like a daydream.

He said she was his life.

He said, "You and the children, you are my life. I don't have any life without you."

He said that he didn't know, that it was the revolution.

In the days of '69, Yunes entered a new phase of his political life. He joined Fatah and became an official in its Western Sector as well as a member of the Southern Lebanon Sector Command Office.

He told Nahilah that hope had reappeared, that he couldn't abandon everything and come back to live with them.

"No, no. I'm not asking you to come back!"

He said he'd thought about it, but what could he do here? How could he earn a living? He said he didn't know a trade and only knew how to live the way he had, but he understood their situation and was there for them, completely.

"I'm here for you," he said.

Nahilah smiled but didn't say anything.

Silence fell.

Time passed slowly and came between them like something solid and unmoving. Yunes tried to break the silence, but the woman's silence stretched in all directions. He'd listened to her and deep down he knew it was true, life had slid past him, without even approaching.

"I swear I didn't . . ."

He didn't complete his sentence and felt the urge to sleep. If only sleep would come and take him from here to there. Sleep was everywhere. The village was sleeping, the trees were sleeping, and Yunes sat in silence in Nahilah's arms.

Nahilah broke the silence. She said Salem was going to be workshop foreman in Mr. Haim's garage and Mirwan was going to work with his brother and learn from him. She said the third boy, Ahmad, was very good in school and wrote poetry, and that Salma helped in the house and was excellent in English, and that the little ones, Saleh and Nezar, were still little.

"Listen, Yunes," said Nahilah. "I want to open a garage for Salem here. Do you have three thousand American dollars to help us?"

"Three thousand!" he said in a hoarse voice. "Me put together three thousand?"

"Never mind. We'll manage. I just wanted to ask you. Don't worry about it. We'll manage as we've managed before. I shouldn't have asked, I know you're not a profiteer, but won't you come to Noor's wedding? Of course you won't come, but the groom's insisting on the horse. His family says he's going to arrive on a purebred Arabian horse and kidnap Noor from in front of the house. It's their custom, and Noor loves him. I'm sure she loves him. They were together in school, and now he works in Acre and plans to move there."

Nahilah told Yunes that the details of life are ordinary and meaningless but had to be taken care of. "Why don't you say anything? Why are you so silent? I swear to you, I don't want anything. I just wanted to get things off my chest and talk. Who do I have to talk to? Before your mother died, God rest her soul, I used to talk to her, but do you think that was easy? When I told her I was going to look for work, she went berserk, and when she saw me in the house studying Hebrew with the children, she trembled with irritation. Your mother lived her life in a world that wasn't connected to the real world. I had to remind her all the time who we were and what misery we were living in.

"How can I tell you about her?

"Poor woman, she didn't know how to calm your father, or how to make his last days easier. She told me he was at the end and that we had to help him to get to the end. Your father was stubborn. He used dust for his ablutions, had no idea where he was anymore, and talked with his sister. Why his sister, I don't know. He'd say something to her, and I'd think he was addressing me, so I'd answer him, and he'd avert his face and say, 'You keep quiet!' Your mother told me about his sister who died giving birth to her first son. It was as if his mind had been wiped clean of everything, and all that was left was his sister. He'd even mistake his wife for her. She'd order him to do something, and he'd obey. Your mother would say to me, 'See how it is at the end, daughter. The wife turns into the sister and the son into the father, and everything's all wrong.'

"And you – when will you become my brother? Let's become brother and sister. That way I can tell you everything, and you can tell me everything. A man can't say everything to his wife, and a wife can't say everything to her husband, but a brother and sister can.

"Come on, speak to me.

"I know you're upset now. I know I shouldn't have told you all these things, but what you don't know is that I'm not upset with you. I swear I'm not. When they announced you'd died and become a martyr, I came back from the prison to the house and put on a funeral that had no equal. I wept every last tear from my body and smeared my face with ashes; I was an exemplary widow. The Israeli interrogator who summoned me a month later said I could be a movie actress. What the interrogator didn't know was that I wasn't acting. In my heart I was convinced I'd become a widow, that you were no longer my husband.

"The military investigator didn't know I wasn't acting. We've been acting for more than twenty years, to the point of taking on our roles and resembling them more and more each day. You're acting over there and I'm acting here. God, it's funny.

"I'm laughing. Why aren't you?

"You're playing your role, and I'm playing mine, and life is draining away.

"Tell me about yourself. Tell me how you live, how you manage, how?

"Me, I've managed to get by through acting. I played the role of a widow and it was well-received, and I played the role of a hero's wife and that went over even better.

"And you, what role do you play over there?

"Did I tell you about the case I brought to the Israeli courts when they refused to register your children in your name? Only Salem and Noor got registered, the others didn't. I brought a case and appointed an Israeli lawyer, Mrs. Beida, and we won. Before Mrs. Beida, I commissioned an Arab lawyer from the Shammas family in Fasouta, but he failed; he wasn't able to prove you were alive. The Israeli lawyer turned the whole thing upside down. She asked them to prove you were dead, which they couldn't do either. The only thing they had to show was the military communiqué in which 'saboteurs' announced your martyrdom, which is a valueless document as far as Israeli judicial practice is concerned, because Israel doesn't recognize the legitimacy of 'saboteur' organizations, so she forced them to issue a judgment in favor of registering the children. This has been my biggest victory here. We forced them to register the children in the name of a man they are pursuing and whose existence they didn't acknowledge. Only on that day did I feel you were my husband, but the feeling faded quickly. How happy I was that day, but you had no idea. How could you have known? You only would come by when the mood struck you, and by the time you finally came, the news was stale. Did I already tell you all this? I don't remember if you ever told me a story as good as mine.

"The story's over now. I'm in my forties, and my life's changing. I'm getting ready to be a grandmother, and that's enough. Shouldn't that be enough to make me unhappy? I feel like weeping all the time, and my tears flow for no reason. My face is going numb, my shoulders hurt, my whole body is falling apart. I feel as though I'm separating from my body, and I'm alone."

Yunes ate a last mouthful, which went down like a knife in his stomach. He put his hands on his legs folded under him and said that he was going to leave again.

"Where to?" she asked him.

"Lebanon," he said.

"No."

She took his hand, left the full plates and the pot of tea, and led him to the cave of Bab al-Shams. She took off her clothes and stood in front of him, waiting. Yunes didn't dare look at her naked body, ignited by desire. She came over to him and started removing his clothes while he stood there, motionless. It was the first time that she initiated things; he felt as though he'd become her plaything, and his virility had disappeared. She made him lie on his back and she spread her hair and breasts and body over him, and when the water of heaven spurted from her, she began to cry.

She got up and put on her clothes; the first threads of dawn's light had started stealing into the cave, and she told him to wait.

She returned at noon.

She returned with a banquet – *kibbeh nayyeh* – a meat pâté – with a topping of *hoseh* – soft cheese, tomatoes, and a bottle of arak.

She set the food aside, heated some water and bathed him. He was like a small child in her hands, playing around in the water, incapable of issuing his usual orders or of making remarks about how hot or cold the water was. She took him to the open space inside the cave, which became a bathroom, ordered him to take off his clothes, bathed him with water and bay laurel soap, dried him and dressed him in fresh, dry clothes. Then they sat down together at the table.

He poured two glasses of arak, drank from his glass and asked her to do the same.

She said no.

She said she didn't like arak. In the past, she'd only drunk to keep him company. She didn't like the smell of arak and the scent of aniseed that wafted from his mouth, especially when he slept with her.

"I used to drink so I wouldn't smell it."

She said she didn't like arak and didn't want to drink any.

He was taken aback. "What? You don't like arak?"

"I hate it."

"And all these years you drank it?"

"I didn't want to upset you."

"All these years you've been drinking something you don't like!"

She nodded.

"I don't understand anything."

She shook her head.

"You don't want to say anything?"

"What is there to say?"

Indeed, what was left to say, after she'd said everything beneath the olive tree? She'd told him she didn't want him anymore, what more was there?

His mind was clouded with only one thought: how had she known? How had she intuited that from now on his visits would be difficult, few and far between? Southern Lebanon was now full of fedayeen, the country was under constant Israeli bombardment, and the borders were almost impossible to cross. To cross the border now required fighting an entire battle. And then there was his age. The war had stolen years from his life, and now he was too old. He was in his late forties and his body was no longer a docile instrument that complied with his desires. He wasn't able to cover those long distances any longer. She didn't know what had happened this time. He'd arrived at the cave at night but didn't go to her right away, as he usually did. He'd felt weak and decided to rest a little before knocking on her window. But, in fact, he fell asleep, awakened at ten the following morning, and spent the day in the cave, waiting for nightfall so he could go to her.

How had she known?

Women just know, thought Yunes as he listened to her. She'd known his visits would become intermittent before stopping, so she'd made her decision. She wouldn't be an abandoned woman; she'd choose her new life deliberately. And now she tells him she doesn't like arak!

Had she forgotten how he'd drunk arak from her mouth? And how after eating she'd washed her hands with arak? Or had she been putting on a show for him, as she had for the military interrogator, the village, her children, and everybody else?

She said she'd prepared this banquet to make up with him and ask him to forget the garage, the dollars, and her stupid requests. She regretted what she'd said the day before, because he was her husband and the crown of her life. She knew this was the only way he could live and was proud of him; she understood that people have to live their lives as they find them.

> *We walked the steps that were written for us,*
> *And the one whose steps are written must walk them.*

"You know," she said, "even after your father had forgotten almost everything and had started living with his sister's ghost, he never forgot his classical poetry. Whenever I wanted him to dig up something from the back of his mind, I'd start by saying the first half of the first line, and he'd sit up straight and recite the two lines without missing a beat, and I could see the words rising up from the well of memory that the years had filled in. His voice would regain its strength, and he'd recite with me:

> *Your errant heart from love to love walks*
> *Never shall the first be worn away*
> *Many a dwelling you shall make your own*
> *But the love for your first home nothing can sever.* *

You've taken your path, and I've taken mine. But you're my husband, and I'm your wife. Please, I beg of you, forget what I said yesterday."

Nahilah said she'd spoken that way because she was afraid for Noor who was about to get married – "May God protect her!"

Nahilah apologized. She said the black veil that had been fogging her vision had lifted. And Yunes, what did he say? Did he explain how difficult the situation actually was in the south? Did he apologize for all those years? Or did he say that he was trying to survive and create a country out of the rubble we call history?

He didn't speak. He drained the last drops of arak from his glass, drinking without quenching his thirst, and let the drink take him. The image of the hero eclipsed the image of the lover, and one story led to another. He spoke of the prisons and the training camps. He spoke of operations in the Galilee panhandle and of the young men the bases were overflowing with and how they rush headlong into death.

He spoke of the Return. He said he'd return with the others. "The nation is not a prison. We shall not return as abject prisoners." And he told her of the revolution he'd been waiting for since the day the Sha'ab garrison had been disbanded and all its members flung into prison. It was near, and he couldn't abandon it.

---

* Verse from a poem by Abu Tammam (9th century).

He spoke and spoke and spoke.

And Nahilah returned to him. She returned to him with every word he spoke, and he could see it. Her face was radiant, her eyes shone, and her hands took the little pieces of bread and transformed them into bite-sized morsels of *kibbeh nayyeh* that she fed to him.

He asked her about Hebrew and if it was difficult.

Of all the things the woman had said, the man picked up only on the question of language. He knew that Palestinian children in Israel learned Hebrew in school, and he knew that his own children were just like the others; but he wanted to talk about his children, so he asked about the language.

Nahilah smiled and said, "*Echad, shtayim, shalosh, arba, chamesh, shesh, sheva, shmone, tesha, eser.*"

"What are you saying?" he asked.

"Guess."

"It's Hebrew."

"Right," she said. "Hebrew's like Arabic. Arabic spoken like a foreign language, if you like, but you have to put in a lot of *ch*'s and *sh*'s. That's how I learnt it. The first thing I learned was the numbers, and then I got so I could understand almost all the words. But the children are much better, God bless them. They speak Hebrew better than the Jews."

She said the language was easy. "The easiest thing is learning their language."

He said he was afraid the children would forget their own language.

"That's their problem," said Nahilah, meaning it was the Israelis' problem, not the Palestinians'. "They don't want us to forget our language and our religion because they don't want us to become like them."

Yunes didn't understand what she meant and started talking about the relationship of the children to their history and their heritage, saying that this relationship could exist only through language. He talked a lot, blending together literature and religion and everything else.

She said he hadn't understood her.

"Listen and try to understand. You don't know anything. Try to listen to things the way I tell them and not the way you imagine them in your head. When I said it's their problem, I meant it's the Jews' problem: We can't abandon our language because they don't want us to do that. They want us to remain Arabs and not to assimilate. Don't worry; they're a closed, sectarian society. Even if we wanted to, they'd never let us."

When you told me, Father, about Nahilah's theory of language, I thought of Isa who wanted to gather the keys to the houses in Andalusia. I wanted to say that we haven't yet understood the fundamental difference. The Castilians didn't persecute the Muslim Arabs and the Jews simply to throw them out, for no expulsion, no matter on how large a scale and how effective, can drive out everyone. The Castilians imposed their religion and their language on the Andalusians, and that's why their victory was definitive; that's why al-Andalus was assimilated into Spain and that was the end of the matter. Here, on the other hand, our keys aren't the keys of the houses that were stolen; it's the Arabic language. Israel doesn't want to make Israelis out of us, it's not imposing its religion or its language on us. The expulsion took place in '48, but it wasn't total. Our keys are with them, not with us.

I didn't say anything because I didn't want to lose the thread of Nahilah's story through digressions, as often would happen.

When I used to ask Yunes about Nahilah, he wouldn't object or refuse to answer. He'd start to answer, then enter the labyrinth of peripheral stories, and Nahilah's story would get lost.

On that occasion, I didn't mention my theory about the keys because I was afraid for the other story, but the other story got lost all the same.

He spoke to me about Hebrew and then fell silent.

"And so?" I asked him.

"And so here we are."

"What happened there, in the cave?"

"I returned to Lebanon, and we built bases in the south."

"What about her?"

"Noor got married and Salem opened a garage and . . ."

"Did you visit her after that?"

"Of course, often. Anyway . . ."

Often and *anyway* was his only response.

"And the cave?"

He didn't tell me about the cave even though he talked a lot that day. He discussed the children's problems and the revolution, which had started to spread throughout Jordan and Lebanon. The two of them talked at length and laughed easily, he would drink and she would fill his glass.

"You're like a bride," he told her.

After he'd finished eating, he was overcome by sleepiness. She covered him with the blanket and gazed at him, her eyes brimming with desire.

"Now?" he asked, and cleared a space for her on the mattress.

"I didn't say anything," she said.

"I'll sleep for a bit," he said.

"You sleep and I'll clean up the cave."

"Wake me in half an hour."

She let him sleep and left. But before he went to sleep, she repeated her invitation with her eyes and he repeated his smile asking if he could sleep for half an hour. She went into the corner of the cave and washed the dishes, and when she came back found him sleeping deeply, so she left him and went home.

When Yunes woke up he didn't find her, and the shadows of evening were spreading over the hills. He found himself filling his water bottle, packing his bag and squeezing into it the two loaves of bread Nahilah had left, and setting off for Lebanon.

Did he go back to see her after the night of the Roman olive tree?

He said he did, but I have my doubts. Yunes' life changed a great deal at that time. Once the revolution grew into an institution resembling a state, Yunes became part of that State. He went abroad as part of the official delegations, phoned his family from various capitals, then became a member of the Fatah Regional Command in Lebanon. His days filled up, especially after the massacres of April 1970 in Jordan and the transformation of Lebanon into the Palestinian Resistance's only refuge following the migration of leadership from Amman to Beirut.

Yunes became part of that huge machine and ceased to be the wandering fedayeen fighter of old, shifting between the Ain al-Hilweh camp in the south and the Shatila and Burj al-Barajneh camps in Beirut. All the same, he was different from the others. He was not seduced by wealth like the majority of the Palestinian leaders; he remained a peasant, as he had been and wanted to remain.

Yunes tried to reconcile his new life with his convictions. It may be that he didn't often succeed, but he preserved his image as Abu Salem, the Wolf of Galilee, who knew the country as no one else did and who had a story like no other.

Was it in that period that his legend began?

I don't know because I didn't know him then. Well, I knew him, but I was young and I couldn't take things in and grasp their significance. I got to know him well from the beginning of the seventies, by which time he'd become a legend. I got to know him as the man who plants his children in Galilee and fights to liberate them.

All the same, I ask myself as I stand here beneath the rain of images covering the bedroom walls, did the legend begin when the story ended? Did he start telling people about Nahilah at the very moment he stopped visiting her?

I don't know.

He said he continued his visits over there until 1978, when in March the Israelis occupied part of southern Lebanon in which they established a dependent ministate to which they gave the name of the State of Free Lebanon. It was just a narrow strip of Lebanese territory that formed a buffer zone between the fedayeen and the settlements of Galilee, which had been exposed to bombardment by Katyusha rockets.

He said the occupation made it impossible to slip across the border, and he began contacting Nahilah and his children by telephone. He spoke to me often of his journeys, and of the three little Nahilahs that were born in Deir al-Asad: Nahilah, the daughter of Noor; Nahilah, the daughter of Salem; and Nahilah, the daughter of Saleh.

He said he would phone all his Nahilahs, that he received their photos by way of a friend in Cyprus and that he lived with them without seeing them; he lived with the photos. "The phone doesn't let you do it, Son. What can you say on the phone? On the phone you can only speak in generalities and clichés. Phone talk isn't talk."

Umm Hassan suggested I send you back over there, and then she died and left me alone with you.

Come to think of it, what do you suggest, Father? There's me, you, and this huge number of pictures hung on the walls of your house. The pictures, I swear, have put a spell on me. They're amazing: smiling girls, boys holding themselves stiffly in front of the camera, and a woman looking into the distance, as if she were gazing at you – waiting for you.

Your life is coming to an end with photos. And what about me? What shall I do with them after you die? I mean, God forbid, I don't want you to die, but if God decides to reclaim what's His – after a long life – what do you want me to do with the photos? Should I return them to your children? Should I bury them with you? Or should I leave them as they are for who-ever comes to live in your house to throw out with the trash?

I don't know.

But I won't be sending you back over there. Even supposing I wanted to send you back, I wouldn't know how, and I don't know if the Israelis would allow it.

And besides, why all the fuss?

Why don't your children ask about you? Did Amna tell them you're dead, and did they already have a funeral for you over there, and was that the end of the matter? Or have they forgotten about you, has the image of the man who knelt and kissed them one by one been wiped from their memories? Or was everything cut off after Nahilah died?

You didn't tell me about the eighth Nahilah.

The eighth Nahilah is *the* woman, Father, and I'm prepared to make changes to the numbering because I know you love magic numbers. So, let's throw out Nahilah number six according to our previous classification and call the Nahilah of the Roman olive tree Nahilah number six, and that makes the Nahilah of the flower basket the seventh Nahilah, the last.

You didn't tell me about that Nahilah. You only said that Salem told you all she was interested in was flowers.

"Her senility's expressing itself through flowers," said the son to the father he didn't know.

"What's all this about flowers?" the man asked his wife from his hotel in Prague, where he was visiting the city with an official Palestinian delegation.

"There's nothing to it. I like flowers and your son makes fun of me and says I'm senile."

After having left his job in Haifa, your son opened his own garage in the village. Business was good, and soon his two brothers, Mirwan and Saleh, went to work with him. Ahmad graduated from the Hebrew University in Jerusalem with a master's degree in Arabic literature and is now preparing his doctoral thesis on the work of Ghassan Kanafani. Nezar is working with Noor's husband as a contractor. Noor is well, except her husband suffers from kidney stones, but the doctor says that his life is not in danger. Salma, the pretty one, is working as a teacher in al-Ramah and none of her flock of suitors has yet found grace in her lovely green eyes.

Why didn't you tell me about the Nahilah that you haven't seen again?

About the woman with the blazing head of white hair who had taken to carrying around a small basket into which she put flowers and little folded scraps of paper on which she wrote the names of those she loved. She'd mix up the flowers with the scraps of paper, warning her grandchildren that she'd put a black mark next to the name of anyone who annoyed her.

That was the game she played with her grandchildren. They'd visit her and she'd spill the contents of her basket onto the ground and ask them to play the basket game with her, and they'd open the scraps of paper and read out their own names and the names of their mothers and fathers, as well as your name, all of your names.

Nahilah believed the basket was her family, and when they brought her back from the hospital to the house, and she was in the throes of the disease, she gave the basket to Nahilah, Noor's daughter, and asked her to leave only three Nahilahs in the basket, because Old Nahilah was going to die. She asked Noor to change the flowers once a week, and each time, she was to change the little scraps of paper with the names written on them.

"Keep the names safe, Daughter, and don't you dare stop writing them and putting them in the basket. This basket keeps the names safe from death."

She took the scrap of paper with her name on it out of the basket and tore it up, and the next day she died.

Don't tell me now about Nahilah's death; I'm not here to listen to sad tales. I'm here to tell you I won't send you back over there. I'll bury you in the camp, in the mosque that's been turned into a cemetery where the young men are buried. Your story will come to an end there, Father. I won't tell little Nahilah that she has to tear up your names and take them out of the basket. I don't believe that little Nahilah has kept up the tradition, for we forget our promises to our dead; we keep them for a few days, and then we forget. I'm sure little Nahilah has forgotten the basket she inherited from her grandmother among her toys, that the basket of flowers ended up like my grandmother's pillow, and that mold will find the scraps of paper on which the woman wrote the names of the ones she loved.

Your Nahilah was careful to rewrite the names when she changed the flowers in the basket. She'd toss the old flowers under the Roman olive tree, burn the names, and replace them with fresh flowers and rewrite the names on new little scraps of paper.

Where are the women?

Where are the two women who used to come?

Where are the friends and comrades?

Where is everyone?

No one.

You are dying now, and there is this no one around you. You are dying in calm and in silence. I make you up as I please and I make myself up in you, I see what you have seen and what I haven't seen myself, I speak of a country I've never visited – a country I entered a few times at night with the fedayeen but never really could see. You told me it was like the Lebanese south, flat and overlooked by low hills, and that it was the epitome of a warm and tender land, which is why it had been ideal for Christ. You can't imagine Jesus Christ without Galilee. This land resembles him and is fitting only for strangers, which is why they call it Galilee of the Nations. The Jews fled to Galilee after the ruin of their kingdom, and we remained in it after the ruin of our history.

You talked to me about its caves and its cactus and its wild animals and its olives that stretch to the horizon. You said Galilee is an island between two seas. In the west there is the Mediterranean, and in the east there is the sea of blue olives. In these two seas, Christ learned how to fish and chose his disciples. A land of fish and olive trees and oil.

You promised to take me with you, and you never did. But I saw everything from the olive groves at al-Khreibeh on the Palestinian border. I saw endless olives and young men who never tired of dying for this land that has become our graveyard and our promise.

And now we're here. Both of us have ended up in this place called Galilee Hospital, which isn't a hospital, as I've told you a thousand times. The hospital is finished, and your illness continues.

"WE'LL CLOSE the hospital before the man dies," said Dr. Amjad, laughing. I don't know what brought him here, it's been ages since he'd stopped by to see you. I was sitting with you after feeding you that yellow food through a tube in your nose, when Dr. Amjad came to talk about the probability of closing the hospital.

He spoke as if he had no idea of what was going on – practically speaking, the hospital is already closed. The first floor has become a warehouse, and on the second floor there are only five rooms left: one for you, a patient, one for me, a doctor, and three others inhabited by new patients I haven't yet found the time to examine.

The patients here don't resemble patients. Two old women and a man around fifty-five. As though the hospital, or what remains of it, has been transformed into an old people's home. Zainab's still here, and the job of looking after the storerooms has been added to her duties. The Syrian guard doesn't guard, the cook doesn't cook, and the operating room has been moved to Haifa Hospital in the Burj al-Barajneh camp. I heard recently that they may close Haifa Hospital, too. As Zainab explained it to me, the cost-reduction plan calls for keeping just one hospital in Lebanon, which will be Hamshari Hospital in the Ain al-Hilweh camp.

You know, things have been turned on their heads. The few surviving Palestinian leaders who migrated to Tunis went back to live in Gaza, where there's an authority, a police force, prisons, everything. That's why they absorb every penny, and there's no need for all these hospitals in Lebanon!

Why didn't you go with them to Tunis?

I didn't because I couldn't. I felt faint in the municipal stadium and went back to the hospital. But what about you? All the fedayeen went, and they ended up with their offices and their bodyguards and their revolution.

Why didn't you go?

Is it true you refused to go and said it was our duty to die in Beirut?

That was a mistake. There's no deciding when to die. We die when we die. Deciding when to die is suicide, madness.

Were you exhausted by it all?

Some people said you'd decided to go back over there after the defeat of '82, but I didn't want to believe it.

You told me it wasn't possible for us to leave Lebanon like the Turkish army. Turn our backs on our people and go? Impossible! We had to stay with the people.

You stayed. Then what?

They slaughtered us the way everyone knew they would slaughter us. And nothing changed. Tell me, why did you choose to be a victim?

Rest assured, I'm not going to send you back now, as a corpse. I'll keep you here with us. Staying was what you chose, and I'll respect your choice. But talk to me about your children and your wife. I don't want the story of Nahilah over again, because I don't know anymore what parts of it are real and what parts are made up.

Do you remember the day you got furious with me because I refused to join the hospital staff – one of the new conditions they imposed on me after the end of the civil war in Lebanon? I refused because I'm a doctor, not a nurse. That day, you insulted me and also railed against your children: "You're all shit! Not one of them has turned out like his father. You, you don't want to work because you're clinging onto your title, Salem is a mechanic, Ahmad's a professor, and Salah's an I-don't-know-what. I didn't beget any real men. Not one of them joined up with us. I was waiting for one of them, just one, who would come and be like me, with me. But they're all like their mother, peasants rooted to the soil. You, too. What does being a doctor matter? The important thing is the work, not the position."

You blew up because your children didn't turn out like you, forgetting that you didn't turn out like your father. Do you understand now how the blind sheikh suffered when you mocked the Sufi gatherings and the sessions of *hadra*?* Your father swallowed his grief. He never once insulted you the way you did us, even though he wanted you to be a sheikh like him, like his father and grandfather. And here you now are, an officer in a slipshod army in a war that never happened. And when it did happen, you said no, this isn't my war. You didn't want to have anything to do with the civil war, not here, and not in Jordan. What were you thinking? That the war would be just as you like them, simple and clear? Were you surprised by the explosion of this Arab world that lost its soul a thousand years ago and today is flailing around in its own blood searching, and failing to find it?

*Ritual invoking the Presence. The *da'ira al-hadra* represents the circle of saints reunited in the Presence, in ecstasy.

> 426 <

What did you expect?

The blind sheikh mourned you and took pity on you.

And when you didn't go to Tunis with the leadership, all of us here took pity on you because you'd become a fragment of the past, a relic, walking among the ghosts of memory.

You don't know your children, or that country you used to contemplate in the blue night through the fissures in your cave. Now I'm going to be the voice of reality, which you've never heard before, as though fate has sent me to tell you your truth that you've taken care to hide away in your basket of stories.

"What is reality?" you'll ask.

I won't answer you by philosophizing and telling you that the reality of a man is his death because I don't like heavy phrases like that. When I read them in a book they convince me that the writer has nothing to say.

Reality, Abu Salem, is what Catherine, the French actress, passed on to me.

Please don't smile. Listen for a moment. I'm not . . . I don't . . . I didn't . . .

Yes, I visited her. I went to the Hotel Napoléon on Hamra Street because she said she wanted to see me before she left. No, it never occurred to me that I might leave everything and go work with them in France. First of all, I don't speak French, second of all, I don't like the theater, and finally, I hate acting.

I thought I'd visit her to get out of this prison. Yes, I feel like a prisoner here. The doors are closed, the light's dim, and there are bars over the windows as though we were surrounded by barbed wire or minefields, or the walls were leaning in on us and melding into one another to suffocate us.

I wanted to get out if only for an hour, and I stayed out all night . . . I don't know. Just be patient, please, I'll get there.

No, it's not what you think. It's serious. Catherine told me something unbelievable, and I read the book and verified that what she said wasn't a lure.

I went to the Hotel Napoléon and asked for her at the reception desk.

They called her on the telephone and I spoke to her; she asked me to wait for her in the lobby.

She came, sat on the edge of an armchair and said she was sorry but she had an appointment with a Lebanese writer who was going to take her to see *Prison of Sand* at the Beirut Theater.

I told her that I'd just come over to say farewell.

She said she needed to talk to me. "Can you come back later?"

"When?" I asked her.

"Tonight," she said. "The play'll be over at ten. I won't have dinner with him; I'll come back and I'm inviting you to dinner."

I said I couldn't stay out that late because getting back to the camp, with all the security barriers surrounding it, was almost impossible at night.

"Please," she said.

"I'm not sure," I said.

As she got up, she said she'd be waiting for me in the lobby at ten.

And we left.

She went toward a man who appeared to be in his mid-forties, wearing glasses and carrying a black leather bag, and I set off with no idea where I was going.

I could've returned to the camp, and that's what I decided to do in fact. But then I thought of the sea and decided to walk a little along the Manara Corniche before going back to the camp.

I got to the corniche and everything opened up. I saw the sea and filled my lungs and heart with the sea air. God, it was delicious! Only we, we who have been released from all the prisons of the earth, can take such pleasure in the taste of the wind. I walked and breathed and took it all in. The sea was every possible shade of blue and I almost wanted to throw myself into the midst of its palette. I ran and walked and danced. I bought some lupine seeds to snack on and sat on a stone bench and watched the people running and striding and strolling. Nobody paid any attention to me. I was alone among them, overhearing snippets of their conversations, which blurred as they drew away and which I'd be trying to continue on my own when new stories would steal into my ears.

Time flowed by without my noticing.

I wasn't waiting for her. Perhaps I was waiting for her unconsciously, but I didn't sit down and wait deliberately. I sat down to sit down, and then I looked at my watch and it said five past ten so I started walking toward the hotel. I walked at a leisurely pace because I was sure I wouldn't find her. The writer would invite her to a restaurant, then woo her and sleep with her. That was their world, and I had nothing to do with it. I arrived at about half past ten to find her sitting on the sofa in the lobby with an empty glass in front of her. She got up and said eagerly, "I was afraid you wouldn't come," and sat me down opposite her.

"What will you have?" she asked.

"Whatever you're drinking."

"I'm drinking margaritas. Do you like margaritas?"

I'd never drunk one in my life, but I said I liked them.

The waiter brought two glasses, the rims coated with salt.

She said she wanted to ask me some questions.

I told her that I didn't know anything about the theater, that I felt strangled inside an enclosed space. I also said the only time I'd seen a play – it was about the history of Palestine – I'd felt stifled by seeing the actors chewing up the Classical language like cud before spitting it out in insipid, repulsive phrases.

She said she'd decided not to take the part. The massacres of Shatila and Sabra couldn't be performed on a stage. She said that she had been terrified when she visited Shatila, and that if she'd accepted the part, she would have felt implicated politically.

"You know, I've visited Israel," she said.

"Really?" I asked coldly.

"Doesn't that surprise you?"

"No," I said.

"You're not upset?"

"Why should I be upset? You visited my country."

"Yes, yes," she said, "I know. But I visited Israel when I was fifteen, and I lived three months on a kibbutz in the north."

"In Galilee," I said.

"Yes. In Galilee."

She said she'd gone there because of the Shoah.

"The what?"

"*Shoah* is a Hebrew word meaning Holocaust," she said.

"I understand," I said and asked if her background was German.

"No," she said, "but all of us" – and here she made a gesture toward her-self and me – "are responsible for the massacre of millions of Jews, don't you agree?"

"Agree to what?" I asked.

"It doesn't matter," she said. "I decided not to take the part. I can't. I can't see the victim as someone turned executioner because that would mean his-tory is meaningless."

I downed my glass, and she ordered me a second drink.

"Are you hungry?" she asked.

"No. Not really."

She said it would be better if we ate something. "Take me into Beirut and choose a beautiful restaurant."

I said I wasn't hungry and quietly started sipping my second drink, since I don't know any restaurants in Beirut, and I didn't have any money on me.

She said she didn't want to perform in that play because reading wasn't the same as seeing.

"You know, Jean Genet's strange. His language is amazing, and there's that ability of his to move from the most savage to the most poetic expres-sion. But the reality's different. I can't do it."

She looked at me with enigmatic eyes and asked where we were going to have dinner.

"I'm not hungry," I said. "I'll finish my drink and go."

She raised her hand, the waiter came over, and she asked him about food. He said it was late and the kitchen had closed, but we could order sand-wiches if we liked.

She ordered a club sandwich for herself and asked me what I wanted. I said, "Anything," and she ordered me a ham-and-cheese sandwich.

For an instant, I imagined myself in a cops-and-robbers film. The lights in the lobby were dim, and Catherine and I were seated in the bar, where there was nobody else. At the bar itself there were three men in black suits who looked like intelligence agents.

I downed the ham sandwich quickly, and she asked me if I wanted another.

"Please," I said.

She called the waiter and ordered another ham-and-cheese sandwich. I would have preferred a club sandwich like hers, but she'd assumed that I liked the first one, since I'd devoured it with such speed.

I ate the second sandwich and felt a little giddy, maybe because of the margaritas or maybe because of the kibbutz story.

I asked her the name of the kibbutz, but she said she couldn't remember.

I asked her if she'd visited the demolished Arab villages in Galilee, and she said she hadn't seen any demolished villages and hadn't known we'd been expelled from our country.

She took a sip and said she was sorry but she wanted to ask me an embarrassing question.

"Go ahead," I said.

She said she'd read something about Iron Brain in a book by an Israeli journalist.

"What is it?" I asked.

"Iron Brain is the name given to the operation to break into Shatila on the eve of the massacre."

"What's it got to do with me?"

"Nothing," she said and fell silent.

She said she'd read in the Israeli journalist's book that nine Jewish women married to Palestinians had been killed in Operation Iron Brain.

"How did you know it was called Iron Brain?" I asked.

"It's in the book. The writer's name is Kapeliouk. Have you read his book?"

"No," I said.

"He describes the deaths of these nine Jewish women in the massacre."

At this point, I felt I'd fallen into a trap. What was this woman saying, and what did Iron Brain mean? No, I swear I'm not paranoid about the intelligence services, and I don't think that everyone who asks questions is in Intelligence. So far I'd understood Catherine, I'd even felt some sympathy for her; she couldn't take the part because she felt responsible for the Holocaust – that was understandable. But this story of the nine Jewish women had a strange smell to it.

She asked if I'd like another drink.

I said I didn't want the drink that was rimmed with salt.

"How about white wine?" she asked me.

"Okay," I said.

She ordered a bottle of white wine, and the waiter came carrying it in a container full of ice. He poured a little into my glass and stood and waited. I didn't know what he wanted, but Catherine gestured to me to drink. I drank and nodded my head, so he poured more into my glass and hers and left.

"Wait a second," she said. "I'll go up to my room and get the book."

I swallowed a large mouthful of wine and stood up to go. I didn't want to discuss the Shatila and Sabra massacres again, and I wasn't going to tell her about Boss Josèph, who I'd heard about from the crazed Lebanese journalist. I swear they're all crazy: They'd invent the news so they could write it. Why did he want to set me up with Josèph? Was it because Josèph was from al-Damour?* Does one massacre justify another? I don't want to make comparisons. I told him I rejected comparisons: Massacres are not supposed to happen, and if they happen, they must be condemned and their perpetrators arrested and taken to court. All the same, I'd gotten involved so I went with him to the restaurant in al-Jemmeizeh, at the bottom of the Ashrafiyyeh district in East Beirut. But, by then, I was half-drunk and wasn't in the mood for a discussion.

I took a last gulp and was getting ready to leave when I saw her coming back, carrying the book.

*Christian city in the south of Lebanon attacked in '76 by the Saika, a pro-Syrian Palestinian militia, leaving approximately 400 civilians dead.

"Listen," she said.

She opened the book and started reading: "In the count of those lost were nine Jewish women who had married Palestinians during the British Mandate and followed their husbands to Lebanon during the exodus of 1948. The Israeli newspapers published the names of four of them."

She closed the book, drank a mouthful from her glass, and asked me if I'd been in the camp during the massacre.

"Yes," I said.

"Did you know those women?"

I laughed out loud. "You've come all this way and given me wine to ask me that? No, my dear friend, I don't know what you're talking about."

"Listen," she said. "I'm serious. Did you know of the presence of Jewish women in the camp?"

"No."

"I'm trying to discover their names. Can you help me?"

"Why?"

"Because this book saved me."

"Which book?"

"Kapeliouk's book. Do you see where I'm coming from?"

"Unfortunately, I don't."

"I told you I went to work on a kibbutz in the north when I was fifteen. I went because I felt guilty. And when I came here for the play, I felt guilty again. Then I came across this book, and it saved me. I stumbled on it here in Beirut – in Antoine's Bookstore on Hamra Street, and I felt a sense of comfort. You know, this book will help me to say to Jews that when they kill Palestinians they're killing themselves, too."

"What has it got to do with me?"

"You're Palestinian, and you have to help me."

"Help you do what?"

"Get hold of the names of those women."

"But it says in the book that they were published in the Israeli papers."

"I want their stories," she said.

"Why?"

"To prove my idea."

"Do you know Hebrew?"

"*Ketsat*."

"What?"

"A little. *Ketsat* means *a little* in Hebrew. Do you know Hebrew?"

"No."

"Why?"

"Because I'm a doctor and not a linguist. Go to Israel, anyway, contact this writer, and he'll give you the names."

"No. I want the Palestinians to tell me about these women's experiences."

"Are you Jewish?"

"No. Why?"

"No reason," I said. "I understand that you won't act in this play so you won't feel implicated. Didn't the tall man say Jean Genet didn't defend the Palestinians, he was just obsessed with death and sex, and that his project as a director was to put on a show that glorified death? You've refused to act in it, and you may be right: In your view, our death doesn't deserve to have a play put on about it. But then you come and ask about nine Jewish women who, you say, or your Israeli writer says, were slaughtered here in the camp. There were more than fifteen hundred people killed, and you're searching for nine!"

"You haven't understood me. Please, tell me, do you believe, as a Palestinian, that what the Israeli writer says is true? Tell me about the massacre."

"What do you want to know?"

"Did you see the massacre with your own eyes?"

I TOLD YOU that I was drinking white wine, the lights were dim, and the noose was around my neck. The wine was going to my head and taking me to places I'd forgotten. It made me think of Jamal the Libyan.

Did you know Jamal the Libyan?

Jamal whose chest was torn open by an Israeli bullet near the Beirut airport during the siege? I don't know why I told her about Jamal. I think his story deserves to be made into a book; if only I'd told it to a great writer like Jabra Ibrahim Jabra, he could have made it into an epic. But Jabra's dead now, and I never met him. All I had in front of me was this French woman half of whose face was hidden behind the bottle of white wine, and I wanted to explain things to her. It didn't matter to me whether she was an actress or a spy. I wanted to make her understand the truth, and all I could think of was Jamal the Libyan. Or no, perhaps I wanted to seduce her. There was the wine, and there was her soft skin, and there was her little head balanced like a little ball upon her neck, and it was night, and for the first time in months I felt my loneliness had been breached.

The man who told the story of Jamal the Libyan wasn't me. It was a man who resembled me.

I saw him do it and observed him closely and was impressed by his way of talking and how he could convert his fear and doubt into a dance of seduction and attraction; how he saw the woman's defenses fall before him, and how taken aback he was at detecting a sort of betrayal as he approached the female body after a long dry spell. I saw him shaking off the humiliations his fear had inflicted on him. By the way, Father, why do fighters, when they feel fear, feel it more deeply than others? If you want to see fear, find a veteran, and put him in a frightening situation; then you'll understand what real fear is.

So there was Khalil, which is to say myself, his fear tossed aside, sitting in front of this French woman about whom he knew nothing, telling her an extraordinary story, one that really deserves to be turned into a novel or a film. The truth is that Khalil Ayyoub had given some thought to the matter. Don't think anyone could know such a story and not get the idea that he might become a writer – though to turn this true story into a novel we'd need at least one military victory so that people would take us seriously and believe that our tragedy deserves to be placed next to the other tragedies our ferocious century has known, while casting the gloom of its final days over us.

We don't deserve our own story, which is why Jamal never told anyone. He fought in silence and died in silence. But what a story it is.

Why, come to think of it, did he tell me his story?

I remember he came to the hospital among the wounded. They brought him in with another man, both covered in blood. The first one looked dead, his blood clotted on his stiff body. I don't know who examined him. Anyway, he was taken to the mortuary in preparation for burial. Then they discovered he was still alive, so they rushed him to the recovery room, and there we discovered he was a poet. The papers that came out in Beirut during the siege published long obituaries about him. When the poet awoke from his "death" and read these, he was delighted beyond imagining. His medical situation was desperate: He'd been hit in the spinal cord and his left lung was punctured, but he lived for two days, which were enough for him to read everything that was written about him.

He said he was happy, that he no longer was afraid of dying because he'd grasped the meaning of life through love woven by words. Ali – that was his name – was the only happy corpse I ever saw; it was as though all his pains had been obliterated. He lived for two beautiful days in his bed surrounded by stacks of obituaries, and by the time he actually died everything had already been written about him, so his second death notice consisted of a few lines and no one paid attention to the time of his funeral. We took him in a procession from the hospital to the camp cemetery – there were only a handful of us.

Jamal the Libyan was wounded along with the poet, fracturing his right shoulder and sustaining several severe chest wounds. This didn't stop him from visiting his friend, the living dead, in the recovery room and weeping over his two successive deaths.

Jamal told me his story in the hospital and I told the tale to Catherine, and here I am now, repeating it to you so I can unravel, for both of us, the meaning of things. I won't lie to you and say that my encounter with this French actress was nothing and ended with the gush of the shower in her hotel room. Something stole into my insides and created a sort of breach, which I wouldn't call passion but which I will say, for the time being, resembled passion.

Jamal the Libyan left the hospital to die, as though it were the fate of this pilot to die on firm ground, not in the sky. His real name, of course, wasn't Jamal the Libyan; the tag "the Libyan" got attached to him because he'd studied at the aviation school in Tripoli in preparation for the formation of the first squadron of the Palestinian air force in exile. The squadron was never formed, and when the Israeli invasion of Lebanon started, the Palestinian pilots from Libya were called to join the defense of Beirut. Jamal died in Beirut, and it was there he told his story.

"Let's start at the end," you'll say.

Okay, I'll do it since I've always preferred to tell the ends of stories before their beginnings. But you'll have to forgive me this time because first I'm going to give you an account of what happened with Catherine. I began with her from the beginning. I didn't tell her, for instance, how Jamal told me his story.

I remember that, when he was speaking about the Israeli army, he said his maternal uncles were all in a dither because they couldn't enter Beirut.

"My uncles are very scared of their soldiers dying. They're sick! And they need psychiatric help!"

I didn't say anything when he mentioned his uncles. At the time I didn't notice because, like tens of thousands of others living in Beirut, I was under continuous Israeli bombardment from air, land, and sea and was suffering from what you might call shell shock.

He said it to give me a chance to stop him at the word *uncles*, and when I failed to notice and got into a political-military debate with him about our likely collapse in the war, he immediately changed the subject and said, "Look, Doctor, you don't know them. I know them better than you because I'm a Jew like them."

"A Jew!" I said, and burst out laughing, sure he was joking.

Jamal wasn't joking, but he wasn't a Jew in the true sense of the word. He said it to give me a jolt and provoke me to question him so he could tell his story.

I didn't tell Catherine the story this way. I began from the beginning. I left things deliberately vague and in limbo to heighten the shock value, and it worked. I didn't make anything up myself – the story's astonishing, and I used it to frame a moment of passion with a beautiful woman in a Beirut hotel on Hamra Street.

We were drinking white wine, and Catherine was seated beside me because when she came back from her room with the book, she'd changed her place and, instead of sitting opposite me, sat down right next to me on the wide sofa. She moved close to me as she read the text so I could see the page she was reading from, but when she finished reading she stayed there.

I was surprised.

Really, the text took me by surprise, and I was on the point of expressing my doubts and saying, as any of us would, that they didn't even want to grant us the benefit of being victims of the massacre but felt the need to skew even that by focusing on the nine Jewish women who'd been slaughtered. But when I remembered Jamal the Libyan, I decided to keep quiet. I swallowed what would've surely appeared ludicrous to that woman, however obvious it seems to you. It was in China that I learned to distinguish between the stupid and the obvious. It takes another culture to let us discover that half the things that seem obvious are simply our own stupidities.

I said to her, "Listen. I'm going to tell you a story about a Palestinian family, and afterward you can draw whatever conclusion you like. But listen carefully."

She said that first she wanted a response concerning these women.

"This story is my response," I said.

And Khalil began.

I can see him sitting in the hotel lobby, the words gushing from his lips and eyes. I see him now as though he were another man, I would have wanted a friend like him because I love people who know how to tell stories.

Khalil began.

Jamal was born in Gaza City, where his father was a notable of the place, a wealthy man who had never been interested in politics, in spite of the fact that Gaza had been badly shaken by the war in '48 and had turned into a city of refugees. The city was overflowing with tens of thousands of those expelled from the areas the Israeli army had just taken over. It almost seemed as though there were no Gazans left in Gaza – Gaza dissolved in a sea of refugees and became the first place to be collectively Palestinian. It was there the Palestinians discovered they weren't groups of people belonging to various regions and villages; the disaster had produced a single people. That's why Gaza became the most important hub of political activity in Palestine's contemporary history. The Communist Party was strong there, it was there that the Muslim Brothers arose, and the first Fatah cells took shape in its camps and quarters. The Popular Front would occupy the city by night, under the command of a legendary figure known as Guevara of Gaza, setting up roadblocks everywhere. It was there that the Hamas and Islamic Jihad movements were born . . .

Ahmad Salim, Jamal's father, lived in the heart of this political and ideological whirlwind that battered Gaza. He never participated in politics, but he permitted his sons, when they became young men, to attach themselves to the Arab Nationalists movement, which had caught on among students.

Jamal, his eldest son, finished his secondary education in Gaza and then studied civil engineering at Cairo University, where he was an activist in the Arab Nationalists movement, which changed its name to the Popular Front for the Liberation of Palestine following the fall of Gaza and the West Bank to Israeli occupation in 1967.

Mirwan, the second son, studied agricultural engineering at the American University of Beirut.

Hisham, the third son, was unable to complete his studies. He was finishing up his secondary education in Gaza in 1967 when everything was turned on its head.

Samira, the only girl and the youngest in the family, was one of the first

Palestinian women to be arrested on charges of forming cells of "saboteurs," as they're called in Israel.

The four children participated enthusiastically in the demonstrations that swept the streets of Gaza in support of Egyptian president Gamal Abdel Nasser and his decision to shut the Strait of Tiran to Israeli shipping, which was the official reason for the Six-Day War.

The war broke out and Gaza was occupied. A period of curfews, of night, and of fear followed.

At the beginning of September 1967, as people in Gaza were searching for ways to initiate resistance, a bomb struck the house of Ahmad Salim.

Jamal said that as war became increasingly likely, his mother began to change. She didn't share her children's enthusiasm for Gamal Abdel Nasser but remained silent, her face flushed with a blackish redness, saying only, "May the Lord protect us, my children!" After the defeat and Gaza's fall to occupation, her silence became heavy and alarming, and her face turned into a dark mask.

That evening, when the entire family was seated around the dinner table, and the mother's silence had imposed a prickly muteness on everyone so that only the clattering of spoons and knives could be heard, the mother broke her silence in a dull wooden voice that seemed to come from far away. She said what she had to say with a strange rapidity, as though the words had been choking her, making her spill them all at once before resuming her silence.

The mother said, "Listen. I want to tell you a secret that your father and I thought would be better to hide from you because it would only create unnecessary problems for you. But things have changed, and you have to know."

The father interrupted her, annoyed, saying there was no reason for such talk. He pushed his plate aside, put his head in his hands and bent over, listening.

"I'm not an Arab or a Muslim. I'm Jewish."

Silence reigned.

Jamal said the food stuck in his gullet and he almost choked, but he didn't dare cough or take a drink. Everything became constricted. Even the September air stopped moving.

Jamal looked at his brothers and sister and saw that they were all examining their plates as though they didn't dare to raise their eyes.

After having dropped this bomb, the mother seemed relieved; the darkness left her face, she sat up straight, and her voice came back to her.

"Your father isn't from Gaza but from Jerusalem, where he belonged to one of the city's rich and notable families. There, in 1939, he met a German Jewess who'd recently migrated to Palestine with her family. Sarah Rimsky. In Jerusalem the girl experienced the difficulties that afflicted many German emigrants: She had a hard time acclimatizing to the laws of the *Yeshuv*, to its values and language. She was eighteen years old, studying German literature at the Hebrew University in Jerusalem. That year she met a man by chance and fell in love with him. She had gone into a shop to buy clothes, and there was a young man, wearing a red fez, working in his father's shop. The relationship was difficult, if not impossible, at first. She loved him but didn't dare declare her love, and he behaved as though he were indifferent. He would sit in front of his shop and wait for her, and when she went by, on her way to the university, he'd say good morning to her in English. She'd reply in German, and they'd laugh. Then things developed. He invited her for Arab pastries at Zalatimo's; she went with him and adored, she said, the smell of orange-blossom water and rose water. They went walking in the streets of the Old City, discovering it together. He said she taught him to see Jerusalem, that he was seeing the city through her eyes. That was his first declaration of love. After a year of a relationship that came into being around the scent of orange-blossom water and the alleyways of the city, they decided to get married – and this was unthinkable. A Palestinian marry an immigrant German Jewess? Impossible, said everyone. But there was no going back.

The girl told her friend she was prepared to get married in secret and run away with him. She suggested Beirut. The young man asked her to be patient and entered into negotiations with his father, which lasted two years.

The girl waited, and the story got out.

One day, the young man arrived with his father's consent, on condition that they leave Jerusalem and go and live in Gaza, where the father had bought his son land and a house.

The crisis ended with their marriage and move to Gaza, where they lived and managed a stretch of orange orchards. What's remarkable is that the young woman adapted quickly to her new situation. She started speaking Arabic with a Gaza accent, embraced Islam and lived in Gaza as a Muslim Arab woman. The name Sarah was not as widespread among Muslims in those days as it is today, though it was not considered unacceptable.

The mother said she'd told her children the truth so they'd know they had two uncles on her side of the family: the first, Elie, a colonel in the Israeli army, and the second, Benjamin, an engineer. Both lived in Tel Aviv.

The father removed his hands from his face and said his wife's relatives had tried to kill her in 1944 – a group of armed Jews had attacked the house and sprayed it with machine-gun fire. The bullets had mostly hit the kitchen, where they believed Sarah would be. He said he'd removed the bullet holes from the kitchen walls but had left one "so we wouldn't forget." He proposed that the children get up so he could show it to them, but none of them moved.

The mother said she was Palestinian and that was her choice, "But you need to know; the Jews are occupying Gaza now, and they won't be going anywhere."

"We'll throw them out," said Jamal.

"How I wish, my son!" said the mother.

"Mon Dieu!" said Catherine. "Is it possible?"

"I didn't invent the story," I said, "which means it's possible. Didn't you just read about it in this book? Did the Israeli journalist make up the story of the nine Jewish women?"

"Of course not," she said.

"There is something mysterious," I said, "but that's not what the story's about."

"They killed her?" asked Catherine.

"No."

"Her brother, the colonel, came and dragged her to Israel?"

"No."

"Like me, Jamal discovered that he was Jewish."

"Like you?"

"No. I mean, I'm not Jewish, just my mother."

"Your mother's Jewish?"

"No, my mother's Catholic, but her mother – her mother's family were Jews. They converted to Christianity out of fear of persecution, then . . ."

"Then what?" I asked.

"I learned the truth from my mother, so I decided to look for my roots and went to Israel."

"And did you find your roots?"

"I don't know. No, not exactly. I discovered that it's not allowed, that we don't have the right to persecute another people."

"We don't?"

"They don't, the Jews don't. That's what I meant."

I told her that Sarah Rimsky's story didn't end with her confession at that family dinner. In fact, that's where it started.

Jamal the Libyan said his mother was changed after her confession. Her smile was gone, the dark spots on her face and neck multiplied, and the family entered the maelstrom of the prison world.

"But I went to see them," said Jamal.

Jamal said he discovered that he wasn't just Palestinian but could be Israeli or German if he so wished. "I went to their house in the Ramat Aviv district in the northern suburbs of Tel Aviv. I knocked on the door and a blond girl of about seventeen, who looked a lot like my mother, opened it. I told her my name was Jamal Salim, that I was the son of Sarah, her father's sister. I spoke to her in English, but she answered me in Hebrew. When I said I didn't know Hebrew, she switched to broken English.

"'Come in,' she said.

"I went into the living room, where she asked me to sit down and went off to tell her father.

"Colonel Elie entered, wearing a brown dressing gown. He stood in front of me and said something in Hebrew.

"'I'm Jamal, Sarah's son,' I said in English as I stood up.

"'You!'"

"'Yes. Me.'"

"I didn't expect him to embrace me, no," said Jamal, "but I did expect that he'd be a little curious, that he might ask how his sister was. Instead, he asked what I wanted.

"'Nothing,' I said. 'I wanted to meet you.'

"'It's been a pleasure,' he said and turned his back to me as though asking me to leave. I stood at a loss in the middle of the spartan living room – no other word fits when you compare their living room to the opulent one in our house. I said I wanted to talk with him a bit.

"'You're an Arab, right?'

"'Palestinian,' I said.

"'What do we have to talk about?'

"'Family matters,' I said.

"'What family?'

"'Our family.'

"'We're not one family,' said the colonel.

"'But you're my uncle.'

"'We're not one family, I tell you. You're a terrorist. I'm sure terrorists sent you here.'

"I burst out laughing and said I'd come to propose a family meeting.

"'Your mother sent you?'

"'No. My mother doesn't know.'

"'So who sent you?'

"'No one.'

"'What's your job?'

"'I'm an engineer.'

"'What kind of an engineer?'

"'A civil engineer.'

"'Where did you study?'

"'In Cairo.'

"'They know how to teach engineering there?'

"'So so. It's not bad,' I said. 'The people who built the Pyramids can build a house.'

"'Your name's Jamal?' asked the girl.

"'Yes, Jamal. And yours?'

"'Leah Rimsky,' she said.

"'A beautiful name,' I said.

"'Do you know Tel Aviv?' she asked.

"'How could I?'

"'Would you like to see it? I could show you around.'

"'Go to your room and let me deal with him,' said the colonel.

"But Leah didn't go to her room, and the interview with my uncle, the retired colonel, was short and brusque. He said he didn't want to see his sister, had no interest in any family meeting, that it was up to us Palestinians to assimilate within the Arab countries ('You're Arabs like the rest of the Arabs') and that he didn't understand our insistence on living in the refugee camps, which had come to resemble Jewish ghettos: 'Go and become Syrians and Lebanese and Jordanians and Egyptians, so that this blood-drenched conflict can come to an end.' I thanked him for his advice and said, 'Thank you, and you too. Why don't you, my dear European German colonel, become assimilated in Europe? Go and assimilate yourself instead of giving me lessons in assimilation, and then the problem will be over. We'll assimilate with the Arabs, you can assimilate with the Europeans, this land will be deserted, and we can turn it into a resort for tourists and religious fanatics from every nation. What do you say?'

"'You understand nothing about Jewish history,' he said.

"'And do you understand anything about our history?'

"At this, Leah intervened and said she was ready to show me around Tel Aviv. We went out. The colonel said nothing and didn't try to stop his daughter from going.

"With Leah I saw Tel Aviv, I discovered that strange society, which I can tell you is difficult to reduce to a few words. No, I didn't go back and visit the colonel. I phoned Leah several times and went out with her, becoming reacquainted with my mother through her. Extraordinary! How is it possible? They'd never met but were so alike in everything – the same laugh, the same gestures, and they liked more or less the same foods. I suggested to Leah that she come with me to Gaza so I could introduce her to her twin, but she said she'd have to think about it."

"And your mother? Have you told your mother?"

"I told my mother I'd visited them, and at first she asked about them eagerly; then the mask reappeared and covered her face.

"'Please, stop visiting them. He's a criminal and will kill you,' said my mother.

"I told her about our discussion about assimilation and her face lit up for a moment, but then she furrowed her brow and said that history was a wild animal.

"After several more outings, Leah stopped answering the phone. Their number had been changed, and I had no other way of getting in touch with her. She'd warned me that her father wouldn't allow her to meet me. Her father changed the number, and she didn't call. Just between us, my uncle, the colonel, was right: After the bus operations, our meetings were no longer possible. Do you remember the bus operations, when the Popular Front planted explosives at bus stops in Tel Aviv?"

"Was that you?"

"I can't claim that honor for myself, but I did take part through surveillance. My outings with Leah were a type of surveillance, and I reported on what I'd seen to the Popular Front cell. The cell was uncovered after a sweep of arrests in Gaza, and they took me to Damoun Prison, where I was sentenced to twenty years on charges of participating in terrorist activities and belonging to a saboteur organization."

Jamal said that prison had brought him relief: "The battering torrent stopped roaring in my head. I was twenty-three years old then and I'm twenty-nine years now, but all the same, when I remember those days before I was arrested and the feelings that raged inside me when I went out with Leah and took her to Jerusalem . . . ! I took her to Zalatimo's, and when I saw her eating and singing and smelling the scent of orange-blossom water I told her about my mother and how my father had managed to seduce her with the help of Zalatimo's pastries. When I remember that now, I feel a loss. Prison let me have a rest. Things are clear there – them and us. We're behind bars, and they guard us. That way there's no confusion. In prison I read all sorts of books, and I learned Hebrew. I thought to myself, When I leave prison, I'll go and visit my uncle and speak to him in his new language.

"My mother came to visit me regularly. My father came with her some-times, but she'd come every week, bringing cigarettes and food. She told me that my brother, Mirwan, had been arrested, too, that Samirah had been held for several days and then released, and that they were thinking about sending Hisham and Samirah to Cairo because they were afraid for them. I asked her why she didn't get in touch with my uncle so he could help to get me out, and she asked me never to mention the subject again. I stayed in prison for five years before I was deported to Jordan."

"And your mother? Where's your mother?" I asked him.

"I haven't gotten there yet. My mother stopped visiting me a year after I went to prison, and my father started coming on his own. He said my mother was sick, that she had arthritis. He brought me letters from her. Her letters were short and said only that I was to take care of myself after I came out of prison. You don't know my mother. I swear no one could've guessed that she was Israeli or Jewish. She was more Palestinian than all the rest of us put together. My father still spoke with his Jerusalem accent, but she became Gazan – a true *ghazzawiyya*. She loved hot peppers, ate salad with-out olive oil, and all the rest. Then my father disappeared, too. Hisham and

Samirah were in Cairo, Mirwan was in prison like me, and my father stopped visiting me.

"Later, a short letter from him reached me via the Red Cross. It said he'd taken my mother to Europe for treatment.

"When I got out of prison, I learned the truth. What a woman she was! And I don't say that because she was my mother. All of us love our mothers and see them as saints, but if you only knew."

"If you only knew," Khalil said to Catherine.

"You could never guess what happened. Sarah didn't go to Europe for treatment. Guess what she did."

"She went to Tel Aviv and returned to her family," said Catherine.

"That possibility has passed through Jamal's mind, but it's not what happened."

"Her brother killed her?"

"Now you're imagining an American film. We can't behave as if we're in American films, even if we like watching them."

"What then?" asked Catherine.

Khalil said Sarah contracted colon cancer, but they discovered the disease too late, after the cancer had spread through her entire body.

"You know how women in our country suppress everything. They don't complain, they refuse to say anything, and barricade themselves in with silence and secrets."

Sarah treated herself at the beginning, and when the pain got bad she went to the doctor. She was admitted to hospital, had three operations, and was sent home after the cancer spread to her bones. She returned home to enter a long period of appalling pain.

One night, when Sarah couldn't sleep because the pain was so bad even though she'd had a morphine injection, she went to her husband's bed, woke him and told him she wanted to talk to him.

The man sat up in bed and listened to the strangest request.

Sarah asked her husband to take her to Berlin and bury her in the Jewish cemetery there.

Her husband told her he was prepared to go any place in the world with her for treatment and that he'd call the doctor in the morning to get the addresses of hospitals in Berlin.

"I don't want treatment," she said. "There is no treatment. I want to be buried there."

Khalil told Catherine that Jamal, as he told the story, was more astonished than he was, as though he were listening, not recounting. He said his father told him later, when they met in Amman a few months before his death, that he'd leave this world in peace because he'd succeeded in making Sarah happy.

"She was like a little girl there," the father said. "Every day we'd go out. I don't know where she found the strength. She took me to the places of her childhood, of which not many remained – but she was happy. It was as though the pain had gone, or a miracle had occurred. After a week she was no longer able to get out of bed. I tried to take her to the hospital, but she refused. Three days later she died, and I buried her there."

Khalil saw the sorrow engraved on Catherine's face. The French actress who wouldn't act in Jean Genet's play was slumped in her chair almost as if she were unconscious.

"Why aren't you drinking?" Khalil asked her.

She looked at her glass and said nothing. Khalil took Catherine's glass and finished it off in one gulp.

Catherine said she was exhausted.

Khalil looked at his watch. "It's three in the morning," he said.

Catherine said she wanted to sleep.

"Now you want to sleep! The night's just beginning. I would like some more wine."

"No. You've had a lot to drink, Jamal," she said.

"Not at all, and my name's Khalil, my mother's name is Najwah, and Jamal died during the Israeli invasion of Beirut."

Catherine got up. Khalil got up.

"How are you going to get back to the camp?" she asked.

"I don't know, but I'll manage."

"You can spend what's left of the night here, in my room."

"In your room . . . No . . ."

"I'm tired and want to sleep. Come up with me."

They went up to her room. Catherine undressed quickly and climbed into bed almost nude. After a little hesitation, Khalil lay down next to her, fully clothed.

"Take your clothes off," she said. "Don't tell me you're going to sleep in your clothes."

He undressed, Catherine turned off the light, and there, in the darkness of the room, which would continue to cling to Khalil's skin, they made love.

Khalil doesn't remember things clearly, but he felt as though he were drowning and caught hold of the woman, who fell on top of him, and they drowned together.

The next morning, as he was opening his eyes, he saw Catherine emerging from the bathroom dressed and wearing a lot of lipstick. He dressed quickly, and they went down to the restaurant, where they ate breakfast like strangers.

She told him she was leaving that afternoon; she was going to the crafts shop near the hotel to buy some presents. He told her he was already late for work at the hospital and would have to get going. Neither one brought up any of the topics of the previous day – they didn't even mention the play again. They finished breakfast and got up from the table. She planted a cold kiss on his cheek, and he left.

AND THAT was all that happened with the French actress.

I told her the story of Jamal, and we slept together. She thought she was sleeping with Jamal the Libyan, who could have been Palestinian or Jewish or German, and I glimpsed in her something of Sarah, who became Palestinian.

Now let's suppose that Catherine had immigrated to Israel, married Jamal, and – after a long life – death had come for her. Where would she have asked to be buried? With her Jewish grandmother, her Catholic mother, or her Muslim children?

Our story has no end.

When Jamal told me his story, I couldn't believe it. He told me because he knew he was going to die; now he's resting in his grave in Beirut while his father's in Gaza and his mother in Germany.

Will the dead be reunited?

Why did Sarah return to the country of her executioners?

"It's the classic relationship between executioner and victim," you'll say.

I'm not so sure. I don't have any strong convictions that would provide me with an answer about a world like the one that drew Sarah toward her German grave.

Jamal told me his father was able to see the joy that reconnecting with the German language gave Sarah. She adored speaking German and would gurgle in it the way a child does.

Are we slaves of our own language?

Is language our land, our mother, and our universe?

Catherine went back to her country. She didn't take the part she was supposed to in the play about the massacre. She left the play to us so we could go on playing the role of the victim. The role has no end, starting from the fall of the man-bird from the heights of the minaret of al-Ghabsiyyeh and the men of Sha'ab who climbed the ropes of rain to their deaths.

The French actress left us to play our role and went back to her country with the story of Sarah and Jamal the Libyan. And, instead of uncovering the names, she lost them. I asked nothing of her; I found myself in bed with her and she spoke to me in French, which I don't understand, and called me Jamal. And when she got up the next day, she put her mask back on and went back to her country.

She was right, but I didn't understand right away.

In the morning, beneath her mask of lipstick, she became another woman. She put on her French mask and planted a glacial kiss on my cheek. She was right: If I'd had a French mask, I wouldn't have taken it off and let myself enter this labyrinth called Palestine. I have no choice because I was born in this labyrinth, nor do you. Jamal the Libyan, his cousin, Sarah, the same goes for an incalculable number of others from here, from over there, or even from outside. We have no alternatives and no masks, and even war no longer provides enough of a mask to conceal the whirlpool in which we're drowning. Them and us. As you see, they've become like us and we've become like them. We no longer possess any other memory.

All the war stories have evaporated, all that's left are the massacres. Are we imitating our enemies, or are they imitating their executioners and pushing us to put on that same mask that camouflaged Dunya's features? You remember Dunya? Dunya's dead now. "It doesn't matter," you'll say. I'll agree – we're all going to die. But Dunya died because she was no longer able to play the role of the victim. That phase is over. The international humanitarian agencies have lost interest in us. Now what they're interested in is the West Bank and Gaza, and Dunya has lost her following. That's why she died.

And you.

I know why you're dying, Father.

You're dying because the story has come to an end with Nahilah's death.

Tell me, why don't you open your eyes and speak as Sarah spoke? Why don't you declare your wish to die over there?

Are you afraid of dying?

Or is it that you don't want your story to end, that you want to leave it open-ended so you can force us to keep on playing the role of the victim for as long as God sees fit?

What do you say?

No, my story's different, and I'll tell it to you from beginning to end. Shams' death is no reason for me to die. No, I won't go out onto the street and ask them to kill me. No, what happened last week was an absolute fiasco. I heard shooting in the street near the hospital, which started shaking with the rattle of the Kalashnikovs. I came running to hide in your room. I was shaking with fear. Now I laugh at myself when I remember how scared I was – I was ready to hide under your bed.

In the morning, Zainab entered your room with a gloating smile.

"What are you doing here?" she asked me.

I said I'd been afraid for you because your breathing was irregular, so I spent the night here.

"Didn't you hear the shooting?"

"No. What happened?"

That was my mistake. When you lie, you discover that you can't correct anything: You're naked. I was naked before Zainab's smile.

"Everyone heard, and Dr. Amjad came from his house to make sure everything was alright and we looked for you. We didn't find you in your room, and Dr. Amjad said you'd run away and told me to get everything ready to move Yunes to the home this morning."

"We won't be moving him," I said.

"As you wish. Go and discuss it with Dr. Amjad. But why didn't you come out of Yunes' room last night?"

"I didn't hear anything. I must have been fast asleep."

"Whatever, Doctor. I can't understand how you couldn't have heard. Maybe you were in a coma. Fear can cause comas," she said as she left.

I ran after her. "Zainab, come here."

"What do you want?"

I asked her about the day before, fear creeping into my voice.

"It was nothing," she said. "A robbery. A bunch of thieves tried to rob the hospital, and when Kamelya noticed them they fired in the air and ran away."

"That's all?"

"That's all. What did you think it was, an assassination attempt? Get a grip! No one's after you. The woman's dead and gone, and if they'd wanted to kill you they'd have killed you. Go back home and get some sleep. What kind of person sleeps next to a corpse when he can sleep at home?"

She called you a corpse! Stupid woman.

It's as though she can't see. No one sees you but me. I said to Amjad –
this was the last time we talked about you – I said to him that I refused to
move you to the home and asked him to come to your room to see for
himself.

"It's your responsibility," he said. "You want him here, let him stay here.
I suggested moving him for your sake." Then he said he refused to examine you himself: "I'm not a forensic physician who examines corpses."

I attempted in vain to explain it to him. He said that what I see as posi-
tive signs are really signs of death. Good God, can't he see how like a little
child you've become? You've grown younger, and the signs of aging have
been erased from your brow and your neck, and your smell is that of a baby.
Even your reflexes are like those of a newborn. The problem is your closed
eyes, which I still put "tears" into. Your eyes are clear, the whites slightly
blue, and your heart's as strong and regular as a young man's.

I told Amjad I could see your improvement in your eyes. I said I could
hear your voice, as though you were waiting for something before coming
out with the words.

"It's all in your imagination," he said.

"No, Doctor, I'm not imagining it. I speak to him and he understands. I
put on Fairouz cassettes for him and see him swimming in his dreams, I play
him Umm Kalsoum and see the desire gushing out around him, I play him
Abd al-Wahhab and Abd al-Halim and see the mist of life curling above his
head."

He said he was sure you'd entered the final phase and he expected your
heart to collapse – it could happen at any instant and carry you off – and
that all my concern for you wouldn't make the slightest difference. You
hadn't died already because your constitution was strong and your heart
excellent – he'd never seen such a pure heart. He used the word *pure* to
mean "regular" but the only true purity is the purity of love, and I'm jealous of you and of your love. I'm jealous of that meeting you had beneath
the Roman olive tree when Nahilah took you to Bab al-Shams and poured

her rain upon you. When I imagine that scene, I see her envelop you like a cloud and then pour her rain upon you. That is the water of heaven, and of life.

How can I convince them you're not going to die? How can I convince myself?

Your childhood drives me crazy and crushes me; I never fathered a child and never knew the beauty that Yunes saw when his son Ibrahim's hair covered the pillow.

Now I've started to understand how a man becomes a father.

Would you agree?

You don't have to agree, Father, because you're my son now. Let me call you "son," please. Think of it as a game. Don't parents play that way with their children, the father calling his son "daddy" and the son calling his father "son"? I'm the same. I carry the same name as your father: He was Ibrahim and I'm Khalil – the Companion. Ibrahim was the Companion of God, which is why we've named Ibrahim's city Khalil, the City of the Companion. That's why, too, the fiercest battles between the Palestinians and the Jews will take place in that city, and for it.

We won't get into the complications of the relationships between fathers and sons. You know I don't care for religious stories, and the name of the sacrifice that wasn't sacrificed – be it Isaac, as the Jews say, or Ishmael, as we say – doesn't concern me. Neither of them was sacrificed, because Ibrahim, peace be upon him, was able to produce a ram. The knife passed over both of their necks without a scratch, so what's the difference?

I don't want to discuss that now. I want you, Son, to see life with your new eyes. Start at the beginning, not at the end. Or start wherever you like. I've told you these stories so you can create a new story for yourself.

I can't imagine the world that's waiting for you. Make it yourself. Make it the way you want to. Make it new and beautiful. Tell the mountain to move, and it will. Didn't Jesus, peace be upon him, say to the mountains, "Move!" Was he not the son who took on the outlines of his father's image when he died on the cross?

Be the son, and let your bed be your cross.

What do you say?

Don't you like the image of the son?

Isn't it more beautiful than all the ones we've drawn during the six months we've spent together here? Come, let's go back to the beginning.

You wanted the beginning, so let's go there.

Listen, I don't know any lullabies. Zainab does. Zainab lost her first-born son in the Israeli air raid on al-Fakahani in '82, and she still sings to him. I see her, when she's all on her own, cradling her arms as though she were carrying a baby and I hear her singing:

> *Sleep now, sleep,*
> *I'll trap for you a dove.*
> *Go, dove, fear not,*
> *I'm only teasing my son.*
> *Come now and sleep.*

Tomorrow I'll go to Hamra Street and buy you Fairouz, and that'll be your sixth birthday present. Now I have to go and make you lunch, and I'll put some orange-blossom water in it. There's nothing like orange-blossom water. It has the most delicious flavor and the loveliest scent. I'll put some orange-blossom water in your lunch, and your birthday meal will be delicious.

THE EXPERIMENT worked. Didn't I tell you?

After I'd bathed you, daubed you with cologne, rubbed you with ointment and dressed you in your sky-blue pajamas, I sat you up at the table and let go of you, and you didn't fall or slump over. You've regained your balance – and it's impossible to balance if your brain is damaged. I left you alone, standing behind you without touching you. Then an idea came to me.

I stood in front of you, took hold of you just below the armpits, and the miracle occurred. It's the first time I've dared to try such an experiment. There are three involuntary reflexes that newborn babies have.

The first is the gripping of the finger. We open the baby's hand and put our finger on it, and the baby closes its palm. I've tried that, and it works.

The second is when we put our finger on the baby's cheek close to its mouth, the baby will start to move its mouth toward the finger, grasp it with its lips and suck on it. I've tried that, and it works, too.

The third, I haven't dared to try. I was afraid you'd fall, and your bones, which have become fragile and soft, might break.

I told Zainab about the two experiments, and she gave me a blank look and didn't say a word. As for Dr. Amjad, you know better than I that he doesn't give a damn. It's a waste of time – medicine's the least of his concerns now. The only thing that interests him about the hospital is how to steal the medicine we get as donations and sell them.

We all know he steals, but what can we do? He's the director, so who can we complain to? *Quis custodiet ipsos custodies*, as they say. I'm not going to start bellyaching, this is the situation we're in, and we have to accept it.

I can't remember if I told Dr. Amjad about those two experiments, but I'm certain his reaction would only be scornful.

The important thing is that I'm happy, and I'm not going to allow anyone to spoil my good mood.

Today I decided to carry out the third experiment, and it was conclusive. I stood in front of you and placed my hands under your armpits and I watched you. Before I began, I raised you up a little, the way you do with babies, then I put you back in the chair and placed my right index finger under your left armpit and my left index finger under your right, and I watched you. I swear, you got up and your feet moved as though they were walking. I saw you walking with my own two eyes. Then I got scared. I grabbed you and put you back in the chair, and I saw pain invade your closed eyes. I picked you up as a mother would her baby – God, how light you've become – I picked you up and put you back on your bed and was overwhelmed with joy.

The third reflex occurred, which means that, from a medical standpoint, you're a child again. You won't progress from sickness to death, as they'd hoped; instead you've become a baby and are starting your life over again.

And that means everything can change.

I have to calculate how old you are now, in your new life. I've decided to calculate from the moment you fell into your coma, which means that as of four days ago, you entered your seventh month.

You've been in the womb of death for seven months, and I have to wait for your birth, which will be in two months.

So here we are at the beginning, like you wanted, and all the torments of childhood await you.

Let's get started.

I spend my time with you, I bathe you, I feed you, and I see you changing before my eyes and feel at peace. I feel my body relaxing, and I sense that I can talk to you about what I feel and be free. You're my son, and fathers don't show fear in front of their sons.

Why, come to think of it, was I ever afraid?

How did fear come to possess me and make me its prisoner? I was afraid of everything, always looking over my shoulder, although no one was behind me. I've lived these long months in nothingness. For six months I've been with you, paralyzed by fear. Your new infancy has just liberated me from it. Fathers aren't allowed to show fear in front of their sons.

My fear is gone.

Do you think I could get you out of here? Why don't we go back to the house? No, we won't go back now; we'll be patient. We'll be patient for two more months, until the birth.

I'm talking to you and I don't believe my eyes.

I was leaning over you when, out of nowhere, Abu Kamal appeared at my side. How did he get in?

"What are you doing here, Abu Kamal? What brought you here?" I asked him to sit down, but he remained standing next to you as though he couldn't hear me.

"What were you saying?" he asked me.

I told him I was treating you.

"Treating him with words?"

"I'm treating him. What business is it of yours? Please, sit down."

But Samir Rashid Sinounou, Abu Kamal, wouldn't oblige. He went over to you, bent over the bed and then drew back. I heard what sounded like a sob and I thought he was weeping, so I put my hand on his shoulder, but then I saw that he was laughing.

"What's this? Incredible! This is Yunes Abu Salem? How the mighty have fallen!"

And he went on laughing.

I tried to grab him by the shoulders and push him out of the room, and I saw his tears. He was laughing and weeping. His tears were streaming around his gaping lips, and his choppy laugh was a sort of cough.

The bald man of about sixty, known in the camp as Eggplant because of his black skin and oblong face, seemed to have lost his balance and dropped his head as though he were about to fall to the ground. I calmed him and made him drink some water.

"How the mighty have fallen," he said. "Is this how a man ends up? This is Abu Salem – God, he's become younger than a suckling child. What kind of illness turns men into babies?"

I took his hand and led him out into the corridor.

"What has brought you here, Abu Kamal?"

Eggplant hasn't visited you before, and I don't believe you were friends; he inhabits a different world and cares only about marriage. He married three times and had ten children, and now he's alone since his third wife died and his two divorced wives refused to come back to him. His children have all emigrated and his life's over, as Umm Hassan said. Umm Hassan felt sorry for him and would visit him and send him food; he was from her village. Abu Kamal is from the Sinounou family, which left al-Kweikat when its people were expelled in '48.

"What brought you here?" I asked.

"Poverty," he said.

When I took him out of your room into the corridor, he stood leaning against the wall, but when he uttered the word *poverty*, he collapsed onto the floor and started his complaint. He asked me to find him a job in the hospital. He said Umm Hassan was a relative of his, he knew the esteem in which I'd held her, and he'd come to ask for work.

"I can do any kind of work. Things are unbearable."

"But Abu Kamal, you know the situation better than I do. Things aren't too good here."

"I don't know anything," he said. "I don't want to die of hunger."

"And your job? Why don't you go back to your old job?"

"What job, Cousin? Is there anyone left in the camp who reads newspapers?"

"Go to Beirut and get a job."

He said he couldn't work in Beirut any longer. The week before, a policeman had stopped him when he was selling papers on the Mazra'a Corniche and asked for his papers. When he saw he was Palestinian, he threatened him and said it was forbidden for Palestinians to work in Lebanon without a permit.

"Now you need a work permit to sell papers, Cousin! So he confiscated the papers and chased me away. He said if I hadn't been an old man he'd have thrown me in jail."

"What about the camp? Work in the camp," I told him.

"You know that nobody here reads newspapers any longer. Anyway, no one has the money to buy them, and people have their television and video now. What am I to do?"

He started talking about his problem with videos, and about how he couldn't see: Everyone else could see, but he couldn't. "They sit around their televisions and run the tape, and they see things I don't. That isn't Palestine, Cousin. Those pictures don't look like our villages, but I don't know what's got into everyone, they're glued to their television sets. There's no electricity, and they still play them, signing up for Hajj Ismail's generator just for the video. They pay twenty dollars a month and go hungry so they can watch the tapes; they sit in their houses and stare at those films they say are Palestine. We're a video nation and our country's become a video country."

Abu Kamal said that after the incident with the policeman he tried to work in the camp. "I opened a news stand, and my only customer was Dr. Amjad, but he didn't pay. He'd take the papers, read them, and return them, while I sat all day long with nothing to do. Can't you find me a job here?"

"Impossible, Abu Kamal. What could you do here?"

"My brother, my friend, I want to eat. I can't go on like this. Are you willing to see your Uncle Eggplant become a beggar? We'll have seen it all! To hell with this miserable life!"

I tried to help him up but he refused.

"Get up, Uncle. Come on, let's sit in the room."

But he wouldn't get up.

"Get up. You can't stay here like this."

He said he didn't want to go into your room because he was afraid.

I told him there was no money and things were tough.

He asked for a cigarette and smoked it greedily, as though he hadn't had one for a long time. I offered him the pack, but he refused it. He accepted one more, smoked it, and went off.

No, before he left, he went into your room to say farewell, and I saw a kind of jealousy in his eyes, as though he envied your long sleep. Then he gave me a few words of support and left the hospital.

I felt so bad for Abu Kamal Sinounou, but what could I do for him? You don't know him so you won't understand why my heart is so heavy. He'd transformed himself from a newspaper seller in Acre into the owner of the largest shop in the camp. Then his shop was destroyed and his life with it; his third wife died, and he ended up alone and poor.

Why are all your stories like that?

How could you stand this life?

These days we can stand it because of video; Abu Kamal was right – we've become a video nation. Umm Hassan brought me a tape of al-Ghabsiyyeh, and some other woman brought a tape of another village – all people do is swap videotapes, and in these images we find the strength to continue. We sit in front of the small screen and see small spots, distorted pictures and close-ups, and from these we invent the country we desire. We invent our life through pictures.

But how did your generation bear what happened to you? How did you manage to block up the holes in your lives?

I know what your response will be; you'll say it was temporary. You lived in the temporary; the temporary was your way of coming to an understanding with time.

You're temporary, and we're video. What do you think?

ABU KAMAL used to sell newspapers in Acre and made his life up as he went along. He was about fourteen when he started. He'd leave al-Kweikat on his bicycle each day and reach Acre some forty-five minutes later, pick up his bundle of *al-Sha'b*,* and sell them. In the afternoons, he carried a big

*Literally: The People.

sign around the streets shouting, "Make it an evening at Cinema al-Burj!" inviting people to buy tickets for *The Thief of Baghdad*, and receiving half a lira for his efforts. Adding this to the lira he'd earned from selling papers, he'd return to his village.

Abu Kamal was known as Eggplant in his own village, too. It must be said, my son, that we brought with us both our nicknames and our real names. Eggplant proved he was wilier than all the rest of Kamal Sinounou's children, however. His three brothers worked with their father growing watermelons, but he found himself a job on his own. He went to Acre, saw a paper seller, and asked if he could work with him. The vendor took him to the Communist Party's Acre office, where he met a short man with whom he came to an agreement to sell the paper.

Abu Kamal wasn't a communist; he wanted to leave the village because he didn't like working in the fields. But it seems that his job selling *al-Sha'b* had its influence on how he spoke, since for the rest of his life he'd mumble certain phrases he'd picked up from the paper's headlines about workers' rights, Arab-Jewish brotherhood, and so on.

When things started to get complicated, he stopped going to Acre and joined the al-Kweikat militia as a bodyguard for Mohammed al-Nabulsi, the only man in the militia who owned a Bren gun. When the village fell and Mohammed al-Nabulsi died, Eggplant found himself part of the wave of people who moved out. They didn't go to Amqa because of the famous dispute between the two villages that followed the rape of a girl from the Ghadban family by an Amqa boy.

All the people of al-Kweikat went to Abu Sinan, and they all took up residence under the olive trees, where they set up their tents of blanket and canvas. They stayed in the fields of Abu Sinan for about a month. I won't go into what we know now about how people went back to their villages by night to steal provisions from their houses whose doors hung askew, and about how Qataf, an eighteen-year-old girl, died from an Israeli soldier's bullet as she was leaving her house carrying the demijohn of oil, her blood mixing with the oil, and about how, and how . . .

"There was nothing left for us to do but pillage our own houses," said Umm Hassan. "Is it possible to steal from yourself? But what else could we do, my son?"

I didn't ask Umm Hassan why they didn't try to take their villages back the way you did in Sha'ab instead of creeping into their houses and stealing from themselves, because I knew her answer would be, "Go on! All that about Sha'ab, and it still fell. Enough nonsense!"

Anyway, Yunes, where were we?

Things have gotten strangely mixed up in my head. Even the names are mixed up. A name will fly away from its owner and settle on someone else. Even names have lost their meaning.

I wanted to say that Abu Kamal tried not to live in the temporary. After Qataf's death and the madness that seized the people of al-Kweikat, everyone left Abu Sinan for Jath, and from Jath in Palestine they went to Rimeish in Lebanon, and from Rimeish to Rashaf, and from Rashaf to Haddatha.

Abu Kamal lived in Haddatha for about two years, working on the construction of the Haddatha-Tibnin road, but he left after a quarrel with his sister-in-law. He then traveled to Beirut, where he worked in construction. He stayed in Beirut for about a month and then went back to Haddatha because of exhaustion and the swelling that had developed in his hip from carrying containers of concrete behind the master plasterer. He returned to discover that the Palestinians had been rounded up and put in the Burj al-Barajneh camp in Beirut. He went to Burj al-Barajneh, but he couldn't find a camp; all he found was a bit of empty land and people sleeping out in the open. A foreign official came, with a Lebanese at his side, and they started distributing tents. They distributed two or three and then stopped for one reason or another.

Those were the days of waiting.

Abu Kamal went back to Haddatha because working with concrete had tired him out, and he found that the Palestinians had been deported to the suburbs of Beirut. The trucks came, they ordered the Palestinians living in Lebanese villages to gather in their squares, and they were transported to Beirut and the north.

That was how they left Lebanese Galilee after their expulsion from Palestinian Galilee.

Abu Kamal didn't grasp the reality of what had happened. Like all of you, like my father, he was led by the feeling that everything was temporary. The temporary led him to work for the Jew, Aslan Durziyyeh, and then toward death.

You lived in the temporary and died in the temporary. You endured unbearable lives and hid yourselves in that never-to-be-forgotten oblivion.

What should I have asked Abu Kamal as he sat there, collapsed, his back against the wall?

Should I have asked him why he'd married three women? Or how his fortune turned after the death of his last wife, Intisar?

Would I have been able to explain to him why his first wife, Fathiyyeh, and his second, Ikram, refused to go back to him?

And how will Abu Kamal live now?

The children have emigrated. They send a little money to the two women, but he's alone, and no one sends him anything. Should I have told him he was paying the price for his behavior? Why should he have to pay? Was the camp destroyed just because he married a third time? His third wife, Intisar, died during the long siege that destroyed our world: Our world wasn't destroyed during the great massacre, when we were buried under corpses; our world was destroyed by what they call the War of the Camps, between 1985 and 1988, when we were besieged from every side. That was when everything was wrecked.

Later we read all that stuff they threw together in a hurry about how the *intifada* in Gaza and the West Bank was born to the beat of the War of the Camps. It may be true – I don't mean to judge history – but tell me, why does history only ever come in the shape of a ravening beast? Why do we only ever see it reflected in mirrors of blood?

Don't talk to me now about the mirrors of Jebel al-Sheikh. Wait a little, listen a little.

In front of me sits Abu Kamal, who I wish would die.

A man who has tried his hand at virtually everything, forging his path through life. He worked in concrete – he left concrete with a hip problem, then at the Jaber Biscuit Factory, before deciding to sell ice cream. Then he opened a café, then a shop, which he named the Abu Kamal Minimarket and where he sold smuggled tobacco and a bit of everything. This man who tried to master life by every means possible, now, however, only inspires pity in me. I'm incapable of imagining a solution for his predicament. How could I possibly find work for him when I am myself, as you know, virtually unemployed? And then this man comes and tells me his two wives have shunned him and are keeping the money his children send from him?

"If I could just get in touch with Subhi," said Abu Kamal. "Subhi's always been kind to his father, but I don't know his address. I went to Fathiyyeh and told her . . . I told her I didn't want anything. You don't know, Son, what it is to be treated like shit by a woman, a woman who was once . . ."

"Shame on you, Abu Kamal. Don't talk that way about the mother of your children."

"But you don't know anything."

He said that Fathiyyeh was humiliated twice. The first time was when he married Ikram, and the second, when Intisar forced him to repudiate his two other wives as a condition of marrying him.

"It was my fault, Son – it was my fault, but I just couldn't resist the Devil. He seduced me and made me accept the woman's conditions, but she died and took everything with her. Now I have nothing. The shop was burnt down, the house is half-destroyed. Can an old man like me live alone? I said I'd go back, I'd go back to my life the way it was before and to the two women who couldn't do enough to serve me. Do you know what Fathiyyeh did when I went to visit her? She stood at her door and began yelling and rousing the neighbors. As though I were a beggar. I didn't go to ask for anything, I went because God had opened my eyes. I said, 'I'll get my wife back, and I'll be decently taken care of. I'll get my children back. God took Intisar and the shop to punish me.' I went to make amends, and all I got was humiliation and abuse. Now I don't have the price of a loaf of bread."

I put my hand in my pocket, but all I found was ten thousand lira. I gave them to him saying it was all I had.

"No, Son, no. I don't beg."

He put out his second cigarette, stood up, and left.

I know Fathiyyeh. That woman – I swear every time I think of Nahilah I see Fathiyyeh's image. A tall, dark woman who covers her head with a white scarf and stands as straight as the letter *alif* – no bending, no shaking, and no stumbling, as though life had passed beside her, not through her.

I don't understand how Fathiyyeh accepted his second marriage. At first, he hid it from her. He bought a house in Burj al-Barajneh, where Ikram lived, and divided his time. He'd spend the night in his first wife's house in the Shatila camp, and he'd spend a portion of the day with his second wife in Burj al-Barajneh. Word got out and Fathiyyeh discovered what was going on. When Abu Kamal returned to the house one day exhausted from work – as he claimed – she raised the subject. A look of uncertainty crossed the man's face, and he thought of denying everything because he was afraid of how she'd react, but instead he found himself telling the truth.

"Yes, I got married," he said. "And that's my legal right."

He waited for the storm.

But instead of getting angry and breaking dishes, as she usually did whenever she had a disagreement with her husband over the smallest of things, and instead of killing him, as he believed she might do, this woman, straight as an *alif*, collapsed and broke in two. She bent over, letting her face fall between her hands, and started shuddering with tears. Fathiyyeh broke apart all at once and never stood upright again until he divorced her.

That same day she made peace with Ikram, and the two women lived in one house with their ten children. As the family hemorrhaged children through the deaths of several boys and the emigration of others, and the marriage of their girls, the women found themselves alone, breathing in the scents of letters sent from far away and chewing over their memories together.

After her divorce, Fathiyyeh came back to life. The slump of her shoulders was erased and they became straight again; the long neck bore its white scarf, and the woman walked the roads of the destroyed camp as though she were flying over the rubble, as though the destruction were a sideshow whose sole purpose was to focus the viewer on the beauty of her commanding height and the splendor of her huge eyes.

Fathiyyeh neither yelled nor roused the neighbors, as Abu Kamal claimed.

She stood at the door, blocking it with her broad shoulders, so Ikram couldn't interfere. She knew Ikram's heart would crumble for the man who'd made her believe that his every footstep shook the earth. She kept Ikram behind her and raised her right hand, straightening her scarf with her left one.

"Out!" she said. "Out!"

He tried to speak, but she put her hand over her mouth to keep her hatred and her shouts in, saying only those two words – "Out! Out!" The man left without daring to speak. He didn't even ask for the address of his son, Subhi, who worked in Denmark. He saw the barrier rise in front of him, and he leaned forward, before turning his back on the door Fathiyyeh had blocked with her body.

And now he comes up with the story that she yelled and humiliated him in front of the camp.

Why do people lie like that?

I'm convinced he believed it himself. I'm convinced that when he told me the story of how he tried to get his divorced wives back, he heard the yells that never emerged from Fathiyyeh's mouth.

Tell me – you know better than I do – do we all lie like that? Did you lie to me, too?

I told you your story with Nahilah as a beautiful story, and I didn't question your version of that last meeting beneath the Roman olive tree. You'll say it wasn't the last and will tell stories of your visits that continued up until 1974, but that meeting was the last as far as I'm concerned and as far as the story's concerned. For after Nahilah had said what she said, there was no more talk, and when there's no more talk, there's nothing.

When there's nothing new and fresh to say, when the words go rotten in your mouth and come out lifeless, old, and dead, everything dies.

Isn't that what you told me after the fall of Beirut in 1982? You said the old talk had died, and now we needed a new revolution. The old language was dead, and we were in danger of dying with it. If we weren't fighting, it wasn't because we didn't have weapons but because we didn't have words.

On that day the words died, Yunes, and we entered a deep sleep from which we didn't awaken until the *intifada* of the people at the interior of the country. Then the papers published the photo of the child with his slingshot and you said to me, "It seems it's begun again." It did indeed begin, but where was it going?

You've never liked this kind of question, even when the self-rule agreement was signed at the White House and we saw Rabin shaking hands with Arafat and we thought everything was over.

You were sad, but not me. I was like someone watching someone else die. And now I can tell you that deep inside I was happy. Death isn't just a mercy, it's happiness, too. This language has to die, and the world manufactured from dead words has to become extinct. I was happy as I watched the end, all while wearing a false expression of sorrow on my face.

Do you remember?

I was at home, we were sitting in front of the television, and you were pulling every last bit of smoke from your cigarette down into your lungs and listening to the American talk. Then you turned to me and said, "No. This isn't the end. There was one end and we got past it. After what happened in '48, there won't be an end.

"During that time, it was the end, my son, but we survived. What's happening now is just a step, anything can change and be turned around."

Your words broke up in front of me and scattered in all directions. Then you went out. You left me alone in front of the television tuned to the American talk. I waited for you until the program came to an end, then I turned it off and went to sleep, feeling that psychic confusion that compelled me to mask my joy with a simulated sorrow.

And now, tell me: How long are we supposed to wait?

Here am I, waiting for your end – forgive me, your beginning – in spite of everything, in spite of the smell of powder that emanates from your room, and in spite of your face, which flows over the pillow like the face of a baby still unformed. I'm here, waiting for the end. No, I'm not in a hurry, and I don't have the slightest idea what I'll do after they close the hospital.

They say they're going to demolish the camp anyway, because the camp isn't the camp any longer – its borders have shrunk, and its inside space, at this point, is up for grabs. I don't know who lives here now – Syrians, Egyptians, Sri Lankans, Indians . . . I don't know how they get here or where they find houses. Soon the bulldozers will come. They say the plan is to demolish the camp and turn the land into part of the expressway linking the airport to central Beirut.

Anything's possible here. Maybe we should start our exile over from scratch. I don't know.

I told you I'm waiting for nothing except the end, and then I don't know. Anyway, it's not important. I asked you about speaking the truth so I could understand why Mr. Sinounou lied about things that didn't happen and then believed his own lies.

No. Not Shams.

I haven't told you anything about her, not because I don't want to, but because I don't know anything. A man only knows the woman he's loved when the talking ends; then he discovers her all over again and rearranges her in his memory. If she dies before that happens, she remains suspended in the fog of memory.

Shams remained suspended because she disappeared in the middle of the talking and left me on my own to discover the infinite senses of things. Shams disappeared into the jungle of her words and left me alone. I don't think all that was an illusion, that I was just a parenthesis in her life, but I don't understand how anyone could be such a chameleon.

My problem with that woman was that I never knew. After having made love, she'd turn into another woman, and it was always up to me to search for the woman who'd been in my bed.

Patience. I'll explain everything. Shams would disappear. She'd be with me, her love too, and then she'd disappear, would take off I don't know where. I'd wait for her and she wouldn't come. Then, when I'd just about given up hope since I had no way of contacting her, I'd find her in my house, a different woman, and I'd have to start all over again.

I'd get lost searching for her. I'd walk the roads, my heart thudding whenever I saw a woman who looked like her. And suddenly she'd knock on my door and come in, her long hair cut short like a boy's, her eyes full of wonder as though she were discovering a place she'd never been in before, reserved, wrapped in modesty as if I were a stranger. She'd start talking about politics, saying that she this and she that . . . I'll spare you her lectures on the necessity of reorganizing ourselves in Lebanon, etc.

When I approached her she'd pull back, shy again. I'd try to take her hand and she'd draw back as though she weren't the same Shams who only a few days earlier had been whinnying in my bed. I'd take her slowly and watch her approaching slowly; then, when I had her in my arms, I'd feel the need to be sure she'd truly returned to me, so I'd whisper in her ear and ask her to say her *ay* that would sharpen my desire, and she'd draw back again.

"I don't want to say it . . ."

She'd move away, sit on the sofa and light a cigarette. I'd wait a little before I'd go back to her. I'd take her hand and start the journey once again, and then I'd hear that *ay* seeping from her lips and eyes. When I took her in my arms, as a man does a woman, she'd twist a bit to one side, hide her face in my neck, let out an *ay* and pull me toward her.

When she was with me I'd forget that she'd disappear in the morning and that I'd have to start the adventure all over again.

My question is, Yunes, where's the sincerity in this relationship?

Is Shams Shams?

Is this woman that woman? Do I know her? Why did the smell of her body cling to mine and the sound of her voice hum in my head?

And by the way, Yunes, why doesn't the lover feel he's a man like other men? Why to prove our masculinity are we forced to take refuge in lies and pretense, stuffing our days with idle talk and boasting of fictitious adventures and then, when we approach the woman we love, we become like women?

Why does something like femininity awaken within us?

It's true, the lover becomes like a woman.

I confessed. Yes, confessed. I tried to explain it to her, but she didn't understand, and even if she had . . . what good would it have done? Even if she'd loved me – and she did love me – or if she'd betrayed me – and she did betray me, then what?

Come to think of it, why did she want to marry Sameh? Why didn't she say she wanted to get married? I was prepared to marry her. I was I don't know what. It's true . . . why didn't I ask her to marry me? I can say now that I didn't dare, that the story she'd told me about her former husband blocked my ability to think, and that her troubles with her daughter, Dalal, stopped me from thinking about marriage.

How do you propose to a woman whose sole concern is to organize the abduction of her daughter? She said she'd have no peace in her life till she'd taken Dalal from Amman and brought her to Beirut, and that she needed a man to help her. And when I said I was at her disposal, I saw a trace of pity in her smile.

"You, my dear, are a doctor, and are of no use. I want a real man. I want a fedayeen fighter."

Was Sameh the man she was looking for?

Didn't she tell me in a satisfied moment, "You're my man"? How could I be her man and not be a real man? And how can you ask a woman to marry you as she's telling you she's looking for another man? But no, I'm not sure, I don't believe she talked about Dalal with anyone but me. She'd forget her most of the time; her daughter would only come alive for her after we'd made love. I'd light my cigarette and take my first sip of cognac, and along would come Dalal and set up an impenetrable barrier between us. Words would die and Shams would become a knot of tears – a woman who'd tell stories about her daughter and curse life and fate. Then suddenly she'd jump up and say she was hungry. I don't know how she didn't get fat. She devoured enormous quantities of food in my presence.

"Why aren't you eating, Qais?"

She used to call me Qais: "You know I'll treat you the way Laila did her Qais. I'll drive you crazy."

But Qais, I mean I, would only eat a little. Once I told her I didn't eat because I was in love. And do you know what her reaction was?

"What an absurd notion! 'Seduction requires strength.' Eat, eat! Love needs food."

I was incapable of eating even though I was hungry. I was like someone who couldn't chew food. It was enough for me to keep her company and look at her devilish eyes stealing glances at me and apologizing for her insatiable appetite.

But maybe not. Maybe the reason I didn't ask her to marry me was that I was afraid of her. Strange. Tell me; don't you think it's strange? Not you – it's impossible to make a comparison with you because Nahilah was your wife and that explains everything. I don't want to trespass on your life.

But why didn't you do what Hamad did?

Like you, Hamad was a fighter in the Sha'ab garrison – don't tell me you don't know him. Umm Hassan told me his story. She said his sister refused to hold a wake for him after he died in her house in Ain al-Hilweh, so the wake was held in Umm Hassan's house in Shatila.

Umm Hassan said they were complete fools: "They say he is Israeli. What does that mean? When we're humiliated and imprisoned for the sake of our children and our land, does that make us traitors?"

I won't tell you the story of Hamad's return to his village in Galilee because I'm sure you know it. I just wanted to say that maybe you also were afraid of love.

Take any love story, Brother. What is a love story? The story we call a love story is usually a story of the impossibility of love. People only write about love as something impossible. Isn't that the story of Qais and Laila, and Romeo and Juliet? Isn't it the story of Khalil and Shams? All lovers are like that; they become a story of unconsummated love, as though love can't be consummated, or as though we fear it or don't know how to tell about it, or, and this is the worst, we don't recognize it when we're living it.

What did Qais Ibn al-Mulawwah do? Nothing. They stopped him from seeing his sweetheart Laila, so he went mad.

> *Didn't you make me a promise, heart,*
> *You'd give up Laila if I did so too?*
> *Behold – I've given up my love for her.*
> *How then, when her name is said, you swoon?*

Nice words and lovely poetry, but the man was crazy and his beloved married another man.

And Romeo, what did he do? He killed himself.

And what about all the other lovers? All of them loved at a distance and lived their love in separation, so they became impossible stories.

Don't you agree?

Is it because love is impossible that every time Shams left me, my mouth would become as dry as kindling?

Was it because I couldn't stand to be parted from her?

Do you know that beautiful verse from the Koran? "They are a vestment for you, and you are a vestment for them." How are we to become vestments for one another – I mean, how are we to become one?

That's what love is, which is why we can't talk about it. We talk only about its impossibility or its tragedy, its victims and its fatalities.

And when lovers are together, it's impossible to describe. In fact, it may be that none of us lives it and that's why we invent reasons why it's kept from us.

It might be that love has no language. It's like a smell. How can you describe a smell? We describe it in terms of what it's not, and we don't give it a name. Love's the same. It has a name only when it isn't there.

I don't mean to belittle the importance of your love for Nahilah. I know that you loved her and that your infatuation was great. I know that she dwelled in your bones. I know that you're dying today because of her.

But why didn't you go back, the way Hamad did?

How was it that Hamad went to prison and succeeded in returning to his house and his wife, and such a possibility never occurred to you?

Don't tell me you sacrificed yourself for the revolution, I don't believe it's that.

Please don't misunderstand me. I don't want to denigrate your history. Your history is my history, and I respect you and honor you and hold you in the highest regard.

But tell me, wasn't there an element of fear of Nahilah in your decision? Didn't you prefer – unconsciously perhaps – that she be where she was and you where you were? That way your story could continue and survive across space and time. Every time you went to see her, you put your life in danger. Every time, you purchased your love at the cost of the possibility of your death. Isn't that extraordinary? Isn't that a story like no other?

Tell me, when you were walking the roads of the two Galilees, of Palestine and of Lebanon, did you feel that your thorn-lacerated feet bore a love story like no other?

As for me, though, what a letdown!

I know my story doesn't deserve to be put alongside yours. I'm just a duped lover; that's what everyone thinks. But no, Shams isn't so simple; you can't sum her up by saying she betrayed me. And "betrayed" isn't accurate. I wasn't her husband, so why did she come to me? If there hadn't been love, she wouldn't have come; if there hadn't been love, her presence wouldn't have bewitched me; if there hadn't been love, I wouldn't have hidden like a dog in this hospital out of fear of revenge. I confess I was afraid and I believed the rumors about the people of al-Ammour vowing to take revenge on their daughter's killers. But that time has passed.

If they'd wanted to kill me, they'd have killed me. I live in the hospital because I've gotten used to it, that's all. I could go back home if I wanted to, but my house is near the mosque and I don't like cemeteries.

None of Shams' family put in an appearance except Khadijeh, her mother. She came to the Ain al-Hilweh camp, took her daughter's things, and went back without making contact with anyone here. I heard that nobody visited to pay their respects. She didn't stay in the camp more than twenty-four hours. She went into her daughter's house, shut the doors and windows, and came out in the morning carrying a large suitcase. She spoke to no one, and at the Lebanese Army barrier at the camp entrance, the one we still call the Armed Struggle barrier, she turned around, spat, and left.

There's nothing to fear. The woman came and went, and I'm here not out of fear but out of habit.

Plus, I want to review my life in peace and quiet.

You want the truth, right?

I'll try to tell you the truth, but don't ask me, "Why did you accept?" – I didn't accept. No, I didn't. And no one consulted me. I found myself in the maelstrom and I almost died, and if Abu Ali Hassan hadn't been there, they would've executed me. That's right, executed.

No, not Shams' relatives, the Ain al-Hilweh camp's militia. They supposed, wrongly of course, that I was the one who instigated her murder to get rid of Sameh and have the woman all to myself. They didn't believe what everybody was saying – that Shams killed her lover herself. They assumed someone else had been involved, and arrested me.

I was too embarrassed to tell you about my arrest. The only thing about it that sticks in my memory is their insulting references to "horns" and the way they treated me as a nobody. But that was what saved me, and it only happened after Abu Ali's intervention. Can you believe it? He intervened on my behalf to make sure that I was humilated. There was no other way out – humiliation or execution. Abu Ali saved me; if it hadn't been for his intervention, they'd have killed me as they killed Shams.

I won't tell you about the interrogation. A man came and delivered a letter from the Ain al-Hilweh militia inviting me to visit them, and I went. They escorted me directly to the Ain al-Hilweh prison, where they threw me in a dark underground vault, full of damp and the smell of decay, and left me.

I rotted in the vault for ten days, which felt like ten years – time got mixed up in my head, and I lived underground as though I were floating on the entire night of my life.

They took me out for the interrogation. A man came holding the kind of pick we normally use for breaking up blocks of ice and started jabbing it into my chest asking me to confess.

He'd stab me with the pick and ask, "What did you do with Sameh, dog?" and I'd ask him who this Sameh was. He'd repeat his question as if he weren't expecting an answer from me.

A stupid interrogator, you'll say.

But no, he was neither an interrogator nor stupid. He was just a criminal. Crime has spread everywhere in our ranks. We've watered it with blood and stupidities. We've wallowed in error, and error has consumed us.

How is it possible?

They arrest you and throw you into the darkness without asking a single question? They throw you into an underground vault where you live with your waste and the next thing you see is an ice pick in your chest. Then they ask you about someone you don't know and don't wait for an answer?

Ten days in nowhere, and if it hadn't been for Abu Ali, God knows how long I'd have remained there. Abu Ali Hassan was a comrade of mine from the days of the base in al-Khreibeh in 1968. He told me later he saved me because he was certain of my innocence. He believed "the whore" had fooled me.

They escorted me to the interrogation and there contemptuous looks and sarcastic smiles fell upon me, and I understood. Instead of being furious, however, and trying to defend my honor, I was afraid for Shams and possessed by a single idea: how to rescue her from their hands. I could read the decision to execute her in their eyes, and I didn't want her to die. At the time I didn't know what life taught me later, that death is the lover's relief.

Nothing can save you from love but death.

If I'd known that, I'd have killed her myself.

At the interrogation, however, I was possessed by fear for her, and instead of going home and back to work when I was released, I decided to look for her to try to save her. I went to the outskirts of Maghdousheh, east of Tyre, where the fighters had established bases. I knew she commanded a military detachment there that carried her name and that she refused to accept orders from the military command in the south because they were directly under the command of Tunis. That's what she'd told me and I didn't believe her, but when I went to Maghdousheh I found out that this time she hadn't lied. There really was an armed detachment known as "Shams' group," but it wasn't at Maghdousheh. I was told they had withdrawn toward Majdalyoun.

I went to Majdalyoun but didn't find her.

I was like a blind man, wandering the roads of the south, searching for her but not finding her. Everywhere I went I was assailed by the same strange looks, as though everyone knew the story.

I searched and found nothing. I crossed Majdalyoun, went to the house they told me was the headquarters of Shams' unit and found it empty – a five-room house surrounded by a garden with fruit trees. I went in and found blankets on the floor, plastic bags, pans, and the odor of rotten food. It looked as though they'd evacuated the place in a hurry without time to organize their departure. I lay down on a blanket and felt like crying. I was besieged with tears, yet I found myself without tears, without emotion, without feeling. Nothing. I existed in the nothing and in tears, and I knew she was lost.

Shams was lost, and I didn't know how I'd fill the gaps in my life without her.

I closed my eyes, squeezed them closed as hard as I could, and the darkness filled up with gray holes and despair overwhelmed me.

My son, Yunes, do you know what it means to feel incapable of living?

Once I told her I couldn't imagine life without her, and she patted my shoulder and picked up Mahmoud Darwish's collected poems and started reading –

> *Take me to the distant land.*
> *Neverending is this winter – wailed Rita.*
> *And she smashed the porcelain of day on the window's iron,*
> *Placed her small revolver on the draft of the poem*

And threw her socks on the chair, breaking the cooing.
She went, barefoot, toward the unknown, and the hour of
my departure had come.

Naked on my bed, she read. The pages gleaming in front of her, her voice bending, branching off, and blushing. I looked at her and failed to understand. I heard the rhythm of her voice mixed with the rhythm of the rhymes, and I saw her body shimmering.

She closed the book and asked, "What's wrong? Don't you like poetry?"

"I like it, I like it," I said. "But you're more beautiful than poetry."

"Liar," she said. "My ambition is to become like Rita as Mahmoud Darwish wrote her. Have you heard Marcel Khalifa's song, "Between Rita and My Eyes There is a Rifle"? I'd like to be like Rita, with a poet coming along and putting a rifle between me and him."

She shot up suddenly and said she was famished and was going to make some pasta.

I didn't tell her I wasn't always that way. I love poetry, I know entire poems by heart. But in the presence of a wild outpouring of beauty, words are no longer possible.

Though in those moments that I spent alone in the house in Majdalyoun, surrounded by traces of her, I could smell the aroma of pasta inside the gray spots dancing in front of my closed eyes, and I felt my death. Believe me, without her I'm nothing – alone with the nothing, alone with what's left of her things, alone with her ghost.

And I sunk into sleep within the odors of decay that fumed from the blankets of that abandoned house.

I slept and floated over mysterious dreams, as though I were no longer myself. I saw her. Shahineh, wearing khaki trousers and a khaki shirt, like Shams. She was caught in the rain. Ropes of rain tied the ground to the sky, and she was standing under a flowering almond tree.

"How can the almond tree flower in the middle of winter?" I asked her.

The branches of the tree shook and the blossoms started to fall. I ran to gather them, and she pointed her rifle at me. "Go back," she yelled. "The Jews are here."

I was a child. No, I became a child. No, I saw myself as a child. Anyway, I started jumping to stretch my body to its normal height because I wasn't a child and it wasn't Shahineh, it was Shams.

"Why are you doing this to me, Shams?" I shouted.

Shahineh said she was going.

I went up to her and the earth started to open up beneath my feet – I was drowning. I was a child drowning in the rain. The huge drops struck me. It hurt.

"Mom!" I cried.

And I saw Shahineh – who looked like Shams – turn her back and disappear into the water.

The dreams are all mixed up in my head now, but when I woke there to the sound of their footsteps, I wasn't afraid. I felt feet kicking me and rifles pointed at my head, so I curled up into a ball to avoid as many of the blows as I could.

They stood me up against the wall and told me to put my hands up. Then they turned my face to the wall and frisked me while I stood like a zombie. I didn't resist because I no longer resisted.

Since the day at the stadium, when I'd decided I wasn't going with the ones who got on the Greek ships, I'd told myself, "Enough."

But where are we to find this enough?

You say, "Enough," and then blind history drags you by the hair back to war.

I said, "Enough," and sunk into the massacre. I said, "Enough," and the War of the Camps encircled me. I said, "Enough," and found myself crucified on the wall of an abandoned house in a village of ghosts called Majdalyoun whose inhabitants had been driven out.

And now I say, "Enough," and I find myself with a child in whom death dances exultantly, as though we were born, and die, in death.

I was standing against the wall, the weariness spreading through me, and with the image of Shahineh in Shams' body as she left me in the rain. Why did she leave me to drown? Is it possible to leave a child calling for help? Even in a dream, it would be shameful. I was standing, the man was patting down my body as though he were detaching my bones, one by one. Then he ordered me to turn and face him. I saw four young men, the oldest not more than twenty. They were like children at play. That's war – it should be like a game; when we stop playing we're afraid, and when we're afraid, we die.

I stood against the wall awaiting my death, but they didn't kill me. Their boss showered me with questions, but I didn't answer. What was I supposed to say? Was I supposed to tell the truth and make myself look laughable and stupid?

When the commander despaired of my face, with its sheen of sleep, he ordered them to take me away. One of them came forward, undid the buttons of my shirt and pulled it up to cover my face. They put me into a Land Rover and took me away. Within the jolts of the furrowed roads, sleep returned to cradle me. I wanted that woman. I wanted to give her the almond flowers I'd gathered for her.

But sleep wouldn't come. I found myself in a dark cell like the one I'd been held in before. My guess is that they'd forgotten about me and left me to live out my three days in prison as though in the belly of death. Now I am Jonah, not you. I lived in darkness for three days without food or water. I was sure they'd forgotten me and that I'd die inside that dark vault, and no one would know what had become of me.

On the third day, however, they took me out of the cell to interrogate me, and the interrogator burst out laughing in my ear.

"So, Mr. Horns!" he said. "What were you doing there?"

I said I'd gone looking for her.

"And why were you looking for her?"

"To understand."

When I said "to understand," the man burst into a long, hysterical laugh and started coughing and choking on his words. Then, in the middle of his coughing and laughing, he gestured for them to throw me out.

So that was how I was twice arrested for her sake and twice released.

I went home, leaving Shams to her fate. Don't say I didn't try to save her. I went home and waited for her death, and she died.

What else do you want to know?

I swear I don't know anything else. All I see in front of me now is a question mark. Why did she come from Jordan? And how did she become an officer in Fatah? And how did she put her military group together?

Questions I don't know how to answer. All I know is that I know nothing.

Do you want to hear the story?

I'll tell you as long as you don't tell me it's unbelievable. Believe first, then I'll tell. I no longer feel the need to determine the truth of stories or the absence of it. None of our stories are believable, Uncle, but does that mean we should forget them?

I believed it because it resembled your story, but your story, and those of Reem or Nahilah in Sha'ab, and Adnan's in prison or in the mental hospital, are all unbelievable stories, yet they're still true. You know them, I know them, everybody knows them.

My question is . . .

No, no. There is no question.

But let's suppose there were a question. The question would be why don't we believe ourselves? Why do I feel that the things that have happened, to me or to others, have turned into shadows? You, for instance – aren't you the shadow of the man you were? And that man – was he a hero, a lie, or an illusion?

I know I disturb you when I throw this kind of question at you, and I know you'd rather be on your own now, because now you're . . . God, how beautiful you are! If you could open your eyes just once to look at yourself in the mirror. An old man opening his eyes and seeing himself as a child, seeing his body liberated from the sack holding his life. You're the one who came up with that theory, remember?

You used to say that the years a man lived were a sack he carried on his back, but we couldn't see it because no one can see his own life. Our life is like a dream: Life trundles us along and time trundles us along and we have no idea. Then suddenly, when we reach forty, we start feeling it, as though time had built up inside a large sack on our backs and were weighing us down.

Do you remember the day you returned to Nahilah, exhausted and wounded, from the Israeli ambush you fell into and by some miracle managed to escape?

You found yourself bleeding in the valley. You picked yourself up and went to her. As you made your way heavily toward the cave, you were certain you were on your way to death. And you didn't feel sorrow. You told me that when you tapped on her window, all the images and memories halted in your eyes, and you saw yourself as a shadow walking toward its shadow.

You came around to find Nahilah before you, covering your head with her white headscarf, wiping your wounds with oil and rocking you as a mother rocks her child. Nahilah tried to remove the bullet lodged in your thigh but couldn't, and you got better with the bullet in its place. I feel it under my fingers now when I bathe you. The bullet is getting bigger and you are getting smaller, there's no need to remove it. We'll let it accompany you to wherever you go off to.

That day you told Nahilah that the sack was getting heavy on your back, you asked her about her sack, she smiled and said nothing.

Nahilah would smile and say nothing, hiding her secret in that broad smile of hers that transformed her eyes into a grove of olives, into night.

That day you told her that age was the cross of man, you talked to her about Christ. She listened to you and loved what you said. She told you that you spoke like your mother, who hid an icon of the Virgin Mary under her pillow.

You told Nahilah that Christ was crucified on wood his own age, years he didn't live, for life is like the cross – in the end we'll find ourselves hung upon it.

Nahilah said you'd started to talk like a philosopher and smiled.

Your sack had started to weigh you down, making you bend. No, your back wasn't hunched, because you were active to the end, but that accursed sack bent your neck a little, and you started to walk with your eyes to the ground.

Look now and see how beautiful and new you are! You've cast it off your back, and your childhood has commenced. You're an ageless child again. The years that were behind you are now ahead of you.

No one will believe me.

I tell Dr. Amjad or Kamelya or Zainab, and they think I'm mad. It's as though they can't see. "Look!" I say, but they don't see. Standing at the head of your bed, Amjad says the danger is now in the heart; at any moment it could fail.

I know more about medicine than he does. I know the chances of a heart attack. But nobody wants to see or believe; even you have become like them. I implore you to open your eyes just one time and look in the mirror, and you'll see the surprise. You'll see how a person can cast the sack of years off his back, return to his childhood, and start over from the beginning.

I told you nothing about our story was believable. Shams, too, is unbelievable. But you have to believe me. I know that in telling Shams' story, I'll kill her. This time Shams will be assassinated by words. All those people who gathered in the hills of al-Miyyeh wi-Miyyeh failed to kill her because she's still alive within me, the betrayal radiating from her hot body and her fingers, as if I were still holding her hand and watching her long, slender fingers, kissing them one by one, igniting her from her fingers.

Shams still burns, Yunes, but it seems the time has come. I feel I have to shroud her in the little sack of years that she carried on her back. I feel the time for her death has come. So I'll tell you the whole story, from the beginning, and I'll bury Shams with words, as we buried Nahilah.

Now it's my turn.

I can no longer hold onto my woman. I have to bury her as people bury their dead and their stories.

Shams' story begins in 1960, when she was born in al-Wahdat camp in Amman. Her father was Ahmad Saleh Hussein, her mother Khadijeh

Mahmoud Ali. Ahmad had married Khadijeh in their village of al-Ammour, in the district of Jerusalem, in 1947. One year later, their first son, Saleh, was born. He died in 1970 in the September battles in Jordan.

Ahmad and Khadijeh found themselves with their baby, Saleh, who wasn't yet a year old, in the throngs of inhabitants of al-Ammour who were expelled from their village in 1948, following the establishment of the State of Israel. The family took up residence in the caves near Bethlehem, as did all the people from the village, and would slip back to the village in search of provisions. Then everything came to a halt because collective border crossings became more difficult, and because provisions had run out, and all the houses in the villages had been destroyed.

In 1950, after a new child – whom they called Ammouri in hopeful memory of the demolished village – had been born, the family moved to the Aydeh camp, in the town of Deir Jasir. There, Ahmad found a job in a pasta factory owned by Abu Sa'id al-Husseini. His wages were a shilling a day, and the shilling was enough because the man used to bring enough pasta back with him to feed the family.

From then on, the family ate only pasta. Even after the factory closed and they moved to the camp in Amman, Ahmad kept making pasta at home. People even called them "the Italians" because all Ahmad talked about in the camp were the virtues and benefits of pasta and the greatness of the Italian people who'd invented it. Ahmad didn't know that pasta was invented by the Chinese, not the Italians, but how could he have?

She was known as "the Italian girl" in Jordan, but it wore off in Beirut, and Shams, who hated pasta as a child, rediscovered it when I fell in love with her. She said that love had brought her back to her Italian roots. All we ate was pasta, except on the rare occasions when I'd cook, in which case I'd make fried cauliflower with *taratur* sauce.

You see, there's nothing unusual about Shams' story so far, except for the pasta. We were all expelled from our villages, we all slipped back into them in search of food, we all stopped doing that after the houses and villages were destroyed, and all of us took whatever jobs we could find.

In 1960, the year Shams was born, Abu Sa'id al-Husseini's factory closed.

It's said he went bankrupt when imported Italian pasta flooded the market and the national pasta industry collapsed because there was no tariff barrier.

Abu Sa'id al-Husseini closed his factory in Bethlehem, and Ahmad found himself out of work with a wife and five children (in the meantime a boy and two girls had been born before Shams). He decided to move from Bethlehem to Amman, to the Ras al-Ain district, where he worked on the stone crushers. Then after two years, he moved to al-Wahdat camp, taking up residence in the development area on the border and building a shack out of sheet metal, where he lived with his family. The house resembled a museum of advertisements of every kind and color. Ahmad Saleh got the metal sheets from the cans discarded in trash heaps along the roads and was not alone in doing so, most of the shacks in the development area were built from sheet metal. People would change the sheets according to the season, since some of them would wear out before others because of their exposure to the elements.

Shams' house looked like an oblong billboard.

Shams said she lived a great part of her life in the multicolored hovel, a house that turned into an oven in summer and a freezer in winter. A father who spoke to his wife only to discuss the need to change this or that wall that was starting to rust. "I lived all my life in dilapidation: The house was wearing out, my father was wearing out, and everything was drenched in water and sun. My father would go off to his work at the stone crushers and return exhausted and at the end of his tether. The only thing he could find to amuse himself was to make pasta and yell at my mother because she hadn't kneaded the dough properly."

Shams said that she remembered those days with a strange tenderness, and she felt alienation for the first time when their house in the camp changed. Concrete arrived and you couldn't change the walls anymore. With the revolution everything arrived, and Ahmad Saleh, whose cousin found him a job in one of the offices of the Popular Front, left his work at the stone crushers and added two new rooms to his house. That was when

Shams said she felt at sea. She was nine when everything in the house changed. The roof stopped leaking, the walls no longer were brightly colored with advertisements, and Shams felt some part of her had died.

Her childhood ended when the house was torn down. Her periods started. Her mother told her she was like all the other girls of al-Ammoura: "We're like that, our girls grow up at nine." Her mother explained everything to her and told her she had to get ready for marriage. Shams waited for a husband.

She waited for him at the UNWRA school.

She waited for him while training at the cadets' camp.

She waited for him as she watched her brother die, hit by a bullet of the Bedouins in 1970.*

She waited for him when she saw her father arrested after the closure of the Popular Front office, before finding himself a job in a pasta factory that belonged to the Alwan family in Amman.

She waited for him as she saw the concrete walls of the house corrode and become like the sheet metal that had enclosed her childhood.

Then came the husband and the nightmares.

How can you expect me to tell you about Fawwaz Mohammed Nassar when I only know him mutilated by Shams' words? When she spoke of him she'd lacerate him: She'd take a small piece of a brown paper bag or a newspaper or a Kleenex or a book and start chewing on it and spitting it out, so I only saw the man drawn on mutilated paper. She would talk and mutilate, and the tears would pour out of her.

Have you ever seen a woman not weeping from her eyes but with everything inside her? Everything in Shams wept as she mutilated Fawwaz Mohammed Nassar and spat out the little shreds of paper she was chewing. And then suddenly she'd wipe away her tears as though it were nothing, as though the woman with tears in her eyes were another woman, and she'd start gobbling the dish of pasta for which she'd made a special sauce of

*Allusion to the Jordanian army, which would recruit heavily from the Bedouin tribes.

cream and basil leaves. She'd eat and sniff the basil and say the smell intoxicated her. She'd eat as though her appetite had exploded inside her. She'd
say she wanted nothing from Fawwaz; she'd just go to Amman, kidnap
Dalal, and bring her back to Beirut.

"I won't start my life without Dalal. Look."

And she'd take a photo from the pocket of her khaki jacket.

"Look how beautiful she is. She's the most beautiful girl in the world."

I'd look. I didn't see the most beautiful girl in the world, only a sweet
child with curly hair and a little brown face devoured by large eyes with long
lashes.

"Look at her eyelashes! How can I leave her with that beast?"

When Shams held Dalal's picture in her hand, she was transformed into
another woman. I'd see tenderness and sorrow and weakness gathered on
her brow, and when I'd try to hold her, she'd push me away as though she
were refusing to share Dalal with me. Then she'd turn to me and say she
needed a man to help her kidnap Dalal. If I tried to tell her this man was
sitting before her, she'd look at me with pity.

"I need a fedayeen fighter, my dear. Not some doctor like you."

Then I'd tell her I was a fedayeen fighter and would talk to her about our
first camps in al-Khreibeh and Kafar Shouba.

"You? Incredible!"

In fact, I made a mistake. I shouldn't have told her how the officer made
me crawl in front of the platoon and how that incident made me lose my
self-respect as a political commissar and as a soldier.

That was an unforgivable slip. I confessed I wasn't brave enough to prevent the officer from humiliating me.

I wanted to be a blank page with her on which she could draw whatever
she wanted. But she wasn't looking for a blank page. Why, then, did she stay
with me? Why was she here with me, and then there with Sameh? I swear
I don't know, I don't understand how the devils that inhabit our bodies
think.

Yes, Yunes. I waited for her until she died. I left the prison and didn't step foot out of my house until after I got word of her murder. I thought she might come to my place to hide. How naïve I was. Rumors had spread through the camp that I'd stayed home to protest my arrest. No. I stayed in the house waiting for her. Ah, if only she'd come! Every part of my body hurt; separation causes pain in the joints, the chest, the knees.

I waited, not to understand what she'd done, but because I loved her. It no longer made any difference to me whether she'd been unfaithful or not. She was what mattered, not me. But she didn't come. I'm sure she wasn't aware I was waiting for her. She was enveloped in her crime, in blood. I can describe her to you, my son, even without having seen her. I can see the red halo around her head, the stains of blood. Ever since we've sunk into our own blood, it has dogged us and tied us to it with a long rope knotted around our necks.

After she died, I left my house and roamed the streets of the camp. I walked like a pathetic revenge taker even though pent up inside me was all the sorrow in the world. I didn't weep for Shams and I'll never weep for her, for all the tears would never be enough. Like an idiot, I walked with my head held high as though I'd taken my revenge.

The rumors started and I took refuge in the hospital out of fear. I was afraid because I knew her; she was a woman capable of killing all her men. She did kill us all – me and Sameh and I don't know who else. Crime is like love: We kill another person just as we love a man or a woman – because they are a substitute for another man or woman.

I was a substitute for two men I didn't know – Sameh, whom I'd never heard of, and Fawwaz, whom I never met. All the same, I was their stand-in. Sameh died, Fawwaz took Dalal, and here I am.

Where were we?

I told you Shams was ready for marriage at nine, and they married her off at fifteen. Fawwaz came along, and he was twenty-four. He married her and took her to Lebanon. But it wasn't Fawwaz who came, it was Abu Ahmad Nassar. He asked for her for his son, Fawwaz, who'd finished his studies in engineering at Beirut Arab University and was working for the

Resistance. Then he took her to Beirut. The girl got to al-Wahdat and became acquainted with her husband in a small house in the Tal al-Za'atar camp, situated in the eastern suburbs of Beirut. She lived a year and a half to the rhythm of bombardments, the explosions of canons, and the rain of bullets.

She said her husband scared her more than the war.

"He'd only have sex with me when we were being shelled. He was the devil incarnate. I never saw him except inside the house. He'd turn up from nowhere covered in dust, having left his position. He'd come to me coated in dust and sweat and take me without taking off his clothes. I never once saw him naked.

"He was an officer in the camp's militia, but I don't know anything about his duties. He never told me.

"His father took me to Beirut; we made an exhausting journey by car from Amman. When we got to the house in Tal al-Za'atar, his father stood at the door and didn't go in. He kissed his son, told him, 'I've brought you the bride,' and left. During the six hours we spent together in the taxi from Amman to Beirut, he didn't speak to me. He sat next to me and didn't say a word. He'd look at me from time to time and say, 'Amazing!'

"My father said I was going to get married, my mother agreed with a nod, and I got married, like a blind woman. Blindly I crossed the distance between Amman and Beirut, and blindly I entered the house of my husband who I didn't know. I found myself standing in the house, holding my suitcase, as if at a railway station.

"'Hello, Shams,' said Fawwaz. 'Come in and take a bath.'

"I went into the kitchen, heated water in a basin that I carried to the bathroom. I washed with the bay laurel soap my mother had put in my suitcase, suggesting I wash myself with it before going in to my husband. I bathed and then entered Fawwaz's world to discover that he wasn't an engineer, or anything at all. He'd come to Beirut to study engineering, then taken a job in a tile factory close to the Mar Elias camp and then forgot all about engineering. With the beginnings of the civil war, he'd joined the Resistance and had been inducted into the Tal al-Za'atar militia.

"I'm not beautiful," she said, "but at Tal al-Za'atar I discovered that I'm a woman in the eyes of men avid for life. There was shelling and war and death; everything was coming apart.

"Fawwaz would go wild with jealousy. I can't describe to you everything he did. At the beginning, he'd bang his head against the wall until the blood ran, he'd sleep with me, and then he'd go back to the wall to bang his head again and again. I didn't understand. 'You're a whore and the daughter of a whore,' he'd say.

"I was scared. I was living through an interminable war, and Fawwaz didn't seem to want it to end. I'd ask him when he was going to go back to his work, and he'd look at me in amazement and say he wasn't an engineer and didn't want to go back to his job at the tile factory.

"'What's wrong with it?' I'd ask him. 'Those things aren't important. My father was a pasta twister, but we still had our dignity. What matters are morals.'

"He'd frown. 'Morals! Whore! I got stuck with a whore!'

"I don't know – maybe he wanted me to be a whore, maybe he was afraid of me, but I didn't do anything. I swear I didn't look at another man. Well, it did happen, but that was much later, during our evacuation from the camp after it fell.

"Do you know what he did?

"He left his position and rushed over to the house. 'Listen to me,' he said. 'I'm going to withdraw with the other fighters. You surrender with the women. We'll meet in Beirut,' and he gave me the address of someone called Karim Abd al-Fattah, Abu Rami, in the district of al-Fakahani.

"'I'll go with you,' I told him.

"'No. This is safer,' he said.

"He looked at me with fierce eyes. 'You're afraid of getting raped!' and he left.

"What can I tell you? Of course I was afraid, and I didn't understand why he wouldn't take me with him. Did he want me to die? What had I done to him? I'd lived through the toughest times with him. You know what life's like during a siege. All we could find to eat were lentils. I lived on my own like a stranger. I'd go to the public water pipe and wait in the line of death: The water was in their line of fire. We called it 'the blood pipe.' I lived alone with nothing to do but wait for him. He'd come, caked with dust and gravel, sleep with me, and leave. He wouldn't eat the lentils I'd cooked because he'd eat with the boys.

"All I wanted was one thing – to go back to my family in Amman. But how could I leave? The camp was closed by the siege. I wanted him to pay attention to me, but I didn't dare ask for anything: He was a fighter and we were at war. Even his visits and his sex were rapid-fire. And every time he slept with me, he'd bang his head against the wall, accuse me of being unfaithful, raving that I was a whore and that my body was a place of evil.

"He came to tell me he was withdrawing and asked me to surrender with the women.

"I knew what I could expect, so I decided to withdraw with the fighters and went toward the eastern edge of the camp. I put on jeans and a green shirt and went to look for Fawwaz. I couldn't find him. It seems he was in one of the first groups to withdraw.

"That was when I met Ahmad Kayyali, who gave me a Kalashnikov and said, 'Come with us.'

"We crossed the Monte Verde, which is full of pines. We walked by night and laid up by day. And there, in the midst of the scattered bullets and the nights of death, I made up my mind to leave Fawwaz. If I lived, I wouldn't go back to him. Ahmad was my first lover. With him I discovered I had a body and that my body deserved the pleasures of life. When Fawwaz had sex with me, he'd say, 'Pleasure me,' but I had no idea how to 'pleasure' him. All I was aware of was his panting on top of me and that thing that penetrated me below, as though it were wounding me. With him I'd reach the edge of pleasure but never get there. Ahmad was different. I asked him to come to me, and I slept with him. We were lost in the forest, we'd left the camp with about twenty fighters, and we walked the entire night. When dawn came, we decided to split up to wait for dark. They started setting off in different directions, but I didn't know what to do. Ahmad took me with him, and we hid on a rocky slope, not daring to breathe. He was around my age, and like all the men, he'd use colloquial mixed with Classical Arabic to make me feel he was serious. He asked me where I was going to go in Beirut. I said, to the house of Abu Rami, Karim Abd al-Fattah.

"'Do you know him?' he asked.

"'No. They gave me his name,' I said.

"'And your family, where are they?'

"'In Amman,' I said.

"'Mine's in Nablus.'

"'Why did you come to Beirut?'

"'To join the fedayeen. And you?'

"I felt tears streaming down my cheeks. Ahmad moved closer to me and put his hand on my head. I said, 'Take me,' and he took me. With him I discovered what it means for a woman to make love with a man. Ahmad disappeared after that; he disappeared at Hammana, when we got to the assembly point. I don't know where he went, I didn't know anything about him. We reached Hammana, he disappeared, and I went down with the groups of fighters to Beirut and considered not going to Abu Rami's house. But where could I go? I thought of going to one of the Fatah offices, but I wasn't a member and didn't carry a card. Stupid – who'd have asked for a card in those days? So I did go to Abu Rami's house, and I didn't find Fawwaz. Umm Rami said he was staying with the boys in the museum district, waiting for me.

"'Go to him now,' said Umm Rami.

"'But I don't know Beirut – I don't know the museum, or anything else.'

"She asked her son, Rami, to accompany me. I got into the orange Renault 12 next to him, and we left. Suddenly, he stopped the car so he could open the back windows; I must have smelled awful. He parked the car in a side street, pointed out a square where people were congregating, and said, 'Over there.'

"I got out, my rifle in hand, and walked among the crowds. I was exhausted and Ahmad's smell went with me everywhere. I looked for Fawwaz for a long time before I found him among the weeping women. Lamenting and wailing, the women had just been dropped off in Lebanese Red Cross vehicles. Women, children, tears, pushing and shoving in front of the missing persons registration office; women telling of rapes, of executions against walls, of bodies being dragged through streets like in Roman times. Fawwaz was in the middle of them. I went up to him until I was almost right in front of him, but he didn't notice me, perhaps because I was wearing trousers and carrying a rifle. I forgot to mention that he'd forbidden me to wear trousers.

"'It's me, Fawwaz.'

"When he saw me, he jumped like a madman. 'I was wrong,' he said. 'I'm crazy. I should have brought you with me.'

"He took me by the arm and lifted the rifle from my hands as though he wanted to toss it aside.

"'That's my rifle. Leave it alone.'

"I snatched the rifle back, and we left. He stopped a car and told the driver, 'To Hamra.' There, near the Cinema Sarola stop, we went into a cheap hotel, where he rented a room on the second floor. As soon as we got inside the room, he attacked me and started tearing at my clothes.

"'Take it easy. I want to wash.'

"He slept with me with Ahmad's smell still clinging to me. I don't know if he smelled the other man, but he hit me. Before that, he'd banged his head against the wall and cursed at me. But in the hotel on Hamra Street, he hit me after he'd had sex with me two times in a row. He said he'd fixed up a house in the camp in Burj al-Barajneh."

Shams lived in Burj al-Barajneh until 1982, in other words, until the fedayeen left Beirut. She led with Fawwaz a wild sort of life that can barely be believed. True, I'm a doctor, or something like it, and true, doctors – through contact with their patients – come to understand the psychologies of their patients, since at least half of all illnesses are psychological in origin. But still I couldn't understand. I asked Shams about Fawwaz's childhood, but what she knew of it didn't provide me with an explanation.

"Did you cheat on him, and he found out?"

She said she never betrayed him except with Ahmad, but Fawwaz made her forget the taste of the love she'd experienced in the Monte Verde.

She said Fawwaz was always afraid of her, always accusing her and repeating that he'd got stuck with a whore, and abusing her because she didn't get pregnant.

"I don't know why I didn't get pregnant in Lebanon and why I did in Jordan, but after the night in the Monte Verde I wanted to get pregnant so I could have a boy like Ahmad. But it didn't happen, and I forgot Ahmad; the only thing I remember was his lips on my breasts – God, how sweet that was! It was the first time a man had taken my nipple between his lips. Fawwaz would rub my breasts and then bite them. But when Ahmad took my nipple between his lips, the waves rose within me and I felt my depths moving toward him and taking him. Fawwaz was nothing like that. He was a beast. He'd crucify me half-naked and say he could only get aroused when he heard gunfire, and I would lay there beneath him as he would fire his gun, terrorized.

Shams thought that's what life was like, and then the Israeli invasion had come and saved her. Fawwaz left with the fedayeen, and Shams went to her family's house in Amman. She found a job in a sewing workshop owned by Mme. Hend Khadir and forgot she was married.

Two weeks later, he came and announced he'd decided to settle in Amman – the revolution was over, he didn't want to go to the camp in Yemen, and he was going back to his original work.

"Meaning you want to be an engineer again?" said Shams sarcastically.

"Shut your mouth!" her mother shouted. "Women don't have the right to make fun of their husbands."

"In al-Wahdat, he no longer needed to fire his gun to become aroused. He stopped beating me and became kind. He'd go to work in his father's shop and would come back in the evenings to eat and sleep. He'd tell me that he'd dreamt that he'd had a son. The poor man didn't know I'd had a diaphragm inserted and wouldn't get pregnant if all the semen in the world were stuffed into my guts. Then I got an infection, so the doctor took out the diaphragm, and Dalal arrived."

IT'S NIGHT and I want to sleep. My eyelids are weighed down with stories. Now I understand why children fall sleep when we tell them stories: The stories infiltrate their eyes through the lashes and are turned into pictures too numerous for the eyes to process. Stories are for sleep, not for death. Now it's time for us to stop telling stories for a while, because one story leads to another, and night blankets the words.

But first tell me, what is the story of that spirit woman and that man who drowned in the circles of the red sun?

That happened at the beginning, but even so, it comes just at the end of the story.

Nahilah explained it to you, it was a simple misunderstanding. You thought she was a spirit, and she thought you were a prophet. You ran away, she knelt down, and Nahilah laughed and laughed.

You told me you named the tree Laila. You used to sleep by day inside the trunk of the Roman olive tree, and when you were with Nahilah you'd talk to her about Laila, and see the jealousy in her eyes.

It was the beginning of the fifties, and Yunes was making one of his trips to Bab al-Shams. That day, he hid inside the Roman olive tree on the outskirts of Tarshiha. When the sun began to set, he came out of his tree and saw something he'd never forget.

He said he'd never in his life forget that woman.

"She was wearing a long black dress, and had covered her hair with a black headscarf. She saw me and came toward me. I shrank back against the tree. I was wearing my long, olive-green coat and carrying my rifle like a stick. The woman was approaching me. She was far away, the sun was in my eyes so I couldn't see her silhouette clearly. I saw a black phantom emerging from among the red rays of the sun and coming toward me. Then, when she was two hundred meters away, she stopped in her tracks as though she were rooted to the ground, knelt down, rubbed her brow with dust, and raised her face toward me. She put her hands together and said something in an Arabic that I wasn't familiar with. Then she rose, stumbling over her long dress. I took advantage of the moment to hide inside the trunk of the tree, slipping inside it with my heart beating like a drum. I stayed inside the trunk until night had covered everything. There was something strange in her eyes. I thought she was a spirit even though I don't believe in spirits; but I was afraid, very afraid."

When Yunes told Nahilah how he'd stood close to his tree, wrapped in the red rays of the sun, and how the spirit woman had appeared to him at a distance and how she was going to carry his mind off like in the stories, Nahilah laughed for a long time.

"A spirit woman! The Yemenis are everywhere. That must have been a Yemeni Jewess."

Nahilah told Yunes about the sobs they'd heard coming from the *moshav* the Yemenis had built over al-Birwa and about the mysterious rumors of children dying and disappearing. She said the Yemeni Jewesses would go out into the fields and lament like Arab women and that she'd started to fear for her children. "If the children of the Jews are disappearing, what will happen to ours?"

"That spirit woman was no spirit," said Nahilah. "She was a poor woman like us who must have lost one of her children. So when she saw you, she probably thought you were a vision of the prophet Elias."

Nahilah laughed at you and called you Elias, saying that with your beard you'd started to look like a Jewish prophet.

You can't forget the scene – a black ray emerging from the red rays of the sun, a woman kneeling on the ground and crying out in a voice to rend the heavens. You thought of her as "Rachel the spirit," and on your way to see Nahilah, you'd enter the Roman tree and invoke the Yemeni woman. You told Nahilah that you were a Yemeni, too. "We come from Yemen. Our tribe migrated from there when the Ma'rib dam collapsed; the dam collapsed and drowned Yemen, and we fled. I'm Yemeni and my sweetheart's Yemeni, I have to look for her."

Nahilah would be a little jealous, but then she'd take you into the space at the back of the cave that she christened "the bathroom," where she'd make you take off you clothes and would bathe you. You'd stand naked and she'd be wearing her long black dress, which would get soaked and cling to her body, kindling your desire, and you'd grab her with the soap still all over you, and she'd slip out of your grasp and say, "Go to your Yemeni woman. I don't care."

I told you about the Yemeni woman to wish you sweet dreams.

I, too, need to sleep so that tomorrow I can try to convince Zainab not to leave the hospital. I don't know anything about Zainab. I've been living with her here for more than six months, and I know nothing. She's been here since the beginning. During these months everything has changed, as you know: Dr. Amjad comes only rarely, I've become head nurse and acting director of the hospital, the nurses have disappeared one after another, the hospital's been converted into a warehouse for medicine, but Zainab's still here, immovable. She limps a little, her shoulders droop, she has a short neck and small eyes. She moves like a ghost and takes care of everything. The cook left so Zainab has become the cook. Nabil went abroad so Zainab took over responsibility for the operating room. The Syrian guard disappeared so Zainab's become the doorkeeper. Zainab is the hospital. I don't care anymore. I spend most of my time with you, convinced that it's no use struggling for the hospital's survival. I had many discussions with Dr. Amjad, and I've tried with Mme. Wedad al-Najjar, the Palestine Red Crescent official in Lebanon, but it's no use.

No one wants this hospital anymore, as though we'd all agreed to announce the death of Shatila.

The camp is besieged from the outside and demolished on the inside, and they won't let us rebuild it. The whole of Lebanon was rebuilt after the war, except here; this testimony to butchery must be removed from our memories, wiped out just as our villages were wiped out and our souls lacerated.

I've lost hope. I said, "If they don't want it, too bad," and I built an imaginary wall around your room and won't let anyone come near you. At first Amjad tried to make me believe that the decision to move you couldn't be revoked, then I forced him to back down. I thought I'd scored a victory, but I discovered he simply didn't care. No one cares. They said, "He'll eventually get tired of it, and if he doesn't get tired of it, the old man will die anyway," and no one expected my treatment method would be so successful. Amjad used to think your death would be a matter of days, and Zainab said you wouldn't see the end of your first month, but here we are, past the sixth and into the seventh. We have to hang on to the end of the seventh month. If we get through the seventh, we'll definitely get to the ninth, and the ninth is where salvation lies. But they don't know. They've shut us in here and left us to rot. If only they knew. I'm certain that no one has the slightest notion of what's going on in this room, here with the world, the women, the words.

I told you Zainab's become everything, meaning nothing. When someone becomes everything it means they've lost their particularity. Zainab's like that: I wasn't aware of her presence beyond the fact that she was present. I didn't ask her for anything. Then two days ago she came to me and said she'd decided to stop working. It never crossed my mind that Zainab could stop working: She exists because she works.

She came to your room and said she wanted to speak to me.

"What, Zainab?"

"No, not in front of him," she said.

"Speak up, Zainab. There are no strangers here."

"Please, Dr. Khalil. I'm afraid to talk in front of him. Please come with me to the office."

I followed her to Dr. Amjad's office, which would have become my office if people took things seriously around here. Zainab went out and returned after a few minutes with a pot of coffee. She poured us both a cup and said that the children wanted her to stop working.

"You're married and have children, Zainab?"

"Of course, Doctor."

"I'm sorry. I never knew."

"'Cripples don't marry,'" she quoted and smiled.

"I'm sorry, I'm sorry. I didn't mean it like that."

"But I'm not a cripple, at least I wasn't a cripple when I got married. This is from Tal al-Za'atar."

"You're from Tal al-Za'atar?"

"I was there. I left with the women, my husband disappeared in the Monte Verde. We walked toward the armed men with our hands in the air, and they fired on us. I was with my children. They were between my legs, and I was trying to cover them with my long skirt. Then a man came, and the firing stopped. We kept going until we reached the armed men, and the Red Cross convoy that had been sent to take us to West Beirut were there. That man came. I don't know why he picked me out of the crowd. 'Over there!' he screamed, but I pretended I hadn't heard and kept going. Then the hot red fluid covered my thigh and bathed the head of my daughter, Samiyyeh, who was still between my legs. I kept going until I made it to the truck. I don't know why he only fired one shot, just one, or why he didn't kill me. These are things I don't understand now, but at the time everything was logical and possible. Our death seemed so logical that we weren't capable of protesting against it. They took me to Makased Hospital, and you can imagine what that did to my children. We reached the museum crossing when they decided to transfer me to the hospital. They put me in an ambulance, and the children started crying. I'd lost half my blood or more but somehow I managed to jump out of the ambulance to stand with my children. Then the nurse understood and let them come with me. At Makased Hospital, they put me in a room with more than ten beds and the children stayed with me. The eldest, Samiyyeh, was twelve and couldn't understand anything, and the youngest of them was three. Five boys and three girls, God protect them. I stayed in the hospital instead of going with the others to al-Damour. It's out of the question! I thought, when I heard they'd decided to house the Tal al-Za'atar people in al-Damour, which had been cleared of its Christian inhabitants. I thought, that's what the Jews did to us, and we're going to do the same to the people of al-Damour? It's not possible; it's a crime. And I stayed in the hospital. There was a doctor there from the Lutfi family in Tyre – do you know him? Dr. Hasib Lutfi? God bless him, he told me I could work in the hospital and found me a small apartment nearby. We lived there, me and the children, until 1982. After the invasion and the massacres, we came to Shatila, and I started working in this hospital. I'm not a nurse, but I learned on the job at Makased Hospital. I came here, and as you know very well, there was no one, so I did everything. But I'm tired, Dr. Khalil. And what are we doing here anyway? You're guarding a corpse and I'm guarding a storeroom of medicine. Also, Shadi, God bless him, is going to send me a visa and a ticket for Germany."

"You're going to Germany? What will you do there?"

"Nothing," she answered. "There nothing, here nothing. But I'm tired. And Shadi's wife – I didn't tell you, Shadi married an Iraqi girl who lives in Germany, a Kurd and political refugee. She arranged asylum and residence for him – a refugee like us, so, like they say, 'Refugees marry refugees,' and she's expecting, so I'll go for the child."

I said I'd feel alone without her.

She said she knew Shams and her husband, Fawwaz, and knew that she was mistreated: "Everyone in Tal al-Za'atar knows how he treated her. He was mad and heartless. It was like a demon possessed him. Could anyone be that crazy about his wife? He was as crazy about his wife as if she were the wife of another man. He told my late husband, Mounir, that he'd fire over her head and around her feet to drive the demons out of her. He was insane, and he drove her insane. He wouldn't let her leave the house or receive anyone either. She didn't dare open the door. We'd knock and she'd yell from inside that no one was there. And Fawwaz didn't sleep at home. He'd sleep with the fighters and would go to her by day, and we'd hear the sound of the bullets and imagine her tears. God knows how she stood it. It was said she'd fled with the fighters. Why did she go back to him? I haven't seen her since the Tal al-Za'atar days, and I haven't heard anything; after all that happened there, people have stopped asking about everyone else. Instead of searching for those who have disappeared, we look for photos of them. I swear we are an insane people, Doctor. The only lesson we've learned from our families is that we shouldn't leave home without our photos. Can you believe it! We were in that Red Cross truck, and I was on the point of death I was bleeding so much. People were piled on top of each other like sardines, and you'd see a woman pull a photo out of the front of her dress and compare it with those extracted from the front of some other woman's dress. It's almost as if we think that by carrying around the pictures of our dead with us, it will save them from death. The photo of Abu Shadi, God rest his soul, has completely faded. I framed it, but photos fade even behind glass. The man disappeared. We know nothing about what happened to him, and I wasn't able to look for him at first – I was in the hospital hovering between life and death, and I had my children with me. Without God's mercy and the generosity of Dr. Lutfi, my children would've been lost, as thousands were. A husband may die or disappear and we get upset, of course. But a child – God forbid!

"Once I got better, I went to al-Damour and met Riyad Ismat, who later was martyred in Tripoli in 1984. Riyad didn't know. I went from office to office in al-Damour but no one could help me in any way. Everyone did, however, assure me he was dead.

"'If he hasn't come back, it means he's dead. They didn't take prisoners in the Monte Verde,' said Riyad.

"Last year I went to the Monte Verde. The war was over, and it was possible to go back there. Samir took me in his car – Samir's my second son, who works as a taxi driver, though God help him if a policeman stops him and finds out he's Palestinian. All Samir dreams about these days is joining his brother in Germany.

"I wanted to see Tal al-Za'atar again. What desolation! It's as though it never existed. I asked people but no one could direct me – nothingness as far as the eye could see. People have forgotten the war and forgotten the camp, and no one dares to say its name. I tried to go in – I wanted to look for my house – but they wouldn't let me. There was a guard of sorts there who said it was prohibited. Anyway, even if I had got in, all I'd have found would have been asphalt: The ground had been completely covered up with asphalt, and everything was black as pitch.

"In the Monte Verde the car traveled the narrow bends. I knew we wouldn't find anything, but I had to do it to honor Abu Shadi's memory. All we found were Syrian soldiers and tanks. Samir asked me where to look for his father's grave; I didn't answer because I wasn't sure that the search was worthwhile, I just wanted to put my conscience at rest. I asked Riyad about the graves – if they'd buried the young soldiers. He said he didn't know, there was no way to know – the bullets had been streaming over their heads and all they'd wanted was to reach Hammana.

"I didn't ask Samir to stop the car, and I didn't feel anything. It was as though those who'd died had been wiped off the face of the earth. War in itself doesn't need graves, because war is a grave. Abu Shadi doesn't have a grave – his grave is war itself. War doesn't call for tombs and headstones, for war is itself a tomb, a tomb in which we live. Even the camp isn't a camp, it's the tomb of Palestine.

"Do you understand? Of course you understand, because you're like me, Doctor. You were born in the camp, or in the grave, and the grave will pursue you to the end of time."

Zainab said she was going to leave us.

"When are you going?"

She said she was waiting for her visa, but that she'd come to advise me to abandon the hospital and stop watching him.

"Who?" I asked her.

"Yunes, Abu Salem."

"What's wrong with him?"

"He's dying, can't you see? Leave him alone. Let him die. Have pity on him! You're forcing him to stay alive."

"But I'm not doing anything," I said.

"You're the one responsible for his condition. Have pity on him!"

"No, Zainab. Please!"

"Let him die. Stop this useless treatment. Can you change the will of God? Leave him in the merciful hands of God and get out of this hospital!"

Then she went back to Shams.

"Your fear of Shams is senseless: No one's going to take revenge on you. What does it have to do with you? She killed her lover and she was killed. Warn the killer that he will be killed. These are the words of God written in His Book. Sameh killed her when he lied to her, she killed him because she wanted revenge, and they killed her to get justice. That's all there is to it. And you aren't so guilty that you should have to bury yourself with this man who's no longer a man. Look at him, it's like he's gone back to being a baby. In the name of God the Merciful, let him die and release us all."

Zainab repeated what Umm Hassan had said: "Where are his family to take him back to his country?"

It's true, Yunes. Why didn't you go back like Hamad?

Don't you know the story of Hamad?

I was told the story by his brother, Mansour, who sells fish in the camp. You love fish. "Ah, how I miss the fish of Acre!" you used to say. What is this blind fanaticism? Mansour told you these were fish from Acre that had been smuggled over and had become refugees like us, but you'd refuse to buy any.

"The fish from Acre's much better. We used to fry it and eat it with thyme *fatayir* and *taratur* sauce. It's Christ's fish. That's where he used to fish, peace be with him."

You said that Christ, peace be with him, never forbade alcohol because he worked with fishermen and sailors: "How can you convince a sailor not to drink? The sea and fishing are impossible without arak and wine. Fish too – you can't eat them without arak, *taratur*, and thyme. The fish of Tiberias are inexhaustible. Fish, Christ, and fishermen – that's Galilee. They don't know Galilee. They're trying to create a fishing industry – can you industrialize the water Christ walked on?

"That's where we'll go back to. Imagine, a whole people walking on water!"

You said that, took a swig, and ask me to pour you more.

"Take it easy, Abu Salem."

"Like hell. Pour the arak and follow me back to Lake Tiberias!"

It was Mansour the fish seller who told me his brother's story. I'd gone to see him on the morning of the feast of Ramadan because I wanted to mark the occasion by eating fish. I found his stall empty. He said he hadn't gone to Tyre to make purchases because of the feast, and he'd gone to the cemetery at dawn to visit his son and had come straight to the shop because he didn't dare go home and sit there with the pictures of his son.

"Over here we die, and over there they have children," he said.

Mansour said he was a fool and that his brother, Hamad, had got away with his life and his children's, too.

You know Hamad, he was your companion in the Sha'ab militia, which was the last to leave Galilee; you were imprisoned together. Then he lived in the Burj al-Barajneh camp. You knew him well – from Tarshiha, the one who always swore by the *kibbeh nayyeh* his wife, Salmeh, made: "*Kibbeh nayyeh* with *hoseh* on top. Meat on meat, my brother. *Kibbeh* underneath and fried meat with onions and pine nuts on top, heaven!"

He said that Salmeh, Umm Jamil, stayed in Tarshiha. He said that *kibbeh* had no taste after he was separated from Salmeh.

Why didn't you do what he did?

Were you afraid of the Jews?

Of Nahilah?

Of yourself?

Truly, Yunes my son, the only thing people fear is themselves. You told me the only thing you were afraid of when you crossed the border was your own shadow, which would stretch out on the ground and follow you.

Do you want to listen to Mansour?

Come on, Mansour. Come tell your story to Uncle Yunes.

He isn't here, of course, but I'll tell you the story as I heard it from Mansour Ahmad Qabalawi, the fish seller, who opened his shop here in Shatila after they closed down the one in Burj al-Barajneh at the entrance to the low-lying neighborhood where people from Tarshiha lived because of differences among the various political groups at the time of the revolution.

Mansour said, "After the fall of Tarshiha, we fled into Lebanon and forgot all about Salmeh and her daughter. It was my fault: The thought of Salmeh never crossed my mind as we were fleeing. It was all shelling and planes and hell let loose, and I wasn't a fighter even though I was in the militia. Between you and me, I was just there to make up the numbers, and when the flight started and the Jews came, I fled with my wife and kids and not once thought of Salmeh and her daughter, Sawsan. Then my brother turned up. He'd spent a year in prison in Syria. He found my tent. Before he could ask, I confessed to him. I didn't tell him she'd died, God forbid. I told him we'd forgotten her and didn't know anything about her whereabouts and that she'd probably stayed in Tarshiha. He called me names, broke the tent pole, and left. Later I learned he'd gone there: He went to Tarshiha and stayed with his wife for a few days. When he returned, we became like brothers again. I don't have anyone but him, and he doesn't have anyone but me. Every time he took off, it would be an adventure. They'd arrest him and expel him. He didn't stay in Tarshiha in secret: He'd knock on his wife's door and would enter in full view of everyone. Each time, they'd arrest him and drag him to the border.

"The last time they arrested him, the Israeli officer who notified him of the expulsion order told him he was absent when the census was made after the establishment of the State, so he was considered an absentee.

"'Well, here I am, Sir. I was absent and now I'm present.'

"'No,' said the officer. 'The absentee is not entitled to be present.'

"'But my wife and children are here.'

"'Take them with you if you like.'

"'But it's my village.'

"They tied him up and threw him out at the Lebanese border. He returned to the camp. He stayed about a year, then disappeared again, and we discovered they'd thrown him across the border into Gaza, and we tied ourselves into knots getting a plane ticket from Cairo to Beirut. Five times he went in and stayed, and five times he was thrown out. The sixth time was the clincher.

"It was in 1957, the morning of the Feast of the Sacrifice. My wife was busy cooking, and the smell of *kibbeh nayyeh* filled the house. He looked at my children and his face ran the gamut of emotions. 'Let's go to Tyre,' he said. I left my wife and my children that day and went with him because I knew him, and I knew nothing could stop him. We went to Tyre, from there to the al-Rashidiyyeh camp, and from there to the house of Ali Shahada from al-Ba'neh. Ali Shahada, who worked as a smuggler, asked for a thousand Lebanese lira to get him to Tarshiha. And a thousand lira in those days was no joke; it was five times the monthly income of a fish-shop owner like me. My brother agreed and said he'd pay over there. Ali, however, asked to see the money before he did anything, and my brother pulled a huge amount of money out of his back pocket, showed it to him, and gave him a hundred lira, saying, 'Here's a feast present for your kids.'

"'Let's go,' said my brother. 'We'll eat lunch first and rest a little.'

"'Then we'll leave right at sundown,' said Ali.

"He slaughtered a rooster for us, and we ate it with rice, drank coffee and chatted. As soon as the sun began to set, my brother, Hamad, set off with the smuggler, Ali, and I went back to Beirut.

"My brother reached his house and stayed there. Thirty years after all this, he got me a permit to visit Tarshiha, and there I found Hamad, living among his children and his children's children. I told him, 'This isn't Tarshiha: Our land doesn't belong to us anymore, and our house isn't ours any longer' – Hamad was living in the house of Mahmoud Qabalawi, whose family live in Burj al-Barjneh today. He told me our house had been demolished along with all the houses in the lower square and that Salmeh had had no choice but to live there. 'I moved in here, but you can tell Jaber, Mahmoud Qabalawi's son, that I haven't changed a thing in their house. When they come back, they can take it, and God bless them.'

"'But it's not Tarshiha, Hamad,' I said to him. 'The Jews are everywhere.'

"Hamad reached his house and stayed a week with his wife before he was seized and deported to the Lebanese border. Before he reached the border checkpoint, he took off his Swiss watch and offered it to the Israeli soldier. The soldier hesitated, then took the bribe, and left Hamad on his own.

"My brother returned and was arrested again. He was convicted as a saboteur, getting eighteen years. He spent nine of those in prison, then they let him out after a series of remissions for good behavior. They didn't know what to do with him because he refused to go to Lebanon – he said he'd rather stay in prison. So they sent him back to his house in Tarshiha."

Tell me, Yunes, why didn't you go back for good?

Why didn't you ever try?

Were you afraid of dying? If you say you were afraid they'd liquidate you, I'll understand, but then don't talk to me about the struggle or the revolution or any of that.

And now, tell me, what will you do when we've got everything fixed and you're born again? Will you lead a new life, or will you return to your old migratory life?

I hear your voice emerging from low-pitched moans. Why the moaning? Your body temperature's normal, everything's tip-top, your heartbeats are more regular than those of a young man; knock on wood. But tell me, if we could run life backwards, who would you prefer to have been – Yunes or Hamad? Or would you prefer a third option, going to Canada, for instance? What do you think – emigrate and leave the whole thing behind?

I know you can't answer. That's why I can ask you so freely, I'm not obliged to defer to you in anything. I know what you'd like to say, but you don't, and that's much better.

Tell me, what should I tell Zainab?

Should I advise her to stay here or encourage her to travel to her son in Germany? Should I promise her that things will get better for the hospital or promise her that her village, Saffouri, will be reborn from its ashes?

I'll tell her to do what she wants.

I see Zainab now for the first time, it's as though for all those long months I'd looked right through her. And now, after she's told me how she was wounded at Tal al-Za'atar, her name is no longer "the crippled nurse," as I would call her to myself; her name is Zainab, Zainab the nurse. Good grief, how long do we need to wear our names for them to become ours! Zainab became Zainab because she told her story. True, she's leaving soon, and true, she informed me when her work here came to an end, and true, if I'd known earlier things would have been different. But that's the way it is. A human being only reveals his name at the moment of departure or, in other words, when the name becomes his shroud. We wrap him in his name and bury him. Now I understand the wisdom of the photos that fill our lives: The victims of the massacres have no names and no shrouds. Their bodies are covered with lime and insecticides before being thrown into a common grave. People disappear because they have no names, they are reduced to numbers. That's the terrifying thing, my son, numbers are the terror. That's why people carry pictures of their dead and their missing, and use them as a substitute for names.

Zainab is not convinced.

She says everything I've done for you was for nothing. If she only knew! But she doesn't want to listen to the story from the beginning, plus I no longer have the energy to tell it. If Zainab had come and listened to your story, she'd have understood I wasn't wasting your time and mine but was buying time and history, for you and for me.

Yes, my son and master, yes.

I'm here because I was under the influence of Shams. I thought I'd flee her ghost and her revenge. I wasn't afraid of real revenge – that one of her family would come and shoot me. No, I was afraid of her.

Your death came and rescued me. You made me a doctor again, you brought me to live with you here in the hospital, and you allowed me to recover my desire for life. Yes, I was incapable of living. The air that entered my lungs felt like knives. I'd feel ants burying themselves in my face and would get dizzy. In clinical jargon, it's called the onset of nervous collapse.

When Shams died, everything inside me died. I became a corpse, and things lost their meaning and taste. Life became unbearably heavy. It was as though I were carrying my own corpse on my back. Who can carry the sack of life when it's filled with forty years of desolation? Who would have the courage?

Amna came, and she told me about you. By the way, where is she now? She vanished, like all your women. This means we've entered the dangerous period, for when the women vanish, it means the end is near. Women only run away when life is extinguished.

Amna left, followed by all your other women. No one remains but me in this collapsing place. There are cracks everywhere – cracks in the walls and cracks in the ceiling; it seems everything is on the verge of collapse.

But I'm not afraid. Everything's collapsing, but I'm here and I'm not afraid.

Strange, isn't it?

Maybe neither one of us has been afraid during these long months we've spent together. We've made a shelter out of words, a country out of words, and women out of words.

I'm not afraid for you, and I won't comment on what Zainab said – don't be angry with her, please: She doesn't understand. She said in the beginning that you'd become young like a baby again, then she added that your shrunken form didn't look human and that I'd created a little monster.

It's as though she can't see.

Never mind; I'm convinced that you're the most beautiful baby, and that's enough, right? And I feel your freedom, too. You can die if you want to. I say, "You can," which doesn't mean I'm suggesting you do so, but you're free, choose to live or to die as you like. Do whatever you feel like doing, for now your truth is inside me.

Tell me a little about your daughter, Noor. What a lovely name! I don't know her, but I feel as though I do, and I long to see her. When you described her to me the first time, I thought you were telling me about Shams. You described her dark beauty and her infinite charm, and you told me about her son, Yunes.

You said you'd received a letter from her announcing the birth of Yunes and that she said all of your children were naming their boys Yunes. That way you'd live among them and would return to them not as one but as a hundred.

You were carrying around the letter and laughing. You read me that passage laughing, then tears started to flow from your eyes. You wept and laughed as though your emotions were crossed and you no longer knew how to express yourself. I promised I'd give you the Fairouz song that's taken from a poem by the Lebanese poet, Bishara al-Khouri, known as Little Akhtal, and I recited the line that opens the song, and you took out a pen and wrote it on the back of the letter:

> *He laughs and cries neither in sorrow nor in joy*
> *Like a lover who inscribes a line of love only to erase it.*

You wrote the line and a white mist arose and clouded your face and eyes, allowing you to escape my gaze; you repeated the ode, the verse swirling around you like water. It was then that I understood the meaning of poetry, and the words of Imru' al-Qais – my grandfather and yours, and the grandfather of all Arabs. For Imru' al-Qais didn't see his own image in the mirror of his beloved's breast; he saw the world, he saw the mist that covered it. And, realizing that he was living inside that mist, he invented words to assuage his shame and confusion. Poetry, my son, is words we use to heal our shame, our sorrow, our longing. It's a cover. The poet wraps us up in words so our souls don't fall to pieces. Poetry is against death – it's both sickness and cure, the bare soul and its clothes. I'm cold now, so I take refuge in poetry, hiding my head in it and asking it to cover me.

Letter in hand, you came and painted a portrait of Noor before reading it. You became like a poet as you read about the hundred Yuneses being born over there, you didn't boast or trumpet your triumph. You wore your triumph and started weeping and laughing, because triumph is not unlike defeat; it is a moment when the soul is exposed from within. You were exposed and wounded, and in ministering to you with Little Akhtal's poem, I poured the voice of Fairouz on your wounds. The mist of poetry covered you and took you to a distant place.

You're now in the distant realm of poetry, the realm of a hundred Yuneses who don't know you're dying, and who don't see the footprints you left behind on the roads of Galilee. Only the forest of oblivion remembers you now.

I PROMISED I'd tell you about Shams, and I didn't. We got to where she became an officer with the fedayeen. How that came about I don't know. I know she went to Jordan after the 1982 invasion of Beirut and her husband, Fawwaz, caught up with her there and worked with his father, who owned a small fabric store in Jebel al-Weibdeh.

Fawwaz quieted down in Amman, the violence that had erupted in Lebanon in the form of bullets fired around his wife's body also disappeared.

"Fawwaz didn't scare me anymore," said Shams. "For six years in Beirut, I can only remember myself as naked, crucified, with bullets exploding around me, and then the man would come to me, erect, boring into my body with a savage shout that emerged from between his thighs. Six years. I knew I'd never get pregnant because what he was doing doesn't make pregnancies. He'd ask me before starting my torture session if I was pregnant, and I'd say no and see his snarl and hear and watch his fury erupt."

She said everything changed in Amman.

"It seems the demon left him, and he became a different man, stammering in front of his father, addressing his mother respectfully and coming to me calmly. We lived in one house with his father, mother, and unmarried sister. Fawwaz became someone other than Fawwaz, and I became pregnant, and Dalal came.

"Three months after Dalal was born, the father died regretting that I hadn't given birth to a boy who'd inherit his name. I paid no attention to his harsh looks or to his refusal to speak to me after Dalal was born; he took to telling his wife and his son anything he wanted to say to me, even when I was sitting next to him. 'Tell her,' he'd say, without uttering my name. But I didn't care. What mattered was that Dalal looked like me, not them. The girl was my daughter, not theirs. God, how beautiful she was! Soon, when I go get her and bring her back here, you'll see the most beautiful girl in the world. I wanted to call her Amal,* because, with her, hope began. But

*Hope.

Fawwaz insisted on Dalal, and I later found out that Dalal was the name of the cousin who'd refused to marry him. His own father had advised his brother not to give Dalal to Fawwaz if she didn't love him; then they stumbled upon me for the no-good son who wasn't an engineer or anything at all. Fawwaz insisted on the name Dalal and his father didn't interfere, so I gave in. I cried because I felt that Amal had died. I named her Amal when she was still in my belly. I'd talk to her and listen to her. I knew from the beginning that she'd be a girl, from the first instant that I felt dizziness, nausea, and thirst. I spent the first three months of the pregnancy sleeping. I'd drink and sleep and talk to Amal. Then they stole the name. Fawwaz said Dalal, I said Amal. But names are not important. Dalal fits her and I've gotten used to it."

Shams told of the great transformation that came about after the death of Fawwaz's father, how the world – and her husband – utterly changed. She said she couldn't believe her eyes.

"The father died of a heart attack, and his son inherited everything. Fawwaz changed. He reverted to being the Fawwaz I'd left behind in Beirut. Instead of trembling before his father, it was now his mother who trembled before him. Instead of stumbling when he walked, it was now his sister who stumbled, and instead of stammering when he talked, we were the ones who stammered. During his father's time, when he came to sleep with me, he'd come whispering, covering my body with his, groping in the dark. Only in Amman, and only in the Amman of the whispering times, did I feel something sexual with him; I felt something move in the depths of me. Then his father died, and the page was turned."

Shams said the situation grew worse and worse. "At first, he stopped paying attention, then he went back to his Beirut ways. He started beating me up, saying he couldn't feel aroused if he didn't hit me. The beatings started light but things progressed, and he began hitting me with all his might while I stifled my screams and my pain out of shame in front of his mother and sister. Then I couldn't control myself anymore; as soon as he beat me, I would start screaming. The scenes multiplied, and I felt I could hear the two women's footsteps outside our door; I imagined them bent over the keyhole, listening and shaking their heads. The sister's handkerchief would fall to the ground and she'd pick it up, looking into her mother's face.

"In the morning he'd leave and I'd be left on my own with the women, not daring to look at them. They behaved as though they were unaware of what went on in our bedroom.

"Once I said something to his mother, and she looked at me with startled eyes. I didn't really say anything, I just said that Fawwaz pursued me at night and I couldn't stand it anymore. She looked at me as though she didn't understand what I was saying and mumbled something about life being like that and I should thank the Lord that he was providing me with a home.

"Umm Fawwaz said I should thank the Lord! Imagine! Thank God for the humiliation and the beatings!

"I don't know whether his mother said something to him or whether things just took their natural course, but after that mistake of mine he became even more brutal and went back to acting out the Beirut scenes. In Amman he couldn't fire his gun: There was a State rather than a civil war – but he transformed the bedroom into a battlefield. He'd spread-eagle me, point his finger like a gun, and fire from his mouth. He'd come up close and start boring into my body with the muzzle of his imaginary gun. I tried to find a solution. I went to see my mother, but all I got from her was, 'Anything but divorce! Divorce costs a woman her reputation.' So I decided to act alone; I decided to run away, but I didn't dare make it happen. Every night, after he'd gone to sleep, I'd draw up my escape plans, and in the morning the plans would evaporate, and I'd find myself one of three women.

"Where was I to run to?

"The West Bank crossed my mind. God, I even thought of going to the Jews! But I was afraid. I didn't know anyone there, and they might throw me in prison. Then I thought of Beirut. I couldn't even stand the sound of the word *Beirut*, but I decided that's where I would go.

"I don't know how I got the words out of my mouth.

"Fawwaz was eating breakfast, sitting alone at the table eating fried eggs and *labaneh*, while we stood – three women hovering around him, ready to obey his every gesture, while he smacked his lips and drank tea. Suddenly, I heard my voice saying: 'Listen. I can't stand it anymore. Divorce me.'

"But Fawwaz went on eating as though he hadn't heard, so I screamed, 'Fawwaz, listen to me. I can't go on. Divorce me.'

"He swallowed what was in his mouth and said in a wooden voice, 'You're divorced.'

"I'm certain he didn't take me seriously, but he said it. I ran to my room, put my clothes in a plastic bag, took Dalal in my arms, and left.

"'Leave the little girl, you whore,' said his mother.

"My body went slack. I'd thought of everything that might happen except for Dalal. His mother came up to me and snatched the little girl from my arms.

"'Go to your family and tell them, Fawwaz divorced me because I'm a whore,' said Fawwaz.

"I'm sure he thought I was going to collapse and weep and implore him to forgive me, but I turned my back on them and left the house. I didn't go to my family. Instead, I walked in the direction of the taxi station to leave for Beirut. I got into a taxi, fell asleep, and didn't wake up until we reached the checkpoint at the Jordanian-Syrian border. Then I fell asleep again and woke to find myself held up at the Syrian-Lebanese border because I didn't have an entry visa for Lebanon. I stood alone after the taxi left me to continue its journey. A man with a Palestinian accent came up to me, and said he could get me to Tripoli, via Homs. At the time, Tripoli was a battle zone: The Palestinian fedayeen, or what was left of them in Lebanon, had congregated in the city, and it was under siege. I gave him everything I possessed. I was carrying forty Jordanian dinars that I'd stolen one by one from Fawwaz's pocket in preparation for my escape."

Shams said she learned about war in Tripoli. She arrived at Fatah's al-Zaheriyyeh office and said she'd come from Jordan to join the revolution.

Mundhir, the official in charge, sent her to join the groups at Bab al-Tabbaneh, where she met Khalil Akkawi, the legendary commander who transformed the poor and the young of Tripoli into little revolutionaries and who was to die later in a savage assassination operation that greatly resembled Shams' murder in al-Miyyeh wi-Miyyeh.

In Tripoli she also met Abu Faris, an assistant to Abu Jihad (Khalil al-Wazir), who, before the fedayeen left the city, appointed her communications officer for Western Sector Command in Tunis, which was responsible for work inside Occupied Palestine.

Shams didn't get on the boats with the fedayeen who left Tripoli in 1984. She said that Tunisia was too far away and she preferred to stay close to Dalal. Abu Faris gave her some money, and she came to Beirut where she joined the Palestinian command center in Mar Elias, and from there slipped into Shatila during the long siege.

Many stories are told about her during that time.

It's said that the Shatila commander, Ali Abu Toq, slapped her in the face in front of the other fighters and told her he was the only commander there.

It's said she succeeded in forming a network to smuggle weapons and supplies into the besieged camp.

She didn't tell me anything about that. I knew her – we'd run into each other in Mar Elias – and I was bewitched by her. Now I don't know, because everything I thought I knew about her evaporated when her murder of Sameh revealed her love for him.

I can say she was an extraordinary woman. She used to tour the Mar Elias camp surrounded by her young men, saying they were members of "Shams' Brigade."

I returned to the camp after it collapsed following the assassination of its commander, Ali Abu Toq, while Shams was transferred to the Sidon area. I returned to find the camp totally disrupted. I participated in the rebuilding of the hospital, and I grew accustomed to the new situation – which you know better than I do so there's no need to get into that. When the fedayeen returned, they weren't like fedayeen. I'm not talking here about the corruption and bribes and quarrels we lived through before the 1982 invasion. I know there was corruption, and we were ashamed of ourselves. But something made us capable of tolerating the situation; let's say there was an issue that was larger than the bribe takers and the crooks. After the fall of the camp, however, everything changed.

In the past, death had been everywhere, and it was beautiful. I know we're not supposed to call death beautiful, but there was a certain beauty there that enveloped us. In the days following the fall of the camp, however, death was naked.

I have no idea how Shams got into the camp after it fell. The Fatah dissidents* had taken over Fatah's offices in Beirut, and only the camps in the south were left. Everyone knew that Shams was against the split, that she worked with Abu Jihad al-Wazir, and that she was loyal to the leadership and accused the dissidents of many things. All the same, she'd come into Shatila without anyone challenging her. She'd come to my house, and we'd spend nights together. I didn't see her often – she was busy all the time, and I had no means of contacting her. She'd come when she wanted and would find me waiting for her.

No, Abu Salem.

No, my beloved child, I wasn't afraid of her, I was afraid of myself. Something suddenly died inside me; when someone we love dies, something dies in us. Such is life – a long chain of death. Others die, and things die inside each of us; those we love die, and limbs from our bodies die, too. Man doesn't wait for death, he lives it; he lives the death of others inside himself, and when his own death comes, many of his parts have already been amputated; what remains is meager.

Before Shams, I was ignorant of this. When she died, I became aware of my amputated limbs and the parts of me that were already buried; I became conscious of my father and my grandmother, even my mother. I saw them as an organ that had been ripped out of me by force.

*Military allies of Syria that had split off in 1983, after the PLO's forces left Beirut.

That's what I was afraid of, and that's why I sought refuge with you.

I wasn't afraid of revenge. Well, maybe I was, but it's not important. I was afraid of dying. Shams died, and I became aware of all the parts within me that had died. I saw death creeping up on what remained of me, and then you came. I didn't want you to die to safeguard that last piece of me separating me from my death. Now I laugh at myself: That last piece of me has become a child. You've become a child, Father, and your smell is like Dalal's, or like that of Ibrahim, your eldest child who died. The decision was Nahilah's. She's the one who decided you shouldn't continue calling yourself Abu Ibrahim. She said, "You're Abu Salem and I'm Umm Salem. We mustn't live with death – the living are better than the dead."

Now I live with your new smell – a fresh smell that invites kisses. The smell of children invites kisses, and you invite me. I hug you and sniff you and kiss you and wrap you up in my voice.

You don't believe me?

For pity's sake, you must believe me! I know she loved me, and you have no right to cast doubt on it. I believed all your stories, the believable and the unbelievable ones. I even believed the story about the ice worms.

At the time, Yunes was on his way to Bab al-Shams. In the morning, he reached his first refuge, near Tarshiha, and lay down beneath the big olive tree he called Laila. He was carrying an English rifle and a bag and was wearing a long green coat.

Yunes was beneath the olive tree when the sun began to set and the reddish light started to spread across the hills of Galilee.

"I'm being unfaithful to you with Laila, my Roman lady," he said to Nahilah.

"I want to see her," said Nahilah.

He promised he'd take her, but he didn't.

"Laila's just for me. She's my second wife. We're Muslims, woman!"

Nahilah would laugh at the man's childishness and say she was going to cut the tree down.

With Laila, he was Yunes.

With the tree, inside whose huge hollow trunk he hid, and in whose shade he slept. A lone tree, set off a little from the olive grove in the countryside on the fringes of Tarshiha. There he could rest and sleep, standing or lying down inside the trunk. There he would organize his thoughts, his plans, his passion, and his body.

Then the tree died.

He spoke of the tree as he would speak of a woman.

He said it died; he didn't say they cut it down.

Why do they cut down the olive trees and plant pines and palms in their place? Why do the Israelis hate the tree of sacred light?

On that day in 1965, after crossing the Tarshiha olive grove, he felt something was missing. He felt lost and couldn't find the tree. The paved road that links Maalot to Carmel had run over Laila.

Yunes said he felt a wild desire for revenge and didn't complete his journey to Nahilah. He returned to Shatila, shut himself up inside, and didn't receive visitors for more than a week. His face was waxy, the tears stood like stones in his eyes. He was in mourning for the tree.

He decided to change his route to Deir al-Asad.

That was when he discovered the route going through al-Arqoub, which three years later – after the 1967 defeat, that is – was to become the main road into Palestine for the fedayeen. The fedayeen discovered al-Arqoub, situated at the foot of Jebel al-Sheikh mountain, and learned how to travel its icy roads. It soon became known as "Fatah Land."

Yunes said Jebel al-Sheikh had enchanted him.

The mirrors of ice.

A mountain that crowned three countries – Palestine, Lebanon, and Syria. "It's the crown of God," he told me.

Yunes said he discovered the route via Jebel al-Sheikh, or Mount Hermon, because Laila was killed. Laila had been his landmark and his refuge. He'd spend the day inside her trunk and when night came he'd slip off toward Deir al-Asad.

"Did you know that the ice has worms in it?" he asked me.

"I discovered them myself," he said. "I took Nahilah ten worms wrapped in a piece of cloth. They're little white worms that look like silk worms. When you pull them out of the ice, they get as hard as pebbles. I told Nahilah they were ice worms; I put one in the water jar and asked her to wait. In less than ten minutes, the water was as cold as ice. Nahilah refused to drink it at first. She said she didn't drink worms. Then she started asking for the worms and giving them away."

Yunes said it was summer. "During the summer, the ice of Mount Hermon becomes like a mirror misted with breath. I slept in the old abandoned house. I don't know what came over me that night. There was no problem with the house: It was an old house that the peasants of al-Arqoub say a Lebanese émigré returned from Mexico and built. They say the man, who was from the village of al-Kfeir, at the foot of the mountain, made a lot of money in Latin America and decided to return to his country when his wife died. He was almost seventy-five years old, and it seems that in his dotage he focused on spiritual matters, saying that on the mountain he'd be closer to God. He chose Jebel al-Sheikh upon which to build his hermitage. He built the house in the Arab style – a courtyard surrounded by five rooms – and announced his intention to found a monastery there.

"How did he find the courage to live there?

"You can't imagine the winter on Jebel al-Sheikh. Winter there, I tell you, is absolute whiteness. Scattered ice dust swirls around and around and covers your eyes. Your bones even become blocks of ice. You become a piece of ice. I only crossed it in winter twice, and both times, when I got to Bab al-Shams, I lit a fire and Nahilah came to put my bones back in place. That's what a real woman is, my son – someone who can put each bone back in its place, warm you up, and let you become yourself again.

"The man, who everyone called al-Khouri,* died before the house was finished, and the ice house became known as "the House of al-Khouri." I don't know if the house was called that because the man belonged to the

* Priest.

Khouri family from al-Kfeir from which hailed many historic personages – such as Faris Bey al-Khouri, a leader of the Nationalist Bloc who became prime minister of Syria, or because he had decided to become a monk and it was given the name in honor of his unfinished monastery project."

That summer day, Yunes reached the house in a state of exhaustion and decided to spend the night there before continuing his journey to Bab al-Shams.

"I was in my room, the only one al-Khouri had completed before he died. Sleep wouldn't come. The August sun was burning the ice, and the ice was burning my face. I was cold and I was burning at the same time. I got up, wrapped myself in a wool blanket, and sat on the threshold above the dry ice. I could feel the worms moving over me. I must have fallen asleep. I awoke to find the ice worms, little white worms, emerging from beneath the crust of dry ice and spreading over my feet. I got up in fright and started stepping on them. On that occasion I didn't wait for nightfall to continue my journey to Nahilah; I traveled by day and God protected me. I don't know how I made it. Nahilah couldn't believe that the ice was full of worms.

"A peasant from the village of Kafar Shouba told me that the ice became wormy when it got old, and that the ice worms were very useful, because they turned water cold.

"I put the worm in the jar and drank, but Nahilah refused at first. Then she started asking me for worms from Jebel al-Sheikh and would distribute them to people in the village – in those days people were poor and no one owned a refrigerator; to cool the water, they'd put it out in jars overnight. Everyone started calling the ice worms 'fedayeen worms.' The whole village knew that I visited my wife in secret. They knew, but Nahilah, God protect her, didn't tell even the children about the cave until the end of her life.

"Salem spoke to me by telephone – you know, over there they can call us, but we can't call Israel.

"Salem said his mother's health was improving and that she'd confided the secret and asked him to go to Bab al-Shams. She told him to visit the cave often to keep it neat and clean. 'Don't let the sheets, towels, and blankets get moldy. It's your father's village, ask him what he wants you to do with it. His home must be kept neat. And when I die, take everything out and close up the entrance with stones. We cannot let the Israelis in there; it's the only liberated plot of Palestinian land.'

"After her death, Salem called me to say that he'd gone into Bab al-Shams, and wanted to know what to do with the things he found. He called it Bab al-Shams on the telephone! No one knew the name of my village except the two of us. There we were on our own, like Adam and Eve, and now along comes Salem and blurts it out!

"He told me about Nahilah's death and then asked me about the cave. I couldn't breathe.

"He said, 'May God compensate you with good health, Dad,' and then he asked me what to do with my things.

"I said I didn't know.

"He said he'd carry out Nahilah's wishes.

"I didn't ask him what her wishes were. I found out forty days later. Salem called and said he'd closed the 'country' with stones. He said he'd gone at night with his son, Yunes, and Noor's son, Yunes, and Saleh's son, Yunes, and Mirwan's son, Yunes . . . they'd gone and closed the country. They'd taken everything out and had divided the things up among them.

"Salem told me, and I didn't manage to utter a word.

"At that moment, I felt my life had ended. Four young men had divided up my clothes, my blankets, my cooking pans, and my books, and closed the country I'd created for my wife.

"Salem said he'd asked the children to keep the secret of the cave.

"'It's Yunes' secret. Leave Yunes in the whale's belly,' he told them, 'and after three days, or three years, or three decades, your grandfather Yunes will emerge from the whale's belly, just like the first Yunes did, and Palestine will return, and we'll call the village that we'll rebuild Bab al-Shams.'"

"No," said Yunes to those who came to pay him condolences, "she isn't dead." But he knew deep within himself that the story was over.

In this last period, he recounted fragments of his stories about Laila, the Roman lady, and the Yemeni woman.

He said the Yemeni woman was wrapped in the red of the sun.

He said he saw himself, with his beard and his rifle that he carried like a prophet's staff, within the circle of sun stretching over the olive groves that extend from Tarshiha to the sea.

He said he became frightened when he saw her kneeling.

He said he hid in the trunk, and all he heard was the word *Elias*.

He said he emerged from the belly of the olive tree and looked for her.

You are Elias, Yunes. It's a new name to add to your others.

I told you the story, my son, so you won't forget that Elias is one of your names. Elias is the prophet of fire, the one who never died. He is the only man to have ascended to Heaven without experiencing death.

Death, as you see, is not a requirement.

Please listen to me.

I know you're tired.

I know you want to die.

No.

You just have to look at yourself to know that your death would be as harrowing as the death of a child; there's nothing crueler than a child's death.

Do you want to die as Ibrahim did?

If only she were here! If only Nahilah were here, she would dress you in Ibrahim's clothes and keep you from dying the way your son died.

But Nahilah isn't here, and I don't know what to do. Still, please, try to get through this seventh month with me, and afterward everything will start anew.

But you aren't listening.

I know you never obeyed anyone but that woman called Nahilah.

Where am I supposed to find Nahilah?

Salem told you that in her last days she couldn't lie flat or her lungs would fill with fluid. She'd sit with her basket of flowers and water next to her. Every day she'd ask Noor's son, Yunes, to go and pick fresh flowers. She'd sit him down beside her and ask him to write out names. She'd put all your names in her basket and recite from the Surah of Light:

God is the Light of the heavens and the earth;
the likeness of His Light is as a niche wherein is a lamp
(the lamp in a glass, the glass as it were a glittering star)
kindled from a Blessed Tree,
an olive that is neither of the East nor of the West
whose oil wellnigh would shine, even if no fire touched it;
Light upon Light;
(God guides to His Light whom He will). *

"Don't forget, children. Recite the Surah of Light at my funeral. I always see him surrounded by light. Come, Yunes, and sit beside me. Ibrahim is waiting for me. We are all descendants of Ibrahim, children. Come, Yunes. Come, Ibrahim."

Nahilah saw her son, Ibrahim, in the form of a man called Yunes, and saw her husband, Yunes, in the form of a child named Ibrahim.

You're his son, not mine, so why are you tormenting me?

Please. I'll go to your house now and will bring back the photos. I'll hang them on the walls of this room. We'll leave the drawing of the Divine Name in Kufic script in the center, and we'll arrange your photos around it. Your photos around the Name, and all of you around Yunes.

I'll go get the photos, and we'll tell the whole story.

The story will be different.

We'll change everything.

I'll hang all the photos here, and we'll live among them.

I'll take down a photo from the wall and will hand it to you, and you'll tell a story. Then I'll choose another photo and a new story will come. Story will follow story.

That way we can compose our story from the beginning without leaving a single gap for death to enter through.

---

* Koran, Surah XXIV, 35.

Now I stand.

I'm alone and it's night.

I stand and speak my last words with you. Talk is no longer possible. The speaking's done, the talk's run out, the story's closed.

I stand, neither weeping nor laughing.

As though your death were in the past. As though you died long ago. As though you didn't die.

I stand, without sorrow or tears.

I stand before this grave. I stand before the mosque turned into a grave by the siege. I bear witness that you placed your head in the earth, closed your eyes to the dust, and left for a distant place.

What then?

Tell me.

Didn't I tell you? Didn't we agree that we had to get through this seventh month? I told you if we succeeded in getting through the seventh month, we'd have outrun death.

Didn't we agree to buy life with these long days and long nights spent in this hospital room, as we told stories and remembered and imagined?

I told you it would cost seven months, and we've made a dent in the seventh month, and your child-features are beginning to take shape. I told you it was the beginning: "We've reached the beginning, Father, and now you'll become a son to me."

Why did you do this to me?

I never intended this to happen.

I decided to leave you for an hour to go get the photos so we could start the story over again. But I didn't make it back until morning. I saw Zainab waiting for me at the door of the hospital. She ran toward me, laid her head on my shoulder, and wept.

I asked her what was wrong, and she shook her head and said, "A heart attack."

Zainab wept, but I didn't.

Amjad wiped his tears as he gave directions for the burial, and I stood there like a stone. As though it weren't me.

Please don't reproach me – you know what happened to me.

I walked in the funeral procession like a stranger, like any one of the dozens who were there. They put you in the hole, they covered you with earth, and no one came forward to say a word. They looked at me, and I lowered my gaze. I was incapable of looking, incapable of speaking, incapable of weeping. It was as though a veil had descended over my eyes, as though I saw without seeing.

I had to wait three days before I found within myself the courage to stand before your grave, in this rain, the night of the camp covering me and granting me speech.

Now I stand, not to apologize but to weep.

I swear the only reason I left was to go to your house and get the photos. I thought I'd go and get the pictures of you and Nahilah and your children and grandchildren, and we'd begin the story. I felt my memory had dried out and my soul had gone dead, and I thought that only the pictures could renew our story.

I'd go to the photos, put them in front of you in the hospital room, and we'd talk.

I thought instead of talking about love, we could talk about the children and grandchildren.

I thought we could tell their stories one by one. That way, with them, we'd make it through these two remaining weeks of our seventh month in death's company and make it into the pains of childbirth.

Isn't that the law of life?

Didn't we agree we'd try to reach the depths of death so we could discover life?

No, I won't leave you on this terrible night.

I thought I'd go for an hour and come back, and I didn't come back.

Forgive me.

Please forgive me.

I left you with the story of Nahilah in her last moments, as she spoke with you and with Ibrahim, calling you Ibrahim and calling him Yunes, her children and grandchildren around her, weeping.

No. I didn't mean to leave you with death, because it was your duty and Ibrahim's to guard Nahilah and accompany her on her final journey.

I wanted a different story.

I wanted to tell you that I believed you when you said you didn't stop going over there after the night of the Roman olive tree, when your wife sat you down and recounted her reality; when she told you that over there you'd become the Jews' Jews, and over here you were the Arabs' Arabs.

I believed you, I swear.

I don't want you defeated and discredited.

I believe you.

After the night of the Roman olive tree, you absented yourself for nine months. Then you resumed your old habits, continuing your journeys over there despite all the difficulties. You didn't stop going over until after 1982, or, in other words, until after the Israeli invasion of Lebanon, when movement inside Beirut became impossible and the trip from Beirut to Sidon a reckless adventure.

That was when you stopped going across Jebel al-Sheikh and they started calling you. You'd talk to them and promise you'd all meet soon in Cyprus or Cairo. That meeting, however, kept getting postponed, as if neither of you wanted it – as if both of you'd agreed, without a word, to avoid the danger of a meeting outside the place you'd created for your meetings. One time it would be you that put it off, another time it was Nahilah, and then she fell ill.

I wanted to talk about this series of visits over there and your trip with Nahilah to Acre, when you went to the Abu Daoud restaurant in the Old City and ate fish and drank arak. It was there that you said to her, as the alcohol went to your head, "It's like they weren't here and had never taken our country. Acre's still Acre, the Jazzar mosque is still where it's always been, the sea and the sea bass and the red mullet and the black bream are still the same. I really feel like going home with you and staying there. What can they do about it? Let what happens happen." When you returned at night, you slipped into Bab al-Shams and spent the night there and forgot your talk of all the different kinds of fish and your plans to stay at home. She left you in the morning and returned at nightfall to accompany you to the outskirts of Deir al-Asad, as she always did.

I was going to tell you about Noor and her son, Yunes, who excelled in his studies in Acre and went to the University of Haifa to study engineering; and about the second Yunes, Salem's son, who is studying business management at Tel Aviv University and is getting ready to marry a Christian girl from Nazareth from the Khleifi family. You blessed the marriage; you told Salem his grandmother used to put an icon of the Virgin under her pillow and that you saw no harm in that, but that the thing that matters is for us to get married and have children.

I was going to tell you about the second Yunes, how you told him that God had blessed us by multiplying our descendants: "Here we are, thrown out of our country in '48, and with only a hundred thousand of us left over there. The hundred thousand have become a million, and the eight hundred thousand who were thrown out have become five million. They bring in immigrants and we have children, and we'll see who wins in the end."

I was going to tell you the stories of the photos, photo by photo, story by story, moment by moment, so we might fool time and not let it kill us.

It's my fault.

Dear God! How did it happen? How did I let it happen? How did I fail to notice? How could I have gotten drunk?

I left her in the morning and told her I had to go to the hospital because my father was sick. She said, "Go. I know all about it."

Apart from that one sentence she didn't say a thing. And we spent the whole night eating and drinking and making love.

What came over me?

Did her ghost come to liberate me, and to let you die in peace?

If only she were here, if only Umm Hassan were here – but she died before you and me. If Umm Hassan had been here, the funeral would've been different. She would've stood and lamented and made everyone weep.

They carried you, and we walked behind them, and they started dancing. The only ones to walk behind your bier were the men of the camp's Sufi brotherhood. They remembered that your father had been a Sufi of their order, so they carried your bier – turning, singing, and dancing. Your bier flew on top of their raised hands and they turned and sang their hymns.

And I walked.

I didn't sway or sing or weep.

I walked like a stranger, as though you weren't my father or my son, as though I hadn't been with you on your secret journey to your secret country.

They carried you and flew with you, singing hymns for the family of the Prophet, and I stood rigidly by.

I was like one who doesn't see.

The taste of that woman was in my soul, the smell of her on my body, her voice enveloped me.

And now you're dead and departing.

Would you like to know what happened to me? What's the point?

Would you like to hear a new story that even its narrator and hero doesn't believe?

We'd decided to stop telling such stories. We'd decided we wanted stories as real as reality.

That's why I went to your house to get you the photos and spread them out in front of you in your hospital room or hang them on the walls and show them to you.

But I failed.

I didn't get to your house, and I didn't get the photos.

I know you want to know, but I feel ashamed. Instead of mourning you and opening my house to receive condolences, I spent the last three days looking for her.

I didn't go to the hospital, and I didn't receive condolences along with Nurse Zainab and Dr. Amjad. Instead I roamed the alleys of the camp like a lost soul and whenever I caught sight of a woman's shadow, I'd run and catch up with her and would look at her for a moment before continuing, the disappointment etched on my face.

I know they think I've gone crazy.

I know what they're saying.

They're saying Khalil Ayyoub lost it after Yunes died. But no! Well, yes, they may be right. I've lost it; yes, definitely, lost it all.

I spent three days searching, I didn't sleep for an instant. I was like someone who's lost his mind. How could she have disappeared? Where had she gone? What was her name? I don't even know her name. I asked her – yes, I did ask. But I don't remember what she said. Did she answer? I don't know.

Maybe she didn't answer. Maybe she smiled, and I nodded my head as though I understood.

For three days I forgot that you were my father and my son. I forgot your death and your life and ran after the ghost of a woman whose name I don't know.

Now I've come back to you.

Forgive me. Pardon me.

I know you'll understand my situation and will accept my apology. After all, you too, spent fifty years running after the ghost of a woman.

Do you know how I returned to my senses?

What saved me was this terrible idea that it was her – yes, her – who had come to force me to spend the night away from you, to steal you from me.

When this terrible idea came to me, I relaxed a little and fell asleep. Then I got up. It was night, and the rain was drumming on my window, so I decided to come to your grave and tell you everything.

I decided it was time for me to weep, mourn, to be unconsolable.

I decided you were dead and that I'd go on with my life without you, without the hospital and without our stories, of which we've only told fractions.

You remember.

When I left you it was seven in the evening, the last of the shadows were disappearing from the horizon. I went to your house for the photos. On my way, I stopped in front of a shop and bought a bag of bread and a little halva thinking I'd have the halva for dinner with a glass of tea.

I took the bag and continued on my way, and there, about fifty meters from your house, I saw her. She was wearing a long black dress, her head was covered with a black scarf, and she had a suitcase in her hand as if she were traveling.

She stood, suitcase in hand, and didn't turn around, as if she were a photograph. When I got close to her, she turned her head in my direction.

"Good evening," she said.

"Good evening," I answered.

"Do you know the house of Elias al-Roumi?" *

"Elias who?"

"Elias al-Roumi," she said.

"There's no one named Elias in the camp," I told her.

"Yes," she said. "Elias al-Roumi."

"So far as I know, there's no one by that name."

"Where are you from?" she asked me.

"From here, from the camp," I said.

"From which village?"

"From al-Ghabsiyyeh," I said.

"I could tell by your accent," she said.

"But I don't have a Ghabsiyyeh accent."

"Yes, you do," she said. "You do without knowing."

"Maybe," I said. "That must be my grandmother's influence."

"Tell me where his house is. I need to deliver a letter from his wife."

I said I didn't know. I told her that she might have mistaken the place; this was the Shatila camp.

* Al-Roumi: The Roman.

"I know, I know," she said. "I've come to Shatila from far away. His wife in Ain al-Zaitoun gave me a letter for him. I have to deliver it and go back because it's already night and I'm a stranger here and know no one."

"I'm afraid that I can't help you, Madame."

I continued on my way toward your house.

I heard her voice behind me, so I went back to her.

"What did you say?"

"Where are the people of the camp?" she said. "Can't we ask one of them? Where's the headman?"

I told her people didn't leave their houses in the evening.

"Why?"

"Because they're afraid."

"Afraid?"

"Yes, afraid. Things aren't too good, as you can see."

"What am I supposed to do now?"

"I don't know."

"I have to deliver the letter and go back. If you could give it to him, I could leave it with you and go."

"But I don't know the man."

"Ask about him."

"I assure you, Madame, there's no one by that name in the camp. The camp's small, and I'm a doctor. I know everyone."

"What's your name, Sir?"

"Khalil. Dr. Khalil Ayyoub," I said.

"Please, Doctor. Help me."

"I'm at your service."

"It seems I'm going to spend the night here. Take me to one of the hotels in the camp."

"You're looking for a hotel in a refugee camp! Impossible. You can go into town. Beirut's full of hotels."

"I don't want to go into town," she said. "I don't have time. I want a hotel here."

"I can assure you there aren't any. I don't know what to say."

"Can't I spend the night here?"

"Of course," I said, "but where? You can sleep in my house, if you like."

"You're married?"

"No."

"You live with your mother?"

"No."

"Sleep in the house of a bachelor who lives alone? Impossible!"

"No, you've misunderstood me. I'll take you to my house, and then I'll go back to the hospital. I'm a doctor, as I told you. I'll drop you off and go."

"Agreed," she said.

And she set off.

She walked ahead of me to the house. The truth is I didn't want to take her to my house; yours was closer. I'd take her to your house, get the photos together, and go. She could sleep there.

She walked ahead of me as though she knew the way to my house, and when we arrived, she stopped in front of the door. I got out my keys, opened the door, and we went in. It was dark, and there was a smell of mold. I struck a match, because the camp's electricity was cut off, and lit a paraffin lamp. Then I saw her. She was sitting on the sofa, her case beside her, her head in her hands, and the slope of her shoulders extended like a shadow that danced on the floor of the room.

"Please make yourself at home," I said. "I'm going. Good night."

"Where are you going?" she asked.

"To the hospital," I said.

"But I'm hungry," she said.

I put the bag I was carrying on the table and said, "Please help yourself." She opened the bag and saw the bread and halva.

"After all that distance, you're going to feed me halva? No. I'll make dinner. Where's the kitchen?"

I picked up the paraffin lamp and led her to the kitchen.

"I hate the smell of paraffin," she said. "Don't you have any candles in the house?"

"Yes, yes." I went to the bedroom to look for the pair of candles I'd hidden in a drawer in case the paraffin ran out. I lit the two candles, placing one in the kitchen and one in the living room.

She opened her case and pulled out a plastic bag.

"Wait," she said.

I sat in the living room to wait for her, thinking the situation over. No, I had nothing in mind: The woman was wearing a long black dress that covered her from head to toe, and her face was half-hidden by her scarf. I can say that I didn't see her. So how?

No, Abu Salem, I had nothing like that in mind.

Then I saw her with a dishcloth knotted around her waist. She started cleaning the house. I tried to help her, but she waved me off. In a matter of minutes – I swear it was minutes, not more – everything was sparkling clean. She was like a magician: She went around the house upending things and cleaning them, and the smell of perfumed soap emanated from every corner.

Then she said she'd make dinner.

"There's nothing in the house. Do you want me to go out and buy things?"

"There's no need," she said. "I have everything."

I was sitting in the living room waiting for the meal when she came out of the kitchen. "You go in and take a bath. I've cleaned everything up for you, but you're not clean."

I picked up the pot of hot water that she'd prepared for me in the kitchen and went into the bathroom. When I came out, she was waiting. Then she disappeared for a few minutes in the bathroom and came out again with her long hair hanging down loose over her shoulders. Black hair, brown skin, large green eyes, a small mouth, a long face, finely sculpted hands, and long, thin fingers.

Beyond description.

I'd never seen a woman so beautiful, or with such presence – it was as though she'd drawn a circle around me from which I couldn't escape.

The strangest thing is that I didn't ask her who she was or what she wanted. At that point I realized the whole story of the letter had been a pretext. Even so, I didn't ask. I was like one possessed, like one revolving in the circle of the Sufi ceremony of remembrance, as if all language had left me and I only knew how to repeat the words, *God! God!*

We sat down at the table, across which she offered me a platter of fried fish.

I couldn't smell oil. How had she done it?

It was a fish banquet – red mullet, sea bass, and black bream – there was also *taratur* sauce and parsley.

"Do you have some arak?" she asked.

"Of course," I said.

I brought over the bottle of local arak and poured two glasses, added water, and offered her one.

"Where's the ice?" she asked.

"Where am I supposed to find ice?" I said. "The electricity's shut off, as you can see."

"On Jebel al-Sheikh," she said, smiling, "he who drinks arak should know where to get ice."

She said she didn't drink arak without ice.

I drank though. I drank my glass and hers and poured myself several more and wallowed in the fish, *taratur,* and arak.

She ate slowly, watching me.

"Good health, good health!" she said.

"Drink!" I said.

"No, I don't like arak."

And I drank until my pores opened and my sinews loosened up. I drank until I felt that my soul had come back to me.

She got up, took the dishes into the kitchen, came back with two glasses of mint tea, and took two small aniseed cakes out of her case.

"Eat one of these," she said. "There's a saying of the Prophet's that goes, 'If you eat fish, eat something sweet afterwards. The one is made for the other.'"

I ate, but I wasn't satisfied. Then I opened my brown bag and brought out the halva and devoured it all.

Then all I remember is her arm around me and me being with her, around her, in her. Revolving and rising and tasting nectar such as I'd never tasted in my life.

How can I describe how she was – her breasts, her waist, the slope of her thighs, her knees, the water that sprang from inside her, her whispers, her kisses, her tongue. It was her, not me. I inhaled her and drank her. I drank her drop by drop and she drank me drop by drop. I'd stop and start, rise like waves and descend with the waves, and never end. The waves were inside me, renewing and reshaping themselves. I was above the wave and inside it and beneath it, and she was the wave and the sea and the shore.

I didn't sleep at all.

I didn't speak. Yes, I spoke – and she put her hand on my lips and silenced me and took me . . . Then how can I . . . Brown-skinned, not white, green eyes, not honey-colored, long hair, not short. I don't know.

That woman, who came from nowhere and stood like a photograph in front of your house, with her black scarf over her head, entered my house and took off her scarf so I could see her hair was pinned up in a bun and thought she must be past sixty, then came out of the bathroom and was transformed.

Her hair was long, her skin dark, her eyes green.

We finished eating the fish, and her skin grew light, her eyes large and black, her dark hair hanging all the way to her knees.

As we drank tea, her body became full, with small drowsy eyes and a complexion the shade of ripe wheat, and she took me.

She started to shimmer and change as though she were a thousand women.

Now I understand.

I want to weep. Please forgive me. I didn't . . . I swear I didn't . . .

The light rose over us. She was still stretched out on the bed, her eyes closed. I got up and put on my clothes. I said to her, "A few minutes. I'll be

> 536 <

back in a few minutes. There's a patient I have to check on and then I'll be back."

She whispered, "I know, I know," and held out her arms as if calling me back to her.

"No. I'm going to the hospital for a moment and then I'll bring you back *kunafa* with cheese for breakfast."

I left her and went to the hospital, and there at the door was Zainab. She hugged me, wept on my shoulder, and grasped my hand to take me to your room, where you were waiting to be washed for burial.

I pulled my hand from hers and told her I'd be back in a moment.

I left the hospital and ran to the *kunafa* seller and asked for two platters. The man looked at me with astonished eyes.

"Condolences," he said.

"May God be with you," I said and snatched the platters from his hand and ran toward the house, imagining her brown arms and her wide eyes and her full lips and her murmurs.

I entered the house, and she wasn't there.

She wasn't in the bedroom, or in the living room, or in the bathroom. The bed was made and everything was in its place.

The kitchen was clean. The smell of mildew filled the house, and the bag of halva was in its place on the table, untouched.

I thought of the suitcase.

I raced through the house, I looked under the bed, I opened the drawers, I searched everywhere, for everything.

I left the house without closing the door behind me and ran through the streets of the camp, peering into the faces of the women, not daring to ask. What could I have asked?

I stopped in front of the halva seller's shop.

The shopkeeper asked me, "What time is the funeral?"

"Now," I said.

"How can it be now? Aren't you going to wait for the noon prayer?"

"Yes, yes, of course we are."

"What time is it?" I asked him.

"Eight in the morning," he answered.

I asked about Elias. "Do you know a man who lives here in the camp called Elias al-Roumi?"

"An Elias – a Christian – here in this camp? Have you lost it, Brother? May God help you, they say you took very good care of him. God will reward you, I'm sure. Go and rest now, then come back for the burial."

I went back to the hospital, and I saw Dr. Amjad wiping away his tears. There were men everywhere, an uproar of lamentation. Amjad said they'd finished washing you, and that the procession would start from the hospital. There was no need to take you to your house.

I left them.

"Where are you going?" asked Amjad.

"I'll be back," I said.

I left them and ran through the streets of the camp. I peered into all the faces, then went back home and looked for her again in the bedroom, the kitchen, the bathroom, the living room.

I sat on the chair in front of the table where the bag of bread and halva still was. I opened the bag and ate a whole loaf with halva, then went to the funeral.

Afterwards, I didn't go back to the hospital.

Zainab told me that Mme. Wedad would be coming to the hospital in the afternoon to inform me of the decision to transfer me to Hamshari Hospital in the Ain al-Hilweh camp because Galilee Hospital was going to close. Zainab said she'd refused a transfer to Tyre: She preferred to stay here, even without work, because anyhow, she was just waiting for the visa from her son.

I said fine, and didn't go back to the hospital.

I wanted nothing, except to find the woman.

Why had she taken me home and fed me fish?

I'm in love.

I burn like a lover, and I die like a lover.

Three days I was alive in death.

Three days before I despaired of death.

And today, Father, I was lying on my bed and I saw her phantom image and I went toward her but she waved me away.

Once upon a time, I saw, as a dreamer sees, that I was in your bed. I was in your room lying in your bed and the photos were swaying on the walls around me, and I saw her. She stepped out of the wall and approached me. I tried to embrace her but she retreated, and then flattened herself against the wall. I looked at the photograph for a while. It was my wife, who'd been in my bed – what was my wife doing in this photo? What was this woman whose name I didn't know doing inside the photo of Nahilah?

I woke with a terrified start and wept.

I didn't weep for Shams as I've wept for you and for this woman.

I didn't weep for my father as I've wept for you and for her.

I didn't weep for my mother as I've wept for you and for her.

I didn't weep for my grandmother as I've wept for you and for her.

I left my house barefoot and ran to your grave.

I'm standing here. The night covers me, the March rain washes me, and I tell you, no, this isn't how stories end. No.

I stand. The rain forms ropes that extend from the sky to the ground. My feet sink into the mud. I stretch out my hand, I grasp the ropes of rain, and I walk and walk and walk

RAINMAKER TRANSLATIONS
supports a series of books meant to encourage a lively reading
experience of contemporary world literature drawn from diverse
languages and cultures. Publication is assisted by grants from the
International Institute of Modern Letters (modernletters.org),
a nonprofit organization dedicated to promoting the literary
arts and literary activism around the world.

Designed by David Bullen Design.
Typeset in Janson Text.
Printed at The Stinehour Press in Lunenburg, Vermont.
The paper is 60lb Mohawk Vellum.